Three fabulous N
talented
intro
international

PENNY JORDAN

Mills & Boon
Presents...

Annie West
Annie Burrows
Margaret McDonagh

100 Reasons to Celebrate

We invite you to join us in celebrating
Mills & Boon's centenary. Gerald Mills and
Charles Boon founded Mills & Boon Limited
in 1908 and opened offices in London's Covent
Garden. Since then, Mills & Boon has become
a hallmark for romantic fiction, recognised
around the world.

We're proud of our 100 years of publishing
excellence, which wouldn't have been achieved
without the loyalty and enthusiasm of our
authors and readers.

Thank you!

Each month throughout the year there will
be something new and exciting to mark the
centenary, so watch for your favourite authors,
captivating new stories, special limited
edition collections…and more!

Mills & Boon
Presents...

Annie West
Annie Burrows
Margaret McDonagh

M&B™ and M&B™ with the Rose Device
are trademarks of the publisher.
Harlequin Mills & Boon Limited, Eton House,
18-24 Paradise Road, Richmond, Surrey TW9 1SR

MILLS & BOON® PRESENTS...
© by Harlequin Books S.A. 2008

The Billionaire's Bought Mistress © Annie West 2008
The Earl's Untouched Bride © Annie Burrows 2008
An Italian Affair © Margaret McDonagh 2008

ISBN: 978 0 263 86587 5

009-0408

Printed and bound in Spain
by Litografía Rosés S.A., Barcelona

Introduction
by
The Sunday Times bestselling author
PENNY JORDAN

This year, 2008, is a very special year of celebration for all those who read romantic novels, write romantic novels or work in the world of romantic fiction. One hundred years after Gerald Mills and Charles Boon founded Mills & Boon Ltd, the company is recognised as a byword for romance the world over.

In this anniversary year, it's really important to look forward to the future as well as back over past achievements, and to showcase some of the marvellous new and talented writers being found and published today, when so many new ways of filling our rare leisure hours are available. New voices, fresh approaches, individual style and sheer flair give the reader choices and keep standards high, and that's why I'm so delighted to be introducing *Mills & Boon® Presents...*

My first introduction to Mills & Boon® romances came via the *Woman's Weekly* magazines passed on to my mother by a neighbour. I would have been about ten at the time, and some of the author names I remember are Mary Burchell and Essie Summers. I stopped reading romance whilst I was at senior school, but then started again when I was eighteen. In those days Mills & Boon books could be borrowed from local corner-shop libraries. The mother of a girl I worked with read them, and I fell in love with them all over again.

My own published writing career began when I was in my late twenties, when I wrote four Regency romances, two air-stewardess romances and a thriller romance for the late agent Desmond Elliott.

Whilst I was writing these books I read in a magazine that Mills & Boon were looking for new writers because they were expanding. I was still an avid reader of theirs – on publication day I used to rush out of work as early as I could to get to the local bookstore to grab my favourites before they all disappeared – and so I plucked up the courage to write my first Mills & Boon. I chose to write the kind of romance I still love best – one with a sheikh hero – and that story was ultimately published as *Falcon's Prey*. I still love writing sheikh books, and I tend to think of them as being very much my 'signature' books.

I used to love going down to London for meetings, as the Mills & Boon offices were then just off Bond Street. On one of these visits my editor at the time insisted on taking me to a shop which specialised in glitzy clothes, where she had bought what she referred to as her 'Harlequin jacket'. After lunch, heady with champagne, and having just met the late Alan Boon, I very unwisely returned to this emporium. I emerged minus a good percentage of my royalty cheque with a frock to end all frocks. No words can do it justice. Think diva 1930s: a body-hugging long dress in stretchy black and silver metallic fabric, with a fishtail skirt from below the knee supported by masses of net petticoat. All the way down the front of this masterpiece was a snake made of 'jewels'. It had add-on full-length sleeves – with mini-snakes to fit over one finger.

Needless to say I never, ever wore it – not even in private.

However, the highlight of these visits was always going down to the area where the new books were stored and being allowed to select my favourites to bring home to read.

I was lucky enough to catch the tail-end of the tsunami of romantic fiction that swept through America in the late 70s and early 80s, when Harlequin Enterprises had acquired Mills & Boon, broadening not just my readership but also the boundaries of my personal world. Prior to writing for Mills & Boon I'd barely travelled at all, but when my first 'big' book came out – *Power Play* in 1988 – Harlequin invited me to attend a 'tea party' in Boston, where I was to speak with another author (an author who is now far more famous than I). I still have the pretty piece of jewellery I bought in Boston, and I have many happy memories of that time. My late husband was with me, and one evening we went to the waterfront with the local PR girl and her hunky boyfriend, whom we teasingly named 'the Italian Stallion' – he was gorgeous! From Boston we went to Toronto, and from there to New York, returning home to the UK on the *QE2*. That trip alone would be enough to make me everlastingly grateful to Harlequin Mills & Boon for the opportunities it has given me to travel and broaden my horizons – personally and professionally.

A PR trip to Ireland followed – a most wonderful experience – then trips to Paris, Hamburg, Prague… It would take me weeks to write about the enormous debt I owe my readers and my publishers for making it all possible.

Here are a few memories of those times. Paris – we stayed in a most beautiful historic hotel in the Place des Vosges, and I will never forget the skill of the translator who accompanied me to a TV appearance (she normally worked at the UN). I met the translators who work on Mills & Boon books, met the French Harlequin team. And there was a fantastic riverboat trip. Despite my lack of French, and her lack of English, a reader was able to convey to me how much our books meant to her 'because of the difficulty of her work' – this work turned out to be nursing the terminally ill. A truly humbling moment.

Hamburg – a restaurant like no other I have ever dined in. The 'show' plates removed between each course were a work of art in themselves. Our hotel had been designed to replicate an English country house, and we were driven everywhere in a Rolls-Royce. The driver was incredibly good-looking, and in true Mills & Boon style he turned out to be the owner of the limousine company!

Prague – meeting the wonderful editorial director there, who later succumbed to cancer.

Many years later I was invited by the Japanese office to visit with fans there, by way of Australia and New Zealand – the trip of a lifetime, and most wonderful.

I have been so very privileged to meet so many special people. Life ebbs and flows, but the loyalty of our readers remains a constant, and we writers are very much aware of that – which is why we all strive so hard to write the very best books we can for you.

Nothing is ever a 'given', and along with my successes I've also had my failures: the grit in the pearl that keeps us striving to be the very best we can be.

I came to romance-writing at a very favourable time. Today new writers have to struggle far harder than I did to become published authors, and I admire them so much for their dedication to their craft.

Harlequin Mills & Boon continue to welcome new talent and to take on new authors, as evidenced by these books. I hope you will be entertained by these three new novels from this trio of exciting and talented writers – Annie West, Annie Burrows and Margaret McDonagh – as they embark on thrilling new careers as romance novelists. They are all being published under different series – Modern™, Historical and Medical™ – all of which offer a quite different reading experience. They are collected together in this one volume to demonstrate the scope and variety of romantic fiction available today, and to offer anyone who hasn't tried all these series recently an opportunity to see what they've been missing.

Annie West is an Australian author whose intense and passionate stories are perfectly suited to Modern™. She creates vivid characters and has a wonderful storytelling ability which, combined with her emotional writing style, makes for a fantastic read.

Annie has a fundamental affinity with Modern romance themes, and in this book you are about to read, *The Billionaire's Bought Mistress*, blackmail and revenge are at its very heart, creating a dark and dangerous edge to the story, setting the scene for a hero who will do whatever it takes to get the vengeance he seeks, and the woman he wants in his bed…

Now, having written five books for the Modern romance series, it's clear that Annie creates heroes who are always dark, brooding, demanding and extremely sexy, whether a powerful sheikh, a gorgeous Greek tycoon, or a ruthless billionaire – and the hero of *The Billionaire's Bought Mistress*, Rafe Benton, is no exception!

Annie Burrows started writing for Mills & Boon® Historical romance in 2006. Her first book, *His Cinderella Bride*, came out in September as a paperback. She sees herself as a character-driven writer, and can't start a story until her characters 'speak' to her.

Her latest book, which you see here, *The Earl's Untouched Bride*, is the story of one woman's struggle with shyness, with a sense that she's out of place and can't handle the manners and mores of Polite Society. She has been rescued from a horrendous marriage by Charles, Earl of Walton, but knows that it was a knight in shining armour moment for him, rather than anything to do with attraction or love. As much as it's a wonderful romance, it's also a coming of age story, in which Heloise (the heroine) finds her own voice and her own independence – an independence which means nothing without the hero's love!

Margaret McDonagh writes for the Medical™ romance series. She says, 'It was a dream come true to finally get the phone call from Harlequin Mills & Boon – one, after twenty years of writing novellas for *My Weekly Story Collection*, Linford Press large prints, serials, and short stories for *People's Friend*, I believed would never happen. I was stunned, tearful, in shock…and *so* excited!'

That first Medical romance from Margaret, *The Italian Doctor's Bride*, went on sale in October 2006. Several more titles have followed, all loosely linked by the fictional setting of Strathlochan in Southern Scotland, with familiar characters popping up again from time to time. Margaret is brimming over with ideas for future characters and books, and she particularly likes writing about close-knit communities and medical professionals for whom caring is more than a job.

Margaret is a very emotional writer, and excels at damaged characters; her heroes – whether British, Scottish or Italian – are always to die for! The reason her work really stood out was her warm and engaging voice. *An Italian Affair*, the novel featured here, is a deliciously sexy story with a big heart; the heroine is a compassionate, unassuming English girl who has her life turned upside down by one irresistible

Italian surgeon!

I very much hope you'll enjoy this collection by these compelling writers, and that you may have found new authors whose books you will seek out and which will give you pleasure in the years to come. In this centenary year of Mills & Boon, I hope you will join me in celebrating the past, present and future of romantic fiction.

Penny Jordan

THE
BILLIONAIRE'S
BOUGHT MISTRESS

Annie West

Annie West spent her childhood with her nose between the covers of a book – a habit she retains. After years preparing government reports and official correspondence she decided to write something she *really* enjoys. And there's nothing she loves more than a great romance. Despite her office-bound past she has managed a few interesting moments – including a marriage offer with the promise of a herd of camels to sweeten the contract. She is happily married to her ever-patient husband (who has never owned a dromedary). They live with their two children amongst the tall eucalypts at beautiful Lake Macquarie, on Australia's east coast. You can e-mail Annie at www.annie-west.com or write to her at PO Box 1041, Warners Bay, NSW 2282, Australia.

Dear Reader,

I still can't quite believe I'm writing a letter to you, one of the many people worldwide who read and enjoy Mills & Boon® romances.

A couple of years ago I was an aspiring writer, dreaming of acceptance. Between you and me, I wondered if I'd ever achieve my dream – to write for Mills & Boon. After all, these were the romances I'd read and loved for years. I started with stories by writers like Violet Winspear, Anne Mather and Anne Hampson, who created aristocratic Spaniards, flashing-eyed Italians and strong, confident Englishmen for me to dream about. I travelled the world in those books, and loved the way they changed with the times as well. I always found passionate tales that packed a wonderful emotional punch. As the years went by I found many new authors – each with their own way of creating a wonderful romance, each telling compelling stories.

When Mills & Boon accepted my first book I didn't believe it. I read the message three times, and made my husband check it before I believed it was true. So you can imagine my thrill at being asked to contribute a story especially for this anthology to mark the Mills & Boon centenary!

The Billionaire's Bought Mistress is my sixth story for Mills & Boon, and my excitement hasn't diminished one bit. I feel privileged to be one of the authors who writes stories for romance-lovers all around the world. Just imagine spending your day fantasising about wonderful heroes and their love lives! Aren't I lucky?

I do hope you enjoy Antonia and Rafe's story, and the other romances contained in this edition. Happy reading in this special centenary year.

With warmest regards,

Annie

With heartfelt thanks to some fine writing friends: Alison, Daisy, Fiona, Heather, Karen and Serena. You've been terrific!

CHAPTER ONE

THE cold rose up from the ground, seeping through Antonia's boots and into her bloodstream as she stood, immobile. Icy air stung her cheeks and caught the back of her throat when she breathed.

Through her dark glasses she surveyed the others. The minister's cheeks were apple-red, and his breath as he spoke came out in white puffs. Most of the small gathering had reddened noses from the crisp wind that swirled flurries of white around their ankles. Antonia watched as they surreptitiously shifted their feet, trying to keep warm.

Stuart Dexter stood farthest away, two spots of colour painting his aristocratic cheeks. She should be furious he was here, but she didn't have the energy even for that.

It was easier to study the mourners than to absorb the minister's sonorous words. The flow of Swiss German was intended to soothe, yet Antonia found no comfort in his platitudes. Despite the coffin being lowered into the dark hole at her feet, she felt divorced from the proceedings.

Her dad wasn't here. Not in that cramped box. She blinked, almost expecting to hear some whispered aside from him, as if he leaned over her shoulder. Some thoroughly outrageous statement, inappropriate but inevitably witty, that would make her lips tilt into a reluctant smile despite the solemnity of the occasion.

She swallowed a sudden constriction in her throat as she reminded herself she wouldn't hear his voice again.

Her beloved, full-of-life, ready-for-anything, daredevil of a father was gone. *He'd left her alone.*

Guilt clutched her heart. She'd failed him miserably. This was her fault.

The chill of the Swiss churchyard was nothing to the deep freeze inside Antonia's body. The cold that spread out from her bones and her heart was every bit as frigid as the air temperature.

Six days since the accident. She was used to the numbness now—even found comfort in it. For she suspected if her heart were to thaw the pain would be unbearable.

She lifted her gaze to the clear alpine sky. Beyond the village Antonia saw the steep white slope of a mountain. Could even make out a zigzag of road, snow poles marking its edges. From here she couldn't see the spot where the car had skidded, slid, and then tumbled down the slope.

A tremor shuddered through her and swiftly she averted her eyes.

Movement caught her attention on the other side of the churchyard. She peered at the figure, now motionless in the blue-black shadow of the church.

He didn't approach, but she sensed his intense regard. The height, the breadth of shoulder, his stance, proclaimed him a man at the height of his vigour. He stood straight and tall. Even from this distance she sensed power, strength, and a solidity that told her he would never meld easily into a crowd.

He moved into the sunlight and Antonia frowned. She'd seen that face before, just last week. *The evening this nightmare had begun.*

She'd agreed to meet Stuart Dexter alone, to discuss his concerns about her father, opting for the safety of a popular bar instead of sharing a meal in his suite. Yet in the quiet foyer he'd groped her, sliding his hands over her as he helped her with her jacket, urging her back to his place for a private 'party'.

Bile rose to her mouth as she remembered the smell of his vodka-laden breath, hot against her face, his heavy hand grasping at her breast.

And over his shoulder the face of this man. A disturbing sky-blue gaze had locked on the pair of them as the stranger's severe features drew tight in supercilious distaste. His eyebrows had crammed together in a black smudge of disapproval.

For an instant she'd thought he was going to flatten Stuart as he grabbed at her and she fought to keep them both upright against his unsteady weight. Stuart had been pawing at her bra by the time she'd finally forced him away.

By that time the stranger had vanished.

What was he doing here today?

His brows were tilted in a V. With his night-dark hair, long black coat and the stark lines of his face accentuated by the slanting morning light, he looked like a disapproving angel, come to supervise her father's interment.

A bubble of something that might have been hysteria rose, threatening her composure. Her dad had joked that he'd never make it through the pearly gates. Despite the wonderful things he'd achieved, he said he'd made too many mistakes and enjoyed life far too much.

Something about the stranger's smouldering intensity, the forbidding set of his jaw and his utterly still posture was uncanny, catching her breath in her raw throat.

He was no angel. That firm, sculpted mouth spoke of experience, not innocence. And despite his dour expression

Antonia had seen in an instant that he was the sort of man who'd draw women like a magnet.

The sound of the minister clearing his throat attracted Antonia's attention. He was winding up the service, watching her expectantly. She forced herself to look down into the chasm at her feet, to the coffin lying at the bottom.

For a moment roiling emotions stirred deep inside. Her eyes prickled hot with the threat of tears.

Then, mercifully, the permafrost of numbness closed round her again. Wherever her father was, it wasn't here.

Bending quickly, she scraped up a little gravel and let it fall. The sound of it spattering against wood was loud in the stillness. Final.

Abruptly she turned and shook the minister's hand, thanking him in flawless German for the service. Then, without waiting to talk to any of the others present, she strode off towards the street.

She felt their eyes on her as she left. Heard their murmurs. And on the bare flesh of her nape a prickling sensation teased her, made her falter in mid-stride.

Antonia didn't turn round. An atavistic sense told her what it was: reaction to the stranger's laser-sharp stare.

Some people liked to gawk. Well, let him. She was beyond caring about anyone else right now.

'Ms Malleson, excuse me.'

Antonia paused, unbuttoning her coat, and looked across to the concierge's desk in a corner of the lobby.

'Herr Weber.' Not the concierge but the manager. She nodded and summoned a vague smile for the man who had been so kind and helpful this past week. 'How are you?'

'Very good, thank you.' His voice had lost its appealing local burr and he spoke formally, with a precision totally unlike his usual warm manner. 'Could we talk, please? *Privately.*'

He looked uncomfortable. The determined set of his mouth was at odds with his normally ready smile.

Instantly Antonia's brain clicked to alert. It was fourteen years since her mother's death—that dreadful time when her father had gone off the rails. But Antonia remembered it vividly. Her father's restless energy, the reckless expenditure—as if he'd been trying to hide his grief in a whirl of new faces and fast living.

Some things stayed with you. Even after all this time Antonia knew instantly the look of a creditor about to demand payment in full. Polite, but worried. Unwilling to broach the unpleasant subject, but grimly determined.

How long had they been here? Frantically she calculated the rate for the suite her father had insisted on and the money left in her account. The result wasn't pretty, but she knew better than to let her concern show.

Damn! She should have been prepared. But in the last few days nothing had seemed to matter. She'd gone through the motions of everyday life in a weird vacuum, barely noticing what went on around her.

'Of course, Herr Weber.' She curved her lips into a more convincing smile as she walked towards the open office door he'd indicated. 'I wanted to speak with you too. I'll be leaving here soon and I'd like to see the account.'

'Ah.' That was definitely relief in his round brown eyes. 'As you wish, Ms Malleson. I understand that you will want to go home now that…'

Now that her father had been buried.

For an instant fierce emotion gripped her heart, squeezing so hard she almost cried out from the pain. Her face froze in rictus paralysis. It took a supreme effort to force the smile back in place.

'That's right,' she murmured at last, her voice husky. 'It's time I went home.'

No need to share the fact that she didn't have a home. That the closest thing she'd had to one in fourteen years had been an English boarding school.

Home had been wherever her dad was. And now…

Herr Weber lowered his voice to a whisper. 'I'm sorry to bother you at this time, Ms Malleson, but I've been fielding calls from a number of businesses. I took it upon myself to say you couldn't be contacted yet, but—'

'It's all right, Herr Weber, I understand.' Her heart plunged. Not just the hotel, then. How many accounts had her father run up?

Suddenly it all clicked into place.

Antonia had been away when her father had received his latest cardiologist's report. She was sure now it had been worse news than expected. Of course her father had kept that to himself. She'd known something was wrong, her father hadn't been himself, but she'd let him reassure her.

Pain twisted low in her stomach.

She should have realised.

She reached out to touch the manager's arm reassuringly. The poor man looked so guilty. It wasn't *his* fault Gavin Malleson had started living extravagantly beyond his means again. Just like in his youth, when he'd been the darling of the jet set, and again when grief for his wife had set him on a downward spiral.

Antonia nodded to the worried man beside her. 'I'm afraid that with my father's accident I've been remiss in settling his accounts.'

'That's completely understandable, Ms Malleson.' The manager bowed his head in a courtly gesture and motioned for her to precede him into his office.

As he closed the door behind them Antonia spied a flicker of movement in the far corner of the foyer. The swing of a black coat, the sure stride of long legs.

The stranger from the funeral.

Her heart hit a faltering beat and then resumed its rhythm. Antonia wondered about the coincidence of seeing him here, in her hotel. Then the door shut and she forced herself to focus on more immediate problems.

Rafe watched the door close discreetly behind them.

So that confirmed it. His first instinct about her had been right. She was short of cash, so she played on her beauty, flashing those dark velvet eyes and cosying up to a man old enough to be her father in order to manoeuvre her way out of trouble. There'd been no mistaking the intimate warmth of her smile, or her hand on the manager's arm, the subtle invitation of her soft, throaty voice as she agreed to a *private* meeting.

Disappointment tasted bitter on Rafe's tongue. And that fuelled his anger. Surely he'd learned all he needed to about avaricious women in the years since he'd made the rich list? He'd been the target of too many gold-diggers, using every trick they could find to snare his interest.

Had he been foolish enough to hope Antonia Malleson was different? One look had made him want to believe that cool, classic beauty was more than skin deep.

Rafe had seen her and instantly wanted her, craved her with a hunger that had stopped him in his tracks. He'd been in the act of shouldering his way to where she stood alone when someone had joined her. A man he knew only too well. Stuart Dexter: twice her age and with a reputation that would keep decent women away. His girlfriends all had one thing in common—a mercenary streak that overcame the revulsion they must feel in his bed.

Since then Rafe had gathered details about this woman who still, to his chagrin, drew his gaze and heated his blood. She lived a life of pleasure, trailing from one expensive resort to another. Obviously she had no qualms about trading on her looks to secure a wealthy lover. Only last week Rafe had seen her and Dexter at a nightclub known for its ready supply of designer drugs. She'd let Dexter half undress her as they'd swayed drunkenly together.

No, she was as shallow as the rest of that crowd. Self-absorbed and greedy.

Just like Stuart Dexter.

Rafe's long-lost, not-at-all-lamented father.

When Rafe had seen her at the graveside this morning, pale and still and composed, she'd been like an ice princess, aloof and remote. As if the loss of her father meant nothing to her. He'd wondered if it could be true what the gossips said: that she was cold at heart. No lasting relationship with a man. No host of female friends.

Then he'd looked more closely. Had that been a hint of vulnerability behind her reserve? She'd looked brittle, as if she held back her grief only by desperate self-control.

And even then Rafe had wanted her.

The hunger he'd felt when he'd first seen her had morphed now into a blood-deep need. Its impact still rocked him, like a pounding blow to the chest.

Lust shouldn't be on his agenda. He had other, more important things on his mind.

Rafe hadn't understood the compulsion to follow her from the churchyard. He'd told himself he wanted to stretch his legs as he walked up the road to the hotel, leaving his rental car behind. It had nothing to do with unwilling concern for a girl who looked to be deep in shock.

But what he'd just seen had dispelled that illusion.

Rafe eyed the closed door to the manager's office and felt a twist of revulsion in the pit of his belly. Obviously the fact that she'd just buried her father meant little to her. Certainly not enough to prevent her playing manipulative games for her own ends.

He turned on his heel and strode out through the entrance.

The cold, distant look he'd seen on her face in the grave-yard summed her up. She wasn't suffering from shock or grief at all.

Antonia Malleson had shown her true colours. And in doing so she'd provided him with a perfect weapon. He had no compunction about using it to his own advantage. The bonus would be the personal satisfaction he'd derive from turning the tables on the beautiful little gold digger.

'I'm sorry, Ms Malleson. Your father's annuity ended with his death. There will be no more payments.'

Antonia sat rigidly upright beside the writing desk. This wasn't news, she told herself. It merely confirmed what she'd suspected. All the same, it was a blow. Her fingers tightened around the receiver.

'I understand,' she said wearily. 'Thank you.'

'Of course,' her father's lawyer explained, in his carefully modulated tone, 'once probate is finalised, as Gavin Malleson's sole heir his assets will pass to you.'

His assets. That almost made her laugh.

Her dad had never been one to scrimp and save. He'd lived lavishly. And if ever there had been money to spare it had gone to the Claudia Benzoni Foundation, the charity he'd established twelve years ago to support victims of the rare cancer that had killed his beloved wife.

Antonia had managed her father's inadequate budget, supplementing it from her summer earnings as a tour guide and interpreter. She knew how little was in his account.

Not for the first time she wished she'd been able to work full-time and put aside some more substantial savings. But her father had needed her, his health deteriorating so badly she'd been scared to leave him alone too long.

'I'm afraid it will take some time to finalise.'

It didn't matter. Her father's legacy consisted solely of debts. She'd contacted the solicitor in the vain hope of finding a way to pay them.

'Thank you very much,' she said. 'I appreciate you clarifying the details for me.'

'I'm happy to help, Ms Malleson. If there's anything else I can do to assist, please contact me.'

Antonia put the phone down slowly. Where did she go from here? The funeral had wiped out her savings. Even when she sold her mother's jewellery she'd have trouble covering the bills. There was more than just the hotel to be paid.

A band of tension clamping tight around her chest reminded her to breathe. The dull throb of pain in her temples sharpened. She stumbled to her feet, knowing she needed to *do* something, if only pace the room.

She was alone in this.

Antonia thought of her dad's car, crumpled and charred at the base of a cliff. A shudder rippled through her.

It was her fault. All her fault.

A sob rose in her throat. She should have *been* there with him. She'd promised to drive him that morning. Had arranged to meet him early. But she'd let him down.

He was dead because of her. Guilt racked her. She clenched her hands, remembering.

It had started with Stuart Dexter. For the last fortnight wherever she'd turned there he'd been, watching her with a hunger that made her skin crawl. She'd only gone out with him that night because she'd fallen for his line about discussing concerns for her father.

She'd fended him off at the nightclub, thought she could handle him. That was before he'd offered to drive her back to the hotel and she'd been foolish enough to agree.

In the dark confines of the car he'd lunged at her, using

his weight and the cramped space to pin her beneath him. He'd tried to force her into intimacy. She'd only just escaped, her shirt torn and her heart pounding in distress and fear. She'd spent the night pacing, wondering whether to call the police, wondering how to tell her dad the man he trusted had attacked her. Eventually sleep had claimed her around dawn, and she'd slept through the alarm. *Slept till the police came to the door with news of her father.*

If only she'd been there that morning there would have been no accident. He wouldn't have died alone.

The walls closed in as horror stifled her breath and blurred her vision.

In a surge of energy she pocketed her key card, grabbed her coat and plunged out of the door. Not bothering with the lift, she hurried down the stairs and into the foyer, desperate to get outside, into the fresh air.

'Careful!' A deep voice growled in her ears. Strong hands on her arms pulled her up short as she catapulted into the hard, warm wall of a masculine chest.

Antonia inhaled a new scent, subtle and spicy, and felt the warmth of it unfurl in her lungs. Her hands splayed against finest cashmere in a deep blue. The heat of his chest penetrated her palms, shocking her into tingling awareness. She hadn't felt anything so warm in a week.

Automatically she went to step back, but his grip held firm, not releasing her. Frowning, she looked up.

At a few inches under six feet, she was usually at eye level with most men. Yet her gaze lifted higher and higher. This man must be over half a foot taller than she was.

But it wasn't his height, or even his impressive shoulders that made Antonia stare. It was the way his azure-blue gaze held hers. Heat shimmered between them, a tangible yet invisible link.

Her eyes widened at the instant connection.

It was him. The man she'd seen at the club that night and again yesterday. He'd watched the funeral. She'd caught a glimpse of him several times before that too, but always at a distance.

A safe distance.

For there was something in his eyes that spoke of danger. A focus, an awareness that panicked her, made her want to thrash out of his hold and flee back to the sanctuary of her room.

Her heartbeat thudded loud in her ears and her breath caught on an indrawn hiss.

It wasn't simply fear of the unknown she felt. Nor even reaction to the absolute focus of his stare. It was the instant realisation that she was *drawn* to him. To this stranger with the bold face now set hard in stern lines.

Emotion swirled and rippled through her. Meeting those eyes was like waking from a foggy dream to face stunning reality.

'You can let me go now.' Her voice was a husky whisper and she swallowed, trying to moisten her dry mouth.

His eyes followed the convulsive movement, and Antonia almost choked as a rush of heat scalded her throat. The air between them sizzled. How could his long silent look be so…aware? So sexually potent?

His gaze trawled up to her mouth and Antonia's breathing grew shallow.

It was her imagination. It had to be. She'd been stared at by lots of men, but she'd never felt anything like this. Obviously her emotions were haywire after the stress of this last week.

Antonia pulled back, as if she could break his hold. Anxiety skittered up her spine as his large hands remained where they were, warmly encircling her upper arms.

Then his eyes met hers, and she realised he'd read her

fear. One dark eyebrow arched up on his tanned face. His hands dropped away.

And still he didn't speak. Belatedly Antonia realised that her hands remained spread across his chest. Her fingers had even curled into the fine wool, as if to anchor her close to the solid wall of muscle beneath. The steady beat of his heart vibrated against her right palm.

Hastily Antonia lifted her hands and stepped back.

Instantly the bustle of new arrivals intruded into her consciousness. The sound of a child giggling, and of a mixture of voices conversing in French, German and Spanish.

There was a blur of movement in the periphery of her vision, yet her gaze remained snagged on his.

'Ms Malleson.' His voice was a deep rumble that prickled the hairs on her nape. 'How fortuitous.'

The skittish impulse to run still pumped through her veins. Antonia ignored it. Despite the disturbing fact that he knew her name, there could be nothing to fear from him here in a busy hotel foyer.

'I'm afraid you have the advantage of me, Mr…'

'Benton. Rafe Benton.'

There was something about his voice that tweaked her curiosity. Not just its richness, but the hint of an accent. Not British, though close. Not American either.

Instinct told her it would be safer not to indulge her curiosity. Far better to put some distance between them.

'Well, Mr Benton, I'm on my way out so—'

'You're going out in that?'

She followed his gaze and saw a blur of white outside the windows. They were in the middle of a snowstorm and she hadn't noticed. No fresh air for her, then. She'd have to pace her room while she worked through her problems.

'Maybe not.' She turned, ready to head up the stairs.

'Wait.' He spoke quietly, yet instinctively Antonia responded to his tone of command. She paused with her foot on the first step.

'I want to talk with you.'

Slowly she turned, unwilling to face that pinioning blue gaze. Then she summoned her courage and met his eyes. His scrutiny seared her but she refused to be cowed.

'I can't imagine why.'

'Can't you?'

'No.'

Maybe with those killer looks and that untamed air he was used to women fawning over him.

Antonia wasn't in the mood. Despite what her uneven pulse might indicate, she wasn't impressed. She'd had enough of men who saw her as a commodity to be possessed.

'Now, if you'll excuse me, Mr Benton, I'll—'

'And what if I don't? Excuse you, that is.'

What? Antonia felt her jaw loosen in surprise. Who did he think he was?

She'd placed that trace of an accent now. Faint but distinctive. This brash stranger was Australian. Yet surely they learned basic courtesy Down Under?

'What's your problem?' she asked bluntly, more bluntly than usual. Something about this man sliced right through the social niceties. Had he been following her?

She glanced across to Herr Weber, busy supervising his staff in the foyer. The sight was reassuring. She only had to call out if she needed help.

Rafe Benton crossed his arms over his chest. The action emphasised the sheer physicality of his big frame. Antonia stood firm against the desire to back away a pace.

'No problem. Not for *me*.'

Had she imagined his emphasis on the last word?

'I have business to discuss with you.'

Ah, that was it. One of her father's creditors. It was almost a relief to identify him as something so mundane— though it meant another bill to pay. For a moment there she'd been really unnerved by his unblinking scrutiny.

'*Private* business,' he reiterated.

Antonia drew a slow breath and stiffened her spine. 'Of course,' she said finally. 'Let's go to the lounge and we can discuss your business.'

He didn't budge, merely shook his head. 'What I have to say is private. The lounge and bar are full of people avoiding the bad weather.'

And there was no privacy to be had here in the foyer.

'Then let's schedule our meeting for later—'

'This can't wait. Your suite is private. We'll go there.' He gestured to the stairs behind her. 'Unless you'd rather take the lift?'

He had a nerve, inviting himself to her room. As if she was in the habit of letting strangers into her private space. Especially strangers like him, who exuded testosterone the way a blaze gave off heat.

'That's not possible.' Her voice was jerky with indignation.

'Oh, I think you'll find it more than possible, Ms Malleson.' His voice lowered to a deep purr that brushed across her skin like velvet. Yet there was an undertone of honed steel. 'In fact, I'd call it advisable.'

She was shaking her head when he reached into his pocket and took out a paper. He held it in front of her.

It was a receipt from a hotel. *This* hotel.

Antonia's jaw sagged as she read it, then reread it. What she saw there turned her pulse into a racing tattoo. Finally, reluctantly, she lifted her eyes to his.

Rafe Benton had paid, in cash, for the suite she and her father had occupied these last weeks. Not only had he covered the outstanding amount, but he'd paid for the rooms up till the end of the week.

'I've bought your debt, Ms Malleson. I think you agree I have a right to see the rooms I've paid for. Don't you?'

CHAPTER TWO

His large hand was firm as he urged her towards the stairs. Antonia dug her heels in. Across the foyer she saw Herr Weber, and lifted her hand to signal for assistance.

The manager caught her glance, but instead of coming to her aid he looked embarrassed, a dull flush colouring his cheeks. Quickly he turned to speak to the concierge.

Slowly Antonia's hand dropped to her side.

'You won't get any help from your admirer Weber.' Rafe Benton's tone was dismissive. 'Once he understood I was paying, he realised you were off-limits.'

Off-limits? Antonia's head whirled as she tried to absorb what he was saying.

'You mean he thinks we're…? That you've paid this because…?'

'It doesn't matter what he thinks,' Rafe Benton said. 'Just that he understands this is between you and me.'

'*What?*' She spun round to face him. 'What is between us? I don't *know* you. Why should you pay for my suite?'

'Why don't we go upstairs and discuss this away from curious ears?'

Antonia saw the tilt of his head towards the other side of the room, where a couple had emerged from the restaurant and watched them with barely concealed interest.

* * *

Rafe looked down into her startled face. There was colour in her cheeks now, and it suited her. No longer the ice queen.

Slowly she turned, and he saw fire spark golden in her brown eyes. Her full, cupid's bow lips primmed into a narrow line of displeasure. Her stare might have shrivelled a lesser man to cinders. It was the sort of look the moneyed elite reserved for upstart underlings.

He repressed a smile as anticipation stirred deep in his belly. And lower.

She'd learn.

It would give him great pleasure to educate Antonia Malleson about the wielding of real power. Call it an added perk, but right now the idea of teaching her a lesson in humility was almost as gratifying as the prospect of his larger, far more important plans.

He was human enough, man enough, to enjoy the prospect of her compliance. Of bending her to his will and his pleasure.

Oh, yes. Already he was looking forward to *that*.

'Let me assure you I have no intention of ravishing you as soon as we get over the threshold.' He watched her eyes widen and her mouth round in astonishment.

'I still don't—'

'I'm not a patient man, Ms Malleson, and I don't have much time. I'll give you a choice. We can sort this out in the privacy of your apartments. Or we can do it right here, within earshot of whoever happens to be passing.'

Of course she capitulated. Yet it was fascinating watching pride war with common sense in those lustrous eyes. She took her time about agreeing. A full thirty seconds. He counted them.

Selfish, shallow, mercenary—just like Dexter. She was the perfect tool for revenge against his father.

But, more than that, Antonia Malleson was fast becoming a very private challenge.

Antonia swiped her room card and pushed open the door, conscious of his looming presence behind her. She told herself he deliberately used his size to intimidate her. A hint of threat hung between them, but she ignored it, assuring herself his aggressive air was intentional—part of his plan to get back the money her father owed.

But if he was a creditor, why pay her account?

Whatever his purpose, he wouldn't harm her. There'd been witnesses to their meeting downstairs. Then she remembered how Herr Weber had avoided eye contact, and a thread of anxiety spun through her.

'Are we going in, or do you intend to discuss our business here in the corridor?'

Antonia's slumping shoulders straightened at the sarcasm in his voice. She entered the room, flicking on the lights, and stood aside, gesturing for him to precede her.

Silently he strode past her, straight to the centre of the sitting room. There he stood, taking in the luxurious suite. The traditional woodwork that teamed surprisingly well with the latest Italian leather lounge furniture. The air of refined yet sumptuous comfort that attracted a steady clientele to this prestigious boutique hotel.

'Very pleasant,' he murmured, glancing at the state-of-the-art entertainment unit that took up one vast wall.

Antonia didn't miss the edge of cynicism in his words, but she had more important things to worry about.

'Who *are* you?' She shut the door and walked across the room to stand watching him.

'I told you. Rafe Benton.' He strolled to the other side of the room and, without asking, straight into a bedroom. She hurried to the doorway, watching him give the luxurious bathroom a cursory glance, then turn his attention to the vast bed with its ivory satin spread.

Her hands curled into fists at his presumption and at the knowledge she couldn't eject him from the premises. He was infinitely stronger than she, and the hard edge to his jaw, the expression on his brooding face, told her she'd be a fool to try pushing him out of the door.

She had no hope of getting him to leave until he'd said whatever he had to say.

'*What* are you, then?' A professional debt collector? He had the daunting power to persuade anyone to cough up money they owed. Yet his clothes were of the finest quality—made to measure, if she was any judge. Besides, he looked like a man used to giving orders, not roughing up recalcitrant debtors.

He slanted an inscrutable look from under dark brows and she stiffened.

'I'm the man who's paid for your accommodation here. That gives me the right to inspect the…premises.'

But it wasn't the premises he was surveying. His gaze dropped from hers, lingered on her lips, then slowly, infinitesimally slowly, travelled down her dark sweater, over the swell of her hips and further, all the way to her boots. That look made her wish she hadn't dropped her overcoat onto a chair. It made her feel that there was nothing protecting her from his inspection.

Beneath the plain cotton of her bra, the comfortable stretch fabric of her top and the light knit of her sweater, her nipples puckered and tightened. Her breasts felt heavy, as if weighted by his look. A strange tingling sensation spread across her chest, and lower.

Panic flared as she tried to rationalise her body's reaction. She couldn't be aroused by his blatant stare, could she?

Then, suddenly, she was looking straight into vivid blue

eyes that had lost their chilly reserve. A jolt of energy sheared through her, tightening every muscle.

'This looks very comfortable,' he murmured, his gesture encompassing the room, but most especially the wide bed right beside him. 'Will we have our chat here?'

'No!' She almost choked on the word. 'We'll use the sitting room.' Antonia spun round and stalked out, ignoring what could have been a low chuckle behind her.

This had gone far enough. No matter who he was, the man had no right to bait her. She went straight to the phone and lifted the receiver.

'I wouldn't do that, if I were you.' Suddenly Rafe Benton was beside her. He didn't reach out, but she stilled.

'Tell me what you want or I'll have the police up here.'

He raised his brows as if in surprise, then nodded. 'All right. Take a seat.'

Without waiting for her, he subsided onto one of the long sofas. The black leather was a perfect foil for the deep blue of his sweater, and for those eyes that surveyed her so steadily.

Antonia put the receiver down and sat on a nearby chair. She perched upright on the edge of the seat.

'I have a proposition for you.'

She frowned. That didn't sound like a creditor.

'Go on.'

'I've paid your account here as a sign of my goodwill.'

Looking at his long body, sprawled so comfortably across the sofa, Antonia read assurance, power and easy confidence. No sign of anything as soft or generous as goodwill. Though in the depth of that suddenly hooded gaze there was something else, and it made her blood pump faster. Some spark of…excitement? No. Anticipation.

'Go on,' she urged, watching him with a wary, unblinking stare.

'I'll be in Europe for the next six months. Mainly in London.' With one outstretched hand he drew lazy circles on the fine-grained leather. His fingers were long, supple and slow moving. For a crazy moment Antonia felt a circle of heat on the bare flesh of her neck, as if he'd touched her.

Her breath shortened, but she sat rigidly still, waiting.

'I'll be working most of the time, but I'll want some company too. Feminine company.'

Antonia's forehead knitted in confusion. He was *lonely*?

She rejected the idea instantly. For all his insolent demeanour, his deliberate rejection of the social niceties, Rafe Benton wasn't the sort to pine for companionship. She'd bet all the money she didn't have that he was usually the centre of attention. He had the indisputable take-charge air of a leader—of someone who didn't give two pins for what others thought or did. His bold looks would bring women flocking to him. All he'd have to do was click his fingers and he'd be surrounded by feminine company.

'I'm afraid you've lost me.'

His lips curved up in a tantalising glimmer of a smile. Just a hint of one. Antonia sucked in her breath as its force hit her and shock waves rippled through her unprepared body.

It wasn't a warm smile, or a friendly one. There was an edge of mockery to it, an almost wolfish sharpness that made him look far too predatory. Yet still she was mesmerised, watching breathlessly as his eyes glittered brighter. Grooves appeared, bracketing his firm mouth, enhancing the strong symmetry of his features.

What would be the effect if he smiled in genuine affection or amusement?

'Ah, then I'll cut straight to the chase.' His fingers stilled against the back of the sofa and she sensed his focus sharpen, though he didn't appear to move a muscle.

'I want you to become my mistress.'

Antonia blinked, focusing on his lips. Had she heard him right? Surely not. It was impossible.

'I'm sorry, I—'

'No need to be sorry, sweetheart. All you have to do is say yes.'

'I…' Her breath escaped on a sigh of disbelief. She curled her hands into fists, pressing her fingernails against her palms, as if that prickling pain could wake her from this bizarre nightmare. 'I don't even *know* you!'

'Ah, I was forgetting. Where I come from I don't have much need of introduction.' He stretched his legs out. 'Rafe Benton. Thirty. Australian. CEO of Pacifica Holdings. I live in Brisbane, but I also have apartments in New York and Tokyo. Bank balance—' his eyes narrowed '—healthy enough to keep you in luxury.'

He paused, as if waiting for her to respond. But for the life of her Antonia was speechless. *Her*, a rich man's mistress? The idea was outrageous.

'I like my women good-looking, intelligent and amenable. I don't have patience for tantrums or tears, and I expect absolute exclusivity. I don't share.' His eyes flashed a warning. 'I want a companion who can hold her own in any social situation: formal dinners, business functions and balls. Someone with the requisite social graces.'

She moistened her lips to speak, to stop him, but he continued regardless.

'My tastes are relatively simple. I expect passion in a lover.' Again that feral half-smile that sent a tingle of warning through her. 'I'm not into anything kinky. Though I'm more than willing to experiment.' His voice deepened. 'In appropriate circumstances.'

The tingle morphed into a shudder as his gaze travelled over her and heat licked her skin. More, a tiny twist of feminine response awakened deep inside her dormant body.

Antonia was appalled.

'In return you'd have six months of living totally at my expense—and I can be very generous if I'm satisfied.'

The glitter in his eyes told her he was talking about sex. What else?

The silence lengthened as Antonia absorbed the shock reverberating through her.

Who the hell did he think she was?

'I'm not some cheap tart,' she blurted out when she eventually found her voice.

'Of course not, sweetheart. I didn't for a moment think there was anything cheap about you.'

'Don't call me *sweetheart*!' Raw fury lent volume to her voice. Her suddenly unlocked emotions roiled to the surface and she felt overwhelmingly, gloriously furious. The ice-cold numbness of the last week had shattered, smashed by a flood of hatred for this arrogant, self-opinionated jerk. She shot to her feet, hands on her hips as she stared down at his rangy form sprawled so indolently before her.

'What do you think gives you the right to insult me like that?'

'Hardly an insult. Simply a business proposition.'

Unbelievable! She'd never met a man with such gall.

Antonia's heart thudded painfully hard, its rhythm jerky and out of kilter.

'Then you can take your business elsewhere. I don't know how things are done in Australia, but you're way out of line here. I'm not for sale.'

Slowly he tucked his long legs under him and rose to his full height. At any other time the force of the warning look in his eyes might have made her step away, but not now. She was beyond anything as mundane as caution.

'Ah. My mistake.' He shrugged those broad shoulders. 'I

overheard some of your conversation with the manager and I know you're short of cash. You have a wait till the next quarter's allowance comes through.' He paused. 'What happened? Did you spend it all on designer clothes and parties? Or do you have more expensive habits? You don't look like a user, but it can be hard to tell.'

His mock sympathy made her grit her teeth. How dared he talk to her like that? She wasn't going to share intimate information with him. Like the fact that she didn't have an allowance and she was virtually destitute.

'My finances aren't your concern. Nor are my habits. But let me put your mind at rest. I don't use drugs.'

'Good. I thought you too intelligent for that. As for the cash…' He raised his hand, as if placating her. 'Of course you won't have a problem paying me what you owe for this luxurious accommodation. Or your other debts.'

'Other debts?' Her indignation bled away.

'Your friend Weber helpfully mentioned your creditors.' His teeth flashed in a ruthless smile. 'I've done you a favour and bought the debts. Now you only have one creditor to deal with: me.'

Antonia's heart plunged. No wonder she'd had trouble tracking down all the money her father owed.

'How much are they worth?'

'You don't know?' One dark eyebrow rose. 'Enough. I'll send you a full account.'

Her throat closed as she saw the implacable light in his eyes. She knew the amount was large—larger than she could manage. And this man was no benefactor.

'Does your silence mean you *can't* pay me?'

'I…' She swallowed her pride, wishing she could tell him to go to hell. 'Are you saying you'll demand payment?'

She held her breath as he surveyed her. A swift, calculating look that made her want to cringe. But she had to face him down. Instinctively she understood that she couldn't let him see how threatened she felt.

'The debt is genuine. Of course it has to be paid.' He paused, and she heard the blood rush in her ears. 'Though if you were my mistress I'd feel obliged to write it off.'

A spasm of shock tightened Antonia's body.

'Why me?' she said abruptly, her head spinning. Surely a man with his looks and wealth didn't need to buy a lover?

He paced closer. Suddenly the room seemed short of oxygen, as if his proximity sucked the air from her lungs.

'I saw you and I wanted you.'

To her horrified disbelief the simple statement evoked a tremor of unwanted excitement, piercing right through the very core of her.

He reached out and stroked his index finger from her temple down her cheek, lingering at the corner of her mouth, where a flicker of response trembled across her nerve-endings. Then he slid his hand down, cupping her chin in his warm palm, raising her face so that she met the full force of his glittering stare.

Her pulse jerked erratically and her breath came in short, distressed puffs that she couldn't control. His spicy scent was heady and enticing, reminding her of the way his hard body had felt when they'd collided. Strong. Masculine. Tempting.

What was happening to her? According to the men she'd dated, she was far too reserved. Too unaffected by the lure of pheromones and a healthy male.

The way her body revved into full awareness, just from being close to Rafe Benton, was unprecedented.

'It's no crime for a man to go for what he wants,' he murmured, his head tilting infinitesimally closer. 'Or would you prefer I dressed this up with pretty words that don't mean anything? Pretend I'm looking for something longer term? Lie to you about my intentions?'

'No!' To her horror, Antonia was mesmerised by the way his mouth moved as he spoke, his lips almost hypnotic while he whispered his outrageous questions. His voice had lowered to a burr that raised the hairs on her arms, as if her body expected…something.

'Good. I prefer to say what I think. It saves a lot of time.' His lips quirked in a way that brought those sexy grooves to the corners of his mouth.

Antonia expelled the breath she'd unconsciously held. Desperately she reminded herself that he was everything she despised: pushy, domineering, acting like God's gift to women. As if she was his for the asking.

'So, Ms Malleson. You don't like what I have to say. But you don't want to pay your debt.' Slowly he shook his head. 'I have to say I'm disappointed.'

Antonia's tongue cleaved to the roof of her mouth as embarrassment heated her cheeks and throat. 'First I need to see the paperwork. Perhaps then we could discuss a schedule of payments?'

His eyes narrowed.

'Did I mention that if you stay as my mistress for six months, not only will I cancel your debt, I'll provide a substantial cash settlement when we part?'

He tilted his head, and for a horrified moment she thought he was going to kiss her. Instead his lips grazed her ear, his breath a hot, disturbingly erotic caress as he whispered a sum so large it made her freeze in disbelief.

'You have to be kidding!'

'I don't joke about my money. Or my women,' he murmured. Then his teeth closed round her earlobe and he tugged gently, provocatively. Instantly darts of fire arrowed to her nipples, her groin, and she caught her breath on an audible gasp. Such a tiny scrape of teeth on flesh and yet she felt branded.

'Don't!' She shoved at his shoulders. It was like trying to push away a boulder.

'Sorry.' He didn't sound at all apologetic. 'Did I hurt you?' His tongue flicked out to soothe the place where his teeth had grazed her.

Something shifted in the pit of Antonia's stomach and her knees began to melt. Her hands curved in against his shoulders, seeking support as she sagged.

'Is that a no?'

She jerked her head away, appalled at this uncharacteristic weakness flooding her. She'd never felt anything like it.

What had he done to her?

His proposition was an insult, his attitude obnoxious. He made her fume at his arrogance. Yet her body responded blatantly, hungrily to his touch.

'I want you to leave. *Now!*'

She felt him straighten, his hand drop from her chin. Yet the warmth of his touch lingered, marking her skin. Belatedly she let go of his shoulders, furious that she had so few defences against his raw physical allure.

'Tell me one thing.' His voice seemed to come from a long way above her.

'What?' Antonia refused to look at him, choosing instead to focus on the blur of white outside the window.

'Why are you refusing me?'

She looked up at that, stunned that he even had to ask. Anger surged again, thankfully replacing that absurd weakness in her blood.

'You think I'm in the habit of sleeping with men for money?'

He shrugged. 'You've been keeping Stuart Dexter company, but you don't have the dewy-eyed look of a woman in love. He must be thirty years your senior. Don't tell me his fatal charm attracted you. It has to be his money. After all—' he flicked a glance around the luxurious room '—you definitely have champagne tastes.'

Antonia took a step back from him, hands grasped together so tightly they shook.

'Well? Are you going to deny it?'

He thought she was *encouraging* Dexter?

The idea was risible. She'd only put up with Stuart's presence because of her father. Dexter was involved in the financial management of the charity that had meant so much to her dad.

Antonia blinked to clear her vision. For two weeks she'd suffered Stuart's leers and his smarmy suggestions for the sake of her father. Nothing else. After what he'd done, just the thought of the man curdled her stomach.

Rafe stared down into her averted face and knew he'd hit a nerve. It didn't take the pulse jerking at the base of her neck or the flat line of her compressed lips to give her away.

He'd seen her rich brown eyes shimmer, over-bright, before she turned her head away.

Vulnerability? From someone mercenary enough to target a wealthy man so she could have an easy life?

He wondered.

No. She was a superlative actress. Playing on a man's sympathy was part of her stock in trade, especially with her damnably beautiful face. She must have used a trick or two to hook Dexter—the man was obsessed with her. It was obvious from the way he watched her every move, with a raw appetite that turned Rafe's stomach.

Yet obviously his father wasn't generous enough with his money, since she was short of cash. No doubt Dexter's looming financial woes were restricting his expenditure. Rafe intended to take advantage of that fact.

Why didn't she accept the proposition he'd just offered

her? That intrigued him. Was she holding out for a better offer?

He'd felt her reaction as he caressed her earlobe. She hadn't been able to conceal the tremor of desire that juddered through her. Her instant, undeniable reaction had been an incredible turn-on. His body had hardened immediately as he'd realised what a sensuous, responsive woman Antonia Malleson was.

'You're not denying it,' he taunted.

'I don't have to justify myself to you,' she snapped, glaring up at him with a razor-sharp look that should have sliced him to shreds. 'You're *nothing* to me.'

'Nothing?'

Call it arrogance, but he couldn't believe her. Even he had been surprised at the intensity of the erotic sizzle between them. Such instant awareness was rare. It fuelled a sudden recklessness in him.

'Oh, no, my fine lady. I wouldn't call it nothing,' he said, bending his head.

'What are you doing?' Her voice was a breathless gasp.

'Clarifying the difference between *nothing* and *something.*'

Her reactions were too slow. By the time she tried to push him away he'd captured the back of her head in one hand. His fingers sank into the satiny invitation of her hair, his other arm wrapping round her waist.

'Relax,' he murmured, already anticipating the heady pleasure of her lips against his. 'This won't hurt a bit.'

CHAPTER THREE

His mouth on hers muffled Antonia's scathing retort.

She struggled against him, but his hold was implacable, unbreakable. The more she tried to get free, the more restrictive was his embrace. A granite cliff would have been more pliable than this mountain of a man.

Who did he think he was, with his outrageous proposition and now his use of superior strength to force a kiss?

Tension spiralled through her as he crowded near, his thighs surrounding hers, his mouth against her closed lips, his hand anchoring her head, one long, strong arm wrapped around her waist.

He was so close, held her so immobile, that she couldn't even get leverage to bring her knee up against him. He contained her struggling form with mortifying ease.

Finally she realised resistance was futile. She held herself stiff as a board, keeping her eyes wide open, refusing to capitulate.

Strangely, it was annoyance she felt. Outrage, not fear. Not like when Dexter had groped her and panic had swelled, making her frantic to escape.

Rafe Benton was more subtle, for all his apparent directness. This man was a wily tactician, a long-term strategist. Not a smash and grab thug like Dexter.

It took her several moments to realise he wasn't using force. His hold was firm, but not tight. His arm at her back held her close, but not brutally so. He seemed content to tease her lips with a gentle, coaxing caress, rather than bruise her into surrender.

All she had to do was stand here, still and unyielding, and he'd stop soon.

She hoped he'd stop soon.

Something about the encompassing warmth of his body threatened to make her relax into his embrace. His lips were surprisingly soft, surprisingly tender.

He took her bottom lip between his teeth, tugging gently, and sensation shot through her, straight down to her breasts, then lower, arrowing to her feminine core.

Antonia started, horrified at the fizz of awareness building in her blood. Like a slow, betraying sizzle.

She pushed her hands against his chest, trying to propel him back, away from her. He was immovable. She splayed her fingers wide and tried again. Nothing. Just the steady beat of his life pulse beneath her fingers.

'Mmm,' he murmured against her mouth. 'Touch me.'

Touch him? She'd give him more than a touch when she'd finished with him!

'I—'

Her pithy retort turned into a mumbled moan as she realised her mistake. His tongue slipped into her mouth as she opened her lips and suddenly the world rocked on its foundations. His arm at her back, his legs surrounding hers, were the only supports keeping her upright.

Antonia's head swam as he delved in, caressing her tongue, her mouth, with a seductively insistent expertise that made warning bells jangle in her ears.

It felt…it felt… Thought atrophied as pleasure mounted. Antonia struggled to escape the fog of sheer physical enjoyment that he'd conjured. She fought not to respond to the slow, evocative caress of his mouth, his teasing tongue, his seductive lips.

She battled the liquid heat of desire that spread through her loosening body and blazed a trail of fire to the secret place between her legs. She squeezed her thighs together, trying to counteract the ache that made her want to melt against him and demand more.

She tried to focus on something else. On the dark gleaming hair, combed ruthlessly back from his face. On the intriguing scent of his skin, spicy, but now overlaid with a hint of musk that made her nostrils flare.

No!

She could withstand this onslaught. Her pride depended on it. Despite the incredible sensations of warmth and pleasure his kiss evoked, the promise of sheer ecstasy.

His hand moved in her hair, tugging at her neat chignon, threading through the long tresses as they tumbled round her shoulders. His touch was leisurely, as if he enjoyed the caress as much as she. He massaged her scalp and her eyelids lowered, her fingers holding onto the soft wool of his pullover.

He bent her back against his arm. Now he had unfettered access, kissing her with a thoroughness that obliterated everything except the recognition of pleasure.

Antonia moaned as his tongue danced against hers and her nipples hardened, eager for the brush of his hard chest. Her eyes flickered shut as she gave herself up to the inevitable, to burgeoning delight. To the sheer comfort of being held safe in strong arms, rocked close against his solid body. To the building excitement of a kiss that was now mutual.

Somehow her hands had slid up and over his shoulders, to lock in the silky softness of his hair, to mould his skull with fingers that trembled. She angled her mouth against his, pressing close as need notched higher and her pulse accelerated into overdrive.

Then, without warning, he stepped away. The lush, sensuous pleasure ended abruptly and cool air rushed in between them. His hands moved to her shoulders, as if he knew she needed support to stand upright.

She resented the fact that she did. Her knees quivered and her legs felt like jelly. A wave of horror flooded her as she realised she'd not only let him kiss her, but had given herself up to his embrace. For a moment she'd even found *comfort* in his closeness!

She looked up at him through slitted eyes and realised he was as cool and distant as before.

All except for the flared nostrils and the pronounced movement of his chest as he dragged in deep breaths.

It was small consolation to see he'd been affected too. She felt dizzy, shocked by his audacity and by the depth of her own response. How could that have happened?

'No, you're wrong,' he murmured, with a smugness that made Antonia want to jam her fist into the hard wall of his abdomen. 'I wouldn't say there was *nothing* between us.' He tilted his head to one side, as if musing. 'In fact I'd say we definitely had something going there.'

Antonia's wrath almost boiled over then. But she knew that any further loss of control on her part would be a victory for this brute.

'You've got to be joking.' It cost her a lot to keep her voice cool and casual, not overplay her hand. 'I was just curious to see if your over-sized ego made a difference to the way you kiss.'

Brilliant fire blazed in his blue gaze and she hurried on, turning to put some much-needed distance between them.

'As for having something going...' She paused, surreptitiously clearing her throat. 'That would be you, Mr Benton.' She stepped away, hoping he couldn't see how badly her legs shook. 'It's time for you to leave.'

Carefully she walked to the entrance and pulled the door open, her hand clammy on the doorknob.

For endless seconds there was no sound but the rapid thud of her pulse echoing in her ears. He didn't move, but stood in the centre of the room, watching her. She refused to meet his gaze. If she did she knew her poise would crumble as a hot tide of mortification flooded her cheeks.

Please. Let him go. Antonia didn't have the strength to deal with him. Not now. Not on top of everything else. Her pride was in tatters and she still reeled from his onslaught on her senses.

Finally he moved, covering the distance between them with a few long-legged strides. He paused in front of her, head inclined towards hers, as if trying to catch her eye.

Stubbornly she resisted. She wasn't a masochist.

The masculine scents of musk and spice tickled her nostrils, and Antonia panicked as a bolt of desire shot through her. She locked her knees to steady herself, waiting.

'As for my proposition—'

'I hope you don't expect me to thank you for that!' She spoke through gritted teeth.

'The offer still stands. For a limited time.' He paused, probably waiting for her to query him or look at him, or, Heaven help her, beg for another of his kisses.

'The suite is paid for till the end of the week. You have two days before you have to vacate. I'll be back then for my money. You can give me your answer at the same time.'

Then he was gone, striding off down the corridor.

Antonia was still trying to come up with a smart rejoinder, something that would put him in his place, when she finally remembered to shut the door.

The problem was she didn't think anything she said *could* cut him down to size. His ego was so massive, his assurance so ingrained, that her feeble ripostes had no impact at all.

His proposition was pure insult. Had he realised how demeaning it was when he'd proposed such an arrangement? Or did he simply not care?

Her pride revolted. More, she felt sullied. She'd been surrounded for so long by people who cared more for their material possessions, their status and having a good time than about fidelity and love. She'd seen too much of the seamier side of life at resorts like this, travelling with small exclusive travel groups.

Her parents' marriage had been like a beacon shining above the dross. The love they'd shared had been wonderful. Long ago she'd vowed to follow their example, to give herself only to the man she loved.

She'd made one youthful mistake. A painful error of judgement that had torn at her self-esteem and her heart. But she'd recovered, all the more determined to hold out for her dream. No second best for her.

Rafe Benton had picked the wrong woman for his plans.

Two days. He had a nerve! He probably expected her to welcome him with open arms just because he kissed like an angel. No, make that a demon. For all his tenderness when he'd held her, Rafe Benton was far too ruthless and sexually experienced to masquerade as a celestial being.

Antonia was totally out of her depth with him.

That was why it was imperative she find a way to cover her father's debt and get out of here. *Quickly.*

Where could she get a significant amount of cash in just two days?

A few hours later Antonia sat in the hotel lounge, pouring tea. Hopefully the steaming brew would warm her. The flash of fury she'd experienced confronting Rafe Benton, the raw anger and—she hated to admit it—the shameful flush of feminine response to his devastating kiss, had long since seeped away.

The creeping numbness of desolation was back, icing up her body and freezing her attempts to think her way out of her problems. A detailed account of money owing had arrived within an hour of Rafe Benton's departure. It confirmed what she'd guessed. She couldn't meet the debt.

She'd contacted her bank, and some other financial institutions, but with no success. Her seasonal work and lack of assets made her a bad risk. She needed another solution—fast.

At worst she'd brazen it out and insist on a schedule of payments. She refused to countenance his proposition.

Antonia was exhausted, her mind turning fruitlessly in well-worn grooves. Despite her efforts to concentrate, she kept circling back to the accident. If only she'd been driving…

It was a relief when her mobile phone rang, dragging her back to the present.

'Antonia? It's Emma.'

'Emma!' Antonia sank back in her chair. What she needed right now was someone to talk to. Her friend Emma had perfect timing. 'It's great to hear your voice.'

'How are you doing?'

She grimaced. 'I'm holding up.'

'I'm sorry I couldn't make it to the funeral. I—'

'Please, don't apologise again. Honestly, no one could expect you to fly out here. You're incredibly busy at the moment. Anyway, I'd rather spend time with you when I get back to England.' Antonia shivered. She never wanted to come back to this place again. 'In the meantime, it's so good to talk to you.'

'Yes. I… We need to talk.' Something about Emma's tone jarred, and Antonia straightened in her seat, the back of her neck prickling in foreboding.

'Is something wrong?' Suddenly this didn't sound like a catch-up chat.

'Yes. Yes, there is.' Emma paused so long Antonia felt the hairs rise on her nape. 'I'm so sorry. You don't need this right now, Antonia, but I can't think what else to do. I'd never forgive myself if I didn't tell you and then…'

'Emma, please. The tension is killing me.'

'Sorry. I just… It's about your father.'

'My dad?' Antonia frowned.

'Yes.' Emma dragged in a deep breath, clearly audible over the line. 'Someone recently withdrew money from one of the Foundation accounts. A lot of money.'

Antonia frowned. What did Emma's work at the Claudia Benzoni Foundation have to do with her father? The Foundation had grown into a significant enterprise, assisting sufferers worldwide and funding medical research. Her father had worked tirelessly to raise money for it. He'd been a contributor, not a beneficiary.

'I'm sorry, Emma. I don't understand.'

'The money is still missing.' Emma's sombre tone set warning bells ringing.

'What do you mean, missing?'

'I mean the withdrawals were unauthorised—totally irregular. They were made using your father's access code.'

Antonia froze, her cup halfway to her lips.

'Antonia? Are you there?'

'I'm here.' Slowly she leaned forward and put her cup on the table. Her hand was unsteady and tea sloshed into the saucer. 'Withdrawals? Plural?'

'Yes. Until eight days ago someone was systematically milking the account.'

Someone using her father's access code.

'You think my father took it.' It wasn't a question. The silence on the line told her exactly what Emma thought.

Yet the idea was absurd. The charity was all that had brought her father back from the brink of grief-stricken self-destruction all those years ago. Despite his conspicuous bonhomie and his avid enjoyment of the good things in life, there were only two things that had kept him going: his love for her and the prospect of saving others from the disease that had snatched away his wife.

'I'm just telling you what I know. The money is gone. I've checked and triple-checked, but there's no mistake. I don't suppose your father…?'

'No! No, he didn't. He wouldn't.' But even as she said it Antonia remembered his reckless expenditure recently, his mood swings and heightened extravagance.

Desperately she shook her head. It wasn't true. No matter how depressed he'd been—and his recent behaviour had surely been a symptom of depression over his rapidly declining health—Gavin Malleson had been an honest man.

It was unthinkable that he'd steal from the one thing that had given his life purpose.

'There has to be another explanation.'

'Of course there is,' Emma said, just a shade too brightly. 'I thought maybe you'd have some idea of what might have happened. Your father didn't mention anything?'

'No. No, he didn't.' Antonia bit her lip against a traitorous wobble. What on earth was going on?

'How much money is missing?' she asked at last.

Her eyes rounded as Emma named an enormous sum.

'You're kidding!'

'I wish. An amount like this won't be overlooked, and there's an audit coming up.'

Antonia's blood froze. 'How soon?'

'In three days. And then there'll be hell to pay.' Emma sounded almost as miserable as Antonia felt. 'You know what this will mean for the Foundation once it's public? Especially since—sorry, Antonia—it does look like your father was responsible.'

'I know,' she responded in a cracked voice.

A few years ago a scandal had rocked another major aid agency with stories of officials skimming money. The allegations of corruption had been unfounded, though there had been sloppy management practices. But the damage had been done. The agency had lost the public's trust and six months later it had closed.

'Even though Dad is dead, the damage would be irreversible,' she whispered.

Gavin had been the Foundation's public face, and the press would lose no time digging up dirt—like his youthful reputation as a profligate high spender. They'd crucify his character, ignoring all the good he'd done later. The public would wonder how long he'd been skimming money.

'The Foundation would be permanently tainted. It might even fold, if it lost the public's trust.'

Antonia's body was rigid with horror as the implications sank in. Her father's reputation in his youth had been appalling. His parents had even disowned him. He'd only found stability when he married. But his attempts as an entrepreneur had failed when his wife died. Since then he'd lived off the annuity his family had settled on him years before. The press would have a field day digging that up, and if word leaked about his recent debts…

Antonia clicked the lock on the door to her suite and tottered across the room, sliding in a boneless huddle into a corner of the nearest sofa.

She was weak from the force of her nausea. She'd been

comprehensively sick in the privacy of the ladies' toilets downstairs as soon as she'd ended the call from Emma. She lifted her knees, wrapping her arms round her legs, hugging tight, as if she could stop the shudders that racked her.

The world had gone mad!

First Rafe Benton, with his outrageous proposition. That had been preposterous, horrendous.

But now it wasn't just debts she had to deal with.

She'd racked her brain to find some plausible explanation for the missing funds. She and Emma had concocted a range of scenarios to account for the withdrawals, each more implausible than the last.

And all the while, despite her obstinate denials, Antonia had harboured a seed of…doubt.

She felt disloyal admitting it. But no matter how hard she tried she couldn't ignore her father's recent erratic behaviour. The extravagant spending. And the fact that the withdrawals had stopped just before her father's death.

No! It wasn't possible! She refused to believe it.

Antonia rocked back and forth, trying to find comfort in the rhythmic motion.

Whatever it took, she had to protect her father's reputation and the wonderful work he'd done. She owed it to him, and to her mother. This was all she had left of them.

The difficulty was, protecting their memories would need far more than a simple belief in her father's honesty. She grimaced and pressed her forehead down against her knees. A few hours ago she'd thought things were bad. She hadn't known the meaning of the word!

Antonia dragged in a deep, shuddering breath. She needed a plan. There must be *something* she could do.

If she could raise the money somehow, then she could cover the charity's loss until the real culprit could be identified.

She needed time to prove her father's innocence. Nothing else mattered. But that meant getting her hands on a small fortune and depositing it with the Foundation before the audit in three days' time.

She had no collateral for a loan.

She had no prospects.

She had an impossible deadline.

How far was she willing to go to save her family name and her dad's reputation? Far enough to accept Rafe Benton's proposition?

Surely she wasn't seriously considering it?

Yet the more her tired, frantic brain searched for solutions, the more quickly she came back to him.

Could she become a mistress? A paid lover for six months to a man whose arrogance and brash ruthlessness raised her hackles? But whose touch, whose kisses, unravelled her?

Whose money she could use to protect her family.

Antonia remembered the searing intensity of his gaze just before he'd kissed her, the unprecedented way she'd responded to him. Instinctively she understood he was far more dangerous than any man she'd ever encountered.

What on earth was she going to do?

CHAPTER FOUR

RAFE stared out of the café window, his espresso untouched, his thoughts fixed again on Antonia Malleson.

Despite her desperate rearguard act, trying to appear unmoved by their kiss, Rafe hadn't been fooled. She'd come alive in his arms as only a truly aroused woman could. The passion between them had accelerated from tentative to dangerously combustible as soon as he'd breached her defences and she'd given up fighting.

The woman packed a hell of a punch. His body was tight, alert at the memory of how she'd felt against him.

Yet she'd pretended she'd felt nothing. Was it pride? He'd shown no finesse, had been almost brutal as he'd told her what he wanted. His previous lovers would have been appalled. But this was different. This woman was one of his father's set, high-living and callous. She was no innocent. Not after the way she'd encouraged his father.

She'd looked down her elegant nose at Rafe as if he'd slid out from under a rock. As if she wasn't used to mixing with anyone who called a spade a spade.

Or as if she was hiding pain.

Where had that thought come from? He frowned. When he'd held her close and tasted her honey-sweetness he'd almost believed he read vulnerability in her face and in the tightly coiled tension of her slim frame.

He dismissed the idea.

Maybe she was embarrassed at not having the cash to cover her accommodation. Dexter must be feeling the pinch already, since he hadn't bailed her out of debt. But money couldn't be a long-term problem for her. She obviously had an allowance that kept her, while others had to work for a crust. No doubt her lovers kept her supplied with luxuries.

Yet, despite all that, Antonia Malleson intrigued him as no other woman had. He rubbed his hand over his jaw.

He needed to remember she was a means to an end. A very beautiful, very tempting means to an end. White hot energy blasted through him as he thought of his mission. Of the scheme he'd put in motion since his mother's death.

As a kid, he hadn't wanted to know the father who'd rejected him before he was born. But the more he'd learned, the more inevitable it had become that there'd be a reckoning with his father one day. Now that day had arrived.

His father: Stuart Dexter. Wheeler-dealer, born with a silver spoon in his mouth. Only Dexter was no example of British *noblesse oblige*. He was selfish to the bone. He'd bartered his family name for a fortune when he'd married. Right after he'd seduced Lillian Benton, his PA, then chucked her out, with no references and no money to help raise their child.

Dexter had expected her to have an abortion. When she'd refused he'd turned his back, threatening legal action for harassment if she tried to see him again.

That was the sort of man Rafe had for a father.

The knowledge ate into him like acid.

Even so, Rafe could have ignored Dexter—except that he'd done far more. He'd all but destroyed Lillian Benton.

Memories of his mother's face, ravaged and gaunt,

haunted Rafe still. His fists clenched as he thought of the damning correspondence he'd found in her papers.

Despite the comforts he'd been able to give her at the end, when his hard work and determination had paid off so spectacularly, Rafe knew Dexter was to blame for what had gone before. *That* was unforgivable.

Ironically, it was his father who had created the opportunity for revenge. He'd made contact, proposing a joint venture. His own company was short of the ready and he wanted Rafe's money, Rafe's expertise, to help him cash in on an opportunity that would pull him out of strife.

He hadn't even bothered to find the connection between Rafe and the woman he'd seduced and then destroyed.

Rafe shoved his coffee away and stood up, too restless to sit. He grabbed his coat and stepped into the street.

A sense of rightness, of satisfaction, settled deep in his chest as he reviewed his plans. It was his duty to put an end to his father's destructive activities. To make him pay for the damage he'd done to Rafe's mother and so many other innocent people. A *family* duty.

Dexter's empire was rocky from too many dubious investments and sheer extravagance. Six months would do it. Rafe had entrusted most of his own business to hand-picked deputies while he devoted himself to the long overdue task of making Stuart Dexter pay.

His father had two weaknesses: money and women. They'd be the key to his revenge.

Shoving his hands in his pockets, Rafe turned down the street, head bent against the chill wind.

When their business was concluded Dexter would be broke and broken, his bank account empty and his ego destroyed. What gorgeous young woman would have him once he was skint?

The *coup de grâce* would be possessing the woman his

father wanted so badly. His current obsession: Antonia Malleson. Rafe would make damned sure that at every party Dexter went to, every function, there she'd be. Close, but always out of reach. Another, richer man's possession.

Rafe's mistress. How sweet the satisfaction when the old man learned she'd rejected him for his own son.

It had been so simple. A phone call from his London office had sent Dexter high-tailing it back there, eager to begin discussions on their joint venture. Since then Dexter had been incommunicado, spending the last few days in meetings he assumed would pave the way to his financial salvation.

With Dexter unavailable to help her, Antonia wouldn't be able to find the cash she owed. She didn't have the resources to withstand Rafe, and the prospect of tapping into his wealth would be irresistible. He'd allowed her time to stew on her decision, but he knew her answer already. He'd left her no alternative. He had her exactly where he wanted her.

Anticipation danced in his blood.

Rafe halted in front of her hotel. It was time to secure the woman who'd make his vengeance complete.

She unlatched the door at his first knock. He'd give her that much: she didn't try to hide.

As the door swung open he felt it again. That surge of power roaring out from his belly, up through his chest, energising his whole body. He looked down into her smooth Madonna face and *knew*. This wasn't just about revenge. Not solely about his plans to bring down his father.

He wanted Antonia Malleson. Wanted her so fiercely the knowledge pounded through him with every pulse of his blood. Even if she hadn't been Stuart Dexter's current fixation, the perfect tool in Rafe's scheme, he'd want her.

With her guarded brown eyes, her mouth a tight line, her

hair scraped into a severe knot and her face wiped clear of emotion, she looked cold and unwelcoming. Yet she was sexier than any woman he could remember. The sizzle of connection as their eyes met sent a jag of heat through him.

How convenient that personal inclination and duty should coalesce in this way.

This was going to be a real pleasure. *His* pleasure.

His gaze flitted down, taking in the high-necked shirt, her jacket, tailored trousers and high heels. She was dressed for business.

Yet the formal clothes didn't conceal the superb length of those slim legs, the curves in all the right places. And more. The inner strength that proclaimed she'd be no push-over but a challenge for any man who took her on.

The combination was tantalising. The touch-me-not air and the seductress body. His blood pumped faster.

He imagined peeling each garment from her till she was nude—all except for those high heels. A flash of pure need rocketed through him, tightening his groin.

'Hello, Antonia.'

'Mr Benton.' She nodded her head and stood back reluctantly to let him enter.

Antonia was glad she had hold of the doorknob. The rumbling caress of his deep voice saying her name made her knees rock. And she was already shaky from the impact of his powerful presence.

She'd screwed up her courage, knowing she had to face him. And still she hadn't been prepared. She'd hoped her reaction to him that first time had been some weird anomaly, brought on by shock and grief.

As she'd looked up into his searingly bright eyes her heart had sunk. It had been no fluke. Even knowing the sort of man he was—one who bought women for his convenience—she couldn't deny her instant physical response to him.

She tried to despise him. But, arrogant as he was, it wasn't contempt she felt.

'So formal, *Ms Malleson*?'

He stopped far too close to her, lingering less than an arm's length away in the vestibule.

She turned and glanced in his direction, careful not to meet his eyes.

'You're here on business, Mr Benton.' She drew a slow breath. 'I reserve my first name for my friends.' Ignoring the way he stilled at her taunt, she gestured to the sofas grouped in the sitting room. 'Please, take a seat.'

Then she turned away, grateful to have her back to him as she fumbled with the doorknob, her palm suddenly slippery and her fingers unsteady.

How was she going to get through this?

She still didn't have an answer. She'd spent the last two nights sleepless. There'd been long, blank periods of grief, when she'd stared dry-eyed and wondered if she'd ever feel whole again. In between she'd grappled with the impossible calculation of the money she needed and the irreparable damage that would be done if she didn't restore it. Damage to her father's name, her mother's charity and to the innocent victims relying on the Foundation.

'Aren't you going to join me?'

She felt his words like a stroke of heat down her spine. Slowly she turned and forced herself to walk into the sitting room. Anxiety knotted her stomach and anger knitted her brow. How dared he sit there, calm as could be?

'Would you like coffee, tea?' Anything to delay the moment of reckoning.

'No, thank you.' Was that amusement in his lazy tone?

'Or something else? Some other drink,' she added quickly, when she saw the speculation in his eyes.

He lolled in his seat, completely at ease, but his gaze was intent. On *her*. Antonia felt like some prized possession up for auction, displayed on a stand for bidders to view. It nauseated her.

Her careful dressing this morning hadn't helped at all. The high heels brought her closer to his height, but that just meant she'd got the full force of his intense gaze when she'd swung open the door. The impact had punched the air from her lungs. Nor did it matter how many layers she wore. She still felt vulnerable with this man.

'I don't want anything.'

He paused long enough for her to remember to exhale, then suck in some more oxygen.

'I'm here for your answer.'

Antonia nodded, and abruptly she was sitting on the sofa opposite him. Her knees had given way. She hoped for her dignity's sake he hadn't guessed how her legs had crumpled.

She spread her hands flat on the leather beside her, trying to anchor herself, the better to fight the trembling weakness that threatened to devour her. It was more than a week since the day her world had rocked off its axis. She had to face the future, no matter how unpalatable. She had a duty to her father's memory. A responsibility.

'You've considered my proposal?'

A flash of sour gallows humour snagged her. It was hardly a proposal. That sounded so respectable—like a promise of marriage. This was definitely a *proposition*, with every sordid nuance the word could convey.

'Yes, I've considered it.' She firmed her lips, horrified at the sound of her voice, raw and unsteady. She cleared her throat and looked at the bright abstract painting on the wall behind him. Anything rather than meet his eyes.

'And…?'

'And…'

Could she do it? Sell herself, her self-respect, her dignity? Her *body*?

No! She couldn't.

There must be another way. Something she'd over-looked. Some avenue she hadn't tried. She'd work tire-lessly till she found it.

The tension locking her neck and jaw eased a fraction as she made up her mind. Relief at her decision eased her muscles and she sank back against the cushions. She still had twenty-four hours to come up with another solution— one that didn't involve giving herself to Rafe Benton.

'Did I tell you your friend Weber directed another couple of creditors my way? Rather *unsavoury* people. *Very* eager to have their debts settled.'

Fear tickled Antonia's nape as his words triggered an old memory, of menacing enforcers visiting her father years ago, after he'd gambled too freely.

'Of course,' he continued smoothly, 'you may have the resources to deal with them. And with any new matters that come to light in future.' He paused. 'No? As far as I can see, Ms Malleson, I'm your only option. And your time has just run out.'

Her shoulders sagged. Who was she kidding?

There *were* no other avenues.

Who'd believe in her father's innocence if there was a trail of debt enforcers clamouring for settlement? She needed help covering those debts, let alone dealing with the missing charity funds.

There was only one way to wipe the slate clean. To ensure that her father's reputation remained intact and her mother's charity safe. Only *she* could fix this.

Her fingers clawed into the soft leather. If only she had the courage of her convictions—

'Do you have an answer for me?'

Antonia snapped her head round at the impatient tone. She zeroed in on his cerulean eyes, hating this man with all the pent-up fear, despair and outrage that swamped her. He was a user, wielding power for his own gratification.

'Yes, I have an answer for you.' Her words were precise, coolly clipped and completely steady.

Antonia stifled the sharp pang of self-loathing that threatened her cut-glass composure. She was determined to lock away her emotions. That was the only way to deal with Rafe Benton. This man would *never* see her vulnerable. She swore it to herself. Whatever happened, she'd be strong.

She tilted her chin up and sent him the sort of chilly stare she'd seen so many wealthy women bestow on insignificant beings like hapless tour guides.

'I accept your offer.'

CHAPTER FIVE

RAFE'S surge of elation was so great he had to smother the smile tugging at his lips.

He had her.

Antonia Malleson had been a constant distraction. He'd been busy communicating with his deputies in Australia and London. But instead of its usual total focus on commercial challenges, his mind had wandered far too often. This woman had disrupted his hectic daytime schedule just as she'd wreaked havoc with his nights.

Now that was over.

He could have what he so desired. The sexy Ms Malleson and the perfect completion of his revenge on Stuart Dexter.

Adrenaline pulsed through his blood. Eagerness.

Never had a woman disturbed him so much. It was amazing, given how little time he'd spent with her. He looked forward to seeing if all her kisses were so incendiary. And more. His blood heated as his mind raced at a vision of her naked in his bed.

He strove to remind himself that the pleasure he felt was because he'd turned the tables on this grasping beauty, making her fit *his* scheme.

'But I have a condition.'

She crossed one leg over another, the pull of dark fabric emphasising the saucy curve of her hip and the length of her thigh.

Instantly heat flared in Rafe's belly, and he lifted his gaze to hers. If they were talking conditions, he couldn't let himself get distracted by pleasures to come.

'Yes? What is it?'

'That bonus you promised me.'

He nodded. He'd decided on the bonus after six months to ensure he had her for the whole period. He intended to parade the fact that she was *his* until the very day he closed Dexter down. Besides, he suspected it would take a full six months to have his fill of her.

'What about it?'

'I want double and I want it up-front.'

His brows rose. She had to be kidding. He'd already agreed to waive her substantial debts. How much did she think she was worth?

Rafe had never paid for a woman in his life. If not for these peculiar circumstances, he'd never have considered it. He had no knowledge of the usual fee structure, but surely the glossy, well-kept women he'd met with their older lovers didn't get such a large bonus?

'Why should I pay you that kind of money?'

She shrugged, her lips softening in the tiniest hint of a pout that made his mouth dry.

'If you want me to agree, that's what it'll cost you.'

'And what do I get for the extra money?'

Her fine brows arched, her dark eyes widening in a show of condescension that would have done a duchess proud.

An insistent voice inside urged him to agree to her terms. Six months with her would be worth every penny.

For the sake of his revenge, of course.

'I would live as your...mistress for six months.' She

spoke calmly, her voice uninflected, as if she were selling a commodity, not herself.

No doubt she had more experience of these arrangements than he did. The realisation brought a twist of sharp sensation to his chest.

'What? No extra perks? No *special* treatment?'

Cool morphed to glacial in a look that should have frozen him to the spot. Obviously his mistress-to-be wasn't impressed. Perhaps she intended to charge by the hour for anything else? Negotiating with her was like taking on a savvy, stony-faced business competitor.

Avidly, Rafe wondered how long it would take to heat her blood to a point where passion took over from mercenary instincts. This woman excited him as no other.

'I'll be your mistress for the period you stipulated. Isn't that what you wanted?'

Of course it was. Though *want* was too bland a word. If she changed her mind, how would he satisfy this…craving?

'You'll live with me in *every* sense? Do as I wish?'

For a moment something flickered in her eyes, something he couldn't define, then she nodded her head abruptly. 'Within reason.'

'Oh, I'm always *reasonable*, Antonia.'

He watched her stiffen at the use of her name. That would have to end.

'All right. I'll give you double what I promised you, spread out in monthly payments—'

'No!'

He watched, fascinated, as a hint of colour appeared on her high cheekbones. It made him wonder how she'd look flushed from lovemaking.

Soon he'd know.

'No?'

She shook her head. 'That won't do. I want payment up-front. Before I leave here.'

'That's asking a lot, don't you think?'

'What? And you're not asking a lot from me?' Her nostrils flared in disdain and her lips primmed. He remembered the taste of her, like honey and raw desire in his mouth. The softness of her hair to his touch. The heat of her body against his.

He'd certainly make sure he got his money's worth out of this transaction—one way or another.

'Fine. Give me your bank details and I'll have the money transferred immediately. Seventy five percent now. Twenty five percent at the end of our arrangement.'

She stilled. He could almost hear her quick mental calculations. Then she reached for her purse and took out a card. He watched her note down the account number. Her movements were controlled, brisk and definite. Almost jerky.

Stress? Could it be?

'You're sure about this?' he found himself asking, amazed at the words emerging from his mouth. It wasn't like him to stymie his own deal.

'Sure that I want that extra payment?' Her lips tilted up in a brittle smile and she laughed—a short tinkle of sound that reminded him, absurdly, of breaking glass. 'Oh, yes, I'm sure. No up-front payment, no deal.'

She leaned over the table towards him, holding out a piece of paper with her account details.

Rafe sat forward and claimed her hand with his own. Her eyes widened and her mouth sagged open a little. At her wrist he felt the flutter of her pulse.

Not so assured, then. Interesting. Antonia Malleson was fast becoming an enigma he wanted to solve.

Or perhaps *unwrap* was a better word.

He encircled her hand, enjoying the feel of her smooth skin, her delicate bones within his grasp.

'I have a condition too,' he murmured, enjoying the immediate flare of consternation in her dark eyes. 'We'll use first names. I refuse to be called "Mr Benton" by my mistress. And I'm sure there'll be times when "Antonia" is more appropriate than "Ms Malleson".'

Colour suffused her cheeks. With her pale gold skin tones it brought a healthy glow to a face that had been too pale, he realised.

The pulse beneath his hand jumped, and he knew they were thinking of the same thing. The pair of them together in bed. This time he did smile, as heady anticipation coursed through his bloodstream.

'First names it is. Now, would you mind releasing my hand? It's uncomfortable, leaning across like this.'

'Of course.' He let her go and took the all-important bank details. Then he stood and walked around to where she sat. 'Shall we seal the arrangement with a celebratory kiss?' That would do for starters.

His words were barely out when she shot to her feet, glaring up at him almost belligerently.

'No. No celebrations until the money comes through.'

Stunned, Rafe stared down at her. Did she expect him to renege on his promise? He frowned. More proof that she'd been hanging around with the wrong sort of men.

'I mean it!'

'Okay.' He raised his hands in a gesture of placation, surprised to hear a note that sounded like panic in her voice. Carefully he scrutinised her, but he couldn't read a thing. That severe expression of calm was back in place, like a mask hiding whatever went on in her mind.

'I'll collect you in the morning, so you'll need to be ready to leave.'

'How long before I get my money?' she countered.

Her avaricious streak was a mile wide. She didn't even bother to hide it. Strange how the idea disappointed him. Yet if she'd been a different sort of woman she wouldn't have agreed to his proposition.

'Within the hour.'

She paused a minute, glancing at her watch. Was she wondering if she had time for some last-minute shopping with his money before she packed?

'Yes. I can be ready.'

'No questions about where we're going?' Surely she'd have to choose what to pack and what to send home?

She shook her head. 'No.'

Rafe narrowed his eyes. She had to be the most uncommunicative woman he'd ever met. And the least curious.

That made her doubly intriguing.

Silently she stood, again looking at something over his shoulder. Whatever it was, it was damned fascinating. Rafe frowned. He'd have thought *he'd* be more interesting to her than some brightly daubed painting. After all, he was the man who'd just bought her for half a year.

The thought cheered him.

'I'll see you at eight sharp, Antonia.'

'I'll meet you in the foyer, Mr Benton.'

He raised a brow. 'We agreed to first names.'

'So we did.' She inclined her head in a regal gesture. 'The agreement will apply *after* you make the payment.'

Vixen! For a moment he was tempted to ignore her supercilious air, tug her into his arms and teach her just who was in control in this relationship.

No one walked over Rafe Benton. He was well past the age of being dictated to. But a streak of selfish enjoyment made him hold back. Let her play her little game for now. It would make her surrender all the sweeter.

'Of course, Ms Malleson.'

He reached for her hand with his, as if to shake it. She tensed instantly, but didn't resist. At the last moment he gave in to the impulse that had gnawed at him since he'd walked into the room. The impulse to taste her again.

He took a pace forward, closing the gap between them as he raised her hand. His eyes on hers, he pressed his lips to the back of her hand and was rewarded with a tremor of response. Her pulse jumped beneath his fingers and he smiled against her skin.

Not so calm and controlled now, madam.

He turned her hand over, keeping his gaze fixed on the shadow of expression that flickered across her eyes. Slowly, oh-so-deliberately, he kissed the centre of her palm, inhaling the heady scent of her warm flesh and her soft cinnamon perfume. It surprised him, as it had two days ago. He'd expected something more sophisticated, more expensive, for a woman in her fast-living, high-spending set. Yet it suited her. It was warm, intriguing, subtly seductive. Dangerously addictive.

Her dark eyes glazed with heat, and gold sparks flared as he licked her palm, drawing the fresh, sweet taste of her into his mouth.

That was better. He felt her pulse race, a quiver of weakness ripple through her, even as his body hardened, ready for the next step towards shared pleasure.

He licked again, more slowly, enjoying the stifled sound of her hissed breath and the knowledge that she was far from immune to him.

She tried to pull her hand away. She wasn't a woman to give anything for nothing—even something as honest and straightforward as mutual passion. For a moment longer he held her hand captive, making sure she understood that the power rested with him. Then he let her fingers slide free.

Rafe straightened, watching the way she cradled her palm within her other hand. As if the sensations he'd evoked had burnt her. How would she react when he kissed more than her hand or her mouth?

Rafe permitted himself a small smile.

'Until tomorrow at eight, Ms Malleson. I'll look forward to commencing our arrangement.'

She made no comment as he strode across the room, opened the door and headed for the stairs.

That afternoon Antonia arranged to repay the Foundation. The transaction would look irregular, but that couldn't be helped. The main thing was that the money would be there. If there were raised brows among the auditors, surely that wouldn't affect the Foundation publicly?

Even with Rafe Benton's cash things would be tight. She'd have to sell her mother's jewellery to cover the few debts he hadn't bought up. But that was the least of her concerns. It was the missing charity funds that had kept her awake each night.

Accepting his offer had been her only choice. But it was worth it, she assured herself the following morning. This was the last thing she could do for her parents.

Antonia blinked back the prickling burn behind her eyes. Strange how emotion side-swiped her when she least expected it. If she'd been going to weep, surely that would have come at the beginning, before the funeral?

She spun away from the window. She had no time for grief. For any emotion. Not if she wanted to survive the next six months. Emotion was a luxury she couldn't afford.

In precisely five minutes she had to go downstairs and meet the man who'd bought her.

A trickle of raw fear slid down her spine and wrapped around her heart, squeezing tight. *What had she done?*

Hysteria threatened at the idea of *her* as a rich man's mistress. She, whose dream wasn't wealth or glamour. Antonia had seen the ultra-rich from far too close. Generally she didn't like what she saw.

She was the cuckoo in the nest. Her dreams were mundane: a home, rather than a succession of hotels. A sense of belonging, a man who'd love her, a family of her own. To study art, then find a job that would give her the security she'd never had because of her dad's wandering lifestyle. She could have left him and pursued her own dreams. But these last few years she'd been so worried about him that she'd put her dreams on hold.

She picked up her bag with a shaking hand and cast a final glance around the room. She'd known grief and despair here, loss and marrow-deep pain, but this place marked the end of her old life.

Sucking in a deep breath, she walked out through the door, closing it with a click that sounded abnormally loud in the hushed stillness. The lift was deserted except for the tall woman with dark hair who stared at her from the mirror on the back wall. One glance at those empty eyes and she turned abruptly to punch the button for the ground floor.

So what if she didn't recognise herself? Wasn't that better? Maybe she could pretend this was happening to someone else, not her?

The doors slid open and she stepped out. The first thing she saw was him.

Rafe Benton looked tall and devilish all in black: trousers, pullover and long coat. His dark hair was combed severely back from his broad forehead. He didn't notice her and she scanned his profile, the cut of his jaw, the angle of his cheekbone and the strong slant of his nose. They made up a formidable whole, compelling rather than handsome.

No hope that he'd changed his mind.

Antonia faltered as the urge to flee caught her. Then his eyes met hers. Electric-blue fire blasted across the space between them and she knew there was no escape.

Wherever she went he'd come after her. There was no mistaking the determination in that face. The flash of possessiveness in those eyes. She repressed a tremor of foreboding as heat licked her skin.

Besides, she'd given her word, taken his money. No one would ever again accuse a Malleson of dishonesty.

She watched his well-shaped mouth curl at the corners. He had a tantalising half-smile most women would find devastating, especially when teamed with those vibrantly blue eyes.

It was all she could do to walk towards him, one foot carefully in front of the other. He held her gaze through every slow, agonising step.

On the periphery of her vision she saw other people in the foyer. Yet the sound of them was muted, drowned out by the heavy pulsing silence between her and Rafe Benton.

'Hello, Antonia.' His smile widened a fraction, as if he relished the sound of her name.

For an instant she baulked. But resistance was pointless.

'Hello…Rafe.' Her voice sounded calm. Yet her heart plummeted as she swallowed the sour taste of capitulation and self-contempt. She'd just crossed an invisible boundary, implicitly accepting his terms. She'd gone from free woman to paid consort.

She'd left her self-respect behind.

Rafe watched her lips shape his name and his satisfaction grew. It was good to see her behaving reasonably. After paying through the nose for her co-operation he wouldn't brook any nonsense.

He felt a punch of desire. She had such a gorgeous mouth. Such soft lips. Perfect. He enjoyed the way she said his name, too, with her neat British accent.

He considered planting a swift kiss on her mouth, a gesture of possession and of need. But he decided against it. He was aware of the other guests, of staff watching them curiously. No. When he kissed her it would be in private, where he could enjoy her sensuality to the full.

'I'm glad to see you're punctual. I'm not a man who appreciates being kept waiting.'

Her look told him she understood that he was talking about more than being in time for a rendezvous. Good.

'Where's your luggage?' He was eager to leave.

'Over there.' She pointed to two suitcases by the concierge's desk.

'That's it?' From his experience of women, there had to be more. These were too modest. 'You've sent the rest of your things home?'

When she didn't answer, he shrugged. He wasn't interested in her luggage. Pleasure stirred at the knowledge she was his. He could put his plans into action.

He turned and put his hand under her elbow, ignoring the way she froze. That would stop soon. Soon she'd be used to his touch, eager for it.

Rafe had no false modesty about his attractiveness or his ability to satisfy women. His lovers were well pleasured. So well, in fact, it was often a problem getting them to leave. He didn't doubt for an instant that Antonia would get as much satisfaction from their liaison as he intended to take.

Besides, despite the wintry reserve she wore like armour, she'd been pliant enough when he'd kissed her. The memory of her soft body melting against his, of her responding to his caresses with her lips and tongue, her hands clutching at his skull, was a clear promise of things to come. A knot of anticipation clenched in his groin.

'Come on. We have a plane to catch.'

She didn't answer, didn't even ask where they were flying, but then he'd specified he wanted a compliant mistress. Rafe had no problem with silence. It made a nice change from so many women he'd met. Like the bimbo who'd set herself to catch his attention in the bar last night. All chatter and cleavage and candyfloss between the ears. Give him an intelligent woman any day.

He glanced down at Antonia. Elegant, reserved, sexy in a way that owed nothing to silicone implants or Botox or even a dazzle of jewellery. Mind sharp as a tack. Tongue to match.

Rafe's mouth kicked up in a smile. Melting that reserve of hers was going to be pure pleasure.

Despite the luxury of his limousine, and the private jet, Antonia couldn't relax. She was too conscious of Rafe beside her, even when he turned his attention to his laptop in flight.

At least he didn't touch her, not like a man touched his mistress. But even his warm grip of her elbow, ostensibly helping her on board, his hand at the small of her back, ushering her through Customs, were enough to keep her on tenterhooks.

The trip passed quickly. She'd checked him out on the internet and she wasn't surprised. The story of his meteoric rise to success in the world of international finance hinted at someone of daunting intellect, determination and impatience. He had the spectacular wealth to make international travel smooth and easy.

Which meant they arrived at their destination far too soon. London. That was a good thing, she told herself, as they stood in the lift of a luxury apartment building. He must be here to work, which meant less time with her.

She'd worried he might take her to some exotic island where there'd be no distractions. Just him and her. All night and all day.

The idea had sent her cold with horror, and hot with something she feared might be eagerness. For she couldn't forget the way he'd kissed her. The warmth and tenderness that had somehow bypassed her guard and left her defenceless and wanting.

'Here we are. Your home for the next six months.'

He ushered her out on the top floor, straight into a massive apartment that looked as if it should be on the cover of some glossy architectural digest. Antonia had a fleeting impression of a lofty space, a vast floor of exquisite parquetry, and a view of the Thames—a perfect backdrop to expensively simple furnishings.

She barely took it in. Instead every nerve strained taut as she focused on *him*, wondering about his next move. The silence between them weighed her down. It was fraught with unspoken expectation. Would he demand—?

'Let me take your coat.' His fingers brushed her and she stiffened, aware that at any moment his touch might grow all too personal. Heaven help her, she'd put herself in a position where she couldn't protest.

'Thank you.' Her voice was a low, grating whisper.

She was wound too tight, like a clockwork toy about to spring apart. Her heart juddered hard against her ribs and she focused on taking slow breaths as he eased her coat from her shoulders and stowed it in a nearby closet.

Then he stood before her, his eyes darkening to a shade she hadn't seen. The intensity of his expression made her breathless, nervous. Expectant. His large hand was warm against her chilled flesh as he tilted her face up. His expression was smug, his eyes alight with a blatant look of ownership that made her blood run cold.

'Alone at last.' He smiled on the words and her heart plunged.

CHAPTER SIX

WHAT had Rafe expected to find as he stared into her beautiful eyes? Bone-melting invitation? A sultry look that told him she was ready and eager for him?

He found neither. There was no welcome, either subtle or blatant. No hint of the attraction that had sparked and sizzled when they'd kissed and she'd transformed in his arms from distant to warm and willing.

Nor was there a trace of the fiery defiance he'd got such a kick out of when they clashed. She was pale, despite her golden olive complexion. There were blue smudges beneath her eyes, and weariness in the slight frown marring her brow. She looked as if she hadn't slept in days.

He hadn't noticed before, because he'd avoided looking. There'd been that first sweeping survey at the hotel, when he'd been rocked by the intensity of his pleasure at seeing her. Later he'd concentrated on work, trying to ignore his hunger for her. He refused to give in to it too soon or too completely. Rafe never gave in to weakness.

Hardly ever.

He bent his head, half expecting her to jerk away. But she stood statue-still. He brushed his lips across hers. For a moment he thought she was going to deny him, and his fingers tightened on her jaw. But her lips were pliant as he slid his mouth along hers. She accommodated him, tentatively shaping to his mouth.

Need rocketed through him as she followed his lead, met his kiss with a gentle response that was somehow more exciting than a full-on passionate embrace.

He deepened the kiss, touching her still only with his hand and his mouth. But the sensation of his tongue sliding against hers, the welcoming heat of her mouth, open for his pleasure, was undeniably erotic.

His for the taking. The knowledge was a naked flame igniting the embers of desire he'd banked down all day.

Reluctantly he pulled away, ignoring the thunder in his blood that demanded he follow through, haul her into his arms and take her to bed right now. His hands shook with the effort of restraint. Despite the clamour of his needy body, this wasn't the time.

'Welcome to your new home.' He searched for a spark of animation in her eyes. Heat to match the fire in his belly.

There was nothing. Her eyes remained blank and remote, shadowed, as if she'd withdrawn behind a wall of secrets.

That annoyed him. *He* was aware of *her* with every sense. Her enticing cinnamon-spice scent filled his nostrils. Her smooth skin was warm satin under his hand. He heard the sound of her breathing, rapid in the silence. And the taste of her, the richest, sweetest flavour in the world, lingered on his tongue, making him hungry for more.

Where had she withdrawn to? How could she be so unaffected?

Rafe was used to women dissolving at the knees when he kissed them. He frowned. It hadn't been a passionate kiss, just a foretaste of gratification to come. But surely he wasn't the only one to feel that scorch of desire? The idea was unthinkable.

'Thank you,' she said politely, as if they were total strangers. 'The apartment looks very pleasant.'

Very pleasant! Was that the best she could do? She looked utterly calm and contained, unimpressed by the obvious luxury of her surroundings. *By him.*

'And so it should be.' His tone was curt. 'It would almost have been cheaper to buy the place than to rent it for six months.'

He glanced dismissively around the room, as if the exquisite oriental rugs, the expensive and elegant furniture, meant nothing to him. Antonia wondered if he'd even noticed the painting opposite the fireplace. It looked like a Chagall, and it wasn't a print.

'If there's one thing you British know how to do, it's charge a premium rate for your bargains, isn't it?'

His laser-bright eyes pinioned her where she stood.

His expression wasn't as warm as a few moments ago, when she'd struggled to maintain some mental distance. His surprisingly tender kiss had undermined her defences and she'd barely managed to maintain her pose of uninterest.

'I only hope I won't be disappointed,' he said, clear challenge in his voice. 'When I pay top dollar I expect the best in *everything*. I don't take kindly to getting anything less than full value for my…purchases.'

Antonia stiffened, jerking her chin from his hand.

He meant *her*. She saw it in his accusing blue eyes.

He'd bought her, and now he expected her to deliver. What would he consider good value? Utter compliance? Enough sexual expertise to seduce and please a jaded appetite? Heaven help her, she wasn't equipped for this.

Nausea rose in her throat, and her skin prickled as white-hot pain encircled her forehead. Antonia swallowed hard, forcing back bile at the idea of giving herself when her emotions weren't engaged. Laying aside her pride and her natural reserve and becoming Rafe Benton's sex toy!

The idea was absurd, but she wasn't laughing. There was an aching hollow inside her. She'd given her word, taken his money. There was no going back.

'You'll also find we have a reputation for honesty in our dealings.' She forced herself to look into the bright glare of his eyes, to face down his cynicism and ignore the whimpering part of her soul that wanted to curl up in a corner and pretend this wasn't happening.

'If it's all right with you, I'd like to freshen up after the journey.' Anything to put some distance between them. If he touched her again, the consequences wouldn't bear thinking about. She'd either go up like flame in his arms, or the safety net she'd built around her feelings would be breached and she'd give in to the pain and fear that crowded so close. Either option was untenable.

'Of course.' Rafe gave a mocking bow. She didn't miss the amused tilt of his lips. 'This way.' He gestured to a wide hall. 'And I'll show you to your room.'

Her room? Was it possible she'd have her own space? Surely a mistress—?

'I prefer to sleep alone,' he said as they walked down the hall, just as if she'd voiced the question aloud. 'You'll have your own bedroom and bathroom.'

Antonia nodded, biting her lip at the edge of hysteria rising inside her. As if this sort of conversation was in any way normal. Her legs moved stiffly, her whole body taut as they approached the bedrooms.

'Here you are.' He gestured for her to precede him.

For the longest moment she hesitated. Crossing this threshold was like crossing her own personal Rubicon.

No. That had been yesterday, when she'd taken his money.

Antonia ignored his narrowed gaze and walked in

She faltered to a stop just inside. She hadn't expected anything like this. To one side was a wall of glass, beyond that the Thames, and the rooftops of central London. Mere mortals couldn't afford vistas like this.

Yet the view barely registered. Instead she took in the room, piece by piece. A huge four-poster bed sat against one wall, each post carved to look like the trunk of a tree. At the top a criss-cross of branches supported a canopy of sheer fabric that draped to the floor. The coverlet was a fantasy of white on white embroidery, topped with plump pillows and a scattering of gold cushions.

The walls were soft ochre, a perfect foil for the timber. In front of a long set of book-lined shelves were a wing chair, with a massive ottoman, plus a sofa. There was a large cabinet that she guessed hid a television, and on another wall a medieval-style tapestry of elegant ladies gathering flowers while their beaux watched from horseback. It had the mellow look of the genuine article.

'It's beautiful,' she whispered, wishing she could think of a better description. The room was wonderful. It felt warm, welcoming, safe. A haven from the outside world.

'I'm glad you approve,' he murmured, his voice a silken skein that unravelled something deep inside her. 'I wondered if you'd prefer something more modern.'

She was aware of him behind her, of the heat of his breath on her neck. Suddenly her delight vanished.

Her gaze darted to the wide bed. This time she didn't see its whimsical fantasy. Just its size. More than big enough for two. She visualised him there, his hair dark against the pure white of the bedlinen. His tanned skin gleaming in the soft glow of the bedside lamps. His long limbs stretched out almost the full length of the bed.

And with him a woman with her mother's thick, wavy hair and dark eyes. A woman with her father's wide mouth and lanky frame. A woman who'd sold herself to keep her father's reputation and achievements safe.

The nausea hit her full force this time, and she hurried across the room to an open door. Sure enough, it was a bathroom.

She nudged the door shut and fumbled the lock closed. Then she was leaning over the sink, trembling arms braced. Her stomach was a roiling mess and acid burned her throat as she struggled to keep her last meal down.

'Antonia! Are you all right?' His voice was sharp.

Probably wondering if she was trying to renege on their deal, she thought waspishly as shudders racked her.

'I'm…fine,' she croaked, as the nausea slowly subsided. Her stomach cramped. Just as well she'd been too nervous to eat.

Eventually she felt steady enough to stand up straight. She longed to kick off her high heels, but she had so few weapons in her armoury, and the additional height gave her the illusion of strength. She was desperate enough to cling even to that hollow illusion. She rinsed her mouth, smoothed back her hair and unlocked the door.

He stood a few feet away, his expression unreadable. An article she'd read about him on the web suddenly sprang to mind. It had described him as brilliant, acute, decisive and unorthodox. He was renowned for his ability to wrong-foot competitors with daring, unexpected moves.

Uneasily Antonia wondered what he was thinking—what he saw as he watched her so closely.

'You're not well.' It wasn't a question.

She lifted her shoulders in a shrug. 'It must have been something I ate,' she lied. 'I'm all right now.'

The harsh lines around his mouth told her he doubted it.

'You need to sit down.' Without waiting for agreement, he put his arm beneath her elbow and pulled her away from the door. Panic shot through her as she thought of that luxurious bed so close, but instead he ushered her to the cushioned wing chair. Gratefully she sank into its comfort. She felt as if she'd aged decades in the last couple of weeks. Sixty-two instead of twenty-two.

'You're shaking,' he accused.

'I told you—I ate something that disagreed with me.'

He sat on the ottoman, elbows on his splayed knees as he leaned towards her. He crowded her space.

'You haven't eaten anything since we left the resort.'

She shrugged. 'I'm just…tired.'

His stare was steady, doubting. He didn't believe her. Sitting so near, the strength of his personality was a potent, palpable force. His distrust was tangible.

'Too tired for sex, you mean? Is that what this is about?'

'I…' Antonia looked away. Had he guessed how she felt? Did he have even a spark of sympathy for her situation?

'If so, you can put your mind at rest.' His tone was harsh. 'I have more important things on my mind right now.' He paused long enough to draw her gaze back to his gleaming eyes. 'Besides, given your reputation for flitting from one man to another, I'm not taking you to bed without protection. I won't run the risk of contracting whatever is doing the rounds.'

Antonia's mouth sagged in disbelief. He made her sound like some undiscriminating street walker. Someone who'd been intimate with countless strangers.

If only he knew! His just-bought mistress was hardly the experienced seductress he obviously expected.

She'd only had one serious boyfriend. Foolishly, she'd believed Peter different from the other rich guys she'd met. Until she'd discovered his idea of an exclusive relationship was ensuring his girlfriend didn't meet the women with whom he had casual sex when she wasn't around. Since then she'd only dated to stop her father fretting that she was lonely.

'Are you always this insulting to your women, Rafe?'

His eyes narrowed as he watched her convulsive swallow. Either she was the best actress he'd come across, or she really was unwell. Yet the way she said his name, in that low, throaty purr, was pure dynamite. Pale and clearly exhausted, and still she made a direct hit on his libido.

'Hardly an insult. I'm just being practical.' Though, as he took in the almost febrile glitter of her eyes and the flush staining her cheeks, Rafe knew he could have been more tactful. 'After all, this is about *your* protection as well. You don't know if I'm clean of disease either.'

'Are you?'

Rafe was surprised to feel heat flare under his skin as her gaze held his.

'Yes, I am.' He was usually very discriminating in his lovers. 'But you shouldn't take my word for it.'

'Oh, I won't.'

Rafe's jaw tightened. What was it about this woman? One minute he felt protective towards her. The next she infuriated him. For a crazy moment he'd even felt a pang of guilt, wondering if he'd been too ruthless, forcing her into this. Until he recalled that it was her own mercenary instinct, her yearning for money, that had led her here.

The only constant was his desire. And her usefulness, he reminded himself. He looked into her gorgeous face and wanted her with a need so strong it carved a hollow in his gut. A need that threatened to overcome his self-control.

Rafe surged to his feet and strode to the door. The news he'd received on the plane, that some New York negotiations had hit a snag and needed his immediate personal intervention, meant he had no time for this now. Business would surely take his mind off this woman and allow him to get his priorities right again.

'I'll leave you to settle in.'

* * *

Two mornings later Antonia checked her make-up carefully, ensuring it hid the ravages of sleepless nights before leaving her room.

She hadn't seen Rafe since their arrival in London. He'd left almost immediately afterwards on business and she'd been on tenterhooks since, wondering when he'd return. When he'd want…her.

Late last night he'd returned. She'd lain, breathing shallow and body stiff, waiting for him to enter her room. But he'd left her in peace. *For how much longer?*

Her stomach churned at the prospect of giving herself to him. Steadfastly she ignored the disquieting idea that though she didn't like Rafe, it was just possible she *did* want him. The damning memory of her capitulation when he'd kissed her made her blood tingle. She hadn't been prepared for the hungry way her body had responded to him.

No! It wasn't true. She didn't want him. She'd never be attracted to a man like that. So domineering. So willing to ride roughshod over others to get what he wanted.

So powerfully compelling.

'Antonia! Looking as lovely as ever.'

She had a fleeting impression of glinting blue eyes and then strong arms swept her up, pulling her close. His heat, the intense masculine scent of his skin, surrounded her as he delved into her mouth, staking his ownership with no preliminaries, no hesitation.

Her head reeled from the sudden sensual onslaught, and she grasped at his shoulders as her knees weakened. He moulded her body against his and she didn't have time to construct any defences. Horrified, she felt a flicker of delight at the way they fitted together, as if this was what she'd missed these last sleepless nights.

He pulled away abruptly, just as she absorbed the taste of him on her tongue, recognised its familiarity. She clung to him a fraction too long—finding her balance, she assured herself. But she couldn't miss the satisfaction in his eyes as he stood back and surveyed her.

His eyes crinkled at the corners and his lips quirked up in a half-smile that was both intimate and devastating.

'I see you missed me too, sweetheart,' he murmured.

'I—' A finger on her lips stilled her denial.

'No, don't spoil the illusion.' For a long moment his gaze held hers and inexplicable warmth traced her body.

'You've got your bag? Good. Come on. I have an early meeting and I want your company on the way.'

'But I can't. I haven't—'

'No buts, Antonia.' He tucked her arm in his and strode to the lift, pulling her with him. 'A man likes his mistress to be amenable. I'm sure you can manage it. Just think of all that lovely money in your bank account.'

His words stiffened her spine. All traces of the strange bone-melting sensation that had so weakened her during his kiss bled away. She stood ramrod-straight beside him in the lift, staring blankly at the control console.

'Not going to ask me where I've been, sweetheart?'

She hated that lazy drawl, the way it curled insidiously deep inside her despite his obvious sarcasm.

'I'm sure you'll tell me if you want to.'

The lift doors opened and she moved to slip her arm free. But there was no escape. He simply snagged her close, his body solid and intimidatingly large beside her.

'Not happy this morning, Antonia?'

'I'm fine.' What did he want her to say? That she enjoyed being treated as a chattel, her movements circumscribed by his whims?

Silently he led her out to a waiting limousine. When they were inside, cut off from the driver by a privacy screen, Rafe turned those laser-bright eyes on her.

'All right, Antonia. What's your problem?'

Her problem? He had to be kidding.

'If you're not happy with our arrangement then say so *now*. I didn't force you into accepting my more than generous offer.' He crossed his arms over his deep chest as he spoke, the picture of male power and annoyance.

Despite herself Antonia felt a thrill of pleasure at having unwittingly provoked him. No, that was too dangerous. Who knew what Rafe Benton would do if pushed too far?

'I refuse to put up with a woman who sulks and pouts her way through a relationship.'

'I—'

'I paid good money for the pleasure of your company, Antonia. And I expect more than this in return.'

Yes, master. Whatever you say, master.

Antonia took refuge in bitter anger. Reality was too unpalatable—for he *had* bought her. She'd made the choice to accept his offer. No matter that she'd been desperate.

'Unless you'd prefer to pay back my cash advance?'

Instantly her defiance waned. That was one thing she simply couldn't do. She'd already spent his precious cash.

'Perhaps you'd better spell out exactly what it is you require,' she said, when she'd found her voice.

Rafe's brows rose as if in astonishment.

'I mean…' she fought down a blush '…when we're not…'

'Making love?' Those two words, uttered in his deep, sultry voice, drew every muscle tight. In revulsion, she assured herself. Not excitement.

'Yes,' she whispered, her throat constricting.

'It's simple, Antonia.' His voice was grim. 'Given the small fortune I've paid for the *pleasure* of your company, you'll be with me whenever I want you from this moment on.'

She stared at him, conscious of the way the wide back

seat seemed to shrink as his gaze clashed and meshed with hers. Of how close he was to her. And of the way her pulse raced at the possessive gleam in his eyes.

'You're mine—bought and paid for.' His voice dropped a notch. The sound of it, like a rumbling purr, made her skin prickle with gooseflesh and her breath stop. 'You'd do well to remember that.'

A wave of energy pulsed between them as his words sank in. Owner and chattel. Man and mistress. Clearly there was no difference in his mind, nor any way out. Antonia absorbed the blow as she had so many others. She told herself she could weather this as she had everything else.

By the end of summer she'd be free. Her own woman. She could take up the career she'd wanted for so long but had delayed in order to take care of her father. She'd start afresh, build a safe, secure life for herself.

'Of course, Rafe.' She paused on his name, her throat closing reflexively, but she forced the word out. Surely it would become easier with time? 'So what did you have in mind next?' She prayed that he couldn't hear the trepidation in her voice.

For a long time he studied her, as if probing for secrets. It was unnerving. He shouldn't be interested in her secrets. He only wanted physical gratification, and the titillating knowledge that she was at his beck and call.

The idea was degrading. But perhaps it offered a way out. If she focused on complying with his whims perhaps she could ignore the welter of emotions that threatened to destroy her composure. If she could divorce her feelings from the need to act the part of his woman, *bought and paid for*, she might just be able to get through this.

'Next I have business to attend to. So you'll have to amuse yourself for the day.' He paused. Was he expecting her to complain? It was all she could do not to grin her relief at the reprieve.

'But tonight we'll go out. We'll be attending a series of engagements from now on. Receptions, dinners and balls. I'll expect you to be *close* at my side for every one.' His brows arrowed into a frown as if he dared her to argue. 'I want an attentive companion—understood?'

'Understood.' She'd hang on his every word.

'One who smiles occasionally.'

She could manage that. Especially if they were at a crowded reception where she wouldn't be caught in the illusion that there was no one but the pair of them in the whole world. When he stared at her so intensely, like now, everything else faded away. It unnerved her.

'No flinching when I put my arm around you. No acting like a scalded cat whenever I touch you.' He was remembering her reaction as he'd marched her to the limousine. Every time he touched her she stiffened.

He was a very tactile man. She'd noticed the way his hand strayed so often to the small of her back, ushering her through a door or into a vehicle. He'd take her arm in his and match his long-legged stride to hers. And each time she'd freeze, horrified at the splintering shards of unwanted awareness arrowing through her at the contact.

She'd wondered whether it was just in his nature to draw close, or if it was an unspoken sign of ownership. For a man so controlled, so calculating, there was a disturbingly sensuous streak to Rafe Benton. Her guess was that he simply enjoyed physical contact. The idea had banished sleep as she tossed in her bed, imagining how it would feel to have those large hands, that body, on hers.

'Antonia?' His tone was impatient.

'Of course,' she murmured. 'No flinching.'

His eyes narrowed, as if he suspected sarcasm.

'I've already mentioned attentiveness,' he warned.

Just as well he had no idea she'd been distracted by thoughts of his touch. His ego would balloon phenomenally if he knew.

'I'll be attentive,' she assured him.

His muffled sigh was the only response. Masculine impatience barely stifled.

'And I want you to look glamorous. No fading into the background.' He dropped his gaze to her grey trousers and jacket, her low-heeled shoes, and his frown deepened.

No doubt he'd want to show off his new trophy. His taste was probably for showy ostentation.

'How formal are these receptions we're attending?'

'Very. Pull out all the stops. My assistant will ring you with details of tonight's engagement.' He watched her closely. 'Why? Is that a problem?'

Rapidly she considered the clothes hanging in her enormous walk-in wardrobe. She had dressy clothes, including a black cocktail dress that she'd worn more times than she cared to remember. But there was formal and then there was formal. She didn't have the sort of outfits Rafe Benton would expect from his mistress. Definitely no ballgowns.

'My wardrobe doesn't currently run to glamorous.'

His instant look of disbelief turned into the hint of a smirk. 'So your luggage was full of sexy lingerie and nothing else?'

'No!' she snapped.

'You disappoint me, Antonia.'

For a moment the gleam in his eyes looked almost teasing. Then it faded.

'You sent your formal clothes home? That didn't show much foresight.'

There was no point in explaining that she didn't have formal clothes. Or a home.

'Well, you've got all day. You can go shopping and pick up something suitable.'

She shook her head. She had no money left for a spending spree—even if she had any longer term use for the sort of designer ballgowns he'd expect her to wear.

'What's the problem now? You've got the whole of London to choose from and a substantial chunk of my money in your account. Surely you can find something suitable?'

Except she didn't have his money. But she wasn't explaining the intimate details of her life to him. Pride was all she had left. Besides, he wouldn't be interested in that, just in her capacity to fill the role of mistress.

'You didn't tell me I'd be expected to buy a whole new wardrobe,' she said, her gaze sliding from his to the busy street as they travelled through the financial district.

Silence. A long silence.

'You really are a greedy piece of work, aren't you, sweetheart?'

She hated it when he called her that. Especially when he used that slow, mocking drawl.

'Haven't you screwed enough out of this deal already?'

'I'm merely pointing out that you didn't specify I'd be expected to outlay for a new wardrobe. Especially the sort of clothes you're talking about.'

He said nothing. Eventually, reluctantly, Antonia gave in to his silent command, turning to meet his eyes. They flashed fire and ice, a potent combination that made her shrink back in her seat.

At last he spoke. 'I can see I should have drawn up a written agreement. It would have saved considerable time. And money.' Each word bit into her flesh. 'So I'm to understand you're unwilling to use your newfound wealth to clothe yourself?'

Antonia met his look, but said nothing.

'You know, I'm in half a mind to have you go naked.'

Her hiss of dismay was loud in the silence. He couldn't be serious. But, reading the sharp disdain in his expression, Antonia realised Rafe Benton might just follow through on that threat. Not in public, but in the privacy of his apartment. Her mouth dried at the very thought.

'Now I think of it, the idea is rather appealing.'

No! Surely he wouldn't.

'Perhaps to you,' she bit out, racking her brain for something to distract him from the idea. 'But if I come down with flu it would interfere with your plans.'

His gaze held hers so long her breathing grew shallow and her heartbeat raced as she waited for his response.

'We couldn't have that, could we? I don't want you flat on your back with illness.'

His searing look and the mocking edge to his voice told her it wasn't the flat on her back bit he objected to. Her stomach cramped.

'All right, Antonia. I'll have my assistant set up a credit account for you to buy your clothes.' The tension was easing slightly from her shoulders when he continued. 'We'll stick to the letter of our bargain, sweetheart. Which means that you'd better deliver precisely what we've agreed. Understood?'

No mistaking the threat in those smooth tones.

Antonia swallowed convulsively. 'Understood.'

'Good. I want you looking spectacular tonight. Don't disappoint me.'

The car swung over to the side of the road and Antonia looked to see they'd parked in front of an imposing office block. This must be where Rafe's office was—

Her thoughts crashed to a halt when she felt his thigh against hers. His hand cupped her jaw and turned her to face him. He was crammed up against her in the corner of the car, pushing her back into the seat as he leaned close.

His eyes glittered as his gaze met hers, then roved her face, settling at last on her mouth. Heat burst through her at the intensity of that look. Heat and expectation. Convulsively she swallowed as unwanted awareness shivered through her.

His thumb swiped across her mouth, tugging her bottom lip down, her mouth open.

'Excellent. I'm glad we understand each other at last.' His breath was a warm puff of air on her lips.

Then his mouth was on hers, his tongue staking blatant claim. His kiss was thorough, deep, flagrantly erotic, even though he kept both hands splayed over her jaw and neck. He didn't paw her, or use his size to subdue her. Yet, to her shock, her body responded, heating with excitement at the sensations spearing through her. He took his time marking his possession. Darts of fire arrowed to erogenous zones she'd not known about as his tongue and lips worked magic.

Melting awareness spread through her, centering in her hollow aching core as he demonstrated a devastating sensual expertise.

His kiss was drugging, an invitation to pleasure unlike anything she'd known. Inevitably Antonia surrendered to the power of it, responding to the dance of his tongue against hers, the overpowering need to answer his caresses.

For long, glorious moments she felt the delicious excitement of pleasure given and shared.

Then he pulled away and she was left bereft, staring into eyes that sparkled with masculine satisfaction and a glint that might even be amusement. He looked completely unmoved and far too smug, while she battled to find her breath and her wits. A horn honked and she started, realising they'd been kissing in a busy street.

'It's a good thing the limo has tinted windows,' Rafe purred, allowing his hand to trail down her throat to her breast in a possessive caress that made her senses sing. And made her want to slam his hand away.

His lips curved into a devilish smile. 'I'm looking forward to tonight.'

CHAPTER SEVEN

SHE didn't disappoint.

That evening Rafe emerged from his suite, shrugging on his jacket, to find Antonia in the sitting room, absorbed in the vista of city lights.

From where he stood there was only one view worth looking at. His nerves pulled to jangling attention. Even wearing a long concealing coat, she was arresting. A red dress flared around her feet, and a glimpse of a stiletto heel caught his interest. He'd yet to see Antonia's legs, but he'd imagined them often enough: bare and silky smooth. A pair of sexy shoes made the picture perfect.

His groin tightened instantly on the thought.

She'd put her hair up again, less severely this time. It looked soft, seductive, as if a single tug would pull those tresses loose to tumble down her back.

Wearing her hair like that was a blatant invitation.

A moment later he'd bent his lips to the warm flesh at her nape, inhaling her exotic cinnamon scent. Was it a perfume or the natural fragrance of her skin? It had an instant impact on his libido. Or maybe it was the feel of her slim, feminine body as he drew her back against him.

She stiffened, then relaxed into his embrace. After the fire that had flashed in her eyes this morning Rafe had expected her to protest more. Perhaps his warning about delivering on her promises had worked.

Whatever. He was too busy nuzzling the side of her throat, sensing the tiny tremors running across her skin, to worry about her motivation. The feel of her so close, so tempting, threatened to divert him from his purpose. Delicious as she was, he couldn't afford to be sidetracked.

'Mink?' he murmured, as he stroked the fur. It was the perfect excuse to learn the shape of her supple body.

'Of course not.' She stiffened again, ramrod straight in his arms. 'It's *faux* fur.'

'You don't approve of wearing animal skins?' he whispered as he kissed behind her ear, not really giving a damn what she was wearing, but wanting to hear her voice again. It had a husky edge that turned him on.

She had other ideas. She tugged out of his arms, spinning round to face him. He had an impression of wide, glowing dark eyes, that gorgeous oval Madonna face, and perfect lips painted a glossy ruby-red.

The impact rocked him. She'd always looked sexy in that cool, classy way of hers. But now she looked *hot*. Red-hot. Those lips were full, sultry, luscious. A temptress's mouth.

Pity about the quelling schoolmarm look. But if she thought it would scare him off she was miles out.

'This is just as warm as fur. It looks as good and it's as soft. Why would I want mink?'

'For the same reason any woman wants to wear an exclusive label. For the prestige. To know that her man has paid a fortune so she can wear something obscenely expensive and flaunt her good luck.'

Her eyes narrowed and her head tilted assessingly.

'You really have a low opinion of women, don't you?'

He shook his head. 'Absolutely not. I've known some extraordinary women. But I'm experienced enough to know that there are plenty who see conspicuous consumption as a badge of honour—proof of their status.'

'Like me, I suppose?' She snapped out the words in bite-sized chunks, and Rafe sensed she'd like to sink those pearly whites into his flesh.

'If the shoe fits, sweetheart.' She was amazingly open about her greed. In his book that meant she had no right to pretend to false virtue. If there was one thing he abhorred it was a woman who pretended affection to get her grasping talons into a man's pocket.

Her nostrils flared disdainfully and she drew herself up straighter. He waited for the inevitable riposte, but instead her features iced over. The vivid light of battle was quenched, replaced by smooth, impassive blankness.

His brows tugged together. He infinitely preferred her sassy to silent. There was a vibrancy about her when she argued, or kissed, that was much more appealing than her snow princess act.

'No argument? No backchat?' he baited.

She curved her lips in the tiniest of smiles. He could have sworn he heard ice crackling at the movement. He faced her haughty look. That was when he realised the sass hadn't disappeared. It was just hidden.

Antonia Malleson was one intriguing woman.

'I thought you specified that you required *compliance* in your mistress.' She paused. 'But, since you raise it, I'd prefer not to be called "sweetheart".'

'Of course…darling. I'm always willing to be *flexible*—especially when it comes to pleasing a woman.'

Something glinted in her eyes. Disapproval? Distaste? Or curiosity?

'You only have to ask and I'll do my best to satisfy you,' he promised.

'I thought that was *my* role. To satisfy *you*.' She tilted her chin higher, as if daring him to contradict her. 'Isn't that why you bought me?'

Dissatisfaction niggled at her description of their arrangement. Strange, he'd never objected to plain speaking before, and it made a refreshing change from the usual female double-speak. Maybe it was because this was the first time he'd *bought* a lover. He was still acclimatising to the concept.

'Pleasure is a two-way street,' he responded. 'You don't think I'd demand satisfaction and not return the favour?'

Her eyes held his without blinking. He couldn't read a damned thing there. Meanwhile he felt the heat of sexual arousal roar into life, igniting his lower body. Just the mention of sex with her did that to him.

'I wouldn't presume to expect anything.' Her tone was clipped, but he spied the telltale pulse at her throat, beating frenetically. Beneath that façade of *sangfroid* she was as intrigued by the prospect of sex as he.

Rafe was tempted to taste that lush mouth. Yet they were late, and he had important business tonight. With the man he'd come to England to destroy. He contented himself with an almost chaste kiss at the corner of her mouth, then pulled back and drew her arm through his.

Strange how much he was looking forward to this evening in her company, and not just the impending prospect of sex. Nor did his anticipation centre solely on the idea of flaunting her in front of Stuart Dexter. Something about his clashes with Antonia Malleson made his blood pump faster. With something more than sexual stimulation.

One day he'd have to make time to figure out what it was.

Forty minutes later Rafe stared into the face of the man who was his father. He felt not one iota of connection, no qualms about activating his plan for revenge.

The memory of his mother's long drawn-out suffering kept his purpose firm. This man was despicable.

Satisfaction warmed him as he read Dexter's body language. An outer gloss of world weariness, a been-there-seen-it-all demeanour. But Rafe was astute enough to know it hid nervousness, even desperation. He smiled.

Dexter interpreted it as encouragement.

'Amazing coincidence, us being at the same ski resort.'

'Amazing,' Rafe agreed, watching Dexter adjust his bow tie. The man was anxious. Anxious enough to drop everything and run back to London the instant Rafe indicated he was ready to talk business. He was desperate for Rafe to bankroll his company's next move. It would be Rafe's pleasure to lend him a hand…straight to ruin.

'So, you're obviously giving this proposal your personal consideration. Excellent.' Dexter smiled. The sort of toothy grin you'd expect from a used-car salesman.

'I always prefer to deal with the man in charge. It saves time,' he continued pompously. 'Forget the clutter of lawyers and accountants. Show me the man at the head of a business, and I'll tell you whether we can deal together.'

'You like to cut through the red tape?'

'Why fetter ourselves with unnecessary clutter?'

'To keep things legal and above board?' Rafe queried.

'Of course. Of course. Yet between like-minded men it's the gentlemen's agreement that counts.'

Rafe nodded, letting Dexter continue his spiel. Was this how he'd separated so many investors from their money? With talk of gentlemen's agreements?

Dexter wasn't precisely a crook—not that Rafe could prove—but he gave the financial regulators a run for their money. His business dealings pushed the legal limits.

But while Dexter had a flair for finance and a reputation for success, he didn't have the discipline to stay on top. For every successful move there were cases of unsound judgement too. In his wake small investors had lost everything, while he slithered out of the morass and started anew.

When you looked at it like that, Rafe had a civic duty to put an end to Dexter's wheeling and dealing. His private revenge would do an immense amount of public good.

It took a moment to realise the other man's patter had faltered, his attention on the other side of the room.

Rafe knew what Dexter had seen. Or rather whom. He stifled a smile at Dexter's absorbed reaction. Securing Antonia as his mistress had been a master stroke.

She'd excused herself as soon as they'd arrived at the Banqueting House in Whitehall. She'd murmured about freshening up, and Rafe had agreed to meet her inside.

Even through the crowd she was easy to spot. Her bright dress stood out like a beacon. His lips twitched. He'd specified that she did not fade into the background. There was no danger of that! Heads turned as she passed, gazes arrested, and Rafe felt a wholly male satisfaction at the knowledge that she was his. Or soon would be.

Then some of the suits parted and he caught a full-length glimpse of her. His heart hammered and his mouth dried. Heat burned along his skin as he took her in.

Hell!

Surely she'd been poured into that dress? He watched the way it hugged her, moving like liquid silk as she moved, covering and yet caressing every curve, every feminine dip and flare. How she managed to walk so serenely through the throng he didn't know. The dress followed the sleek contours of her waist, hips and thighs, only widening at the bottom, to flirt around her feet as she moved.

She was dynamite. Sex on a pair of teetering high heels. His blood pressure rose just at the sight of her,

Suddenly he wanted to forget about this evening's commitment and head straight back to the apartment.

Leaving Dexter gawping, he shouldered his way through the crowd that clustered about her. All male, he noticed.

Her eyes met his, and he could have sworn he saw uncertainty in her expression. But it must be a trick of the light. This was no hesitant damsel. A woman who could wear that dress with insouciance was sexually confident and supremely sure of herself. A siren, not a shrinking violet.

She'd been silent on the way here, as on their trip to London. He'd actually pondered whether he'd done the right thing, bringing her tonight. It wasn't long since she'd lost her father. Rafe had even wondered if his assessment of her had been too simplistic. Maybe she *was* grieving.

But no mourner dressed like that. It wasn't grief she felt as she played up to all the male attention. If she had anything else on her mind, it was only devising her next ploy to part him from his cash.

Rafe had to use force to push his way through the men crowding closest around her. He frowned. You'd think they'd never seen a woman before.

'Antonia.' His voice sounded unexpectedly rough.

'Rafe.' She looked up at him and curved her lips into the slightest of smiles. Its impact thundered through his chest. This was the first time her smile hadn't held sarcasm or superciliousness. The effect was hypnotic. Dimly he realised she was only delivering what he'd demanded. The appearance of intimacy. But that didn't lessen the effect.

He reached out and took her hand, drawing her near, staking his ownership.

Strange how the avid attention of every male in the place annoyed him. He always dated gorgeous women, so he was used to envy. This should be no different.

'Quite an entrance you've made,' he whispered. 'If this

is your idea of *not fading into the background*, I'd love to see what you'd do if I asked for *eye-catching*.'

She shrugged one shoulder, and he watched the slinky material move with her body. It didn't matter that it covered her from neck to toe. This was gift wrapping any man would itch to rip away.

Rafe wanted to stroke the fabric, to feel her heat and her delicious curves through it. But he had a purpose in bringing her here: to show her off to Stuart Dexter. To show him that she was beyond his reach now.

His jaw hardened at the sudden, sickening memory of her and Dexter together at that resort nightclub. Dexter's hands pawing at her, his body pressing into hers.

Had Dexter's obsession with her been due to the fact that he'd yet to get her into his bed?

Or had they been lovers? Had she displayed that sultry body for Rafe's father? An invisible vice squeezed the air from his lungs at the thought.

'Come on,' he urged in a voice of gravel. He put his arm round her. 'There are people I want you to meet.'

His hand touched flesh. Bare, warm, satin-smooth. Rafe stilled. His fingers splayed over the indentation of her spine, then slid lower to the dip of her waist. The only fabric he encountered was a narrow lacing, presumably keeping the dress from slipping straight off her.

She met his look steadily, her eyebrows raised just a fraction, as if in query.

What was she wearing? There was precious little to the front of the dress, despite the fact that it covered everything. He'd assumed at least it would have a back.

He lowered his voice. 'I'm wondering how much this dress cost if you thought I could only afford half of it.'

He surprised a smile out of her—a genuine one this time. It was glorious, intriguing, and far too short.

'Believe me, Rafe...' She paused on his name and his skin tingled at the sound of it on her tongue. 'You can afford it. You said you wanted glam, and this *is*.'

It was more than glam. It was sinfully sexy. Beyond provocative, it was downright blatant. He knew exactly what message it sent to every male in the vicinity. That was why he had to stifle the urge to bundle her back into her concealing coat.

Rafe frowned as he ushered Antonia into the penthouse. In the thick silence, he pondered what had gone wrong.

Showing off Antonia as his woman had worked like a charm. Dexter had all but salivated over her in his eagerness to get close. Nor had Rafe missed the glint of chagrin, of anger, in the other man's face as he watched them together.

Antonia had been superbly indifferent, cool and haughty, deigning to respond to Dexter only when absolutely required. That had made Dexter fume even more.

To Rafe's astonishment, she'd even made a show of nestling close to his side, cosying up, so he'd spent most of the evening with his arm wrapped round her. She'd been a distracting armful. His mind had kept wandering as he'd touched her bare back and tried to concentrate.

But, instead of triumphing at Dexter's frustration, Rafe had spent the evening unsettled and increasingly annoyed. Men had clustered around Antonia like dogs around a juicy steak. Those she hadn't seduced with her here-I-am-take-me outfit, she'd charmed. Rafe had spent the evening keeping the wolves at bay.

Not how he'd planned to spend his time.

Who'd have expected her to converse so knowledgeably with one of the National Gallery's most august patrons about the venue's remarkable ceiling? Who cared that it was the only such painting by Rubens still in its original location? Or that there'd been a *simply marvellous* recent exhibition of Dutch masterpieces?

Rafe had been stunned. He'd assumed her area of special expertise was designer labels.

'I don't know how you can stay up so late socialising and then put in a full day's work,' Antonia said, as he shut the apartment door behind them. 'Unless you have a late start tomorrow?' She knew she was babbling, but here, suddenly alone with him, she was aware only of his silent looming presence. And of the proximity of the bedrooms just down the hall. Tension held her rigid.

She'd spent the whole day trying not to think about this moment. She'd had two days' reprieve from his bed. She'd be a fool to expect any more.

'No late start. It will be a normal working day.'

She felt his eyes on her, grazing heat across her skin. Instead of meeting his look, she turned towards the kitchen. Maybe a cup of tea would soothe her nerves.

'Not so fast.'

Antonia stiffened at his harsh tone.

Not now. Please not now.

She was dizzy with fatigue. Grief and anxiety still kept her awake each night. Then there'd been tonight's shock. Her flesh crawled as she remembered being confronted with Stuart Dexter, Rafe's business associate.

She'd taken refuge in Rafe's presence, sidling closer to his protectively large body. She'd known Dexter wouldn't try anything while she was with Rafe, despite the thwarted fury she'd read in his expression. It had been weak of her, relying on the Australian's greater strength, but it had got her through the evening.

'I'm awfully tired.' And her head was beginning to throb. A stress headache.

'Nevertheless, we need to talk.'

Talk? Relief eased her taut shoulders.

He stalked round to stand before her, hands thrust in his trouser pockets, legs planted wide. There was a hint of dark shadow on his jaw that another woman might think enhanced his sexy appeal. She shoved aside the recollection of how his skin's intriguing scent had tickled her senses all evening.

Antonia watched Rafe's jaw harden, his blue eyes flash a warning signal. Just like when she'd walked into the reception tonight. Then she'd experienced a dangerous thrill, knowing she'd surprised him, punctured his self-assured certainty that he was in control of everything. But her delight in standing up to him had long since faded.

'That dress. I don't want to see you in it again.'

That caught her full attention. It was the last thing she'd expected to hear.

It had taken all her resolve to wear this dress. She'd known that if she didn't meet Rafe's demands head-on, with sheer bluff, she'd sink into self-pity. She couldn't afford that if she was to survive the next six months.

She'd made her bed—oh, how she hated that expression—and she had to lie in it. That didn't mean she'd let him browbeat her into submission. Her body might be his to possess, but she was determined he'd know she still had a mind and a will of her own.

She couldn't hide her new mistress status, so she'd decided to flaunt it, and show Rafe his temporary ownership meant nothing. She'd found much-needed strength tonight in the gesture of defiance. It had helped her keep her chin up despite the knowing looks and quizzical murmurs.

'You don't like it?' She lifted one eyebrow, her headache fading as combative energy sizzled.

'I expect you to draw a distinction between looking glam-

orous and looking…overly provocative.' There was an edge
to his words that told her he wasn't happy.

Good. Nor was she. She shrugged off her long coat and
draped it over a chair, feeling his eyes on her.

She shouldn't enjoy baiting him so much. It was far too
dangerous. But his glowering disapproval sparked an inexplicable recklessness in her. And surely that was better than
sinking into despair.

'The most glamorous fashion designs *are* provocative.'

'I want you looking classy,' he bit out. 'Not like some
cheap hooker.'

'Goodness.' Deliberately she widened her eyes. 'The
prostitutes in Australia must be very well dressed. This is
from a *very* exclusive boutique.' One of the few that sold
quality fashion second-hand at knock-down prices.

Old habits died hard. It wasn't the first time she'd
stretched her budget by snaffling a bargain there. But let
Rafe think she'd spent a fortune on his credit card. That was
what he'd expect.

'Don't play the innocent with me,' he growled. 'You
know what I mean.'

'Frankly, I don't. You wanted me to look eye-catching,
so I wore red.' She raised her hand and ticked off one finger.
'You wanted glamorous. This dress is designed on classic
lines.' Another finger ticked off. 'You wanted something appropriate for tonight. This is a formal dress, and unique to
boot.' Tick.

'What about the back of it?'

She tilted her head to one side consideringly. 'You're
surely not telling me, as an experienced man of the world,
that a little bit of bare skin is a problem?'

'More than a little.' He spoke through gritted teeth.

Antonia shrugged. 'You'd see more on any beach. And
besides, it's just my back. No cleavage, no bare legs.'

With a single stride he closed the space between them. His azure gaze was so bright it should have scorched her, but after the emotional turmoil of the last few days she must be immune. Suddenly she was reckless, beyond fear.

'No arguments, Antonia. You won't win.' He glared down at her as if he'd like to shake her into submission. And still the unexpected surge of energy kept her from caring.

'No more backless dresses. Understood?'

'Yes,' she drawled, refusing to be cowed. 'Master…'

Somehow she wasn't at all surprised when he yanked her close and took her mouth in a punishing kiss.

CHAPTER EIGHT

THE sensation of slamming up against his raging heat, his powerful body, his simmering anger, obliterated Antonia's sassy insolence instantly.

How could she even *pretend* to be provocative when every nerve in her body was in shock at the sensations bombarding her?

She felt the clamp of his hands, his arms binding her close, his broad chest crowding her so she couldn't breathe. His tongue plunged into her mouth, possessing her intimately with the brazen confidence of ownership.

The contact lasted only a few moments then, abruptly, he released her. She rocked back on her heels, stunned by his withdrawal, dragging in deep, shocked breaths.

Heat flared in his stunning eyes and her heart plummeted. Her pulse throbbed a frantic beat.

Staring into those eyes, she knew with a sinking heart that it had come. *The moment of reckoning.*

Anger churned inside Rafe. He'd been patient, civilised, more than reasonable. She'd tested his goodwill to the limit. She'd even distracted him from his purpose. These last few days, his mind had wandered from his tricky negotiations and his plans for Stuart Dexter's ruin.

He'd promised to attend the reception tonight, especially as he'd known it would make Dexter sick with jealousy to see him with Antonia. Yet all evening he'd wanted nothing more than to be alone with her.

Satisfaction tinged his annoyance. Now they were—*completely* alone.

Wordlessly he reached for her hand. It was cool, like his mistress. The woman who'd milked him so expertly of his money. It was about time she gave something in return.

Her eyes met his, questioning. He swung her round and strode down the hall to her room, pulling her with him.

'Rafe?' She sounded breathless. He liked it.

Switching on a light, he drew her inside. Lamplight caught the fluid slide of slinky material over her breasts. Teasing little witch! This was going to be a real pleasure.

He placed her hand at his waist. Instantly tremors rayed out under his skin, shooting down his leg and into his groin. Her hand was slim, delicate, feminine. He couldn't wait to find out how it felt on his bare flesh.

'You had a pleasant time this evening?' he said, revelling in a moment's anticipation.

'I…yes. Thank you. Did you?' Her tone was thin, as if her mind were elsewhere. As if his conversation was of little interest. She fixed her gaze over his shoulder.

But he *was* significant. He'd paid for her delightful company—as she'd remember soon enough.

'It wasn't bad.' He slid his palm across her hand, where it rested on his jacket, enjoying the soft texture of her skin warming beneath his, the imprint of her hand on his body. 'But the night's not over yet.'

Looking into the velvet depths of her eyes, he was suddenly tired of this cat-and-mouse game. He knew what he wanted and he was going to get it. *Now.*

'So, Antonia.' His voice lowered to a deep murmur that

drew her skin shivery tight. 'I do believe it's time to consummate our arrangement.'

His bright gaze drew her in, like a helpless moth to a flame. He had her now, and he revelled in the knowledge, in the sheer masculine greed for sexual satisfaction.

Antonia gulped down the clogging distress blocking her throat. She wasn't a helpless victim. She refused to be. The only way she could prevent herself from sinking into helpless despondency was to play the part she'd signed on for. Become his willing mistress and hope to salvage her autonomy by thinking of this purely as a mechanical, physical thing. By divorcing her emotions.

A wave of desolation roared through her.

No! She'd pick up the pieces later, when she was alone.

Antonia's breath snared as she watched him shrug out of his jacket and toss it over a chair. Then he reached for his midnight-blue bow tie. Seconds later it hung loose, a tantalising adornment to his strong, bronzed throat.

Deft fingers flicked open the first few shirt buttons, leaving her staring at a V of bare flesh.

Panic should set in now. Revulsion at what she was about to do.

But instead of horror Antonia discovered something else as Rafe lifted her hand to his chest. Shock reverberated through her at the raw explosion of need ricocheting inside her. What was happening to her?

Involuntarily her fingers splayed wide across the hard, cushioned muscles of his chest. As if she could absorb his masculine essence, the potent life force that emanated from him. It roused her dormant body to instant awareness and a welling sense of longing.

'Yes. Touch me, Antonia.' Rafe gathered her to him, his hands gliding down her back, dipping to follow the indentation of her spine. Then lower, to curve over her buttocks and squeeze. His body was all heat and hardness, his erection blatant against her.

Perversely, she felt no repugnance, no hesitation, only a strange urgent hunger that spiralled tight within her.

How was it possible?

Rafe tilted his hips and a rush of moist heat pooled between her legs.

She wanted him—welcomed his brazen arousal!

Urgent sensations she'd never before known ran riot through her. Each nerve clamoured for more: of his touch, of his body, of his heat that warmed her as nothing ever had.

'Yes, like that,' he urged. Then his head blotted the lamplight and he took her mouth. Behind closed eyes Antonia was aware of him with every inch of her body. She drew his heady musk scent deep into her lungs, experienced the raw power of his sensuality as he melded her against him, kissed her till her head spun.

She told herself she responded because she had no choice. But it was a feeble lie. She wanted—

Strong hands on her shoulders pried her away from him. Glittering eyes the colour of paradise stared down at her as she fought to regulate her breathing. Her pulse raced, her body trembled with the force of unaccustomed desire. If he could do that to her with just a kiss…!

'Take your clothes off,' he said, pushing her back.

Antonia blinked, stunned by his abrupt tone, missing his embrace.

He sat down, and she realised they'd moved across to the bed without her realising. He spread his arms wide on the coverlet and leaned back, bracing himself on his hands.

'Strip for me,' he ordered.

Wordlessly she stared at him, searching for a trace of humour, a hint that he was kidding. She waited.

His mouth curled up at one side in a parody of a smile.

His eyes wore a hooded expression of salacious intent, of impatience—like a petulant sultan, growing annoyed with a recalcitrant concubine.

He was serious. One dark brow rose in mocking interrogation. It was the look she'd dubbed his fallen angel expression. Haughty, challenging, utterly superior.

That's what you get for taunting a man like Rafe Benton. He'd probably stored up the memory of each time she hadn't toed the line, hadn't jumped instantly to his bidding. Now he intended to make her pay.

First he'd humiliate her. Then he'd sate himself in her body. Horrible crawling embarrassment slithered across her skin, leaving it tight and cold. She wanted to wrap her arms about herself and hide from that despoiler's gaze. But she couldn't escape.

He was opening his mouth, no doubt to reiterate the order, when, with a sudden desperate energy, she reached for the shoulders of her dress, wrenching them down her arms with total disregard for the delicate fabric. She shrugged out of both sleeves till the dress hung from her waist.

The air was cold, raising gooseflesh on her skin. She felt her nipples tug into tight peaks. Whether from the chill, or the fact that he surveyed her with proprietary intensity she didn't know. He must be aware of her reaction. It would be visible even beneath the red bra that had been designed to match the delicate laces at the back of the dress.

Antonia couldn't watch him as she lowered the side zipper then pushed the fabric down over her hips. She let her eyes glaze to an unfocused blur. It was easy with moisture pricking them.

She had to shimmy out of the clinging dress, but eventually managed to push it down till it slid to pool around her feet. Ice-hot shame seared her.

Gingerly she stepped to one side and bent to undo the tiny straps on her shoes.

'No! Leave them.' His voice seemed hoarse, but Antonia knew it was just that she couldn't hear properly over the rushing sound in her ears.

She fixed her eyes on the sheer curtains tied beside the bed as she lifted her hand to the front clasp of her bra. Her fingers shook so much she couldn't undo it.

She bit the inside of her cheek as she tried to steady herself. No matter how he tried to humiliate her, she refused to let Rafe Benton know how well he'd succeeded. She couldn't let him guess how much this cost her.

Mortification filled her as she realised how unthinkingly she might have given herself if only he'd continued kissing her. She'd been putty in his hands.

And he'd known it. But obviously that hadn't been enough for his jaded tastes. He'd needed to torment her too.

'Come here,' he ordered. 'There are some things a man prefers to do himself.'

Every muscle froze to rigidity. Bad enough to provide the floor show. But the idea of his hands on her body…

Her stomach cramped in a spasm of pure dismay. She ignored it and stepped close, till she stood within the V of his spread legs. The heat of his body curled around her, but it couldn't warm her. She was chilled to the marrow.

Lifting her chin, she kept her eyes fixed on the swathe of bed curtains. Maybe if she didn't look she could pretend this wasn't real.

But the feel of his long fingers deftly flicking open her bra was all too real. Antonia sucked in a breath as he slid the straps off her shoulders and it fell away.

Silence.

She squeezed her thighs tight together, trying to stop the trembling in her legs. Cool air caressed her breasts, and despite her best intentions she drew a deep shuddery breath that pushed her nipples forward towards him as he sat so still and silent.

What next? Was she supposed to discard her knickers too? Heaven help her, she had no knowledge to draw on here.

'You really are beautiful, aren't you?' he whispered roughly. 'But obviously you know that.'

It sounded like an accusation. Antonia frowned. What did he want her to say?

Then all thought suspended as his hands closed on her breasts, cupping them, moulding, massaging. Her breath was a hiss of desperation as unfamiliar sensations shot through her.

'You like that?' No mistaking the satisfaction in his gravel-deep tone.

But Antonia didn't answer. She was too busy stiffening herself against the strange laxness that had attacked her muscles. She wasn't going to fall in a heap at his feet, no matter how insidiously wonderful the feelings he evoked.

His thumb and forefinger tightened, tweaking her right nipple, and a jolt of fiery heat shot straight through her.

'Ah, you're very sensitive.'

She hated his smug tone almost as much as she hated her body's betrayal. How could she respond when he was so callous in his treatment of her?

She'd always believed that she'd only respond physically to a man if she were in love with him. Or believed herself to be, as she had with Peter. How appallingly little she knew about herself.

'So I think you'll like this.'

Antonia jumped as his mouth closed on her nipple.

'Steady,' he murmured, and she felt his lips on her sensitive skin. One strong arm wrapped around her back to hold her close against him. His other hand was warm and surprisingly gentle, cupping her breast as he sucked.

Antonia's knees threatened to buckle at the scorching comet of heat and need that burned its way across her consciousness. Her eyes fluttered shut and she swayed towards him, pressing into him, revelling in the ecstasy of his mouth working her flesh. It felt…unbelievable.

Not so unbelievable as the unmistakable flood of moist arousal at her core. Again she tensed her legs, this time trying to counter the warm gush. She didn't want to be turned on. She *shouldn't* be. And yet undeniably her body was responding to his ministrations. He ran his tongue over the underside of her breast and all her muscles clenched.

'Open your eyes,' he demanded.

She opened them to slits against the light.

'Now look at me.'

Slowly, reluctantly, Antonia tilted her head down. Dark hair, blazing blue eyes, that long angular nose and… She reached out and grabbed his shoulders, needing to anchor herself. She watched his teeth nip at one rosy peak then move to the other. He licked her breast, from bottom to top, his eyes never leaving hers. Her fingers tightened like claws on the muscles of his shoulders as darts of pure desire shot with lightning force through her.

From under straight black brows his knowing eyes surveyed her, watching the effect of his caresses. There was nothing she could do. She couldn't dissemble. Not when she was melting at every deliberate touch, each gentle bite. He drew her nipple into his mouth and sucked hard, and she felt it straight through her belly, between her legs, in every erogenous zone in her body.

A low moan sounded in her ears and she realised it must be her. Yet she could barely care when he worked such magic on her.

Finally he raised his head, still watching her. Her breasts throbbed and it was all she could do not to thrust them forward, wordlessly demanding more.

'Now it's your turn,' he said. 'Undress me.'

The pulse drumming between her legs was almost strong enough to drown out her silent cry of denial.

But where could she go? Rafe would only haul her back. And the shaming truth was that, despite the humiliation of being ordered to please him, Antonia was excited by the experience. Secretly thrilled by the sweet torment of his mouth and hands on her breasts. Desperately eager for more, if more meant an ease to the compulsive urge for intimacy.

Her hands shook as she removed his cufflinks, but she got them out and dropped them into his waiting palm. He reached out and put them on her bedside table, along with something he drew from his pocket. Square foil packets. Several of them.

Her eyes rounded. Surely they wouldn't need so many?

'I like to be prepared,' Rafe said as he surged to his feet before her. This close his spicy musk scent tickled her nostrils. The sharp tang of it was different, more pronounced than before.

He lifted her hands to his half-open shirt. Now her movements were less clumsy. Maybe because with each button she revealed more of his dark bronze chest and torso.

Her mouth dried as she took in the masculine perfection slowly being revealed. She tugged his shirt out and spread it wide. A fuzz of dark hair crossed his pectorals. In the lamplight its shadow highlighted the pronounced definition of his muscles.

She'd known he was strong, but somehow he seemed bigger, more solid, without the layers of his suit and dress shirt. He was completely, blatantly masculine.

Antonia pushed the fine cotton from his shoulders and

let it fall, aware of him with each straining nerve. She trembled, caught within his potent physical aura, her heartbeat erratic. If Rafe Benton hadn't been a corporate high-flier he'd have made a fortune as a male model. Her gaze trailed down his body and every inch was perfection.

'There's more,' he urged, in a dark, teasing voice.

Antonia blinked, jerked out of her abstraction. Still she refused to look him in the eye. She knew her limits.

Instead she knelt before him to undo his shoelaces. He'd enjoy that, no doubt, the sight of her obeisance. Desperately she tried to ignore his looming presence, but it was impossible. She felt too vulnerable.

Too soon his shoes and socks were discarded and she straightened, wobbling only slightly on the high heels. For a heartbeat she hesitated, steeling herself, then made herself reach for his belt. Her knuckles brushed his abdomen and the smooth skin that was pure invitation. It was like touching electricity—shock waves roared through her. For a moment her senses swam, then she noticed his reflexive movement—the drawing in of muscle, the tightening of skin. She paused, wondering.

Slowly she undid the buckle and loosened Rafe's belt. Then she reached for the fastening of his trousers, slipping her fingers inside, against the hot satin of his skin. Again that instant reaction. This time she could almost swear she heard a swift intake of breath.

The realisation buoyed her. Not so one-sided, then, despite Rafe's arrogance. Her hand was almost steady as she tugged the zip down, then pushed his trousers to the floor.

'And the rest,' he urged, his voice a low whisper.

Tentatively Antonia reached out and tugged his boxers down. There was a moment of delay as the fabric caught on his erection, but he helped her, freeing himself from the shorts and thrusting them impatiently out of the way.

Antonia tried not to stare, but it was impossible. Rafe Benton was beautiful all over. And the sight of his arousal, rampant and ready for *her*, was shamingly exciting.

Hurriedly she shifted her gaze, to find him tearing open one of the foil packets.

Her eyes darted to his face, taking in the stark lines of concentration there, the taut control. For all his measured movements, Rafe looked like a man on the edge.

'Here.' He pressed the condom into her hand and sat down on the bed.

'You want me to…?'

'Why not?' His smile was frayed. 'Practice makes perfect, and I'm sure you've had plenty of practice.'

Antonia gritted her teeth at the calculated insult. 'You may be surprised to discover that I've never…' She paused and swallowed. 'Never done this before.'

'What? Never fitted a condom?' His tone was incredulous. Then his eyes narrowed and he sat forward a little. 'Or are you trying to tell me you're a virgin?'

Flaming heat washed Antonia's face as she shook her head. 'No. Not that.' Though in truth she was only barely experienced.

'Good. I wouldn't like to think you'd added lying to your other accomplishments.' He leaned back and fixed her with a gimlet eye.

The self-satisfied, smirking—

'I'm ready when you are,' he taunted.

That much was obvious, she thought sourly. More than ready. So ready that she was nervous, wondering about the mechanics of this. She was tall, but he was so well endowed. Was that squiggle of tension in her stomach fear or excitement? She blanked her mind, trying not to think about it. Trying not to think about anything.

'Come on, Antonia. You do it this time and I'll do it next.' He smiled a wide, white taunting grin. 'I'm an equal opportunities lover.'

That stiffened her spine, Rafe saw. Not that it needed straightening. She was the perfect picture of haughty disdain. Even standing there in nothing but lace panties and the sexiest shoes he'd ever seen, she had the bearing of a queen. He watched her perfect high breasts sway as she knelt and his breath stopped deep in his lungs.

If he didn't have her soon, he'd explode. The combination of her cool touch-me-not air and the incredible sensuality of her response to his lightest caress had him groping for control. He'd had to pull back, establish some mental distance, so he didn't do something stupid like take her instantly, with no preliminaries and no precautions.

Antonia Malleson was the hottest woman he'd ever met. The sound of her husky voice moaning as he sucked at her breast had shorted something in his brain, welding shut the door on what was left of his self-possession.

He couldn't remember ever wanting a woman with quite this level of desperation.

Her slim fingers touched him and thought fled. He held his breath as tentatively, softly, her fingers fluttered over him. She fumbled with the condom, paused and tried again.

He wasn't breathing. His hands were clamped into the bedding and his body was tight as a high wire. Why hadn't he listened when she'd said she'd never done this before? She was killing him by degrees. It was sheer erotic torment having her touch him. Damn his need to score points with his taunting.

Afterwards Antonia couldn't recall exactly what happened next. It was a blur of rapid movement, of shockingly intimate, wonderful sensation. Within seconds, it seemed,

Rafe had finished the job she'd barely begun, stripped away her shoes and her underwear, and she was caught in that mesmerising electric gaze.

She felt it flare again—the same heat that had pulsed between them when they'd met. A scorching force that rocked her to her core. She tried to hang on to her anger but her focus was shifting.

'No more games,' he growled. Then his arms were around her and he pulled her onto the bed, his body warming hers, his hands creating fire with each slow swipe.

He took her face in his palms and kissed her. Not in a show of strength or domination this time but, it dawned on her, in mutual delight.

Her fear and even her fury fled as he coaxed, cajoled, tempted her into responding. She didn't recall giving up the fight to stay distant, whole, separate. For Rafe set about seducing her with expert caresses, whispered words of encouragement, and a look in his eyes that no woman could resist. That expression—intense pleasure, sultry invitation and something else that looked remarkably like tenderness—bypassed the last of her weak defences.

His hands were those of a lover: sure, gentle and knowing. He palmed her inner thigh, up one leg and down the other, slowing each time to touch her just...*there*, where her need burned brightest. He lingered, stroked, his caresses languorous, then purposeful. And through it all his eyes held hers captive.

Soon her body was alight with a blaze of desire. She welcomed him as he braced himself above her. There was no thought now of pride or honour or shame as she slipped her hands round his back, sliding them across his slick, hot skin. There was just this moment.

He paused, his chest heaving above her, the coarse hair

on his legs tickling her thighs. His warmth, his musky scent, his power encompassed her.

'Ready?' he surprised her by asking.

It didn't occur to her to say no. For this was what she wanted. Whether it was right or wrong, she craved this intimacy now with every particle of her being.

Wordlessly she nodded, and an instant later the world turned over, rocked off its axis by the sensation of his possession, their oneness. She had a moment only to absorb that stunning new reality and then it started, a trembling rush of heat that forged out through her body, tightening each muscle and sinew, shocking her with its intensity.

Antonia clutched at him wordlessly and he responded with another slow, deep thrust right to her core that unleashed the floodtide of exquisite sensation. Her eyes fluttered shut as her body found ecstasy. And through it she carried the image of his sky-blue eyes, heard his husky voice urging her on and on.

Then, just as she reached an impossible peak of pleasure, that perfect rocking movement faltered and he climaxed too. His body shook with the force of it, his guttural cry reverberated in her ears and she felt him pulse within her.

Antonia pulled him close, wrapping her arms tight round him as she sank into the bed, blanketed by his solid weight. Against all logic, she experienced a sense of rightness. It should be impossible. Yet what they'd shared was remarkable, mind-numbing. In the aftermath of bliss she didn't have the energy to question it.

After a few moments he moved, rolling onto his back, keeping her clamped to him as if he couldn't bear the thought of breaking that embrace any more than she could.

She felt safe in Rafe's arms, as if the grief and pain of the everyday world had been magically banished. Their hearts beat together, their urgent breaths in sync.

She tried to tell herself this was just sex. Better sex than she'd had with Peter. Better sex than she'd dreamed possible. Yet thinking it and believing it were two different matters.

An inner voice told her that it had just changed her life. Antonia closed her ears to it. That wasn't hard to do as Rafe lifted her chin with long fingers that shook just enough for her to notice. They stared at each other, and Antonia realised his eyes were glazed with the same shock that filled her. The same wonder. No trace now of the cocky autocrat who'd ordered her acquiescence to his whims.

'Antonia.' Even his voice sounded different—a raw, husky whisper.

Then he was kissing her, slowly, gently, as if she was the most precious thing in his world. She gave herself up willingly, reciprocating with caresses of her own.

The lamp was still on when she woke out of a haze of comfort, her body weighted with pleasure. Something had changed. The intense heat that had cradled her was missing.

Blearily she narrowed her eyes against the light, glancing at the bedside table with its litter of torn wrappers. It looked as if they had used them all.

A tiny thrill spiralled through her belly at the memory of how well loved she'd been. Of how perfect Rafe had made it for her, responding to needs she hadn't been aware she possessed.

She reached out a hand to him, realising she couldn't feel him against her. Abruptly she turned her head, hearing movement. She frowned as an invisible weight pushed down on her chest. Her breath seized under the pressure.

Rafe stood at the foot of the bed, his clothes a tumbled bundle in his naked arms. He looked gorgeously male, the lamplight gilding each powerful curve and plane of his body and glinting off the dark sheen of his rumpled hair. His surprisingly soft hair, through which she'd tunnelled her hands as they'd made love time after time.

Something like tenderness welled inside her.

Then his eyes met hers, and her pulse pounded loud in her head. He looked *different*. Gone was the intimacy, the shared pleasure of the past few hours. Instead his gaze was sharp, like honed steel.

'What are you doing?' Her voice was a ragged whisper as she spoke over rising foreboding.

'Collecting my clothes.' His forehead puckered, as if he was surprised at her question.

'Why?'

'I don't expect you to do my laundry, Antonia. I'm sure such domesticity wouldn't suit you.' His tone was cool, collected, matter-of-fact. Totally unlike the man who'd just shared her bed and what she'd thought in her innocence had been the most profound mysteries a man and a woman could experience together.

Her heart dipped. 'Why not?' Already she knew she wouldn't like the answer.

She was right.

'Because your talents obviously lie in other directions.' His gaze roved from her hair, loose around her shoulders, down the rumpled coverlet, to encompass the whole of the vast four-poster bed. His mouth curved up in a slow, satisfied smile that iced her veins.

'Sleep well.' He turned towards the door.

'Where are you going?' She couldn't keep the sharp edge from her voice.

Rafe paused and looked over his shoulder, his expression closed. 'I told you when we arrived, Antonia. I sleep alone. I'll see you tomorrow.'

The light clicked off and darkness enfolded her.

She'd just been dismissed. Used by the man who'd paid for her services, put firmly in her place, then set aside.

It was as if he'd slapped her across the face.

Reality crashed in, negating the joy they'd shared, the unexpected sense of peace she'd discovered in their intimacy. He'd smashed her fragile fantasy, reminding her this was a business transaction. *A sordid arrangement. Not a new beginning.*

Pain welled in all the places his touch had thawed.

She felt like a prostitute.

CHAPTER NINE

ANTONIA stared out of her bedroom window, her mind straying inevitably to Rafe. And how she'd morphed in his arms into a woman she didn't know.

Heat flooded her as she recalled their encounters. Her skin drew tight and tingling at the images shifting in her brain. Images of them entwined together, of the desire blazing in his eyes as he undressed her, of the eager way she'd matched his demands with a ravenous hunger of her own.

It had been a revelation. Despite her pride, her anger, her confusion, she could never resist him. Each time he drew her close her resistance crumbled and she grew willing, even wanton, in his arms.

There must be a sensible explanation. Maybe sex with Rafe was a physical outlet for the turmoil of raw emotions she'd clamped a lid on for so long. Heaven help her if her response had anything to do with genuine attraction.

Attraction? To the man who'd purchased her to warm his bed? She told herself that was impossible.

She frowned. Each night she played the part of devoted mistress, accompanying him to some society event and then later spending hours satisfying his more personal needs. He was a demanding lover, and a generous one. To her shame she found herself eagerly anticipating their lovemaking. It would be too easy to allow her own physical satisfaction to blind her to the fact that this was a business arrangement. He still left her to sleep alone. Never bothered to check if she was awake before leaving early for the office. It was his PA who called each day with details of that night's outing.

No, this was a thoroughly cold-blooded deal. She fitted a convenient niche in life. That was all.

A numbing fog enclosed her as she watched rain spatter the windows. Grief was still a yawning dark void inside. She was trapped in a role that outraged every sensibility, and there was no escape.

The wintry weather matched her mood: dull and listless. Even the solace of tears eluded her. She was closed up— her emotions, even her grief, locked away.

The only time she felt a spark of heat and life was when Rafe baited her into indignation or anger.

Or when he made love to her.

'Antonia. Are you ready?' Rafe's voice pulled her out of her reverie.

Hurriedly she scooped up her jacket, her beaded evening purse and opened the door, ignoring a skittering sensation that might be excitement. No, it was simply that she didn't want him entering her room.

'Ready,' she said, not quite meeting his eyes. He looked superb in evening dress. The contrast between the suave suit and his rugged handsomeness inevitably sent a twinge of awareness scooting through her.

Slowly he surveyed her and she held her breath, hating the way excitement pumped her blood faster.

'You look fantastic.' He took in her sleeveless top and trousers in slinky black threaded with gold.

His eyebrows rose as he saw her sandals: pure mistress material, with gossamer straps of rhinestones and four-inch spiked heels. One look had told her they were perfect for the role she was playing.

'And…' his lips tilted up in wry appreciation '…you have the sexiest feet.' His voice was a rich, low rumble that caressed her skin.

Astonishment froze her. She recognised with dismay the skirl of excitement his words evoked. She tensed.

'I'm glad you like glitter. I've brought you something I think you'll enjoy.' He stepped into the room, proffering a velvet case.

A gift? A second look confirmed her initial impression. There was no mistaking the jeweller's box. The zing of secret pleasure she'd felt at his arrival disintegrated.

'Aren't you going to open it?' He sounded more impatient than amused now.

Reluctantly she took the case and lifted the lid. Inside was a brilliant rope of stunning yellow diamonds. A long strand shaped as a pendant and a matching bracelet.

'You hired them?' she asked dully.

'No.' Even without looking up she could hear the frown in his voice. 'I bought them for you to wear tonight.'

'Thank you,' she said woodenly.

He wanted to flaunt his mistress and his wealth for all to see. He'd sell the pieces when she was gone. After all, she was expendable.

This reminder of their commercial arrangement hit her like a body-blow to the stomach. Antonia felt the last tattered shreds of her self-respect rip away as his big square hand dipped into the box and lifted the necklace. Her muscles cramped and her fingers tightened like claws on the plush velvet of the jewel case.

'You haven't worn any jewellery since we came to London.' No missing the question in his tone.

'No,' she said, her eyes fixed on this symbol of her degradation. 'It's not really my style,' she lied.

'Now, that surprises me.'

She darted her head up and found his gaze raking her, as if he could strip her bare of secrets. She shivered at the intensity of that look, feeling far too vulnerable.

'Your complexion is perfect for gold,' he said, with all the conviction of a man who'd no doubt adorned his previous mistresses with baubles and pricey trinkets. 'Like that pendant you wore in Switzerland. Opal, wasn't it?'

'Yes,' she said quickly and ducked her head, pretending interest in the diamonds. Why did he have to remember that? It had been her mother's favourite piece and Antonia had sold it with the rest of her jewellery. That had been her first act when she'd had a day alone in London.

A familiar ache began deep inside her—a burgeoning pain she battled to repress. All she had now of her mother was memories. She really was utterly alone.

'Here, let me,' he murmured. Deftly he clasped the bracelet around her wrist, then moved behind her to lower the pendant onto her bare neck. The icy metal burned her flesh like a brand. A brand of his possession.

His hands moved from her nape to her shoulders and he turned her to face the full-length mirror on the other side of the room. She concentrated on the sparkling necklace rather than the image of his tall body framing hers.

'Nothing to say, Antonia?' No mistaking his impatience.

'It's very beautiful,' she said, knowing it was the truth, but sickened at the realisation he'd bought her as easily as he had the jewellery.

What had she become?

Rafe looked at the reflection of her set face and wondered what in hell was wrong with her.

'Most women would be excited about a gift like that,' he prompted, annoyed that he'd let her get to him again.

'I'm sure you're right. It must have cost a lot of money.' She said it as calmly as if she didn't give a damn for the price—which he knew to be a lie. The thought infuriated him.

'Most women would show their thanks in a tangible way.' A kiss, even a smile would be a start.

He was tired of the way she clammed up, as if an impenetrable barrier cut her off from him. They only communicated when she let down her guard because he'd taunted her into a dispute. Then he'd see the vibrant woman behind the blank façade.

Or when they made love. Then it was as if she were another woman. Real and passionate and just as needy as he. Then the desire between them was so strong, so compelling, he had a hard time matching her to the aloof beauty who kept him at arm's length.

'I'm sorry. I've disappointed you.' He watched her reflection form the words. Her lips seemed curiously stiff.

She turned round to face him and he looked down into guarded dark eyes. Not even a flicker of satisfaction there. She must be the most cold-blooded woman he'd ever met. Yet a disturbing niggle in his gut told him she wasn't that straightforward.

Slowly Antonia lifted her arms. He caught the spangle of gems on one wrist as she looped her hands behind his head. Her fingers cupped his neck and his breathing quickened.

'How would you like me to thank you?' Her voice had that husky quality he loved. The throaty roughness that signalled her arousal. Only this time instinct told him it was some other emotion he heard in her voice.

Her lips touched his. Pliant, warm, enticing. Instantly, inevitably, heat roared through him.

'With a kiss?' The movement of her lips against his was an erotic invitation, and the feel of her leaning close sent his pulse thundering.

'Or something more?' She pulled back a fraction, letting cool air slide between them. He saw her tilt her head to look at her watch. 'We're due there in forty minutes. I don't know how important this reception is tonight.' Her eyes met his unblinkingly. 'Do you want to be on time?'

Rafe frowned at the sudden twist of discomfort in his stomach. It was the way she spoke, so cold-bloodedly, as if it made no difference to her whether they left now or whether he tumbled her back onto the bed.

He knew that wasn't true. He knew for a fact she was *always* satisfied with his loving. He made sure of it. She was as interested in their sex-life as he was, damn it!

He had no explanation for the crawling heat that spread under his skin. She couldn't have reinforced more clearly that he'd purchased her for his pleasure. To his chagrin, he discovered he wanted more. He wanted her willing and wanting. An equal partner, not a bought one.

He reached round and took her hands in his, dragging them from his shoulders and holding them before him. The gems of her new bracelet were hard and cold against his palm.

'No! You've done enough.' His tone was rough and her eyes widened.

Which was the real Antonia? The fiery seductress or the cold-as-frost woman calmly offering herself in recompense for the thousands of pounds worth of diamonds on her wrist?

He'd seen the golden fire in the stones and instantly thought of the way her eyes blazed when they made love. The purchase had been pure impulse. One he now regretted.

'Come on,' he grated. 'It's time we left.'

* * *

Two hours later Rafe looked down at the gorgeous woman beside him, baffled. Gone was the reserve that for one crazy moment he'd thought might be pain. Her mood had swung to one of hectic gaiety. She chatted animatedly, drawing men to her side effortlessly with her wit and her smiles.

Never before had he felt so wrong-footed. When he asserted his presence, made her acknowledge him, she devoted her attention to him with generous smiles, a hand on his sleeve, sparkling glances from lustrous eyes.

Yet her apparent intimacy felt unsatisfying. False. As if she were a consummate actress playing a game.

Annoyance twisted his mouth to a grim line. He'd counted on her acknowledging the powerful attraction between them by now. But she pretended it didn't exist.

'Let's dance,' he murmured in her ear, simultaneously drawing her aside.

'Dance?' She faltered to a stop.

'Yes. It'll give your admirers a chance to wipe the drool off their faces.'

Her brows arched. 'You're exaggerating.'

'I never exaggerate.' He swept a look down as he led her to the dance floor. He should have paid more attention to what she was wearing earlier, but he'd been preoccupied with her puzzling lack of response to the diamonds. It hadn't been until they'd arrived at the business awards ceremony that he'd seen the way her trousers swung as she walked, parting in long side-slits to reveal the perfection of her legs. She was barely decent.

If it weren't for the fact that he was giving a speech soon he'd take her straight home. But at least in a slow dance her outfit wouldn't draw too many eyes. Rafe pulled her close, loving the feel of her soft body against his.

'I had an interesting conversation with my PA today.'

'You did?'

'Yes. There was some confusion with a couple of credit accounts, and she checked the expenditure on the one you've been using.'

Antonia raised her head at that, stiffening in his embrace. 'You've been checking up on me, you mean!'

He ignored that. Why the hell would he check up on a card he'd made available for her use?

'She said there'd been very little spent, despite the glamorous outfits you've been wearing.' His hand slid over the silky fabric at her back. She felt so good.

'And?'

'Why are you being so frugal with my money?' In the dimmed lighting it was hard to read her expression, but she was avoiding his eyes.

'I hadn't realised it was compulsory for me to be extravagant.' Her response was flippant.

He pulled her close, so she was flush against him. After a moment's resistance he felt her relax. His lips curved up in satisfaction.

'There's no need to get on your high horse. I'm not annoyed, just curious.'

She shrugged. 'Why spend a fortune on clothes I'm not going to keep?'

'Of course you'll keep them. They're yours.' Anger roughened his voice. Was she implying he'd take them from her when they parted?

She shook her head. 'In case I want to hook myself another wealthy man? No, thanks.'

Satisfaction jabbed him at the knowledge she wouldn't wear any of her sexy outfits for anyone else. Until he realised she'd probably demand any future lover bought her a complete new wardrobe. The very idea of Antonia with another man sent tension spiralling through him. His hands tightened on her and she looked up at him. Those dark eyes of hers were mesmerising, almost enough to distract him.

'How are you keeping the bills so low, Antonia? You might as well tell me. I'll find out eventually.'

Her chin jerked up as if he'd aimed a body-blow. Had he hit a nerve?

She turned her head and stared past his shoulder, as if the milling crowd held her interest.

'I bought them from a few places I know. They deal in second-hand fashion.'

Rafe couldn't believe his ears. He'd summed her up as too proud, too haughty, ever to stoop to wearing someone else's garments.

'You can pick your jaw up now,' she said tartly. 'It's not that unusual, you know. Lots of people do it.'

But he'd never imagined her to be one of them. 'I know.' Hell, he'd done it himself years ago. 'But why take the cheap option when you have access to my money?'

Was there ever a more puzzling woman?

'Habit, I suppose.' Her voice was so low he had to lean close to hear her.

'You've done this before?'

'It's nothing to be ashamed of!' She paused, as if waiting for him to change the subject. But he was intrigued.

'Go on.' He could feel her body stiffening again. But he'd question her all night if he had to.

'Money has always been tight. All right?' She glared at him, her mouth a flat line. 'My father never learned to econ-omise, and the places we lived…well, there was rarely a cheap option.' She drew in a deep breath. 'Now, can we leave this?'

'Of course. On one condition. From now on you buy new. Understood?' No woman of his was going to wear hand-me-downs. He'd worked too long and hard to escape all that.

For a charged moment she held his gaze. Then abruptly she nodded. Strange how her capitulation felt like a victory. This information merely confirmed what he knew about her constant need for money. She moved in circles where wealth was taken for granted, but she had trouble keeping up appearances. No wonder she was on the make.

Yet there was something else here too. Something he couldn't quite put his finger on. If she was so greedy, why hadn't she taken advantage of his money and spent lavishly on herself?

He shook his head and pulled her to him, revelling in the feel of her delicious curves moving against him.

Would he ever understand this woman?

Antonia gave herself up to the heady pleasure of Rafe's embrace. The rhythmic swaying movement seemed so intimate. When he held her like this she felt absurdly safe and content. Almost…cherished.

The idea was ridiculous. But every so often, like now, she sensed there was another side to him. Apart from the demanding tycoon and the expert lover.

Why had he insisted on her buying new clothes for herself? Was it pride—he didn't want his mistress in second best? Or was it generosity?

He'd been generous in giving her the diamonds too. And she was pretty sure now that he had no idea how insulting she'd found the gift. He'd looked so stunned at her reaction. Almost hurt.

Hah! As if that were possible. Her being able to hurt the mighty Rafe Benton.

Yet there were other things that made her wonder about him. His unfailing politeness to staff, from doormen to waitresses. He treated them with the same courtesy he bestowed on the wealthy guests at functions like tonight's.

His easy camaraderie with his chauffeur, the back and forth discussion on anything from football scores to politics and the achievements of young grandchildren.

In her experience, most mega-wealthy people preferred to forget that the people who drove them, or served them in some other way, were real people with lives of their own.

'That woman tonight,' she said suddenly, remembering the gorgeously dressed older woman. 'Barbara Havers.'

'Yes? What about her?' His voice came from just above her, muffled in her hair. She shut her eyes, enjoying the illusion of warmth and intimacy it engendered. She'd never enjoyed dancing with any man the way she did with Rafe.

'Is she an old friend?'

'I never met her before tonight. Why?'

'You got on so well, I wondered.' She paused, choosing her words carefully. 'Some people find it difficult or embarrassing at first, having a conversation with someone in a wheelchair.' She remembered the last stages of her mother's illness, when strangers would instinctively turn away from the frail seated figure.

'More fool them. It's the person, not the chair, you speak to.' There was something in his voice that made her raise her head.

His face looked curiously set, his jaw hard.

'My mother was in a wheelchair for years,' he said at last. 'So I know exactly what you mean.'

Was? Past tense? Had she recovered, or was she…? Antonia didn't have the nerve to pry.

'You spent a lot of time with her?'

'I was her primary carer for years.' His mouth thinned to a flat line and he stepped back as the music ended. Cool air rushed between them. Antonia felt curiously bereft.

The lights were turned up and she read grimness in his eyes. Bad memories, then. Something squeezed tight inside her at the sight of his pain; fellow feeling, perhaps. She too had personal experience of caring for an ailing parent, and of loss.

Instinctively she reached out and put her hand on his arm.

For a moment he stood still, looking down at her hand on the fine cloth of his jacket. Then he turned, obviously not wanting in her sympathy.

'Come on. It's time to take our seats.'

CHAPTER TEN

RAFE sat at the conference table, watching an audio-visual presentation. He hadn't taken in a single fact. He'd been on edge all day. All night. He hadn't slept since leaving Antonia's room last night.

A month since they'd become lovers and still the novelty hadn't worn off. She was endlessly fascinating. Far more so than this presentation.

If he wasn't careful she'd distract him from his scheme for revenge. That would be disastrous. It was past time his father paid for his sins.

Yet all day his thoughts had centred on the woman he'd left curled in bed. She was an intriguing mix of vamp and innocent. That first night it had been patently obvious she wasn't as sexually experienced as he'd assumed, though she had the sensual power to rob him of coherent thought.

She was a riddle: the woman who grabbed every penny she could and yet was unmoved by diamonds that cost a fortune. Who was happiest discussing art history with some ageing expert. The woman who'd once encouraged Dexter's intimacies and now shrank from him every time they met.

The woman who'd given Rafe the best sex of his life.

Had her initial coldness been an act to pique his curiosity? He sure as hell hoped so. He'd never met a woman who had the power to arouse him so completely or quickly.

Yet memories flashed into his head. Of her soft eyes, wide and wary. Of her taut self-possession. Of the way she'd almost dare him to take her, refusing to initiate intimacy herself. Then his certainty would crumble a little and something like guilt would crack his complacency.

He had no reason for guilt. He'd offered a deal and she'd taken it. A business transaction and a mutual pleasure. She couldn't deny that. So often he brought her to the brink of ecstasy, then waited till she begged for completion. He needed to hear her husky-voiced pleas, see the stunned delight in her dark eyes, knowing that no other man had ever satisfied her the way he did.

Their first time together had been spectacular. He'd been so aroused just by the sight of her stripping, and then by the feel of her velvet-soft skin against his, that he'd climaxed almost straight away. But to his amazement that excitement had never faded. Each time was like the first. Better, even, as he learned what pleased her most, so she became willing and wanton in his arms.

Last night he'd wanted to stay with her, wrapped in her sleek warmth, caressed by her long silky hair, hearing the soft sound of her breathing, reliving the ecstasy of their coming together. Anticipating the next time.

Yet in the afterglow of sexual satisfaction he'd read danger. He could so easily be tempted to spend even more time with her. Already she stole his attention when, as now, he had important business to attend to.

No, she had her place in his life—temporarily. It would be unwise to give her more. He sat straighter, resolving to concentrate on the presentation.

A few minutes later he glanced at his watch, calculating how long before he could wrap up his meeting.

* * *

Rafe arrived home early. She'd be getting ready. He couldn't remember where they were going. Some reception where he could remind his father that he, Rafe, possessed the woman the older man wanted. Each hungry, frustrated stare Stuart Dexter directed at Antonia was balm to Rafe's soul. Revenge was sweet and it could only get better.

Perhaps she was in the shower. His thoughts strayed to an image of water sluicing lovingly over each curve, of it sliding down the perfection of those long, long legs.

His body grew taut. He flung his briefcase onto a side table, tugged his coat from his shoulders and threw it onto a sofa, then strode down the hall.

He found her in the bathroom, her back to him. She was fully clothed, but the sight of her pulled him up short. His breath punched from his body as shock rippled through him.

Impossible that she could go *anywhere* dressed like that. Yet she could wear it for him any time—privately. He'd revel in watching her. For the few minutes before he stripped her naked.

His gaze trawled down sleek black leather, fitted like a glove over her narrow shoulders and even narrower waist. The flare of her hips was accentuated by the wide belt she wore over tight-fitting leather trousers. Rafe eyed the perfect curve of her buttocks, searching for evidence of underwear but finding none. Heat shot to his groin.

Her legs looked impossibly long and sexy. Once again she was wearing heels so high she looked like a…

A mistress, he realised as she met his gaze in the wide mirror. A very expensive, very sexy mistress.

She'd done something to her eyes, darkening them. They looked exotic and blatantly sensual. Her lips were red, glossy, a pout straight from one of his erotic dreams. Around her throat was a narrow ribbon of black velvet that emphasised the pure, delicate line of her throat and managed to draw attention down to the zip of her jacket, undone just enough to hint at the inviting abundance below.

His libido roared into full gear.

He read some fleeting expression in her eyes. Surprise perhaps, but then the blankness he'd come to hate shuttered it. He'd never met a woman so controlled, so apparently impervious to him—at least until he got her naked.

'You're home early.' She didn't even turn to face him, much less offer a greeting.

Rafe wondered if he should renegotiate their contract. How much would he have to pay to get a welcome kiss when he came home? Though maybe wives did that, not mistresses.

'My meetings ended earlier than expected.' Because he'd cancelled the last one, eager to get back and see her.

'Then you'll have plenty of time to get ready for tonight.' She turned her attention to the mascara she was applying, dismissing him.

But Rafe wasn't a man to be dismissed. He paced forward till he was flush behind her. She froze, then slowly lifted the mascara wand to her face.

He put his hand on her buttock and felt her stiffen. Warm leather, soft female, and nothing, he'd swear, between them. The realisation sparked all sorts of salacious thoughts. He slid his hand down, enjoying the knowledge that she was his for the taking. This delicious, tantalising witch of a woman was his alone. She was one hell of a temptress.

'That's a sexy new outfit,' he murmured, swaying forward to shadow her body. 'Did you buy it to celebrate?' A month of mind-blowing sex was an excellent reason to party. He especially approved of the gift wrapping. He eyed the zip of her jacket, with its tantalisingly large tab.

'Celebrate?' She looked at him in the mirror, her eyes wide and questioning. 'Is this some special occasion?'

Rafe's mouth firmed as he watched her expression of apparent confusion. She knew what he was talking about. He could read the knowledge in her oh-so-innocent look.

He shrugged, noting how her eyes fixed on the rise of his shoulders in the mirror. She tried to hide the fact, but Antonia was as fascinated by him as he was by her.

'Not particularly.' He lowered his other hand to cup her bottom, squeezing gently till she squirmed and put down the mascara. She felt so good. His fingers massaged the backs of her thighs then slid higher again. Oh, yes!

'It's almost a shame that I'm the only man who'll ever see you in this.' He leaned forward to nip her on the nape. His hands slid round her hips and arrowed down to the V of her legs, to the heat there. He nudged her legs apart with his thigh, planting himself intimately close.

'But I'm wearing it tonight,' she protested.

Slowly he shook his head. 'Absolutely not.' He lifted one hand to her jacket zip and tugged, exposing her bra and bare torso. 'If you went out in that you'd cause a riot.'

She swatted at his hand, yanking the zip back up. 'But I'm already dressed.' Flashing dark eyes met his in the wide mirror and he felt a surge of excitement, as he always did when they argued.

'Then you can just get *undressed*.' He lifted his hands to the back zip of her trousers and eased it down, enjoying the view of her naked cheeks. He'd been mistaken. She was wearing a tiny wisp of a thong. He hooked a finger underneath it and traced her bare flesh, enjoying the tremor she couldn't hide.

Urgently now, he shoved her leather pants down, then reached round to tug her jacket undone. It was the work of a moment to undo the front catch of her bra so her unbound breasts spilled into his waiting palms. He pressed himself against her backside, his erection pushing against her. Scorching heat roared through his bloodstream.

Soon, very soon, he'd be inside her. He surged close, tilting his hips forward, anticipating his release. In the mirror he watched his tanned fingers massage the ultra-soft skin on the underside of her pale breasts. There was something about the sight of her naked flesh against his that was incredibly erotic. He could barely wait. He fished a condom from his pocket.

Quickly he released his trousers and tore the packet.

'Are you sure you want to do this now?' Antonia's voice was cool. 'You don't want to be late tonight, do you? I thought it was some important event we were going to.'

Rafe paused, meeting her eyes, reading the veneer of boredom in her expression. With her raised eyebrows, the angled chin, her nostrils flaring as if in distaste, she was the picture of suffering patience.

In contrast, he was randy as a teenager, his need urgent and unbridled. Yet Antonia was apparently unmoved. Damn it, she was doing it again—distancing herself, pretending she had no interest in sex, or in him. Each night he had to break down that brittle shell to the passionate woman she hid so well.

His mind filled with the image of him standing behind her, pushing her forward so she was fully exposed to him. He'd thrust into her depths till he was sated, her breasts cupped in his hands, his lips on the soft skin of her neck. Completion would be swift and glorious. But it would end with her looking down her supercilious nose at him.

She was deliberately goading him. As if she *wanted* him to find his pleasure without her. As if she didn't want to sully herself with anything as honest as lust.

'Not as important as this, lover.' He spun her round to

face him, enjoying her surprise. Then he bent down, dragging off her shoes and tugging at the tight trousers till finally he'd wrestled the leather away from her.

'Now, where were we?' He enjoyed the flash of near panic on her face as he yanked off her belt, then slid her jacket fully open. He reached down to the scrap of fabric covering the juncture of her thighs. The slight ripping sound as he tore it away was loud in the quiet room.

'Ah, that's right. *Here*, I think.' He slipped a finger down between her legs, unerringly finding the sensitive bud he sought.

A quiver rippled through her, but she stood stock still. He probed further, delving inside, then stroking out again, again and again, until he felt the sway of her lower body pushing into his touch. No mistaking her arousal now. The scent of feminine musk teased his nostrils, urging him on. He lowered his head to her breast and was rewarded with a gasp of delight.

By the time he straightened her eyes were glazed, hot and feverish under heavy lids. This was how he wanted her. Warm and wanton and ready. He hoisted her up onto the wide bench below the mirror.

'Lift your legs,' he ordered.

As soon as her thighs closed around his hips he positioned himself against her, then pushed deep inside till he was anchored at her very core.

Antonia blinked, trying to clear her eyes of excess moisture. She couldn't believe it had happened again. Each time she steeled herself to resist, reminding herself that it was just sex. Crude, unvarnished physical lust. Yet each time she caved in, giving herself up to the magic of Rafe's touch as if afraid she'd never experience it again.

Aftershocks of pleasure rippled through her and she sank

bonelessly into Rafe's hard torso, grateful for his arms holding her tight as she came back down to earth.

No matter how often she told herself she despised him, he still overcame her resolve with just a few caresses, or that sultry low murmur of his voice as he whispered outrageous suggestions in her ear.

Where was her backbone? Bad enough that she'd sold herself as his mistress. Did she have to enjoy her own downfall quite so much? Hot distress filled her.

Pride demanded that she remain unmoved, yet Rafe could bend her to his will with shaming ease.

She'd thought tonight at least she'd stand firm. She'd woken this morning to realise she'd shared herself with him for precisely a month. The knowledge had left a bitter taste in her mouth.

Tonight's outfit had been another gesture of defiance. Futile, perhaps, but important to her—a sign of her autonomy. She spent her time pandering to his whims, ignoring the pointed jibes of people who saw her as fair game now she was so obviously Rafe's possession. People who knew what it meant when she wore his glittering jewels yet obviously didn't hold his affection. For he never pretended she was anything more than a convenient companion.

Antonia had lost count of the questions about the size of her allowance. And the lewd suggestions from men wanting to offer her a *private arrangement* when Rafe tired of her.

Her self-respect had been shattered and her pride tarnished. She bluffed her way through by pretending to an insouciance she didn't feel. Yet inside she felt stripped to the bone. Her soul shrivelled every time she had to face those knowing looks and lascivious stares.

What would her parents have said if they'd known what she did for their sakes? They'd have been horrified.

But she'd saved what was really important: her father's

memory and her mother's charity. She'd heard from Emma at the Foundation that the auditors had found some unusual transactions, but that officially no further action was being taken since the money was there and her father's access code was no longer valid.

So it was all worthwhile. She had to believe that.

'Hold on tight.' Antonia felt Rafe's words against the side of her neck as he lifted her up in his embrace. Automatically she held on till they reached the bed and fell together onto its wide expanse.

Still he didn't release her.

'I'll go and find something else to wear,' she said, eyes fixed on his squared chin just a few inches away.

'No.'

'No?' Startled, she raised her eyes to his. His gaze was intent, his brow furrowed, as if he tried to solve a knotty problem.

'No. We're staying here. And I'm going to make long, slow love to you until you forget how to scowl.' He lifted his hand to her face, his touch infinitely gentle, not at all like the ruthless man who'd just stripped her in the bathroom. Or the man who walked away from her each night after she'd given him what he wanted.

Antonia felt his fingers slide along her brow, smoothing the lines of her frown. His other hand caressed her cheek in a slow motion that felt like tenderness.

'But I—'

'No buts, Antonia. You don't want to go out tonight, do you?'

Helplessly she gazed up at him, fearing he could read far more in her face than she could in his. But for once the determination that had held her steadfast these past weeks had drained away, leaving her tired and vulnerable.

Of course she didn't want to go out. She was the envy of

a lot of women, yet it grew harder each day to overcome her sense of shame, of failure, that she hadn't been able to find another way to protect her family.

Worse still was the guilty knowledge that she enjoyed the perks of her position far too much. If she wasn't careful she'd become addicted to the feel of his strong arms round her, to the sound of his lazy drawl when he made love to her.

Then where would she be, when the time came to go her own way? She should be focusing on her plans for the future, not his impressive lovemaking.

She shook her head.

'Good.' His mouth curved up in a thoughtful smile that made her heart beat faster.

His lips closed on hers, coaxing a response with their slow, luxurious caress. It felt as if he had all the time in the world and nothing on his mind except her. If she believed in fairy tales she'd even be tempted to think he cared, just a little.

Antonia's last coherent thought before she succumbed to his slow seduction was to wish she was gullible enough to believe it would all turn out right in the end.

CHAPTER ELEVEN

THAT was the night everything began to change.

The differences were so subtle that sometimes Antonia wondered if she imagined them. Despite her attempts to remain aloof, they seemed to be building a relationship.

A flush warmed her cheeks now, as she hurried through the lunchtime crowd. Sex was still a vital part of what they shared. Each day her inhibitions dissolved further as he teased and tempted as well as demanded. Rafe had an un-inhibited sensuality, and a generosity when it came to sharing pleasure that was fast destroying her defences.

Yet there was a sense of growing closeness, of a sharing more intimate than physical caresses.

That evening when he'd taken her hard and fast in the bathroom had been the first time he'd stayed the night with her. She'd woken at dawn in the warm cocoon of his arms. Her sense of wellbeing and contentment had been a revelation. It had felt different between them, as if this time he'd shared something more than the hard perfection of his body and his erotic expertise. Something of himself.

After the lacerating pain of those earlier nights, watching him leave her room, she hadn't been able to help reading significance into his decision to share her bed. It was as if he took comfort in her company, as she did in his, especially in the early hours when grief had previously kept her awake and hurting.

Now he spent every night with her, holding her close, giving her the solace she'd so long desired. Under his tender ministrations the ice around her heart had begun to fracture and thaw, just a little.

Rafe even *sounded* different. He was less ready to jump to negative conclusions. He listened more, and she sometimes found him watching her with a curious expression that made her wonder what he found so fascinating.

They went out less, often spending a night in with a meal he had ordered and a fine bottle of wine. They'd chat about almost anything: travel, movies, politics. Afterwards Rafe would say he needed to work, but somehow he'd never open his laptop and they'd end up in each other's arms.

Even when they went out, to some grand dinner or elegant soirée, there was a change. No longer did she feel like a trophy, cold-bloodedly displayed to complement Rafe's power and prestige. Instead he introduced her to people he thought might interest her, especially those with an interest in art. She'd discovered Rafe Benton could be charming, attentive, witty— the sort of man she'd *choose* to spend time with.

He'd even steered her clear of Stuart Dexter more than once, since she'd let slip how much she disliked the man. Rafe's brows had risen, and for a moment he'd looked doubtful, but from then on she'd seen far less of Dexter.

If Antonia wasn't careful she'd find herself liking this new Rafe far too much.

She was smiling as she turned in to the cosy Italian restaurant. She knew she shouldn't set too much store by the change in him, in *them*. Yet after the pain of the last months her bruised soul responded to his warmth, his wit, his tenderness, with a yearning she couldn't repress.

'Antonia.' Suddenly he was there, and her heart flipped

over at the impact of his rare smile. He was so handsome, and more charismatic than any man she'd ever met.

Her hand trembled as he lifted it to his lips. Blue eyes fixed on hers as he turned her hand over and pressed his mouth to the underside of her wrist. His tongue, erotically inviting, ran over the sensitive pulse point and tendrils of desire instantly wove round her.

'Rafe!' She tugged her hand away, afraid that she'd melt into a puddle of longing right there in the restaurant.

The glint in his eyes told her he knew precisely the effect he had on her. His hand was possessive at her back as he steered her to their table. Strangely, she didn't mind that proprietorial gesture nearly as much as she once had.

'I approve of the skirt,' he said as he sat beside her in a secluded booth. Underneath the table he planted his hand on her knee, pulling up the fabric till his broad palm touched sheer stockings. Antonia shivered at the pleasurable sensations that radiated in whorls of heat from his touch.

'Rafe, no. Someone will see,' she hissed.

His lazy smile as he stroked her inner thigh was deliciously wicked, reminding her of the way they'd spent the night, locked in each other's embrace. She wished they had more than just this lunchtime gap between his meetings.

'Please,' she said. 'Not here.'

'No?' he teased. With one final caress, he smoothed her skirt and lifted his hand to close around hers on the table. Any bystander would look at them and think they were a couple in love.

With a sudden pang Antonia wondered exactly what it was Rafe felt for her. Something more than lust, she was sure. The question haunted her days.

She shied away from examining her own feelings. They were far too complicated, and her innate sense of self-preservation warned against delving.

Surely these confused emotions were a good reason to concentrate on planning her future? In a few months she'd be a free agent, able to pursue those dreams she'd put on hold while she looked after her father. She'd work as a guide till she could start the Art History course she'd set her heart on, and then find a permanent job and a little place of her own somewhere.

Why didn't the idea seem as appealing as it used to?

'Are you hungry?' Rafe asked. His knowing gleam told her he wasn't just talking about food. His smile scrambled her thoughts.

She nodded. 'I'm always hungry when I come here. It has the best Italian food in London.'

He raised his brows.

'Really. It's marvellous.' It had been her mother's favourite restaurant, and she cherished memories of it.

'Antonia! *Ragazza mia bella! Come stai? Dove sei stata?*' Antonia looked up into familiar coal dark eyes and felt a grin spread across her face.

'Domenico!' She let herself be drawn up into brawny arms, blinking back sudden tears. Domenico was the owner and head waiter, someone she'd known since birth. He was a big man, and his bear hug squeezed her breathless. It was a sensation that took her straight back to her childhood.

'*Sto bene. E tu, Domenico?*'

'*Cosi cosi,*' he answered, gesturing with his flat hand and chuckling.

Rafe listened to the rapid exchange in Italian. Another facet of his lover he hadn't known about. She really was a mystery. He'd never known a woman so close-lipped about herself.

As he watched the older man hug her tight, and saw her laughing response to something he'd said, Rafe knew a sudden, unprecedented surge of envy. Antonia never looked at *him* like that, with her expression utterly unshadowed.

Even in the throes of passion she held something of herself back. He'd barely tapped into her secrets. Secrets that each day it seemed increasingly important for him to uncover.

Now she glowed with joy. The sight of her radiant beauty stole his breath. Antonia had always been lovely, even when she put on the ice queen act or tried his temper with her provocative attitude. Now he saw her bone-deep beauty. The sun itself seemed to shine from her smile.

He wanted that look for himself.

'Aren't you going to introduce me?' he said, getting to his feet and slipping a possessive arm around her.

She turned, and the warmth of her smile slid through him, deep into his chest.

'Rafe, this is Domenico Licarta, a friend of my parents. Domenico, this is Rafe Benton.'

'Mr Benton, it's good to meet you. I see you're looking after our Antonia. It's been a difficult time for her.' His grizzled eyebrows drew together as he turned to her. 'I was so sorry to hear about your father.'

Antonia nodded, her lips pursed in a wobbly line. 'It was sudden.' Her voice was husky with emotion. 'He'd had bad news from the cardiologist. Worse, I think, than he let on… You know what he was like.'

Her voice trailed off and Rafe watched her swallow jerkily, her eyes over-bright.

'At least this way it was quick,' she said. 'I don't think he could have coped with becoming an invalid.'

Rafe's arm tightened, drawing her close. Something punched low in his belly at that hitch in her voice. He barely listened to Domenico's murmurs of condolence as he absorbed the evidence of Antonia's grief. There was no mistaking it. He was all too familiar with the anguish of loss after the death of his mother.

Rafe frowned, remembering her hard-as-nails composure in Switzerland, the comments he'd overheard about her aloofness, and his conviction that she was too cold-blooded to experience true sorrow at the loss of her father.

Yet he could feel it now in her taut frame, in the tiny tremors running through her body as he held her against him. Each breath she dragged in was just a little unsteady as she smiled crookedly at the big, concerned Italian.

Rafe experienced a jolt of dismay. Had he been so arrogant, so wrapped up in his own plans for revenge, that he hadn't looked properly? Hadn't read the grief behind the icily composed face she presented to the world?

Hell! If he'd missed that, what else had he missed?

'Sit, sit.' Their host was gesturing to their booth seat. 'No need for a menu. I'll bring you a special meal. Only the best for my little Antonia and her friend.'

Snapping dark eyes met his from under beetling brows, and Rafe knew the Italian was taking his measure.

'Thank you. Antonia has been telling me you have the best food in London.' He pulled her down beside him, taking her cool hand in his, automatically chafing it warm.

The other man nodded, accepting the compliment as his due, then with one final inquisitive glance bustled off towards the kitchens.

'You have a fan,' Rafe murmured, watching her drawn face closely. It was a relief to see her lips curve up in a smile and know he'd coaxed it from her.

'Actually, Domenico was a fan of my mother's.'

'Really?'

She nodded and gestured to a wall. It was covered with pictures of famous guests, all flanked by a smiling Domenico and others whom Rafe guessed were family members.

'That one in the centre, third row down.' She pointed to

a portrait of a dark-haired woman with a face that would stop traffic. 'That's my mother, Claudia Benzoni.'

'The actress?' Rafe had seen some of her films, though they'd been made when he was just a kid. The experts called them classics of Italian cinema. In his youthful enthusiasm he'd been too busy appreciating the female star to notice their artistic significance.

'That's right.' No mistaking the warmth in Antonia's voice. Or the wistfulness.

Rafe remembered hearing about the actress's untimely death from a rare form of cancer years ago. It had stuck in his mind because it had happened about the time his own mother's illness had taken another turn for the worse.

'She was beautiful,' he said. 'Almost as lovely as you.'

Antonia turned, her expression astonished. He took in her large eyes, her lush mouth, her classic beauty, and felt something tug deep inside him. A need to banish the shadows from her eyes.

Rafe put his finger under her chin, revelling in the soft texture of her flesh, and tilted her face up. He leaned forward and pressed a slow, tender kiss to her lips.

When Rafe kissed her like that, Antonia's mind ceased to function. Instead she was simply *aware*. Of him, of the steady acceleration of her pulse as desire built, and of a warmth that was more of the spirit than the body.

How could that be, when their relationship was based on sex? It was at times like this she felt something significant developing between them. Rafe was fast becoming important to her.

He broke the kiss and she stared dazedly into eyes the colour of heaven. When he smiled at her so intimately, his lips tilting up in a little twist of shared pleasure—

'Here you are,' Domenico boomed as he strode to the

table. 'The best *stracciatella* outside Italy. I guarantee it.'
He placed two steaming bowls on the table and stood back,
grinning in anticipation.

Hastily Antonia sat back in her seat, flushed at being
caught out, so absorbed in Rafe's kiss.

'Thank you, Domenico. It's my favourite.'

He nodded. 'Of course. You think I'd forget?' He looked
across at Rafe. 'Try it. You've never tasted anything like
Mamma's *stracciatella*.'

Antonia picked up her spoon and leaned close to the
aromatic dish. Instantly memories flooded her. She took a
spoonful and closed her eyes for a moment. Heaven!

'As good as ever, Domenico! Wonderful.' She looked at
Rafe, apparently hesitant beside her. 'Try it,' she urged.

She watched Rafe taste the soup, then swallow, the
movement of his strong, corded neck fascinating her.
Whatever was happening to her, it was serious if she found
herself diverted just by the sight of the man eating!

'Antonia's right.' Rafe nodded his appreciation.

'You sound surprised,' Antonia ventured as Domenico
moved away to serve another table.

'I don't like soup,' he said. 'But this is better than most.'
He spooned up another mouthful.

Antonia frowned. She knew people who disliked the
taste of various foods, but a dislike of soup? Intriguing.

'That's…unusual,' she ventured.

Rafe shrugged. 'When for years it's virtually all you
have to eat, it begins to pall.'

'Were you sick? Did you need a light diet?' Antonia
found it hard to imagine him as anything but superbly fit.
But he never spoke of the past, only the present.

'No, it was simply our staple diet. Nutritious, easy to
prepare, and very, very cheap,' he said, his voice holding a
bitter note.

Antonia frowned at his words. His family had been short of cash?

He caught her staring. 'You find that surprising?'

'I... Well, I suppose I'd assumed your family was well off.' After all, he was so supremely confident of his power, arrogantly at ease with his extreme wealth. He seemed like a man born to money.

Rafe smiled, a brief twist of the lips that reminded her of the hard derision that had been so obvious in him when they'd met.

'Born with a silver spoon in my mouth?' He shook his head. 'Anything but.' He sat back in his chair. 'There was just me and my mother. She was good at what she did—she was an executive assistant—but it was hard finding a job that gave her time to bring up a child too. She settled for one with flexible hours, but the downside was lower pay. It was always a struggle.'

'Your father didn't contribute?' She supposed she shouldn't pry, but it was so rare for him to open up about his past she couldn't prevent the question.

'My *father*?' No mistaking the dismissal in *that* tone, or the seething flare of emotion in Rafe's blazing eyes. 'He washed his hands of us before I was born. He didn't give a damn if we lived in poverty. Or even if we lived.'

Antonia stiffened, shocked at his words and by the rabid loathing she heard. Surely Rafe was exaggerating? But as she saw the expressions flit across his granite features, his mouth compress into a forbidding line, she realised he was speaking the truth as he saw it.

What sort of man could be so unfeeling towards his own flesh and blood? Antonia's parents had been deeply in love and had shared that love with her. How lucky she'd been.

'It must have been hard on one salary,' she murmured.

Rafe raised his eyebrows. 'Lots of families manage on

one wage,' he said. 'Our problem was that my mother couldn't keep her job, not full-time. She was diagnosed with a degenerative illness.'

He thrust a hand through his dark hair in a gesture that hinted at uncharacteristic vulnerability and made Antonia want to reach out to him.

'She fought it every step of the way, but it was rough going. Even before she was confined to a wheelchair she was often too exhausted or sick to work. There was a never-ending barrage of medical bills on top of everything else.'

'How did you manage?' Antonia was appalled that she'd inadvertently blundered into such a painful memories.

Rafe shrugged. As she watched his expensively tailored jacket pull tight over those wide shoulders, Antonia wondered about the innate strength and determination that had got him to the very pinnacle of the business world.

'Any way we could. I held down a string of jobs even as a kid. We grew our own produce, and I became an expert at making ends meet.' He shook his head. 'One of the first things I did when I started making real money was take her out for the best steak and seafood meal I could afford. I still remember the taste of it.'

Antonia's fingers closed around his sleeve. 'You don't have to…' She gestured to his bowl.

'What? I don't have to finish my soup?' The brooding intensity of his expression was banished by an unexpected flash of humour. 'It's okay, Antonia. I'm not so damaged by my past that I can't manage a bowl of the stuff.' His gaze held hers for so long his smile faded and his expression slid back into taut lines. 'Right now I'm more interested in knowing how I came to tell you all this.'

He looked truly discomfited by the extent to which he'd

opened up about his childhood. She guessed he'd view the sharing of personal information as a weakness.

'Perhaps I'm a good listener?' She tried to lighten the atmosphere.

'Perhaps.'

He reached out and cupped her chin in his hand, staring into her eyes. The intensity of his regard warmed her right to the core, just as his touch heated her skin. This close, she felt she could almost drown in the cerulean depths of that compelling gaze.

'Or,' he murmured in that low, rough suede tone that always sent a shiver through her, 'perhaps you're a witch.'

They spent the rest of the meal ostensibly concentrating on the superb food. They spoke little, yet to Antonia it seemed that their silences were companionable.

Between courses Rafe pulled her in close against his solid warmth and asked about her own childhood. What had it been like growing up with an Italian movie starlet for a mother? Where had they lived?

Antonia told him about her early years, surprised to discover how easy it was to talk with him. It was good to relive the memories, as if by recalling them she affirmed the importance of the parents she'd lost.

By the time they'd finished their meal and were drinking coffee Antonia was replete and relaxed. She refused to think about anything other than the comforting feel of Rafe's arm around her and the sound of his voice, deep enough to burr her skin into gooseflesh.

She felt so good. Better than she'd felt in a long, long time. Even before her father's accident she'd felt as if she was spinning frantically on a wheel, working when she could to supplement their income, but worrying when she was away from him, for his heart condition and his mood swings had concerned her. Then, at the resort, with Stuart Dexter hanging around and her fear for her father notching up by the day, she'd been on tenterhooks.

'Ready to go?' Rafe asked.

Reluctantly she nodded and gathered her bag. She'd prefer to stay here all afternoon, but it wasn't possible.

It was late by the time they were out on the pavement, after saying their farewells to Domenico and his family, and promising to return soon.

Antonia frowned at her watch. 'I didn't realise we'd be so long. Do you have meetings this afternoon?'

'Nothing that can't be deferred,' he said, 'for something more important.'

She tilted her head questioningly. 'More important?'

'Yes.' Slowly his mouth curved into a smile. The full force of it weakened her knees. 'I can think of several things I'd rather do—if you're agreeable.'

The glint in his eyes was easy to read. Rafe was thinking about the two of them naked. The realisation sent a rush of liquid heat through her.

'But your meetings…' She'd learned in these past weeks that *nothing* was more important to Rafe than his current business project. It was all-consuming.

'It can wait.' He paused. 'If you want.'

Antonia had never heard Rafe sound hesitant. But there was no mistaking the question in his expression, or the waiting stillness of his big frame.

He was asking if she wanted intimacy. *Asking*.

Previously, even when he'd coaxed, teased or dared her into sex, *he'd* made the decision and had acted on it.

Now the decision was hers.

Was it stupid to feel that this was somehow momentous? Surely she was reading too much into it? Nevertheless, she felt far more than physical desire, more than anticipation, as she slipped her arm through his and whispered, 'Yes'.

Fifteen minutes later they were in a fourth-floor bedroom in the nearest hotel. Rafe had called his office to cancel his meetings while he strode down the street at a fast clip, shepherding her along beside him as if he had to keep her close. He'd organised a room in record time, and once they were alone divested them both of their clothes with a speed that left her breathless and excited.

The urgency of his actions, the intensity of his expression as his hands swept over her, stole her breath. She wondered if they'd even make it to the bed.

Yet once he yanked the coverlet away, and they were lying on crisp linen sheets, Rafe slowed. The urgency was still there. She could sense it in his rough breathing, the heavy thud of his pulse and the fine tremor of his hands. It was an urgency that matched her own. She shifted, restless and wanting, stroking her palms over him, clutching him close, wanting more. Needing *him*.

He had other plans. For long minutes—for hours, it seemed—Rafe stroked, kissed, nipped, and caressed the whole of her, from her face to her feet. He brought her to the brink of completion again and again, and then moved on to pleasure her elsewhere.

Never had she reached such a fever-pitch of desire. He was so focused on her: her pleasure, her responses, her needs. She felt a connection with him as never before.

At last he gave in to her hoarse pleas and positioned himself above her. Antonia looked into his face: proud, tense with restraint, yet so tender. She felt the hard knot inside that she'd lived with for so long melt and ease.

She felt whole.

With a single slow surge of power he brought them together. Antonia opened for him, taking him deep inside, revelling in the ecstasy that was already welling up and exploding through her.

'Rafe! I…' Her words died and she hung on tight to his slick, powerful body as they moved together. He was her reality, her world, her safety net. Everything spun away into glorious, mind-numbing bliss.

It was only much later, as she lay wrapped close in his arms, the fuzz of his chest hair under her cheek, his broad palm splayed possessively on her hip, that Antonia realised what it was she'd been going to say.

Rafe. I love you.

CHAPTER TWELVE

'You like it?'

Antonia stared at the small box Rafe had just pressed into her hands and blinked back absurd tears. The brooch was gorgeous. Elegant, stylish, and so *her*. She stroked the silver, noting the loving detail in the small artist's palette and brush.

'It's lovely. Absolutely perfect,' she murmured.

How different from the diamonds he'd bought her. This was another one-off piece, designed by a master. Yet it had been chosen for *her*. It wasn't gaudy glitter obtained solely to show off Rafe's bought woman.

Antonia's chest squeezed tight as warmth trickled through her, filling even those places in her guarded heart that had remained frozen until now.

'Why did you—?'

'It reminded me of you,' he answered, his voice an intimately soft rumble. 'I saw it and I had to have it for you. Here, let me.' He took the piece from her.

She looked up, noting the way his brows crinkled in concentration. The firm line of his jaw that only a few hours ago had rubbed against her cheek as they'd made long, slow love in the dawn light. The fan of dark eyelashes that hid his eyes as he looked down.

After three months Rafe's face was so familiar. So dear. She couldn't prevent the welling tenderness as she stared up into those features she'd once thought so hard.

Now she knew another side of him. Her lover could be a generous, protective, caring man. He made her forget that he'd pushed her into intimacy as part of a business arrangement. Their relationship felt like anything *but* business. She'd even started hoping that one day he might reciprocate her feelings. The love that had at first so terrified her and now was her secret delight.

She wasn't mistaken. He felt *something* for her. She knew he did. Could it ever be love? Was she fooling herself, dreaming they had a chance of happiness?

Inevitably her mind shifted to the tiny changes she'd noticed recently. The slight tenderness in her breasts, the delay in her monthly cycle. They meant nothing...probably. They'd been so careful—though she knew these things could happen... A whisper of excitement shivered through her. What if Rafe really did care? And what if...?

'There. Perfect.' Dazzling bright eyes met hers, and a shaft of heat pierced her heart.

'Aren't you going to look?' Despite his light tone, his expression was serious, intent.

Hope surged and she forgot her doubts, for now.

'It's stunning,' she said as she turned to the mirror. Antonia lifted a hand and stroked the metal tentatively.

'I'll treasure it.' *Always* she added silently. 'Thank you, Rafe.'

'It was entirely my pleasure.'

The sight of his tall frame beside hers and the glimmer of approval in his eyes filled her with delight. *Yes*. Surely she was right and he felt this spark between them?

'I thought it would appeal to your artistic soul.'

Rafe met her look in the mirror and felt a punch to the

abdomen. The sight of her smiling at him like that, so open, so radiant, did the strangest things. He'd been jealous of those smiles that day she'd directed them at Domenico Licarta. Now he had them for himself. He felt a greedy delight that told him it would be a long time before he tired of Antonia.

The six months he'd arranged with her wouldn't be enough. Maybe he'd invite her to holiday in Australia after his business here was complete.

He lifted a hand and stroked his knuckles down her cheek. Inevitably the contact sent desire swirling through him. No matter that they'd just spent the night and half the morning together naked. He couldn't get enough of her.

'Have you ever done any painting yourself?' He slipped in the question, needing to divert his thoughts lest they end up in the hotel's king-sized bed again. He had a specific reason for bringing Antonia on a weekend in the country. But first they had to make it out of their room!

She shook her head, and her hair swirled around her shoulders, loose and inviting, just the way he liked it.

'I tried, but I have no talent. Just enough of an eye to begin appreciating what I see.' She stroked the brooch gently, as if it were a living thing. 'I plan to enrol in an Art History degree one day. Then, if I'm lucky, I'll get a job in a museum or a gallery, or an auction house.'

Rafe stared. A job? More than that—a job in a field that, from the little he knew, was difficult to break into. One that required years of dedicated study.

He frowned. She'd never mentioned a career. He'd thought she was content to live off the allowance her family had no doubt left her. If she wanted to supplement her income, surely there was something easier, especially with her looks?

'Is this a new idea?'

'No.' She shook her head and her cloud of dark hair slid round her, its fresh scent filling his nostrils. 'It's what I've always wanted.'

'So why have you left it so long?'

Her hand dropped from the brooch. 'My father needed me. He was sick and lonely, despite all his socialising. He needed someone to look after him. There was only me.'

Abruptly she turned, and walked across the room to where her coat and bag lay on the end of the bed.

'Are you ready to leave?'

Rafe's eyes narrowed. She was changing the subject. Because he'd reminded her of her grief, or because she was lying? But why lie? Antonia had always been up-front. She didn't shy from confrontation, and she'd never hidden her blatant interest in his cash.

Yet the woman he'd got to know wasn't simply the grasping siren he'd pegged her for. She was far more complex.

Who was she? In some ways she was still an enigma. He wished he'd taken the time to find out at the beginning instead of focusing all his energies on revenge.

'Yes, I'm ready.' He thrust the puzzle from his mind, vowing to revisit it soon.

'I know this place!' The sight of a long formal carriageway tugged Antonia from her pleasant haze. Drifts of daffodils, rows of huge elms, and in the distance a glimpse of the rhododendron garden to one end of a lake.

Every year the Claudia Benzoni Foundation's gala charity lunch was hosted here, in one of Britain's loveliest privately owned heritage homes. She'd received her invitation weeks ago, but hadn't for a moment supposed she'd be able to get away from London to attend.

Rafe glanced at her briefly before he changed gear to guide the sports car over an ornamental bridge.

'I thought you'd want to attend the fundraiser for your mother's charity.' He paused. 'Why didn't you tell me about it? I only found out when I received an invitation.'

Antonia shrugged. 'I assumed you wouldn't leave London for something that wasn't…relevant to your business. I know how important your work is.' Nor had she imagined he'd be happy for her to come alone. Rafe wanted her near.

His mouth pursed at her words, as if she'd said the wrong thing. But it was true. He was single-minded about his business, except lately, when she'd dared to dream there might be something else occupying his thoughts.

'You could have asked.'

'Thank you, Rafe.' Tentatively she touched his arm. 'I appreciate you bringing me here.' She'd been sad at the prospect of missing the event, which had always been a high point for her and her father. 'It was thoughtful of you.'

More than thoughtful. It was a wonderful surprise.

He flashed her another quick glance, then lifted one hand off the wheel to close over hers, clamping her hand against his taut muscles.

'My pleasure, lover.' His expression was pure male speculation. 'I'll look forward to your gratitude later.'

Antonia smiled at the laughter in his voice even as answering need burst into life inside her at the promise in his tone. She loved Rafe's teasing as much as his blatant desire and his tender gestures.

She glanced out of the window, seeing the carpet of bulbs and the swelling buds on the trees. Spring had arrived. Suddenly she realised the arctic grip around her heart had eased too. The ice-hard barrier that had kept her apart from the world had melted.

She felt Rafe's touch on her hand and realised she wasn't alone any more. It felt good.

* * *

Hours later, Antonia excused herself and headed for the restroom. It had been a wonderful day, and a relief to see the Foundation thriving despite the near-calamity of the theft. A quiet word with one of the officials had assured her that Gavin Malleson's name was safe.

She'd spoken to acquaintances, and some of her father's friends, and it hadn't been nearly the chore she'd feared receiving their condolences, for Rafe had been at her side.

The man was a puzzle. She'd been dumbfounded when Rafe's name had been announced as a sponsor, with a pledge for a staggering amount. He'd been chagrined as applause had swelled through the room, then he'd shrugged and murmured that it might encourage others to donate.

The door to the ladies' room was just ahead when she heard someone approach rapidly from behind.

'Antonia Malleson,' said a voice she knew. 'And without her minder. How unusual!'

Antonia stared up into Stuart Dexter's gaze and felt something like fear chill her blood.

'In here, my dear.'

Before she knew it, he'd swung her round into an open doorway. She wrenched her arm free, tugging away. Too late she realised that had taken her further inside a small sitting room. Dexter was between her and the now closed door.

'What do you want?' She resolved to stand her ground, but as he paced close and she read his salacious expression she found herself backing away.

'What do I want?' His lip curled. 'What I've always wanted. I'm not used to being denied. I almost had you where I wanted you before. But then you found a way to refill the Foundation's coffers and pay your father's debts.' His gaze trawled down her in a leer that made bile rise in her throat.

'Refill the coffers?' Antonia gaped as his meaning sank

in. 'It was *you* who took the money! You who made it look like my father had…' Shock made her sway. And relief. *It hadn't been her dad.*

This was the confirmation she'd wanted for so long. But hard on the heels of relief came guilt. Despite her denials there'd been moments when she'd wondered, when she'd doubted her father.

'A temporary embarrassment of funds made it desirable. But it's not something you'll ever be able to prove.' Dexter shrugged, looking totally unmoved. 'I'd intended to use the situation to persuade you that we should spend more *quality* time together. I was going to help you out if you agreed to be a little more accommodating.'

He stretched out a hand and she shoved it away, aghast at what she was hearing.

'Unfortunately business took me away just when I'd hoped—'

'What? To blackmail me into your bed?' Antonia's breath came in ragged gulps and her blood fizzed with adrenaline.

Those cold eyes stripped her bare and she shuddered.

'But my son beat me to it, didn't he?' Dexter's tone was ugly. 'One sniff of his money and you were straight into his bed. No prudish scruples with *him.*'

What? Disbelief hollowed her churning stomach. She stared, dumbfounded, as his words tumbled through her brain.

Dexter took advantage of her shock to step close, crowding her back so she had nowhere to go.

'Your son?' She choked the words out.

'Of course. Didn't Rafe tell you? How remiss of him. He hasn't mentioned it to me either, but I found out and obviously he knows. Why else go into business with his old man?'

Her Rafe? Dexter's son? The idea was laughable.

But she wasn't laughing. She was staring, stricken, into the face before her and seeing physical similarities.

No! It couldn't be true.

But the shape of the head, the angle of the nose, the strong flyaway eyebrows that gave Rafe his fallen angel look... For the first time she recognised them in the man before her. The shock was like a stab to the chest.

'I don't believe it.' She tried to convince herself.

'Believe it,' Stuart Dexter said.

He lunged forward, pinioning her against a bureau while he tugged her jacket from her shoulders, hauling it down to her elbows and hampering her frantic attempts to escape.

'You've no idea how hard it's been to stand on the sidelines, watching him monopolise you.'

'No!' It was a shriek of horror and fear as Antonia realised he had her trapped, his extra body weight working for him as he pawed her. Desperately she fought him. 'Rafe will kill you!'

'No, no.' Stuart mouthed the words against her now bare shoulder, then bit down till she flinched. 'Like father, like son, you know. We can keep this little arrangement in the family. My prospects are looking up. I'll be able to keep you in style once he's finished with you. What do you say?'

Antonia's gorge rose in her throat as his words sank in. He squeezed, groped, tugged at her clothes. The room lurched around her as her head swam. She grabbed his shoulders and shoved.

This couldn't be happening! She shut her eyes against the sight of his excitement and summoned all her strength to hold him off. His mouth was on her neck. His hands—

'Not an edifying sight,' drawled a dark familiar voice, and abruptly the weight of Dexter's body was removed.

Antonia swayed, finding herself suddenly alone. She snapped open her eyes.

'Rafe!' He was here. Relief weakened her knees and instinctively she reached out, needing his support.

She couldn't believe her eyes when he stood unmoving, glowering, his hands clenching in spasms at his sides. His jaw was locked and fury vibrated from him in waves. She felt as if just one unwise word would make him explode.

Her hand crept to her throat, fingers splaying protectively. What was going on?

Out of the corner of her eye she saw Stuart Dexter stumble to his feet from the sofa where he'd been shoved. He stayed there, out of Rafe's reach, adjusting his tie.

'Rafe?' She stepped towards him and his brows rose. She faltered as she read his gaze, and something slammed shut deep inside her. Antonia had never thought to see him look at her so again.

She drew in a trembling breath and pulled her jacket into place with shaky hands. Rafe's coldly disapproving gaze ripped her defences bare.

'Sorry, Rafe.' Antonia heard Dexter as if from a distance. 'But I'm only human, and your little lovebird's been casting out lures.' He shrugged his jacket straight. 'You need to talk to her about it. Personally, I'd—'

'I don't give a damn what you'd do,' Rafe said in a voice like crushed glass as he swung round to face Dexter. 'Get out of here now, before I *really* hurt you.'

Over her thundering pulse Antonia heard the deadly intent in his words. She shuddered. Violence was in the air, like the smell of lightning on a stormy summer afternoon. She reached out and steadied herself on the back of a nearby chair.

She'd never seen anything like Rafe's barely bridled fury. It terrified her.

'We were just renewing an old acquaintance.' Dexter's joviality couldn't hide the fear that shook his voice.

Rafe took a single stride towards him and suddenly Dexter was scurrying out through the door, his bravado deserting him in the face of Rafe's glowering wrath.

The lock clicked and Rafe swung round to face her.

Antonia lifted her chin, refusing to be cowed by his terrific scowl. *She* wasn't the one who had to explain herself. Even now she searched for some sign that Dexter had lied, that Rafe wasn't his son. But since he'd planted the idea her conviction had grown with each moment.

Rafe hadn't been straight with her. He'd lied about his identity. Why? What else didn't she know? Foreboding filled her. He seemed a stranger once more.

'You just couldn't keep away from him, could you? So much for not liking him.' He paced towards her till his big frame took up all her vision and his heat encompassed her.

What? Antonia gaped at him. He couldn't believe *that*!

'What was he giving you? Cash? Jewels?' Rafe bit the words out with a savage gnashing of his teeth. The accusations slammed into her, sharp and deadly as knives, plunging straight into her heart.

She opened her mouth on a silent gasp of agony as they hit home and the foolish hopes she'd harboured bled away to nothing. How could he care for her when he didn't *trust* her? When he believed her lacking even in common decency?

She'd wondered what Rafe thought of her. Now she knew.

Anguish twisted inside her. She was grateful for the chair's support. It prevented her crumbling to the floor.

'Nothing to say, Antonia?' Rafe goaded. 'Are you so brazen that you didn't think I'd mind sharing? I specified exclusivity in our agreement. Remember?'

There was a crack of sound as Rafe intercepted her palm, just inches from his cheek. The shock of that connection juddered down her arm. His hold was so tight she should feel pain, but the sensation was eclipsed by the jagged agony of her slashed hopes.

Rafe tugged her close till she was flush against him, her breasts brushing him, his thighs surrounding hers. Nausea welled as she realised their intimacy had always been a sham. He wanted her physically, but clearly he despised her, thought she was mercenary and moral-free.

Nothing had changed. How could she ever have thought…?

'Let me go.' Her voice was a raw whisper.

She thought he hadn't heard. Then, finally, he released his death grip. Her arm dropped to her side, her knees buckled, and she crumpled into the chair.

CHAPTER THIRTEEN

RAFE paced, fighting the red mist of rage that had descended the moment he'd walked into the room.

How had he been gullible enough to believe in her?

He'd been a fair way to convincing himself that Antonia wasn't motivated by money. He'd been almost sure...

But obviously that was wishful thinking. She wouldn't have been in Dexter's arms for anything other than the promise of cash.

How long had it been going on?

He thudded his clenched fist down on a broad window-sill at the end of the room.

He'd allowed himself to believe that Antonia was more than she'd seemed at first, that she cared for him. He'd *allowed* himself to fall for her lies. What a fool!

The sight that had met him as he opened the door was emblazoned on his brain and he couldn't think past it. Antonia in Dexter's arms, her hands on his shoulders. His mouth on her neck. Rafe couldn't believe he'd stopped at hauling the bastard off her. Every impulse had urged him to pound Dexter till he was a bruised and bloodied heap.

He feared what he might do if he succumbed to the impulse for blood. It was only that which had given him the strength to hold back.

Knowing Antonia had been in another man's embrace made him want to vomit. Or rage. Or commit violence.

His fist slammed down again on the sill and pain radiated from the point of impact. Rafe welcomed it. Anything to drag him back to the present, away from the lurid image branded into his brain.

He turned, needing an outlet for the angry energy shooting through him. Something glittered on the carpet. He frowned, identifying it as the trinket he'd given her. The brooch she'd accepted with such apparent pleasure.

He strode straight past it and stopped in front of her. He was itching for an argument. Antonia owed him that much, since he didn't trust himself to confront his father without killing him.

'What have you got to say for yourself?'

She refused to look up, remaining stubbornly silent.

Rafe's chest heaved with barely suppressed fury. He needed an outlet for his wrath. He shoved his fisted hands into his pockets and stared down at her.

Her head was downcast, but he could see she was pale. Ashen, even. Her features were so still he could barely make out her breathing. Her hands were clasped in her lap, their hold so tight her fingers were white.

Rafe frowned as, unbidden, memory blindsided him. Antonia by her father's grave. So controlled, so cold he'd thought she felt nothing. Only later had he discovered it was a façade she'd adopted to hide the pain deep inside.

A shard of doubt pierced his certainty.

'Look at me,' he ordered.

She didn't move.

'Antonia!'

When she refused to meet his gaze he cupped her chin in his hand. Her flesh was cool to the touch. He lifted her head. Drowning brown eyes met his. They were huge, staring blindly as if she didn't see him.

Foreboding corkscrewed through him at that vacant look. His certainty crumbled a fraction. But he'd been fooled by her before. He wouldn't be gulled a second time. Especially now he knew how potent were her feminine wiles.

'Haven't you got something to say to me?' He was damned if he was going to let her off the hook.

'Is it true?' she whispered, and he had to lean forward to hear her. 'Are you Stuart Dexter's son?'

Rafe straightened, his hand falling away from her.

'What the hell's that got to do with anything?' He wasn't here to recount his life story.

'So it's true.' Her voice was devoid of inflection, and her face could have been that of a beautiful, lifeless mannequin. Her eerie detachment made Rafe's neck prickle. If this was a con job it was remarkably effective.

'Don't you think you owe me an apology?' All that mattered was that he'd found her in his father's arms.

'What for?' There was a spark of energy in her voice this time. 'For not having the strength to fight him off? For not screaming loudly enough?'

Rafe scowled down at her. 'You weren't screaming.' Though even as he spoke he remembered the muffled sound of *something* through the solid door.

Her chin tilted higher in a look he hadn't seen in weeks. The ice queen was back.

'If you can't tell the difference between a lovers' tryst and sexual assault, that's not my problem.'

Sexual assault? She had to be kidding. She must have known what Dexter wanted when she'd come in here with him.

'Or do you think I'd willingly submit to *this*?' She yanked her jacket back to reveal a gaping tear in her dress. There was a livid red mark, already purpling, on her slim shoulder, and one at the base of her neck. Bite marks.

It was like receiving a stupefying blow to the stomach. Rafe's belly cramped as he absorbed the shock.

'No!' She shrank back in her chair, jerking her jacket back over her shoulder as he reached out instinctively towards her, to soothe his fingers over the broken skin.

Rafe froze, reading fear in her eyes. Of him? He'd never touch her in anger. Hadn't he waited to master his emotions before confronting her?

'Don't...touch me,' she whispered. It took only the desperate plea in her husky voice to convince him.

In that instant the last of his rage bled away, leaving Rafe stranded in the knowledge of his own inadequacy. He hadn't protected her. He'd raged at her when he should have held her close and comforted her.

His mind raced back to the moment he'd pulled Dexter away and she'd stood alone, hair mussed and dress dishevelled. There'd been a light in her eyes when she'd seen him. He recognised it now as relief. And desperation in her voice. Yet in his fury he hadn't looked or listened properly. He'd seen Antonia in his father's arms and fury had ousted common sense.

A leaden weight pressed down on his chest, seizing his lungs so his breath laboured. *Guilt.*

He hadn't believed her when she'd needed him.

Rafe hunkered down. She avoided him, looking to one side. Undeterred, he took her hands in his. They were shaking. Antonia was in shock.

'It's all right,' he murmured, pitching his voice low, as he would to a frightened child. 'You're safe now.'

Silence.

'I'm sorry, Antonia. I went crazy when I saw him with you.' He paused. 'I should have believed you immediately.'

She turned and looked at him. But there was no connection there. No softening. Nothing.

'Did you hear me?' There was desperation in his voice. 'I believe you. I know you weren't willing.'

Rusty laughter cracked the air. 'Well, thank you for that, Rafe. You can't imagine how good that makes me feel.'

Rafe frowned as he heard the hint of hysteria. The tremor in her hands was growing worse. He straightened and lifted her in his arms, tucking her in close.

'Come on, Antonia. It's time to go home.'

Home. The word echoed in Antonia's head as she dried herself after the longest, hottest shower in history. She felt as if she'd never be clean again. Though whether from Stuart Dexter's filthy touch or Rafe's razor-sharp accusations, she didn't know.

Silly how she'd begun thinking of the apartment as home, despite her lifelong yearning for a little house. Some place with a garden, neighbours, a sense of community—the things she'd missed out on as she'd traipsed around Europe with her parents.

This could never be home.

Despite the fact that Rafe had turned up the heating, Antonia donned warm trousers, a soft flannel shirt and a thick sweater. The cold had got into her bones.

He was waiting in the sitting room. Even knowing what he thought of her, realising how pathetically far-fetched were her fantasies of love and trust, her heart pattered faster at the sight of his strong profile.

'Antonia. There you are.' He strode over, but halted a few paces away, his expression unreadable. 'I made coffee.' He gestured to the low table in front of a massive suede sofa. A pang of sensation pierced her as she remembered making love with him there one evening, when he'd been so urgent they hadn't made it to the bedroom.

She sat in a nearby chair and poured herself a steaming mug. Mercifully, her hands didn't shake any more.

'Thank you,' she said, and turned to look out at the vista of London spread before them. She'd miss this view, she realised dully.

She sipped the strong coffee. So much nicer than the sickly sweet tea he'd pressed on her earlier.

'We need to talk.' He sounded grim.

'Yes.' She'd spent the trip back to London psyching herself for the discussion they had to have. His brooding silence in the sports car should have made her a nervous wreck, but she'd been so grateful he hadn't wanted to talk then.

'I'm sorry,' he said, sitting on the sofa, leaning forward to catch her eye. 'Truly sorry. I don't know what got into me. I found you together and I just saw red.'

He was genuine. She could see it in his eyes. But it was too late for apologies. What good was sorry when he'd revealed how little he truly thought of her?

'Can you forgive me?'

'It doesn't matter now.' He didn't trust her. He saw her only as a possession he'd bought and which he didn't want to share. *That* was what mattered.

She shrugged and changed the subject. 'It's true. You're his son, aren't you?'

'Yes.' Rafe leaned back in his chair, looking as weary as she felt. 'He's my father.'

'And?' She waited, knowing there was more.

'I'd never seen him until a few months ago,' he said in a cool voice. 'He was the reason I went to the Alps.'

She remembered Rafe's adamantine hardness when they'd met, his sense of urgency. In her naïvety she'd put it down to his determination to get what he wanted: her in his bed. Now she wondered.

'You know what my…father is. A vulture personally,

and professionally too.' He shot her a direct look. 'I don't know how he got involved in your mother's charity, but take my advice and have him removed. His practices are dubious, if not downright criminal.'

'Go on.' She sensed Rafe was prevaricating. As if he didn't want to talk about this.

He got to his feet and stalked over to the windows, his hands in his trouser pockets.

'My mother was his PA—young, naïve, but very, very good at her job. He poached her from a colleague and then set about seducing her.' He paused. 'She was in love, swept off her feet. She was waiting for his proposal when she learned he was marrying someone else. Someone with enough money to keep him in the style he wanted.'

Rafe turned and shot her a quick look from under lowered brows. 'That was when she shared the news she'd been waiting to break to him—that she was pregnant.'

Antonia's heart sank. She knew already where this was heading. 'How old was she?'

'Just twenty.' He turned to stare out into the distance, his broad shoulders hunched. 'He told her to get an abortion. Once that *inconvenience* was out of the way they could continue their affair, despite his new bride.'

Antonia shuddered, knowing Dexter was that callous.

'She refused, so he turned her away without a reference. He put it about that she was unstable and had been caught ripping off the petty cash account. He blackened her name so she couldn't work here. Not in the finance sector.'

Rafe paced.

'Mum got as far away as she could. She started afresh in Australia. But she had a difficult pregnancy and no family support. She kept working when she shouldn't have, saving for when the babies arrived.'

'Babies?'

'She was expecting twins.'

Something about the silence at the end of that sentence prevented her from asking more.

'Unfortunately she overdid it, working till she was exhausted. She collapsed on the job, succumbing to a virus. The result was complications and the early onset of labour. Only one child survived.'

He seemed so detached, yet Antonia could detect a wealth of pain in him.

'She blamed herself for my brother's death till the day she died. She felt guilt for something that wouldn't have happened if she'd had proper care and support!'

Antonia heard his grief, and sensed his loss was still raw. She wanted to reach out to him, but she didn't dare.

'We had a decent life. Short on cash, but happy.' He paused. 'Then she was diagnosed with a degenerative illness. It was long, slow and painful.'

Antonia's heart squeezed as she remembered the look on his face when he'd talked of being his mother's carer. Her instinct was to put her arms round him, despite today's events. But he'd never looked more distant.

'I vowed I'd make lots of money and find a cure for her.' His lips twisted in a self-deprecating curl. 'Unfortunately a cure wasn't possible, but at least her last years were comfortable.'

Rafe tasted bitter defeat on his tongue at the thought of how useless his wealth had been. For all his hard work, his determination, his sheer *refusal* to have her give in, she'd slipped away, worn out too early by stress and overwork even before the illness took her.

He stared at the cityscape, not seeing it, remembering instead the information he'd uncovered. Of how Dexter had not only discarded her but been deliberately culpable in exacerbating those years of pain. He'd shortened her life.

'Recently I discovered she'd been in touch with Dexter. Once during her pregnancy, pleading with him to take her back. She loved him, despite what he'd done.'

He paused, still finding that hard to stomach. But then what did he know of romantic love? Just enough never to trust in it! It was a delusion for the unwary.

'He threatened legal action. It was a masterpiece of bluff. If she'd pursued a paternity suit he'd have had to acknowledge me, but it wasn't money she wanted.'

He paused, his fists hardening. 'She wrote later, when she found out how ill she was. She was terrified she'd die while I was young, with no family to take me in. She'd discovered he had no legitimate children and suggested he build a relationship with me against the day she was gone.'

Rafe shook his head in disbelief, knowing she'd swallowed her pride and asked for financial assistance that time, since it had been such a struggle to support her son.

'His answer was curt to the point of insult.' Rafe was still amazed Dexter's lawyers had let him send something so inflammatory. 'He even despatched some goons to make sure she got the message to leave him alone.'

Rafe recalled the late-night visit by dark-suited men with lethally determined voices. He'd been a kid, but he'd stood by his mother, refusing to leave. He'd looked into their grim faces and understood genuine menace for the first time. They hadn't resorted to physical violence. They hadn't needed to. Their intentions had been clear.

That night Rafe and his mother had left their rented home of more than a decade, taking only what they could carry, giving up the friends and the job that had supported them.

'For the next few years we kept on the move, in case Dexter's *associates* looked us up again. Without consistent care or a permanent job my mother's health deteriorated faster than it should. That was Dexter's fault.' Even now the word *father* tasted like poison on his tongue.

He swung around to meet Antonia's compassionate gaze.

'If he'd had a skerrick of common humanity she wouldn't have had to work herself to the bone in dead-end jobs. She'd have had the strength to fight for her life.'

His words tailed away in futile regret. Nothing could bring his mother back. But he could sure as hell make the man who'd betrayed her then hounded her to an early grave pay.

'I came to Europe to get revenge on Stuart Dexter.'

Antonia saw the cruel glitter of pure hatred in his eyes. It was a face that scared her. A remorseless face, belonging to a man driven by the most destructive of emotions. No trace of the warm, caring man she'd thought she'd discovered.

How had she fooled herself that he felt tenderness for her? This man wasn't capable of it. *Nothing* was as important to Rafe Benton as revenge. There was no place in his life for anything as positive as a loving relationship. She'd never *meant* anything to him. Not really. She was merely a convenience.

Her chest tightened as she realised how pathetic she'd been, dreaming of a future together. Their shared joy if, perhaps, her instincts here right and she was pregnant.

She shuddered. Even if there *was* a baby, there'd be no shared joy, no mutual love. No happily-ever-after. How could she expect him to love her child when he was wrapped up in hate and vengeance?

That was no sort of father for any child.

Pain radiated out through her numb body, bringing it to aching life.

'And me?' Her voice was hoarse. 'Where do I fit in?'

Rafe focused on her, as if seeing her for the first time. He sat down opposite her and drew a deep breath.

'I saw you with Dexter—saw how obsessed he was,' Rafe murmured, in that voice which still had the power to unravel her. 'Only two things matter to him. Wealth and satisfying his libido. He goes to extraordinary lengths to pursue any woman he's set on possessing. It's a fixation.'

Rafe waited, as if watching for her reaction. But hurt held Antonia so taut she knew her face was immobile.

'Go on,' she breathed.

'I planned to use that to destroy him: remove his wealth, his business, his reputation. In just a few more weeks Dexter will be insolvent.' Rafe paused, his gaze shifting. 'And I decided to take the woman who currently means more to him than his long-suffering wife ever could. The woman who lets him fantasise that he's young and virile again.' Sky-blue eyes met her. 'I took you.'

Shock exploded inside. It felt as if he'd punched a hole right through her.

Rafe had *never* wanted her for herself! Even the blast of attraction she'd felt when they met had been one-sided. She'd just been a lever to tip the scales in his favour—a tool for revenge.

Her breath caught in her chest and she had to focus on drawing more oxygen into her body as her head spun.

The lovemaking they'd shared, the intimacy she'd believed meant far more than sex, had been just a perk to him. If you paid for a woman—even one chosen because your *father* had the hots for her—why not make the most of her?

In her weaker moments she'd almost been tempted to find his single-mindedness in pursuing her exciting. That a man wanted her so much should be testimony to the strongest of attractions, if only physical.

Yet even *that* had been a sham.

A ball of hot, choking emotion rose in Antonia's throat.

Bile burnt the back of her mouth as she grabbed the arms of her chair in a panicked grip. She would *not* break down now. Not in front of him.

Frantically she searched his face for a sign of remorse. She found only rigid determination.

Antonia gagged over the swelling nausea.

'You're like him,' she whispered. She hadn't wanted to believe it. The knowledge was a death knell to all her fragile hopes.

Rafe lifted one dark satanic brow, looking more like Dexter than ever. Searing pain lanced her breast and she knew it was her heart breaking. She'd deluded herself into believing this was a man she could love.

'You're just the same. *Like father, like son.*'

'You've got to be kidding! I'm nothing like that bastard.' Disbelief held Rafe motionless.

He who'd worked his way to success through sheer effort, determination and a well-honed natural talent. He who'd never broken the law in his life, never shirked a responsibility.

'Didn't you hear what I said?' He surged to his feet. 'Don't you understand yet what sort of man Dexter is?'

'Oh, I understand all right. Believe me, the likeness between you two is so blinding I wonder I never saw it before.' Her face was pale as milk, but her eyes flashed topaz fire.

Rafe shook his head. If he responded to that insult he'd say something he'd regret. What had got into her?

'I'm sorry, Antonia. I know this is a shock to you.' That had to be it. She was traumatised from Dexter's attack. Not thinking straight. He'd bruised her ego, revealing how she'd been part of a bigger plan. He shoved his hand through his hair, realising that perhaps he should have trusted her with some of the truth a little earlier.

She laughed—a horrible, jerky sound that jarred every nerve alert. Hysteria? No. She was too calm for that. Too calm all round. A flicker of anxiety flared in his gut.

'Don't apologise,' she said, with all the hauteur of a princess. 'It's a relief finally to hear the truth and know exactly where I stand.'

Rafe frowned, disliking that tone. 'There's more to it than that—'

'I'm sure there is. No doubt your revenge took months of planning. You must have worked hard at it. But I've heard enough.'

She got to her feet so slowly he wondered if Dexter had injured her in their scuffle.

'Are you all right?'

Her brows arched, and for a moment a shadow of emotion flashed across her face. Then it was gone, hidden behind that distant demeanour he'd worked so hard to break down.

'I'm fine,' she lied, tipping her jaw to the defiant angle he knew so well. The way she stood, gripping the back of her chair with hands as tight as talons, the way she swayed slightly, as if unsteady, gave her away.

He took a step towards her.

'No!' The raw emotion in her voice stopped him in his tracks. 'Don't touch me.' It was a plea, not an order.

'Antonia.' He lowered his voice to a soothing murmur. 'Let me take care of you.' She needed him to look after her. And, damn it, he wanted to, despite her defiant air. He couldn't bear to see her like this.

'You've got to be joking.' Her mouth thinned to a flat line of distaste that pulled him up short. 'I'd as soon trust myself to your father's ministrations.'

'Now, hold it right there! You're getting ridiculous!' That anyone, particularly the woman with whom he'd shared so much of himself, could seriously compare him to Stuart Dexter was the ultimate insult.

'Ridiculous, am I?' Antonia jammed her hands on her hips and glared at him.

Despite his annoyance, he couldn't help appreciating the superb picture she made. She was glorious when roused. Rafe felt a tug of desire tighten his belly and thighs.

'You're both utterly selfish. So absorbed in getting what *you* want that you don't give a damn about the consequences for anyone else.'

'That's pure fantasy.' Anger burred his voice and he made an effort to relax. 'Dexter is amoral. His only interest is in pleasing himself.'

She shook her head. 'And you're not? You have this grand plan for vengeance and you do whatever it takes to make it work. *Use* whoever you must. The fact that you're taking advantage of innocent people—'

'Hardly innocent,' he murmured, furious at being challenged on a point of honour. 'Much as I admire you, lover, you *did* agree to my terms, didn't you? It was *your* choice to take up my offer and accept my money.'

The money she'd screwed out of him, he reminded himself bitterly. Though lately that hadn't seemed to matter. Now, though, the thought of it fuelled his anger.

'My *choice*? I never had a choice. You were blackmailing me with those debts.'

Rafe stilled. Yes, he'd bought her debts. Yes, he'd held them over her head, determined to persuade her to agree. But it hadn't been that which had made her comply. It had been the lure of more money that he'd promised. That and the attraction that had blazed like wildfire between them. No matter how she'd tried to deny it, there'd been no mistaking that sensual pull.

'Just like your father. He was going to use blackmail too.'
She stared at him, unwavering, and something dropped
inside him at the look in her eyes. 'He stole from the
Foundation and made it look like my father had done it.
That's why I was so desperate for money. To pay back the
missing funds.' Her mouth twisted in a spasm that drew
Rafe's belly tight. 'My father wasn't around to protect his
reputation, so I had to do it for him.'

Aghast, he stood silent, absorbing her words. Dexter had
done that? Put her in that position?

'That's why you wanted the money up-front?'

She nodded. 'I needed it straight away so I could transfer
it before an audit.'

'Why didn't you tell me?' he blazed. 'If I'd known...'
Rafe's words petered out as he realised she couldn't have
known he'd have helped her out even though she was a
stranger.

'Why would I tell *you*, another man trying to force me
into sex?' Anger slurred her words, she spat them out so fast.
'You'd only have used it to your advantage somehow.'

'That's preposterous.' But ice slid down his spine as he
realised how untenable her position must have been. How
much she'd needed a champion. How he'd taken satisfaction in forcing her to submit to his plan and his wishes.

Silence reigned as he met her glowing eyes and read the
truth and the disdain there. It was a new and unsettling experience to feel as if perhaps he deserved it.

'No. What's preposterous is that I didn't see the connection between the two of you before. You're both ruthless and
self-absorbed. He steals and lies to get what he wants, and
you've spent months totally absorbed in plotting revenge,
using whatever means you can to win.'

She paused long enough to heave in an uneven breath.

'You're both blackmailers. Your father views women as

sex objects and so do you. Where do you get off, offering a complete stranger money to sleep with you?'

Rafe's skin tightened as she aimed her words like darts. Dull heat spread across his neck.

'How do you think it feels, knowing that the man I've been…intimate with was only motivated by revenge?'

His stomach muscles clenched at the way she said 'intimate', as if it was something dirty.

'He said it today,' she continued remorselessly. *'Like father, like son.* He seemed almost proud of it.' She rubbed her hands over her arms, as if to counter a chill that Rafe couldn't feel. 'He was offering to keep me in style once you'd tired of me. *Keep me in the family.'*

Nausea rocked him, a sucker punch to the gut. When Rafe got his hands on his filthy excuse for a father…

'Where are you going?' It took him a moment to realise she was walking away.

'I'm leaving. I'm not staying to serve out my time. If you've got a problem with that, sue me. I never want to see you again.'

Every instinct told him to go after her, to comfort her, to explain. But his clamouring need for her was overridden by the stark truth written in her face.

She hated him. And with cause. Even the attraction between them, the sexual awareness that had been his excuse for forcing her into intimacy, seemed ephemeral now. It had held him in its thrall and he'd persuaded himself she'd felt it from the first too. But she hadn't…

Rafe spun on his heel and strode out of the apartment. He had no idea where he was going. Nowhere would be far enough to escape the appalling truths she'd revealed.

CHAPTER FOURTEEN

ANTONIA sipped her orange juice in the warm Italian sunshine and let her eyelids droop as she relaxed for the first time, it seemed, in weeks. She'd arrived early for her appointment, and these few moments of peace in the villa's private courtyard were just what she needed.

This last trip had been demanding—a whistlestop tour for an extended-family group. Pity the money bulging in their wallets hadn't made up for their unpleasant personalities.

If she could afford it she'd give up this job and find something else. But she didn't have time. She needed to get some money behind her, quickly. Antonia slid a hand over her still flat stomach and felt tears spring to her eyes as regret welled for all that might have been. For the dream she'd once cherished—her, Rafe and their baby, a loving family.

She'd had no choice. She'd done the right thing in leaving. How could she have stayed with a man who'd given himself over to the poisonous fantasy of revenge? Who'd used her so heartlessly? So cold-bloodedly?

How could a man like Rafe, intelligent, clever, warm and caring behind the tycoon façade, have fallen into that trap? No matter how appalling Stuart Dexter's behaviour, why hadn't Rafe been able to see that pursuing vengeance was turning him into the sort of man he despised?

Then there was the small fact that he didn't love her. Would never love her. Familiar pain twisted inside as it had every day since she'd left him. Every empty day since he'd let her go with not a word of protest. Part of her had expected him to follow, to sweep her into his arms and refuse to let her leave. But he hadn't cared enough.

She sobbed herself to sleep every night, crying for what she'd never have. The wall of protective ice round her heart had finally broken and she felt raw from grief.

Yet now she had a reason to be strong. She needed to pull herself together and concentrate on the future.

Rafe stood in the shadows of the courtyard, watching her. She was even more beautiful than he remembered, her profile perfection, her body sheer invitation, even covered in the sedate suit she wore for work.

How would she react when she found her new client was the man she'd spurned a month ago?

His stomach churned; his pulse hammered. The sensation had become familiar these past weeks, as he'd come to terms with what she'd said and realised how small were his chances of persuading her to come back. He was a desperate man.

Abruptly he stepped out of the shadows and into the sunlight. He couldn't take this waiting any longer.

'Antonia.'

'Rafe?' The shock of hearing his voice jerked her out of her reverie. It was *him*, standing right in front of her. Eyes bluer than the sky stared down at her from that face she knew so well.

Her heart accelerated into an uneven tattoo at the stunning picture he made, gilded by sunlight. He was all masculine angles and hard planes, tall and powerful and utterly magnetic. She barely stifled the need to reach out to him.

How pathetic was she?

'I missed you.' His voice, deep and warm, rumbled across her skin, and a flitter of joy shivered through her.

I missed you too. But she couldn't say it.

'I'd have thought you'd have another woman to warm your bed by now.' Anguish ripped through her at the idea, but she needed to remind herself to stay firm.

He shook his head, eyes never leaving hers. 'I'm not interested in any other woman. You must know that.'

Antonia was silent. He'd let her walk out of his life without a word of protest. If he'd cared he'd have tried to persuade her to stay. She knew the truth. He'd never really wanted *her*. That knowledge was a cold, suffocating weight on her chest, making it hard to draw breath.

'I've done my time as your mistress. I'm not going back to that.'

'I didn't for a moment think you would.'

Antonia's heart nosedived. He'd confirmed it, as she'd known he would—he didn't want her back.

Why did it hurt so much, hearing it from his lips? She bit down on a suddenly trembling lip.

'Why are you here?' Every moment he stood there it grew harder to maintain this shell of composure. She feared she couldn't keep up the pretence. Not when her heart was breaking at seeing him so close, so unattainable. She knew she shouldn't want him, but was unable to suppress the craving.

He dragged out a chair and sat in front of her. His knees almost brushed hers. His powerful hands flexed on his thighs. The scent of his skin reached her, making her nostrils flare and her nipples tighten.

No! It was too much. She made to stand.

'Wait.' His hand hovered close to hers.

'I'm here to meet a client.' Antonia looked at her watch. Surely she had the time right? The message had said ten. The housekeeper expected her.

'I know.' That was all he said, but suddenly she knew. It was *Rafe* who had requested her for this job. Rafe who'd booked a personalised tour through Italy.

'Marcus Paulson—'

'Is my agent.' He paused. 'I knew if I made the arrangements myself you wouldn't agree to meet me.'

He was dead right. Even now, knowing what he was, how he'd used her, she found herself wanting to stay.

'I have to go. I can't—'

'I need to talk to you, Antonia.' His eyes clouded, as if this was as painful for him as for her. 'To explain.'

Automatically she shook her head.

'Please.'

The single word stilled her movements and she subsided in her chair. There was such sincerity in his expression, a rough edge of discomfort in his voice. The problem was that even now she could barely resist him.

'Thank you.'

For a moment she thought he was going to reach out, and her heartbeat revved. She told herself it wasn't disappointment she felt when he didn't.

'I'm sorry,' he said at last. 'Sorry for everything. You were right. I behaved terribly. As bad as my…father. Worse, I prided myself that I was dealing out justice for his sins, yet I didn't see the damage I inflicted. On you.'

He thrust his hand through his immaculate dark hair in a gesture that made him look oddly vulnerable. Silently Antonia cursed herself for responding to it, for wanting to reach out to him.

'I forced you into an impossible situation and there was

no excuse. I let my bitterness cloud my judgement. I convinced myself you were the sort of mercenary party girl I despised. The sort of woman I've been fending off for years. I should have guessed the truth. You were too honest, too decent for that.' He drew in a long, slow breath. 'I treated you abominably.'

'I…' What could she say? That in her heart she'd already forgiven him? She blinked back tears, unable to prevent the wish that she'd met him *now*, not when he'd been obsessed with vengeance.

'Don't cry, Antonia.' He took her hand and chafed it. His touch felt so good she didn't have the strength to tug out of his hold.

'I'm not crying.' She reserved that for the lonely solitude of her single bed.

Silently he reached out and stroked her cheek. She felt dampness there and was horrified. She'd been so determined that he'd never see her weak.

'Of course you're not.' He pulled out a large white handkerchief and wiped her cheek as she blinked back the welling tide. 'You've been so brave, Antonia, so strong.'

She almost convinced herself she read approval in his cerulean gaze. A glow of warmth sparked inside her.

'I need to tell you about Stuart Dexter.'

Her shoulders slumped. He'd come to talk about Dexter?

'It took me a long time to deal with the truth,' Rafe said. 'I'd been fixated on revenge—though I called it justice—for so long it was hard to shift my perspective.' His mouth twisted in a grim line. 'You did that for me. When you told me I was like him I couldn't believe it. I didn't want to believe it.'

His hold tightened but she didn't complain. She'd longed to take back the accusation almost as soon as she'd made it. Even then she'd known it wasn't true. Rafe had an inner core of decency Dexter had never possessed.

'It was only when I discovered you were right about the man I'd become that I realised I had to drop it.'

'You've given up your pursuit of him?' It seemed unbelievable. Rafe had been so single-minded.

He shrugged. 'Not completely. After what he did to you I couldn't let him walk away scot-free, so I compromised.'

Antonia's brows puckered. 'I don't understand.'

Rafe smiled, and she saw a trace of the ruthless tycoon in that satisfied expression.

'I stopped trying to play God. Dexter's in so much difficulty he'll go under soon without me interfering. But I made sure the information my team had dug up on his dubious business practices was available to the authorities. They were eager to see the documentary evidence.' Rafe leaned towards her, his expression serious. 'Let them bring him to justice. There are more important things in life. I wash my hands of him.' He paused. 'Unless you want to press charges for assault? If you do, I'll back you all the way.'

She shook her head. The last thing she wanted was to revisit the past.

'I knew the damage he'd done my mother, and how he'd tried to manipulate and then force you. It made me wonder what life had been like for the woman he married.'

Antonia blinked. 'It did?'

His mouth thinned to a sombre line. 'I realised how lucky my mother had been despite everything. Being married to my father would have been infinitely worse.'

His gaze grew unfocused, as if he saw things she couldn't, and Antonia realised how devastating it must be for a man of Rafe's pride to acknowledge a louse like Dexter as his father.

She wrapped her fingers around his in a tiny gesture of comfort. Instantly his eyes zeroed in on hers in a look that made her feel hot. She tried to slip her hand away, but his hold tightened. Was that a satisfied curve at one corner of his mouth, or just her imagination?

'What did you do?' she asked, suddenly breathless.

He lifted his shoulders in an offhand movement. 'There wasn't much I could do. I made sure the house was in his wife's name, so she'll have somewhere to live when he loses everything else. And I secured an annuity for her.'

'You did that? You don't even know the woman.'

'We've met,' he said. 'And it was the least I could do. Call it a family duty to pick up the pieces in his wake. Besides, it felt…right.'

'Oh, Rafe.' Emotion welled. He really *had* changed.

'What?' His brows arrowed down as he watched her.

'I'm glad.' Even though it made the pain of knowing he'd never want her even more poignant.

'Really?'

His look was so intense it stripped away the last of her defences. She couldn't afford to let him guess how she felt about him. All she had left was her pride.

'Yes. I'm pleased for you. You can move on.' She hitched her chin higher. 'And so can I.'

For what seemed a full minute he stared into her eyes, as if probing everything she tried to hide.

'In that case we can talk about this tour.'

She jerked back in her seat.

'You're not serious!' He couldn't expect her to escort him around Italy on a month's personalised tour. That would be too cruel.

She'd have to deal with him in the future. The secret she carried made that inevitable. But not now. Not yet. The pain was still too raw. She wasn't ready.

'I've never been more serious about anything,' he murmured, capturing her other hand and holding it in his.

Antonia felt the blood pulse fast through her hands, through his, their heartbeats in time.

'Spend the next month with me?'

She shook her head so vigorously she felt her hair slide loose of its pins. 'I can't.'

'Why not? Wouldn't you enjoy a holiday together, getting to know each other properly?'

'No!' Antonia was aghast. She wanted it too much. Already knew him too well. That was the problem. She couldn't bear to be with Rafe, knowing her feelings weren't reciprocated.

'Not even if I told you I loved you?'

Her eyes rounded in astonishment and her heart faltered. She didn't have time to absorb his words for suddenly he moved, pulling her up into the circle of his arms. She tried to back away, but his embrace was like warm steel, keeping her close.

'I don't believe you.'

'I love you, Antonia. Believe it. Have I ever lied to you?'

'But when…?'

'Ages ago. I didn't know it was love. I thought it was plain old-fashioned lust. It wasn't till you walked out on me that I realised I'd lost the one thing that made my life whole.'

The hunger, the pain in his eyes almost convinced her.

'But you didn't come after me.'

'Would you have taken me?' He shook his head. 'You needed space. And I needed to make some changes before I came after you. You painted a frightening picture of what I'd become. How could I ask you to take on a man like that? I needed time to sort myself out.'

Antonia felt a ripple of excitement deep inside. Could it be true? She tried to think sensibly about what he said but cogent thought was almost impossible. Then she looked into his dear, stern, worried face and realised he was absolutely serious.

Rafe loved her!

'Say you'll come, Antonia. Give me a month to show you how much I love you. A month to convince you that you care for me too. *I know you do.*' His gaze was mesmerising.

'I do,' she whispered. 'I love you, Rafe. I—'

'Antonia…' His lips closed on hers, and any thought of speech fled. All the dialogue they needed was here, in their entwined bodies. He held her so close, yet so tenderly, his hands sliding possessively over her as if he'd never get enough of her. There was magic in their kiss, in the hot, slow dance of their tongues, in the luscious sharing of intimacy. Antonia gave herself up to the ecstasy of being in the arms of the man she loved. And who loved her.

'I don't deserve you,' he whispered against her lips, when they finally broke apart to gasp down some air.

'Don't be absurd.'

'It's true.' Blue eyes bright with passion met hers. 'But I'm not saint enough to deny myself. I wanted you from the moment I saw you, and I'll *never* let you go.'

'Rafe. You don't have to say that. I know it was just because Dexter wanted—'

His finger on her lips stopped her. 'Let's not mention him again. But as for wanting you, my darling, you should know that revenge was just the excuse I needed to make a move on you. Even if he hadn't been there I'd have pursued you. I saw you and I wanted you. I had to have you. And nothing's changed except that now I understand how much you mean to me.'

When Rafe looked at her like that Antonia found it hard to breathe. Burgeoning joy robbed her of words. He'd wanted her from the first? Just as she had wanted him?

'Say you'll marry me,' he demanded. 'We'll make this our honeymoon. When it's over we'll look for a house together—anywhere you want.'

She shook her head, still stunned at the sight of her determined lover so needy, so…desperate. Emotion swirled deep inside as she met his eyes.

'Antonia. You can't refuse!' His voice was raw with shock. His hands tightened possessively.

'No, I'm not refusing.' Her voice was uneven, whether with tears or welling laughter she didn't know. 'I'd love to marry you, Rafe.'

He pulled her close, his eyes glittering as he bent to kiss her. But she held him off, reaching out to take his hand and slip it between them to rest low on her belly.

'The sooner we get ready for this little one's arrival, the better.'

'A baby?' He was still for heartbeat, then he scooped her up in his arms and twirled her round, his deep laugh echoing across the wide courtyard. Antonia had never heard a more joyous sound.

'Have I told you how wonderful you are, Antonia?'

She grinned, the last of her doubts dissolving like shadows at midday. 'I didn't do it by myself, you know.'

He stopped, his eyes meeting hers unerringly. 'I love you, Antonia Malleson.'

'And I love you, Rafe Benton.'

There in the citrus-scented sun, the words sounded like vows. The echo of distant church bells rose in the air. For a long moment they stared into each other's eyes, feeling love surround them. Then Rafe turned with her in his arms and strode towards the open doors.

'Where are we going?'

The devil was in his eyes as he smiled down at her. 'To anticipate our honeymoon.'

* * * * *

THE EARL'S
UNTOUCHED
BRIDE

Annie Burrows

Annie Burrows has been making up stories for her own amusement since she first went to school. As soon as she got the hang of using a pencil she began to write them down. Her love of books meant she had to do a degree in English literature. And her love of writing meant she could never take on a job where she didn't have time to jot down notes when inspiration for a new plot struck her. She still wants the heroines of her stories to wear beautiful floaty dresses, and triumph over all that life can throw at them. But when she got married, she discovered that finding a hero is an essential ingredient to arriving at 'happy ever after'.

Dear Reader,

It was such a thrill to be asked to contribute to this anthology, celebrating one hundred years of publishing from Mills & Boon.

Recently I had the opportunity to look at some cover pictures from the very earliest publications. As a lover of all things historical, I found it fascinating that it was fairly easy to date each book, simply by the style of the cover art. The glamour of the 1920s and 30s was replaced by a more patriotic and earnest tone during the war years. Then came a profusion of bright colours which reflected the hopes of a nation emerging from austerity and rationing.

Whatever decade we live in, though, one thing is certain. Though our lifestyles may change, the deepest needs of each human being remain the same. Each of us longs to feel valued – loved for ourselves, just as we are.

The hero and heroine of my contribution to this anthology are both painfully aware of their own deficiencies. So aware that it is hard for either of them to believe another person can truly love them. I hope you enjoy reading their story, which is set against the turbulent times France and England had to face when Napoleon escaped from Elba and tried to re-establish his empire.

Annie Burrows

Readers may contact Annie Burrows via her website: www.annie-burrows.co.uk

To my parents,
who taught me to love reading.

CHAPTER ONE

GIDDINGS opened the door to find His Lordship standing upon the step, his face set in such rigid lines a shiver went down his spine. It was a relief when the Earl of Walton looked straight through him as he handed over his hat and coat, turning immediately towards the door to the salon. Thank God young Conningsby had taken it into his head to pass out on one of the sofas in there, instead of staggering back to his own lodgings the previous night. It was far better that it should be a man who could answer back, rather than a hapless member of staff, who became the butt of His Lordship's present mood.

But Charles Algernon Fawley, the ninth Earl of Walton, ignored Conningsby too. Striding across the room to the sideboard, he merely unstoppered a crystal decanter, pouring its entire contents into the last clean tumbler upon the tray.

Conningsby opened one eye warily, and rolled it in the Earl's direction. 'Breakfast at Tortoni's?' he grated hoarsely.

Charles tossed the glass of brandy back in one go, and reached for the decanter again.

'Don't look as though you enjoyed it much,' Conningsby observed, wincing as he struggled to sit up.

'No.' As the Earl realised the decanter was empty, his

fingers curled round its neck as though he wished he could strangle it. 'And if you dare say I told you so…'

'Wouldn't dream of it, my lord. But what I will say is—'

'No. I listened to all you had to say last night, and, while I am grateful for your concern, my decision remains the same. I am not going to slink out of Paris with my tail between my legs like some whipped cur. I will not have it said that some false, painted jilt has made the slightest impact on my heart. I am staying until the lease on this apartment expires, not one hour sooner. Do you hear me?'

Conningsby raised a feeble hand to his brow. 'Only too clearly.' He eyed the empty decanter ruefully. 'And while you're proving to the whole world that you don't care a rap about your betrothed running off with some penniless artist, I don't suppose you could get your man to rustle up some coffee, could you?'

'Engraver,' snapped the Earl as he tugged viciously on the bell-pull.

Conningsby sank back into the sofa cushions, waving a languid hand to dismiss the profession of the Earl's betrothed's lover as the irrelevance it was. 'Judging by the expression on your face, the gossip-mongers have already been at work. It's not going to get any easier for you…'

'My mood now has nothing whatever to do with the fickle Mademoiselle Bergeron,' he snarled. 'It is her countrymen's actions which could almost induce me to leave this vile charnel house that calls itself a civilised city and return to London, where the most violent emotion I am likely to suffer is acute boredom.'

'But it was boredom you came to Paris to escape from!'

He let the inaccuracy of that remark pass. Staying in London, with his crippled half-brother, had simply become intolerable. Seeking refuge down at Wycke had not been a viable alternative, either. There was no respite from what ailed him there. The very opulence of the vast estate only served as a painful reminder of the injustice that had been perpetrated so that he could inherit it all.

Paris had seemed like the perfect solution. Since Bonaparte had abdicated, it had become extremely fashionable to hop across the Channel to see the sights.

Leaning one arm on the mantelpiece, he remarked, with an eloquent shudder, 'I will never complain of that particular malady again, I do assure you.'

'What is it?' Conningsby asked. 'What else has happened?'

'Another murder.'

'Du Mauriac again, I take it?' Conningsby's face was grim. The French officer was gaining a reputation for provoking hot-headed young Englishmen to duel with him, and dispatching them with a ruthless efficiency gleaned from his years of active service. And then celebrating his kill by breakfasting on broiled kidneys at Tortoni's. 'Who was it this morning? Not anybody we know, I hope?'

'On the contrary. The poor fellow he slaughtered before breakfast today was a subaltern by the name of Lennox.' At Conningsby's frown, Charles explained, 'Oh, there is no reason why you should know him. He was typical of all the others who have fallen by that butcher's sword. An obscure young man with no powerful connections.'

'Then how…?'

'He served in the same regiment as my unfortunate half-brother. He was one of those young men who constantly paraded through my London house, attempting to rouse him to some semblance of normality.' Sometimes it seemed as if an entire regiment must have marched through his hall at one time or another, to visit the poor wreck of a man who had once been a valiant soldier. Though few of them paid a second visit after encountering his blistering rejection. Captain Fawley did not want to be an object of pity.

Pity! If only he knew! If he, the ninth Earl, had been injured so badly, there would be not one well-wisher hastening to his bedside in an attempt to cheer him. On the contrary, it would be vultures who would begin to hover, eager to see who among them would gain his title, his wealth…

'At least he was a soldier, then.'

'He never stood a chance against a man of Du Mauriac's stamp, and the blackguard knew it! He sat there laughing about the fact that the boy did not look as though he needed to shave more than once a week! And sneered at his milk-white countenance as he faced him… God, the boy must have been sick with fright.'

Charles smote one fist into his palm. 'If only Lennox had asked me to be his second, I would have found a way to stop it!'

Conningsby eyed him with surprise. The only thing he had known about the Earl before his arrival in Paris was that, upon coming of age, he had caused a ripple through society by ousting his guardians from his ancestral home and subsequently severing all connections with that branch of his family. He had not known of a single man who dared claim friendship with the chillingly insular young lord. In Conningsby's capacity as a junior aide at the English embassy, he had dutifully helped him to find these lodgings in the Rue de Richelieu, and generally smoothed his entry into the social scene. It had been quite a surprise, the previous night, when the Earl had reacted as any man might on discovering the beautiful Parisienne to whom he had just proposed had run off with her lover. He had gone straight home to drown his sorrows. Though his head had proved stronger than Conningsby's.

'Couldn't have backed down, though, could he?' he ventured sympathetically. 'Wouldn't have wanted to live with an accusation of cowardice hanging round his neck.'

'Somebody should have found some way to save Lennox,' the Earl persisted. 'If only…'

He was prevented from saying anything further when the butler opened the door. 'There is a visitor for you, my lord.'

'I am not receiving,' Charles growled.

Giddings cleared his throat, and eyed Conningsby warily, before saying diffidently, 'The young person insists you would wish to see her.' He stepped forward and, in a voice intended only for his master, said, 'She says her name is Mademoiselle Bergeron.'

Charles felt as though he had been punched in the stomach.

While he struggled to draw breath, Conningsby, who had remarkably acute hearing, rose gingerly to his feet. 'She has in all probability come to beg your forgiveness…'

'She shall not have it!' Charles turned to grasp the mantelpiece with both hands, his shoulders hunched. 'I shall not take her back. If she prefers some artist to me, then she may go to him and welcome!'

'But there may have been some dreadful mistake. Let's face it, my lord, the Bergeron household last night was in such a state of turmoil, who knows what may have been going on?'

They had gone to escort Felice to a ball, where the engagement was to have been announced. They had found Monsieur Bergeron slumped in his chair, as though all the stuffing had been knocked out of him, and Madame Bergeron suffering from a noisy bout of hysterics upon the sofa. The only clear piece of information either of them had been able to glean was that she had turned off the wicked maidservant who had aided and abetted her ungrateful daughter to elope with a nobody when she could have married an English earl.

The Earl was breathing rather rapidly. 'I am not safe to

see her.' He turned back to face the room, his entire face leached of colour. 'I may well attempt to strangle her.'

'Not you,' Conningsby assured him.

The Earl looked at him sharply, then straightened up. 'No,' he said, his face freezing into a chillingly aloof mask. 'Not I.' He went to one of the fireside chairs, sat down, and crossed one leg nonchalantly over the other. 'You may show Mademoiselle Bergeron in, Giddings,' he said, keeping his eyes fixed on the door.

Conningsby got the peculiar impression he had just become invisible. And, though he could tell the Earl would not care one way or another, he had no intention of becoming a witness to the impending confrontation. It was one thing helping a man to drown his sorrows in a companionable way. Hell, what man hadn't been in a similar predicament at one time or another? But becoming embroiled with some hysterical Frenchwoman, with his head in its present delicate state, was asking too much! He looked wildly round the room for some other means of escape than the door through which Mademoiselle Bergeron would shortly appear. The only other exit appeared to be through the windows.

It took but a second to vault over the sofa on which he'd spent the night and dive through the heavy velvet curtains.

'Mademoiselle Bergeron,' he heard Giddings intone, as he fumbled open the shutter bolts.

Charles experienced a spurt of satisfaction when she paused on the threshold, her gloved hand fluttering to the heavy veil draped from her bonnet.

Instead of rising to his feet, he deliberately leaned back in his chair and crossed his arms, eyeing her with unremitting coldness. She squared her shoulders, taking one faltering step forward. Then, to his complete astonishment, she broke into a run, flying across the room and landing upon her knees at his feet. Seizing his hand, she pulled it to her face, kissing it through the veil.

Impatiently, he snatched it back. Whatever she had been up to last night, he was not prepared to unbend towards her without a really good explanation. And probably not even then. To feel such strong emotions that they could reduce you to the state of mind where not even copious quantities of alcohol could anaesthetise them was something he did not care to experience again. He was just about to tell her so when she knelt back, lifting the veil from her face.

'Oh, thank you, milord! Thank you for letting me in. I was so afraid! You have no idea how unpleasant it is to walk the streets unescorted with feelings running so high…'

Charles reeled back in his seat. 'You are not…not…'

'Felice? No.' The young woman who knelt before him returned his look rather defiantly. 'I regret the deception, but I did not think you would agree to see anyone but her today. And so I led your butler to believe I was she. And, indeed, the deception was not so very great. You were expecting Mademoiselle Bergeron, and I am Mademoiselle Bergeron…'

'You are entirely the wrong Mademoiselle Bergeron,' he snapped. How could he have mistaken the much shorter and utterly plain Heloise for her beautiful, glamorous, and entirely captivating younger sister? He couldn't blame the bonnet, though the peak of it did protrude from her face by over a foot, nor the heavy veil that was suspended from it, though it had concealed her features. He had wanted to see Felice, he acknowledged painfully. He had clung to the faint hope that there had been some dreadful mistake, and that she had come to tell him that she wanted no other man but him. And so he had seen what he wanted to see. What kind of fool did that make him?

Heloise swallowed nervously. She had been expecting a

little antagonism, but the reality of facing a man whose heart had been broken was altogether more daunting than she had supposed it would be.

'No,' she persisted. 'I do not think you will find that I am when you hear what I have to propose…'

'I cannot imagine what you hope to accomplish by coming here and prostrating yourself in this manner,' he began angrily.

'Oh, no—how could you, when I have not yet explained? But you only need to listen for a very few minutes and I will tell you!' Suddenly very conscious that she was still kneeling like a supplicant at his feet, she glanced about the room.

'May I sit upon one of these so comfortable-looking chairs, my lord? This floor it is most hard, and really I do not see that you can take me at all seriously if I do not make some effort to look more rational. Only I did not know what was to become of me if you did not let me in. I was followed all the way from the Tuileries gardens by a contingent of the National Guard of the most vile manners. They refused to believe at all that I am a respectable female, merely visiting a friend of the family who also happens to be an English milord, and that they would be entirely sorry for accusing me of the things they did—for why should I not be entirely innocent? Just because you are English, that does not make me a bad person, or unpatriotic at all, even if I am not wearing either the white lily or the violet. If they are going to arrest anyone, it should have been the crowd who were brawling in the gardens, not someone who does not care at all that the emperor has gone, and that a Bourbon sits on the throne. Not but that they got the chance, because your so kind butler permitted me to enter the hall the moment he saw how things were, and even if you would not see me, he said there was a door to the back through the kitchens from which I could return home, after I had drunk a little something to restore my nerves...'

The Earl found he had no defence against the torrent of words that washed over him. She didn't even seem to pause for breath until Giddings returned, bearing a tray upon which was a bottle of Madeira and two glasses.

She'd risen to her feet, removed her bonnet and gloves, and perched on the edge of the chair facing him, twittering all the while like some little brown bird, hopping about and fluffing its plumage before finally roosting for the night.

She smiled and thanked Giddings as she took the proffered drink, but her hand shook so much that she spilled several drops down the front of her coat.

'I am sorry that you have been offered insults,' he heard himself saying as she dabbed ineffectually at the droplets soaking into the cloth. 'But you should have known better than to come to my house alone.' Far from being the haven for tourists that he had been led to believe, many Parisians were showing a marked hostility to the English. It had started, so he had been reliably informed, when trade embargoes had been lifted and cheap English goods had come on sale again. But tensions were rising between die-hard Bonapartists and supporters of the new Bourbon regime as well. If factions were now brawling in the Tuileries gardens, then Mademoiselle Bergeron might well not be safe to venture out alone. 'I will have you escorted home...'

'Oh, not yet!' she exclaimed, a look of dismay on her face. 'For you have not heard what I came to say!'

'I am waiting to hear it,' he replied dryly. 'I have been waiting since you walked through the door.'

Heloise drained the contents of her glass and set it down smartly upon the table that Giddings had placed thoughtfully at her elbow.

'Forgive me. I am so nervous, you see, I tend to babble

when I am nervous. Well, I was only nervous when I set out. But then, after the incident in the Tuileries, I became quite scared, and then—'

'Mademoiselle Bergeron!' He slapped the arm of his chair with decided irritation. 'Will you please come to the point?'

'Oh.' She gulped, her face growing hot. It was not at all easy to come to the point with a man as icily furious as the Earl of Walton. In fact, if she wasn't quite so desperate, she would wish she hadn't come here at all. Looking into those chips of ice that he had for eyes, and feeling their contempt for her chilling her to the marrow, Heloise felt what little courage she had left ebb away. Sitting on a chair instead of staying prostrate at his feet had not redressed their positions at all. She still had to look up to meet his forbidding features, for the Earl was quite a tall man. And she had nothing with which to combat his hostility but strength of will. Not beauty, or grace, or cleverness. She had the misfortune to have taken after her mother in looks. While Felice had inherited her father's even features and long-limbed grace, she had got the Corbiere nose, diminutive size, and nondescript colouring. Her only weapon was an idea. But what an idea! If he would only hear her out, it would solve all their difficulties at a stroke!

'It is quite simple, after all,' she declared. 'It is that I think you should marry me instead of Felice.'

She cocked her head to one side as she waited for his response, reminding him of a street sparrow begging for crumbs. Before he could gather his wits, she had taken another breath and set off again.

'I know you must think that this is preposterous just at first. But only think of the advantages!'

'Advantages for whom?' he sneered. He had never thought of little Heloise as a scheming gold-digger before.

But then nor had he thought her capable of such fluent speech. Whenever she had played chaperon for himself and her sister she had been so quiet he had tended to forget she was there at all. He had been quite unguarded, he now recalled with mounting irritation, assuming, after a few half-hearted attempts to draw her out, that she could not speak English very well.

Though the look he sent her was one that had frozen the blood in the veins of full-grown men, Heloise was determined to have her say.

'Why, for you, of course! Unless... Your engagement to Felice has not been announced in England yet, has it? She told me you had not sent any notice to the London papers. And of course in Paris, though everyone thinks they know that you wished to marry Felice, you have only to say, when they see me on your arm instead of my sister, "You will find you are mistaken," in that tone you use for giving an encroaching person a set-down, if anyone should dare to question you, and that will be that!'

'But why, pray, should I wish to say any such thing?'

'So that nobody will know she broke your heart, of course!' Her words, coupled with her look of genuine sympathy, touched a place buried so deep inside him that for years he had been denying its very existence.

'I know how her actions must have bruised your pride, too,' she ploughed on, astonishing him with the accuracy of her observations. Even Conningsby claimed he had not guessed how deep his feelings ran until the night before, when, in his cups, he'd poured out the whole sorry tale. But this girl, of whom he had never taken much notice, had read him like an open book.

'But this way nobody will ever guess! You are so good at keeping your face frozen, so that nobody can tell what you are truly feeling. You can easily convince everyone that it was my family that wished for the match, and that they put Felice forward, but all the time it was me in whom you were interested, for I am the eldest, or—oh, I am sure you can come up with some convincing reason. For of course they would not believe that you could truly be attracted to me. I know that well! And if any rumours about a Mademoiselle Bergeron have reached as far as London— well, I have already shown you how one Mademoiselle Bergeron may enter a room as another. Nobody else need know it was quite another Mademoiselle Bergeron you had set your sights on. If you marry me, you may walk round Paris with your head held high, and return home with your pride intact!'

'You are talking nonsense. Arrant nonsense!' He sprang from his chair, and paced moodily towards the sideboard. He had ridden out malicious gossip before. He could do so again. 'The connection with your family is severed,' he snapped, grasping the decanter, then slamming it back onto the tray on discovering it was still empty. He was not going to be driven from Paris because a few tattle-mongers had nothing better to talk about than a failed love affair. Nor would anything induce him to betray his hurt by so much as a flicker of an eyelid. 'I see no need to restore it!'

He turned to see her little face crumple. Her shoulders sagged. He braced himself for a further outpouring as he saw her eyes fill with tears. But she surprised him yet again. Rising to her feet with shaky dignity, she said, 'Then I apologise for intruding on you this morning. I will go now.'

She had reached the door and was fumbling her hands into her gloves when he cried out, 'Wait!' His quarrel was not with her. She had never given him a moment's trouble during the entire time he had been courting Felice. She had never voiced any protest, no matter where they had dragged her, though at times he had been able to tell she had been uncomfortable. All she had done on those occasions was withdraw into the shadows, as though she wished to efface herself from the scene completely. That was more her nature, he realised with a flash of insight. To have come here this morning and voiced that ridiculous proposition must have been the hardest thing for her to do. It had not been only the brush with the National Guard that had made her shake with fright.

He had no right to vent his anger on her. Besides, to let her out alone and unprotected onto the streets was not the act of a gentleman.

'*Mademoiselle,*' he said stiffly, 'I told you I would ensure you returned to your house safely. Please, won't you sit down again, while I get Giddings to summon a cabriolet?'

'Thank you,' she sighed, leaning back against the door. 'It was not at all pleasant getting here. I had no idea! To think I was glad Maman had turned off Joanne, so that it was an easy matter for me to sneak out without anyone noticing.' She shook her head ruefully. 'It is true what Papa says. I am a complete imbecile. When I had to pass that crowd in the Tuileries, I knew how stupid I had been. Then to walk right up to the door of an Englishman, on my own, as though I was a woman of no virtue…'

Seeing her tense white face, Charles felt impelled to check the direction of her thoughts.

'Please, sit down on the sofa while you are waiting.'

She did so, noting with a start that her bonnet still lay amongst its cushions. As she picked it up, turning it over in her hands as though it was an object she had never seen before, he continued, 'Whatever prompted you to take such drastic steps to come to my house, *mademoiselle*? I cannot believe you are so concerned about my wounded pride, or my—' He checked himself before alluding to his allegedly broken heart.

She turned crimson, suddenly becoming very busy untangling the ribbons of her bonnet. Her discomfort brought a sudden suspicion leaping to his mind.

'Never tell me you are in love with me!' The notion that this plain young woman had been harbouring a secret passion for him, while he had been making love to her sister under her very nose, gave him a very uncomfortable feeling. 'I had no idea! I did not think you even liked me!'

Her head flew up, an arrested expression on her face when she detected the tiniest grain of sympathy in the tone of his voice. 'Would you marry me, then, if I said I loved you?' she breathed, her eyes filled with hope. But as he returned her gaze steadily she began to look uncomfortable. Worrying at her lower lip with her teeth, she hung her head.

'It is no good,' she sighed. 'I cannot tell you a lie.' She sank back against the cushions, her whole attitude one of despondency. 'I'm not clever enough to make you believe it. And apart from that,' she continued, as Charles settled into his favourite fireside chair with a profound feeling of relief, 'I confess I did dislike you when you first came calling on Felice and she encouraged your attentions. Even though Maman said I was letting the family down by making my disapproval plain, and Felice insisted I was being a baby. But I couldn't help feeling as I did.' She frowned. 'Although, really, it was not you at all I did not like, so much as the idea of you. You see?'

He had just opened his mouth to reply that he did not see at all, when she continued, 'and then, when I got to know you better, and saw how much you truly felt for Felice, even though you hid it so well, I couldn't dislike you at all. Indeed, I felt most sorry for you, because I knew she never cared for you in the least.'

When she saw a flash of surprise flicker across his face, she explained.

'Well, how could she, when she had been in love with Jean-Claude for ever? Even though Maman and Papa had forbidden the match, because he has no money at all. I really hated the way you dazzled them all with your wealth and elegance and seemed to make Felice forget Jean-Claude.' Her face brightened perceptibly. 'But of course you hadn't at all. She merely used your visits as a smoke-screen to fool Maman into thinking she was obeying her orders, which gave Jean-Claude time to make plans for their escape. Which is all as it should be.' She sighed dreamily. 'She was not false to her true love.' She sat up straight suddenly, looking at him with an expression of chagrin. 'Though she was very cruel to you when you did not deserve it at all. Even if you are an Englishman.'

Charles found himself suddenly conscious of a desire to laugh. 'So, you wish to marry me to make up for your sister's cruel treatment of me? In fact because you feel sorry for me—is that it?'

She looked at him hopefully for a few seconds, before once more lowering her eyes and shaking her head.

'No, it is not that. Not only that. Although I should like to make things right for you. Of course I should. Because of my sister you have suffered a grievous hurt. I know you can never feel for me what you felt for her, but at least your pride could be restored by keeping the nature of her betrayal a secret. It is not too late. If you acted today, if you made Papa give his consent today, we could attend a function together this evening and stop the gossip before it starts.' She looked up at him with eyes blazing with intensity. 'Together, we could sort out the mess she has left behind. For it is truly terrible at home.' She shook her head mournfully. 'Maman has taken to her bed. Papa is threatening to shoot himself, because now there is not to be the connection with you he can see no other way out.' She twined one of the bonnet ribbons round her index finger as she looked at him imploringly. 'You would only have to stroll in and say, "Never mind about Felice. I will take the other one," in that off-hand way you have, as though you don't care about anything at all, and he would grovel at your feet in gratitude. Then nobody would suspect she broke your heart! Even if they really believe you wanted to marry her, when they hear of the insouciance with which you took me they will have to admit they were mistaken!'

'I see,' he said slowly. 'You wish to save your family from some sort of disgrace which my marrying Felice would have averted. That is admirable, but—'

The look of guilt on her face stopped him in his tracks. He could see yet another denial rising to her lips.

'Not family honour?' he ventured.

She shook her head mournfully. 'No.' Her voice was barely more than a whisper. 'All I have told you is part of it. All those good things would result if only you would marry me, and I will be glad to achieve all of them, but—' She hung her head, burying her hands completely in the by now rather mangled bonnet. 'My prime reason is a completely selfish one. You see, if only I can persuade you to marry me, then Papa would be so relieved that you are still to pull him out of the suds that he will forget all about compelling me to marry the man he has chosen for me.'

'In short,' said Charles, 'I am easier to swallow than this other fellow?'

'Yes—much!' she cried, looking up at him with pleading eyes. 'You cannot imagine how much I hate him. If you will only say yes, I will be such a good wife! I shall not be in the least trouble to you, I promise! I will live in a cottage in the country and keep hens, and you need never even see me if you don't want. I shan't interfere with you, or stop you from enjoying yourself however you wish. I will never complain—no, not even if you beat me!' she declared dramatically, her eyes growing luminous with unshed tears.

'Why,' said Charles, somewhat taken aback by her vehemence, 'would you suspect me of wishing to beat you?'

'Because I am such a tiresome creature!'

If it hadn't been for the fact Heloise was clearly on the verge of tears, Charles would have found it hard not to laugh.

'Papa is always saying so. So did Gaspard.'

'Gaspard?'

'My brother. He said any man fool enough to marry me would soon be driven to beat me. But I feel sure…' her lower lip quivered ominously '…that you would only beat me when I *really* deserved it. You are not a cruel man. You are not cold, either, in spite of what they all say about you. You are a good person underneath your haughty manner. I know because I have watched you. I have had much opportunity, because you never took the least notice of me when Felice was in the same room. And I would not be afraid to go away with you, because you would not ever wish to beat a woman for sport like he would…'

'Come now,' Charles remonstrated, as the first tears began to trickle down her heated cheeks. 'I cannot believe your papa would force you to marry a man who would be as cruel as that…'

'Oh, but you English know nothing!' She leapt to her feet. 'He would very easily sacrifice me to such a man for the sake of preserving the rest of the family!' She was quivering from head to toe with quite another emotion than fear now. He could see that. Indignation had brought a decidedly militant gleam to her eye. She was incapable of standing still. Taking brisk little paces between the sofa and the fireplace, she did not notice that she was systematically trampling the bonnet, which had fallen to the floor when she had leapt to her feet. It occurred to him, when she stepped on it for the third time, that her sister would never have been so careless of her apparel. Not that she would have been seen dead in such an unflattering item in the first place.

'And, besides being so cruel, he is quite old!' She shuddered.

'I am thirty-five, you know,' he pointed out.

She paused mid-stride, running her eyes over him assessingly. The Earl's light blue eyes twinkled with amusement from a face that was devoid of lines of care. Elegant clothes covered a healthily muscled physique. His tawny hair was a little disarrayed this morning, to be sure, but it was neither receding nor showing any hint of grey. 'I did not know you were as old as that,' she eventually admitted with candour.

Once again, Charles was hard put to it not to burst out laughing at the absurdity of this little creature who had invaded the darkness of his lair like some cheeky little song bird hopping about between a lion's paws, pecking for crumbs, confident she was too insignificant to rate the energy required to swat her.

'Come, child, admit it. You are too young to marry anyone!'

'Well, yes!' she readily admitted. 'But Felice was younger, and you still wanted to marry her. And in time, of course, I will grow older. And by then you might have got used to me. You might even be able to teach me how to behave better!' she said brightly. Then, just as quickly, her face fell. 'Although I very much doubt it.'

She subsided into the chair opposite his own, leaning her elbows on her knees. 'I suppose I always knew I could not be any sort of wife to you.' She gazed up at him mournfully. 'But I know I would have been better off with you. For even if you are as old as you say, you don't…' Her forehead wrinkled, as though it was hard for her to find the words she wanted. 'You don't smell like him.'

Finding it increasingly hard to keep his face straight, he said, 'Perhaps you could encourage your suitor to bathe…'

Her eyes snapped with anger. Taking a deep breath, she flung at him, 'Oh, it is easy for you to laugh at me. You think I am a foolish little woman of no consequence. But this is no laughing matter to me. Whenever he comes close I want to run to a window and open it and breathe clean air. It is like when you go into a room that has been shut up too long, and you know something has decayed in it. And before you make the joke about bathing again, I must tell you that it is in my head that I smell this feeling. In my heart!' She smote her breast. 'He is steeped in so much blood!'

However absurdly she was behaving, however quaint her way of expressing herself, there was no doubt that she really felt repelled by the man her father thought she ought to marry. It was a shame that such a sensitive little creature should be forced into a marriage that was so distasteful to her. Though he could never contemplate marrying her himself, he did feel a pang of sympathy. And, in that spirit, he asked, 'Do I take it this man is a soldier, then?'

'A hero of France,' she replied gloomily. 'It is an honour for our family that such a man should wish for an alliance. An astonishment to my papa that any man should really want to take on a little mouse like me. You wonder how I came to his notice, perhaps?' When Charles nodded, humouring her whilst privately wondering why on earth it was taking Giddings so long to procure a cab to send her home in, she went on, 'He commanded Gaspard's regiment in Spain. He was…' An expression of anguish crossed her face. 'I was not supposed to hear. But people sometimes do talk when I am there, assuming that I am not paying attention—for I very often don't, you know. My brother sometimes talked about the Spanish campaign. The things his officers commanded him to do! Such barbarity!' She shuddered. 'I am not so stupid that I would willingly surrender to a man who has treated other women and children like cattle in a butcher's shop. And forced decent Frenchmen to descend to his level. And how is it,' she continued, her fists clenching, 'that while my brother died of hunger outside what you call the lines of Torres Vedras, Du Mauriac came home looking as fit as a flea?'

'Du Mauriac?' Charles echoed. 'The man your father wishes you to marry is Du Mauriac?'

Heloise nodded. 'As commander of Gaspard's regiment, he was often in our home when my brother was still alive. He used to insist it was I who sat beside him. From my hand that he wished to be served.' She shuddered. 'Then, after Gaspard died, he kept right on visiting. Papa says I am stupid to persist in refusing his proposals. He says I should feel honoured that a man so distinguished persists in courting me when I have not even beauty to recommend me. But he does not see that it is mainly my reluctance that Du Mauriac likes. He revels in the knowledge that, though he repels me, my parents will somehow contrive to force me to surrender to him!'

Heloise ground to a halt, her revulsion at the prospect of what marriage to Du Mauriac would entail finally overwhelming her. Bowing forward, she buried her face in her hands until she had herself under control. And then, alerted by the frozen silence which filled the room, she looked up at the Earl of Walton. Up until that moment she would have said he had been experiencing little more than mild amusement at her expense. But now his eyes had returned to that glacial state which had so intimidated her when first she had walked into the room. Except…now his anger was not directed at her. Indeed, it was as if he had frozen her out of his consciousness altogether.

'Go home, *mademoiselle*,' he said brusquely, rising to his feet and tugging at the bell pull. 'This interview is at an end.'

He meant it this time. With a sinking heart, Heloise turned and stumbled to the door. She had offended him somehow, by being so open about her feelings of revulsion for the man her father had decided she should marry. She had staked everything on being honest with the Earl of Walton.

But she had lost.

CHAPTER TWO

IT CAME as something of a shock, once the door had closed on Heloise's dejected little figure, when Conningsby stepped in over the windowsill.

'My God,' the man blustered. 'If I had known this room overlooked the street, and I was to have spent the entire interview wedged onto a balcony when I fully expected to be able to escape through your gardens...'

'And the curtains were no impediment to your hearing every single word, I shouldn't wonder?' The Earl sighed. 'Dare I hope you will respect the confidentiality of that conversation?'

'I work for the diplomatic service!' Conningsby bristled. 'Besides which, no man of sense would wish to repeat one word of that absurd woman's proposition!'

Although Charles himself thought Heloise absurd, for some reason he did not like hearing anyone else voice that opinion. 'I think it was remarkably brave of her to come here to try to save her family from ruin.'

'Yes, my lord. If you say so,' the other man conceded dubiously.

'I do say so,' said the Earl. 'I will not have any man disparage my fiancée.'

'You aren't really going to accept that outrageous proposal?' Conningsby gasped.

Charles studied the tips of his fingers intently.

'You cannot deny that her solution to my…uh…predicament, will certainly afford me a great deal of solace.'

'Well,' said Conningsby hesitantly, loath to offend a man of Lord Walton's reputation, 'I suppose she is quite a captivating little thing, in her way. Jolly amusing. She certainly has a gift for mimicry that almost had me giving myself away! Had to stuff a handkerchief in my mouth to choke down the laughter when she aped your voice!'

The Earl stared at him. Captivating? Until this morning he had barely looked at her. Like a little wren, she hid in the background as much as she could. And when he had looked he had seen nothing to recommend her. She had a beak of a nose, set above lips that were too thin for their width, and a sharp little chin. Her hair was a mid-brown, without a hint of a curl to render it interesting. Her eyes, though…

Before this morning she had kept them demurely lowered whenever he glanced in her direction. But today he had seen a vibrancy burning in their dark depths that had tugged a grudging response from him.

'What she may or may not be is largely irrelevant,' he said coldly. 'What just might prompt me to take her to wife is that in so doing I shall put Du Mauriac's nose out of joint.'

Conningsby laughed nervously. 'Surely you can't wish to marry a woman just so that some other fellow cannot have her?'

The Earl returned his look with a coldness of purpose that chilled him. 'She does not expect me to like her very much. You heard what she said. She will not even be surprised if I come to detest her so heartily that I beat her. All she wants is the opportunity to escape from an intolerable position. Don't you think I should oblige her?'

'Well, I…' Conningsby ran his finger round his collar, his face growing red.

'Come, now, you cannot expect me to stand by and permit her father to marry her off to that butcher, can you? She does not deserve such a fate.'

No, Conningsby thought, she does not. But then, would marriage to a man who only wanted revenge on her former suitor, a man without an ounce of fondness for her, be any less painful to her in the long run?

Heloise gripped her charcoal and bent her head over her sketchpad, blotting out the noise of her mother's sobs as she focussed on her drawing. She had achieved nothing. Nothing. She had braved the streets, and the insults of those soldiers, then endured the Earl's mockery, for nothing. Oh, why, she thought resentfully, had she ever thought she might be able to influence the intractable Earl one way or another? And how could she ever have felt sorry for him? Her fingers worked furiously, making angry slashes across the page. He had coaxed her most secret thoughts from her, let her hope he was feeling some shred of sympathy, and then spurned her. The only good thing about this morning's excursion was that nobody had noticed she had taken it, she reflected, finding some satisfaction in creating a most unflattering caricature of the Earl of Walton in the guise of a sleekly cruel tabby cat. She could not have borne it if anyone had found out where she had been. It had been bad enough when her *maman* had laid the blame for Felice's elopement at her door—as though she had ever had the least influence with her headstrong and pampered little sister!

With a few deft strokes Heloise added a timorous little mouse below the grinning mouth of the tabby cat, then set to work fashioning a pair of large paws. Folly—sheer folly! To walk into that man's lair and prostrate herself as she had!

There was a knock on the front door.

Madame Bergeron blew her nose before wailing, 'We are not receiving visitors today. I cannot endure any more. They will all come, you mark my words, to mock at us...'

Heloise rose to her feet to relay the information to their manservant before he had a chance to open the door. Since her seat was by the window, where she could get the most light for her sketching, she had a clear view of their front step.

'It is the Earl!' she gasped, her charcoal slipping from her suddenly nerveless fingers.

'It cannot be!' Her papa sprang from the chair in which he had been slumped, his head in his hands. 'What can he want with us, now?' he muttered darkly, peering through the window. 'I might have known a man of his station would not sit back and take an insult such as Felice has dealt him. He will sue us for breach of promise at the very least,' he prophesied, as Heloise sank to the floor to retrieve her pencil. 'Well, I will shoot myself first, and that will show him!' he cried wildly, while she regained her seat, bending her head over her sketchbook as much to counteract a sudden wave of faintness as to hide the hopeful expression she was sure must be showing on her face.

'*Noo!*' From the sofa, her *maman* began to weep again. 'You cannot abandon me now! How can you threaten to leave me after all we have been through?'

Instantly contrite, Monsieur Bergeron flung himself to his knees beside the sofa, seizing his wife's hand and pressing it to his lips. 'Forgive me, my precious.'

Heloise admired her parents for being so devoted to each other, but sometimes she wished they were not quite so demonstrative. Or that they didn't assume, because she had her sketchpad open, that they could behave as though she was not there.

'You know I will always worship you, my angel.' He slobbered over her hand, before clasping her briefly to his bosom. 'You are much too good for me.'

Now, that was something Heloise had long disputed. It was true that her mother should have been far beyond her father's matrimonial aspirations, since she was a younger daughter of the *seigneur* in whose district he had been a lowly but ambitious clerk. And that it might have been reprehensible of him to induce an aristocrat to elope with him. But it turned out to have been the most sensible thing her mother had ever done. Marriage to him had saved her from the fate many others of her class had suffered.

The affecting scene was cut short when the manservant announced the Earl of Walton. Raising himself tragically to his full height, Monsieur Bergeron declared, 'To spare you pain, my angel, I will receive him in my study alone.'

But before he had even reached the door Charles himself strolled in, his gloves clasped negligently in one hand. Bowing punctiliously to Madame Bergeron, who was struggling to rise from a mound of crushed cushions, he drawled, 'Good morning, *madame, monsieur.*'

Blocking his pathway further into the room, Monsieur Bergeron replied, with a somewhat martyred air, 'I suppose you wish to speak with me, my lord? Shall we retire to my study and leave the ladies in peace?'

Charles raised one eyebrow, as though astonished by this suggestion. 'Why, if you wish, of course I will wait with you while *mademoiselle* makes herself ready. Or had you forgot that I had arranged to take your daughter out driving this morning? *Mademoiselle—*' he addressed Heloise directly, his expression bland '—I hope it will not take you long to dress appropriately? I do not like to keep my horses standing.'

Until their eyes met she had hardly dared to let herself

hope. But now she was sure. He was going to go through
with it!

'B…but it was Felice,' Monsieur Bergeron blustered.
'You had arranged to take Felice out driving. M…my lord,
she is not here! I was sure you were aware that last night
she…'

'I am engaged to take your daughter out driving this
morning,' he continued implacably, 'and take your daughter
I shall. I see no reason to alter my schedule for the day. In
the absence of Felice, Heloise must bear me company.'

For a moment the room pulsed with silence, while
everyone seemed to be holding their breath.

Then Madame Bergeron sprang from the sofa, darted
across the room, and seized Heloise by the wrist. 'She will
not keep you waiting above ten minutes, my lord.' Then, to
her husband, 'What are you thinking of, not offering his
lordship a seat? And wine—he must have a glass of wine
while he is waiting!' She pushed Heloise through the door,
then paused to specify, 'The Chambertin!'

While Monsieur Bergeron stood gaping at him, Charles
strolled over to the table at which Heloise had been sitting
and began to idly flick through her sketchbook. It seemed
to contain nothing but pictures of animals. Quite strange-
looking animals, some of them, in most unrealistic poses.
Though one, of a bird in a cage, caught his attention. The
bedraggled specimen was chained to its perch. He could feel
its misery flowing off the page. He was just wondering what
species of bird it was supposed to represent, when something about the tilt of its head, the anguish burning in its
black eyes, put him forcibly in mind of Heloise, as she had
appeared earlier that day. His eyes followed the chain that
bound the miserable-looking creature to its perch, and saw
that it culminated in what looked like a golden wedding ring.

His blood running cold, he flicked back a page, to a

scene he had first supposed represented a fanciful scene from a circus. He could now perceive that the creature that was just recognisable as a lion, lying on its back with a besotted grin on its face, was meant to represent himself. The woman who was standing with her foot upon his chest, smiling with smug cruelty, was definitely Felice. He snapped the book shut and turned on Monsieur Bergeron.

'I trust you have not made the nature of my interest in your elder daughter public?'

'Alas, my lord,' he shrugged, spreading his hands wide, 'but I did give assurances in certain quarters that a match was imminent.'

'To your creditors, no doubt?'

'Debt? Pah—it is nothing!' Monsieur Bergeron spat. 'A man may recover from debt!'

When Charles raised one disbelieving eyebrow, he explained, 'You English, you do not understand how one must live in France. When power changes hands, those who support the fallen regime must always suffer from the next. To survive, a man must court friends in all camps. He must be sensitive to what is in the wind, and know the precise moment to jump…'

In short the man was, like Talleyrand, '*un homme girouette*', who was prepared, like a weather vane, to swing in whichever direction the wind blew.

Somewhat red in the face, Monsieur Bergeron sank onto the sofa which his wife had recently vacated.

'So,' Charles said slowly, 'promoting an alliance with an English noble, at a time when many Parisians are openly declaring hostility to the English, was an attempt to…?' He quirked an inquisitive eyebrow at the man, encouraging him to explain.

'To get one of my daughters safely out of the country! The days are coming,' he said, pulling a handkerchief from his pocket and mopping at his brow, 'when any man or woman might go to the guillotine for the most paltry excuse. I can feel it in the air. Say what you like about Bonaparte, but during the last few years I managed to hold down a responsible government post and make steady advancements, entirely through hard work and capability. But now the Bourbons are back in power, clearly bent on taking revenge on all who have opposed them, that will count for nothing!' he finished resentfully.

Charles eyed him thoughtfully. Monsieur Bergeron feared he was teetering on the verge of ruin. So he had spread his safety net wide. He had encouraged his pretty daughter to entrap an English earl, who would provide a safe bolthole in a foreign land should things become too hot for his family in France. And he had encouraged the attentions of his plain daughter's only suitor though he was an ardent Bonapartist. Every day Du Mauriac openly drank the health of his exiled emperor in cafés such as the Tabagie de la Comete, with other ex-officers of the Grand Armée. Much as he disliked the man, there was no denying he would make both a powerful ally and a dangerous enemy.

Finding himself somewhat less out of charity with his prospective father-in-law, Charles settled himself in a chair and stretched his legs out, crossing them at the ankles.

'Let me put a proposition to you.'

Monsieur Bergeron eyed him warily.

'I have my own reasons for not wanting my…er…disappointment to be made public. I wish, in fact, to carry on as though nothing untoward has occurred.'

'But…Felice has run off. That is not news we can keep quiet indefinitely. It may take some time to find her, if you insist you still wish to marry her…'

He made an impatient gesture with his hand. 'I am

finished with Felice. But nobody knows for certain that it was her I intended to marry. Do they?'

'Well, no…'

'Then the sooner I am seen about in public with your other daughter, the sooner we can begin to persuade people that they were entirely mistaken to suppose it was Felice to whom I became engaged.'

'What are you suggesting?'

'Isn't it obvious? Since Felice is out of the picture, I will marry your other daughter instead.'

'But—but…'

'You can have no objections, surely? She is not contracted to anyone else, is she?' He held his breath while he watched the cogs whirring in Monsieur Bergeron's head. Heloise had spoken of proposals to which she had not agreed, but if her father and Du Mauriac had drawn up any form of legal agreement things might be about to get complicated.

'No, my lord,' Monsieur Bergeron said, having clearly made up his mind to ditch the potential alliance with the man whose star was in the descendant. 'She is free to marry you. Only…' He slumped back against the cushions, closing his eyes and shaking his head. 'It will not be a simple matter of substituting one girl for the other. Heloise has so little sense. What if she won't agree? Ah!' he moaned, crumpling the handkerchief in his fist. 'That our fortunes should all rest in the hands of such a little fool!'

Charles found himself rather indignant on Heloise's behalf. It seemed to him that it was Felice who had plunged her family into this mess, but not a word was being said against her. And, far from being a fool, Heloise had been the one to come up with this coldly rational plan which would wipe out, at a stroke, all the unpleasantness her sister had created.

'I beg your pardon?' he said coldly.

'Of course our family owes it to you to redress the insult my younger daughter has offered you. But I pray you won't be offended if I cannot make Heloise see reason.'

His brief feelings of charity towards the older man evaporated. He had no compunction about forcing his daughter into any marriage, no matter how distasteful it might be to her, so long as he stood to gain by it. If Charles hadn't already known that Heloise was all for it, he would have turned away at that point and left the entire Bergeron family to sink in their own mire.

'I am sure she will do the right thing,' he said, in as even a tone as he could muster.

'That's because you don't know her,' her father bit out glumly. 'There is no telling what the silly creature will take it into her head to do. Or to say. She is nowhere near as clever as her sister.'

Charles eyed Monsieur Bergeron coldly. He had encouraged Felice to ensnare him when she'd never had the slightest intention of marrying him. Heloise, for being, as she put it, too stupid to tell a lie, was castigated as being useless. On the whole, he found he preferred Heloise's brand of stupidity to Felice's sort of cleverness.

'A man does not look for a great deal of intellect in his wife,' he bit out. 'I am sure we shall deal well together. Ah,' he said, as the door opened and Heloise and her mother returned to the room. 'Here she is now, and looking quite charming.' Walking to her side, he bowed over her hand.

'Pray, don't overdo it,' she whispered, her eyes sparking with alarm.

Tucking her hand under his arm, and patting her gloved hand reassuringly, he smiled at her mother, who had also hastily donned her coat and bonnet. 'I am sure you will agree there is no need for you to act as chaperon, *madame,* since the news of my engagement to Heloise will soon be common knowledge.'

Her jaw dropped open as she reeled back. 'You wish to marry Heloise?' she gasped.

'Why not?' he retorted. 'I have already settled the matter with your papa,' he turned to inform Heloise. 'He thinks your family should make recompense to me for the insult your younger sister offered me. Since I have rather got used to the idea of returning to England with a bride, it might as well be you. And, before you raise any foolish objections, let me inform you that I expect your full co-operation.' He bent a rather stern eye on her. 'I have no wish to appear as an object for vulgar gossip. I do not want anyone to know your sister jilted me. You will explain, if you please,' he said, turning once more to Madame Bergeron, 'that naturally you are upset by Felice's running off with a totally unsuitable man, but that it has no bearing on the relationship which already existed between me and her older, better-behaved sister.'

The woman plumped down onto the sofa next to her husband.

'People have grown used to seeing the three of us about together over the last few weeks. And while Felice was always the more flamboyant of the two, if we but stick to our story we can easily persuade people that it was Heloise all along who was the object of my interest. She is much better suited to becoming my countess, since her manner is modest and discreet. What man of breeding would want to take an outrageous flirt to wife?'

'Heloise,' her father now put in, rather sternly. 'I hope you are paying attention to what his lordship is saying. As a dutiful daughter you must do all you can to protect the honour of this family. I expect you to submit to me in this, young woman! You will keep your mouth shut about how far things went between Felice and his lordship, and you *will* marry him.'

Meekly bowing her head, Heloise replied, 'Whatever you say, Papa.'

Not wishing to linger any longer with that pair of opportunists, Charles ushered Heloise to the door.

She stayed silent, her head bowed to conceal her jubilant expression from her parents, until they were outside. Her eyes ran over the smart two-wheeled carrick Charles had procured for the occasion with approval. She had recognised the vehicle the moment it had drawn up outside. He had borrowed it once before, from another English noble who had brought it over to Paris for the express purpose of cutting a dash in the Bois de Boulogne. When Charles had taken Felice out in it, he had hired two liveried and mounted servants to ride behind, ensuring that everyone knew he was *someone*, even if he had picked up his passenger from a modest little dwelling on the Quai Voltaire.

Borrowing this conveyance, which he could drive himself, giving them the requisite privacy to plan their strategy whilst contriving to look as though they were merely being fashionable, was a stroke of genius.

He tossed a coin to the street urchin who was holding the horses' heads, and handed her up onto the narrow bench seat.

'You were magnificent!' she breathed, turning to him with unfeigned admiration as he urged the perfectly matched pair of bays out into the light traffic. 'Oh, if only we were not driving down a public street I could kiss you. I really could!'

'We are already attracting enough notice, *mademoiselle*, by driving about without a chaperon of any sort, without the necessity of giving way to vulgar displays of emotion.'

'Oh!' Heloise turned to face front, her back ramrod-straight, her face glowing red with chagrin. How could she have presumed to speak in such a familiar fashion? Never mind harbour such an inappropriate impulse?

'You may place one hand upon my sleeve, if you must.'

His clipped tones indicated that this was quite a concession on his part. Gingerly, she laid her hand upon his forearm.

'I have decided upon the tale we shall tell,' he said, 'and it is this. Our alliance has withstood the scandal of Felice's elopement with an unsuitable young man. I am not ashamed to continue my connection with your family. After all, your mother came from an ancient and noble house. That your sister has lamentably been infected by revolutionary tendencies and run off with a nobody has nothing to do with us.'

The feeling of happiness which his put-down had momentarily quelled swelled up all over again. She had known that if anyone could rescue her it was the Earl of Walton! He had grasped the importance of acting swiftly, then taken her rather vague plan and furnished it with convincing detail. She had always suspected he was quite intelligent, even though he had been prone to utter the most specious drivel to Felice. What was more, he would never let her down by making a slip in a moment of carelessness, like some men might. He was always fully in control of himself, regarding men who got drunk and made an exhibition of themselves in public with disdain.

Oh, yes, he was the perfect man to carry her scheme through successfully!

'I was planning to announce my engagement officially at Lady Dalrymple Hamilton's ball last evening.'

'I know,' she replied. It had been his decision to make that announcement which had finally driven Felice to take off so precipitously. She had hoped to keep him dangling for another week at the very least. Heloise worried at her lower lip. She hoped Felice had managed to reach Jean-Claude safely. Although he had gone ahead to Switzerland, and secured a job with a printing firm, he had planned to return and escort Felice across France personally.

'No need to look so crestfallen. I do not expect you to shine in society as your sister did. I will steer you through the social shoals.'

'It is not that!' she replied indignantly. She might not 'shine', as he put it, but she had mingled freely with some of the highest in the land. Why, she had once even been introduced to Wellington! Though, she admitted to herself with chagrin, he had looked right through her.

He glanced down at the rim of her bonnet, which was all he could see of her now that she had turned her head away.

How shy she was. How hard she would find it to take her place in society! Well, he would do all he could to smooth her passage. It was her idea, after all, that was going to enable him to salvage his pride. He would never have thought of something so outrageous. He owed her for that. And to start with he was going to have to smarten her up. He was not going to expose her to ridicule for her lack of dress sense.

'Deuce take it,' he swore. 'I'm going to have to buy you some more flattering headgear. That bonnet is the ugliest thing I think I've ever seen.' He leant a little closer. 'Is it the same unfortunate article you trampled so ruthlessly in my drawing room this morning?'

She looked up at him then, suddenly cripplingly conscious of how far short of the Earl's standard she fell. 'It is practical,' she protested. 'It can withstand any amount of abuse and still look—'

'Disreputable,' he finished for her. 'And that reminds me. While we are shopping, I shall have to get you a ring.'

His eyes narrowed as a look of guilt flickered across her

mobile little features. No wonder she did not attempt to tell lies, he reflected. Her face was so expressive every thought was written clearly there.

'What is it?' he sighed.

'First, I have to tell you that I do not wish you at all to take me shopping!' she declared defiantly.

'You are unique amongst your sex, then,' he replied dryly. 'And what is second?'

'And second,' she gulped, the expression of guilt returning in force, 'is that you do not need to buy me a ring.' Holding up her hand to prevent his retort, she hastened to explain, 'I already have a ring.'

He stiffened. 'Our engagement may not have been my idea, *mademoiselle*, but it is my place to provide the ring.'

'But you already have. That is—' She blushed. 'The ring I have is the one you gave Felice. The very one that made her run away. She gave it to me.'

'The ring…made her run away?' He had chosen it with such care. The great emerald that gleamed in its cluster of diamonds was the exact shade of Felice's bewitching eyes. He had thought he was past being hurt, but the thought that she found his taste so deficient she had run to another man…

'Yes, for until that moment it had not been at all real to her,' he heard Heloise say. 'She thought you were merely amusing yourself with a little flirtation. Though I warned her over and over again, she never believed that she could hurt you. She said that nobody could touch your heart—if you had one, which she did not believe—and so you made the perfect smokescreen.'

'Is that estimation of my character supposed to be making me feel better?' he growled.

'Perhaps not. But at least it may help you to forgive her. It was not until you gave her that ring that she understood you really had feelings for her. So then of course she had to run away, before things progressed beyond hope.'

'In short, she would have kept me dangling on a string indefinitely if I hadn't proposed marriage?'

'Well, no. For she always meant to go to Jean-Claude. But she did not mean to hurt you. Truly. She just thought—'

'That I had no heart,' he finished, in clipped tones.

Inadvertently he jerked on the reins, giving the horses the impression that he wished them to break into a trot. Since they were approaching a corner, there were a few moments where it took all his concentration to ensure they were not involved in an accident.

'Oh, dear.' Heloise was gripping onto his sleeve with both hands now, her face puckered with concern. 'Now I have made you angry again, which is precisely what I wished not to do. For I have to inform you that when we are married, if you forbid me to contact her, knowing that I must obey I will do so—but until then I fully intend to write to her. Even if she has wronged you, she is still my sister!'

The moment of danger being past, the horses having been successfully brought back to a brisk walk, she folded her arms, and turned away from him, as though she had suddenly become interested in the pair of dogs with frills round their necks which were dancing for the amusement of those strolling along the boulevard.

'Ah, yes,' he replied, reaching over to take her hand and place it back upon his own arm. 'You fully intend to bow to my every whim, don't you, once we are married?'

'Of course! For you had no thought of marrying me until I put the notion in your head, so the least I can do is be the best wife you would wish for. I will do everything I can,' she declared earnestly. 'Whatever you ask, I will do with alacrity!' Pulling herself up short, she suddenly frowned at him suspiciously. 'And, by the way, why did you suddenly change your mind about me? When you made me leave, you seemed so set against it!'

'Well, your proposal was so sudden,' he teased her. 'It took me by surprise. Naturally I had to consider…'

She shook her head. 'No, I may have surprised you, but you had made up your mind it was an absurd idea.'

'So absurd, in fact,' he countered, 'that nobody would credit it. Nobody would believe I would take one Mademoiselle Bergeron merely to save face at being embarrassed by the other Mademoiselle Bergeron. And therefore they will have to believe that you were the object of my interest all along.'

When she continued to look less than convinced by his complete about-face, he decided it was high time he regained control of the conversation.

'Now, getting back to the ring. May I enquire, although I somehow feel I am about to regret doing so, why your sister left it with you? The normal practice, I should remind you, when an engagement is terminated, is for the lady to return the ring to the man who gave it to her.'

'I had it with me when I came to visit you this morning,' she declared. 'I was going to return it to you for her if you should not agree to my suggestion.'

'Indeed?' His voice was laced with scepticism. 'And yet somehow it remains in your possession. How did that come about, I wonder?'

'Well, because you were so beastly to me, if you must know! I told you the deepest secret of my heart and you laughed at me. For the moment I quite lost my temper, and decided I should do with it exactly as Felice said I ought to do! For you are so wealthy it is not as if you *needed* to have it back, whereas for me…'

She let go of his arm again, folding her own across her chest with a mutinous little pout which, for the first time in their acquaintance, made Charles wonder what it would be like to silence one of her tirades with a kiss. It would probably be the only way to stop her once she had built up a head of steam. Something in the pit of his stomach stirred at the thought of mastering her militant spirit in such a manner. He shook his head. It was not like him to regard sexual encounters as contests of will. But then, he frowned, when had he ever had to do more than crook his finger for a woman to fall obediently in line with his every whim?

'I take it you meant to sell it, then?'

Heloise eyed his lowered brows contritely.

'Yes,' she confessed. 'Because I needed the money to get to Dieppe.'

'Dieppe?' He shook himself out of his reverie. 'What is at Dieppe?'

'Not what, but who. And that is Jeannine!'

'Jeannine?' he echoed, becoming fascinated in spite of himself. 'What part does she play in this farce, I wonder?'

'She was Maman's nurse, until she eloped with Papa.'

'There seems to have been a great deal of eloping going on in your family.'

'But in my parents' case it was a good thing, don't you think? Because even if they were terribly poor for the first few years they were married, since my grandpapa cut her off entirely, she was the only one to survive the Terror because her family were all so abominably cruel to the *menu peuple*—the common people, that is. Jeannine was cast out, but she married a *fermier*, and I know she would take me in. I would have to learn how to milk a cow, to be sure, and make butter and cheese, but how hard could that be?'

'I thought it was hens,' he reflected.

'Hens?'

'Yes, you said when you married me you would live in

a cottage so that you could keep hens. Now I find that in reality you would rather milk cows and make cheese.' He sighed. 'I do wish you would make up your mind.'

Heloise blinked. Though the abstracted frown remained between his brows, she was almost sure he was teasing her. 'I do not wish to milk cows at all,' she finally admitted.

'Good. Because I warn you right now that no wife of mine will ever do anything so plebeian. You must abandon all these fantasies about living on a farm and tending to live-stock of any sort. When we return to England you will move in the first circles and behave with the decorum commen-surate with your station in life. You are not to go anywhere near any livestock of any description. Is that clear?'

For a moment Heloise regarded the mock sternness of his features with her head tilted to one side. She had never been on the receiving end of one of these teasing scolds before. Whenever he had been playful like this, she had never been able to understand how Felice could remain impervious to his charm.

'Not even a horse?' she asked, taking her courage in both hands and deciding to play along, just once. 'I am quite near a horse already, sitting up here in your carriage.'

'Horses, yes,' he conceded. 'You may ride with me, or a suitable companion in the park. A horse is not a farm animal.'

'Some horses are,' she persisted.

'Not my carriage horses,' he growled, though she could tell he was not really the least bit cross.

The ride in the fresh air seemed to be doing him good. He was far less tense than he had been when they set out. Oh, it was not to be expected that he would get over Felice all at once, but if she could make him laugh now and again, or even put that twinkle in his eye that she could see when he bent his head in her direction to give her this mock scold, she would be happy.

'What about dogs, then? What if I should go into some drawing room and a lady should have a little dog. Must I not go into the room? Or should I just stay away from it? By, say, five feet? Or six?'

'Pets, yes—of course you will come across pets from time to time. That is not what I meant at all, you little minx!'

Pretending exasperation he did not feel, to disguise the fact he was on the verge of laughter, he said, 'No wonder your brother said I should end up beating you. You would drive a saint to distraction!'

'I was only,' she declared with an impish grin, 'trying to establish exactly what you expected of me. I promised to behave exactly as you would wish, so I need to know exactly what you want!'

He laughed aloud then. 'You, *mademoiselle*, were doing nothing of the kind.' Why had he never noticed her mischievous sense of humour before now? Why had he never noticed what an entertaining companion she could be when she put her mind to it? The truth was, he decided with a sinking feeling, that whenever Felice had been in the room he'd had eyes for nobody else. With her sultry beauty and her vivacious nature she had utterly bewitched him.

Flicking the reins in renewed irritation, he turned the curricle for home.

CHAPTER THREE

His eyes, which a moment ago had been twinkling with amusement, had gone dull and lifeless. It was as though he had retreated into a dark and lonely room, slamming the shutters against her.

She was positively relieved to get home, where her *maman* greeted her with enthusiasm.

'I never thought to have secured such a brilliant match for my plain daughter!' she beamed. 'But we must do something about your attire,' she said as Heloise untied the ribbons of the one bonnet she possessed. 'He cannot want people thinking he is marrying a dowd.'

Hustling her up the newly carpeted stairs to the room she had shared with Felice, her mother grumbled, 'We do not have time to cut down one of Felice's gowns before tonight. If only I had known,' she complained, flinging open the doors to the armoire, 'that you would be the one to marry into the nobility, we could have laid out a little capital on your wardrobe.'

Nearly all the dresses hanging there belonged to Felice. From the day the allies had marched into Paris the previous summer, what money her parents had been able to spare had been spent on dressing her sister. She had, after all, been the Bergeron family's secret weapon. She had flirted and charmed her way through the ranks of the occupying forces, playing the coquette to the hilt, whilst adroitly managing to hang onto her virtue, catapulting the family to the very heart of the new society which had rapidly formed to replace Napoleon's court.

'Nobody could have foreseen such an unlikely event,' Heloise replied rather dispiritedly, hitching her hip onto her bed.

She worried at her lower lip. What was her sister going to do now? She had left carrying only a modest bundle of possessions, and her young husband would not have the means to provide either the kind of dress allowance she had enjoyed for so long, nor the stimulating company of the upper echelons of society.

Heloise sighed. 'What about the lilac muslin?' she suggested. It was quite her favourite dress. She always felt that it made her look almost girlishly attractive, though the underskirt, which went with the full, shorter overdress, was embroidered about the hem with violets. Surely she could not be taken for a supporter of Bonaparte if she appeared in public on the arm of an Englishman?

'Where is His Lordship taking you tonight?' her *maman* enquired sharply.

'To the theatre first, and then on to Tortoni's for ices.'

Her mother clicked her tongue. 'Muslin to the theatre? I should think not!' she snapped, entirely overlooking the political symbolism of the violets, Bonaparte's emblem. 'When Felice went to the theatre with him she wore the gold satin!'

'I cannot compete with Felice, Maman,' Heloise remonstrated. 'Nor do I think it would be wise to try to be like her. Do you not think he might find it in poor taste if I did?'

'I had no idea,' her mother remarked sarcastically, 'that you had such a grasp of what is in men's hearts.' Flinging a bundle of Felice's discarded gowns to the bare boards, she gripped the iron foot-rail of the wide bed the girls had shared. 'Don't, I beg of you, do anything to make him change his mind about marrying you.'

'He has only taken me to save face,' Heloise pointed out. 'I know he still loves Felice. Nothing I do will matter to him.'

Her mother regarded the bleak look that washed over her daughter's features with concern.

'But you are going to be his wife, you foolish creature!' Coming round the side of the bed, her mother took her hand, chafing it to emphasise her point. 'Listen to me! And listen well! You will be going away to live in a foreign country, amongst strangers. You will be utterly dependent on your husband's goodwill. So you must make an effort to please him. Of course he will never fall in love with you—' she made a dismissive gesture with her hand '—the sister of the woman who betrayed him. Not even if you were half so beautiful or clever as she. But at least you can try not to antagonise him. You must learn to behave in a manner worthy of the title he is going to bestow on you. He will expect you to dress well and behave well, as a reflection of his taste. You must never embarrass him by displaying any emotion in public.'

He had only just informed her that displaying emotion in public was vulgar. So her mother's next words took on a greater power.

'Above all, you must never clamour for his attention if he does not wish to give it. You must let him go to his mistresses when he is bored with you, and pretend not to notice or to mind.'

A great lump formed in her throat. He would, of course, be unfaithful. She was the one who had instigated this marriage, and though he was disposed to go through with it, she knew only too well that it was not because he found her attractive.

How could he? Even her mother, who loved her as well as she was able, referred to her as her plain daughter.

'Mistresses?' she whispered, a sickening vision of a lifetime of humiliation unfolding before her.

'Of course,' her mother replied, stroking her hand soothingly. 'You are not blind. You know that is what men do. All men,' she said grimly, her thin lips compressing until they were almost white. 'Just as soon as they can afford it.'

Heloise's stomach turned over at the implication of her mother's words. Even her papa, who behaved as though he was deeply in love with her mother, must have strayed.

'If he is very considerate of your feelings he will conduct his affairs discreetly. But I warn you, if you make any protest, or even show that you care, he will be most annoyed! If you wish him to treat you well, you must not place any restrictions on his little *divertissements*.'

'I have already informed him that I will not interfere with his pleasures,' Heloise replied dully. And when she had told him that she had meant it. But now the idea that he could hasten to the arms of some other woman, when he could barely bring himself to allow her to lay her hand upon his sleeve, was unbelievably painful. Rising to her feet swiftly, she went to the open armoire. 'What about the grey shot silk?' she said, keeping her face carefully averted from her mother. 'I have not worn that for some time. I don't think His Lordship has ever seen me in it.'

Heloise did not particularly like the dress, for it had bad associations. The first time Du Mauriac had asked her father if he might pay his addresses to his oldest daughter, he had been so proud that she had captured the interest of a hero of France that he had sent her to the dressmaker with the instruction to buy something pretty to wear when her suitor came calling. She had been torn. Oh, how pleasant it had been, to be able to go and choose a gown with no expense spared! And yet the reason for the treat had almost robbed her of all joy in the purchase. In the end she had not been able to resist the lure of silk, but had chosen a sombre shade of grey, in a very demure style, hoping that Du Mauriac would not think she was trying to dress for his pleasure.

'It is not at all the sort of thing Felice would have worn,' her mother remarked, shaking her head. 'But it will do for you. I shall get it sponged down and pressed.' She bustled away with Heloise's best gown over her arm, leaving her to her solitary and rather depressing reflections.

He had never seen her dressed so well, Charles thought with approval, when he came to collect her that evening. The exquisitely cut silk put him in mind of moonbeams playing over water. If only her eyes did not look so haunted. He frowned, pulling up short on the verge of paying her a compliment.

For the first time it hit him that she did not really wish to marry him any more than he wished to marry her. And she looked so small and vulnerable, hovering in the doorway, gazing up at him with those darkly anxious eyes.

She needed solid reassurance, not empty flattery.

Taking her hand in his, he led her to the sofa.

'May I have a few moments alone with your daughter before we go out?' he enquired of her parents. They left the room with such alacrity he was not sure whether to feel amused at their determination to pander to his every whim, or irritated at their lack of concern for their daughter's evident discomfort.

Heloise sank onto the sofa next to him, her hand resting limply in his own, and gazed up into his handsome face. Of course he would have mistresses. He was a most virile man.

She would just somehow have to deal with this crushing sense of rejection the awareness of his infidelity caused her. She must learn not to mind that he frowned when he saw her, and stifle the memories of how his eyes had lit with pleasure whenever Felice had walked into a room.

'Heloise!' he said, so sharply that she collected he must have been speaking to her for quite some time, while she had not heard one word he had said.

Blushing guiltily, she tried to pay attention.

'I said, do you have the ring?'

Now he must think she was stupid, as well as unattractive. Her shoulders drooping, she held out her left hand obediently.

'Hell and damnation!' he swore. 'It's too big!'

'Well, you bought it for Felice,' she pointed out.

'Yes, and I would have bought you one that did fit if only you'd told me this one didn't! Why in God's name didn't you tell me, when I raised the subject this afternoon, that this ring was not going to be any good?'

'Because I didn't know it wouldn't fit. Although of course I should have known,' she ended despondently. Felice had long, strong, capable fingers, unlike her own, which were too slender for anything more strenuous than plying a needle or wielding a pencil.

'Do you mean to tell me that you had an emerald of this value in your possession and you were never tempted to try it on? Not once?'

'Oh, is it very valuable, then?' She looked with renewed interest at the jewel which hung from her ring finger. In order not to lose it, she knew she was going to have to keep her hand balled into a fist throughout the evening. 'I was not at all convinced it would get me all the way to Dieppe. Even if I'd managed to find a jeweller who would not try to cheat me, I fully expected to end up stranded halfway there.'

Her reference to her alternative plan of escaping Du Mauriac turned his momentary irritation instantly to alarm. He would do well to remember that he held no personal interest for her for his own sake at all. He was only providing the means, one way or another, for her to escape from an intolerable match with another man.

'Well, you won't be running off to Dieppe now, so you can put that notion right out of your head,' he seethed. Damn, but he hoped her distress was not an indication she was seriously considering fleeing from him!

Though he could see she was scared as hell of him right now. And no wonder. She had entrusted him with her entire future, and all he could do was berate her over the trifling matter of the fit of a ring!

'Come, now,' he said in a rallying tone. 'We struck an honest bargain this morning. It is in both our interests to stick with it.' He took her hands between his own and gave them what he hoped was a reassuring squeeze. 'We are in this together.'

Yes. She sighed. And so was Felice. He would never be able to keep from comparing her, and unfavourably. Just look at the way he was coaxing her out of the sulks in that patronising tone, as though she were a petulant child.

'It is easier for you,' she began. He was used to disguising his feelings behind that glacial mask he wore in public. But she had never been any good at dissembling.

'Why do you suppose that?' he said harshly.

'Because I won't know what to say to people!' she snapped. Had he forgotten already that she had told him she was hopeless at telling lies?

'Oh, come,' he scoffed. 'You ran on like a rattle in my drawing room this morning!'

'That was entirely different,' she protested. 'It does not matter what you think.' They were co-conspirators. She had no need to convince him she was anything other than herself.

Charles swiftly repressed the sharp stab of hurt these words inflicted. Why should he be bothered if she did not care what he thought of her? It was not as if she meant anything to him, either. He must just accept that playing the role of his fiancée was not going to be easy for her.

'Very well,' he nodded, 'you need not attempt to speak. I will do all the talking for us both. Providing—' he fixed her with a stern eye '—you make an attempt to look as though you are enjoying yourself tonight.'

'Oh, I am sure I shall—in my own way,' she assured him.

She loved studying how people behaved in social situations. Their posturing and jostling both amused and inspired her with ideas that went straight into her sketchbook the minute she got home.

A vague recollection of her sitting alone at a table littered with empty glasses, a rapt expression on her face as she observed the boisterous crowd at the *guingette* that Felice had dared him to take her to, sprang to Charles' mind. He began to feel a little calmer. The theatre was the best place he could have chosen for their first outing together *à deux*. She would be content to sit quietly and watch the performance.

Then she alarmed him all over again by saying mournfully, 'It was a stupid idea. I wish I had never mentioned it. Nobody looking at the two of us together will ever believe you wish at all to marry me.'

'Well, they will not if you carry on like this!' It was bad enough that Felice had jilted him; now Heloise was exhibiting clear signs of wanting to hedge off. What was wrong with the Bergeron sisters? He knew of half a dozen women who would give their eye teeth to be in their position. Why, he had been fending off females who wished to become his countess since his first foray into society!

'You came up with this plan, not I. And I expect you to play your part now you have wheedled me into it!'

'Wheedled?' she gasped, desperately hurt. She had not wheedled. She had put her proposition rationally and calmly...well, perhaps not calmly, for she had been very nervous. But he was making it sound as though she had put unfair pressure on him in some way.

'If that is what you think—' she began, sliding the ring from her finger.

His hand grabbed hers, thrusting the ring back down her finger.

'No, *mademoiselle,*' he said sternly, holding her hands captive between his own, his steely fingers keeping the ring firmly in place.

She took a breath, her brow furrowing in preparation for another round of argument.

There was only one sure way to silence her. And Charles took it.

She flinched when his lips met hers, rousing Charles' anger to new heights.

What was the woman doing proposing marriage if she could not even bear the thought of kissing him? Leaving go of her hands, he grasped her by the nape of the neck, holding her still, while he demonstrated his inalienable right, as her betrothed, to kiss her as thoroughly as he pleased!

Charles had taken her completely by surprise. She didn't know what to do. No man had ever kissed her before. Du Mauriac had tried, once or twice, but she had been expecting it from him, and had always managed to take evasive action.

But she didn't want to evade Charles, she discovered after only a fleeting moment of shock. What she really wanted, she acknowledged, relaxing into his hold, was to put her arms about him and kiss him back. If only she knew how!

Well, she might not know anything about kissing, but there was nothing to stop her from putting her arms about his neck. Uttering a little whimper of pleasure, she raised shaky hands from her lap and tentatively reached out for him.

'My God,' he panted, breaking free. 'I never meant to do that!'

Leaping to his feet, he strode to the very far side of the room. Hearing her little cry of protest, feeling her hands fluttering against his chest in an attempt to push him away, had brought him to his senses.

'I can only offer my sincere apologies,' he ground out between clenched teeth. He could not think what had come over him. What kind of blackguard chose that particular way to silence a woman?

He had accepted intellectually that one day he would have to get his heirs by Heloise. But judging from her shocked recoil it had been the furthest thing from her mind.

The fierce surge of desire that even now was having a visible effect on his anatomy was an unexpected bonus. When the time was right, he was going to enjoy teaching his wife all there was to know about loving.

Until then he must exercise great restraint. He would have to get her used to the idea of him before broaching the subject of heirs. He already knew how shy she was, and had realised she would need to feel she could rely on him. How could she do that if she was worried he was going to pounce on her at any moment?

'You need not fear that I shall importune you in that way again,' he grated, his back still turned to her while he desperately fought to regain mastery over his unruly body.

Heloise pressed her hand to her bruised lips, her heart

sinking as swiftly as it had soared when he had seized and
kissed her so excitingly. Why had he done it if he was now
adamant he would not be doing it again? Had it only been
some sort of experiment? To see if he could stomach
touching her as a man should want to touch his wife? If so,
it was evident he regretted giving in to the impulse.

It was a while before he could bear to so much as turn
round and look at her! But at least it gave her the time to wipe
away the few tears that she had been unable to prevent from
trickling down her cheeks. For she would never let him see
how humiliated his rejection made her feel. If he did not wish
to kiss her, then she would not beg for his kisses. Never!

She got to her feet, determination stiffening her carriage.
She would never let him suspect—not by one lingering
look, one plaintive sigh—that she… She faltered, her hand
flying to her breast.

No, this was too appalling! She could not be in love with
him. She *must* not be in love with him. She was certain she
had not lied when she had denied being in love with him that
morning. Her feelings could not have changed so swiftly
during the course of one day. Just because he had strolled into
the drawing room and swept all her problems away with his
marvellously insouciant declaration of intent to marry her.
Not because she had felt a momentary rapport with him while
they had gently teased each other during their carriage ride.

And yet she could not deny that since her *maman* had
broached the subject of his infidelity she had been eaten up
by jealousy.

No, that was not love! It was wounded pride that made
her eyes smart so. It had to be.

Her abstracted air, coupled with the Earl's barely tamped
down lust, created quite a stir when they entered the theatre
arm in arm.

As soon as they were seated, Charles tore off a corner of the programme and wedged it under her ring. 'That should hold it in place for now.'

'Thank you,' she murmured, keeping her face averted. It was stupid to feel resentful because he was being so practical about everything. She sighed.

'*Mademoiselle*,' he murmured, 'I am about to put my arm along the back of your chair, and I do not want you to flinch when I do it.'

A shiver slid all the way down her spine to her toes at the warmth of his arm behind her shoulders. With him so close, every breath she took filled her nostrils with his clean, spicy scent. Though his arm was not quite touching her, she remembered the strength of it, holding her captive while he ravaged her mouth. She felt weak, and flustered, and utterly feminine.

'I promise I shall not do anything you will not like. Only I must sometimes seem to be…how shall I put it? …lover-like when we appear in public. I shall not go beyond the bounds of what is proper, I assure you.'

No, she reflected with annoyance. For he'd found kissing her such an unpleasant experience he had vowed never to do it again! This show of being 'lover-like', as he put it, was as much of a performance as what was going on upon the stage. But then, she reflected bleakly, she had known from the outset that all he wanted from her was the means to salvage his pride.

'Y…you may do what you like,' she conceded, feeling utterly wretched. 'I understand how important this show is to you.' Turning towards him, so that their faces were only a few scant inches apart, she declared, 'It was for this reason that you agreed to marry me, was it not? So that nobody would suspect you had been hurt. I think the worst thing you could endure is to have someone mock you.' Raising one hand, she laid it against his cheek. 'I trust you,' she said, resolving that, come what may, she would never be sorry to have given him this one source of consolation. 'However you decide to behave tonight, I will go along with it.'

Charles found it hard not to display his hurt. Go along with it, indeed! She could not conceal how nervous he made her. She was drawing on every ounce of courage she possessed to conceal her disquiet at his proximity. She had shuddered when he put his arm round her, tensed up when he had whispered in her ear.

Was it possible, he wondered, his heart skipping a beat, that she found him as repellent as Du Mauriac?

Regarding her nervously averted eyes, he refused to entertain that notion. She had come to him, after all. He had not put any pressure on her. She was just shy, that was all. He doubted many men had so much as flirted with her, let alone kissed her. She was as innocent as her sister had been experienced.

His expression bland, he murmured, 'We should take advantage of our relative privacy to organise the practical details of our wedding, don't you think?'

The sooner he secured her, the sooner he could stop worrying that she might run away.

By the end of the first act, by dint of keeping their heads close together and keeping their voices low, they had managed to agree upon a simple civic wedding. Conningsby, upon whose discretion he relied, would serve as his witness, and her parents would support Heloise. It would take next to no time to arrange it.

They had also managed to create the very impression Charles had sought. The audience, agog with curiosity, spent as much time training their opera glasses upon the unchaperoned young couple who appeared so intent on each other as they did upon the stage.

Heloise ordered a lemon ice once they finally managed to secure a table at Tortoni's. But she did not appear to be enjoying it much. She was still ill at ease in his company. The truth was that much of the behaviour upon which she had to judge him might well have given her a false impression of his character.

He shuddered, recalling that excursion beyond the city boundaries to the *guingette*, where ordinary working people went to spend their wages on food, drink and dancing. Felice had made it seem like such fun, and in its way it had been. But Heloise, he suddenly realised, watching as she daintily licked the confection from her spoon, had not only refused to join in the hurly-burly, but would never have cajoled him to attend such a venue. He would have to reassure her that he would never so browbeat her again.

'Since I have been in Paris,' he began, frowning, 'I have done things I would never consider for a minute in London. Things that are breaches of good *ton*.'

Heloise tried not to display her hurt that he should regard marrying her as a breach of ton. She already knew she was not at all the sort of wife an English earl ought to marry. His infatuation with Felice would have been much easier for society to forgive, given that she was so very enchanting. But nobody would be able to understand why he had picked up a plain little bourgeoise like her, and elevated her to the position of Countess.

'Allow me to be the first to congratulate you,' a voice purred. Dropping her spoon with a clatter on the table, she looked up to see Mrs Austell hovering over their table, her beady eyes fixed on Felice's emerald ring. 'Though I had heard…' She paused to smile like a cat that had got at the cream, and Heloise braced herself to hear whatever gossip had been noised abroad concerning the Earl and her sister. 'I had heard that you were going to make an announcement at the Dalrymple Hamilton ball.'

'Circumstances made it impossible for us to attend,' Charles replied blandly.

'Ah, yes, I hear there was some unpleasantness in your family, *mademoiselle*?'

Laying his hand firmly over hers, Charles prevented her from needing to answer. 'Mademoiselle Bergeron does not wish to speak of it.'

'Oh, but I am the soul of discretion! Is there nothing to be done for your poor sister? Too late to prevent her ruination, I suppose?'

'Oh, you have the matter quite out. The affair is not of that nature. The young man fully intends to marry my fiancée's sister. Has done for some considerable time. It is only parental opposition that has forced the silly children to feel they needed to run off together in that manner.'

Heloise marvelled that he could appear so unconcerned as he related the tale. Deep down, she knew he was still smarting. But it was this very *sang-froid* she had factored as being of paramount importance to her scheme. Why should she be surprised, she chastised herself, when he played the part she had written for him so perfectly?

'A little embarrassing for me to have an escapade of that nature in the family,' he shrugged, 'to be sure. But it is of no great import in the long run.' With a smile that would have convinced the most cynical onlooker, Lord Walton carried Heloise's hand to his lips and kissed it.

'Of course I never held to the prevalent opinion that you would make the younger Mademoiselle Bergeron your wife,' Mrs Austell declared. 'A man of your station! Of course you would prefer the more refined Mademoiselle Bergeron to her flighty little sister. Though I must warn you—' she turned to Heloise, a malicious gleam in her eye '—that you ought not to make your dislike of Wellington so apparent when you get to London. They idolise him there, you know. If anyone were to catch a glimpse of that scurrilous drawing you made of him…' She went off into a peal of laughter. 'Though it was highly entertaining. And as for the one you showed me of Madame de Stael, as a pouter pigeon!'

'I collect you have had sight of my betrothed's sketch-book?'

'Felice handed it round one afternoon,' Heloise put in, in her defence. 'When a few ladies connected with the embassy paid us a visit.'

'Oh, yes! Such a delight to see us all there in her menagerie, in one form or another. Of course, since the one of myself was quite flattering, I suppose I had more freedom to find the thing amusing than others, to whom *mademoiselle* had clearly taken a dislike.'

At his enquiring look, Heloise, somewhat red-faced, admitted, 'I portrayed Mrs Austell as one of the birds in an aviary.'

With a completely straight face, Charles suggested, 'With beautiful plumage, no doubt, since she always dresses so well?'

'Yes, that's it,' she agreed, though she could tell he had guessed, even without seeing the picture, that all the birds portrayed on that particular page had been singing their heads off. If there was one thing Mrs Austell's set could do, it was make a lot of noise about nothing.

'And dare I ask how you portrayed Wellington?'

But it was Mrs Austell who answered, her face alight with glee. 'As a giraffe, if you please, with a great long neck, loping down the Champs-Elysées, looking down with such a supercilious air on the herd of fat little donkeys waddling along behind!'

'For I see him as being head and shoulders above his contemporaries,' Heloise pleaded.

'Oh, I see!' Mrs Austell said. 'Well, that explains it. Have you seen your own likeness among your talented little betrothed's pages, my lord?' she simpered.

'Why, yes,' he admitted, feeling Heloise tense beneath his grasp. 'I feature as a lion in a circus, if you please.'

'Oh, of course. The king of the beasts!' she trilled. 'Well, I must not take up any more of your time. I am sure you two lovebirds—' she paused to laugh at her own witticism '—would much rather be alone.'

'As soon as you have finished your ice,' Charles said, once Mrs Austell had departed, 'I shall take you home. Our "news" will be all over Paris by the morning. Mrs Austell will convince everyone how it was without us having to perjure ourselves.'

He was quiet during the short carriage ride home. But as he was handing her out onto the pavement he said, 'I trust you will destroy your sketchbook before it does any more damage?'

'Damage?' Heloise echoed, bemused. 'I think it served its purpose very well.'

'There are pictures in there that in the wrong hands could cause me acute embarrassment,' he grated. He had no wish to see himself portrayed as a besotted fool, completely under the heel of a designing female. 'Can I trust you to burn the thing yourself, or must I come into your parents' house and take it from you?'

Heloise gasped. She had only one skill of which she was proud, and that was drawing. It was unfair of him to ask her to destroy all her work! It was not as if she had made her assessment of her subjects obvious. Only someone who knew the character of her subject well would know what she was saying about them by portraying them as one type of animal or another.

It had been really careless of her to leave that sketchbook

lying on the table when she had gone up to change. She had not been gone many minutes, but he had clearly found the picture she had drawn of him prostrate at her sister's feet, while she prepared to walk all over him. And been intelligent enough to recognise himself, and proud enough to resent her portrayal of him in a position of weakness.

He was not a man to forgive slights. Look how quickly he had written Felice out of his life, and he had loved her! Swallowing nervously, she acknowledged that all the power in their relationship lay with him. If she displeased him, she had no doubt he could make her future as his wife quite uncomfortable. Besides, had she not promised to obey his slightest whim? If she argued with him over this, the first real demand he had made of her, she would feel as though she were breaking the terms of their agreement.

'I will burn it,' she whispered, her eyes filling with tears. 'I promised you, did I not, that I would do my best to be a good wife, and never cause you a moment's trouble? I will do whatever you ask of me.' However it hurt her to destroy that which she had spent hours creating, the one thing in her life she felt proud to have achieved, her word of honour meant far more.

'Heloise, no—dammit!' he cried, reaching out his hand. That had been tactless of him. He should have requested to examine the book, and then decided whether to destroy the one or two sketches which might have caused him some discomfort. Or he should have been more subtle still. He should have asked if he could keep the whole thing, and then ensured it was kept locked away where nobody could see it. Not demand her obedience in that positively medieval way!

But it was too late. She had fled up the steps to her house, the sound of her sobs sending a chill down his spine.

How had the evening gone so wrong? He had decided she

needed reassurance, and what had he done? Bullied and frightened her, and sent her home in floods of tears.

If he carried on like this she might still decide to run away to her farm in Dieppe. And where would that leave him?

HELOISE gazed wide-eyed around the mirror-lined interior of the most expensive and therefore the most exclusive restaurant in Paris.

'Most people come to Very Frères to sample the truffles,' Charles had informed her when they had taken their places at a granite-topped table in one of the brilliantly lit salons.

That seemed inordinately foolish, considering the menu contained such a staggering variety of dishes. 'I will have the *poulet à la* Marengo.' She leaned forward and confided, 'Although it is much cheaper in the Trois Frères Provencaux.'

'You do not need to consider the expense,' he pointed out. 'I am a very wealthy man.'

Heloise shifted uncomfortably as his gaze seemed to settle critically upon her rather worn lilac muslin. 'I am not marrying you for that.'

'I know,' he acknowledged. 'But you must admit having a wealthy husband will make your lot more tolerable.'

'Will it?' she replied in a forlorn little voice. She really could not see that it mattered how wealthy her husband was when he was in love with someone else. Someone he could not have. And when she would only ever be a poor second best.

'Of course,' he replied briskly. He had decided to make amends for his overbearing attitude the previous evening by spoiling her a little. And demonstrating that he was prepared to consider her feelings. 'I appreciate that you may find certain aspects of marrying me more uncomfortable than I had at first assumed.' If he didn't want her bolting to Dieppe, he would have to persuade her that marriage to him would be nothing like the picture she had painted of being chained down by Du Mauriac.

'I shall not forbid you from pursuing your own pleasures.' He did not want her worrying he would be forever breathing down her neck. 'Nor shall I expect you to hang on my arm.' He would not force her to any event that she would rather not attend. He knew that her rather retiring nature might make it hard for her to hold her own with some of the people with whom he routinely crossed swords during the course of his public life. However, he did not want her to feel he saw her shyness as a failing. 'It is not done for a man to be seen about too much with his wife,' he explained. 'And though we must live in the same house, there is no reason we may not live virtually separate lives.'

Her heart fluttered in panic. It sounded as if he meant to deposit her in some house in a foreign country, where she knew nobody, and leave her to fend for herself.

'D...don't you want people to think we have a true marriage?'

He felt touched that she could still think of his image, when she must have so many reservations about the new life she was about to embark upon.

'We must be seen about together occasionally, yes,' he acknowledged. 'Just once every se'en night or so should be sufficient.'

She bit her lip. She could hardly complain if he could not face wasting more than one evening a week on her. Hadn't she rashly declared she would go and live in a cottage and keep hens if he did not wish to be burdened with her company?

'Do you have a house in the country, my lord?' she asked. The hens were seeming increasingly attractive.

'That is far too formal a way to address me now we are to be married,' he countered, puzzled by her abrupt change of subject. He had done what he could to put her at ease. Now it was time to take things to a more intimate level. 'You had best call me Walton. Or Charles.'

'Ch…Charles,' she stammered, the familiarity of his name catching on her tongue.

'And may I call you Heloise?'

She nodded, rendered speechless at the warmth of the smile he turned on her for acceding to this small request.

'I hope you will like Wycke.'

'Wycke?'

'Although I have a house in London, where I reside whilst Parliament is in session, Wycke is my principal seat, and it is where…' Where the heirs are traditionally born, he refrained from finishing. Regarding her upturned, wary little face, he wondered with a pang if there would ever come a time when he would be able to tackle such a delicate subject with her.

Though, legally, he already had an heir.

'There is one rather serious matter I must broach with you,' he said firmly. It was no good trying to shield her from everything. There were some things she would just have to accept. 'I have someone…residing with me in Walton House—that is, my London home.'

Heloise attacked the tender breast of chicken the waiter had set before her with unnecessary savagery. She had wondered just how long it would be before he raised the topic of his mistress. Of course she would not voice any objections to him visiting such a woman. But if he expected her to let his mistress carry on living with him, then he was very much mistaken!

'Indeed?' she said frostily.

'He is not going to be easy to get along with, and on reflection I recommend you had better not try.'

He? Oh, thank goodness—not a mistress.

Then why should she not try to get along with this guest? Heat flared in her cheeks. Of course—she was not good *ton*, and this person was clearly someone whose opinion he valued.

'Whatever you say,' she replied dully, taking a sip of the *meursault* that had somehow appeared in her glass when she had not been attending.

'And, while we are on the topic, I must inform you there are several other persons that I do not wish you to associate with.'

'Really?' she said bleakly. She was not good enough to mix with his friends. How much more humiliation did he intend to heap on her? 'Perhaps you had better provide me with a list?'

'That might be a good idea,' he replied in an abstracted manner. In marrying him, Heloise would become a target through which his enemies might try to strike at him. It would be unfair to leave her exposed when, with a little forethought, he could protect her. Some people would take great pleasure in making her as uncomfortable as possible simply because she was French. Others would be livid that she had thwarted their matrimonial ambitions towards him. 'Those you need to be wariest of are certain members of my family.'

She knew it! He was downright ashamed of her! What further proof did she need than to hear him warn her that his own family would be her bitterest enemies?

'You see, I have severed all connection with certain of them—'

Catching the appalled expression on her face, he pulled up short.

'Beware, Heloise,' he mocked. 'Your husband is a man notorious for being so lacking in familial feeling that even my closest relatives are not safe from my cold, vengeful nature.'

She was so relieved to hear that his forbidding her to mix with these people was not because he was ashamed of her that she could easily dismiss the challenge aimed at her with those bitter words. Whatever had happened in the past was nothing to do with her! It was her future conduct that mattered to him.

'Of course I would not have anything to do with people who would say such things about you,' she declared, with a vehemence that shook him.

'Your loyalty is…touching,' he said cynically.

'I will be your wife,' she pointed out with an expressive shrug, as though matrimonial loyalty went without saying. Her declaration effectively stunned him into silence.

'Shall we stroll awhile?' he eventually recovered enough to say, when they had finished their meal.

Heloise nodded. At this hour of the evening, the brightly lit central quadrangle of the Palais Royale would be crowded with Parisians and tourists looking for entertainment of all sorts. From the restaurants in the basements and the shops beneath the colonnade, to the casinos and brothels on the upper floors, there was something in the arcades to cater for all tastes. Strolling amongst the pleasure-seeking crowds would be one way of demonstrating that he was not in the least broken-hearted.

They had barely stepped outside when she heard an angry and all too familiar voice crying, 'Hey, Heloise—stop!'

Looking across the square, in the direction from which the voice hailed, she saw Du Mauriac bearing down on them like an avenging whirlwind.

To her consternation, rather than retreating into the relative safety of the restaurant, Charles continued to stroll nonchalantly towards the most dangerous man in Paris.

'Didn't you hear me calling you?' he snarled, coming to a halt directly in front of them. His black moustache bristled in a face that was mottled red from wine and anger. Heloise tried to detach her hand from Charles' arm. The waiters would not deign to help, but many of the diners in Very Frères were Englishmen, who would be bound to come to their aid if she could only get to them.

But Charles would not relax his grip.

Eyeing the lean figure of her former suitor with cool disdain, he drawled, 'My fiancée does not answer to strangers shouting in the street.'

'Fiancée!' Ignoring Lord Walton, Du Mauriac turned the full force of his fury on the slender form cringing at his side.

'Y…yes,' she stuttered.

'Do not let this fellow unsettle you, my sweet. I will deal with him.'

'Your sweet?' The Earl's endearment drew Du Mauriac's fire down upon himself. 'She is not your sweet. Everyone knows you are in love with her sister! Not her! What could a man like you want with a little mouse like her?'

'Since you speak of her in such a derogatory manner,' he replied stiffly, 'it is clear you care little for her either. So what exactly is your problem?'

'You have no notion of what I feel for Heloise. Before you came to France, with your money and your title, she was going to be my wife! Mine! And if she had an ounce of loyalty she would be mine still. But it is the same with so many of her sort. They can wear the violet on their gowns, but their heart is filled only with greed and ambition.'

The confrontation between a slender officer in his shabby uniform and an obviously wealthy Englishman, in the doorway of such an exclusive restaurant, was beginning to attract the attention of passers-by.

'I collect from your agitation,' Charles said, finally relinquishing his vice-like grip on her hand, so that he could interpose his own body between her and Du Mauriac, 'that you were once an aspirant to Mademoiselle Bergeron's hand?'

Heloise was too shocked by these words to think of running for help. Charles knew exactly how things had stood between them. So why was he pretending differently? Oh, she thought, her hands flying to her cheeks. To conceal her part in the plot! He was shielding her from Du Mauriac's wrath. Her heart thudded in her chest. It was wonderful to know Charles was intent on protecting her, but did he not know Du Mauriac would calmly put a bullet through a man on far flimsier quarrel than that of stealing his woman?

'I fully understand,' Charles said in an almost bored tone, 'if the harsh words you level at this lady stem from thwarted affection. Being aware that you French are apt to be somewhat excitable, I also forgive you your appalling lapse of manners. Though naturally were you an Englishman it would be quite another matter.'

Du Mauriac laughed mockingly. 'I insult your woman and you stand there and let me do it, like the coward you are. What must I do to make you take the honourable course? Slap your face?'

The Earl looked thoughtful. 'You could do so, of course, if it would help to relieve your feelings. But then I would be obliged to have you arrested on a charge of assault.'

'In short, you are such a coward that nothing would induce you to meet me!'

Heloise gasped. No gentleman could allow another to call him a coward to his face. Especially not in such a public place.

But Charles merely looked puzzled. 'Surely you are not

suggesting I would wish to fight a duel with you?' He shook his head, a pitying smile on his face. 'Quite apart from the fact I do not accept there is any reason for us to quarrel, I understand your father was a fisherman of some sort? I hate to have to be the one to break it to you, but duelling is a *gentleman's* solution to a quarrel.'

'I am an officer of the French army!' Du Mauriac shouted.

'Well, that's as may be,' Charles replied. 'Plenty of upstarts are masquerading as gentlemen in France these days. I,' he said, drawing himself up a little, 'do not share such republican ideals. A man is a gentleman by birth and manners—and frankly, sir, you have neither.'

Du Mauriac, now completely beside himself, took a step forward, his hand raised to strike the blow that would have made a duel inevitable. And met the full force of the Earl's left fist. Before he knew what had hit him, the Earl followed through with a swift right, leaving the notorious duellist lying stretched, insensible, on the gravel path.

'I am so sorry you had to witness that, Heloise,' the Earl said, flexing his knuckles with a satisfied smile. 'But it is well past time somebody knocked him down.'

Heloise was torn by a mixture of emotions. It had been quite wonderful to see Du Mauriac floored with such precision. And yet she knew he was not a man to take such a public insult lying down. At least, she thought somewhat hysterically, only while he was unconscious. As soon as he came to he would be hell-bent on revenge. If he could not take it legitimately, by murdering the Earl under the guise of duelling with him, then he would do it by stealthy means. It would be a knife in the ribs as he mounted the steps to the theatre, or a shot fired from a balcony as they rode along the boulevard in the borrowed carrick. She could see the Earl's blood soaking into the dust of some Parisian street as she held his dying body in her arms.

She burst into tears.

Putting one arm around her, Lord Walton pushed a way through the excited crowd that was milling round Du Mauriac's prone form.

It had been a tactical error, he acknowledged as he bundled her into a cab, to deal with Du Mauriac while she was watching. Gentlemen did not brawl in front of ladies. Displays of masculine aggression were abhorrent to them. But it had seemed too good an opportunity to pass up! Wellington had forbidden officers of the occupying forces to engage in fisticuffs in public places. He had stipulated that the sword was the weapon of gentlemen, and Du Mauriac had taken advantage of that order to murder one young Englishman after another. Only a man like Walton, who was exempt from Wellington's orders, was free to mete out the humiliating form of punishment that such a scoundrel deserved.

But witnessing what an aggressive brute she was about to marry had clearly devastated Heloise. By the time they reached the Quai Voltaire she had worked herself into such a pitch he had no option but to carry her into the house and hand her over to the care of her mother, while he went in search of some brandy.

'He will kill him, *Maman*,' Heloise sobbed into her mother's bosom. 'And then he will take his revenge on me. Whatever shall I do?'

'We will bring the wedding forward to tomorrow,' her mother said, comforting Heloise immensely by not decrying her fears as groundless. 'And you will leave Paris immediately after the ceremony.'

'What if he should pursue us?' Heloise hiccupped, sitting up and blowing her nose.

'You leave that to me,' her mother said with a decisive

nod. 'He has plenty of enemies who want only a little push to move against him, and we can keep him tied up long enough for you to escape France.'

'But I thought you wanted me to marry him!'

'And so I did, my dear.' Her mother absently stroked a lock of hair from her daughter's heated forehead. 'When I thought you could get no other suitor, and when I thought Bonaparte's ambition would keep him away from Paris, fighting for ten months of the year. But I would never have permitted you to go on campaign with him. Besides,' she concluded pragmatically, 'Bonaparte is finished now. Of what use is a man like Du Mauriac when he has no emperor to fight for?'

The moment Charles heard Madame Bergeron suggest that, due to Heloise's state of nerves, it might be better to bring the wedding forward, he completely forgot his determination that nothing would induce him to leave Paris before the lease on his apartment had run its course. Nothing mattered except making sure of Heloise.

'I will go and order the removal of my own household,' he said, rising from his chair and pulling his gloves on over his bruised knuckles. It would take some time to pack up the house and arrange transport for his staff. But he could leave all that in Giddings' capable hands. He could most certainly leave immediately after the wedding ceremony. It only required his valet to pack an overnight case.

At first he assumed that once she had spoken her vows, and signed all the necessary documents, he would feel easier in his mind. But it was not so. Every time he glanced at the tense set of her pale face he wondered if she still considered the dairy farm at Dieppe a preferable option to being leg-shackled to a man of whom she was growing increasingly afraid. He was not being fanciful. She had admitted almost as soon as they had set out that she had left her one decent dress behind because it brought back bad memories.

It was the one she had been wearing the night he had forced that kiss on her.

Before long, he realised he was not going to be able to relax until he had her on board ship and out into the Channel. While they were in France there were innumerable ways for her to wriggle out of his grasp.

It was a great relief when, about ten miles out of Paris, her head began to droop. She couldn't have slept a wink the night before to be sleeping so soundly in the jolting carriage. She must have been scared stiff of leaving her family and her country behind, and going to live amongst strangers. She made no demur when he tucked her wilting form against his shoulder, and once he was certain she was fully asleep he took the liberty of putting his arm round her, and settling her into a more comfortable position. She was so tiny, tucked against his heart. So frail a creature.

Surely there must be some way he could get her to see he was not a monster? Just a man who wanted to be her friend and protector. But how? When so far all he had done was bully and frighten her?

She did not wake until well into the afternoon.

'Where are we?' she yawned, pushing herself upright.

'Abbeville. Since you were sleeping so soundly, I took the opportunity to press on. We have been able to cover far more ground than if we had needed to keep stopping to see to your comfort.'

His matter-of-fact tone brought her sharply to her senses. For a blissful moment, as she had come awake within the cradle of his powerful arms, she had mistaken the fact that he had allowed her to use his broad chest for her pillow as a mark of tenderness.

'You will have your own suite of rooms tonight,' he said,

plunging her deeper into gloom. Of course he would not want any real intimacy with her. Their marriage was only for public show.

She was not very much surprised when a meal was brought to her own little parlour, or when she ate it alone. He had barely spoken a handful of words to her all day. On seeing the meagre amount of luggage she had packed, instead of appreciating her ability to travel light he had made a sarcastic comment about having to arrange credit at various smart outfitters once they arrived in London. After that Charles had turned from her and gazed fixedly out of the window.

The hotel was naturally first class, and the maid provided to help her prepare for bed was both efficient and friendly. But Heloise knew she would not sleep a wink, no matter how soft the feather mattress was. She had dozed in her husband's arms nearly all day, and now she was wide awake—and as troubled as she had been the night before.

She had nobody but herself to blame for her predicament. She had approached Charles and offered to be the means by which he could salve his wounded pride. She should not feel offended that he cared so little for her that he would not even fight a duel when she was insulted in a public square. Besides, she had not wanted him to fight a duel. She could not bear to think of him being injured or, worse, killed on her account.

She would not be able to rest properly until he was safely in England, where Du Mauriac would not dare follow, she reflected, chewing at a fingernail.

Anyway, she had worked out, during the long sleepless hours of the previous night, that the quarrel in the Palais Royale had not been about her at all, no matter what words the men had used. Charles had clearly known far more about Du Mauriac than she had told him, else how would he have been able to sneer at his parentage? And another thing—it

had only been when she had told him Du Mauriac was the
suitor she wished to escape that he had shown any inclination to take her proposition seriously.

She shivered at the cold, calculating way Charles had
behaved. He must have studied Du Mauriac closely to have
taken the very course which would hurt him most. He had
stolen his woman, refused to acknowledge him as a social
equal, then knocked him down in a public place, rendering
him an object of ridicule.

She drew the coverlet up to her chin, the cold seeping into
her very soul. Felice had said he had no heart. He had
warned her himself that his nature was so cold and vengeful
he could sever the ties to his own family without a qualm.

No. She shook her head. Felice had been wrong. And when
Charles himself had informed her of his nature there had been
something in his eyes—almost as though he was taunting her
with the description she had heard applied to him so often.

His treatment of Du Mauriac had been cold and vengeful,
that was true. But Du Mauriac was a vile man who fully
deserved all that Charles had done to him. And as for that
business about cutting ties with the family who had raised
him…well, yes, that did sound bad. But, knowing what she
did of Charles, she would not be a bit surprised to learn that
it was they who had done something dreadful, and that
rather than expose them he'd let the gossip-mongers make
what they would of it all.

She was startled out of her reverie when someone pushed
her bedroom door open. This might be a first-class inn, but
clearly some people lodging here had no manners. She was
just opening her mouth to scream her objection at having
her room invaded when she realised it was only Charles,
entering not from the corridor but from a connecting door
to another bedroom.

'I am not a monster, Heloise,' he sighed, stalking towards

her. 'You do not need to clutch the sheet up to your chin as though you fear I mean to ravish you. I can assure you, nothing is further from my mind.'

Relief that it was not some stranger about to assault her had her sagging into the pillows. Though his words rankled. Did he think she was a complete fool? She knew all too well that when he wanted a woman he would go to one of his mistresses.

'I only came to inform you of the fact that I will not be making demands of that nature upon you. I said from the start that you are far too young to be married at all, leave alone face motherhood.' He bent over her and placed a perfunctory kiss on her forehead. 'Goodnight, Lady Walton,' he said.

'Goodnight, Charles,' she replied, betraying by only the very slightest quiver in her lower lip her feeling of humiliated rejection.

She would not cry until he had left the room. He detested any display of emotion. She could only imagine how disgusted her complete breakdown the night before must have made him. But it probably accounted for his distant behaviour with her today. She must not make the mistake of showing such lack of breeding again. Even if he never came to care all that much for her, she would do her utmost to be the kind of wife he wanted—compliant and undemonstrative.

To prove that she could do this, she tried a shaky smile. To tell the truth, she did feel a measure of relief. She was totally unprepared for a wedding night with a husband who regarded her as a necessary evil. Or to endure the ordeal of being deflowered by a man who would regard it as a duty to be performed in the cold-blooded way he seemed to live the rest of his life.

Lord Walton ripped off his cravat the moment he entered his room, and flung it aside to land he knew not where. He felt as though he could not breathe. God, how scared of him she had looked! And how relieved when he had told her he had no intentions of claiming his husbandly rights!

He strode to the side table and poured a measure of brandy into a tumbler. Then slumped into a chair, staring into its amber depths. He would find no solace there, he reflected, swirling the liquid round and round, warming it to release its fragrant fumes. The one time he had attempted to use alcohol as an anaesthetic it had failed him miserably. All it had done was make him feel sorry for himself. He had spouted the most maudlin nonsense to a virtual stranger, and woken with a thick head in the morning. He would need a clear head the next morning. If they could make an early enough start they would reach Calais and be sailing for home on the evening tide.

Providing Heloise did not fly from him during the night. Starting to his feet, he crossed to the chamber door. And paused with his hand on the latch.

Perhaps the gentlemanly thing to do would be to let her go.

Heloise deserved a man who could love and nurture her, not scare and bully her.

Dammit, why was it so impossible to behave rationally around her? He ran a hand over his brow.

Seeing her sitting in that bed, chewing her nails like a frightened, lonely child, had made him want to take her in his arms and comfort her. But he knew it would not have worked. He was the last person she would want to seek comfort from. He was the worst of her problems. Besides, the feel of her slight body, snuggled trustingly against his in the coach, had filled him with most unchivalrous longings. Right this moment he wanted her with a ferocity that made him disgusted with himself.

God, what had he done? What was he to do?

Determined to prove she was capable of behaving correctly, Heloise sat bolt upright in the carriage all the way to Calais.

In spite of the fact she had spent most of the night crying into her pillow, she was not going to repeat the mistake of yielding to exhaustion and falling asleep on a husband who seemed to regard any form of touching as an intrusion on his personal dignity.

She had served her purpose—giving him the opportunity to take revenge on Du Mauriac and concealing the chink in his armour that was his love for Felice. And now he did not know quite what to do with her.

He was avoiding her as much as he could. When they got to Calais, he left her in the carriage while he arranged their passage, then installed her in a private parlour to await the sailing while he went off for a walk. On the few occasions when he had deigned to speak to her, he had done so with such icy civility she just knew he regretted giving in to the rash impulse to marry her.

And who could blame him? No one was more unsuitable to be the wife of such a man than she!

By the time he came to inform her it was time to embark, she was trembling so badly she had to cling to his arm for support.

Just as they reached the companionway, a messenger dashed up to them. 'Countess of Walton? Formerly Mademoiselle Bergeron?' he panted.

When she nodded, he reached into his pocket and pulled out a letter. 'Thank heaven I reached you in time.' He grinned. 'Urgent, the sender said it was, that I got this to you before you left France.' His mission complete, the man melted back into the crowd that thronged the quayside.

'You had better open it at once,' she heard Charles say, and he pulled her slightly to one side, so that they did not impede other passengers from boarding.

'It is from my mother,' she said, after swiftly scanning the few lines of hastily scrawled script. 'Du Mauriac is dead.'

Translating for Charles, she read, "'...the Royalist officials sent to arrest him employed such zeal that many Bonapartists rushed to his aid. In the ensuing brawl, somebody stabbed him. Nobody knows yet who it was...'"

She clutched the letter to her bosom, her eyes closing in relief. Charles was safe.

'What violent times we live in,' Charles remarked, wondering why it felt as though the dock had lurched beneath his feet.

Heloise had only married him to escape Du Mauriac's clutches. What a pointless gesture she had made. If only she had waited a few days, and not panicked, she would not have had to make that ultimate sacrifice.

'Dear me,' he observed. 'You need not have married me after all.'

CHAPTER FIVE

OH, POOR Charles! He was already smarting from taking on
a wife he did not really want, and now he had learned that
at least part of his reason for doing so had ceased to exist.

But, instead of betraying his annoyance, he held out his
arm and said in an icily polite voice, 'Will you come aboard
now, madam?'

Oh, dear. She gulped. How he must wish he could just leave
her on the quayside and go back to England alone. But he was
too honourable even to suggest such a thing. Laying her hand
upon his sleeve, she followed him up the gangplank, her heart
so leaden in her chest she wondered it could keep beating.

He showed her to the cabin he had procured for the
voyage, then informed her that he was going on deck. His
face was frozen, his posture rigid, and she ached for his
misery. It hurt all the more to know she was the cause of it!

Charles hardly dared breathe until the last rope was cast
off and the ship began to slide out of the harbour. She had
not made a last desperate bid for freedom. Even when the
coast of France was no more than a smudge on the horizon,
she remained resolutely belowdecks.

Avoiding him.

He paced restlessly, heedless of the spray which repeat-
edly scoured the decks.

His conscience was clear. After a night spent wrestling with it, he had deliberately given her several opportunities to give him the slip during the day. Why had she not taken them? She was not staying with him because she was avaricious, nor was she all that impressed by his title.

The only thing that might explain her resolute determination to stick to their bargain was the fact she had given her word. Did it mean so much to her? He pictured her eyes, burning with zeal when she had promised to be the best wife she knew how to be, and accepted that it must.

It was a novel concept, to link a woman with integrity. But then Heloise, he was beginning to see, was not like any woman he had ever known.

Below decks, Heloise groaned, wishing she could die. Then he would be sorry. She whimpered, reaching for the conveniently positioned bucket yet again. Or would he? No, he would probably just shrug one shoulder and declare that it was a great pity, but after all he could always marry someone else. It was not as though he cared for her—no, not one jot. How could he, to leave her to endure such suffering alone?

Not that she wanted him to see her in such a demeaning state, she amended, heaving into the bucket for what seemed like the hundredth time.

Oh, when would this nightmare be over? How long before she could leave this foul-smelling cupboard and breathe fresh air again?

Never, she realised, after an eternity had rolled and pitched relentlessly past. Though she could hear the sounds of the hull grating against the dock, of officers shouting commands and sailors running to obey, she was too weak to so much as lift her head from the coarse cotton pillow.

'Come, now, my lady,' she heard her husband's voice say,

none too patiently. 'We have docked. It is high time to dis-embark—Good God!'

The evidence of Heloise's violent seasickness finally caught his eyes.

'Go away,' she managed resentfully when he approached the bunk, stern purpose in his eyes. He was a brute to insist she get up and move. Later, once the ship had remained steady for several hours, she might regain the strength to crawl. 'Leave me here to die,' she moaned.

'Nobody has ever yet died of seasickness,' he said briskly, swinging her into his arms. It was amazing how cheerful he felt to discover it was seasickness which had kept her below-decks, when he had been imagining her lying there weeping for her lost freedom. 'I know it must have been unpleasant for you, but you will be right as a trivet once you get upon dry land.'

'Unpleasant?' she protested. 'I have never suffered anything so horrid. How could you be so cruel as to force me to go to sea in a storm? I think—' she hiccupped down a sob '—that I hate you.'

'I am sure you don't mean that,' he reproved her mildly. Although he wasn't at all convinced. 'Besides, the sea was scarcely more than a bit choppy.' He consoled himself with the reflection that, even if she did hate him, nothing but the direst distress would ever induce her to endure another sea voyage.

He had planned to push on to London straight away, but he could not force Heloise to travel in her weakened state. He told the coachman to stop at the first hotel that could offer a suite of rooms.

He left her to herself for as long as he could. But when night fell concern for her had him knocking on her door and marching in before she had time to deny him admittance.

She was sitting up in bed, looking much better. Indeed, the nearer he got to the bed, the rosier her cheeks grew…

He checked in the middle of the room, biting down on a feeling of irritation. Did she think he was crass enough to insist on his marital rights, after she had been so ill? But before he could begin to defend himself Heloise blurted out, 'Oh, I am so sorry, Charles, about what I said.'

'What exactly that you said are you apologising for?' He frowned, drawing a chair to her bedside and settling himself on it.

'For saying that I hate you! I thought you meant to force me to walk off that ship and try to behave like a lady, when all I wished to do was die. I never guessed you were going to pick me up and carry me. And I had spent the entire voyage cursing you, so it was hard to get myself out of thinking that everything was entirely your fault. Indeed, at that precise moment I think I did hate you. But of course now I have calmed down I fully accept it is not your fault that I have seasickness. And you weren't at all cruel to force me to go on that ship. It would only have been cruel if you had known how ill I would be—and how could you, when I never knew myself? For I have never been on a ship before!'

'Nor will you ever set foot on one again,' he said with determination.

She shuddered. 'Indeed not.'

He paused. 'You know, of course, that means you can never return to France.'

They eyed each other warily as the import of his remark sank in, each convinced the other must regret this truth, and each equally determined to conceal their hurts.

It was Charles who ended the impasse, by leaning back, crossing one leg over the other, and declaring, 'Since you do not hate me at this precise moment, perhaps this would be a good time to discuss our mode of life together?'

Recalling the way he had indicated he wished her to

keep herself amused, and not interfere with his no doubt
hectic social life, Heloise forced herself to nod, waiting to
hear what further layers of humiliation he meant to heap on
her.

'I don't wish to raise any speculation about my marriage
by appearing to pack you off to the country as though I did
not like you.' She would have to live with him in London, just
to begin with, to prevent any speculation regarding their
union. Not that he cared what people said about him. But he
did not want her exposed to the sort of malicious gossip that
was bound to hurt her. 'The season has not yet properly
begun, but that will give you time to procure a suitable
wardrobe and settle into your new role. I expect it will take
you some time to find your feet, socially speaking, but until
you have acquired your own circle of acquaintance I will
ensure you always have a trustworthy escort to any event you
may wish to attend.

'Naturally, I do not expect you to understand the British
political system. All I expect from you is to be charming to
those I introduce as my political allies, and reserved towards
my opponents. Even though you may not like them, I shall
expect you to be hospitable to the more important party
members to whom I shall make you known, and their wives,
when I have occasion to invite them to any of my homes.
Do not worry, however, that I shall expect much of you as
a hostess. I have excellent staff running all my properties,
and a sterling secretary to whom you may apply, should you
find yourself floundering in the political shoals.'

Heloise listened to that patronising little speech with
growing indignation. If it would not give rise to the very
speculation he wished to avoid, he would as soon pack her
off to one of his country houses. Her poor little brain was
no match for the intricacies of the English political system.
She was not to interfere in the management of any of his

households, which were all running exactly as he wished. And if she had any questions, he wished her to apply to his secretary rather than bother him!

'Heloise?' he prompted, when she had been sitting in simmering silence for several minutes. He sighed. She clearly felt overwhelmed by the idea of being a leading figure in society. 'You must tell me if there are any gaps in your education which may cause you difficulties.' He had no intention of throwing her in at the deep end and letting her sink or swim as best she could.

'G…gaps?' she gasped, flashing him a look so indignant even he could not misinterpret it.

'Don't fly into the boughs with me,' he retorted, annoyed that she should cling to her hostility when he was doing all in his power to smooth her entry into society. 'If you cannot dance then I need to know, so that I may engage a dancing master for you. If you cannot ride then there is no point in me acquiring a horse for you to show off its paces in the park. I would instead purchase a barouche, or landaulet, and employ extra grooms to take you about.'

Her cheeks flushing, she hung her head. 'I beg your pardon, my lord,' she said, as humbly as she could. She had to admit he was trying to make the best of a bad job. He was prepared to employ as many staff as it would take to ensure she would be able to carry off the role he expected her to play. Just so long as he didn't have to be personally involved.

'I have learned to dance,' she flashed at him. 'Though you probably never saw me stand up whenever we went to balls in Paris. For not many men have ever asked me to dance, and when I was with you it was in the role of chaperon, so it was not at all appropriate. As for the horse, it is true that I cannot ride.'

'Should you like to learn?'

'Do you wish me to?'

'I should never object to any activity which would give you pleasure, Heloise,' he said wearily. It was clear that he was not going to win his wife's trust overnight. And her mention of how he had neglected her, whilst showering attentions on her sister, reminded him she had a deep well of resentment from which to draw. 'I bid you goodnight.'

He placed a chaste kiss on her forehead and retreated before things deteriorated any further. She might declare she did not hate him, but she had withdrawn sufficiently to start calling him 'my lord' again.

All he could do was keep sufficient distance for her to forget to regard him as a tyrant, whilst maintaining a watchful eye on her. She would learn, eventually, that she could trust him.

Wouldn't she?

London was not at all like Paris. The streets and squares through which their carriage passed were so clean and orderly, giving an overall air of prosperity. She frowned. Although perhaps it was just that her husband inhabited one of the better areas. This, she surmised as the carriage drew to a halt outside an imposing mansion, whose doorway was flanked by two massive pillars supporting a portico, was probably the equivalent of the 'court' end of Paris. There were probably overcrowded and dirty alleys somewhere. It was just that as an English countess she would never set foot in them.

A footman dressed in blue and silver livery handed her from the coach, and she entered her new home on her husband's arm. Oblivious to the interested stares of the servants who had gathered to greet their new mistress, Heloise gazed in awe at the lofty dimensions of the hall. A marble staircase swept upwards, branching at a half-landing to serve the two wings of the first storey, then continued up by several more flights, as far as she could see. Light flooded in through a domed skylight at the very top. Walton House reminded her of one of the better hotels in Paris, though it was shocking to think one man lived here alone. In Paris, a house like this would be divided into several apartments, which would be leased to tourists to provide an income for the impoverished nobles who clung to the upper floors.

An upper servant approached, bowing. 'Begging your pardon, my lord, but Captain Fawley has requested the honour of making the acquaintance of your Countess.'

'Has he, indeed?' Handing over his gloves and hat, Charles wondered what new start this might be. 'How does the Captain fare today?'

'Restless, my lord,' the footman replied, wooden-faced.

'My lady,' Charles said to Heloise, placing his hand under her elbow. 'A word in private, if you please?'

Drawing her into a little ante-room, he shut the door to ensure total privacy. 'I have little time to explain, but I would request a further favour of you. I had planned on sparing you the worst of Captain Fawley's temper, but on this one occasion I would ask that you bear me company and back me up in whatever I say. Can you do that for me?'

'This Captain Fawley…he is the man you wished me not to meet, who lives here with you?'

'I have no time to explain it all, but the salient facts are these: Captain Fawley is my brother. He hates me. He hates the fact that since he was invalided out of the army he has been forced to depend on me. I fear he will use your presence in my life as an excuse to try to strike out on his own. He must not do so, Heloise.' He took her by the shoulders, his eyes burning with an intensity she had never seen before. 'He must stay in Walton House!'

'Of course I will do whatever it takes to prevent him from

leaving, if that is your wish,' she replied, though it all seemed very strange to her. Whatever could have gone wrong between them? Was this to do with the rift Charles had referred to before, with certain of his family?

'Robert—that is Captain Fawley—occupies a suite of rooms at the rear of the house, on the ground floor,' he explained as he steered her out of the little ante-room and across the hall. 'His condition when I first brought him back from the Peninsula made it imperative that he not have to attempt stairs. Also, I had hoped that installing him in these particular rooms would encourage him to make free of the place. They have a private entrance, leading to the mews, which would have made it easy for him to come and go as he pleased.'

They reached a set of panelled doors, upon which Charles knocked. To her surprise, he did not simply enter, but waited until the door was opened by a stocky servant, dressed in a plain black coat and stuff breeches.

'Ah, Linney,' Charles said, 'I believe Captain Fawley has expressed an interest in meeting my bride?'

'Indeed he has, m'lord,' the stocky man replied, his own face as impassive as her husband's. Why, then, did she get the impression that both of them saw this as a momentous occasion?

It took Heloise's eyes a moment or two to acclimatise to the gloom that pervaded the room she walked into. Lit only by the flames of a roaring fire, it was clearly the domain of a man who did not care what his visitors might think. Her nose wrinkled at the smell of stale sweat, unwashed linen and general neglect that hung in the overheated room. Unfortunately, it was the exact moment her eyes came to rest on a figure sprawled on a scuffed leather sofa, to one side of the soot-blackened fireplace.

For a second her heart seemed to stop beating. The man

who regarded her with piercingly hostile black eyes was so very like Gaspard that she uttered a little cry and ran to him, her hands outstretched.

Leaning on his shoulders, she planted a kiss on each cheek, before sitting down next to him. When he flinched, she said, 'Oh, dear—should I not have done that? I have embarrassed you. It is just that you are so like my own dear brother.' In spite of herself, her eyes filled with tears. 'Who I will never see again. But now I find my husband has a brother, so I have a brother again, too.'

Somewhat overcome, she reached into her reticule for a handkerchief. While she was busy blowing her nose, she heard Charles cross to the fireplace.

'You haven't embarrassed me as much as I fear you have embarrassed yourself,' Captain Fawley snarled. 'Linney, perhaps you would be so good as to draw back the curtains?'

In silence, the manservant did as he was bade. Sunlight streamed in, illuminating the livid burns down one side of the Captain's face, head and neck, which the length of his unkempt hair did little to conceal. The left sleeve of his threadbare jacket was empty; the lower part of his left leg was also missing.

Perplexed, Heloise said, 'Why will drawing the curtains make me embarrassed?'

Captain Fawley laughed—a harsh noise that sounded as though it was torn from his throat. 'You have just kissed a cripple! Don't you feel sick? Most pretty women would recoil if they saw me, not want to kiss this!' He indicated his scarred face with an angry sweep of his right hand.

But, 'Oh!' said Heloise, her face lighting up. 'Do you really think I am pretty? How much more I like you already.'

The stunned look on Captain Fawley's face was as nothing compared to what Charles felt. Her face alight with pleasure, Heloise really did look remarkably pretty. He could not think why he had never noticed it before. Her eyes sparkled with intelligence, she had remarkably thick, lustrous hair, and a dainty little figure. She did not have the obvious attractions of her sister, but she was far from the plain, dull little creature he had written off while his eyes had been full of Felice. 'Captivating', Conningsby had said of her. Aye, she was. And she would be a credit to him once he had her properly dressed.

There was a certain dressmaker in Bond Street whose designs would suit her to a tee…

'You cannot mean that!' Robert began to curse.

A few minutes of such Turkish treatment was all he would permit Heloise to endure, then he would escort her to the safety of her rooms.

'Why not?' Unfazed, Heloise untied the ribbons of her bonnet and placed the shapeless article on her lap. Charles had a vision of wresting it from her hands, throwing it off a bridge into the Thames, and replacing it with a neat little crimson velvet creation, trimmed with swansdown.

'Well, because I am disfigured,' Captain Fawley said. 'I am only half a man.'

She cocked her head to examine him, in the way that always put the Earl in mind of a cheeky little sparrow. She missed nothing—from the toe of Robert's right boot to the puckered eyelid that drooped into the horrible scarring that truly did disfigure the left side of his face.

'You have only lost a bit of one leg and a bit of one arm,' she said. 'Not even a tenth of you has gone. You may think of yourself as nine-tenths of a man, I suppose, if you must, but not less than that. Besides—' she shrugged '—many others did not survive the war at all. Gaspard did not. I tell you now, I would still have been glad to have him back, and nothing would have prevented me from embracing him, no matter how many limbs he might have lost!'

'But you must want me to leave this house,' he blustered. 'And once an heir is on the way—' he rounded on Charles '—you can have no more excuses to keep me imprisoned here!'

Before he could draw breath to reply, Heloise said, rather stiffly, 'Is it because I am French?'

'Wh...what?'

'You reject my friendship because I am French. In effect, all this nonsense about being disfigured is the flim-flam. You don't want me for your sister.'

Faced with an indignant woman, Captain Fawley could do nothing but retreat from his stance, muttering apologies. 'It is not your fault you are French. You can't help that. Or being married to my half-brother, I dare say. I know how ruthless he can be when he wants his own way.' He glared up at Charles.

'Then you will help me?' Again, her face lit up with hope. 'Because Charles, he says it is not at all fashionable for a husband to hang on his wife's arm all the time. I have heard in Paris all about the season in London, with the masquerades, and the picnics, and the fireworks, which he will not at all want to take me to, even if I was not his wife, because such things are all very frivolous and not good *ton*. But I would like to see them all. And he said I may, if I could find a suitable escort. And who would be more proper to go about with me than my own brother? And then, you know, he says I must learn to ride...'

'Well, I can't teach you to ride! Haven't you noticed? I've only got one leg!'

Heloise regarded his left leg with a thoughtful air. 'You have only lost a little bit of the lower part of one leg. You still have your thigh, and that, I believe, is what is important for staying in the saddle. Do I have that correct? You men grip with your knees, is that not so? Whereas I—' she pulled a face '—must learn to ride side-saddle. I will have to hang on with my hands to the reins, and keep my balance while the creature is bouncing along…'

'Well, there you have it!' Captain Fawley pointed out. 'You have both hands. I have only one, and—'

'Oh, don't tell me you are afraid of falling off!' she mocked.

Charles suddenly felt conscious of holding his breath. For weeks before he had gone to Paris he had known Robert had regained most of his health and strength. There had been nothing preventing him from getting out and resuming a normal life but his own black mood. Had they all failed him by tiptoeing round his sensibilities?

'A brave soldier like you?' Heloise continued relentlessly. 'You are full of…of… Well, it is not polite to mention what you are full of!'

Captain Fawley turned for support to his brother. 'Tell her, Charles. Tell her that I just can't—'

Charles cut him off with a peremptory wave of his hand. 'You had as well give in graciously. Once she has the bit between her teeth, there is no stopping her. You cannot argue with her logic because it is of that singularly female variety which always completely confounds we mere males.' So saying, he swept her a mocking bow.

Robert sank back into the cushions, looking as though he had been hit by a whirlwind. Heloise was still watching him, her head tilted to one side, a hopeful expression on her face. And all of a sudden the dour cripple let out a bark of genuine laughter.

'I quite see why you married her, Walton.'

'Indeed, she left me no choice.'

'Very well, madam. I will come with you when you start your riding lessons,' he conceded. Then he frowned. 'Since I expect we will both fall off with monotonous regularity, I recommend we take our lessons early in the mornings, when nobody will be about to see us.'

She clapped her hands, her face lighting up with joy. Something twisted painfully inside Charles. Nothing he had ever done or said to her had managed to please her half so well.

'I dare say,' he said brusquely, 'you would like to see your rooms now, madam wife, and freshen up a little?'

Heloise pulled a face at Robert. 'What he means, no doubt, is that I look a mess, and that also he wishes to take me aside to give me a lecture about my appalling manners.'

'No, I am sure not,' Robert replied, regarding the stiff set of Walton's shoulders with a perplexed frown. 'Your manners are delightfully refreshing.'

Heloise laughed at that, but once they had quit Captain Fawley's suite she turned anxious eyes on her husband.

He made no comment until he had taken her to the suite of rooms he'd had his staff prepare for his bride. On sight of them, Heloise gasped aloud. She had her own sitting room, with a pale blue Aubusson carpet upon which various comfortable sofas and chairs were arranged. Her bedroom, too, was carpeted almost to the wainscot. With a smile, Heloise imagined getting up in the morning and setting her bare feet on that, rather than the rough boards of the little room she had shared with her sister. No shutters on any of the windows, she noted, only heavy dark blue velvet curtains, held back with self-coloured cords.

'I hope you like it—though of course if there are any alterations you wish to make, you have only to say.'

Heloise spread her hands, shrugging her utter bewilderment at such opulence. 'How could I not like this?' she managed to say, when it became apparent that her husband was waiting for her to say something.

It seemed to have been the right thing to say, for some of

the tension left his stance. 'I will ring and ask for refreshments to be served up here in your sitting room,' he said, crossing to the bell-pull beside the chimney breast. 'You may rest assured I shall not intrude upon your privacy. This is your domain. Just as the rooms downstairs are Robert's. The only time I shall enter, save at your express invitation, will be to bid you goodnight. Every night,' he finished sternly.

So that the servants would believe they were a normal husband and wife, she assumed. She sighed as a group of them came in and laid out the tea things. She supposed she should be grateful he wanted things to look right. At least she would get to see him once each day. Otherwise, the place being so vast, they might not bump into each other from one end of the week to the other.

Once the servants had retreated, Charles said, 'Come, Heloise, I can see you are bursting with questions. I have a little time to spare to indulge your curiosity before I must be about other business.'

There was no point in questioning their living arrangements. She had promised not to be a nuisance. But she would like to know what on earth had happened between the two Fawley brothers for them to come to this.

'Why does your brother accuse you of imprisoning him here? Is this something to do with the rift in your family you spoke of to me?'

'You do not need to have tea served if you do not like it,' he remarked, noticing the grimace of distaste with which she had set down her teacup after taking only one sip. 'The kitchen can provide anything you wish for.'

'Don't you wish to tell me? Is that why you talk about tea? If you do not want me to know about your family secrets then you only need to say, and I will not pry any further!'

'That is not the issue!' This was not a topic he found it easy to discuss. She would have to make do with a succinct account of the facts. 'Robert's mother was my father's second wife,' he bit out. 'In their zeal to protect me from her influence, when my father died the people he had nominated my guardians sent her back to her own family—with a modest annuity and penalties attached should she try to inveigle herself back into my life.'

'What was she, then, Robert's mother?' Heloise asked, fascinated. 'Something scandalous? An actress, perhaps, or a woman of easy morals?'

Charles smiled grimly. 'Worse than that, in the opinion of my stiff-rumped maternal relatives. She was a doctor's daughter.'

At Heloise's complete bafflement, he continued, 'She was, with her middle-class values, the kind of person who might have influenced me into thinking less of my consequence than they thought I should. They reminded me that my real mother was the Duke of Bray's granddaughter, and set about instilling me with pride in my true lineage. Rigorously.'

Heloise shook her head. What a miserable little boy he must have been. But worse was to come.

'I did not even know that I had a brother until, when I came of age, I began to go through all the family papers with my lawyers, instead of just ratifying them as my guardians assumed I would. I discovered that Robert had been born some five months after my father's death. Instead of having him raised with me, and acknowledged as second in line to my inheritance, they consigned him to the care of his mother's family. By the time he was sixteen, so vehemently did he hate my mother's relations that he began to refuse even the meagre allowance they had arranged for him. Instead he requested they purchase him a commission, so that he could make his own way in the world without having any need for further contact with relatives who had made no secret of the fact they wished he had not been born. Which they did—hoping, no doubt, that his career would be short and bloody. It was not long after that when I discovered his existence. And by then he was beyond my reach. He neither wanted nor needed anything from the brother he had grown up hating.'

'Oh, Charles,' she said, her eyes wide with horror. 'How awful. What did you do?'

He looked at her with eyes that had grown cold. 'I did as I was trained to do. I acted without emotion. I severed all connection with those who had systematically robbed me, my stepmother and my brother of each other.'

'And what,' she asked, 'happened to Robert's mother?'

'She scarcely survived his birth. The story he had from his family was that she died from a broken heart, at the treatment meted out to her whilst she was still in shock at being widowed.'

No wonder Charles appeared so hard and cold. The one person who might have taught him to embrace the softer emotions had been ruthlessly excised from his orbit. Then his relatives had taught him, the hard way, that there was nobody upon whom he could rely.

No wonder he had been able to shrug off the loss of a fiancée with such panache. Her betrayal was nothing compared to what he had already experienced.

And yet, in spite of all that, he had never stopped reaching out to the brother who repaid all his overtures with bristling hostility.

'Oh, Charles,' she cried, longing to take him in her arms and hold him. Tell him he was not alone any more. She was there.

She had begun to stretch out her hands towards him

before recalling what a futile gesture it was. She could not be of any comfort to him, for he was only tolerating her presence in his life. Besides, he had already expressed his dislike of her propensity for being demonstrative.

'I am so sorry,' she said, swallowing back the tears she knew he would disparage, and folding her hands in her lap with a feeling of resignation. He had only confided in her so that she might understand the situation, and not create further difficulties with his brother.

He made that very clear by turning on his heel and stalking from the room.

What further proof, thought Charles, seeking the solitude of his own bedchamber, did he need that she now considered him more repulsive than Du Mauriac? Even though her heart had been moved by his tale, she hadn't been able to bring herself to so much as touch his arm through his coat sleeve. But she had run to Robert and managed to kiss him. On both cheeks.

CHAPTER SIX

'I HAVE brought my bride to you for dressing,' the Earl informed Madame Pichot, upon entering her establishment the following morning. 'She needs everything.'

Madame Pichot's eyes lit up. 'Walking dresses, day dresses, ballgowns, nightrail?' She swallowed. 'A court dress?'

'Naturally.' By the time such a grand toilette was complete, and Heloise had practised walking in the hoops, he would have found someone to present her in Queen Caroline's drawing room. It was not so great a hurdle as obtaining vouchers for Almacks. If she offended one of the six patronesses of that exclusive club, or if they decided her background failed to meet their exacting standards for membership, she would never be truly a part of the *haut ton*.

Noting Heloise's rather worn coat and battered bonnet, Madame Pichot ventured, 'I could have one or two items delivered later today, or possibly first thing tomorrow. Just to tide milady over, of course…'

The Earl nodded acquiescence. Heloise would find it easier to think of herself as an English countess once she shucked off the serviceable clothing of a French bureaucrat's daughter.

'In future, should we require your services, you will present yourself at Walton House at my wife's convenience.'

'Of course, my lord,' replied the dressmaker, somewhat startled by the statement Heloise knew had been made primarily for her benefit. Whatever had been her habit formerly, a countess did not deign to visit a dressmaker's. She sent for such people to wait on her in the privacy of her own home.

'My wife will wear pastel colours. Rose and powder-blue—and, yes, this primrose satin would suit my wife's colouring.' He fingered one of the swatches an assistant had brought for his inspection.

'Oh, but with *madame*'s dark hair and eyes, she could wear striking colours. This crimson would look ravishing.'

'I don't want her going about looking like a demi-rep,' he curtly informed the somewhat abashed modiste.

Heloise had just taken a breath to object and say that she was quite capable of selecting her own gowns, thank you very much, when her mother's warning rang loud in her memory. He would want her to look the part she had persuaded him she could play. That he had no confidence in her dress sense might be somewhat insulting, but then, he was the one picking up the bills. Feeling like a child's dress-up doll, she meekly tried on the few gowns that were already made up, and had never been collected by other clients, while Charles and the modiste between them decided which could be altered to fit, and which did nothing for her.

A trip to a milliner followed, and then to the bootmakers, where she had her feet measured for a last.

'You must be growing tired,' Charles eventually declared, when all his efforts to spoil his wife had met with supreme indifference.

Felice would have been in ecstasy to have had so much money spent on a wardrobe of such magnificence, not to mention his undivided attention in selecting it. But Heloise, he was coming to realise, cared as little for such fripperies as she did for him. He was not going to reach her by showering her with the kind of gifts that would win most women over.

'I have other business to attend to for the rest of the day,' he told her. 'But I shall be in for dinner this evening. Will you dine with me?'

Heloise blinked in surprise. He had spent hours with her today already. She had assumed he would have something better to do with his evening. But he had actually asked her to dine with him!

Struggling to conceal her elation, she had just taken a breath to form a suitably controlled reply when he added, 'Or would you rather remain in your room?'

Was that a veiled way of telling her that was what he wished her to do? Did he hope she would take the hint?

Well, she was blowed if she was going to take all her meals in her rooms as if…as if she were a naughty child!

'I will dine with you,' she said, with a militant lift to her chin.

As though she were about to face a firing squad, he thought, hurt by her response to a simple invitation.

'Until tonight, then.' He bowed, then stalked away.

The evening was not a success. Charles made polite enquiries about how she had spent the rest of her day, while they sat sipping sherry in an oppressively immaculate ante-room. He looked relieved when the footman came to inform them dinner was ready. She soon realised this was because they would no longer be alone. A troupe of footmen served a staggering variety of dishes, whisked away empty plates, poured wine, and effectively robbed the event of any hint of intimacy.

Her heart did begin to pound when Charles leaned forward, beckoning to her, indicating that he wished to whisper something to her. Only to plunge at his words.

'At this point it is the custom for ladies to withdraw. I shall join you in the drawing room when I have taken some port.'

Feeling humiliated that he'd had to remind her of this English custom, Heloise followed one of the younger footmen to a vast room that was so chilly her arms broke out in goose pimples the moment she stepped over the threshold. She sat huddled over the lacklustre fire for what seemed like an eternity before Charles joined her.

'Should you like to play cards?' he suggested. 'Some people find it helps to pass the time until the tea tray is brought in.'

He could not have made it clearer that this was the last way he wished to spend his evening.

'I enjoy cards as little as I care to pour that vile drink, which is fit only for an invalid, down my throat,' she replied rather petulantly.

'Most husbands,' he replied frostily, 'take themselves off to their clubs, where they find companionship and amusements they cannot find at home, leaving their wives free of their burdensome presence.'

As Heloise stormed up the stairs, she decided never to set foot in that horrible drawing room again. If Charles would rather go off to his club, then let him go! She did not care, she vowed, slamming her sitting room door behind her, almost knocking over one of the silly little tables dotted about the floor as she stormed across the room to fling herself onto the sofa.

She glared at it, and the collection of ornaments it held with resentment. She hated clutter. She would have to get a footman to move it against the wall, out of the way. After all, Charles had said she could do as she pleased up here.

A militant gleam came to her eye and she sat up straight. He had meant she could decorate as she pleased. But she could do much more than that. She dared not ask him for a proper drawing table, knowing how much he disapproved of her sketches, but if, under the pretext of reorganising her rooms, she had that one large desk moved to a spot between the two windows, to catch the maximum daylight…

Her spirits began to lift. Drawing was more than just a hobby to her. She could lose herself for hours in the fantasy world she created on paper. It had been a solace to her in Paris, where she had been such a disappointment to her parents. How much more would it comfort her here in London, as an unwanted bride?

Her fingers were already itching to draw Madame Pichot, with her peculiar accent that would only pass for French in England. She reminded her of a drawing she had seen in the Louvre, of a creature whose eyes stood out on stalks and which was said to change colour to match whatever type of background it walked across.

Though how she was to locate a really good shop where she could buy pencils, paper and brushes without Charles finding out, leave alone how she would pay for her materials, would pose quite a problem.

It was very late when Charles came up to bid her goodnight, as he had warned her he would do.

'Do you have everything you need?' he enquired politely.

'Yes, thank you,' she replied in an equally polite tone, her fingers plucking listlessly at the quilt.

'Then I will bid you goodnight,' he said, barely brushing his lips across her forehead.

Heloise glared at his back as he left, barely suppressing the urge to fling some pillows at it. She was not a child for him to come and kiss goodnight in that insufferably condescending manner! She was surprised he did not tuck her in and pat her on the head while he was about it!

But the sad truth was she was as inexperienced as a child.

She had no idea how to encourage her husband to regard her as a woman rather than a girl. And there was no female to advise her. Her worst fear was that if she did try to breach his reserve she might only succeed in alienating him completely. She heaved a sigh as she sank down under the covers. At least *he* appeared content with the present situation.

Several evenings passed in an equally unsatisfactory manner before Heloise discovered a chink in Charles' armour.

When they met before dinner, and he enquired, as he always did, how she had spent her day, she told him that several outfits had arrived, and she had spent the afternoon trying them on.

'Was the riding habit among them?'

'Yes, and it is…' She bit her tongue. The pale blue gown with its silver frogging had instantly put her in mind of his servants' livery, and had made her crushingly aware that he only regarded her as just one more of his chattels. 'It is very pretty,' she finished in a subdued tone.

'If you are still determined to learn to ride, I could arrange for you to begin lessons with Robert tomorrow morning.' He frowned into his sherry glass for a few seconds, before saying softly, 'I bought him a lovely bay mare, very soft about the mouth, for Christmas. He has never even been to look her over. I shall be for ever in your debt—' he flicked her a glance '—if you could goad him into taking some form of exercise.'

'Of course!' she cried, immensely flattered that he had entrusted her with such an important mission. 'He must not stay in those dark rooms and moulder away.'

The rigid formality of the dining room was completely unable to dampen her spirits that night. For now she had a plan. If she could be the means to help poor Robert get out of his rooms, Charles would be pleased with her. Riding lessons would only be the start. He could take her shopping for art supplies. And, though he might be sensitive about his scars, surely she could get him to take her to Vauxhall Gardens to watch the fireworks one evening? Buoyed up by the prospect, she received her husband's goodnight kiss with complaisance. Even though he was dressed in his evening clothes, and clearly on his way out.

One day, she vowed, snuggling down beneath the covers, he would take her with him on one of these forays into London's night life from which he had so far excluded her. If all went well with Robert in the morning, it might be quite soon!

The sound of the outer door slamming, not once, but twice, roused Charles from the pile of invitations he had been poring over in his study early the next morning. As the season got under way, more and more people were expressing an interest in meeting his bride. But he had no intention of exposing her to this collection of rakes, cynics, and bitches, he vowed, tossing a handful of gilt-edged invitations into the fire. It said something about his social circle that he thought it unlikely he would ever find a house into which he could take his vulnerable young bride without risk of having her confidence ripped to shreds.

'Stop right there!' he heard Robert bellow, just as he emerged from the study. Heloise, the back of her powder-blue riding habit liberally stained with mud, was fleeing up the stairs.

She did not even pause, but ran along the corridor to her rooms, from whence echoed the sound of yet another slamming door.

Robert, red-faced, had stopped at the foot of the staircase, clutching the newel post.

'Problems?' Charles drawled softly.

Robert spun round so swiftly the heel of his false leg slipped on the marble floor and he nearly lost his balance.

'Go on, then—order me to leave your house!' he panted.

Charles leaned against the doorjamb, folding his arms across his chest. 'Why do you suppose I should wish to do that?'

'Because I have insulted your bride,' Robert flung at him. 'I swore at her. Comprehensively and at length! You must have seen that she was crying when she fled up the stairs!'

Frowning, Charles pushed himself from the doorframe and advanced on his brother. 'If you have insulted her, it is for you to put right. This is your home. I shall not evict you from it.'

Glowering, Robert spat, 'And just how do you propose I make the apology? Crawl up all those stairs?'

Charles regarded the false leg his brother had, for the first time to his knowledge, strapped onto his mangled knee joint. Heloise was amazing. She had only been here a matter of days, and already she'd cajoled Robert out of his rooms, into his false leg, and onto the back of a horse.

'No,' he mused. 'Until she calms down, I dare say all that will happen is that she will inform you she hates you. Far better to wait until she has had time to reflect on her own part in your quarrel. I suggest you join us for dinner tonight, and make your apologies then.'

'Dinner?' Robert blustered. 'I had as well crawl to her suite now as to attempt ascending to any other rooms on the upper floors!'

'Then I will order dinner for the three of us in the little salon,' he replied, indicating a room across the hall. His heart beating with uncomfortable rapidity, he waited for Robert to protest that nothing would make him sit down and eat with the man who had been instrumental in causing his mother's death. Instead, he only glared mutinously before hobbling back to his own rooms and slamming the door behind him.

Upstairs, Heloise was blowing her nose vigorously. It was no good feeling sorry for herself. That her first riding lesson had been such a fiasco was not what upset her the most, though that had been bad enough. What really hurt was her failure to gain any ground with Robert at all. Charles would be so disappointed with her.

Startled by a tap on the door, she blew her nose again, annoyed to find her eyes were watering afresh.

'May I come in?'

Charles stood in the doorway, ruefully regarding his wife's crestfallen appearance. 'Was it the horse, or my brother?'

Waving admittance to the footman who hovered behind him, bearing a tray of what looked like His Lordship's finest brandy, Charles advanced into the room.

'I thought you might feel in need of a little restorative,' he explained, as the young man placed the silver salver on an elegant little table beside the sofa she had flung herself on when first she had come to her room. 'And, since I know of your aversion to tea, I thought I would supply something more to your liking.'

'You are m...most k...kind,' Heloise half sobbed, as Charles stooped to pick her riding hat up from the floor, where she had flung it not five minutes before. The feather that adorned the crown had snapped. He ran his fingers over it with a frown.

'Why is your hat on the floor? Is your dresser not in attendance?'

'I have not rung for her. I don't want her!' she snapped. Since he was already disappointed in her, she had nothing to lose by admitting she could not live up to his exacting standards. 'If I wish to throw my hat on the floor and…and stamp on it, then I have no wish to have her tutting at me as though I am a naughty child. It is my hat, after all, and I can do with it as I see fit!'

Instead of reprimanding her for her childish outburst, he merely smiled and remarked, 'I'll buy you another one,' tossing the crumpled headgear to the footman as he exited the rooms.

'I don't want another one,' Heloise said, perversely irritated by his magnanimity in the face of her tantrum. 'I am never getting on another horse again as long as I live.'

'I thought you scoffed at people who disliked falling from horses. I seem to remember you saying—'

'Yes, I remember very well what I said. If the horse had been trotting, or even walking, it might not have been so humiliating. But the horrid creature was standing perfectly still when I fell off. If I can fall off a stationary horse, which is being held at the head by a groom, I cannot think how much worse it will be should the brute try to move.'

'Are you badly hurt?' Charles frowned, suddenly wondering whether her tears and her evident discomfort might stem from more than wounded pride. 'Should I send for a doctor?'

So, after a perfunctory check, he was going to palm her off on another person? If they had the relationship a husband and wife ought to have, he would be running his hands over her bruises right now, assuring himself that nothing important was damaged. Instead of which he had handed her a drink, with a mocking smile twisting his lips.

'I don't need a doctor.' She sighed. I need a husband. A husband who would put his arms round me and tell me everything is all right, that he is not ashamed of his stupid little wife, or disappointed in her failure to help poor Robert.

Mutinously, she went to the bellrope and tugged on it viciously. 'I wish to change out of these clothes now,' she informed him. 'And take a bath. Unless there is anything else you wish to say to me?'

Charles bowed politely, remarking, 'Only that I hope, when your temper has cooled a little, you will endeavour to mend fences with Robert. I have invited him to dine with us this evening. It is the first time that he has agreed to do so. I would not wish it to be his last.'

Heloise glared at the door through which he departed. Not a word of thanks for her efforts, abortive though they had been. Only a stern warning to watch her behaviour at dinner this evening, so as not to offend his precious brother any further. He had not even bothered to find out what the boor had said to upset her!

Nothing she ever did would please him.

Very well, then, she would start pleasing herself. She tore at the silver buttons of her riding habit with trembling fingers. She would dismiss the horrible dresser who looked down her nose at her. As a pair of housemaids came in, carrying towels and cans of hot water, she eyed them speculatively. Her husband seemed to employ dozens of staff. If she could not find one amongst them with whom she could strike up a tolerable relationship, then she would advertise for an experienced lady's maid and begin to conduct interviews. If nothing else, it would give her something to fill the endless monotony of her days.

And as for tonight… Oh, Lord! She sank into the steaming fragrant water of her bath and bowed her head over her raised knees. Charles would be watching her like a hawk. Robert would resent her for being the catalyst that had forced the two men to eat at the same table. She would be like a raw steak being fought over by two butcher's dogs.

By the time she entered the little salon Robert and Charles were already there, sitting on either side of the fireplace, sipping their drinks in a silence fraught with tension. Both, to her surprise, looked relieved to see her.

'I believe I owe you an apology,' Robert said, struggling to his feet.

She merely raised one eyebrow as she perched on the edge of the third chair which had been set before the hearth.

'All right, dash it! I *know* I owe you an apology. I should never have used such language to a female…'

'Not even a French female?' she replied archly, accepting the drink the footman handed to her. 'Who is not even of noble birth, is an enemy of your country, and most probably a spy to boot?'

Flushing darkly, Robert muttered, 'If I said any of those things to you this morning…'

'If?'

'All right. I admit I said a lot more besides the swearing I have reason to apologise for! But don't you think it is pretty disgusting behaviour to laugh at a cripple?'

'Oh, I was not laughing at you, Robert.' Heloise reached a hand towards him impulsively, her eyes filling with tears. 'No wonder you got so cross, if that was what you thought. It would indeed have been the most unforgivable behaviour if that was so!'

'But you were laughing…'

'It was the horse! When you went to climb onto him from the right side it looked so surprised. I have never seen such an expression on an animal's face before.' A smile twitched her lips at the memory. 'And it turned to stare at you, and it tried to turn round to place you on what it thought was the correct side, and the groom was dodging about under its head, and you were clutching onto the saddle to stop from falling off the mounting block…'

'I suppose it must have looked pretty funny from where you were sitting,' Robert grudgingly admitted. 'Only you have no idea how I felt—too damned clumsy to mount a slug like that, when I've always been accounted a natural in the saddle.'

'I'm sorry, Robert. But you have to admit I received just punishment for my thoughtlessness.'

He barked out a harsh laugh. 'Aye. You should have seen her, Walton. Laughed herself right out of the saddle. Lost her balance and landed on the cobbles at my feet…'

'With you swearing down at me while I was struggling to untangle all those yards of riding habit from my legs…'

'And the grooms not knowing where to look, or how to keep their faces straight…'

'It sounds better than the pantomime,' Charles put in dryly. 'Ah, Giddings, it is good to see you back with us. I take it your presence indicates that our dinner is ready?'

Charles had tactfully arranged for the meal to be brought to a small round table set in the alcove formed by the bay windows, so that Robert had very little walking to do.

Linney took a position behind Robert's chair. When Charles' footman approached him with a tureen of soup, the man took it from him, ladling a portion into a bowl for his master himself. For the first time it occurred to Heloise just how difficult it must be to eat a meal with only one arm, and how demeaning it must be for a man in his prime to have to rely on someone else to cut up his food for him. How he must hate having others watching the proof of his disability.

Desperate to introduce some topic of conversation—anything to break the strained silence which reigned at the table—she asked Giddings, 'Did I not meet you in Paris?'

Although he was somewhat surprised to be addressed, the butler regally inclined his head in the affirmative.

'How was your trip back to England? I hope your crossing was smooth?'

'Indeed, once I was at sea I felt heartily relieved, my lady,' he unbent enough to admit.

'Did you dislike France so much?'

The butler looked to his lordship for a cue as to how he should answer. Instead, Charles answered for him.

'You have evidently not heard the news, my lady. Bonaparte has escaped from Elba. On the very eve of our marriage, he landed at Cannes with a thousand men and began his march on Paris.'

'Damn the fellow!' Robert put in. 'Has there been much fighting? King Louis must have sent troops to intercept him?'

Charles again gestured to Giddings, which the butler interpreted correctly as permission to tell his tale himself.

'The last I heard, every regiment sent for the purpose of arresting him joined him the minute they saw him in person.'

'It is no surprise, that,' Heloise said darkly. 'He has a way with the soldiers that makes them worship him.'

'By the time I reached Calais,' Giddings continued, 'fugitives from Paris were catching up with me, telling tales of the desperate measures they had taken to get themselves out of the city before he arrived. The price of any sort of conveyance had gone through the roof.'

'Thank heavens we married when we did,' Charles remarked. 'Else we might have been caught up in that undignified scramble.'

'Is all you can think of your precious dignity?' Robert retorted. 'And how can *you*—' he rounded on Heloise '—be so bacon-brained as to worship that Corsican tyrant?'

'I did not say *I* worship him!' Heloise snapped. First Charles had made light of the convenience of their marriage, and now Robert had jumped to a completely false conclusion about her. 'Do you think I want to see my country back in a state of war? Do you think any woman in France is ready to see her brothers and sweethearts sacrificed to Bonaparte's ambition? It is only men who think it is a fine thing to go about shooting each other!'

'Now, steady on, there,' Robert said, completely taken aback by the vehemence of her reply, and the tears that had sprung to Heloise's eyes. 'There's no need to fly into such a pucker...'

'Not at the dining table,' put in Charles.

'Oh, you!' She flung her napkin down as she leapt to her feet. 'All you care about is manners and appearances. Men in Paris might be fighting and dying, but all you can do is frown because I speak to a servant as if he is a real person, and say what I really think to your so rude beast of a brother!'

'This is neither the time nor place—'

'When will it *ever* be the time or the place with you, Charles?' she cried. Then, seeing all hope torn from her— not only for her marriage, but also for her country—she burst into sobs and left the room.

For a few moments the brothers sat in an uneasy silence.

'Dammit, Walton,' Robert said at last, flinging his spoon down with a clatter. 'I didn't mean to upset her so.'

'I dare say she is anxious over the safety of her parents,' Charles replied abstractedly. Did she really think he was so shallow all he cared about was good manners? 'Giddings, give Her Ladyship an hour to calm down, then take a tray up to her room. As for you—' he turned to Robert with a cool look. '—I suggest you finish your meal while you consider ways to make amends for insulting my wife and making her cry for the second time in one day.'

CHAPTER SEVEN

'CHARLES, you will never guess what has happened!' Heloise greeted her husband, when he came in to bid her goodnight several nights later.

She was not clutching the sheets nervously to her chest for once, Charles observed. Sadly, the robe which matched the gossamer-fine nightgown she wore was fastened demurely across her breasts, rather than lying provocatively across the ottoman. Though she was getting used to him visiting her room, she had no intention of inviting him into her bed.

Still, it was a small step in the right direction. There were other indications that she was gaining confidence in her position as his wife, too. She had ordered some lower footmen to rearrange her furniture without asking his permission. She had dismissed the dresser and the maid he had engaged for her. Then, as though wondering just how far she dared push him, she had promoted the scrubby little girl who cleaned the grates and lit the fires to the position of her maid.

She had then gone to Cummings and asked how she might go about doing some personal shopping.

Was that what had put the sparkle in her eyes tonight? Discovering from his secretary what a generous allowance he had arranged for her to have?

He took his seat at her bedside with a vague feeling of disappointment.

'Robert is going to take me to Vauxhall Gardens to see the fireworks! Is that not wonderful?'

His disappointment evaporated. Her pleasure stemmed from mending a quarrel with his brother rather than a so far concealed streak of avarice.

'He said that he cannot take me anywhere by daylight, but if we kept to shadowy walks, so that nobody can raise objections to the state of his face, it might not be too bad. Charles, this is something I do not understand.' Her brow puckered with confusion. 'Nobody looks askance at a soldier on the boulevards of Paris, no matter how grotesque his injuries!'

'But you have had conscription in France for many years. Everybody feels more personally involved in the war. Anyone's brother or husband could easily suffer the same fate as those poor wretches.' He sighed. 'Heloise, you must understand that most people are basically selfish. They come to town to enjoy themselves. They want to gossip and flirt and dance. Seeing a man like Robert is a reminder that life can be ugly and brutal. And they don't want reminders that outside their charmed circle men are fighting and dying to ensure their freedoms.'

Heloise felt a twinge of guilt. She herself had become so preoccupied with her husband, and how she could win his approval, that she had not spared Bonaparte a thought for days.

'I trust you have not fixed tomorrow evening for your outing to Vauxhall?' Charles frowned. It had suddenly occurred to him that it would look very odd if her first outing in public was taken in the company of her brother-in-law. He rapidly reviewed the entertainments available to him for the next evening.

And wondered why he had never thought of it before.

'You will be accompanying me to the theatre.' It had worked well for them in Paris. Why should it not work here?

'I...I will?' Finally, *finally* he was going to permit her to appear in public as his bride!

And people would look at how small and plain she was, and wonder why on earth he had married her when he could have had any woman for the lifting of his finger.

Charles watched the joy drain from her face.

'Is the primrose satin ready?' he asked tersely, refusing to voice his hurt.

It was not her fault she regarded an outing with him as a duty to be borne, when a trip to Vauxhall Gardens with his half-brother filled her with eager anticipation.

When she nodded, he said, 'Wear it tomorrow.' Without further comment, he gave her the kiss which was always the prelude to leaving her room.

It was only after he had gone that she allowed herself to feel resentful that he had not bothered to thank her for getting Robert to venture out of doors. Nobody else had succeeded in so much as rousing him out of his rooms for months. But could Charles unbend towards her enough to applaud her achievement? Not he!

But she still, foolishly, studied his face for some sign of approval as she descended the stairs the following evening, dressed according to his dictates. She felt a little uncomfortable in the high-waisted gown which would have left her arms completely bare were it not for the matching gloves that came past her elbows. The neckline glittered with the most intricate beadwork Heloise had ever seen. The motif of thistle-heads and leaves was picked up in the self-coloured stitching on her gloves, and repeated around the three flounces on her skirts.

'Come into my study for a moment before we leave,' he said, crooking his finger imperiously. His guarded expression told her nothing. 'I have something I wish to give you.'

She followed him, her stomach feeling as though a nest of snakes had taken up residence there. She was thrilled he was taking her out, desperate to be a credit to him, terrified she would let him down, and agonisingly conscious of every single one of her physical deficiencies.

Walking to his desk, he opened a large, square leather case which had been lying on it, and pushed it towards her across the polished mahogany surface. Inside, nestling on a bed of black velvet, was a parure consisting of necklace, bracelet, earrings and an aigrette of pale yellow gems, in a rather heavy and elaborate setting of gold. From another box, which he produced from his pocket, he took a matching ring.

'I wished to have given you this sooner, but on returning to London and examining it I found it needed cleaning.'

'Oh?' Her eyes filled with tears as he slid the ring, which fitted perfectly, onto her finger. He had bought Felice a ring that matched her eyes. When he had given it to her, he had said no jewel could compare with them. He had merely had some old baubles he'd had to hand cleaned up for his plain and undeserving wife.

Still, at least she understood now why he had ordered her to wear the primrose satin. There were not many fabrics that could complement such unusually coloured gems as the ones he lifted from the box and fastened in her ears.

'Perfect,' he said, standing back to admire the effect of the earrings glittering against the curtain of his wife's dark hair.

Heloise stiffened her spine, stifling her momentary pang of self-pity. She had always known she was a second-best wife. Of course she would only get second-hand jewels!

What had she expected? That her husband would begin to act out of character and forget that she was not the woman he had wanted to marry?

He was being very kind, considering the way she had acted since being installed in his home. He had never, for example, upbraided her for the scene she had created at dinner, when she knew such behaviour was what he deplored above all else. He had merely sent her food up to her room.

Because he was, she suddenly realised, a kind man underneath those chillingly controlled manners. It was why she had never really been able to stay afraid of him for longer than a minute at a time. Why she had been able to confide in him from the very first. She had even been secure enough to give way to the childish temper tantrums that her brother had predicted would drive any husband to give her a beating.

Charles would never beat her. He did not, she saw with a sinking heart, care enough about her to lose that glacial self-control.

'I couldn't have you going out without any jewellery, could I?' he said, fastening the necklace round her throat.

'No, I suppose not,' she replied. He might not care about her much, but he cared about his own reputation. His Countess could not appear in public without adequate adornment. The dress, the jewels—they were just the costume that made her look the part she was playing.

Charles was rather perplexed by Heloise's response. He had just hung diamonds worth a king's ransom around her neck, and instead of going into raptures she seemed weighed down.

Could she be nervous at suddenly having so much wealth displayed upon her person? She had never owned much jewellery before.

Nor wanted it. She had not even been tempted to try on the emerald ring that had been her sister's.

'These are yours by right as my wife, you know, Heloise.' The set of yellow diamonds had been in his family for generations, handed down to each new bride upon her wedding—except for the ring, which was given upon the occasion of the betrothal. 'It never felt right that you had to wear that ring I bought in Paris.'

'I shall never wear it again,' she vowed. It must remind him of all he had lost! And while she had been complaining to herself of all that she did not have, she had entirely forgotten that her husband was still trying to recover from his broken heart. He was so good at disguising his emotions that it took moments like this to remind her how much he must still be hurting.

'What are we going to see at the theatre tonight?' she said, deciding that he would be more comfortable if they talked about trivial matters.

'The *beau monde*,' he quipped, taking her arm and leading her to the door. He was glad he had taken that moment to reassure her. Now that she had got over her initial reluctance to accept the family heirlooms, she might even be able to enjoy herself a little. 'As in Paris, we go to the theatre to see who is in the audience, not what is being performed upon the stage. I expect that during the intervals persons wishing for an introduction to my new Countess will besiege our box. They will probably think,' he remarked dryly, 'that they will be able to get to me through you. I hope you will not be taken in.' He frowned. 'It would be best if you did not associate with anyone without checking their credentials with me first.'

Heloise was virtually silent all evening. At first, Charles wondered if he had said something to offend her. She had lifted her chin as he'd handed her to her seat, and stared fixedly at the stage throughout the first act. Fortunately, this had left her oblivious to the stir her appearance, decked in the Walton diamonds, had created.

Gradually, he recognised that this was the Heloise he had first become acquainted with. The quiet, reserved girl that nobody noticed. Who observed but did not participate. This public Heloise was a far cry from the termagant who yelled at his brother, flounced out of rooms, slammed doors, and rattled on without pausing to draw breath.

He welcomed her return when they got into the carriage to go home.

'Charles,' she breathed, leaning forward and tapping his knee with her ivory-handled fan. 'Who was that dreadful man—the great big dark one who accosted us in the corridor during the interval?'

He smiled wryly. He had assumed it would be easier to control exactly whom he permitted to approach her if they went for a stroll, rather than sitting passively in their box and letting the importunate besiege them.

'Lord Lensborough,' he replied, no doubt in his mind as to who she meant.

The Marquis had stood directly in their path, blocking their progress. And when he had said, 'Allow me to felicitate you upon your marriage,' his hostility had been unmistakable.

'Is he one of the family you won't speak to because of what they did to Robert?'

'Far from it. If anything, he regards himself as Robert's champion. His own brother, who serves in Robert's former regiment, was so concerned about the Turkish treatment I would mete out, he wrote begging Lensborough to watch over him.'

'Oh. I am so sorry.' Heloise laid one gloved hand upon her husband's sleeve.

'For what?' It was ridiculous, he reflected with a frown, that his spirits should lift just because she had forgotten herself so far as to reach out and touch him.

'That people should so misunderstand you. What do they think you mean to do with Robert? Is he not your brother? Your heir?'

'Alas, from Lord Lensborough's reaction this evening, I fear they suspect that I mean to cut him out by siring an heir of my own. Through you.'

'Well, that just goes to show,' she said, snatching back her hand, remembering his reaction when she had made such an impulsive gesture once before, 'how silly they are.' Couldn't they see how devoted Charles was to his brother? Didn't they understand how outraged he had been by the way his guardians had tried to cut him out of the succession?

Charles sighed. The reminder that she would one day have to face this distasteful duty as a wife had brought about an instant withdrawal.

But at least when he went to her room later, to bid her goodnight, she seemed to be in good spirits.

'Thank you for this evening, Charles,' she said prettily, when he bent to bestow a chaste salutation on her forehead. 'I did enjoy it.'

'Really?' He frowned. 'I thought you seemed…abstracted.'

'Oh, well…' She fidgeted nervously with the ties of her robe, her cheeks flushing pink as she averted her eyes from his.

Ah! She was relieved it was over. But she did not wish to wound him by confessing as much.

She wanted him gone. Very well, he would oblige her! He would not force his unwelcome presence on her a moment longer. Turning on his heel, he stalked from the room.

Heaving a sigh of relief, Heloise flung back the covers and went to the desk which she had converted to a drawing table. She had nearly given the game away then. It was just that there had been so many odd people at the theatre. And the knowledge that there was, at last, a fresh sheaf of drawing paper and a selection of really good-quality pencils hidden in a box beneath her bed was like a tonic fizzing through her veins. Now that she was a countess, with an army of staff at her disposal, she did not have to search the shops for what she wanted. She simply sent her maid, Sukey, with a list, and *voilà*! After an hour or so the girl returned with exactly what she requested! And, since Sukey was so grateful for the meteoric rise in her status, she would rather cut her own throat, she had breathed dramatically, than ever betray Her Ladyship's confidence.

Heloise only felt a small twinge of conscience for continuing with a pastime Charles frowned upon. So long as he did not find out, it could not hurt him.

And so many ideas had flooded to her while she had been studying the crowds tonight. *Beau monde!* She scoffed as she pulled a stool to her desk and lit the two lamps she had placed there for moments such as this. There was nothing *beau* about the manners of some of those people! They ignored the efforts of the actors upon the stage for the most part, which was rude, since they had clearly gone to a great deal of effort for the entertainment of an audience that was interested only in its own members. Except for certain of the men, when the pretty young dancers came on. Then it was all tongues hanging out and nudging elbows, and comments which she was certain were coarse, though fortunately she had not been able to hear them. And as for that obnoxious marquis, who harboured such uncharitable thoughts towards both Charles and herself…well! She had seen the plump little blonde sitting beside him in his own private box, giving him sheep's eyes. A woman who was clearly not his wife. And he had the temerity to look askance at *her*!

Dawn was filtering through her curtains before Heloise began to yawn. Her excitement had driven her to fill page after page with initial sketches. Later, when she had the interminable hours of daylight to fill, she would add the detail and bring the scenes to life with judicious touches of watercolour paint. Yes… She yawned again, sloughing off her robe and letting it drop to the floor. There was much to be said about an evening spent at the English theatre.

And tonight the pleasure gardens of Vauxhall would provide even more material for her portfolio.

Robert was to dine with them both before taking her out. Charles had sent a note to inform her.

This time there were no arguments. There was scarcely any conversation at all. It was as though all three of them were determined to say nothing that might spark another confrontation.

Eventually, Charles remarked, 'I shall not be dining at home for the next few evenings, Lady Walton. I warned you before we married that I have an interest in politics. And at this particular time, with Bonaparte on the rampage again, you will appreciate that I must be busy in the affairs of my country.'

Of course she understood. In Paris, it was in the private salons of influential hostesses that statesmen decided which line they were going to take in public. Similar meetings must go on in London.

She nodded. Robert scowled.

She was not surprised when, the second they got into Walton's private carriage, which he had put at their disposal for the outing, Robert blurted, 'He's not going to back those fools who want to try and appease Bonaparte, is he?'

'I do not know,' she shrugged. They never talked about anything. 'All I know is what you heard him say. Charles will be too busy to bother with me for a while.'

Robert looked perplexed. 'I'm sure he did not mean that. You must admit, Bonaparte escaping like that, and winning over the army that was sent to arrest him, has caused the deuce of a panic all over Europe.'

She turned bleak eyes in his direction, though she could only make out his silhouette. Somehow, in the darkness of the jolting carriage, it was easy to let her hurt spill out. 'It is not a question of him suddenly being busy. He has never wanted to spend more time with me than he has to.'

'Cold-hearted wretch,' she heard Robert growl.

'No, you must not say such things,' Heloise protested. 'Really, he is most kind to me…'

'Kind! To leave you alone in your room, night after night, while he goes out on the town? Oh, don't think because I stay in my rooms I don't know what goes on in this house. The way he neglects you. Look.' He leaned forward, his earnest expression illuminated for a second as they passed under a street lamp. 'I may not be able to introduce you to the elevated set my brother belongs to, but I do have friends in town. You'd probably enjoy yourself a deal more with them, anyway, than at the stuffy *ton* gatherings Walton frequents. I'll…' He drew in a breath, as though steeling himself to go on. 'I'll introduce you to them. I will not,' he stipulated, 'escort you to picnics, or go boating, or anything of that nature. But once you get to know a few people you'll have no shortage of invitations to all the sorts of things females of your age enjoy.'

Sitting back, and running a hand over his perspiring brow, he grumbled, 'Why Walton hasn't seen to it himself beats me.'

Heloise was torn. On the one hand she wanted to defend

Charles' actions. And yet there was no doubt she could use Robert's misapprehension to get him to renew contact with the friends he had shut himself away from for far too long.

It would take something as radical as his ingrained hatred for his brother for him to run the gauntlet of public reaction, she began to realise as the evening wore on. She lost count of the number of dandies who lifted their lace handkerchiefs to their noses as they sauntered past, eyes swiftly averted. She grew furious with the females who placed troubled hands to their breasts, as though the very sight of Robert was too distressing for their delicate sensibilities. She was beginning to wish she had not dragged Robert out and exposed him to such a cruel and humiliating reception.

Spying a bench, positioned in a secluded nook for the convenience of clandestine lovers, Robert limped to it and sat down heavily. His false leg might have been fashioned by the most skilled craftsman Walton could hire, but learning to walk in it was clearly no easy matter.

'Oh, Lord,' Robert moaned. 'Here comes another one of 'em.'

Heloise sat forward, to look round Robert and see who he meant, and spied Lord Lensborough strolling towards them, the plump blonde on his arm.

'I thought he was your friend.'

'No,' replied Robert shortly.

As he drew level with them, Lord Lensborough paused, eyeing them closely.

'My lady,' he said, bowing slightly. 'Captain Fawley. How…interesting to see you here, of all places.'

The blonde giggled, alerting Heloise to the fact that his sneering words could as well mean this particular secluded bench as Vauxhall Gardens. Beside her, she felt Robert stiffen.

'A word in private, if you please, Lensborough?' Robert growled.

The Marquis sloughed the blonde from his arm, taking a seat on the far side of Robert. The blonde seemed inured to such cavalier treatment, wandering off a few paces without expecting to be introduced, let alone take part in the general conversation. Indignant on her behalf at such rudeness, Heloise got to her feet, deciding she would go and introduce herself.

'Hello,' she said, offering her hand to the startled blonde.

Warily, she looked to Lord Lensborough for her cue. But since he had his head close to Robert, and they were engaged in such deep conversation that they were oblivious to what she might be doing, she protested, 'You didn't ought to be talking to the likes of me—a great lady like you.'

'Well, if I did not I would be sitting being ignored. Since you are being ignored as well, we might as well amuse each other, don't you think?'

The blonde smiled uncertainly.

'I saw you at the theatre yesterday evening, did I not?' Heloise asked, since the blonde still seemed unwilling to initiate any conversation.

'Yes, and I saw you too. With your husband. The Earl. Ever so nice you looked. That gown was from Madame Pichot's, wasn't it?' When Heloise nodded, she went on, 'Oh, I should love to have a gown from her. Your husband is ever so generous, ain't he? Mrs Kenton was always saying it, and when I saw those rubies he gave her…' She trailed off, suddenly looking guilty. 'I shouldn't be mentioning the likes of Mrs Kenton, or what your husband gives her,' she continued, hanging her head. 'Jasper is always telling me I talk too much…'

'It is of no matter to me.' Gritting her teeth, Heloise smiled bravely at Lord Lensborough's ladybird. 'Men of his rank always have mistresses.'

When the nameless blonde smiled in obvious relief,

Heloise knew that the simple creature had just inadvertently revealed the name of Charles' mistress. She had always known he would have one. But it was a shock, all the same, to find out her name at a moment when she was least expecting it.

Feeling a little sick, she turned back to Robert.

'I wish to return home now,' she said, pointedly ignoring the Marquis, who had so far done the same to her.

'I shall be only too glad to take you. I'm devilish tired.'

To her surprise, as Robert struggled to get up, the Marquis also rose to his feet, and made her a respectably deep bow. Pinning her with an intent look, he said, 'I have issued an invitation to you and my young friend for an evening at Challinor House. Quite informal. A little supper, some hands of cards…'

Though she felt certain the last thing the Marquis wanted was to have her enter his home, she also knew he had Robert's welfare at heart.

'I don't mind taking you to play cards at Lensborough's,' Robert admitted gruffly. 'But not the supper.'

She winced at the memory of Linney cutting up Robert's food for him. 'It sounds delightful. I love above all things to play cards,' she lied.

Her ineptitude at the card table was one of the faults for which her father had frequently berated her. But people were so fascinating when they forgot company manners to concentrate on their game. Far more interesting than the little pieces of board she held in her hand, or the points she should have been counting in her head. However, Robert needed to believe she wished to play, and wanted his escort.

Bowing to her with a tight smile, the Marquis gathered up his companion and took his leave.

Neither of them was very talkative on the way home. Robert's face had the waxy pallor of a man close to exhaustion. And Heloise was wrestling with the turbulence of her thoughts.

She was not sorry, now, that she had let Robert think badly of Charles. It would motivate him to take her out, so that she could make her own friends. Which would leave Charles free to live his own life.

With his Mrs Kenton.

Somehow she would learn to cope. At least if she concentrated on helping Robert to regain his self-esteem it would stop her wallowing in her own unhappiness. It would be her mission, she decided, squaring her shoulders.

It was not until they made to go their separate ways, in the hall of Walton House, that he turned to her and said, in a voice hoarse with emotion, 'My brother is a prize idiot not to see what a treasure you are. If he won't treat you as he should, then, dammit, I will!'

'Oh, Robert,' she said, rather tearfully. Nobody could force her husband to grow fond of her. 'It is enough that you agree to take me out now and again. I have been...' She paused as her breath hitched in her throat. 'So lonely since I came to London.'

Impulsively, she flung her arms round him, almost causing him to overbalance.

'I say—steady on!' Robert laughed.

'I cannot help it,' she declared with feeling. 'You are the only friend I have.'

Neither of them heard the door to the small salon close quietly as Charles withdrew behind it. He had been a little anxious all evening about how Heloise would cope with his irascible brother. Given the way things usually turned out whenever Heloise tried to 'help' his brother, he had been preparing to go and pour oil onto troubled waters. He had not, he thought, recoiling from the scene he had just witnessed, expected to see his brother make a declaration of that sort to his wife—nor for her to respond so enthusiastically!

Nor had he expected the searing pain that left him gasping for breath.

For a few moments he gripped the edge of the mantel, leaning his forehead against the cool marble and taking deep, steadying breaths, while his heartbeat gradually returned to something like normal.

Why in Hades was he so upset?

It was not as if he was in love with Heloise. It was a proprietorial thing. That was all. He had always felt the same disgust when one of his mistresses had shown affection for another man while under his protection.

Had he made it clear to Heloise, when laying down the terms of their union, that, while he was willing to let her lead her own life, he would not tolerate her taking a lover? At least not until after she had given him an heir.

It probably hurt all the more that it was his own brother who had so effortlessly breached the defences he had lain siege to weeks ago. He laughed bitterly. All he'd had to do was trim his hair, put on clean linen, and take her to watch some fireworks!

He strode to the salon door and flung it open. The scene he had witnessed was only the opening round in the dance that went on between a man and a woman. He would have to make Heloise understand that it must progress no further, he thought, as he pounded up the stairs to her room.

He gave only a peremptory knock before striding into her bedroom. She was not yet in bed, but standing by her dressing table in the act of disrobing.

At his entrance, the maid uttered a little shriek, her hands flying to her cheeks. Heloise's gown, already half undone, slithered to the floor, leaving her standing in just a flimsy chemise. She had already removed her shoes and stockings.

He had never seen so much of her. Slowly, his blood thickening, he examined every perfect inch of her—from her flushed cheeks, down her slender arms, past her shapely calves and ankles to the ten naked toes she was curling into the soft blue carpet. She was exquisite. And he wanted to stake his claim right now.

'Sukey,' she said in a reedy voice, 'hand me my wrap, then you may leave us.' Whatever Charles wanted must be important for him to be displaying such an uncharacteristic lack of manners.

His eyes flicked upwards. She was fastening the belt tightly, with fingers that trembled.

Moodily he paced to her desk, looking blindly at the sheets of paper scattered on it, seeing only the anxiety in her eyes when he had invaded the sanctuary of her bedroom.

'I am writing a letter to my sister,' she said, breathy with panic as she gathered the loose pages and stacked them neatly together before he got a chance to glimpse any of the sketches she had been working on lately.

Stuffing the pages into a drawer, she turned to him warily.

'You did not forbid me, so I have written several times. I suppose that now you will tell me I must stop?' she finished gloomily.

She still thought of him as a tyrant, he realised, reeling from her. Hadn't he made any progress with her at all? If she still believed he would forbid her contact with her family, no wonder she turned to his brother for comfort.

'Heloise,' he ground out, seizing her by her shoulders, 'didn't I tell you that all I want is for you to be happy as my wife?'

'N…no, you didn't,' she stunned him by stammering.

'Of course I did!' He paced away from her, running his

fingers through his hair. He had made it absolutely clear, on more than one occasion. Hadn't he? 'Well, I am telling you now!' he exclaimed.

Why, when he had just told her he wanted her to be happy, was she shrinking from him like that?

There must be something he could do to drive that scared look from her face. Perhaps he could begin by reassuring her that he did not, as she assumed, frown on her corresponding with her sister.

'If you want to write to your sister, of course you may. Has Felice replied to your letters?' he said, in as calm a tone as he could muster. 'How is she?'

'She reached Switzerland safely, and—' she swallowed, loath to be the one to break the news '—she has married Jean-Claude.'

Charles struggled to find something else to say. How did a man go about gentling a nervous female? He didn't know.

He only knew that he had to get out of here before he tore the damned wrapper that she was clutching to her throat like a shield from her perfect, enticing young body, and proved conclusively that he was the monster of her imagination.

Muttering an oath, he beat a hasty retreat.

'Whatever has got into His Lordship?' Sukey said, as she emerged timidly from the dressing room, where she had taken refuge. 'I've never seen him in such a pucker.'

'I have no idea.'

All she did know was that for the first time since their marriage he had not kissed her goodnight. No. Tonight, with thoughts of Felice running through his mind, he could not bear to touch her at all.

He was probably already on his way to his Mrs Kenton, to seek the solace his unappealing wife was too naïve to know how to offer.

'No idea,' she repeated dully.

CHAPTER EIGHT

'I DO NOT agree!' Heloise returned her soup spoon to the bowl, the consommé untouched.

Robert glowered at her across the table. 'I suppose you think all the other European nations should just let Bonaparte take up where he left off, then?'

'That was not what I said!'

It was at moments like this that she was at her most attractive, Charles reflected, sipping his wine. And he only ever saw her this animated these days when Robert was around.

On the few occasions she could spare time from her increasingly hectic social life to accompany him to a ball, or rout, she behaved with extreme modesty and decorum.

He got the 'public' Heloise.

Not this vibrant, intelligent woman who held such passionate views.

She picked up her spoon again, her mind so fully locked in the tussle with Robert she didn't notice that she spattered droplets of consommé across the snowy damask tablecloth.

'I just meant that there might not need to be another war. There has not been any fighting in France…'

'Only because anyone who might have opposed Bonaparte's return has turned tail and fled. Why do you think he's amassing an army, you silly goose? Do you think he means to march them up and down the Champs-Elysées to entertain the tourists?'

'There are no tourists left in Paris,' Charles pointed out pedantically. 'They have all run for their lives.'

Heloise and Robert turned to stare at him, his wife's face creased with frustration, his brother's lip curling in contempt.

Flicking his finger to Giddings, Charles indicated it was time to remove the cooling soup and bring on the next course.

To all intents and purposes things could not be progressing better. He had wanted Heloise to make her own way in society. He had wanted Robert to get well.

He had not imagined the two events, taken in tandem, would make him feel like an intruder in his own home.

'There was no need for the tourists to flee,' Heloise said to him carefully. 'Your Whig politicians are pressing to make the treaty with Bonaparte…'

'While the allies gathered in Vienna have just declared him an outlaw!' scoffed Robert.

Charles frequently heard them bickering like this when they returned home of an evening. He was growing increasingly resentful that it was Robert with whom she felt easy enough to speak her mind. But that was nothing to what he felt when he heard them laughing together.

What kind of fool resented hearing his wife enjoying herself? Or watched his own brother's return to health and vigour with a sense of dread?

His lips twisted in self-mockery as he dug into a dish of lamb fricassee.

Heloise took only a small portion of the stew, which was on tonight's menu so that Robert would have at least one dish from each course that he could manage for himself. She glowered at him as Linney spooned onion sauce onto his plate. She wished Charles would not invite Robert to dine with them quite so often. He ruined all her attempts to impress her husband with her increasing grasp of British politics. She had spent hours poring over the newspapers and questioning Cummings, to no avail. Robert took her up on every point, arguing with her until she became hopelessly enmired and tripped herself up. Confirming her husband's opinion she was the greatest idiot he had ever met. She only had to see the mocking way he was smiling now to know what he thought of her intellectual capabilities.

Well, she would soon wipe that smirk off his face!

'So—this masquerade you take me to at the Opera House this evening. Will it be very disgraceful?'

She had the satisfaction of causing Robert to choke on his wine. He had lectured her at length upon the importance of *not* telling her husband where they were headed tonight. Charles would strongly disapprove of his wife disporting herself at a venue where ladies of quality simply did not venture, he had warned her.

'Of course it would be,' he said hastily, 'if anyone was to find out you had gone there. But I've taken all the precautions necessary to protect your reputation. We will both be wearing masks and cloaks, and travelling in a plain carriage.'

Though he addressed the last part of this to his half-brother, Charles' face remained impassive.

'I say, you don't mind me taking Heloise there, do you?' Robert put in uneasily.

'If it amuses her to go to such places—' he shrugged '—who am I to deny her? I have told her she may enjoy herself exactly as she pleases.'

She felt as if he had slapped her. Robert was always saying how generous it was of her husband to leave the

Walton coach and driver at her disposal, but she knew better. He didn't care how many servants he had to pay to keep her out of his hair. Oh, he went through the motions of squiring her to at least one event 'every se'en night or so', as he'd put it, 'for form's sake'. But she knew, from the very way he carried himself on those occasions, that he was not enjoying her company.

'Well, then,' she said, rising to her feet and tossing the napkin to the table, 'I shall go and fetch my cloak. Tonight, Robert, you will get the proof that all I have been saying is correct.'

Charles went cold inside. Had he just inadvertently given his wife the go-ahead to commence an affair with Robert by saying she could do as she pleased?

He heard Robert's chair scrape back, heard him mutter that he would wait for Heloise in the hall, but all he could see was her face—the defiant look in her eyes as she said, 'Tonight, Robert.'

Sweat broke out on his brow.

Tonight.

Around him the footmen were clearing away the dishes, removing the cloth, pouring the port.

He had instinctively known they couldn't be lovers. Not yet. Apart from the fact Robert was scarcely fit enough, Heloise was not the kind of woman to break her marriage vows so quickly.

She had never been able to deal in deceit. Her father had said it was because she was too stupid, but he liked to think it was because she was too honest.

But if he didn't do something to put a spoke in Robert's wheel it would happen. How could Robert not desire her when she turned those flashing eyes up at him, or laughed at one of his sarcasms? She was so full of life. It was all any man could do to keep his hands off her. And she was clearly growing increasingly fond of him. It was only natural. They were far closer in age, their tastes seemed to mesh…

He was damned if he was going to sit at home and let his brother seduce his wife out from under him!

Leaving his port untouched, he rose from the table and, like a man on a mission, made his way up to his rooms. He had purchased a domino and mask for a private masquerade himself, the previous autumn. If his valet knew where to lay his hands on the outfit, he would track his wife and brother down at the masquerade and observe them undetected. The grotesque devil's mask that would cover his upper face was of red satin, matching the lining of the black velvet domino. He would look nothing like his usual civilised, conventional self in that disguise. Hell, he scarcely recognised himself any more. What kind of jealous fool stalked his wife and spied on his half-brother?

After the dire warnings Robert had given her, Heloise was surprised to discover the Opera House was not the shabby, ill-lit lair of her imagination, but a rather elegantly appointed theatre. Four tiers of boxes, decorated in white and gold, surrounded a stage upon which people in a variety of disguises were dancing.

'It's still not too late to turn back,' Robert urged her. 'So far you have not stepped over that invisible line which separates you from scandal. But if you set so much as a toe across it, I warn you, you will unleash consequences so dire…'

She tossed her head. 'I am no coward, to cringe at the threat of these vague consequences! But if you are afraid…'

Robert drew himself up. 'If I am wary, it is not on my own account, I assure you.'

'Isn't it?' she taunted. 'Isn't it truly the prospect of the rejection of females that has you quaking like a blancmange tonight? For I cannot believe you are suddenly afraid of

what Charles might do—not after some of the places you
have been taking me to…'

'Only because you asked me to!' he protested, twitching
her simple black domino over her evening gown. 'For God's
sake, if we are going to stay, keep yourself covered up,' he
urged, taking her arm and tugging her towards one of the
boxes on the lowest tier. 'And don't do anything or say
anything that might give anyone a clue as to who you are.
If you think you can shock Walton into taking more notice
of you, you need your head examining!'

She almost laughed aloud at Robert's misapprehension.
She had long since given up any hope of making Charles
regard her with anything more than bored indifference.

But Mrs Kenton was a different matter.

She was not going to permit That Woman to sneer at her
and pity her and crow over her for being the one who had
Charles in her bed every night!

It had been Nell, Lord Lensborough's plump blonde
mistress, who had introduced the two women one evening,
when Heloise had gone unaccompanied to a small party
being held by one of Robert's friends. At the last minute he
had confessed he was not feeling up to it, but, at the look
of disappointment on her face, had told her there was
nothing to stop her going alone.

From the outside, the house had looked completely respectable. It had only been once she had stepped inside she'd
realised she ought not to have gone. The guests had nearly
all been young, single military gentlemen, who had already
been growing rather boisterous. She had intended to say hello
to her host, a Mr Farrar, and slip away, when Nell had come
bounding up to her. The dear silly creature had noticed her
looking a little flustered upon coming into a room of virtual
strangers without a male escort, and decided to look after her.
Being slightly foxed, she had seen nothing untoward in in-

troducing her to the statuesque brunette who'd stood at her side. For a split second neither lady had been sure how to react.

It had been Heloise who had recovered first. Later, when she had gone over the evening's events, she had been proud of the way she had behaved.

She had smiled gaily, holding out her hand to Mrs Kenton, who had been looking as if she wished to strangle poor Nell.

'Is it not fortunate for us both that Charles is not here? This is exactly the sort of scene which he would dislike above anything!'

'Indeed he would,' Mrs Kenton had replied faintly, taking Heloise's hand in a limp grasp.

Seeing Nell's brow finally pleating with concern, Heloise went on, with false bravado, 'I assure you, I do not in the least mind meeting the lover of my husband. It is only what I expected when I married an Englishman. It would be silly of me to pretend I do not know he has a mistress.'

And now that she had seen her she could understand exactly what drew Charles to this woman. Although she was a good deal older than Felice, she had the same dark hair, the same graceful carriage, even a sultry set to her lips that put her strongly in mind of her sister when she was not in the best of moods.

'At least he does not have two, like Lord Wellington,' she prattled on. 'Or parade them about in public while shunning his poor little wife. Why he brought her to Paris at all nobody could in the least guess, if he meant to humiliate her in that fashion!' Finally she paused to breathe, desperately hoping the bright façade she had adopted was successfully hiding her despondency.

For Mrs Kenton was wearing the ruby necklace. The stones were magnificent, gleaming like fire against the woman's milk-white skin, the large, central stone dipping provocatively into a cleavage that made Heloise fully conscious of her total inadequacy to compete in the bedroom stakes.

'Although I suspect, myself, that he wished to prove he had beaten Bonaparte upon all suits, and probably had no idea he had hurt her. Men!' she finished on a false laugh, fluttering her fan before her flushed cheeks.

'It is very…open-minded of you to say so,' Mrs Kenton said, with a puzzled frown.

'Oh, no—I am a realist, me. And it seems silly to pretend not to know how the world works.'

A knowing expression flickered across Mrs Kenton's face. She purred, 'Or to pretend that you don't mind?'

Heloíse responded with a shrug. 'Why should I mind?'

The older woman's eyes narrowed on the parure Heloise was wearing, her expression growing positively feline.

'Why, indeed? He is such a generous man that any woman with an ounce of sense would always forgive his little…lapses.' She leaned forward conspiratorially. 'You are wise to pretend not to mind about me, my dear, just as I shall pretend not to mind about you. The one thing he cannot abide is a woman making a fuss. He hates to feel he might be losing control of a situation.' She chuckled—a low, throaty sound. 'Well, you know how far he takes his *desire* for mastery.' She fanned herself, raising her eyebrows meaningfully. 'My, I grow heated just thinking about his skill between the sheets. It more than compensates for the coldness of his public manners, as I am sure you would be the first to agree.'

Heloise turned and stalked away. Round one had definitely gone to the courtesan. Though she wanted nothing more than to leave the party at once, she refused to let it look as though Mrs Kenton had driven her away.

The second bout was fought with rather more subtlety. Mrs Kenton followed Heloise to the lady's retiring room, where she had been trying to hide until a sufficient amount of time had passed to make it look as though she was not running away.

Pretending she did not know anyone else was in the room, Mrs Kenton remarked to Nell, who was with her, 'Isn't it a good thing that Walton's poor little wife is able to look after herself?'

Nell blinked owlishly, hiccupped, and subsided onto a sofa.

'Otherwise, who knows what would become of her? Everyone knows he is bored with her already.'

'Well, I like her,' Nell protested.

'As do I!' Mrs Kenton quickly put in. 'Which is why I feel so sorry for her. He never goes anywhere with her if he can avoid it. One can only wonder why he married her in the first place!'

That remark had struck her to the core. Charles had only married her to save face, and at her own suggestion. But it had been to no avail. The whole of London could already see that it was a mismatch!

Well, one thing they would not see. And that was a bride who was not completely content with her lot. Heloise had determined there and then to prove to the whole world that nobody need feel in the least sorry for her. Particularly the patronising Mrs Kenton. From that moment she had taken pains to attend the sorts of places she was most likely to run into the woman, and demonstrate that not only did she know exactly what she was to her husband, but that it didn't affect her in the least. She would show them all she was a sophisticated Parisienne, well acquainted with, and impervious to, the base nature of men.

This bravado had carried her, over the next few days, to

all sorts of places she had not enjoyed visiting in the least. But she would not back down. Not while that woman flaunted the rubies her husband had given her, while all she had to show for the marriage were some antiquated crystals he'd got out of a cupboard and dusted down so she would not look as though she had nothing! And if she could face down her husband's mistress at every turn, Robert could learn to deal with his own demons.

'Robert,' she said now, more gently, laying a gloved hand on his arm, 'your limp will not deter a woman who has a good heart.'

'Nor my face?' he scoffed.

'Ah, but tonight it is covered.' She reached up to adjust the set of his white velvet mask, which matched her own. 'Any woman you approach will see only your eyes, burning with admiration for her. She will see how determined you are to approach her, and she will think, My, how he must want me. You will not give her commonplace flatteries about the colour of her hair, or the magnificence of her figure— *non*! You will tell her that no other woman has such beauty of spirit. You will see beneath the trappings to the very heart of her. And her heart, it will be in your hands before the end of the very first dance.'

'I shall sound like a complete coxcomb if I dish out that kind of cant,' Robert grumbled. 'Then I'll probably catch my false leg in her skirts and trip her over.'

'Ah, no! The coxcomb is the one who pays tribute too prettily, not meaning half of what he says. You will let your lady see that you need her. Every woman wants to feel she is the only one who can answer the needs of her lover's heart.'

'Sounds like a load of hokum to me,' huffed Robert from the dark corner of the box where he was hunched. 'Shall I prove it? Shall I do as you have suggested, and make a complete fool of myself?'

'That,' replied Heloise with some asperity, 'was the whole reason for coming to a masked ball. So that you could try out the technique on some girl who does not in the least matter to you, rather than make the cake of yourself before your friends. There!' Heloise took his arm and indicated a female in a pink domino, who was casting them an occasional look from a box directly across the stage from where they sat. 'She is looking your way again. Go and ask her to dance!'

The masked damsel shot him a coy look, before turning away and fanning herself with vigour.

'Hell, what have I got to lose?' Robert finally said, pushing himself out of the chair.

It was not until he had left her alone in her box that Heloise realised just how vulnerable she was to the attentions of the masked revellers who leered at her over its edge. This was not the first time since embarking on her private little battle with Mrs Kenton that Heloise had felt completely out of her depth. But it was the first time she had sensed she could be in real danger. Even in private gaming hells there was a code of conduct which ensured her personal safety. But here the drunken bucks who made free with the females clearly felt they had the right to do so. For the type of females who came to such a place did not expect the same consideration as would a lady of quality. Indeed, she had not seen any woman here display reluctance towards any advances made upon her.

It was quite terrifying when a large male, clad in a black silk domino topped with a red devil's mask, stepped over the edge of the box without so much as a by-your-leave.

The domino parted as he took the chair beside her, revealing the stuff knee breeches of a tradesman.

'All alone, my pretty?' he slurred. 'How about a kiss?' He lurched forward, assailing her nostrils with gin fumes.

'*Non!*' she gasped, shrinking back into her chair.

'French, hey?' the stranger responded, cocking his head to one side. 'Not a good time to be a Frenchwoman in London, is it? Though you are the prettiest one I've ever seen. Let me see you better,' he said, reaching for the strings of her mask.

'You must not!' she cried, rapping him over the knuckles with her fan. It was imperative that her mask remain in place. Charles would be furious if he ever found out she had revealed her face at such a place as this!

'Why not?' The man chuckled, his hands dropping to her waist. 'It's what you've come here for, isn't it? To have a little fun?'

In a panic now, Heloise struck out at his devilish mask with her fan. He caught her hand easily, his reflexes surprisingly quick for a man whose slurred speech indicated he was heavily inebriated.

She could not think how to get rid of him. Admitting she was a respectable married woman would do no good. He would not believe her. Respectable married women did not come to places like this. Not without their husbands.

If he knew she was the Countess of Walton, with a husband renowned for his vengeful nature, he would stop trying to paw at her like this! But she could not betray Charles by using his name! Nobody must ever know that she had disgraced him by coming to a place like this!

In desperation, she mentioned the only threat which she thought might hold sway with the drunken buck.

'I am not here alone! I am here with my…' Even if she mentioned her brother-in-law, it might give her assailant a clue as to her true identity. In spite of his domino and mask, it was impossible to disguise the full nature of Robert's injuries. Anybody who knew anything about the upper classes would have heard of the maimed soldier who lived with his half-brother and the French wife. 'My lover!' she declared, hoping this man had not seen Robert limp off towards the far side of the stage.

'Lover, is it?' the stranger hissed. 'Pretty careless of him to leave you here unprotected, then, wasn't it?' He placed his arm along the back of her chair, propping his leg up against the door of the box as he did so, effectively penning her in with him. 'I don't think he would care all that much if I stole a kiss or two…not if he's the fellow I saw going to the refreshment room with the little tart in the pink domino a moment or so ago.'

Heloise's breathing grew ragged. Robert could *not* have abandoned her! He would not do such a thing!

'You lie! He would die for me! And he was a soldier. If you dare to touch me he will kill you!'

The man's eyes glittered coldly through the slits in his mask. 'He would have to catch me first,' he sneered. 'Is that how you came to be his lover? He fought in France? Is that it? And brought you back with him? Spoils of war…' Almost casually, the hand which was not gripping her shoulder fumbled its way under the silken folds of her domino.

'*Non!*' she cried, trying to push his hand away. 'It was not like that!'

'What was it like, then?' His hand headed unerringly towards her breast. She couldn't believe how strong he was. It took both her hands and all her determination to prevent him from reaching his destination, and even then she was not convinced he hadn't stopped for some obscure reason of his own.

'It is none of your business!' she panted, seizing his wrist as his questing hand altered the angle of its exploration under the concealing folds of her domino, this time sliding to the low neckline of her gown, from whence he slipped it inside her bodice. 'Stop this! Stop it at once!' she shrieked, leaping up out of her chair with such haste that the neckline ripped. 'Oh!' she sobbed, pressing herself to the back of the box, her hands clutching at the torn edges of her gown. Thank heaven Sukey was utterly loyal to her. She would never be able to give a satisfactory explanation to Charles if he ever found out she had come home with the front of her gown torn. 'You will pay for this!'

'Since I'm paying, I may as well get my money's worth,' the man said, lunging at her.

He grasped her by the elbows, his body pressing hers into the thick crimson curtains that shrouded the shadowy depths of the box as his mouth crashed down on hers.

It was an angry, demanding kiss, and quite terrifying. Outraged, Heloise struggled against him with all her strength.

Until something quite unexpected happened. As the stranger's hands embarked on an assured exploration of her feminine contours, she began to compare him with Charles. He was of the same height and build, and though his voice was coarse, and his clothes that of a much poorer man, the eyes which glittered from behind the devilish mask were of a similarly cool blue.

If only Charles would kiss her like this. She groaned, and then, for a few crazy seconds, found herself pretending this man was her husband, and that he wanted her. She stopped struggling, sagging back into the suffocating folds of the drapery, her whole body trembling with a kind of sick, guilty excitement.

If only Charles would caress her like this! Would be so wild with desire for her that he would kiss her in a public place, even peeling the torn fabric of her dress away and pressing his lips to the exposed skin beneath as this man was doing now. She moaned. Oh, if this man did not stop soon, she would fling her arms round his neck and kiss him back!

And why should she not? Charles was doing something like this, maybe at this very moment, with the beautiful Mrs Kenton!

At the thought, a whimper escaped her throat.

The stranger's head jerked back. For a moment he simply stood, gazing down at her, his chest heaving with each hoarse breath he took. And then he astounded her by reaching out, almost tenderly, to brush away a tear that was trickling down her cheek.

She did not even know at what point during the assault she had started to cry.

'Aren't you going to slap me?' he mocked, withdrawing slightly.

Heloise grabbed the chair back as the world seemed to lurch crazily, flinging her completely off balance.

'Non,' she grated, shaking her head. 'I deserved it.' She had just responded lustfully to a drunken stranger's lecherous groping! 'I am a slut,' she gasped in shock. Sinking to the chair, she buried her face in her hands and burst into tears.

CHAPTER NINE

HELOISE flinched when a large male hand landed clumsily on her shoulder.

'Oh, Robert!' She sighed in relief on recognising it was his form looming out of the shadows, and not her assailant's. 'P…please take me home!'

She was still shaking with reaction, unable to form coherent replies to any of Captain Fawley's questions until they were safely shut inside the coach and on their way home.

On hearing the bald facts, Robert became so angry it was all she could do to prevent him turning the coach round and hunting the man down.

'It was my fault—all my fault,' she insisted. 'I never want to go to such a place again.'

'I did not want to go in the first place,' he retorted. 'From now on let me decide where we go, if you must go out with me and not your husband!'

As if she had any choice! The mere mention of her husband's neglect sent her into fresh floods of tears. When they reached Walton House she was in no state to argue when Robert steered her into his rooms, sat her firmly on the sofa, and pressed a drink into her hands.

'If you think you fared badly,' he drawled, easing himself

onto a chair opposite her, 'you should hear what I suffered at the hands of the Pink Domino.'

She was sure that he was inventing more than half of the amusing story he went on to tell her, but by the time he had finished, and her drink was all gone, she had stopped shaking.

She even managed a wavering smile for him when, a little later still, she reached the half-landing and looked down to see him standing in the hallway, watching her with a troubled frown.

'I will be fine,' she assured him.

Though she did not believe the lie herself.

From then on, guilt and shame hung over her like a pall wherever she went, no matter how gaily she forced herself to smile.

If it were not for the importance of pushing Robert back into the circle of friends who were restoring him to health and vigour, she would have stayed in her rooms. Preferably in bed, with the covers drawn up over her head.

But she could not let him down too. She might be useless as a wife, but at least she was doing Robert some good.

She glanced across the crowded, stuffy room to the group of young men surrounding him tonight, earnestly discussing the latest news from France. Surreptitiously she crept away to find a quiet corner, where she could nurse her bruised spirits in relative peace.

Heloise did not notice the malevolent look Mrs Kenton arrowed her way, but the Honourable Percy Lampton did. Swiftly he made his way to Mrs Kenton's side.

'We have not spoken before—' he began.

'I am free to speak to anyone,' Mrs Kenton interrupted him, 'since I broke with Walton.'

Percy Lampton was a younger scion of the side of the

family she had been strictly forbidden by Charles to have anything to do with, if she valued her position.

'Even his wife?' Lampton said snidely. 'I don't think he would like to hear how you've been tormenting her.' He clucked his tongue reprovingly. 'Letting her think you are still in his keeping. In fact, I wonder at your daring. It can only be a matter of time before Walton finds out what you have been about, and when he does…'

'Are you threatening me?' She wrenched her eyes from Heloise to glare at him.

'Far from it.' He sidled closer. 'I am just wondering how far you would be prepared to go in your quest for revenge. It is revenge you want, is it not? Though why you feel entitled to seek it…' He shook his head in mock reproof. 'You must have known he would marry eventually. And that it could never be to a woman like you.'

Tears of chagrin stung her eyes. 'It would not have been so bad if she had been beautiful, or wealthy, or even from a good family. But to think he cast me off for *that*!' She gesticulated wildly in Lady Walton's direction.

Snagging a glass of champagne from a passing waiter, Lampton drew Mrs Kenton into a small antechamber.

'And what am I left with?' she continued, having downed the drink in one gulp. 'I was completely faithful to him, let other opportunities slip through my fingers for him, and now I have to start all over again…'

'In direct competition with nubile young nymphs like Nell.' He nodded sympathetically.

'I am still an attractive woman!' she spat at him.

All he did was raise one eyebrow, and she subsided. They both knew her career was in terminal decline.

'If it is any consolation to you, I happen to know that Walton married as he did purely to spite my family. Before he took off for Paris there were moves afoot to bring him back into the fold.' He smiled wryly. 'We had exactly what you described—a beautiful young woman of good family, who was also incidentally in our pockets—lined up to marry him. Is it so surprising he went off and married the first plain, poor foreigner he came across? She is Walton's little rebellion, nothing more. It must be obvious to you that Walton has no strong feelings for her personally. He has done the bare minimum required to stem speculation by arranging her presentation and squiring her to a few *ton* events. But on those occasions the chilliness of his demeanour towards her has been marked.'

'Has it?' Mrs Kenton had never actually seen them together, since she did not have an entrée to the upper echelons of society.

'Most marked.' Lampton grinned. 'And can you wonder at it? She is teetering on the verge of social ruin, coming to places like this. All she would need is one little push…'

Her eyes flashing with malice, she purred, 'What do you want me to do?'

'May I join you?'

Heloise looked up in annoyance. Just because she was sitting on her own, why did men assume she would welcome their attention? Did she have a sign pinned to her gown, saying 'This woman is a slut. Feel free to insult her?'

'I would prefer you did not,' she huffed, snapping her fan open and waving it before her face.

'Ah, I see you recognise me,' the man said cheerfully, taking the vacant seat beside her. 'But don't you think it a little silly to carry the feud so far? I can understand why Walton should not wish to have anything further to do with his mother's relatives, given their shoddy behaviour towards his brother,' the man persisted, 'but I had nothing to do with all that. I had not even been born!'

'You are of the family I am not supposed to acknowl-edge?' she guessed, examining his face properly for the first time. There was a strong resemblance, now she was looking for it. He was of the same height and build as Charles, though a good few years younger. His eyes were the same clear, pale blue, fringed with golden lashes. As they rested steadily on her, something about the coldness of his regard began to make her feel uneasy. And then, over his shoulder, she noticed Nell looking from one to the other of them, before scuttling off, wringing her hands in distress.

'Come, my lady,' he said, leaning closer. 'Why shouldn't we be friends? It is not as if your husband even has to know. I dare say he does not know the half of what you get up to, hmm?'

The knowing tone of his voice, the way he slid one arm along the back of her chair while extending one leg so that she felt trapped by his body, was jarringly familiar. Could this be the man who had kissed her at the masquerade?

'I am sure he does not know you attend bachelor parties alone, or that Captain Fawley has introduced you to gaming hells, does he?'

His smile was predatory, chilling her to the core. He must have been watching her every move, just waiting for the opportunity to strike.

'P…please, sir,' she begged him. 'Do not persecute me like this!'

'Oh, Lady Walton—there you are!' a female voice cut in.

Looking up, Heloise saw Mrs Kenton standing over them, with Nell hovering anxiously behind her.

'I have been looking for you everywhere. Have you forgot you promised to partner my friend at cards?'

'Oh, yes,' she replied, jumping hastily to her feet. She glimpsed a scowl marring the stranger's handsome features as she made her escape.

'Have you no sense?' Mrs Kenton hissed, as soon as they were far enough from her persecutor for him not to hear. 'Consorting with your husband's enemies? Don't you know how foolish it is to antagonise a man of his temperament?'

'I didn't know who he was when he sat down!' Heloise protested. 'And anyway, I tried to make him go away.'

'That was not what it looked like from where I was standing,' Mrs Kenton sneered. 'He had his arm round you! And you just sat there!'

What was she supposed to have done? Heloise had no experience of men approaching her with such determination and lack of respect.

Mrs Kenton would have known exactly how to put him off, a little voice whispered in her head. No! No, she would rather die than ask That Woman for advice. It was bad enough to suffer the humiliation of having to thank her for coming to her rescue. Which she could scarcely bring herself to do.

'I did not do it for you,' Mrs Kenton replied. 'But for Nell. She seemed to feel it was her fault Percy Lampton had cornered you. But if you will choose to loiter in secluded corners, what can you expect? Look, if you don't want predators like Lampton pawing at you, the thing to do is stay in full view, preferably in the company of several other people, engaging in some innocuous pastime like playing cards.'

She dragged Heloise into the card room, indicating the small knots of players grouped around the various tables. Plastering an alluring smile to her face, she approached two gentlemen who appeared to be waiting for her.

'Good evening Lord Matthison, Mr Peters,' she said, ushering Heloise towards the green baize table. 'I hope we have not kept you waiting too long?' Smoothing her skirts, Mrs Kenton took a seat opposite the older of the pair, a florid-faced, bewhiskered gentleman with a claret-stained cravat.

His companion, a dark, lean young man, regarded Heloise through world-weary eyes. 'May I hope you are at least a competent player?'

Heloise shrugged as she took her seat opposite him. Much as she hated to admit Mrs Kenton was correct, she would feel safer waiting for Robert in here, pretending to play cards, than falling prey to men like Lampton. 'I do not know. What game do we play?'

'Whist,' the whiskered gentleman grinned. 'And Lord Matthison boasted he could beat me, no matter who Mrs Kenton found to partner him!'

'Oh,' she sighed in relief. If her partner was such a good player, her lack of skill would not matter. 'I have never played whist before, my lord. Is it difficult to learn?'

Lord Matthison gave Mrs Kenton a hard look, before going through the rules with Heloise. They seemed fairly simple, and for the first few hands Heloise did not let her partner down too badly. She even managed to win a few tricks.

But then Lampton strolled into the room, a drink in his hand, and took up a position by the fireplace, from where he could observe her play at his leisure.

The looks he sent her were lascivious enough to make her squirm in her seat. She no longer doubted he was the man from the masquerade—the man to whom she had responded so shamefully! The longer he stood there, leering at her, the more worried she grew that he would use that interlude against Charles, somehow.

But what could she do to stop him?

'I think it is time to call it quits,' she eventually heard Lord Matthison drawl. 'It serves me right for not specifying that I could win were I partnered with any male. In future, miss,' he growled at her, 'you might try to remember that if you lead with a trump, your partner will assume you have a fist full of them. My congratulations, Peters—' he bowed to Mrs Kenton's partner '—on rolling me up so effectively.'

'Did I make you lose a lot of money?' Unsure of the value of what they had just lost at cards, Heloise began to chew at her lower lip.

'No more than I can afford,' he said shortly. 'And I hope the same goes for you. Though, judging by the pile of vowels Peters is holding, you may have to pledge your jewels until you can wheedle the cash from whichever poor sap paid for that expensive gown you have on.' Flicking her one last contemptuous look, Lord Matthison strode from the room, leaving her cringing on her chair.

He thought she was someone's whore! She hung her head. What else was a man to think, when it had been Mrs Kenton who had introduced them?

'Your bracelet,' she heard Mrs Kenton urging her in an undertone. 'Leave that as security until you can raise the ready.'

Still cringing at what she had led her whist partner to think, she peeled off the bracelet and dropped it onto the mound of IOU's she had written.

'How much is the total?' she asked.

'Five hundred guineas!' Mr Peters beamed.

'What the deuce—?'

At the sound of that voice, Heloise looked up to see Robert limping towards her, his face drained of colour.

'Heloise, you have never lost your bracelet at play?'

'It is just a pledge against what I owe,' she protested. 'I will get it back when I pay this gentleman.'

'You will oblige me by giving me your address,' Robert grated. 'I will deal with the matter on the lady's behalf.'

'With pleasure.' Peters grinned, scribbling on the back of a scrap of paper.

Robert did not speak to her again until they were safely tucked into Walton's closed carriage.

'I can't believe you dropped that bracelet on the table like that!'

'But I had run out of money. And I did not like to put any more vowels down. It is not as if the bracelet is all that valuable…'

'Not valuable! You little idiot! It is a family heirloom. A totally irreplaceable part of the Walton parure!'

'Y…yes, I suppose it would be difficult to match those funny yellow crystals…'

'They're not crystals, Heloise. They're diamonds. Extremely rare, extremely fine yellow diamonds.'

'I had no idea,' she admitted, beginning to feel a bit sick. 'But I have not really lost it. We can get it back when you pay Mr Peters what I owe.'

Robert subsided against the squabs, looking relieved. 'That's right. God!' He laughed. 'I wondered how on earth you had the nerve to wear those baubles at some of the places I took you to! I thought it was because you wanted to make Mrs Kenton jealous…' He shook his head ruefully. 'When all the time you had no idea…' He grinned. 'Never mind—it could be worse, I suppose. How much did you lose tonight, by the way?'

'Five hundred guineas.'

Robert went very still.

'What is the matter? Is that a great deal of money? I am not perfectly sure how many guineas there are to the pound, but I know it is not twenty. That is shillings…' She faltered. 'Or is that crowns?'

'I had thought I could bail you out,' he grated, 'if you had any difficulty raising the cash. But there's nothing for it now.

You are going to have to go to Walton and make a clean breast of it. You have lost a small fortune at play, and left a priceless heirloom as security against the debt. Only a man of his means will ever be able to redeem it. My God,' he breathed, 'he'll kill you. No, he won't, though—he'll kill me! He'll know you've no more notion than a kitten how to go on in society. It's all my fault for not taking better care of you. I've taken you to the lowest places, let you consort with prostitutes—and not just any prostitutes, oh, no! He will think I did this on purpose. And just when… Oh, hell.' Suddenly he looked very weary.

'Then we must not tell him!' She could not let Robert take the blame because she had been such a fool. 'There must be some other way to find the money. I have an allowance which I draw from Cummings. He might let me have an advance against next quarter!'

Robert shook his head. 'The only way to get hold of that kind of money in a hurry would be to go to a money lender. And for God's sake don't do that! Once they get you in your clutches, you'll never get out. No, there's nothing for it. We'll have to throw ourselves on Walton's mercy.'

'No,' she moaned, burying her face in her hands. It was not just a question of the gaming debt and losing the bracelet. She knew, once Charles looked at her in that cool, superior manner of his, that it would all come tumbling out. How jealous she was of his relationship with Mrs Kenton. This was precisely what her mother had warned her she must never do—behave like a jealous, possessive wife! And she had promised, too, that she would never cause him any trouble. She had broken the terms of their agreement twice over. He would never forgive her.

The carriage drew to a halt and a footman let down the steps. Her heart was in her mouth as they entered the hall together. It seemed the inevitable end to a disastrous evening when, just as she had taken off her cloak and handed it to a servant, the door to Charles' study swung open and he appeared in the doorway.

'Tell him now,' Robert murmured into her ear. 'The sooner you get it over with, the better for all of us.'

'Tell me what?' said Charles, advancing on them. 'Whatever it is you have to tell me had better be told in my study.' He stood to one side, inviting them into his domain with a wave of his arm.

Robert limped forward immediately.

'Care to join us, Lady Walton?' said Charles.

She had never felt so scared in all her life. But it would not be fair to let Robert face her husband alone. It was not his fault she had been stupidly goaded into gambling away a fortune by Charles' mistress. It had been her own stubborn pride that had done that. Not that she should have known who Mrs Kenton was, anyway. And Robert was right. Charles would blame him for that, too. There would be another fight between the two men, and the rift between them, which had begun to heal, would be ripped even wider. She could not let it happen.

Garnering all her courage, she followed Robert into the study, and joined him beside the desk.

Charles took the chair behind it, and gazed upon them with cool enquiry.

Neither of them could tell how fast his heart was beating as he braced himself to hear what he assumed would be the confession of their affair. He had not needed to question Heloise for long when he had trapped her in that box at the masquerade. She had confessed that Robert was her lover. Though she'd clearly felt guilty, bursting into tears and castigating herself for her loose morals, hearing the confirmation of his suspicions from her own lips had stunned him. He had reeled away from her in agonising pain and found himself somehow back here—waiting, as had become his habit, until he knew she was safely home.

They had both gone to Robert's rooms, rather than parting at the foot of the stairs as they normally did. It had been some considerable time before she had emerged, with a little smile playing about her lips as she floated up the stairs. Robert had stood in the hallway, gazing up at her, with a calculating expression on his face.

'Well?' he rapped out, when they had stood shuffling their feet and exchanging guilty looks for several minutes.

'I have taken Heloise to several places you would not like—' Robert began.

'The truth is,' Heloise blurted out, determined not to let him sacrifice himself for her, 'that when we went to that horrid masquerade some man assaulted me!'

Robert turned to her with a look of exasperation on his face. 'Hang on, Heloise, that's not—'

'No, Robert! Let me tell this my own way!'

With a shrug, he fell silent.

'Robert only left me for a minute or two unprotected, I promise you. It was not his fault. It was mine. I insisted that he ask a young lady to dance, since he had the idea that no woman will ever accept him with the injuries he has taken. And while he was engaged with her this man, whom I have never seen before, took me in his arms and…kissed me.'

'Did you enjoy the experience?' Charles enquired coldly.

Heloise gasped as though he had slapped her.

'What sort of question is that?' Robert put in, aghast. 'She was naturally terribly upset! The point is, I had no business taking her to such a place…'

'Is this all?' Charles enquired politely, looking down at a sheaf of papers on his desk. Frowning, he moved the top sheet, as though something of interest had caught his eye. Certain that they were about to confess what had gone on between them behind closed doors, under his very roof, he was filled with such cold fury he could not bear to look at either of them. The only hope left to him was that he might be able to salvage his pride by masking his true state of mind while he waited for the blow to fall.

'Yes, that is all!' Heloise flung at him, her face white with fury. 'Come, Robert. You can see that to him it is nothing!'

She flounced out, Robert hard on her heels.

'Heloise! Wait!' Robert cried.

She paused halfway up the stairs and glared down at him.

'I told you we would have to find another way!' she whispered, aware that the door to Charles' study was not properly closed.

'You haven't confessed the whole yet—'

'What would be the point? I would die rather than tell him what happened tonight. Besides, if he finds out I have thrown away something you say he values so highly, he will banish me to the country—or put me aside altogether...'

'No, he won't. A gentleman doesn't divorce his wife over—'

'Gentleman! I do not even know what you mean by that term any more. Except that it is a nature that is cold and proud and unapproachable! I will not beg him to rescue me ever again! I wish I had not done so in the first place! Du Mauriac is dead, after all, and I would have been able to stay with my parents, who, though they think I am an imbecile, at least let me draw what I wish!'

While Robert's brow pleated in perplexity at this statement he found incomprehensible, in his study Charles clutched his head in his hands.

He had known from the start that she should not have carried on with the marriage once Du Mauriac was out of the picture.

Stifling a groan, he went to the study door and closed it.

'I will find a way to raise the money myself!' Heloise declared defiantly, storming off up the stairs.

In his study, Charles paced the carpet, too agitated even to pause to pour himself a drink. It would not soothe him, anyway. Nothing could ever ease the agony of hearing Heloise declare she wished she had never married him.

He had done all in his power to reconcile her to her position. To demonstrate she need not fear him he had allowed her more freedom than even the most besotted of men would accord their bride. He had put no pressure on her to conform to his requirements, imposed no restrictions on her movements, no matter how close she had sailed to the wind. And for what?

As he passed the window, he caught sight of his reflection in the panes of glass. Could this wild-haired, wild-eyed man really be him? Within two months of being married his wife had reduced him to this?

He should never have kissed her. That had been his greatest error. Now that he knew what she felt like under his hands, his mouth, he could more readily imagine his brother's hands shaping her breasts, his brother's mouth plundering her soft, responsive lips.

A strangled cry escaped his throat as he whirled away from the reflection of a man whose blood was infected with a form of madness. For no sane man would experience such rage, such despair, such self-disgust! Where was the cool, untouchable man who had always believed that to give way to strong emotion was a sign of weakness?

He flung himself into his chair, dropping his head to his hands. He had to get a grip on himself.

Straightening up, he drew several long, deep breaths through flared nostrils.

He *must* look at this situation dispassionately. The facts were these: his wife, for whom he felt more than he had ever imagined he could feel for any woman, did not return his affection.

Second, in spite of his forbearance, she had decided to humiliate him by taking a lover before providing him with an heir.

Decided? He shook his head. Heloise was too impulsive a creature to decide upon such a course of action. She had just followed her heart. She had been brought up by parents who had eloped in the teeth of opposition, and had applauded her sister for jilting him for the sake of her 'true love'. She had not meant to betray him. In fact, letting him know she was going to that masquerade could have been a cry for help. She had known she was on the slippery slope to adultery, and her tender conscience had been troubling her.

But as for Robert... His fist clenched on the arm of the chair. Robert was getting the perfect revenge. Cuckolding his despised brother under his own roof, secure in the knowledge there would be no divorce to expose him for the scoundrel he was. And if Heloise fell pregnant Robert's child would inherit the property from which he had been excluded. For Walton would be obliged to acknowledge the bastard as his own if he wanted to shield Heloise from disgrace.

And he did. He lowered his head, his face contorted with anguish. He would not permit her to run off with Robert and live a hand-to-mouth existence as the whore of an invalid on a meagre army pension.

He got to his feet and strode to the door. He must tell her, and tell her now, that he would not permit that. Though she might not think so, she would do far better to give up her foolish dreams and accept her lot. She was staying with him!

He took the stairs two at a time, flung open the door to

her suite, and crossed the darkened sitting room to her bedroom.

When she saw him, her eyes widened with apprehension. It infuriated him to see her draw the sheet up to her chin, as though he were the villain of the piece! Losing control of the ragged edges of his temper, he strode to the bed, ruthlessly yanking the covers from her fingers.

'You are my wife—' he began.

'Yes, I know, and I am so sorry! I never meant to—'

He laid his fingers to her lips, stopping her mouth. He did not want to hear her confess what he had already worked out for himself. She had only followed where her heart led.

'I know you couldn't help yourself.'

Beneath his fingers, her lips parted in surprise. 'You are not angry?' Had Robert told him everything after she had left? 'Oh, Charles,' she sighed, tears of remorse slipping down her cheeks. 'Can you forgive me?'

Cupping her face between his hands, he brushed those tears away with his thumbs. Could he forgive her? Wasn't that asking rather too much? With a groan of anguish, he gathered her into his arms and buried his face in her hair.

And suddenly he knew, with blinding clarity, that if he could have her once—just this once—then his future would not be so unbearable. For he could make himself believe that any child she bore might be his.

And so he pushed the nightgown from her shoulders, grating, 'Just this once. Just tonight.'

'Yes,' she sighed, winding her arms about his neck and sinking back into the pillows.

It was her guilt that motivated her to offer him this comfort, he was sure. But he was desperate enough to take whatever he could get. Swearing to himself that he would never take advantage of her in this manner again, he followed her down and for the next few moments let his hot need of her sweep aside all his scruples. He forgot everything but Heloise: the sweetness of her lips, the softness of her skin, the heat of her breath pulsing against his throat.

And then, searing his soul like a whip cracking into naked flesh, the sound of her agonised cry as he took her virginity.

CHAPTER TEN

CHARLES could not credit that he had been so wrong about her.

'I beg your pardon,' he said lamely. Where was the rule of etiquette to cover an occasion like this? 'If I'd had any idea you were a virgin…'

She had been lying beneath him with her eyes screwed shut. Now they flew open, full of disbelieving hurt, as though he had struck her.

'Of *course* I was a virgin!' How could he think she would break her marriage vows? Didn't he know she would rather die than be disloyal to him in any way?

The shuttered expression on his face only added to her feeling of humiliation. She had imagined that he had finally come to her bed because he had begun to find her desirable.

Instead it had been an expression of his contempt. He thought she was the kind of woman who…

'Ooh!' she cried, pummelling at his shoulders. 'I hate you! I hate you!'

He reared back, appalled at the mess he had made of things.

Pausing only long enough to snatch up his clothes, he fled from her bedroom, chastened, sickened and shaken.

He might just have destroyed whatever slim chance there had been to make something of their marriage.

He sank to the floor, his back pressed to his bedroom door, his clothing bundled up against his chest.

'Heloise,' he groaned. 'My God, what have I done?'

Alone in the dark, Heloise rolled onto her side, drew her knees up, and let the tears flow.

He must have heard rumours about the places she had been, the company she had kept, and jumped to the worst possible conclusion.

And why wouldn't he? It was only what Lord Matthison had deduced within minutes of meeting her.

Dawn found her gritty-eyed from weeping. When Sukey came in with her breakfast, her throat was so hoarse she could barely croak a dispirited dismissal.

How could she eat anything, when she'd just had her last shred of hope ripped from her? And what was the point of getting dressed and going out, acting as if her life had meaning any more? He had come to her bed. For whatever reason, he had finally decided to make her his wife in fact as well as in name—and what had she done? Lashed out at him. Told him she hated him. Driven him away.

She lay under a black cloud of despair until noon, when Sukey came back, bearing yet another tray of food.

'I told you to leave me alone,' she sighed wearily.

'Begging your pardon, my lady, but His Lordship insisted you had something to eat when I told him you wasn't getting up today.'

His feigned solicitude ground her spirits still lower. Even though he regarded her as an infernal nuisance, he would always fulfil his responsibilities towards her in the most punctilious fashion. Appearances were everything to Charles.

He would not want the servants to know there was anything amiss between them. He most definitely would not want her confiding in Sukey that she wished she had never set eyes on him.

Forcing her lips into a parody of a smile, she murmured, 'How thoughtful,' and propped herself up on the pillows so that Sukey could place the tray across her lap.

For appearances' sake she picked at the food while Sukey drew back the curtains, tidied the room, and poured water into her washbasin. The sound made her aware of how sticky and uncomfortable she felt. She could at least cleanse herself, put off her ruined nightgown and dress in clean clothes.

In some ways, she thought some time later, sitting down at the dressing table so that Sukey could comb out her tangled hair, this would be the perfect time to go to him and confess what a scrape she was in. It was not as if he could possibly think any worse of her.

Could he? Her heart twisted into a knot at the prospect she could sink any lower in his estimation.

No, she would not tell him about the bracelet. Somehow she would get it back. She lifted her chin and met her own eyes in the mirror. He would not divorce her. Robert had been adamant about that. So she had a lifetime to reverse the poor opinion he had formed.

And, judging by the way things had gone between them so far, a lifetime would be how long it would take.

Still, Robert was so much better. She need not go anywhere with him again. Though most of his friends were completely respectable, if not of her husband's elevated status, women like Mrs Kenton hovered on the fringes of his world. She had no intention of locking horns with her again. She would just stay in her rooms if Charles did not require her presence at his side. If she grew really bored she would take the occasional walk in the park, with Sukey. And a footman for good measure. She would put Mrs Kenton right out of her mind, and concentrate on being such a model of rectitude that even Charles would be able to see he had misjudged her.

And in the meantime she would cudgel her brains until she came up with a way of raising enough money to pay off her gambling debts and recover the bracelet. Before Charles noticed it had gone missing.

She dismissed Sukey, needing to be alone to think. After pacing the floor fruitlessly for a while, she went to her desk and pulled out her supply of paper from under the layers of petticoats in the bottom drawer. 'Five hundred guineas', she scrawled across the top of a fresh sheet. How on earth could a woman honestly raise such a sum without going to money lenders?

As her mind guiltily replayed the way she had accumulated the debt, her hands instinctively began to portray that fateful game of whist. She drew herself first, as a plump little pigeon, being plucked by a bewhiskered gamekeeper with a smoking gun at his feet. In the background she added a caricature of Percy Lampton as a pale-eyed fox, licking his lips from his vantage point in a hedge whose leaves bore a marked resemblance to playing cards.

Suddenly she came out of that reverie which often came over her when she was sketching. People—artists like Thomas Rowlandson, for example—made a living by selling cartoons. She had seen them in bound copies in Charles' library, and lying around the homes of Robert's bachelor friends. Depictions of sporting heroes, or lampoons of political figures were very popular. She recalled how amused the ladies from the embassy in Paris had been by the sketchbook that Charles had forced her to burn.

Her heart began to beat very fast. She dropped to her knees and scrabbled through the second to bottom drawer, where she stashed her finished works. Whenever she returned from an outing with Charles, she sketched the people who had particularly amused or annoyed her. Politicians, doyennes of society, even the occasional royal duke had all fallen victim to her own very idiosyncratic interpretation of their foibles. If only she could find someone to publish them, she was sure she could make money from her drawings!

She pulled them all out and rolled them up together, then went to the fireplace and tugged on the bell to summon her maid. She would need string, brown paper, and a cab. She was most definitely not going to turn up at a prospective employer's door in the Walton coach, with her husband's family crest emblazoned on the panels. Not only would that advertise her predicament, but his driver would be bound to report back to Charles where he had taken her. She hoped Sukey would know where to find a print shop, so that they could give an address to the cab driver.

Oh, Lord, she was *still* engaged in activities of which he would disapprove. She pressed her hands to her cheeks, taking a deep, calming breath. It would not be for much longer. Once she had paid off this debt she would never do anything Charles might frown at. Never again.

Charles twirled the pen round in his fingers, staring blindly at the rows of leatherbound books which graced the wall of the library opposite his desk. He had never felt so low in his life. Until now he had always been sure that whatever he did, no matter how harsh it might seem to disinterested observers, was the right thing to do.

He could not understand now, in the clear light of day, what had driven him to act in such a reprehensible, nay, criminal fashion last night.

If only he could go to her and beg her forgiveness. Wrap

her in his arms and at least hold her while she wept. And he knew she was weeping. Sukey had whispered as much to Finch, the youngest of his footmen, when she had taken the untouched breakfast tray back to the servants' hall. He could not bear to think of her lying up there alone, with no one to comfort her. But he was the very last person she would wish to see this morning.

At midday he had insisted Sukey check on her again. To his great relief Heloise had nibbled on some toast and drunk most of a cup of chocolate. She had then risen, washed her puffy eyes in cold water, and donned her long-sleeved morning gown with the apricot lace flounces. Finch had yielded this information to Giddings, who had informed His Lordship when he brought a cold collation—which Charles had not ordered—to the library, from where he could not find the energy to stir.

Mechanically, he bit into the slice of cold mutton pie Giddings had slid onto his plate, only to leap up at the sound of small feet crossing the hall, followed by the noise of the front door slamming.

Wiping his mouth with his linen napkin, he strode into the hall, Giddings at his heels.

'Where has she gone?' Charles barked at Finch, who froze in an attitude of guilt by the console table.

'I am sorry, my lord, I do not know.'

'She did not order the coach,' Giddings mused. 'She must not intend to go far.'

Charles was barely able to restrain the impulse to race upstairs and check her cupboards, to see if she had packed her bags and left him. Good God, losing Felice was as nothing compared to what it would be like if Heloise should desert him.

Barely suppressing the panic that clutched coldly at his stomach, he fixed a baleful stare on the hapless Finch, and asked, 'What was she carrying?'

'Umm…' Finch thought for a moment. 'Well, nothing as I can recall. Though Sukey had what looked like a long sort of tube thing.' He frowned. 'Might have been a parasol, wrapped up in brown paper.'

A parasol? A woman did not run away from her husband armed only with a parasol, whether she had wrapped it in brown paper or not. He ran a shaky hand over his face as he returned to the relative sanctuary of his library. He could not go on like this. Whether she could believe in his remorse, whether she could ever forgive him, or even understand what had driven him to say what he had, was beside the point. He had to tell her he would accept whatever terms she cared to name so long as she promised not to leave him.

It was late when she returned. He decided to give her only sufficient time to put off her coat and take some refreshment before going up to her room with the speech it had taken him all afternoon to perfect.

Five more minutes, he thought, snapping his watch closed and returning it to his waistcoat pocket.

He looked up, on hearing a slight noise from the doorway, to see Giddings making an apologetic entrance.

'Begging your pardon, my lord, but there is a man who insists you will want to see him. When I informed him you were not receiving, he told me to give you this.' Giddings laid a rolled-up piece of paper on the desk, concluding, 'He is awaiting your answer in the small salon. I would have left him in the hall, but he insisted that the matter was of the utmost delicacy, and that he did not wish Her Ladyship to see him.'

Charles' hand shot out to unroll the single sheet of drawing paper. He could see, after one glance, that it was his wife's work.

It was the night he had taken her to the theatre. The boxes that overlooked the stage were populated by various creatures, though the one which leapt out at him was a sleek black panther, with one paw upon the neck of the sheep who shared his box. It was Lensborough to the life, and the sheep undoubtedly the silly young lightskirt he currently had in keeping. The stage was populated by a flock of sheep, too, with ribbons in their curly fleeces, and all of them with wide, vulnerable eyes. The audience that filled the pit comprised a pack of wolves, their tongues hanging out as they eyed the helpless morsels penned on the stage.

Was this what Sukey had been carrying this afternoon when she had gone out with Heloise? Not a parasol, however disguised, but this picture, rolled up just as Giddings had presented it to him? And, if so, where had she taken it—and who was the man who had brought it back to him?

For the first time that day Charles recalled that Heloise had other troubles than being married to a man she'd grown to hate. Last night Robert had tried to make her tell him what they were. Instead of listening to her, he had totally lost his head and driven her away, confirming her opinion that he was 'cold and proud and unapproachable'.

'Send the fellow in,' he ordered Giddings. Seating himself behind the desk, he schooled his features so that they revealed nothing of his inner turmoil. That this man had one of his wife's sketches and had dared to use it as a calling card was enough to set his back up. If the scoundrel was in any way connected with whatever it was that was troubling his wife, he would soon learn he had made a bad mistake. Charles would destroy him. Slowly, painfully and completely.

'Mr Rudolph Ackermann,' Giddings announced, somewhat surprising Charles. This man was a reputable publisher, not the sort he would have expected to dabble in blackmail.

'Thank you for agreeing to see me,' Ackermann said, coming to stand before the Earl's desk. 'I apologise for the unorthodox method I employed—' he indicated the sketch that lay on the desk between them '—but I needed to get your attention.'

'You have it, sir,' Charles replied. 'State your business.' He did not invite the man to sit. Nor did he ask Giddings to bring in refreshments before dismissing him.

'Your wife came to my offices on the Strand this afternoon,' Ackermann began, the second the door closed behind Giddings. 'I would not have admitted her had she not brought her maid along. Indeed, at first, I assumed she wanted to make a purchase.'

He ran a finger round his collar, clearly growing uncomfortable under the Earl's hostile scrutiny.

'Instead, she produced a bundle of her own work, and asked me if I would pay her for them, and for as many more as would be needed to make up a volume for public sale. Since she was clearly a lady of quality, I thought it best to humour her by pretending to examine her drawings. I was amazed at how wickedly comical they were. For a while I got quite carried away with the notion of actually bringing out a book along the lines of *The Schoolmaster's Tour*. We even discussed calling it *The French Bride's Season...*' His voice faltered under the Earl's wintry stare.

'Of course,' he blustered, 'I came to my senses almost at once.' He sighed, looking wistfully at Heloise's sketch of her night at the theatre. 'I realised that such a scheme would be abhorrent to a man like you.' He cleared his throat. 'Not that she told me her real name. Indeed, I was only completely sure of her identity after my clerk returned—that is, the lad I sent to follow her home—and he told me the address of the house she came into.'

The Earl's eyes bored into Ackermann's. 'You say my wife brought you a bundle of her work? I assume you are now going to tell me you hold the rest in safekeeping?'

Ackermann looked relieved. 'Precisely so. If I had not persuaded her that I would buy them all she would simply have taken them to another publisher. Someone who might not share my scruples.'

'Scruples?' the Earl repeated, his lips twisting into a cynical sneer.

'Yes.' Ackermann's face set in implacable lines as he finally understood what the Earl was implying. 'My lord, my business relies on the goodwill of men of your class. If I were to expose your wife to scandal I know full well you would break me. I have taken what steps I could, in good faith, to prevent Lady Walton's actions from coming to light. I gave her a modest payment, to ensure she would not think of going to someone who might enjoy seeing you humiliated...'

'A modest payment?'

'Five guineas.'

'You make a poor sort of blackmailer if all you require of me is five guineas.'

Ackermann looked as though he was hanging onto his temper by the merest thread. 'Whoever may be blackmailing your wife, it is not I. Though she is clearly trying to raise a large sum of money in a hurry.'

Charles stroked his chin thoughtfully. He took another look at the sketch, then at Ackermann's indignant posture, recalling his wife's distress in this very room the night before.

'How much money did she say she wanted?'

'Five hundred guineas.'

For several minutes Charles said nothing.

Heloise was in need of five hundred guineas, but she

found him so unapproachable she would probably rather die than ask him for anything. Especially now.

And yet... He tapped on the arm of his chair thoughtfully. If he could somehow supply her with the funds she needed, in such a way that he did not appear as the tyrant of her imagination...

'Take a seat, Mr Ackermann,' he said. 'While I spell out exactly what I wish you to do for me.'

CHAPTER ELEVEN

HELOISE did not know whether to massage her aching wrist or rub at the frown that felt like a hot knife welded between her eyebrows. She had sat up all night, putting finishing touches to any half-started sketches she could find, so that she could impress Mr Ackermann with her industry at this morning's interview.

Although if he was only going to give her five guineas per drawing, she had realised just as she was climbing into the cab, she would have to sell him another ninety-nine to clear the debt. It would take her months to raise five hundred guineas this way. Even if he agreed to buy everything she ever drew, which was hardly likely.

She slumped back into the grimy leather seat, chewing at her lower lip. She still had Felice's emerald ring. Charles had said it was quite valuable. Since she was never going to wear it, it might as well go the way her sister had originally intended.

And, since she was never going out again, she would not be needing all the expensive gowns Charles had bought her. In Paris she had thought nothing of going to peddlers of second-hand clothes. There was bound to be a similar market in London. Particularly for beautifully embroidered creations from the salon of Madame Pichot.

By the time the cab reached its destination Heloise was drawn tight as a bowstring. Since it was a bad business tactic to reveal her state of nerves, she pulled her shoulders down and raised her chin as she took a seat in Mr Ackermann's office. The drawings she had left with him the day before were already spread across his desk. He took her latest offerings, slowly perusing every single page.

Little shafts of hope streaked through her every time his lips twitched in amusement. He hovered for the longest time over her depiction of her presentation. At first glance it looked as though she had drawn a lily pond, surrounded by reeds amongst which elegant herons were poised, eyeing the fat carp drowsing in the shallows. The puffed-up toads squatting on their lily pads were easy enough to identify. It took him a little longer to work out which personage each fish or bird represented.

'Is this all you have?' he eventually asked her.

'Yes, but I promise you I can produce as many as you wish. I will work every hour of the day and night...'

'No, no.' He held up his hand to stop her. 'I shan't need any more.'

When her face fell, he swiftly explained, 'I am willing to give you five hundred guineas for what we have here.'

She gasped, pressing her hands to her cheeks as he slid an envelope across the desk towards her. 'You are giving me all the money now? Just like that?'

'Just like that,' he replied, with a wry twist to his mouth.

She grabbed the envelope before he changed his mind, and tried to stuff it into her reticule. It would not fit. Even folded, it was far too bulky. She clutched it to her bosom, bowing her head as a wave of faintness washed over her. It was terrifying to have so much money on her person. What if she lost it? She had to get home and hand it over to Robert at once. She leapt to her feet and made blindly for the door.

Once there, she turned back, gasping, 'I am sorry if I appear rude, but so large a sum of money…'

The strangest look flitted across his face. It was almost as though he pitied her. But his brisk, 'Good morning,' as he began to tidy her drawings from his desk-top was such a businesslike dismissal she decided that in her nervous state she must have imagined it.

As soon as the door had closed behind her, the Earl of Walton emerged from his place of concealment. Sparing only a second to nod his acknowledgement to Mr Ackerman for playing his part so well, Charles set out in hot pursuit of his wife.

He hated resorting to following her like this. But how else was he to find out why she needed five hundred guineas? He had abandoned the idea of simply demanding an explanation almost as soon as it had occurred to him. He would not give her any further grounds for accusing him of bullying her.

It was not long before it became apparent she was going straight home. He bit down on a feeling of frustration as he watched her climb the front steps. He might have to shadow her movements closely for some time before discovering what she intended to do with the money.

He slipped into the hall so soon after her that the footman did not even have time to close the door behind her.

And saw her disappearing into Robert's rooms.

She had flown straight to him!

It always came back, somehow, to Robert.

A series of images flitted in rapid succession through his brain. Heloise embracing Robert in this hall, telling him he was her only friend. Heloise wafting up the stairs with a smile playing about her lips after the masquerade.

Given her family's propensity for eloping at the drop of a hat, he could only draw one conclusion.

Thrusting his hat into the hovering footman's out-stretched hands, he strode across the hall, pushing Linney aside as he plunged into his brother's rooms hard on his wife's heels.

And caught her holding out the envelope containing the money—his money—to Robert.

They both froze, looking at him just like two children caught with their hands in the biscuit barrel.

A vision of her in some French farmyard feeding chickens flashed into his mind. Robert emerged from a shadowy doorway, put his arm about her waist and kissed her cheek. She smiled up at him, the picture of content-ment...

Charles could not bring himself to say a word. He felt as if he was teetering on the edge of an abyss, and one wrong move would send him hurtling eternally downwards.

Until this moment he had not really believed she hated him. She had said it once before, in the heat of the moment. When she had calmed down, she had admitted she had not really meant it.

But here was the evidence she could not bear to spend another moment as his wife.

It was his own fault. He had treated her abominably. He had left her shaking and crying at the masquerade. No wonder she had turned to Robert for comfort. He had prac-tically driven her into his arms. And, worse, he had flung his mistrust in her face at the worst possible moment...

He drew in a ragged breath. This time, no matter what it cost him, he would hold his anger in check until he had learned the truth. All of it. Whatever it might be.

Only then would he deal with it—or rather find a way to survive losing both his brother and his wife in one fell swoop.

Like an automaton, he crossed the room to the fireplace

and propped himself against the mantel, folding his arms across his chest.

Eyeing Robert, who was reaching for the crutches that were propped on the arm of the sofa on which he sprawled, he ground out, 'I think it is high time someone told me exactly what is going on.'

'Tell him, Lady Walton,' ordered Robert, letting the crutches fall.

'I cannot!' Heloise stood rooted to the spot, the money clutched in her hands, large tears welling in eyes that stared at him piteously from a pinched white face.

'Then I will,' Robert declared, pulling himself to a more upright posture. 'It's no use trying to hide it from him any longer. The game's up.'

'Robert!' she cried, rounding on him as though he had betrayed her.

'It is far better for Charles to act for you in this matter,' he went on mulishly. 'I said so from the start.'

Act for her? These were not the words of a man contemplating eloping with his brother's wife. Nor was his exasperated tone in the least lover-like. A great weight seemed to roll from Charles' shoulders.

'Perhaps you would find it easier to confide in me if I were to tell you that I know you were trying to sell your drawings, and that it was, in fact, I who supplied the publisher with the five hundred guineas in that package?'

Heloise let out a strangled cry, dropping to a chair and covering her face with her hands. She should have known no businessman would pay so much money for the dozen or so drawings she had given him. They were probably not worth a sou!

'I can see I have been even more stupid than usual,' she said, turning the packet over in her hands.

She would have to tell Charles everything. And then he

would be so angry with Robert. He would say things that might alienate them from each other for ever. They were both of them so deucedly proud! Insults, once spoken, would not be easily retracted or forgiven by either. And it would all be her fault.

Perhaps if she could tell Charles alone, and he had time to calm down before confronting Robert…

'Robert,' she said, getting to her feet and dropping the mangled package onto the cushion beside him, 'you know what to do with this. Charles—' She turned to him, lifting her chin. 'If you will spare me a few moments, I will tell you the whole.' She took a few steps towards the door. 'In my sitting room.'

To her great relief, not a second after she quit Robert's rooms, she heard Charles' tread on the staircase behind her.

'Please—won't you sit down?' She waved him to a chair to one side of the fireplace once she had dismissed Sukey. Nervously, she perched on the one opposite. 'I p…promised you before we married that I would not be any trouble to you at all, but I have got into such a terrible mess! I do not know where to start.'

'Start with the pictures,' Charles said grimly. 'I should very much like to hear why you felt obliged to run round town selling your work for a paltry sum…'

'It is not a paltry sum. Robert said it was a small fortune!'

'Well, I have a large fortune at my disposal. For heaven's sake, Heloise, am I such an ogre that you cannot even apply to me for funds when you need them?'

'It is not at all that I think you are an ogre. But that I have broken my word and did not want to admit it. Nor why I broke it! I have done all that is reprehensible. And then I lost all that money at cards…'

'Gaming debts.' Why had he never considered that she might have been fleeced at cards? He shook his head. 'I have

even made you think I would not meet your gaming debts,'
he said bleakly.

Wringing her hands, she plunged on. 'I am the imbecile.
Maman warned me I must not mind about your mistresses,
but when I saw her, with those rubies you chose for her, and
her air of such sophistication, while I had only those horrid
yellow stones… But then Robert said they were diamonds,
and priceless, and I knew how angry you would be that I
was such a ninny—but how could I know?' She got to her
feet then, pacing a few feet away before turning to exclaim,
'You said you had got them cleaned, and handed them to
me as though they meant nothing. I thought you could not
bother to go out to a jeweller and buy anything just for me.
I did not know,' she sniffed, dashing a solitary tear from her
cheek, 'I swear I did not know how valuable that bracelet
was, and if I had known what a vile place the Opera House
was I would never have made Robert take me there. He
warned me, but I would not listen, so it was entirely my own
fault that horrid man kissed me—'

'Just stop right there!' Getting to his feet, Charles crossed
the room and took hold of her firmly by her shoulders.

He had considered once before that there might be only
one way to stop his wife when she was in full flow.

He employed it now. Ruthlessly, he crushed her lips
beneath his own, knowing she would not welcome the kiss,
but completely unable to resist. When he thought how close
he had come to accusing her of infidelity again… He shuddered. Thank God he had managed to rein in his abominable
jealousy!

'Ch…Charles,' was all she could manage, in a strangled
whisper, when he finally pulled away. Why had he kissed
her when he was clearly very angry with her?

As he looked down into her distraught face, he knew he
still had a long way to go. Though she had not been planning

to run off with Robert, he had still been the one she had run to in a panic, assuming she had nowhere else to turn.

Gently, he tugged her to sit beside him on one of her prettily brocaded sofas.

'Heloise,' he explained, 'anyone can get badly dipped at cards. You should have just told me.'

'I was too ashamed,' she admitted. 'I knew I should not have been playing at all, when I am so useless at counting, but when Mrs Kenton looked at me with such contempt I felt I had to prove I could be as good as her at something! And then, because it was the house of one of Robert's respectable friends, and not a gaming hell like some we had been to, I was not on my guard. And nobody told me a guinea was worth more than a pound!' she complained, as though the injustice of this had just struck her. 'Why must you English have crowns and shillings, and guineas, and everything be so complicated?'

'That is the second time you have mentioned Mrs Kenton,' Charles said sternly. 'Would you mind telling me how you came to make her acquaintance?'

Determined to protect Robert as far as she was able, Heloise said, 'Nell introduced us.' When Charles looked puzzled, she explained, 'Lord Lensborough's mistress. They are friends.'

'Yes, but how came you to be acquainted with a woman like Nell—if that is her name?'

'Why should it not be her name? She is entitled to a name, like any other person. Just because to earn her living she has to—'

Charles took the only certain method of silencing his wife once again.

'If you cannot keep to the point, madam wife, I will have to keep kissing you, you know.' He wanted more than anything to rain kisses all over her dear little face. But her reaction told him she would not be receptive to such a demonstration of affection.

She disentangled herself from his arms, her cheeks flushing mutinously. So he kissed her to punish her, did he? A perverse excitement thrilled through her veins. She only had to defy him, then, and he might kiss her again! Oh, if only she were not so determined to clear her name and prove she was not the amoral hussy that Englishmen all seemed to assume, just because she did not follow the stricter rules their society imposed on Englishwomen.

While she was still dithering between his kisses and his contempt on the one hand, or his respect with coldness on the other, he said, quite sternly, 'Heloise, you should not be socialising with women like Nell and...Mrs Kenton...'

'No, Maman warned me that I must pretend not to know about your mistress. But this was absurd when we walked into each other. How am I supposed to ignore a woman who is standing right in front of me?'

Felice would have done it with relish, he reflected. She had a way of cutting people, a haughty tilt to her head sometimes when she took offence at something said to her, that had made it easy for him to envisage her as his Countess. She would have had no trouble ripping his discarded mistress to shreds. She could easily have become the sharpest-clawed of all the tabbies in town. He swallowed suddenly on the frightening prospect. But Heloise—his sweet, good-natured, straightforward little pea-goose—needed his support and his care in a way Felice would never have done. A feeling of hope warmed his veins. She had based at least some of her actions on a couple of misapprehensions about him. If he could clear those up, perhaps he could begin to redeem his character in her eyes.

'Heloise,' he said, steeling himself for the kind of conversation a man as fastidious as himself should never have to have with his wife, 'Mrs Kenton is not my mistress.'

'Don't lie to me, Charles! Everyone knows those rubies she flaunts were a gift from you.'

'She *was* my mistress. That much is true. But, for your information, those rubies were my parting gift. I gave them to her before I left for Paris. And now we will not mention her again. In that I have to agree with your *maman*. I should not have to discuss my mistress with my wife.'

Heloise did not question how she knew he was telling the truth.

But that cat had deliberately made her think the relationship was current!

Indignantly, Heloise leapt to her feet, pacing back and forth as she assessed how the woman had deliberately played on her insecurities, taunted her into playing beyond her means, and finally goaded her into parting with the bracelet she must have known was priceless.

'Oh!' she cried in vexation, flinging herself back onto the sofa. 'She has made a complete fool of me.' Suddenly sitting up straight, as another thought occurred to her, she exclaimed, 'And *he* was in it too! Percy Lampton!'

'Lampton?' Charles grated, his hackles rising. He might have known the Lamptons would do their utmost to hurt his chosen bride.

'Yes—he persecuted me until Mrs Kenton and her game of cards seemed like a perfectly reasonable means of escape. And he kissed me, too!' she concluded, remembering the assault at the Opera House.

'He *what*?'

A shiver of dread ran down his spine. Apparently Lampton would stop at nothing. Oh, he no longer feared Heloise would stray into an adulterous affair. He must have been mad to suspect her integrity for so much as a second!

But a ruthless swine like Lampton would only have to get her into a compromising position, arranging things so that there were witnesses, and his wife's reputation would be in tatters.

It was no use hoping she would suddenly start trusting him enough to listen to any warning he had to give her. The only sure way to keep her safe would be to remove her from that man's reach altogether.

'We will have to leave London.'

He would take her down to Wycke, his principal seat. And while they were there he would make sure she spent at least some part of each day in his company. There were so few other distractions to amuse a city-bred girl like Heloise that she would soon welcome any company—even his. He would rein in his absurd jealousy, treat her with the kindness and consideration a young bride deserved, and maybe, just maybe, she might come to regard him as a patient, devoted husband rather than the unapproachable tyrant of her imagination. God, how he wanted to kiss her again! If only she didn't freeze whenever he took her into his arms, and then look at him with those bemused, wounded eyes when he let her go.

'I just need to clarify one point,' he said. 'Will the money you gave Robert today clear all your outstanding debts, or is there anything else I should know before we leave town?'

'Th…that is all,' she stammered, amazed that he was taking it all so calmly.

He nodded, relieved that she had at least had someone she could turn to for help—but, dammit! He swore to himself, rising to his feet. He should have taken better care of her!

She tensed as he turned his back on her. Did that outward calm only conceal a deep disgust of her failings?

'I am sorry, Charles—' she began.

He rounded on her, a strange gleam in his eye. '*You* are sorry?'

Her heart sank as she saw he was not going to accept her apology. He was not going to give her a chance to prove she had learned a valuable lesson and would never behave so foolishly again. He was just going to pack her off to the country, where she could not do his reputation any damage.

'I suppose,' she muttered mutinously, 'I should thank you for not threatening to cast me off without a penny.'

He flinched as though she had struck him. 'You are my wife, Heloise. A man does not cast his wife off for being a trifle expensive. I might scold, or preach economy, or...' Manfully, he strove to gentle his voice. 'The truth is, you are the least expensive female I have ever—' He broke off, cursing himself for this tactless turn of phrase.

But it was too late.

Stiffening proudly, Heloise replied, 'Yes, in that I should have listened to Mrs Kenton. She told me how generous you are.'

Damn Mrs Kenton, he thought, slamming himself out of the room. If she was here now, he would be sorely tempted to wring her neck!

Heloise watched a Dresden shepherdess on a console table beside the door rock dangerously before settling on its plinth. Could she never learn to control her tongue when she was with Charles? He had told her it was not suitable to speak about his mistress, and what had she done? Dragged her straight back into the conversation again.

No wonder he felt he had no option but to pack her off to one of his country estates. It was she, after all, who had put the notion into his head when she had suggested they should get married! She had actually *offered* to go and live in the country and keep chickens.

Uttering a cry of pure vexation, she seized the hapless

shepherdess and flung her against the closed door, shattering her into hundreds of tiny shards. Nobody would ever be able to glue her back together again.

She knew her eyes were puffy from weeping. She knew her face was blotchy. She would much rather have stayed in her room than face her husband's disapproval so soon after that last devastating scene.

But Giddings had told her they would be dining *en famille* in the small salon tonight. And once Charles had deposited her in his country house and come back to town it might be months before she saw him again. As hard as it was to endure his presence, writhing inside as she was with humiliation, it would be far worse to sit alone in her room, knowing he was in the house and still, ostensibly, within her reach.

Charles and Robert were already there, standing on either side of the fireplace, so engrossed in conversation they did not appear to notice she had come in.

At least her time in London had not been a complete waste. When she had first come to England they had barely been able to stand being in the same room. Now, as they fell silent, turning to look at her with almost identical expressions of distaste on their faces, she could see that disapproval of her flighty, irresponsible ways had united these two proud men in a way that perhaps nothing else could have achieved.

'I am pleased we are all able to dine together tonight,' Charles said, as Finch proffered a tray containing a single glass of the sweet Madeira wine she had recently developed a taste for. 'This may be the last time we are all three together for some time. I am taking Lady Walton down to Wycke as soon as all the travel arrangements are in place,' he informed Robert.

'Sloughing me off?' his brother replied bitterly. 'Not that I can blame you, I suppose.' Eyeing Heloise with open hostility, he tossed back his drink, then held his glass out to Finch for a refill. 'Oh, don't look at me as though you're some puppy dog I've just kicked,' he growled, when her eyes filled with hurt tears. After downing the second drink, he sighed, rubbing his hand wearily across his face. 'Best sit down to dinner and forget I said anything.'

A wooden-faced Giddings pulled out her chair, assisting her to take her place when, in response to Robert's remark, Charles gave the signal to commence dining.

They ate their minted pea soup in silence. Heloise could think of nothing to say that wouldn't make everything ten times worse. She kept stealing glances at her handsome, enigmatic husband, a sense of awful finality lining her stomach with lead. While she had been dressing for dinner she had analysed every aspect of his behaviour towards her. She could better understand his attempt to consummate the marriage now she knew he had not, after all, been availing himself of Mrs Kenton's services. Assuming she was experienced, he had decided he might as well try her out 'just the once'. But, from the rapidity with which he left the room afterwards, it was clear she had fallen way short of his exacting standards.

And the fact that he did not seem to mind too much about the gambling debt must be because he was glad she had finally given him the excuse he needed to send her away. He had said they must spend some time in London just at first, to silence gossip. Well, now that time was at an end, and who could wonder at him taking her to the country and leaving her there?

He was only just recovering enough from his disappointment with regard to Felice to be thinking about having another woman in his bed. But once she was installed at Wycke he could come back to London and trawl through the women thronging Covent Garden, just as the other men of his class did.

She briefly wondered what he would look like with pea green soup dripping down his supercilious face. Perhaps fortunately for her, Giddings cleared away her bowl before she had summoned up the courage to indulge her vengeful daydream.

Linney leaned over Robert's plate to cut up the collop of veal that comprised the second course, provoking Robert into thumping his one clenched fist on the tabletop. His wine glass went flying, splattering scarlet liquid all over the pristine white tablecloth, onto his plate, and into the nearby dish of béchamel sauce.

'Dammit, dammit, *dammit*!' As he tried to push himself to his feet, Finch, who had sped to the scene with a cloth to mop up the spill, inadvertently blocked his clumsy manoeuvre. Linney caught him as he bounced off the strapping young man's frame, deftly deflecting him back into his seat. Then, without so much as a raised eyebrow, calmly carried on cutting up his master's veal.

'You'll feel much better, if you'll forgive me for saying so, sir, once you've got on the outside of some meat,' Linney observed. 'Been overdoing it today, he has, my lord.' He addressed Charles. 'Dashing all over town, knocking himself up, and getting into a pucker over the news.'

'Thank you, Linney. When I want you to speak for me, as well as cut up my food and put me to bed,' Captain Fawley stormed, 'I'll let you know!'

For the first time since she had come into the salon Heloise stopped thinking about her own problems and noticed that Robert looked really ill.

'Robert, what is the matter? Why have you been dashing all over town? Oh, please say it was not on account of my—'

'The news which has upset Robert, I believe,' Charles interrupted, hoping to avoid having his wife's gaming debts discussed before the servants, 'is—'

'Hell and damnation! Will you all stop trying to speak for me as though I'd lost my tongue along with an arm and a leg and my looks!'

'I beg your pardon,' Charles replied, calmly cutting up a portion of his own meat and spearing it neatly with his fork. 'By all means, repeat before my wife the news you related to me earlier.'

'Well, dammit, so I will!' he retorted. 'Grey lost the vote,' he told her. 'The government has finally decided to send British troops to support the forces the Prussians, Russians and Austrians have already assembled to put a stop to Bonaparte's ambitions. Britain is, in effect, at war with France again.'

He glared at her so ferociously that Heloise felt obliged to say, 'I know I am French, Robert, but I am not your enemy…'

He snorted in derision. 'But you're the only French citizen I'm likely to get anywhere near. Wellington and Bonaparte are finally going to meet, every able-bodied ex-soldier is volunteering, and what am I doing? Running errands for a French-born—'

'I think you have said enough,' Charles said.

Robert struggled with himself. 'Lady Walton,' he eventually said, 'it is not your fault you are French. I dare say the truth is that Linney is right. I have done too much today—knocked myself up. But if you had heard the way those fools were prating in the clubs! Laying odds on the chances of Wellington beating Bonaparte as though it was a cockfight! And all my friends, joining up and saying their farewells, and I'm stuck here—a useless wreck of a man. I just want to hit someone! I don't particularly care who. And

I can't even do that,' he finished, glaring down at the empty sleeve which Linney had pinned neatly out of the way for dinner.

'Truth of the matter is I'm not fit company tonight, and I should never have come to this table,' said Robert, signalling to Linney to help him from his chair. 'I'll return to my rooms and stop casting a blight on your evening. Lady Walton.' He bowed to her. 'I carried out your little commission, as you requested. I gave the package to Charles. I apologise for my filthy temper, and my boorish manners. And I trust you will enjoy your visit to Wycke.'

Heloise's mind began to race. 'Charles,' she said, turning to him the minute Robert had left, 'it cannot be good to go away just now and leave Robert all on his own. He might sink back to the way he was when I first came here.'

If she could postpone her exile, even for a few days, surely she could come up with some way to prove to Charles that he need not banish her? Even if it was only a stay of execution, she would at least have had a few more days with him.

'No,' he said, with such finality it dashed all her hopes to the ground. 'My mind is made up.' He had to remove Heloise from the dangers London posed for such an innocent. 'We will leave in the morning.'

She sat like a stone, picturing her lonely, loveless future, while the servants efficiently cleared away Robert's place-setting. In a space of minutes it was as if he had never been in the room. Even his chair was removed and placed against a wall, where it blended in amongst its fellows. Charles would no doubt have his servants eradicate all traces of his errant wife from this house just as efficiently.

'Do you require any help with your packing?'

She blinked. Charles was set on his course. She had no doubt that if she tried to resist he would order these efficient minions of his to pack her things for her. She had a brief vision of Giddings wrapping her in brown paper, securing her with string, and stuffing her into a trunk.

'No,' she said, folding her napkin neatly and placing it beside her still half-full plate. 'But what of Robert?' It had occurred to her that her exile might be easier to endure if she had a friend to share it. 'I cannot bear to think of him alone in those gloomy rooms. Could he not come with us?'

Charles set down his knife and fork. If Robert came with them it would ruin everything! He wanted Heloise to himself.

'Robert has a standing invitation to view Wycke any time he pleases. He is my heir, if you recall. But he does not care to go,' he warned her.

Heloise went cold inside. Charles had just reminded her he had no further use for her—not even to provide him with an heir. He wanted Robert to succeed him.

Frantically she grappled for something, anything, that might still win her a tiny place in her husband's good graces.

What if she could get Robert to travel to Wycke? Would that not please Charles? It had to be worth a try. For as things stood she was never likely to set eyes on him again. Once he had settled her into her new home he would feel free to pick a fresh, pretty new mistress, and within a month he would have forgotten all about her.

'I am finished here,' she said, pushing herself to her feet.

On legs that felt like cotton wool she left the salon and wove her way across the hall to pound on Robert's door. She had to persuade him to come to Wycke. It was her last chance to show Charles she had some worth as a wife.

CHAPTER TWELVE

'GOODNESS!' Heloise exclaimed, leaning over Robert to peer through the window on his side of the carriage. 'How much land does Charles own?'

'More than half of Berkshire, I believe, besides swathes of land just outside London, and several minor estates dotted about the country.'

She sat back, a troubled frown on her face. 'I only meant how big is this estate of Wycke? It has been more than ten minutes, I think, since we drove through the lodge gates.'

'We have been driving through Walton's lands for the past hour and more,' Robert explained.

'All those farms and fields...the village we just passed through...'

'Did you not notice the name of the inn? The Walton Arms? The very vicar of the church is in your husband's pocket.'

He owned a village. And paid the priest. He was—she shuddered—the local *seigneur*. Just like her infamous grandfather.

She had always known Charles had a grand title. He had told her he had a vast fortune. But she had never fully comprehended what it all meant until this moment.

Feeling very small, and very helpless, Heloise turned to

look out of her own window, so that she could keep her feeling of shock from her travelling companion. And caught sight of Charles, mounted on his favourite hunter, breaking away from the cavalcade that was winding its ponderous way along the carriage drive and making for a belt of trees on top of a small rise. Did the house lie in that direction? In the middle of a forest?

She swallowed down a feeling of panic. He was going to abandon her here in the middle of all this countryside, with not a soul to talk to for miles.

The carriage wound round a right-hand bend, revealing yet another feature of Wycke's extensive grounds. On her side of the carriage the ground sloped down to a shimmering silver lake, containing an island complete with yet more trees, and a ruined castle.

It was a relief when the coach veered away from what looked suspiciously like the very sort of place a man would lock away an unwanted wife, and rolled along an avenue bordered by neatly clipped shrubbery.

The house itself was huge, naturally, and built of stone the colour of fresh butter.

'Oh, hell,' muttered Robert.

Following his gaze, Heloise registered that in order to reach the front door they were going to have to ascend a flight of about twenty steps.

By the time they stepped through the glass-paned double doors and into a bright, airy lobby, Robert's face was the colour of whey.

'Walton,' he gasped, addressing the figure emerging from a green baize door to the rear of the hallway. 'Beg leave to inform you…'

But before he could finish, his eyes rolled back in his head. With a grunt, Linney took his dead weight, lowering him gently to the cool, marble tiled floor. Heloise dropped to her knees beside them, her hands frantically tearing away Robert's neck cloth.

'Finch! Wilbrahams!' Charles barked.

Heloise briefly lifted her head, registering her husband striding towards them with his jacket flying loose, his riding crop in his hand, closely followed by two footmen in the familiar blue and silver livery.

'Get Captain Fawley to his rooms!'

With Linney's help, the footmen manhandled Robert's dead weight towards a set of mahogany doors to the right of the grand staircase.

When Heloise scrambled to her feet and made to follow them, Charles caught her by the arm. 'Leave him to Linney,' he snapped. 'Your duty lies elsewhere.'

For the first time she noticed that the hall was crowded with servants, all of whom were watching her with avid curiosity.

From among them stepped a grey-haired lady, severely garbed in black bombazine.

'The staff wish to extend a warm welcome to your new bride, my lord,' she said dropping a respectful curtsey, though the expression on her face did not match her words.

Heloise was suddenly aware that as she had knelt to help Robert her bonnet had come askew, and that in rising she had caught her heel in her skirts, tearing loose a flounce. Her face felt sticky after the journey, and she was convinced there must be at least one smut on it.

'This is Mrs Lanyon, our housekeeper,' Charles said, his fingers curling more tightly round her arm. He guided her along the line of servants as the housekeeper proceeded to name each and every one, along with their position.

Charles could not seriously expect her to remember the names of an entire regiment of household staff? Could he? Never mind the additional brigade of grooms and gardeners.

'And now I shall conduct you and your personal maid to your suite of rooms, my lady,' Mrs Lanyon intoned. 'There will just be time to refresh yourself and change for dinner,' she added, sweeping up the dark oak staircase. 'We have held it back against your arrival on this one occasion, although normally, of course, we do not keep town hours at Wycke.'

Heloise meekly followed, mortifyingly aware of the staff nudging each other and whispering behind their hands.

'I trust this is to your satisfaction, my lady?' Mrs Lanyon said, upon showing her into a set of rooms on the second floor.

'I am sure it is,' Heloise replied, loosening the ribbons of her bonnet. There had been something in the woman's tone that almost dared her to make any criticism. 'If you would show me where I may wash?'

Mrs Lanyon led the way across what Heloise had to admit was a very pretty, feminine sitting room, and opened a door. 'Your dressing room.'

'What a lovely washstand,' Heloise said inanely.

The top was of pink-veined marble. Standing upon its gleaming surface was a floral-patterned washing set, comprising ewer and basin, and a dish holding a cake of soap sculpted into the shape of a rose. Pristine linen sheets were draped in readiness over a free-standing towel rail.

'I shall feel so much better after a wash,' she said, removing her bonnet and unbuttoning her spencer in the hope that Mrs Lanyon would take the hint and leave her in peace.

'Shall I send up some refreshments?'

'A glass of lemonade would be very welcome.'

'Lemonade,' Mrs Lanyon echoed faintly. Then, as though pulling herself together, 'If that is what you wish…'

'It is,' Heloise insisted, barely resisting the urge to stamp her foot. It had been a horrible day. Charles had been in one of his most unapproachable moods all day, the coach had been hot and stuffy, making the journey extremely uncomfortable, and she had discovered that her husband was not just Charles at all, but a man as important and influential as a French *seigneur*. This woman's thinly veiled disappointment in her new mistress was the last straw.

Only when she heard the door shut behind her did she permit herself to sink onto a striped day bed and toe off her sweat-stained pumps.

'Oh, Sukey,' she groaned, pressing her fingers to her throbbing temples. 'Did you ever see such a place? Or so many servants?'

'No, my lady,' she agreed, in a voice that was slightly muffled since she was peering into the wardrobe. 'Shall I pour the water for your wash now?' she asked, shutting it, and running her hand reverently over the beautifully carved door panels.

'You had better,' Heloise replied, prising herself from the sofa and padding to the dressing room in her stockinged feet. 'I dare not be late for dinner. You heard what that woman said. "We don't keep town hours at Walton."'

Sukey giggled as Heloise imitated the woman's voice almost perfectly.

'What shall I lay out for you to wear?'

'Whatever looks the least crumpled,' Heloise replied as Sukey went to work on the hooks of her gown. 'Oh, that feels so much better,' she sighed, as she peeled gown and stays from her perspiring body.

It felt better still to sponge herself all over with cool, delicately scented water. When she went back into the sitting room, wrapped only in a linen bath sheet, she found a tray containing lemonade and a plate of freshly baked biscuits on a little occasional table. Both were delicious, and very welcome.

'I've laid out that light yellow silk gown for dinner,'

Sukey said, emerging from another door, which Heloise could see led to a bedchamber. She felt a queer tightening in her middle at the possibility there might be a door somewhere that connected her suite to her husband's rooms, just like in London. Should she ask Sukey? Or just go and look for herself later on? So it would not seem as though she had given the matter any thought?

'Since it has been such a hot day, I thought you would want something cool to wear.' Sukey explained her choice. 'But I've put the gold silk shawl out as well, in case it gets chilly later on.' She picked up Heloise's hairbrush. 'Shall I start on your hair while you finish your drink, to save time? And if I bring the plate of biscuits to the dressing table you can carry on eating, too.'

'A good idea,' said Heloise, settling on the low-backed chair.

'It's going to take me a month of Sundays to remember the names of all the people who work here,' Sukey muttered through a mouthful of hairpins.

'Me also,' agreed Heloise with a rueful smile.

'And have you ever seen so many trees? Not but what we don't have trees in London, but at least they are in nice straight lines along the side of the road, where they give shade in the summer,' she grumbled, swiftly working the brush through Heloise's tangles. 'I reckon they must be downright gloomy when it rains.'

'Do you dislike it so much here?' Just because she was doomed to misery, it was not fair to condemn her maid to the same fate. She felt a flicker of panic. 'If you want to return to London…'

'I dare say I will get used to it!' Sukey said hastily. 'I didn't mean to complain. I'd much rather be a lady's maid, even if it is stuck out here in the middle of all this nothing, than go back to blacking the fires in London!'

'I don't expect you will go back to blacking fires—not now you've become a lady's maid,' Heloise reproved gently. 'You have learned to do it so well! At least, I think you have.' She frowned. Then, seeing Sukey's downcast expression in the mirror, she explained, 'You see, I never had a maid—not before I married Lord Walton. In Paris I shared a room with my sister, and we used to help each other dress and do each other's hair.'

Absentmindedly, she nibbled on a biscuit. She had no experience with servants at all, if truth be told. In London, once she had discovered that Charles disliked her chatting to Giddings as though he were a real person, she had tried to ignore them. They had all helped her by taking care to be as unobtrusive as possible. They had certainly never all stood in one place at the same time, and stared at her as though she was some kind of fairground exhibit. Why had he not warned her they would all turn out to greet her like that? And why had he not told her what she should say? She had seen the expression of disapproval on his face when she had been struck dumb by the onslaught of all that curiosity. And she had felt the scorn emanating from Mrs Lanyon's stiff back as she had led her way up the stairs.

'I hope you won't leave me, Sukey,' she said, suddenly reaching for her maid's hand over her shoulder. She needed at least one ally amongst all these strangers.

'Of course I'll stay. It's not as if we'll be down here for ever, is it? Old Giddings was explaining to me that though His Lordship comes down here regular, he never stays for long. We'll soon be back in town, dressing you for parties and the theatre and the like!'

Charles never stays for long. She sighed, replacing her half-eaten biscuit on the plate. But she doubted very much whether she would ever see London again.

* * *

Just when he'd thought the day could not possibly get any worse, Charles discovered dinner had been laid out in the state dining room.

Nothing could have been more daunting to a woman like Heloise. His place was at the head of the table, while she sat at its foot, some twenty feet distant. There was no point in even attempting any sort of conversation.

He barely managed to stifle the irritation that had dogged him all day, reminding himself that the staff had clearly gone to a great deal of trouble to impress his new Countess. The meal was a culinary triumph. And he was sure Mrs Lanyon had not intended to intimidate Heloise the minute she stepped through the front door. It was just, he realised, that his guardians had inaugurated a devilishly formal atmosphere at Wycke. And he had never bothered to dismantle it. When he was in residence his focus was on the land, and his tenants. He did not care enough about household management to bother altering a routine into which he fell without thinking.

He should have given Heloise a hint, though, about how to deal with that welcoming party. He had meant to, but when he had gone out to the coach and seen Robert sitting in it he had been so angry that the only way to avoid an unpleasant scene had been to have his hunter saddled up and claim he preferred to ride in such warm weather. So instead of spending the journey warning Heloise that their housekeeper liked to do things 'properly', he had flounced off in a right royal huff. He should have been pleased that she had somehow cajoled Robert into finally accepting an invitation to come and view the place where he should have grown up.

All he could think of was that his plans to get Heloise to himself had been ruined. He would have to divide his time between wooing his reluctant bride and initiating his recalcitrant brother into the ways of Wycke. And in giving way

to anger he had done them both a disservice. Not only had
Heloise's inadvertent recoil offended Mrs Lanyon, but he
had not taken sufficient care of a man who was still far from
well. It would probably take Robert days to recover from
the journey down here.

He rose to his feet when Heloise left the table, morosely
noting how swiftly she fled his presence.

He had the devil of a job on his hands with both Heloise
and Robert. And, he reflected, gulping down port that should
really have been sipped and savoured, he was damned if he
knew how to proceed with either of them.

Heloise took the stopper from the perfume bottle she had
found on her dressing table and sniffed tentatively. It was
floral, but with an underlying hint of musk that was quite
sensual. She dabbed a little onto each wrist, and behind her
ears. Then, feeling very daring, between her breasts.

She had already dismissed Sukey, claiming with complete
honesty that she would not need her any more. For seducing
her husband was a thing a woman had to do for herself.

During dinner she'd had ample opportunity to study her
distant spouse and form a plan. He seemed very much at
home here, in this house that ran with the precision of a
clockwork toy. He was not the sort of man to break any habit
he had formed without good reason. So she could probably
expect him to come and bid her goodnight.

Gazing along the length of polished mahogany that had
symbolised the vast gulf that separated them, she had noted
that he was able to enjoy the meal for which she had little
appetite. He was a healthy man in his prime, with healthy ap-
petites—at least one of which had not been met since they had
married, so far as she could tell. And they were miles from
anywhere. And he was not the sort of man to dally with the
housemaids.

Which was why she had got Sukey to fetch her most revealing nightdress under the pretext that it was a very sultry night. And doused herself with the only perfume she could lay her hands on.

Finally, with great daring, she arranged herself in what she hoped was a seductive pose on top of the covers.

And waited nervously for Charles to come to her.

It was hard to resist the instinctive desire to preserve her modesty by pulling the covers over herself when she heard the knock that presaged his arrival. Her sense of vulnerability increased when he strode into the room fully dressed.

His reaction was not what she had hoped for either. He glanced only briefly to where she knew her nipples were just visible through the filmy fabric of her nightgown, then, his jaw tightening, fixed his eyes firmly on her face.

'I must apologise,' he said, sitting on the chair beside her bed and crossing his legs as though he had not noticed she was barely decent, 'for the reception you received from the staff. Mrs Lanyon meant well. I was remiss in not preparing you for the formality with which things are done here,' he added, thinking of the dreadful atmosphere at dinner. 'Mrs Lanyon has ruled the roost for a long time.'

Far too long. It was well past time some changes were made. Mrs Lanyon presided over the routine his guardians had inaugurated. But he could remember that Wycke had had a far more relaxed, happy atmosphere when his father had been alive.

'I hope you will make whatever changes you feel are necessary to make this a comfortable home.'

Heloise bit her lower lip. Before they had married he had told her that his staff were efficient, and that he did not want her altering anything. That had been before he had discovered she was such a liability he would not be able to tolerate living in the same household. That he was now granting her permission to make whatever changes she wished here at Wycke, so that she could be relatively comfortable in her exile, was a generous concession on his part.

'You must be tired,' he said. 'It's been the devil of a day.'

He kissed her swiftly, and left so abruptly he might just as well have slapped her.

It was only after he had gone that she worked out what she should have done. When he had bent to kiss her she should have put her arms about his neck and kissed him back. Not on the lips, she had not the courage to be so brazen. For if he had recoiled from such a kiss she would have died of the humiliation. But she could have given him an affectionate peck on the cheek. She frowned. Though he had warned her he did not like displays of affection.

Oh, damn the man! She knelt up and flung a pillow at the door through which he had retreated. Then buried her face in her hands. The barriers which separated them were impenetrable. Especially since he bolstered them every way he could. She should just give up before she totally humiliated herself.

Charles' mood the next morning was even blacker than it had been the night before. Heloise had looked so tempting, lying on her bed in that confection of lace and moonbeams, that it had been all he could do to keep his hands off her. The wary look on her face had reminded him just in time what a disaster that would have been. The speech he had spent so long carefully preparing had evaporated like morning mist at the sudden hot flare of lust he'd had to disguise by sitting down quickly, crossing his legs, and clasping his hands in his lap.

He'd spent a sleepless night, remembering how she had looked reclining on that bank of pillows and wishing he could be beside her. Racking his brains to think of some way he could achieve that goal.

While he had been shaving, he'd had a brainwave. For a couple of days he would have Heloise to himself, while Robert was recovering. He could make a start by showing her over the house. And while he was doing that he would persuade her that it might be a good idea to learn to drive the estate gig. The narrow seat of the two-wheeled vehicle could only accommodate a driver and one passenger. They would have to go out on their own. He would have to take hold of her hands to teach her how to use the reins. She would get used to him touching and holding her, under the guise of accepting instruction, and slowly she would cease to feel threatened by him. When they reached that point he would slide his arm about her waist, or her shoulder. He would inform her that her bonnet was most becoming, and drop a kiss on her cheek…

A less contained man than he would have whistled on the staircase as he went down to breakfast.

And would then have thumped Giddings for informing him that his bailiff was already waiting for him in the estate office.

Why had he forgotten that he always spent his first day at Wycke going over the estate accounts? And damn the place anyway, for its relentless routine which ground any hope of spontaneity into the dust!

Heloise checked on the threshold of the breakfast room when she saw the thunderous expression on his face. A stickler for good manners, he got to his feet and bade her a gruff good morning, but it was evident he had not expected her presence at the breakfast table.

The room was far nicer than the one where they had dined the night before. It was smaller, for one thing, and the floor-to-ceiling windows gave a view over a gravelled parterre in the centre of which an ornamental fountain played. The table was round, and lacked formal place-settings. If Charles had not retreated behind his newspaper, indicating his preference for solitude, she could have sat next to him.

'I had thought you might like a tour of the house this morning,' he said, as she helped herself to some chocolate from a silver pot which stood on a sideboard. 'Unfortunately I have pressing estate business to see to, else I would have taken you around myself.'

'It is of no matter.' Heloise shrugged. She would have years to explore this horrid house, and would probably come to detest every inch of it. 'I will go and make a visit with Robert, see how he does. And after I shall take a walk through the gardens.'

'I have another suggestion,' he put in hastily. He had to wean her from the habit of turning to Robert. 'Have Mrs Lanyon take you over the house this morning. She knows far more about its history than I, in any case. She has made quite a study of it. And, you know, it would be a good opportunity to get on terms with the woman.' They had not got off to a good start. 'You are going to have to deal with her on a regular basis…'

Yes, Mrs Lanyon was to be her jailer! Breaking open a bread roll with rather more force than was necessary, Heloise considered her husband's advice. It was bad enough that she was going to have to live in this wilderness, let alone with a woman who despised her. One who wielded such immense power over the staff as well.

'You are right,' she sighed.

'Then I shall arrange it. Also,' he added in a deceptively casual tone, 'one day soon, since the estate is so large and you do not ride, I shall teach you to drive a gig. Then you will be able to get around more independently.' He studied her downbent head with a growing feeling of disquiet. It was almost as if she sensed his suggestion was merely a ruse to get her alone, and was thinking of excuses to put him off. 'It would be a great pity to be restricted to the house when there are so many delightful vistas just a short drive away,' he went on, in some desperation. 'Once you become proficient I should not object to you driving yourself into the village on occasion—provided, of course, you took your maid.'

Heloise could hardly swallow her bread and honey for the lump which formed in her throat.

He might not be able to feel any affection for her, but he was clearly not going to leave her here until he was fairly sure she had the means to be comfortable. He was intent on smoothing her way with the formidable Mrs Lanyon, and had come up with a plan to ensure she had a degree of freedom when he was no longer there.

Though he did own a village, and held the lives of so many people in the palm of his hand, he was by no means a tyrant. His strict sense of duty ensured he looked out for the welfare of all his dependants, be they tenants or injured and estranged brothers, or ill-chosen wives. How could she help loving him?

She sighed. It would take a remarkable woman to earn his regard. She did not know why she had even thought it was worth trying.

There was no point in her wearing transparent nightgowns and dousing herself with perfume to try to titillate his manly impulses. Or trying to worm her way into his busy life by interrupting him at the breakfast table when he clearly would much rather be reading his paper. She would revert to the routine they had set in London and keep out of his way, as she had initially promised.

She lifted her chin, laying what remained of the honeyed crust on her plate.

'You do not need to teach me to drive. I shall get Robert to do it. It will do him good to get out in the fresh air. Besides, I am sure he wants to explore the estate, but nothing would let him admit as much. If he has the excuse of having to look after me, it will mean he can get out as often as he wants.'

He was still groping for some objection to her very logical suggestion when she rose from her chair and glided from the room without a backward glance. Somehow she had managed to slip through his fingers yet again.

'And now we come to the portrait gallery,' Mrs Lanyon intoned.

She certainly knew a great deal about Wycke, and the family who had lived there since it had been built, in the latter days of Queen Elizabeth. She liked nothing better, she had confided on collecting Heloise from her rooms, than showing interested parties around.

Wycke was mentioned in guidebooks, and visitors to the county always put it at the very top of their itinerary, she had further declared, with pride.

'This is the first Earl,' she said of a life-sized portrait of a man with a ruff round his neck and a fierce expression on his face that put Heloise in mind of Robert.

Each successive Earl and Countess Mrs Lanyon introduced her to gazed down at her with varying degrees of disdain.

'The late Countess of Walton,' Mrs Lanyon said, jerking Heloise out of her introspection.

'Which one?' she dared to ask, her interest reviving for the first time since 1724.

'I mean to say, is it the Earl's mother, or his stepmother?'

Mrs Lanyon drew herself up to her full height before saying frostily, 'His mother, naturally. She was the grand-daughter of the Duke of Bray.'

She looked as though she might have been, Heloise mused. The weight of generations of breeding sat heavily on the slender shoulders of the young woman who looked out of her gilded frame with a somewhat pained expression. The glossy curls which peeped from under the brim of her hat were of a similar colour to Charles' hair, and her eyes were blue, but her mouth had a petulant droop to the lips that she would never associate with him.

'My grandfather,' Heloise blurted in a spirit of rebellion, 'was among the very first to go to the guillotine.' Her father might be only a government functionary, but her mother's blood was as blue as any of these ancestors of Charles'.

'Dreadful!' gasped Mrs Lanyon, her hand flying to her throat.

'Yes, he was. He doubled the taxes during a period of famine, causing great hardship to the peasants. Something that Charles,' she declared with conviction, 'would never do.'

Having finished her tour of the house, Mrs Lanyon handed her over to Bayliss, the head gardener. Thoroughly oppressed by so much history, and aware she had spoken too controversially for Mrs Lanyon's comfort, Heloise was glad to get out of doors.

To her dismay, the Walton family, and in particular the ladies, pursued her through the grounds. A knot garden was the work of the first Countess; a rose garden was the inspiration of the third. She could see why the place attracted visitors, for it contained a great deal that was beautiful. But it was more like a museum than a home.

Spying a familiar figure lounging on a south-facing stone terrace, Heloise escaped from her guide.

'Robert!' she cried, running up the steps and bounding to his side. 'You are better today, yes?'

'Just sitting out enjoying the fresh air,' he groused. 'Don't go pestering me to go anywhere today, because I have no intention of stirring from this terrace. Which is mine, by the way.'

'How do you mean, yours?' She sat on a wooden bench next to him, her eyes alight with curiosity.

'I mean just that. The windows behind me lead directly into my rooms. Nobody is supposed to disturb me out here. Do you know you have to walk across I don't know how many lawns to get to those steps you ran up?'

'Only too well!' she snorted. 'For I have walked across them. Oh,' she said, suddenly registering what he had said, 'you wish me to leave you alone.' From his eyes she met the hostility of generations of Waltons. 'I understand.'

Leaping to her feet, she ran back down the steps and, without knowing where she would end up, headed away from the house. Anywhere, she fumed, blinking back tears, as long as she was out of everyone's way! She blundered through a dense shrubbery to emerge on the lip of an embankment. To her amazement she discovered she had come out just above the curving carriage drive, and that beyond it a flower-sprinkled meadow undulated down to the lake.

Perhaps the grounds were not so large as she had first assumed. She would never have guessed, when she had driven along this particular stretch of the drive the day before, that she was so near the house.

She eyed the ruined tower on the island in which she had imagined Charles might lock her away. He might just as well. The servants had despised her on sight, and now even Robert, whom she thought of as a brother, had said he wanted her to stop pestering him.

Very well! She would not pester Robert to teach her to drive after all. She would get one of the grooms to do it. And prove to Charles that she did not need him—no, not for anything.

And then he could go back to London and forget all about her.

And she…no, she would never forget Charles. She would spend every minute of her long, lonely exile wondering what he was doing.

And who he was doing it with.

CHAPTER THIRTEEN

CHARLES paused in the doorway of the state dining room, which tonight was looking its most magnificent. The staff had polished the massive epergnes to mirror-brightness, filling them with banks of freshly cut flowers that filled the air with their perfume. A footman was going round lighting the candles already. Once he had finished, the china and crystal would glitter like jewels set against the yards of spotless damask linen tablecloth.

'It all looks splendid—as ever,' he said to his house-keeper. Within a week of his arrival Mrs Lanyon had reminded him that he always sent out cards of invitation to his neighbours. It was just one more tradition he wished he had never allowed to become set in stone. 'Though in future you should expect Lady Walton to oversee events of this nature.'

Fortunately for her, Mrs Lanyon refrained from making the comment which would have brought her instant dismissal. Though the way she pursed her lips told him exactly what she was thinking. Heloise had played no part in the organisation of this dinner whatsoever. Whenever Mrs Lanyon had consulted her, she had replied she must do exactly as she wished.

Though it hurt to think she disliked him so much she

could not even pretend to show an interest in his social life, he could not be angry with her. Being on display for his neighbours would be an ordeal for a woman of her shy, retiring disposition. If he could only have thought of a way to cancel the dinner without insulting his neighbours he would have done so. But in the end he had decided it would be better to just get the thing over with as soon as possible. Far better for them to find out that his wife was a little gauche than for them to imagine she was unfriendly.

He had never been so irritated by the number of obligations his position brought him before. But since they had come down to Wycke every chance he might have had to get closer to Heloise had been thwarted by estate business in one form or another.

Still, he had dealt with all the most pressing business now. And once this annual county dinner was over he could devote himself almost exclusively to wooing her.

As he went along the corridor to the red salon, he wondered what lay behind her decision to get Grimwade, the head groom, to teach her to drive rather than Robert. Strolling to the window that overlooked the carriage drive, he rubbed his hand across the back of his neck. To his knowledge, Robert had not stirred from his rooms since his arrival, although Linney assured him his master was recovering nicely from the journey. He barely repressed the urge to fling the window open. Though the room felt stuffy, the air outside was even hotter, and heavy with the threat of an approaching storm. He hoped it would not break too soon. The last thing he wanted was for his guests to be stranded, so that he would be obliged to offer them hospitality.

'Do I wear the Walton diamonds?' Heloise was anxiously asking Sukey. 'Or will it look as though I am showing off?'

One did not dress so elaborately in the country. Even she

knew that. Which was why she had chosen the simplest evening gown she had. But, since she had no other jewellery, it was either wear the Walton parure or nothing. She did not think Charles would wish her to look dowdy.

Though how could she look anything else? She had neither Felice's emerald eyes, nor the voluptuous figure of Mrs Kenton. With a small cry of distress, she whirled away from the mirror.

'Don't be nervous, my lady,' Sukey said brightly. 'You are the highest-ranking lady in the district, and nothing anyone might think will alter that.'

She was right. The women she'd seen wearing the Walton diamonds in portrait after portrait might disapprove of her, but she was as much the Countess as any of them. Because Charles had married *her*. Not the graceful Felice, nor the experienced Mrs Kenton, but plain, naïve little Heloise Bergeron.

Anyway, these hard cold stones were all she had to prove this marriage was real. Especially since the arrival of her monthly courses, a few days earlier, had robbed her of even the faint hope that she might have conceived a child during that one brief coupling.

Straightening her shoulders, she walked across to the table on which the ancient jewel case squatted. 'I will wear the diamonds,' she said. 'All of them.'

She did not care if anyone thought she was overdressed. She clipped the earrings to her earlobes with a grimace. Though she wanted to make a good impression on the people who would form her new social circle, she had an even greater need to bolster her flagging self-esteem.

Before long she was ready to join Charles in the red salon, where Mrs Lanyon had told her he always greeted his dinner guests.

He looked magnificent in his evening clothes. He was

always so immaculately dressed, so correct in all his behaviour. She itched to reach up and tousle his neatly brushed
hair, to mar that perfection which threw all her own faults
into stark relief. When his guests started to arrive, and saw
them standing side by side, they were bound to wonder at
the Earl having made such a mismatch.

The breath hitched in Charles' throat as she trailed slowly
across the room to join him beside the empty hearth. She
was so lovely. The simply cut gown she had chosen became
her slight figure far more than some of the fussy creations
he had seen adorning the so-called leaders of fashion in
London. And with the diamonds glittering about her throat
and wrist she looked every inch the Countess.

He was on the verge of telling her so, when she began to
twist her hands together at her waist. He had got used to
seeing her drooping disconsolately about the place, but this
new symptom hurt him abominably. She could not bear to
come within three feet of him!

He turned from her abruptly. It took him a moment or two
to get himself in hand. And then he found he was standing
by the sideboard. He did the only thing that came to him
which might just help her. He poured a small glass of
Madeira and carried it back to her.

Heloise tossed it back, wondering in what way she had
failed to measure up this time, for him to walk away from
her with such a grim expression. Had it been a mistake to
wear the full parure? Had it reminded him of how very
nearly she had lost part of it? Or did he just think she was
overdressed? And if he thought so what would his guests
think? Perhaps she should run back upstairs and change? Oh,
but there was no time. The front door was being opened, she
could hear Giddings greeting someone, and already there
was the sound of more wheels crunching over the gravel
drive.

Her heart pounding against her ribs, she held out her empty glass to Finch.

'Get me another,' she pleaded, avoiding her husband's gaze. It was bad enough knowing she disappointed him without encountering the full wintry blast of his eyes.

The room rapidly filled with about thirty people who had known Charles and each other all their lives. There was only one person amongst them who did not totally overwhelm her. Her name was Miss Masterson, and her father was a retired colonel. Heloise empathised with the way she sought out a corner away from the more ebullient guests, and made sure the circulating footmen did not overlook her. When Charles had gone back to London she would call on the girl, who looked as if she was of a similar age, and see if she could make a friend of her. If, that was, she could bear to enter the house of the Colonel and his bulldog-faced wife.

'Hoped to be able to meet your long-lost brother,' Colonel Masterson was booming at Charles, as though he was yards away across a parade ground. 'Military man, ain't he? Was hoping to have a jaw with him about developments in the Low Countries. Wellington's been given charge of the allied armies, d'you know? Got it from Viscount Brabourne on his way through to his hunting box in Wiltshire. Damned shame we're at war with your wife's country again. Though I'm sure,' he said turning towards her, 'you want to see Bonaparte brought to book, eh? Must support the Bourbons. Walton wouldn't have married you unless you was a Royalist, now, would he?'

'You are mistaken,' she replied, cut to the quick by his barely concealed speculation as to what on earth could have induced an Earl to marry her. 'I am very far from being a Royalist.'

She did not realise that she should have taken the time to

explain she despised fat Louis and his inept government almost as much as she detested Bonaparte's ruthless efficiency until she heard the Colonel confide to his wife, in what he must have thought was a whisper, as they were processing to the dining room, 'Outrageous! He's brought a Bonapartist amongst us!' His wife managed to hush him, but she could not stop him casting suspicious looks her way throughout the meal.

Lord Danvers, who was sitting to her right at the foot of the table, opened the conversation over the soup by enquiring if she hunted.

She made the fatal error of confessing that she could not ride at all.

'Not ride?' He looked at her as though she had confessed to a crime.

Swiftly she tried to vindicate herself. 'It is considered unpatriotic, in my country, to keep a horse. Like our sons and brothers, they belong to the army of France.' The malevolent glare this comment drew from Colonel Masterson suggested he now believed she must have come to England for the sole purpose of winkling state secrets from her husband. Now he would never allow her to befriend his daughter.

After that, the conversation at the foot of the table became painfully stilted. And yet Heloise dreaded the moment when she would have to rise, signalling it was time for the ladies to withdraw. While they were confined to their seats and occupied with their food only the nearest handful of guests could attack her. She had the feeling that once she got to the music room it would turn into a free-for-all.

Lady Danvers fired the opening salvo.

'Do you play the pianoforte, Lady Walton?' she cooed. 'Or perhaps the harp? Or have you arranged something particularly French—' she tittered '—to entertain the gentlemen when they join us?'

'No,' she replied bluntly. She did not ride, she did not play any musical instrument, and she did not have a lively personality. She sighed. And if only it were true that she had ensnared her husband by the sort of French naughtiness this abominable woman implied.

With a triumphant gleam in her eye, Lady Danvers went to the sofa where Lady Masterson was sitting, settled beside her, and murmured something in her ear that caused the older lady to regard Heloise with even deeper hostility.

'Perhaps our dear Countess has other talents,' suggested the vicar's wife. 'We are all good at something. Even if it is only the art of putting the poor at ease when visiting. Or the clever arrangement of flowers. Or embroidery. Or…' Looking more and more desperate as Heloise shook her head at every suggestion the kind lady put forward, she eventually subsided.

'You mean to tell me you have no accomplishments whatever?' Lady Danvers drawled.

'I do not tell you that at all,' Heloise snapped, her patience finally running out. 'I am an artist!'

'An artist?' Lady Danvers quirked one eyebrow in distinct mockery. 'You mean you dabble about with paint?'

'No, I draw,' she replied, her heart suddenly plunging to her dainty satin slippers. Charles would hate it if these people ever found out she had tried to make money from the sale of her work. Work of which he strongly disapproved.

'But I do not have a portfolio to show you. It was lost…' Well, at least most of it was 'lost', burnt, actually '…when I left France.'

'Oh, how disappointing,' drawled Lady Danvers sarcastically. 'I am sure we have missed a rare treat.' She exchanged a knowing smile with Lady Masterson.

Heloise gasped. The woman was accusing her of being a liar to her face!

Lydia Bentinck, one of a trio of elderly spinsters, sniffed loudly before saying, 'There is more to being a lady of quality than being able to draw, or play the piano, or ride a horse. I have always held that good manners are an absolute prerequisite.' She looked pointedly at Lady Danvers. 'So sadly lacking in many these days.'

Lady Danvers' eyes snapped with fury. While she struggled to find a suitably cutting come back, Diana Bentinck turned to Heloise and enquired, 'What sort of drawings do you do?'

'People. I do sketches of people.'

'Oh, how charming. Would you do a sketch of me and my sisters? I should love to have a likeness. Or would it take too long?'

She was on the point of refusing, out of deference to Charles' views, when she caught sight of Lady Danvers' lip curling in derision.

'I would be glad to sketch you,' she declared defiantly. 'Please to take seats close together, while I find some materials.'

By this time one of the other ladies, a Mrs Goulding, had taken a seat at the piano, and while Heloise unearthed some sheets of writing paper from a desk drawer she began to pick out the bare bones of a Haydn sonata. From her reticule, Heloise produced the sliver of charcoal which she was never without. While the Bentinck sisters fluttered about the three chairs they had decided to pose on, arguing as to which order they should sit, either by age or by size, and whether one should stand behind the other two to make an interesting group, Heloise's nimble fingers flew across the page. By the time they were settled she was able to walk over to them, holding out her finished work.

'Why,' exclaimed Lydia, 'this is quite remarkable!'

Three grey heads bent to examine the sparse lines on the

creamy vellum. They could see Lydia standing over her two seated siblings. Diana was holding out her hand, palm upwards, while Grace had her head tilted to one side, a pensive frown knitting her brows. Though each pose denoted a certain amount of conflict, each woman was also expressing a strong affection for the other two, so that the overall impression was one of harmony.

'I cannot believe you did that so quickly!' Diana Bentinck cried.

'It was not so quick.' They had been bickering gently for several minutes, and she had always found it a simple matter to reproduce an accurate physical likeness.

'I am sorry that it is only on writing paper…' she began.

But, 'Oh, no!' the three sisters cried simultaneously. 'This paper has the Walton crest on it. What a lovely reminder it will be to us of a delightful evening spent at Wycke!'

The vicar's wife had now sidled up to her. 'Oh, I should love to have a sketch drawn by you, Lady Walton,' she gushed.

'As you wish,' Heloise replied, picking up her charcoal.

Fortunately, she had not had time to study these people too closely, and so link them inextricably in her mind with some member of the animal kingdom. So she managed, with some application, to repress her imagination and stick to a strictly literal likeness of her next subject. The resultant sketch was exclaimed over, passed round, and generated such excitement that several other ladies asked if she would do their portraits too.

She became so deeply absorbed that she noticed neither the passage of time nor the arrival in the music room of the gentlemen. All she did see, when she handed Miss Masterson her finished sketch, was the smile which lit up her face.

'Do I really look like that?' the girl exclaimed, running a finger wonderingly over the smudged lines of her portrait. Her face clouded. 'I think you must have been flattering me.'

'Not in the least,' Charles said, startling Heloise. She'd had no idea he was standing behind her chair. 'My wife never flatters her sitters. She has the knack, though, of putting something of the subject's personality in beyond the physical likeness. Perhaps that is what you recognise in your own portrait, Miss Masterson?'

Heloise did not know what to make of this remark. Perhaps his oblique reference to the way she habitually portrayed people as the animals they reminded her of was a warning to behave herself?

'You must do my son,' Lady Masterson said. 'Now that you have managed to make my stepdaughter look so fetching.'

Heloise hesitated. She would have been thrilled at winning over one of her major opponents so easily, were she not so scared of offending Charles. Warily, she looked to him for guidance. But his expression gave her no clues.

She pulled a fresh sheet of paper from the drawer of the writing desk as young Thomas Masterson took the seat his older sister had just vacated.

Why did she never think about the consequences before acting? she berated herself. It had been just the same in that stupid card game. Only tonight it had been Lady Danvers who had goaded her into losing her temper and acting in a way that was guaranteed to displease Charles. Gripping the charcoal tightly, she paused to examine the young man's features for a moment or two before setting to work.

Charles watched in fascination as her fingers flew across the paper. He had never seen her drawing before. She had pitched her work this evening in a way that was guaranteed to please their guests. His heart swelled with pride. She could so easily have taken revenge for the various snubs she had borne earlier, by accentuating the uglier aspects of her neighbours. Instead, she brought out the best in them. She had even managed to make the dreary Miss Masterson look interesting, transforming her habitually vacant stare into the dreamy reverie of a *savant*.

She was so talented. He ached to tell her so. He pondered how best to word the compliment, savouring the knowledge that it was the very one he could pay her that would please her.

And while they were on the subject he must ask her pardon for forcing her to burn that sketchbook. If she could forgive him that one transgression… His heart-rate picked up dramatically. Had he finally found the key that might unlock his wife's heart?

He could hardly wait for the last of his tedious guests to leave so that he could make his declaration.

'I am sorry you did not have an easy time of it this evening,' he began, his expression sobering as he recalled Colonel Masterson's rudeness, and imagined the barbed comments he was sure the spiteful Lady Danvers must have let fly. 'But I believe most of our guests went away having been tolerably well entertained.'

His words struck at her like a blow from a fist. Though she had very nearly disgraced him, he seemed to be saying, his neighbours had been gracious enough to overlook all her inadequacies.

'Then may I go to my room, now?'

'Very well,' he conceded, battening down his eagerness to put his new plan of action in train. He followed her into the hall and watched her ascend the stairs. He would give her a few minutes before following her, and then…

'A word, if you please, Walton!'

Robert's harsh voice abruptly shattered his fantasies. He

turned to see his half-brother emerge from the shadows beneath the bend in the great staircase.

'Ashamed of me, are you?' Robert began, with no preamble.

'I beg your pardon?' Why did he have to pick such an inappropriate moment to pick a quarrel? 'You'd better come into my study.'

Striding past his brother, he flung open the door and went in. He was not going to participate in any kind of a scene in the hall, where angry words would echo up to the rafters.

'What is it?' he said with impatience, going from habit to the side table on which rested a decanter of fine cognac and several glasses.

'I want to know why you excluded me tonight,' Robert began, stumping angrily along in his wake. 'Why the devil drag me down here if all you do is shut me away like some...?'

Abruptly his words petered out as he caught sight of the portrait that hung above Charles' desk.

'That's my mother!' he exclaimed in indignation. 'Why have you got a picture of my mother in your study? Why isn't she up in the gallery with all the reputable Waltons?'

'When have *you* been up in the picture gallery?'

Robert looked a little discomforted, but did not admit that he had bribed Finch to show him round at times when he knew neither Giddings nor Mrs Lanyon nor Charles would discover he had done so.

'Well, I am glad you have been exploring your home, though had I known you wished to do so I would gladly have been your guide...'

'Oh, would you?' he sneered. 'When you hide me away from your neighbours as though you are ashamed of owning such a brother!'

'I have done no such thing! I had nothing to do with the arrangements. Heloise…' He frowned. She had left the whole thing to Mrs Lanyon. Did the housekeeper have a problem with Robert's presence in the house? Might she even have some lingering loyalties to the Lamptons?

'Oh, hell,' said Robert, casting himself into a chair and easing the position of his wooden leg with his good hand. 'My cursed temper! I've upset her. I wondered at the time…though normally when I rip up at her she gives it me back threefold.'

'Here.' Charles pressed a glass of cognac into his hand and settled behind the desk.

'I wish you wouldn't be so damned reasonable all the time,' Robert grumbled. 'If only you would shout back at me just once in a while, instead of being so…icily polite, I shouldn't feel so…so…'

Charles shrugged one shoulder. 'My guardians did a sterling job of raising me after the pattern of my own mother's irreproachable forebears. Although…' he swivelled in his chair to gaze at the portrait that hung there '…when I gaze upon your mother's face I can remember a time when things were very different here at Wycke. It was only from the day they ousted her it became this cold, inhospitable mausoleum. They told me she had abandoned me.' He took a large gulp of the cognac. 'I was eight years old. She was the only mother I had ever known. She had always seemed warm and loving, to both me and my father. Suddenly it was as if I had never known her at all. How could a woman turn her back on a child who had just lost his father?'

'She didn't!' Robert defended her. 'They sent her back to her family and then threw all their weight into crushing her spirit!'

'For which crime I shall never be able to forgive them.' His eyes grew so cold that Robert took a swig of his cognac to counteract the chill that pervaded the whole room.

'You should have grown up here, with me. We should have climbed trees, fished in the lake, and played at Knights and Saracens in the ruined tower. If your mother had been here she would have made sure I went to school rather than being walled up here with a succession of tutors.'

'I never appreciated you may have felt like this.' Robert frowned into his glass. 'I always assumed that the quarrel you started with the Lamptons when you came of age was to do with money...'

'Money! Oh, no. They were always scrupulously honest when it came to my finances. It was something far more valuable they robbed me of.' His eyes returned to the portrait of the dark-haired woman smiling down at her boys. 'Something irreplaceable. My childhood.'

After an awkward pause, Robert managed to mumble, 'Grown up in the habit of hating you, but I have to concede of late you have been very generous to me...'

Charles made a dismissive gesture with his hand. 'I have done nothing but restore what should always have been yours. How our father managed to make such a botch of his will...'

It was the opening he had longed for since the day he'd discovered he had a brother. As the level in the brandy bottle steadily dropped, the two men managed to discuss, for the most part relatively cordially, the woman they had both called mother, and the events that had led up to her tragic demise.

By the time Charles went upstairs and softly entered his wife's room she was fast asleep.

'Oh, my darling,' he murmured, bending to kiss her sleep flushed cheek. 'Thanks to you, my brother has been restored to me.'

Gently, he brushed one stray lock of hair from her forehead, before retreating to his own room. If she did not come down for breakfast in the morning he would send a note, requesting she join him in his study as soon as she was awake. He had learned a valuable lesson from his long, and painful interview with Robert. His brother had attributed nefarious motives to all his actions. It was not until he had spelled out exactly why he had taken what steps he had that Robert had finally managed to let go of years of resentment.

He needed to have just such a conversation with his wife.

Heloise stared at the curt little note she held in her hand with a sinking heart. Charles requested her presence in his study as soon as she woke. Pushing her breakfast tray to one side, she swung her legs out of bed. He must be so angry with her for flouting his wishes the night before. She did not wish to make him any angrier by keeping him waiting. She went straight to her washroom, pulling off her nightgown and tossing it aside in her haste to begin her toilette.

'Please to lay out my clothes while I wash,' Heloise said, when Sukey gaped at the sight of her mistress pouring water into the basin for herself. 'My green cambric walking dress.'

She was halfway down the stairs before she wondered what on earth she was doing. She could well imagine what he wanted to say to her. He was ready to go back to London. And, since she had let him down so badly, he had no intention of taking her with him. She had lived in dread of this moment ever since they had got here.

She stood, clutching the banister for support, as tears began to roll down her cheeks.

Stifling a sob, she hitched up her skirts and, instead of meekly going to the study, she ran down the passage that led to the back of the house and fled into the gardens.

And she kept on running. From her pain, from her loneliness, from her sense of utter failure. Across the lawns, through the shrubbery, down the bank and across the meadow. Only when she reached the lake did she veer from her course, following the shoreline until her strength gave out and she crumpled to the ground, giving way to the misery she had bottled up for so long.

She had no idea how long she lay there, curled up like a wounded animal, her utter misery cloaking her in a dense shroud of darkness.

It was only when the first great fat drops of rain began to strike her back that she sat up, suddenly aware that the darkness was not only inside her. The storm which had been hanging over Wycke for days had finally broken. She gasped as rain struck the ground around her like a hail of bullets, spattering her dress with sandy ricochets.

Her first instinct was to seek shelter. But she could not bear to go back to the house. She could see herself standing before Charles' desk, her hem dripping water onto his polished floor, her hair hanging in rats' tails round her face, while he informed her, his lip curling with disdain, that he never wished to set eyes on her again.

She pushed herself to her feet and made her way back to a wooden footbridge she remembered running past. It led across a narrow strip of water to the island on which stood the ruined tower. She would wait there until the storm had passed.

Maybe by then Charles would already have left Wycke, so that at least she would be spared the ordeal of suffering his dismissal in person.

Stumbling over a large piece of masonry half hidden by nettles alerted her to the fact she was nearing her goal. She lifted her head, brushing back the streamers of wet hair clinging to her face. The tower stood defiantly amidst the mounds of crumbling stones, all that remained of what might once have been an impressive set of fortifications. It still possessed a door, though it was almost completely obscured with a tangled growth of ivy. Grabbing the iron ring that served as a latch, Heloise turned it and pushed with all her strength.

The door yielded by perhaps two feet, grating over the stone-flagged floor within. She squeezed inside, grateful to have found shelter so quickly. It was dry inside, though almost pitch-black. Only the faintest glimmer of light filtered in from a source far above her head. It originated from the head of a wooden staircase, set into the outer wall of the tower.

She wrinkled her nose at the smell of decay that hung in the air. What was she doing in this dark, dirty ruin, when she could be sitting before a nice warm fire in her pretty sitting room, sipping hot chocolate? She could at least be comfortable, even if she would not feel any less miserable.

She wrapped her arms round her waist as a shiver racked her body. The rain had soaked right through her dress and flimsy indoor shoes in a matter of seconds. Charles would think she was an idiot for running in here instead of returning to the house.

Well, she *was* an idiot! She had been told as much for as long as she could remember. She sniffed. But the most foolish thing she had ever done was fall in love with a man that even a child could see should never have married so far beneath him!

And the worst of it was she had no right to admit she was miserable because he did not love her. Love was never supposed to have been part of the bargain they had made.

She wiped her hand across her face, not sure if it was rain or tears that were running down her cheeks, as a gust of wind blew in through the partially open door. She retreated from the storm, deeper into the gloom, and felt a sharp stab of pain in her shin as she stumbled over a broken chair which was lying on its side next to a battered wooden trunk.

Perhaps she would be better off up on the next floor, where it was a bit lighter. And there might not be so much rubbish lying about, she thought, making for the stairs. There was a metal railing fixed into the wall, onto which she clung as she tentatively began to climb. After only a few steps the air began to feel fresher, and as her head came onto a level with the upper floor, she saw that the room was indeed a great improvement on the rubbish tip the ground floor had become. Though the floor was a bit dusty, there were several pieces of quite sturdy-looking furniture, arranged to face a floor-to-ceiling window which, though grimy, was fully glazed.

She was just congratulating herself for making the decision to explore, when without warning the step upon which she had just placed her foot gave way with a sharp crack. Her foot went straight through, and if she had not been clinging to the handrail she would have fallen. Shaking with shock, she pulled her leg carefully up through the splintered tread.

Then realised, with horror, that it was not just her body that was shaking. The whole staircase was quivering under her weight.

And then, with a sound that reminded her of the ship's timbers creaking as the craft had plunged its way across the Channel, the whole structure parted company from the wall.

CHAPTER FOURTEEN

CHARLES pulled his watch from his pocket and frowned as it confirmed what he already knew. It had been three hours since Sukey had put his note into Heloise's hands, and still she had not come to him.

'You sent for me, my lord?'

Charles looked up to see Giddings standing in the doorway.

'Yes.' He snapped his watch shut and tucked it back into his waistcoat pocket. 'Have luncheon served in the breakfast parlour, and send someone to find out if Her Ladyship will be joining me.'

Perhaps she was unwell. Although, if that were the case, surely she would just have replied to his note with one of her own, apprising him of the fact.

No, he could not shake the conviction that this prolonged silence was a message in itself. He sighed. It had been too much to hope that he could put things right with his brother and his wife on the same day.

He went to the window, leaning his forearm on the sash as he gazed out at the rain which had begun to fall not long after Robert had left in the family coach, bound for London. He accepted that Robert needed time on his own, to come to terms with the new understanding they had reached in the early hours of the morning. And when Robert had haltingly given his reasons for wishing to return 'home', his heart had leapt, knowing that this was at last how he thought of his rooms at Walton House.

He turned at the sound of a knock on the door.

'Begging your pardon, my lord,' said Giddings. 'But Sukey does not seem to know Her Ladyship's whereabouts. Apparently she dressed in a great hurry and left her rooms quite early this morning, as soon as she received the note Your Lordship sent her.'

Charles felt as though a cold hand had reached into his chest and clamped round his heart. It could not be a coincidence that Heloise had disappeared the same morning his brother had returned to London.

'Will that be all, my lord?'

'What? Oh, yes—yes,' he snapped, dismissing his butler with a curt wave of his hand.

He had been standing in this very room, he recalled, the last time he had received news that had rocked his world to its foundations. Though he had only been a child, and standing on the other side of this desk, when his maternal uncle had told him he was never going to see his stepmother again. He stared blindly at the desk-top as he felt that same sense of isolation closing round him all over again.

His stepmother had kept a little singing bird in a cage in the sitting room that now belonged to Heloise. He had been able to hear it singing clear up to his schoolroom. But not that morning. When she had left she had taken it with her, and a dreadful silence had descended on Wycke.

And now, though Heloise had never really belonged to him, her absence would reverberate through every corner of his existence.

How could she have betrayed him like this? How could Robert?

He drew in a deep breath, forcing himself to sit down and consider his situation rationally.

Though jealousy would have him believe his wife was the kind of woman who would run off with another man, his saner self knew her better than that. Though she had made her marriage vows in haste, and soon come to regret them, he could not believe she would break them so easily. Her conscience was far too tender. Look how she had berated herself for supposed lack of morals that night he had kissed her at the masquerade, when she had still been a virgin!

No, if she had left with Robert, it was not to embark on an affair.

She could not do it.

The only thing that would ever induce her to break her marriage vows was if she fell in love with someone else. And there was no evidence to indicate she had done so.

And as for Robert... No, he could no longer believe that he would deliberately conspire against him either. What he could imagine was Heloise going to him and begging him to take her back to London, where she would be safe from her cruel husband. A man would have to have a heart of stone to refuse her.

He would give her a few days' respite from his loathsome presence before following her to London. Though follow her he would. For he would not be able to rest until he could look her in the face and tell her...

He sucked in a sharp breath as the truth hit him. He had fallen in love with his wife. Fallen. He groaned. What an apt term! A fall was something you had no control over. It happened when you least expected it. It shook you up, and took your breath away, and it hurt. God, how it hurt. Especially when the woman you loved could not bear to be in the same room—nay, the same county!

What was he to do now?

Why, he mocked himself, take luncheon as if there was nothing the matter, of course. It was what he did best—act as though nothing touched him.

He went to the breakfast parlour, sat down, and methodically worked his way through the food that was set before him.

When at last he rose from the table, he went to the windows. For a while he just watched the rain trickling down the panes, observing how it was drowning his entire estate in tones of grey. But at length something impinged on his abstracted mood. There was a thin plume of smoke rising from the trees on the island. Who on earth would be foolish enough to try lighting a fire, on his private property, in such weather as this?

His heart quickened. He knew only one person foolish enough to be outside at all on a day like today. He could not begin to imagine what Heloise was doing out on the island, nor did he question how he was so certain she was the one responsible for raising that defiant plume of smoke. He only knew he had to get to her.

Flinging open the French windows, he strode along the parterre, vaulted over the stone parapet, and broke into a run. He sprinted across the lawns and through the shrubbery, skidding down the slope and landing in an inelegant heap on the carriage drive.

He scrambled to his feet and pounded his way across the bridge, not stopping until he reached the foot of the tower, from which, he had soon realised, the smoke was rising.

'Heloise!' he roared as he forced his way through the half-open door. 'What the devil do you think you are doing in here?'

'Charles?'

He looked up to see her head and shoulders appear over

tho lip of the upstairs landing. It took him only a moment to work out what must have happened. All that remained of the staircase was a heap of rotten timbers scattered across the floor.

Heloise's face looked unnaturally white, and her hair was plastered to her face. Just how long had she been stranded up there, alone and afraid? When he considered how he had tucked into a hearty luncheon, bitterly imagining her guilty of all manner of crimes…

'I'll soon have you down from there!' he vowed, looking wildly about for something he could use to climb up to her. He had to get her to safety, take her in his arms, and wipe that agonised expression of dread from her face.

There was a chest which he knew contained croquet hoops and mallets, a table kept specifically for picnics on the island, and several chairs and other boxes used for storing all manner of sporting equipment. Hastily he piled them up against the wall where the stairs had been, and began to climb.

'Oh, take care!' Heloise cried, when the pyramid of furniture gave a distinct lurch.

'It is quite safe, I assure you. Give me your hand and I will help you climb down.'

She shook her head, backing away. 'Charles, I don't think I can…'

He was just about to offer the reassurance he thought she needed when his improvised staircase separated out into its component parts. The chest went one way, the chair another, and he gave one last desperate push upwards, to land sprawled at his wife's feet on the upper landing.

Before he could do more than push himself to his knees, Heloise had flung her arms around his neck.

'Oh, thank heaven you made it safely! I was so afraid you were going to fall,' she said, pulling back just far enough to be able to gaze up into his face. Her eyes were full of concern.

Charles looked down into her tear-streaked face with a sense of wonder. She cared about him. Oh, maybe not as much as he cared for her, but nevertheless…

Taking ruthless advantage of her momentary weakness, he wrapped his arms about her and hugged her to his chest.

'I am fine,' he said, and in fact he could not remember when he had ever felt better. 'But what about you? Are you hurt?'

'Only a graze on my leg where my foot went through the stairs.'

'Let me see.' As he pulled her onto his lap, he suddenly registered that she was wrapped in what looked like a large, dusty sheet.

'What on earth is this?' he asked, pushing a swathe of material away from her leg. He winced as he saw the gash on her shin, and the blood which smeared her skin right down to her toes. Her bare toes.

'It is a curtain. I hope you do not mind, but I was so wet and cold, and I did not know how long it might be until somebody came to rescue me, and then I found the tinder box, and there was already some kindling in the grate, and I am sorry, but I also smashed one of the chairs, but only the littlest one, to get a fire going…'

Looking over her shoulder, he saw various items of feminine attire draped over a semicircle of chairs arranged in front of the fireplace. A muddy gown, a dripping petticoat, torn stockings…

His hand stilled.

'Are you completely naked under that curtain?' he asked throatily.

She nodded, her cheeks flushing. 'That is why I could not have climbed down to you. I was going to explain that if I let go it would just fall away, for I have no pins to secure it, nor a belt…'

She had simply wrapped the curtain round her shoulders like a cloak, and was maintaining her modesty only with the greatest difficulty.

'Your feet are cold,' he said, having forced his hand to explore in a downward direction, when all it wanted to do was slide upwards, underneath the curtain. Her ankles were so slender, he noted, gritting his teeth against the sudden surge of blood to his groin. He could almost encircle them with his fingers.

The rest of her was not cold at all—not any longer, she thought. As his hand gently stroked her injured leg, it sent fire coursing through her veins, making her feel as though she was melting from the inside out.

'And I fear I am making you wet again,' he said, suddenly pushing her off his lap.

Guilty heat flooded her face as she wondered how on earth he could know what his touch was doing to her. But when he stood up and stripped off his jacket she realised he had not been saying what she thought he had at all.

For as he draped it over the back of the chair which already held her stockings, he remarked, 'My waistcoat is a little damp, too, but apart from my neckcloth—' which he deftly unwound and hung beside her petticoat '—my shirt is quite dry.'

Her mouth went dry when he untied the laces and pulled it over his head.

'Here,' he said, holding it out to her. 'Put this on. You will be more comfortable and…er…secure than wrapped in that curtain. Which looks none too clean, by the way.'

She got up and moved towards him. The flickering fire-light seemed to caress the planes of his face, the powerful sweep of his shoulders. His hair was a little mussed from having pulled off his shirt, his shoes were caked in mud, and his breeches were grass-stained. For the first time since she had met him he did not look in the least forbidding.

As her eyes strayed to the enticing expanse of male flesh bared to her avid gaze, her lips parted. Instead of taking the shirt he was holding out, she found herself reaching out to touch the very centre of his chest. The hair which grew there was coarse and slightly springy. His body was so intriguingly different from hers. Where she had soft mounds of flesh, he had slabs of hard muscle. Her hand slid over, and down, until Charles abruptly stopped her exploration by clamping her hand under his own.

'What are you doing?' he rasped.

Shocked at her own temerity, she tried to pull her hand away. But he would not let it go. Keeping it firmly pressed to his waist, he declared, as though in wonder, 'You want me!'

She could not deny it. But nor dared she admit it, only to suffer the humiliation of being rejected all over again. She turned her face away, biting down on her lower lip as she wondered how on earth she was going to come up with an explanation for what she had just done.

'You don't need to be shy with me. I'm your husband,' said Charles, taking her chin firmly between his thumb and forefinger and turning her face upwards. 'If you really do want me, I will be only too happy to oblige.' He smiled, and lowered his head to kiss her.

His mouth was so gentle. For the first time he was kissing her as she had always imagined a lover would kiss his woman.

And it was all she could ever have dreamed of. As he let go of her hand to pull her closer she slid it up his side, finally feeling she had permission to explore the rugged contours of his body. He was so big, so powerful. Yet so gentle as he lifted her and laid her down on a rug by the hearth.

She basked in the wonder of his touch, not even registering the moment he unwound the curtain from her body until he reared up to gaze down at her nudity.

It was too much for her. Shyly, she pulled a corner of material over her hips, stammering, 'I cannot...we cannot...it is broad daylight! Somebody might discover us!'

'Nobody will even think of beginning to search for us until we do not appear for dinner,' he pointed out. He could not bear it if she were to draw back now. 'We have hours. Hours and hours...' he murmured, bending to kiss her into submission again. But she was no longer so pliant under his ministrations.

Eventually he knew he would have to make some concession to her shyness. In desperation, he got up, went to the window, and tore down the one remaining curtain.

'Here,' he said, draping it over them both as he lay down beside her. Though he would have enjoyed being able to look at her while they made love, the most important thing was that he got her past this first hurdle.

She wrapped her arms tight about his neck, pressing her lips to his throat as though in gratitude, and he sighed with contentment.

She had been so scared when he had got up and walked away, a frown on his face as though he had grown impatient with her. It was such a relief when he came back she could have wept. She would make no more foolish protests. Whatever he wanted to do, whatever he asked of her, she would comply.

Even though to begin with she felt a little shocked that there were so many places on her body he wanted to kiss, or lick, or nip with his teeth, or pluck at with his clever, sensitive fingers.

But before long he'd roused such a tide of sensation in

her that it swept all modesty aside. She writhed and moaned, kicking the curtain away as her whole body throbbed with heated pleasure. Then his fingers plucked once more, sending her shooting high into a realm of such exquisite sensation she cried aloud at the glory of it.

'Ah, yes,' he murmured into her ear. 'You liked that.' He was elated by her response. He had hoped she might grant him some concessions eventually, after a long period of wooing. He had been prepared to play on her sense of honour, reminding her she had a duty to give him heirs, if nothing else worked. Yet she had just yielded completely. And it was typical of her to give so much when he deserved so little. Especially considering how he had insulted her on the night he had taken her virginity. He should have been gentle and considerate of her inexperience. Instead of which...

'I was less than chivalrous last time,' he ground out. 'I will not be so careless of your needs in future, I promise you.'

She was so beautiful, lying in sated forgetfulness in the aftermath of what he knew must have been her first orgasm.

'But I have needs of my own,' he said, moving over her and into her, revelling in the soft warmth of her welcome.

Her eyes fluttered open as he began to move gently, her hands lifting to his waist as, unbelievably, she began to respond to him all over again.

He forced himself to go slowly, introducing her to the next level of lovemaking with an entirely different repertoire of moves.

'Charles!' she cried, and he felt her throbbing with release.

Hearing his name rise to her lips as she came to completion was all that was needed to send him tumbling over the edge. And, when he was spent, a feeling of such intense peace washed over him he dared not say one word for fear of shattering their first experience of harmony.

It took Heloise quite a while to come back down to earth. Charles had given her such intense pleasure. She could never have imagined her body was capable of anything so wonderful.

She turned her head to look at him. He had fallen asleep. Not surprisingly, she smiled. For he had done all the work.

'He likes to have the mastery between the sheets,' she remembered Mrs Kenton gloating, fanning her face, and just like that her joy was snuffed out. He was always like this in bed with a woman. It was nothing special to him.

And, she recalled, a feeling of sick dread cramping her stomach, he had only done this to 'oblige' her. She had approached him, blatantly stroking his chest, with her mouth hanging open at the sight of his semi-nudity. He knew they would not be rescued for hours, so it had seemed like as good a way to pass the time as any other. And he had needs, as he had pointed out as he had taken what was on offer.

She turned onto her side, pulling the curtain up over her shoulder, wondering why she should feel so cross. After all, not many nights ago she had worked out for herself that he would need a woman soon, and then made that spectacularly unsuccessful attempt to seduce him. She should be crowing in triumph, not blinking back tears. For she had got what she wanted, had she not?

It made her feel even more cross when he awoke with a smile on his face. When he saw that she was sitting hunched in front of the fire, the curtain clutched to her chin defensively, he cheerfully broke up another chair, tossing the pieces onto the fire until it was ablaze. It annoyed her that he was so much more successful at coaxing warmth from a fire she had only managed to get smoking damply. And it made her resentful when he began to tell her all about how this room had been used by former countesses to take tea, since it overlooked a particularly pleasing view of the lake, as though she were a guest he had to entertain.

It was a relief when, as dusk fell, she heard footsteps approaching the tower. Charles went to the landing, informing the servants who had come looking for them what had happened, and telling them to fetch a ladder. Hastily, while his back was turned, she fumbled her way into her damp clothing under cover of the dusty curtain.

Charles wished there was something he could do to ease his wife's discomfort. He could see she felt guilty for having enjoyed herself so much with a man she did not love. She had only married him to escape the horrific subjugation she would have suffered at Du Mauriac's cruel hands. It was futile to point out that plenty of people enjoyed the sexual act without any emotional involvement whatsoever. What they had just shared fell far short of her ideal.

She had succumbed to a fleeting moment of desire. Probably brought on by relief at surviving a frightening ordeal. He had disrobed before her, she had already been naked, and nature had taken its course.

He wanted to tell her that this mutual attraction was only the beginning. That love could grow from here. But she did not look as though she would be receptive to anything he had to say—not yet. She was clearly quite annoyed with him for taking advantage of her moment of weakness.

But he was not in the least repentant. They were lovers now, and there was no going back. She could not pretend his touch repelled her any more. They could have a good marriage. For even if she did not love him, he loved her— more than he had thought it was possible to love any woman, he reflected, as he helped her down the ladder. He would show her, he vowed, sweeping her up into his arms when she made to leave the tower on her own two feet, how good marriage to him could be. No bride would ever be as spoiled as she would be.

Ignoring her shocked gasp, and the amused looks of the two footmen who were holding the ladder, he kissed her, lingeringly, full on the mouth. And quelled her feeble protests that she was capable of walking back to the house.

'You are far too weak to make the attempt. You have not eaten anything all day. And you spent the entire afternoon making love.'

She subsided into his arms with that mutinous little pout he was beginning to love so much, saying not a word until he laid her down on the sofa in her own sitting room.

And then, when she drew breath to make the first of what he was sure would be a litany of complaints, he forestalled her.

'Sukey! See that Her Ladyship has a hot bath, and tend to the grazes on her shins. Then put her to bed and bring her some hot soup, bread and butter, and some of that apple pie she enjoyed so much at dinner the other night, if there is any left. And don't forget a pot of hot chocolate. I,' he said, dropping a kiss on his wife's parted lips, 'will return when I have had my own bath and a shave, and put on clean clothes. And, Giddings?' He turned to address the butler, who had followed them up the stairs on seeing the bedraggled state of his master and mistress. 'No visitors for the next two—no make that three days.'

'Very good, my lord.'

'And don't glare at me like that,' he advised Heloise. 'I have dealt with all the most pressing estate business, I have given my duty invitation to the neighbours to meet my Countess, and now I am entitled to enjoy my bride.'

Heloise let out one cry of vexation as Giddings turned, red-faced, from the room. First he had made it obvious to those two grinning footmen what they had spent the afternoon doing, and now he had scandalised Giddings with a statement of what he intended to spend the next few days doing. Where had all his rigidly correct behaviour gone, just when she could have done with it to spare her blushes?

Though in many ways she enjoyed his attention over the following week, just as much as he seemed to be enjoying hers, she never quite got rid of the feeling that it could not last. In desperation she grabbed what happiness she could, whilst privately waiting for the axe to fall.

It fell one morning while they were at breakfast, and Charles was reading one of the newspapers he had couriered up from London daily.

'My God,' he breathed, his eyes scanning the printed columns. 'There has been a battle.' Though he lowered the paper, it was as though he was looking straight through her. '*The* battle—the decisive battle. The losses have been disastrous.'

'Wh…who won?'

'Nobody.' His face was grim. 'The cost in human life was too great to call it a victory for Wellington. The losses from Robert's regiment alone…' He appeared to pull himself together. 'I will have to return to London. He should not be alone to deal with this.'

She went cold inside. He was going back to London. Just as he had always planned.

She could not let him walk out of her life like this. Not without a fight! Before they had become lovers she had fled out into the gardens rather than humiliate herself by confessing he was the centre of her universe. But now the thought of trying to survive without him was even more unbearable than the prospect of begging for a tiny place in his life.

'Please,' she began hesitantly. 'Please let me come with you.'

She saw disbelief in his eyes, and her heart began to thunder. She was breaking the terms of their agreement.

'Yes, I know I promised I would never cause you any trouble. But really, truly, I will not get in your way. I might even be able to help you,' she argued in desperation. 'I managed to help Robert before when nobody else could! Surely I could be of more help in London than stuck down here in the middle of nowhere? Please, Charles, let me try. Let me come with you. Don't leave me here alone!'

CHAPTER FIFTEEN

'LEAVE you here?' Charles frowned. 'Why would I do that?'

'B…but that was why you brought me down here! Because I had become too much trouble in London…'

'Because you had been *having* too much trouble in London,' he corrected her. 'I hoped that by the time we returned we might have come to a better understanding. So that you would feel you could come to me when you were in a scrape.'

'You never planned to leave me here?' Her eyes filled with tears. 'Truly?'

'I have never lied to you, Heloise,' he replied sternly. 'I never will.'

'But you were so angry…'

'Yes, I was angry the day we travelled down here. But that was not your fault.'

'Oh, but it was. I promised I would never give you any trouble, and I was in such a tangle…'

'I hold myself responsible for that. I should have taken better care of you. I knew there would be people that would try to hurt you in order to score off me, and I did nothing to protect you. Can you forgive me?'

'F…forgive you? There is nothing to forgive!'

He felt shamed that she should take such a generous

attitude. Most women who'd found themselves tied to such an unsatisfactory husband would have done nothing but complain. Some would even have taken a lover—for consolation if not revenge.

Yet she seemed to be poised for him to mete out punishments for the most trifling faults… He blinked, remembering the day she had first come to him with her proposal. She had assumed from the very first that he would find her so irritating he would end up beating her.

She had no idea of her own worth.

And as yet he had done nothing to demonstrate just how much he valued her.

But all that was about to change…

'Well, now we have that misapprehension cleared up, we should make all haste to leave. Both of us,' he said firmly.

She scurried from the breakfast room as though his remark contained some kind of threat. She was so ready to believe the worst of him, he sighed. Just as Robert had been.

She had declared she found him cold and proud and unapproachable.

It was true that he had an abhorrence of expressing his feelings, especially when they were as turbulent as the ones Heloise aroused in him. Fortunately, he had already taken steps to show his regard for her.

But it was not just his reserve or her own lack of self-esteem he had to counter. As he climbed into the carriage beside her, and caught the expression of trepidation on her face, it hit him afresh that her plea to return to London was not in any way due to a wish not to be parted from *him*.

She had only spoken of her desire to help Robert. And when he reflected how miserable she had been during her stay at Wycke, it was perhaps only natural she should want to return to the city. He frowned as the carriage rumbled through the lodge gates and out into the lane. Her dislike of the place was yet another hurdle he would have to overcome. For he had a duty to his tenants and neighbours to visit the place more than once each year. And he was not going to leave Heloise alone and unprotected in London while he dealt with estate business. Besides, his heirs would be born there. And he wanted them to grow up there. He could picture a brood of perhaps three or four, tumbling over their mother's lap under the shade of the yew tree on the south lawn. Heloise would be such a good mother—loving and loyal.

He reached for her hand abstractedly, raising it to his lips and kissing her fingers as he focussed on how he was to bring about a state in their marriage where she would look up and smile as he approached, rather than shrink from him in expectation of a scold, as she did now.

The regime at Wycke would have to change before they visited again. Of that he was certain. He did not know if he should go so far as dismissing Mrs Lanyon, but sadly he feared that might be necessary. She seemed to harbour some kind of grudge against Robert, and, though he had always appreciated her efficiency in the past, he now saw that she was singularly lacking in compassion. A kinder woman would have helped Heloise grow accustomed to her position, instead of increasing her feelings of inadequacy.

He had not been aware how long they had been sitting in silence until he heard Heloise sigh. It struck him forcibly that if it had been Robert sitting beside her she would no doubt have been chattering away merrily. He turned to look at her, noting the dejected slump of her shoulders. Except for a few brief moments when she forgot herself, in his arms in bed, that air of sadness hung round her like a persistent mist.

He drew in a sharp breath, turning away from her to look out of his own window as he felt a stab of fear that he might never be able to totally lift it. Even if she grew content with what he could offer her, it would never be the grand passion she had so admired her sister for harbouring for that penniless young engraver. Her parents had eloped, too, setting love above their personal safety. Whatever understanding they eventually reached, would it always seem like a poor substitute for the real thing?

Well, he might never move her heart to any great degree, but he could prove his solid worthiness.

He cleared his throat. 'When we return to London, things will not be between us as they were before.'

She turned to look at him, a little frown pleating her brow.

'There is no need to look so alarmed. It is your well-being that I am thinking of.'

He would need to deal with Lampton and Mrs Kenton in person before he could permit Heloise the same degree of freedom she had enjoyed before.

It was not just the personal vendetta the Lamptons held against him that might prove dangerous to her, either. After the losses incurred at Waterloo, there might well be some antagonism towards her simply because of her nationality. Until he had tested the waters for himself, and made sure she would be absolutely safe, he was not going to permit anyone anywhere near her.

Nor, to begin with, would he be free to escort her anywhere. The political map of Europe was going to change radically, if he was any judge of matters, and, while he had no intention of forcing Heloise to cross the Channel so that he could participate fully in negotiations, he could be busy laying the groundwork for those who would go in his stead.

'It might be a good idea if, just at first, you did not move about too much in society.'

Was there anything more annoying, she thought, than

being told to act in a way she had already decided upon for herself? Why, it had been weeks since she had determined to be such a model wife that she would scarcely even venture out of doors! She knew she ought to be grateful that he was permitting her even a tiny place in his life, yet the longer he lectured her about what she was and was not permitted to do, and trotted out excuse after excuse for why he would be behaving much as he had done before, resentment began to smoulder inside her.

Charles noted that the nearer they drew towards London, rather than being reassured by his promises to take far better care of her than he had done before, she looked increasingly strained.

'Is something worrying you?' he eventually asked her.

Smiling determinedly to conceal her increasing feelings of resentment, she replied, 'Of course there is! I worry about Robert. It is for him that we return to London after all,' she reminded herself.

Charles was glad to get out of the carriage when at last it pulled up outside Walton House. He knew she was not in love with Robert, yet to hear of her concern for another man filled him with such unreasonable jealousy that it was all he could do to keep it leashed.

Heloise drooped into the house in his wake. He seemed so relieved the journey was finally over. Oh, he had tried manfully to be what he seemed to think she would want— holding her hand, forcing himself to make conversation to keep her amused. As though she was a child and he a rather stern guardian, pointing out that he was going to be busy with important matters of state, and she must behave herself until he had a few minutes to spare!

He surged into the house, making straight for Robert's rooms. Just before he reached his door, he turned, as though recalling her tiresome presence, and said, with an exasperated expression on his face, 'I think you should go up to your rooms, Lady Walton, while I see how my brother fares. I cannot say when I may join you.'

She lifted her chin as her heart sank even lower. 'Of course.' Whatever had made her hope he might appreciate having his silly little wife at his side? Or that she might be able to help him through this crisis? He just wanted her to keep out of his way.

'I will see to my unpacking. As long as Robert is being cared for, that is all that matters.'

He turned from her so swiftly she was sure he had already relegated her from his thoughts. As he pushed open Robert's door, she caught a glimpse of booted feet sprawled at ungainly angles, and empty bottles lying on the floor.

She caught her breath. She really was silly to feel slighted because Charles did not dance attendance on her when his beloved brother was going through such a terrible time.

Feeling slightly ashamed of herself, she went up to her rooms.

'There is a parcel for you, my lady,' said Sukey, as soon as she saw Heloise trail in.

Frowning, Heloise went to the bed, on which the flat, square package lay. She did not think she had any orders outstanding with the modiste. Wondering what it could be, she tore open the brown paper wrapping to find it was a leatherbound book.

She opened it at random, and gave a gasp of surprise. She was looking at one of her own sketches. Crossing to the desk by the window, she laid the book out flat and flipped through the pages.

'These are all mine!' she said to Sukey, who was peering over her shoulder. All the drawings she had left with Mr Ackermann were bound, here within these beautifully tooled leather covers. Just as though they were the work of a real artist.

She turned back to the very first page, and read the words: '*A collection of original watercolours, penned by the hand of Lady Heloise, beloved wife of Charles, 9th Earl of Walton…*'

Beloved wife? She ran a trembling finger over the printed words. This flowery language was not at all the kind of thing Charles would ever say, never mind cause to have written. He must have left the exact choice of words to the printer.

'Charles,' she whispered, wishing with all her heart that the words were true.

It was scarcely half an hour later that he came in and found her sitting on the bed, the book clasped in her arms and tears streaming down her face.

'Don't you like it?' He felt as though an iron fist had squeezed his heart. He had been so sure she would love seeing her work professionally bound.

'Like it?' she raised tear-drenched eyes to his. 'I love it. Did you…?' She stopped, shaking her head. If he had not meant the words, she did not want to hear the denial from his own lips. Far better to cling to the illusion that he felt some affection for her than to have her dreams shattered.

Hesitantly, Charles took a step towards the bed. 'I wanted to do something to demonstrate how sorry I am for forcing you to destroy that other sketchbook. It was quite wrong of me.'

'Oh!' Her head flew up, her eyes looking curiously wounded.

He clasped his hands behind his back. He would have thought his apology would comfort her. Perhaps it had only reminded her what an unfeeling brute he could be.

'I was acting completely out of character that night,' he admitted. 'My state of mind at that time was not… That is, Heloise…' He swallowed, searching for the words that would convince her, once and for all, that he was not the tyrannical bully he had shown himself to be during those few mad days in Paris. 'You have a remarkable skill. I admire it greatly. I have no wish to stifle your talent. I know I made a great deal of fuss, saying I did not want people to see your work, but that is not how I feel about it now. Now I have come to know you better, I know you would not do anything to embarrass me, or the name of Walton.'

'Not deliberately!' she cried, kneeling up and moving towards him, her hands outstretched. 'I did not mean to make a spectacle with your neighbours at Wycke…'

'You did not!' he vowed, taking the final step that brought him within touching distance. Taking her hands in his, he said, 'I was proud of the way you managed to make some of the most cantankerous, narrow-minded provincials look like rational, attractive people. With only a stub of pencil and some rather ancient writing paper!'

'Truly?'

He sat on the bed next to her, drawing her hands close to his chest. 'Heloise, when will you learn that I never say anything I do not mean? In fact, the next time we go to the country I hope you will spend some time making sketches of my favourite vistas. It is long past time that I put up some original artwork in this place.' His gaze flicked round the un-inspiring collection of oils that graced her walls, and he grimaced. 'Your work would at least have the bonus of being amusing.'

'I draw people, though, not scenes,' she protested.

He cut her off with a smile. 'You do scenes. And you capture the atmosphere of a place. Have you forgot this?' He leaned down and flicked through the pages of the book until he came to the depiction of their first night at the theatre. 'Looking at it brings back the atmosphere of that night so vividly I can almost smell it.'

'But it is the people that create the atmosphere…'

He shook his head. 'Heloise, you have more talent than you give yourself credit for. I know you focus on the people, and regard the background only as the setting for your caricatures, but even in the few strokes you begrudged the curtains round Lensborough's box you captured the very texture of the velvet. If you wanted, you could capture not just the scenery of my home but its very essence. When you know it better. I feel sure that even now, should you decide to draw the ruined tower…'

Their eyes met and held as they remembered that afternoon they had become lovers. The book slid to the floor, forgotten, and they moved into each other's arms.

'I shall ring and have supper sent up,' Charles said, much later. 'There is no point in dressing for dinner now. And we would be eating it alone, wherever we took it. Robert is in no fit state to appear before you, my love.'

Rolling onto his side, he propped himself on his elbow.

'We had no need to fear that Robert would suffer alone. While the bells rang out all over London to celebrate the nation's victory, those who could not stand the pain of their bereavement gravitated to his rooms and made a valiant attempt to drink my cellars dry. You may be surprised to hear Lord Lensborough himself is one of those currently nursing a hangover down there.'

Heloise was beyond making any response. He had praised her work, taken her to bed in broad daylight, and called her his love. Yet downstairs Robert and his companions were mourning the shameful waste of so many young male lives. It was wrong to experience any measure of happiness when so many were grieving.

'I will visit with him tomorrow,' she declared. Tonight was just for her and Charles.

'Tomorrow will be soon enough,' he agreed, making her

heart soar. 'Robert's rooms are no fit place for a lady at the moment. But now he knows we have returned, it may be the push he needs to begin sobering up. And his friends will feel they may safely leave him now that we have come home.'

Her brief moment of joy dissolved. Charles was not thinking of how delightful it would be to have a romantic supper in bed with her. His priority was still Robert's well-being.

'You are not upset, are you, that I will be otherwise engaged tomorrow?'

As if she were a spoiled child who had to be constantly amused!

She lifted her chin. 'I do not need you to dance attendance on me,' she declared proudly. 'Even when I first came to London, did I not manage to amuse myself?' Flushing darkly, she added, 'Perhaps that is not such a good thing to remind you of. But I will do better now. I will not go to gaming hells, or masquerades, or gamble with military gentlemen again, I promise you!'

'Even if you should do all of those things,' Charles declared, 'I should not banish you to the country. If you get into any sort of trouble you must tell me straight away, and no matter what you have done I will help you.'

'I have just told you,' she snapped, 'that I won't get into trouble!'

'Well, we'll see, shall we?'

Crestfallen that he still assumed she would get into some sort of trouble the minute his back was turned, she rolled over and pretended to go to sleep.

Over the next few days Heloise was carried along by a determination to prove to Charles that in spite of his misgivings she *could* behave herself when the need arose.

She usually slept in until quite late. For, although she

scarcely saw Charles during the hours of daylight, whatever time he came home, he never failed to come to her bed.

Once she had washed and dressed, she liked to take an airing in the park, although she made sure both Sukey and a footman always properly escorted her. When she returned there was always some little gift from Charles for her to unwrap—proof that he was appreciative of her efforts to reform. She spent the hours before dinner either reading the poetry, or pressing individual blossoms from a posy—or, once, attempting to put together the cleverly designed portable easel he had purchased. And she spent the hours after dinner waiting impatiently for him to come home.

She might even have felt a measure of contentment if only she'd had Robert to keep her company during the long, dull evenings. But whenever she went and knocked on his door there was always already a group of grim-faced young men sprawled about the rooms, and a distinct aroma of alcohol in the air. The fact that all conversation ceased the moment she walked in made her feel increasingly awkward about intruding. He had friends about him. That was the main thing. And who better than those young men, with military backgrounds, who could understand far better than she could what he was going through?

She was selfish to wish he would at least let her in for half an hour, so that she had someone to talk to. She sighed now, picking up the latest novel that Charles had sent her. Did she not have so much more now than the last time she had been in London? She might not go out, but then she had not really enjoyed many of her outings anyway. Particularly not once she had locked horns with Mrs Kenton.

She shivered, applying herself to words that she had a vague recollection of reading before. It was not an easy story to get into, but she wanted very much to be able to tell Charles that she was enjoying it. Even though she was having difficulty working out what the story was supposed to be about, she sighed. Still, though the story itself was not very interesting, she did love the fact that Charles had bought it for her. He was so generous.

'…so generous that it quite makes up for the coldness of his public manners…' she heard Mrs Kenton whispering.

That Woman! The moment her mind strayed in her direction, her words flooded her mind with her poison all over again.

She shut the book with a snap, and went into her bedroom. She would sketch until Charles came home. That always made her feel better.

But though she sat at her drawing desk, and took the charcoal in her fingers, her mind remained devoid of inspiration. She could not think of a single thing she wanted to draw. She had not been anywhere or seen anyone since returning to London to fire her imagination at all.

There seemed to be nothing but a great emptiness all around her. When Charles came in, far earlier than she had expected, she was so relieved to see him that she flew into his arms. She knew he would not rebuff her these days. On the contrary, he seemed only too keen to strip her naked and kiss and caress every inch of her, until she was mindless with pleasure and he was completely exhausted.

She looked down at him, as he lay sleeping beside her later, a troubled frown creasing her brow. If only she had never met Mrs Kenton. For then she would be completely happy, thinking that the way he behaved was an indication that he felt something for her. But she *had* met Mrs Kenton, and she knew that he took similar pride in his performance in bed, no matter which woman shared it.

And, on reflection, she could not read very much into the fact he sent her gifts every day, either. Mrs Kenton had told her how generous he was to his mistresses.

He had never given her a single thing before he had taken her to his bed. With a pang of shock, she realised that, far from being a mark of his approval, those gifts were more like payment for services rendered.

He was treating her just like he would treat his mistress!

No, on second thoughts he was not even treating her so well as that. At least a mistress got an outing every now and again. She had met Nell in the theatre, and at Vauxhall Gardens, and although everyone said Lord Lensborough was a hard man, even he had given Nell her own carriage and pair to drive about in the park.

She sat up, hugging her knees to her chest as she grew more and more upset. He had said before they married that as his wife she would move in the first circles. But she didn't. She never went anywhere. It was as if he was ashamed of her!

She could barely look at him when he rose the next morning to be about his business. Business which, she thought huffily, he could as well conduct at home, if he had a wife he trusted. If he really was engaged in politics. She sniffed. For all she knew he could be out carousing with his friends, or even trawling Covent Garden for a new mistress.

'Heloise?' he said gently, noting the stiff set of her shoulders under the blankets. 'I can see you are not happy with me this morning.' Or indeed any morning. 'This state of affairs cannot continue.' Fortunately he would be able to conclude his involvement in party affairs today. And then he would be able to devote himself entirely to getting his wife to admit that being a partner in a marriage of convenience was not the end of the world. 'When I return tonight, you and I need to have a serious talk.'

She shut her eyes tight on the wave of pain that assailed her. She had known it! She had known it from the first! She had only ever been a poor substitute for Felice, and now he could not even continue to use her as he would use a mistress. He was tired of her.

Had he already found her replacement? Was that where he went every night, when he said he was engaged in state affairs? *Affaires*, more like! And she, rather than demanding he treat her with respect, had welcomed him into her bed whatever time of the night he rolled in, with open arms, like the lovesick fool she was! She should have known when she'd had to go to such lengths to seduce him that he would not stay faithful for long. If he had ever found her in the least bit desirable he would have made the first move!

'In the meantime, I should like you to have this.' He went to his jacket, which was hanging on the back of a chair, delved into the pocket, and extracted a black rectangular box. 'I had meant to give it to you last night, but…' He smiled wryly at the memory of her flying to his arms, and more or less dragging him into bed.

'Don't remind me!' she flung at him waspishly.

He frowned as he approached the bed, where she was sitting with her knees hunched up, a mutinous glare on her face. He faltered, wishing with all his heart that she did not feel so ashamed of experiencing desire without love.

'Here,' he said, proffering the jeweller's box.

Until now, the gifts he had bought her had been trifling things, meant to amuse her and remind her he was thinking of her, though he could not be with her. But he had never forgotten her face when she had spoken about the Walton diamonds. She had thought he did not care because they were old. She seemed to have thought that if he cared about her he would have bought her something new. And so he had sought to redress that error in the purchase of these pearls. Pearls for purity. For she was the purest woman he had ever known. Besides which, he could not wait to see how the ear drops would look against the glorious silk of her dark hair.

As he opened the box to reveal the long strand of perfectly matched pearls, her eyes widened in horror.

'How dare you?' she cried, drawing back as though he was holding out a snake. 'I won't be treated like this! No—not one minute more! Oh, yes, I know I promised I would not stop you from amusing yourself, however you wished, but I have to tell you that I cannot keep to that stupid bargain we made one minute longer!'

He went cold with dread as he heard her telling him their marriage was over. And all because he had given her pearls? He looked down at the box, lying open in his hand, wondering where he had gone wrong this time.

He was about to find out. Flinging the covers aside, Heloise rose from the bed, completely forgetful of her nudity, and advanced on him, her eyes spitting fire.

'I am your wife! Your *wife*!' She swiped at the box, knocking it from his nerveless fingers. 'And if you think you can pay me off with pearls, when even that Mrs Kenton got rubies, you are the greatest imbecile! And I know you never made *her* stay within doors, not to mingle with your so perfect friends. Even poor little Nell gets trips to the theatre every now and again. And you think, you *really* think, that I will walk out of your life quietly after you give me the kind of jewels that a mother would give to her daughter when she makes her first curtsey in society? Well, I tell you, *no*! I am not going back to Wycke, and I am not going to sit at home any more while you go out and amuse yourself without your embarrassing wife hanging on your arm. And if you think I am going to do nothing while you set up another mistress, then you are very much mistaken. If you dare…if I find out where you are keeping her…I shall…I shall…'

For much of the tirade Charles had been too bemused to take in more than the fact that she was furiously angry and gloriously naked. But at last some of her meaning began to percolate through.

'What,' he said, his heart pounding, 'will you do, Heloise, if you find out where I have set up my mistress?'

'Oh!' She drew back, as though him saying it made it real. Her eyes filled with tears. She began to shake. 'I shall do something terrible,' she whispered, her face grim. 'Of that you can be sure.'

'Thank God,' he sighed, drawing her into his arms. She loved him. She must do to be experiencing such fierce jealousy. It was a feeling he recognised only too well.

'No!' she whimpered, struggling to break free. 'You shall not subdue me with your kisses again. I won't let you. I hate you!' she cried, raising her fists to beat at his chest.

'No, you don't,' he countered. 'You hate feeling weak and helpless under the force of your feelings. But your feelings for me are not hatred. Ah, no—don't cry, my little love,' he crooned, scooping her up and carrying her back to bed. 'I have not set up a mistress. I promise you,' he said, kissing her forehead.

'You…you have not?' she hiccupped, frowning up at him through tear spiked lashes.

'Of course not. Why ever would you think I would do such a thing?'

'Well, I know you are only putting up with me…you only married me, after all, to save face so that no one would know Felice broke your heart. I…I know you will never love me like you loved her.'

'That much is true,' he said dryly. 'For I was never in love with her at all.'

'What? That is not true. When she ran off with Jean-Claude your heart was broken!'

'Actually, no, it was not. Not in the least. The truth,' he said ruefully, 'as you pointed out with such perspicacity at the time, was that she had severely dented my pride. You see,' he said, taking her hand, 'Felice was such fun to be with. I had never met anyone like her before. When I was with her she made me feel as though there was something about me as a person that she valued, since she made no secret of the fact she despised the aristocracy as a class. She was not forever hinting that she wanted me to buy her things, either.' He shook his head, a frown clouding his brow. 'And I was in a peculiarly vulnerable state of mind at the time.'

Though Heloise still seemed oblivious to her state of undress, he felt obliged to reach down and pull the coverlet up, tucking it round her shoulders as he considered the best way to explain.

'I had suffered a series of shocks. Discovering I had a brother. Learning that the men I had trusted throughout my youth had perpetrated a crime against him and my stepmother…and then finding that I was totally unable to escape their pernicious influence!' He laughed bitterly. 'I could cease seeing them, but I could not undo my training. No matter how much I wished it, I could not find the least desire to behave with anything less than complete decorum. And then I took Robert into my home and endured his scorn, while seeing how very much he was valued by his friends… In the end I fled to Paris looking for…well, I don't know what I was looking for, to tell you the truth. I only know that for a while I felt that Felice was the answer. She made me feel as though I could slough off all that I had been and make a fresh start. It was my dreams of becoming a better man she stole, not my heart, Heloise.'

He stopped fussing with the coverlet and looked her straight in the eye as he confessed, 'My heart belongs to you, Heloise. It is a poor, stunted thing, I know. But, such as it is, it beats for you alone.'

'But when…? But how…?' She sat up, an intent expression on her face. 'When you brought me to London you left me utterly alone. After giving me a long list of things I was not supposed to do and people I was not to talk to, as though I was a complete nuisance!'

He took her face between his hands. 'Do you know how much it hurt that you never understood?' He took a deep breath. 'You always put me in mind of a little bird. And when I saw that picture you drew of yourself, chained in an intolerable marriage, I knew I did not want it to be like that between us. I know I said a lot of damn fool things at the start, but once you were mine I did not want you to feel you were caged, or chained. I wanted you to be able to fly free and come to me because you wanted to come to me, not because I compelled you.'

'I...I thought you did not care what I did. And I felt as though my heart was breaking. Because I loved you so much...'

'You said you didn't!' he protested, rearing back. 'When you suggested we get married...'

'I don't think I did—not at that precise moment. Or perhaps I had not allowed myself to, because I thought your heart belonged to my sister. But by the afternoon, once I knew you were to be my own husband, I could not bear the thought that you might want any other woman. And then, when I feared Du Mauriac would kill you, then I was sure. I was so scared! I had to get you away from France to safety, no matter what it cost me!' She reached up and stroked his cheek, her expression full of remembered concern. 'I told myself I would not care if you never loved me back so long as you were safe. Oh, but when we got to London, and you were so cold, I made such a fool of myself trying to win your approval,' she finished ruefully.

'You were trying to win my approval with all that time you spent with Robert?' he groaned. 'While I was trying to show you how tolerant I could be, letting you do as you liked!'

'Oh, don't be tolerant any more, then,' said Heloise. 'It made me so unhappy!'

'Very well, since you ask,' he growled. 'From now on I shall be the most intolerant—' he kissed her hard on the lips '—jealous—' he pulled her down until she lay flat on her back '—possessive husband that ever drew breath! In fact I will never let you out of my sight again. When I think of the torment I suffered when I thought you planned to leave me...'

She looked perplexed. 'When was that? I never thought of leaving you!'

No... The day he feared she had run back to London with Robert she had in fact been stuck in the tower. And the day he had assumed she was trying to raise money to elope with him she had been trying to sell her pictures to pay off her gambling debts. Even in France, when he had thought she would want to flee an intolerable marriage, she had already been in love with him!

She had never thought of leaving him. Nor had his stepmother, come to that. And at that revelation something inside him seemed to unfurl and blossom. He felt tears prick his eyes. Somewhat appalled, he blinked them away, before burying his face in the silken cocoon of her hair.

'I love you,' he said, for there was nothing else that summed up so neatly the enormity of what he felt at that moment.

Her answer, 'I love you too,' was exactly what he needed to hear.

Some time later, she whispered, 'And you promise you really won't send me away and take a mistress?'

'I would not dare,' he groaned, rolling onto his back and pulling her into his side. 'Besides, you would not let me— would you?'

'How could I stop you if you really wanted to?'

He chuckled. 'Are you serious? Don't you know how powerful you are?'

'Powerful? Me?' she squeaked.

'Yes, you. You have been able to mould me like putty in your hands from the first moment you set your sights on me. When I had vowed to have nothing whatever to do with your family you persuaded me to marry into it. I had decided nothing would induce me to leave Paris until my lease expired, and scarcely a day later you had me racing for the coast like a lunatic. And worst of all, when I had always believed love was a debilitating emotion from which I would never suffer, you wrung it from my stony heart. Nobody else could have done it.'

'Are you sorry?' she asked in a small voice.

'Sorry?' He snorted. 'I have never been more glad of anything in my life. You are my life, Heloise,' he said softly. 'The light of my life. If you had never bullied me into marrying you I would have been the coldest, loneliest man in London. Instead of which…' He paused, his eyes suspiciously bright with moisture. 'Ah, don't talk any more,' he groaned. 'Just kiss me.'

'With all my heart,' she sighed. 'With all my heart.'

* * * * *

AN ITALIAN
AFFAIR

Margaret McDonagh

Margaret McDonagh says of herself: 'I began losing myself in the magical world of books from a very young age, and I always knew that I had to write, pursuing the dream for over twenty years, often with cussed stubbornness in the face of rejection letters! Despite having numerous romance novellas, short stories and serials published, the news that my first "proper book" had been accepted by Harlequin Mills & Boon for their Medical™ line brought indescribable joy! Having a passion for learning makes researching an involving pleasure, and I love developing new characters, getting to know them, setting them challenges to overcome. The hardest part is saying goodbye to them, because they become so real to me. And I always fall in love with my heroes! Writing and reading books, keeping in touch with friends, watching sport and meeting the demands of my four-legged companions keeps me well occupied. I hope you enjoy reading this book as much as I loved writing it.'

www.margaretmcdonagh.com
margaret.mcdonagh@yahoo.co.uk

Margaret McDonagh's next novel,
Virgin Midwife, Playboy Doctor, **is due out in July 2008 from Mills & Boon® Medical™.**

Dear Reader,

Welcome to this new authors' anthology, celebrating Mills & Boon's centenary. One hundred years of bringing pleasure to generations of readers around the world. That's some achievement!

It was always my ambition to write for Mills & Boon, and I am thrilled to find myself living the dream, and awed at sharing shelf-space with established writers I have long admired. I will never forget the day I received the call to say my first title, *The Italian Doctor's Bride*, had been accepted. It was the best Christmas present ever! My wonderful editor believed in me, and continues to help me fulfil my goals as a Mills & Boon author. To have my sixth title included in this anthology to mark the centenary and launch out into a new one is an honour, a special experience.

If you are new to Medical™ romances, I hope *An Italian Affair* will tempt you to read more – there is a wide variety of themes and settings, by some wonderful writers. Do try the exciting 2008 Penhally Bay continuity series. I hope you will enjoy my books, and will make a return visit to my fictional world of Strathlochan in beautiful rural Scotland. You will be very welcome.

Love,

Margaret

www.margaret.mcdonagh@yahoo.co.uk

To my very special editor, Joanne…
Thank you so much for believing in me
and for giving me the chance
to fulfil my dreams.

To Fiona J…
Thank you for your support
and for all your kindness and care.

And Happy Centenary to Mills & Boon…
Thanks for the enjoyment and opportunities
offered to readers and writers
around the world.
Here's to the next hundred years!

PROLOGUE

A WOMAN'S scream—high-pitched and fearful—shattered the silence.

Sebastiano Adriani paused, his purposeful stride faltering, his gaze scanning the dark, narrow streets for the source of the sound. Concerned, he changed direction, heading further away from home to investigate. He could spare a few moments to ensure no one was in serious trouble.

In the early hours of the morning, Florence was quiet. Only a few street cleaners were in evidence, along with an occasional couple who lingered to embrace as they made their way home after a romantic night out. The July air was laden with sultry summer heat, so Seb had removed his tie, unfastened the top button of his shirt, and slung the jacket of his Armani suit over one arm. Despite the lateness of the hour, he had chosen to walk back to his expensive but impersonal apartment not far from the hospital. Both the exercise and the solitude appealed to him.

He had spent a pleasant enough evening escorting Lidia di Napoli, first to dinner at one of the city's finest restaurants, which boasted three Michelin rosettes, and then to an open-air classical concert. Not his normal taste in music, but Lidia, an attractive young actress, had pouted prettily and begged him to accompany her. Her pout had been less appealing later in the evening, when he had been called back to the hospital. A *pro bono* patient he had operated on that morning—a young man who had needed major and intricate facial reconstruction following a traffic accident—had taken a sudden and unexpected turn for the worse. Seb's presence had been needed urgently. To the relief of the medical team, the young man was now stable but under constant observation in intensive care.

Lidia had been vocally displeased at the abrupt end to the evening, and had still been complaining as he had paid a taxi to take her home…alone. If she hoped to see him again, she would need to learn that nothing and no one came before his work. Not that he would have stayed with her, regardless of the unsubtle inducements she had been offering since he had collected her from the theatre at the end of rehearsals for her new play. He never spent the night in any woman's bed—and never allowed a woman in his.

Thankfully, due to the latest political scandal to take Florence by storm, the paparazzi had been absent from the restaurant, tracking down more lucrative prey elsewhere. For once his evening, and his companion, had failed to attract media attention, and he had been able to eat dinner and attend the concert without being bothered. He was grateful. Unlike the women who tried to be seen on his arm, who sought to use his name to further their own, he had no desire to feature in the gossip columns.

Hearing raised voices, Seb increased his pace, cutting through a nearby *piazza* into a warren of narrow streets just as another scream alerted him to the panicked woman's location. Rounding a corner, he saw a man, dressed all in black, hit his victim in the face and begin dragging her struggling form towards a recessed doorway.

'*Arresto!*' Shouting at the man to stop, to leave her alone, Seb ran to the woman's aid. '*Lasci il sua solo!*'

Pushing the sobbing woman roughly aside, the assailant refocused his attention. Cautious, but unafraid, Seb faced the man. He knew how to look after himself. The outward veneer of polish and sophistication he now wore with ease, as one of Europe's most successful reconstructive plastic surgeons to the rich and famous, failed to mask his origins. The boy from the streets, who had survived on his charm and his wits, had never been entirely banished.

Jockeying for position, Seb placed himself between the attacker and the distressed woman, keeping her safe in the doorway behind him. Despite the paucity of light, Seb scanned the man's build and face, memorising every detail and distinguishing feature he could for later identification: the scar bisecting his chin, the letters tattooed in red across the knuckles of each hand, the row of gold studs outlining one ear. Never taking his attention from his opponent, Seb tossed the woman his mobile phone and instructed her to call the police. He had hoped the man would back down, but he appeared undaunted, moving swiftly, the sudden flash of a knifeblade a silvery menace in the shadows.

Adrenalin pumped through Seb's veins. Watchful and wary, he dodged to the side as the man lunged towards him, the knife extended. With his jacket wrapped around his right arm, Seb used the padding to deflect the next attack as the knife slashed sideways through the air. The fabric ripped. But not his skin. Yet. His heart was thudding under his ribs. Dimly, he was aware of the woman crying on the phone, giving their location, begging for help, but his sole focus was on the knife. Again the man came towards him. Again Seb attempted to deflect the blow. The material afforded scant protection, and he winced as the knife sliced across his wrist and bit into the heel of his right hand. He could feel the blood welling from the wounds, flowing hot and sticky down his palm and between his fingers.

In the distance came the wail of a siren, but the man refused to retreat, feinting one way and then the other in an attempt to get past Seb and reach the woman. She screamed again, pressing back into the corner of the doorway. Thinking only of protecting her, Seb stepped in front of the man once more. Keeping his voice calm, he told him to give up, reminding him the police were coming. The sirens were ever louder.

'Rinunziare. La polizia sta venendo.'

Swearing profusely, the man lunged forward a final time. As the knife came towards his face, Seb instinctively raised both arms to shield himself, the razor-sharp blade cutting through his left forearm near the inner elbow before slashing across his right wrist and palm. Seb kicked out, catching the man off balance. The attacker staggered back, cursing violently before he regained his footing. Then, with the police closing in, he ran from the scene, disappearing into the darkness.

Ignoring his own problems, Seb turned to check that the woman was all right. 'Signora, come sta?'

'Bene. Grazie, Signor, mille grazie.' The woman sobbed her thanks. 'Dio! Siete sanguinando!'

Seb already knew he was bleeding. Assured that the woman was physically unharmed, he dropped to his knees, anxious to attend to his wounds, to stem the blood and keep his hands—the tools of his trade—elevated to reduce any swelling. His injuries produced a worrying mix of pain and numbness. And he couldn't perform the actions he intended. His left arm felt heavy and sluggish, refusing to transmit his commands to his hand. His right wrist was slack, and the thumb and index finger of his right hand wouldn't move, couldn't grasp the tissues the woman handed him.

He had not been scared before.

Now he was.

CHAPTER ONE

'I AM sure we found the right place, Gina. The special place I shared with my Matteo.'

Gina McNaught heard the emotion in her grandmother's familiar accented voice. A mixture of wistfulness, anxiety and longing brought a gleam to faded hazel eyes, while a fierce determination radiated from the elderly lady's increasingly frail frame. Once long ebony hair was now short and grey—more evidence of the relentless march of time. Smiling against the melancholy realisation that there might not be many more years, Gina took one work-roughened hand in hers and gave a gentle squeeze. She knew what this journey meant to her grandmother…knew how important it was that they located the exact spot depicted in the faded black and white photograph now resting on the table in front of them.

The photograph, and the story accompanying it, had intrigued and enchanted Gina since she had been a young child. She never tired of hearing how fate had brought her Italian grandmother and her Scottish grandfather together, how Maria Tesotto and Matthew McNaught had met on a deserted beach…and had fallen in love.

'There was no villa there in those days,' her grandmother continued, lost in her memories. 'But it is still secluded, unspoilt…and the name gives it away, no? Back then, people referred to the rock in the sea as Lancia del Nettuno—Neptune's Spear. You can just see it in the picture. And now we find Villa alla Roccia del Nettuno. The Villa at Neptune's rock. Gina, it *has* to be right.'

'I'll find out, Nonna. I promise.'

'You do so much for me, *ragazza mia*. Maybe too much, no?' she asked with a sad smile.

'Of course not,' Gina reassured her. 'You mean the world to me.'

One increasingly arthritic hand cupped her cheek. 'And you to me. But I worry that you have given up so much of your own life for me…and for your grandfather. Since we left that damp old council house in Glasgow and came to live with you in your lovely cottage in Strathlochan you have spent all your time caring for us and making our lives comfortable when you are not working at the hospital.'

'Nonna—'

'I know.' Her grandmother forestalled the interruption. 'You see your friends. You love your job. But there is more to life, Gina. We never wanted you to end your relationship with Malcolm because of us.'

Gina ducked her head to hide her gaze. No way would she ever tell her grandmother the vicious, hurtful things Malcolm had said. 'It wasn't like that, Nonna. Things had run their course.' They had certainly been over when she had discovered that Malcolm's understanding of family and her own were so widely divergent.

'But it's four years, and you've not dated at all! I want you to be happy—as happy as I was for all those years with my Matteo. I want you to find that special man who is right for you. You should be meeting men, having fun, thinking of your own needs.'

Perhaps it was being back on Elba, where her own happiness had begun, that had put these ideas into her grand-mother's head. 'I'm fine, Nonna.'

It was a long time since she had allowed herself to have needs, or to indulge in dreams of her own. Real life hadn't worked out that way. Not for her. And maybe, having grown up with the fairytale, she couldn't bring herself to settle for anything less. She had made her choices and she had no regrets…even if she could scarcely remember how it felt to be a desirable woman.

'Now you give up your holiday time and organise this trip, obliging the whim of an old woman.'

The words pulled Gina from her reverie. 'That's non-sense and you know it,' she rebuked softly. 'Besides, I have always longed to see Elba. What better place could we come together?' She smiled, but the reason for their visit here took the gloss off her pleasure, as did the sadness that dulled the light in her grandmother's eyes.

'That is true. And you would have found a way to bring me here no matter what, keeping the promise you made to me and your grandfather. This means so much to me.'

'I know, Nonna.' Gina hid her worry about the toll this trip might take on a woman troubled by her aging, arthritic body, not to mention the emotions involved by returning to the place she held so dear while bearing the loss of the man who had been her world for fifty years. 'Will you be all right resting here on your own if I go back and see if someone has returned to the villa?'

Her grandmother patted her hand. 'Do not fret. I am fatigued after our long hours of travel yesterday, that is all.'

The journey, entailing a flight from Scotland to Pisa, and then a train ride to Piombino, the port on the Italian mainland from where they had caught the ferry to Portoferraio, Elba's capital town, had been exhausting. And it had not ended until they had travelled to the unspoilt western end of the mountainous island, where Gina had booked a room at an inexpensive bed and breakfast run from a private house. The twin-bedded room was small, basic, but comfortable…all she could afford on a tight budget.

It was also close to Capo Sant'Andrea, a name her grandmother remembered, believing it to be near their ultimate destination. Gina wasn't surprised her grandmother, now seventy years old, was feeling the strain—especially as she had insisted they begin their search for the right location along the stretch of the north-west coast first thing that morning. Thanks to the taxi driver's local knowledge, they had struck lucky and found the hidden cove containing Neptune's Spear. Gina could only hope that her grandmother would not be disappointed with the rest of her quest.

'I'll go and make enquiries.' Rising to her feet, Gina collected her bag. 'My mobile phone number is on the pad, and Signora Mancini has it, too. She'll be here if you need anything.' She was grateful to their kindly landlady, who had volunteered to maintain a discreet watch while Gina was out. Her grandmother nodded, masking a couple of coughs, and Gina frowned, unable to dismiss a twinge of unease. Bending, she kissed a soft, wrinkled cheek, sending up a silent wish that her outing would be successful. 'I'll do my best for you, Nonna.'

'You always do. Bless you, *ragazza mia.*'

Moisture shimmered in wise hazel eyes and Gina forced a smile, blinking back the answering tears that pricked her own darker eyes. 'I'll see you soon.'

Keen to cut costs where possible, Gina declined the taxi that had been necessary that morning with her grandmother's decreased mobility. Instead, she hired a bicycle and rode back along the narrow, winding roads of the cape towards the villa their search had identified earlier in the day.

All her twenty-eight years money had been tight, but what the McNaughts had lacked in material things had been more than compensated for with an abundance of love, care and support. She had revelled in being able to return that love and care by having her grandparents live with her for the last four years, seeing them benefit from Strathlochan's cleaner air, cosier conditions and sense of community. Any thought that she had put a part of her life on hold to do it she pushed to the back of her mind. She had made her choices and had never had a moment of regret. Now, though, her grandfather was gone, and the pain of his loss stabbed through her. Her grandparents had never been able to return to Italy together, but she had vowed to help her grandmother see this through.

With only her nursing salary, it was a struggle to pay all the bills, to cover her mortgage and to meet her grand-mother's needs. The elderly lady's pension was a pittance and, despite a lifetime of hard work, her grandfather had been able to leave little behind in support. She had a small amount left in an emergency fund, but Gina prayed she wouldn't need to use it—and that Nonna Maria wouldn't find out that she had cashed in her savings to pay for this Elban pilgrimage.

Coming to a halt at the entrance to the villa, Gina paused a moment. Taking in a breath of clean air, she marvelled at the landscape, at the way chestnut woods swept down the hillsides to the coast. All was quiet. She stared at the sign on the gate across the drive that led to a home hidden from view amongst the trees. Villa alla Roccia del Nettuno. The Villa at Neptune's Rock. For her grandmother's sake, Gina hoped this was the right place—and that the owner would be understanding of the unusual request she had come here to make.

Closing the gate behind her, Gina pushed the bike up the

rough driveway. She was glad she had worn trainers with her denim shorts and cut-off T-shirt, but when the villa finally came into view she worried that she was too casually dressed to make the right impression. Whoever lived here clearly didn't have money worries.

'Wow!'

She stared in admiration. Long and low, the palatial villa had a classic Elban red-tiled roof, while the walls were painted a pale creamy yellow. The garden was lush, the hilly terrain and native woodland lending perfect seclusion and privacy to the setting. The sound of birds and the faintest rustling of a breeze in the trees were the only noises to impinge on the silent stillness of the afternoon. Gina immediately felt at peace here, experiencing a strange sense of belonging. She wasn't given to fancy, but she wondered if she was close to the place that was so special to her grandparents, if she somehow sensed their spirits here, reaching across the ages.

Shaking her head at such a notion, she propped her bike against the wall, took her bag from the basket and hooked the strap over her shoulder. She walked to the front door, disappointed when no one answered her ring of the bell.

Undecided, she hesitated. They had come a long way, and this mission was important to her grandmother. She couldn't give up now. Perhaps she should wait for someone to return. She could leave a note, asking for the owner to phone, but she would rather explain her purpose for coming here in person. Feeling guilty for trespassing, she walked around the side of the villa. It was huge, a U-shape around a rear terrace, and it looked as if her whole cottage would fit into a couple of rooms here. The spacious terrace had a large table, comfortable chairs and recliners, plus an outdoor cooking facility. Near the far end was an artist's easel and equipment, but she didn't venture across the terrace to inspect the canvas. It was the view over the rocky cliffs and the sea that held her attention and took her breath away. She had never seen anything so stunning—and that was saying something, given the spectacular scenery around Strathlochan.

Drawn despite her caution, she followed a path through the shrubs which led to steep stone steps that marked the way down to a sheltered beach far below. This must be where Maria and Matthew had walked together fifty years ago, before the villa had been built. She had to go down there. Had to see for herself the precious cove, the rock formation shaped like Neptune's spear, the spot where her grandparents' love had been born.

It was a daunting trip down the uneven cliff steps, and Gina knew that if this did turn out to be the right place there was no way her grandmother would be able to manage the journey down. Once on the small crescent of beach, protected by the curving cliff walls, she had her first proper glimpse of the rock feature that rose from the water a distance offshore. Irregular, and surrounded by other rock forms, it did, indeed, look like a massive trident...Neptune's three-pronged spear...just as her grandparents had described so vividly and with so much fondness.

Gina absorbed the solitude, the natural beauty, amazed by the clarity of the water, a glistening mix of emeralds and azures. Sitting down, she wrapped her arms around her knees. The September sunshine was hot on her skin, and she tipped her head back, closing her eyes, imagining the moment her grandparents had met, the secret romantic rendezvous that had followed, their determination to marry despite Maria's parents' dissent. Maria and Matthew had made it work, had survived the hardships to enjoy a lifetime of devotion. All thanks to that one chance meeting on this tiny Elban beach.

Elba. The name had a magic to it. A magic sparked to life in her childhood as her grandmother regaled her with stories of this special place. Gina would never forget the moment yesterday when she had seen Elba for the first time. The mountainous outline of the island, jutting from the blueness of the sea, had shimmered into her vision and grown into reality. All her life she had been captivated by the romance, the fairytale, the joy and love that coloured her grandparents' memories of this place. She had been determined to come— one day. Now she was here. But in these circumstances?

Frowning, she turned her thoughts to the reason for bringing her grandmother back to Elba. She was concerned that the emotion would be too much, but her grandmother was determined, and Gina would never break the promises she had made. Lulled by the peacefulness of the surroundings, she relaxed, some of the tension and responsibility she had shouldered for so long draining from her.

The soft swell of the sea under the sun cast shifting light over the rock formation, highlighting a myriad of colours and textures. At that moment, as she stared towards the mythical symbol, it seemed as if the very sea-god himself appeared from behind the rocks, swimming towards the shore with an easy stroke before rising from the water. Gina gasped, startled from her reverie, wondering for a moment if the apparition was real or a figment of her imagination.

He certainly looked real as he removed his mask and snorkel and waded towards the beach at a slight angle away from her. The sheer masculine perfection of him held her spellbound. As she watched, he ran the fingers of his free hand through jet-black hair, shedding water, sweeping the strands back from an arresting, impossibly handsome face. A face that could have been sculpted from the surrounding granite by the hand of a master craftsman. Yet he was un-doubtedly flesh and blood...human and all male. Gina couldn't drag her gaze away from his athletic physique, appreciating the broad shoulders, the bronzed skin on which a sheen of water glistened, the supple muscles, and a chest dusted with dark hair trailing in a narrow line over a flat abdomen to his navel. Black swim-shorts sat low on his hips, the wet fabric clinging to strong, leanly muscled thighs.

As he strode through the shallows to the beach, Gina felt overheated, sure she would melt on the spot. Then he looked up, stilling as he noticed her for the first time. The breath trapped in her lungs as their gazes met. Her sea-god changed direction, walking purposefully towards her, the touch of his gaze firing her blood and tightening her stomach. With more haste than grace, Gina scrambled to her feet as he closed the last of the distance between them.

'*Buongiorno, signorina.*'

His accented voice was throaty and attractive, the warm huskiness of it sending prickles of awareness down her spine. Gathering her scattered wits, she answered in Italian.

'*Buongiorno.*'

It was hard to believe possible, but close up he was even more gorgeous than her first impression had suggested. Around six feet tall, she guessed he was in his early thirties. A day's growth of beard shadowed a strong, masculine jaw, while his mouth was sultry, beautifully shaped, his lips deliciously kissable. He had eyes the colour of liquid caramel, deeper than hazel, but not as dark a brown as her own, and they were framed by impossibly long sable lashes and gentle laughter lines.

Unable to resist the temptation, her gaze slid down to inspect his bare torso…strong shoulders, perfect chest, and a taut abdomen and belly. The way water droplets drizzled in slow motion down his dusky skin mesmerised her. She was so close to him that when she breathed in she inhaled the teasing scent of the sea, mingled with his woodsy male aroma. She had to fight the overwhelming urge to reach out and touch him.

Startled by her impulsive desire, Gina took a step back, her gaze lifting to his face, finding that he appraised her with equal thoroughness. Her breathing was uneven, her pulse raced, and her flesh tingled as if he had physically touched her. Alarmed, she retreated another pace. How long was it since she had appreciated an attractive man? How long since anyone had made *her* feel attractive and womanly?

'This is a private beach, *signorina.*'

The softness of his voice failed to mask the challenge and thread of accusation. 'I'm sorry,' she murmured, keeping to Italian, caught off guard by his sudden appearance as well as by her spontaneous reaction to him.

'How did you find it? What are you doing here?' he queried, folding his arms across his chest.

'Um…' Gina hesitated, distracted by the way his muscles flexed as he moved. She forced herself to remember why she was here, determined to get back on track. 'Does the beach belong to the people who own the villa?'

Suspicion appeared in watchful eyes. 'Why does this interest you?'

'I need to talk to the owner.'

The man observed her for a moment, his expression unreadable. 'The villa is not for sale.'

'No. No, that's not it. I…'

'The property is owned by a family from Florence,' he informed her as her words trailed off. 'They are not expected to return to the island for some time.'

'So you take care of the place for them?' she mused to herself, wondering how much to confide in him, deflated as the prospect of a successful outcome began to crumble and the fulfilment of her grandmother's hopes began to fade.

A speculative glint appeared in his eyes. 'Tell me why you want to talk to them.'

'It's private.'

'Maybe I can help you.'

She regarded him warily. His presence made her feel breathless and shaky. 'If you'll tell me how I can contact the owners, *that* would help.'

'Come on up to the villa. We will talk. You will tell me why you want to find them, and I will consider giving you the information you need,' he suggested, tempting her with a lifeline to keep her promise to her grandparents alive.

Gina bit her lip, thinking of her grandmother and the reason they had come all this way. She couldn't let her down. And, with only a few days available to them before their return to Scotland, time was short. As caretaker, and with access to the owners of the beach, there was a chance this man could help her achieve her aim and grant her grandmother's appeal. Instinct warned her that spending more time in his company wasn't sensible, but it seemed she needed to work with him.

Her decision made, she nodded. 'All right. But I can't be too long. Someone is waiting for me.'

A man?

Seb frowned, wondering why the possibility bothered him so much. It was true that this unknown woman immediately intrigued him, with her mix of mystery and understated sexiness. Emerging from his swim to find the stranger on the beach had been a surprise—one he planned to explore to the fullest. Her presence made him suspicious. She had yet to explain how she had found the secluded villa, what she had been doing on the private beach, or what she wanted with his family. That she assumed him to be the caretaker could be genuine. He scanned her soul-deep brown eyes, searching for the truth. Or it could be the ruse of a clever journalist to lull him into a false sense of security and get a story on him. He had been tricked before. This time he would not let down his guard…or let this woman out of his sight…until he knew more about her and her motives.

Not that having her in his sight was a hardship. Far from it. He indulged in another leisurely perusal. In her mid to late twenties, and above average height, she had sultry dark eyes and flawless skin. Her hair was constrained in a loose braid that fell almost to her waist, its colour a rich deep brown, glinting with auburn highlights in the sun. He wanted to free it from its restraint and see the thick, lustrous waves in all their glory. Her facial features were strong yet feminine: a well-defined jawline with a hint of stubbornness in the set of her chin, high cheekbones, small, straight nose, and the kind of mouth that could tempt a man to wickedness…pouting, rosy-red lips demanding to be kissed with thorough abandon.

He was bored with the artificiality and falseness of the women he usually came into contact with, and this woman's natural freshness and apparent lack of affectation appealed to him. So did her shapely figure. Here was a woman with generous curves. Curves that were all her own, not fashioned on an operating table. She was voluptuous, earthy, comfortable in her skin. No wedding or engagement rings, he noticed, disconcerted by the rush of male satisfaction and possessiveness that observation brought. Indeed, she wore no jewellery or adornments at all…save for a simple narrow-banded silver watch around her right wrist.

Totally feminine, she stirred his interest as no other woman had ever done. But was she genuine? Could he trust her? Time would tell. For now, he wasn't anywhere near ready to let her go. Until he knew for sure who she was and what she wanted he would follow the maxim of keeping his friends close and any possible enemies closer.

Seb would have enjoyed a much longer inspection of her delectable body, but she readjusted the position of her canvas shoulder bag, then turned and headed towards the age-old steps cut into the cliff that led back up to the villa. Seb followed, appreciating the back view nearly as much as the front. Her faded denim shorts were cut well enough for him to enjoy the delicious swell of her rear, and short enough to allow a generous view of smooth, pleasingly rounded thighs. She moved a few steps up ahead of him, and he could admire gently muscled calves and trim ankles. Closing the distance between them, lured by the sway of her hips and the gentle bob of the plait hanging down her back, he resisted the temptation to brush his fingertips across the tantalising band of golden skin exposed between the low-slung shorts and the hem of her short-sleeved top. He was further intrigued by the small tattoo of a leaping dolphin at the base of her spine.

They were not quite halfway up the rough climb when a loose patch of ground came away under the woman's foot. Seb reacted instinctively to her startled cry, thankful he was close enough to catch her as she slipped precariously towards the edge. His heart was thudding as he dragged her back with him, holding her close as they leaned on the cliff wall for a moment, catching their breath.

'Thank you,' she gasped, resting against him, one fist closed around the strap of her bag, her other hand clinging to the rock face.

'Are you all right?'

She nodded. 'I'm fine.'

Still neither of them moved. Enjoying the feel of her in his arms, Seb was in no hurry to let go. One forearm rested under the lush fullness of her breasts, their plumpness, firm but soft, pressing against him. He could feel that the rapid thud of her heart matched his own. And as he breathed in he inhaled the scent of vanilla and sweet, sun-warmed woman. Sexy and arousing. Her body was athletic, strong, yet softly feminine. His free hand had settled at her bare navel, his fingertips brushing the silkiness of her skin.

Loosing her hold on the rock, she turned in his arms, on a level with him due to the incline of the steps. Their gazes locked. Time stopped. Seb's gaze dropped to her mouth. The urge to kiss her was almost irresistible. Almost. But suspicions still nagged at him. He didn't yet know if he could trust this woman. It took a huge effort of will to control his compulsive rush of desire, but he reluctantly released her and put a few inches of distance between them.

'We should move on,' he told her, cursing the unevenness of his voice.

Sooty lashes lowered to hide the expression in dark brown eyes. 'Yes.'

'Be careful how you go.'

As she turned from her rescuer and began making her way up the remainder of the steps to the top of the cliff, Gina intended to heed the warning. And not just in terms of watching her footing. Her reaction to the man himself was troubling. Her heart hammered and every particle of her thrummed—more from the feel of his body pressed against hers than from her stumble on the uneven ground. His strength, his heat, the male scent of him, had combined to make her light-headed. The warmth of his palm and the touch of his fingers on her bare skin had set her aflame. For one wild moment, when she had looked into those inscrutable eyes, she had thought he was going to kiss her. Even more disturbing was her yearning for him to do so. How long had it been since she'd been kissed?

Grateful to reach the safety of the path, she headed back towards the villa, conscious of his presence behind her. She felt shaken by her intense and instant attraction to the stranger who had emerged so unexpectedly from the sea. A tremor rippled through her as he rested a hand at the small of her back and guided her towards the expansive rear terrace with its incredible views.

'Make yourself comfortable, *signorina*.' His voice was polite but guarded as he gestured towards the chairs. 'Excuse me while I change. When I return, we will talk.'

'And you'll help me get in touch with the villa's owner?' she interjected, reminding him of her purpose, determined not to be defeated.

A smile played at his mouth, but suspicion still lurked in his eyes. 'We will see.'

The comment made Gina realise that she might have to confide more than she had intended if she hoped to gain his co-operation.

She watched him stride to the villa and disappear through a doorway. A sigh escaped her. She felt edgy, unsettled, and whilst she knew in part it was because of the importance of her mission here, she also knew that most of her jitters were due to the immediate desire she had experienced the moment she had met her enigmatic host. There was no denying her response to him, nor the masculine interest in his eyes as he had looked at her. She was shocked, because those few moments of mutual interest had cracked open a shell she had thought firmly constructed, awakening things she had tamped down and rejected for herself when she had made the decision to put her grandparents' needs before her own. Maybe she was allowing the setting and the fairytale of their romance here to go to her head. That was all it was, she consoled herself. When she saw the man again things would be fine, the momentary aberration would have passed.

Unable to keep still, she set her bag on the table, then

walked to the balustrade wall, leaning on it to admire the sweep of coast laid out before her. Curiosity bettered her, and she moved along to the artist's easel she had noticed earlier, stepping closer to inspect the canvas. The work was unfinished but impressive, the style unusual. She was no expert, but the clever use of abstract blocks making up the seascape appealed to her. She wondered if her sea-god was the artist, or if someone else lived here with him. A woman?

A noise alerted her that she was no longer alone. Embarrassed at being caught snooping, she spun round. Several things hit her at the same time. Any hope that her reaction to him had been a passing fancy was instantly discounted. Dressed in leg-hugging jeans and a black T-shirt, the man was darkly attractive and dangerously exciting, his impact no less disconcerting now he was fully dressed. He had taken time for a quick shave, but he was just as ruggedly appealing as before, with an untamed air that did strange things to her hormones. Hormones that were meant to be in retirement, or at least a long hibernation.

Carrying two glasses containing some kind of fruit drink, he was frowning as he approached. Instead of setting them both down together, he put the glass in his left hand on the table before transferring the second from his right hand to his left. Puzzled by his awkwardness, she noted the way he attempted to flex his right wrist, index finger and thumb, as if experiencing problems with movement, maybe numbness or pain. It was as she neared him that she noted for the first time the fresh scars that marred his skin…three across the palm, heel and wrist of his right hand, one on his left forearm near his inner elbow.

Her caring nature rose to the fore, and she wanted to help, to comfort, but one look at the challenge and flare of angry pride in his eyes kept her questions and her concern unspoken. Experience as a trauma nurse helped her mask her emotions and interested speculation. Ignoring what she suspected he would see as his weakness, she made no comment and sat down.

'Thank you for the drink, *signor*.' She smiled, taking a sip of the tangy mixed berry juice from the glass nearest her. 'It's very refreshing. The weather is still so warm here.'

He inclined his head, a momentary flash of puzzlement crossing his expression before he drew out the chair next to her and sat far too close, heightening her intense awareness of him. 'You are welcome. And now that you are officially my guest, and I am to try to help you, we should introduce ourselves.'

'Yes, of course.' Setting down her glass, suppressing a shiver of anticipation at the thought of touching him again, she held out her hand. 'My name is Gina. Gina McNaught.'

'I am pleased to meet you, Gina.'

The way he said her name caused a fresh tingle of desire to chase along her spine. Then his hand sought hers, and every nerve-ending was focused on his touch, on the way his strong but graceful fingers curled around her own, the pad of his thumb brushing across the back of her hand like a caress. As her palm was all but swallowed up in his, she felt the jagged lines of the scars he had suffered, wondering again what had happened to him.

'And your name is…?' She faced him, hoping her voice had been steady and he wouldn't realise the effect he had on her.

For a moment he returned her gaze in silence, the expression in his eyes unreadable save for a glimmer of that masculine pride and challenge. 'I am Sebastiano Adriani.'

CHAPTER TWO

NOT a flicker of recognition showed in Gina's eyes at the mention of his name, Seb noted. Either she genuinely had no idea who he was, or she was an exceptionally good actress. He was not prepared to take any chances. Why had she come here? *Was* she a journalist out for an exclusive story? Or a woman on the make, wanting to use his name, his money, to further her own ends?

When he had gone inside to change his clothes, he had glanced out the front door, expecting to find the car Gina had arrived in. Hoping for clues, maybe a Florentine number plate that could suggest she had followed him here, he had been surprised to discover instead a rented tourist bike propped against the wall. It added to the woman's mystery. And it crossed his mind that the bike could be a crafty prop. Life had taught him to be cynical and untrusting.

Gina refused to fit into a convenient box in his head. Nothing about her and her sudden appearance on the beach made sense. Nor could he explain her reaction to his awkwardness with the drinks. He knew she had noticed the scars that reminded him at every moment of how his life had changed. Most people in the last weeks had shied away from touching him—even talking to him. They either refused to mention what had happened, as if that would make it go away, or they patronised him, treating him like an invalid. Gina was different. She had not fussed, had not been embarrassed, and had not hesitated in instigating the handshake.

Needing time to think how to handle this situation, how to draw out the information he needed to know from her while giving nothing of himself away, he followed her lead and settled back to enjoy the view. But as he reached out to pick up his drink his hand locked again. It happened sometimes, often when he was least prepared for it. He hated it. Hated even more for his clumsiness to be witnessed.

As he cursed under his breath, Gina calmly rescued the glass and set it back on the table. Seb froze as she boldly took his right hand in both of hers. Since the incident that July night in Florence, people had pitied him, or smothered him, unable to face the reality. He braced himself, but Gina surprised him by tackling the issue head on.

'How long has it been, Sebastiano?' she asked, stripping away his defences with the exquisite gentleness of her touch, the understanding, concern and complete lack of pity in her eyes.

'Seb,' he corrected, thrown off balance by this woman. His voice sounded rough, and he tried to shut his mind to the vivid memories of that night. 'Seven weeks.'

Gina refused to back down. 'What happened?'

Unable to comprehend why he was telling her anything at all, he found himself playing down his role in the incident, passing off his injuries as an accident while going to the aid of the woman being attacked. From her expression, Gina knew there was more to it, but she didn't press him. Dark thoughts assailed him as he recalled how he had staved off blows to his face and body, but at the expense of the knife slicing through his hand and arm. The resulting loss of sensory and motor function, while not impacting significantly on his normal daily existence, was sufficient to prevent him from carrying out the intricate surgery that was his life.

In his heart he had known from the moment he had knelt on that dark street as the police had arrived and the frightened woman had fussed over him that he was finished as a surgeon. All he had been able to focus on was his hands, and the fear that no matter how quickly he got to hospital the damage was done. He had been right. He would never operate again.

Throughout his time in plaster he had gone along with family and colleagues who had assured him everything would be all right. Inside he had known it would not. His moment of selflessness had robbed him of the thing that mattered to him most. His career was over. Many other things were over, too, he allowed with cynicism. How many so-called friends had faded away these last weeks? How many celebrity clients had blanked him now he was no longer of use to them? How many women, like vain, fickle Lidia di Napoli, once eager for the kudos of being associated socially with him, had vanished like rats deserting a sinking ship? He was no longer the darling of Florentine society. Only the media, eager to capture the gory details of his descent from the pinnacle of his profession, still chased him.

As soon as he had been able to cope alone, he had left his aunt and uncle's house and come to the family villa on Elba, to escape the press and decide what the hell he was going to do with the rest of his life. Here on the island he could be himself. No one bothered him. The locals knew and respected the family, guarding their privacy. And, thankfully, the press had never found this place. Or had they? Did that explain the presence of his unexpected visitor?

'It must have been a terrible experience, Seb.'

Gina's comment interrupted his runaway thoughts, and his suspicions about her intensified. 'You could say that.'

Unfazed by his sarcasm, she studied his scars. 'Nerve and tendon damage?'

'Yes.'

He started as one finger brushed across the scar on the inside of his left forearm near the indentation of the elbow. The feather-light touch sent darts of awareness shooting through him.

'Does this cause you problems, too? Was the ulnar nerve cut here?'

'Why?' Who *was* this woman? Did she know more about him than she was pretending? 'What do you know about it?'

Dusky lashes lifted and dark brown eyes looked into his own, a self-deprecating smile curving her tempting mouth. 'Sorry. I'm being nosy. I didn't mean to intrude. It's an occupational hazard. I'm a senior staff nurse, and until a few days ago I worked in a busy accident and emergency department.'

That explained her knowledgeable questions, Seb allowed, but left more of his own unanswered. She was a nurse who had recently worked in trauma. Had she known where he was and thought to…what? Care for him? Heaven forbid. Or was she hoping to find a new job working on his team? She would be out of luck. He no longer *had* a team. Seb opened his mouth to tell her it was a waste of time, looking to him to aid her career, but it seemed her inquisitiveness had not yet ended.

'Are you having physio? Keeping up the mobility is important, as you'll find you can regain more sensation and movement for many months yet.' She awarded him another smile, her fingers sure but gentle as they explored his hand. 'I'm sure your surgeon has already told you that. Injuries like this weren't unusual in the department I worked in, and I know how frustrating it can be in the early stages of recovery. Don't lose heart on there not being more improvement to come. Are you the artist?'

'Sorry?' Her chatter and her sudden change of subject amused and vexed him at one and the same time.

Gina gestured across the terrace to his unfinished canvas, and he remembered she had been looking at it when he had come out of the villa. 'Is the painting yours?'

'Yes. I wanted to see if I could still handle the brushes. I can't grip properly, so I've had to change my style, but—'

Seb broke off, annoyed with himself for revealing more to this woman. How did she *do* that? How could she slip inside his protective shell and make him say things, do things, he never would with anyone else? Realising she was still holding his hand, that he was allowing her to do so, he frowned and removed it, even more cross with himself for missing her touch.

Undaunted by his gruffness, she took another sip of her drink. 'The painting is different, but in a good way. Interesting. Atmospheric.'

'You like it?' Surprise drew the question from him.

'It's amazing. Cleverly done with those abstract blocks or zones. You've captured the sharpness of the natural light and the vivid colours of the island to perfection. Do you sell a lot to tourists?'

'No.'

'You should. I'm sure your work would be very popular.'

Watching her, Seb wondered if she was as uncomplicated and as innocent as she seemed. Did she really believe him to be the villa's caretaker—a man who sold a few paintings to supplement his income? It could be a front, a cover for why she was here, but gut reaction nagged at him that she was telling the truth. He would be checking out her story once he learned more about her, but she was so open, so completely without guile, that it would surprise him were she not genuine. Having been caught out before, however, he couldn't take any chances now.

Determined to wrest back control of this situation, he set about asking some questions of his own.

'You said you worked in trauma. Are you here looking for a new job?' He watched her closely as she absorbed his words.

'No, not at all.' She tossed her braid over her shoulder. 'I start in my new role as soon as I get home.'

Her smile increased in wattage and did curious things to his insides. He wondered whether he would wake up any moment and discover this strange interlude had been some surreal dream—that Gina was a figment of his imagination. So much for taking charge of things. Sitting forward, he rested his forearms on his knees.

'And where is home, Gina?'

'Strathlochan.' His confusion must have been obvious because she laughed. 'It's in Scotland.'

That threw him. As did the place name. Why did Strathlochan sound familiar? He had never been to Scotland. But his cousin Riccardo had. He made a mental note to check the connection with him later. Several other facts hit him at the same time. Gina's surname should have registered with him before, yet her colouring betrayed a Latin ancestry, and she spoke Italian like a native. He needed to probe more deeply into this intriguing woman's background, and get to the bottom of just what she had been doing on the villa's private beach.

'You do not live on Elba?' Seb questioned, and Gina sensed his surprise.

'No. I've always lived in Scotland,' she confirmed, keeping to Italian. 'I'm only here for a short holiday.'

'Your Italian is perfect,' Seb countered, in proficient if accented English.

'As is your English.' She was startled by his fluency. Knowing she would have to divulge more about herself if she was to secure his help, she continued. 'I have Italian ancestry, but I have never been here before.'

His watchful gaze held her captive. 'You are enjoying Elba? The island is beautiful, no?'

'Very beautiful.'

She couldn't look away from him to appreciate the coastal view. His nearness and his attention were potent, firing her blood and increasing the awareness she had felt from the first moment she had seen him. She remained curious about his injuries, convinced there was more to the incident than he had told her. He'd put himself in danger to go to someone's aid, and no matter how much he tried to play down his involvement, that said a great deal about him in her view. But the pain, anger and confusion evident in his eyes attested to the fact that he had yet to come to terms with the effect his loss of motor and sensory function had had on his life.

It must be hard for him as an artist, worrying whether he would be able to use his hands again. She would like to reassure him, but he put up barriers, retreated behind his pride. He was not a man to share the troubled feelings she sensed boiled inside him. Besides, it was none of her business. After today she would probably never see him again. A wave of sadness and regret overwhelmed her at that realisation.

'So, Gina,' he said now, reclaiming her attention. 'We were going to discuss why you are here.'

Nervousness gripped her. 'Yes, we were.'

'Why now? Why this beach? You cannot see it from the road, so how did you know it was here?' he pressed, and although his voice was warm, the challenge was unmistakable.

'I was looking for the rock called Neptune's Spear. When there was no reply at the villa, I decided to wait in case someone came home so I could talk to them. The temptation to go down to the beach and see if I had the right place was too much to resist. I had no idea you were down there swimming,' she explained, meeting his gaze, seeing a mix of curiosity and wariness in his eyes.

He regarded her for a long moment in silence. 'How did you know of the rock? Why is it that you wish to contact the owner of this villa?'

'It's a long story. A personal one.' She hesitated, wondering how to handle the situation. 'And it's not really mine to tell.'

'Then whose is it? You said you were here on Elba with someone?' he queried, his expression guarded.

'My grandmother.'

Surprise replaced the suspicion in his voice. 'Your *grandmother*?'

'Yes.' What had he been expecting her to say? And had she imagined that flash of relief that had crossed his face? It had happened too quickly for her to be certain. Pushing aside fanciful notions, she took a deep breath. 'Nonna Maria is Italian. Elba, and the beach at Neptune's Spear in particular, are special to her. She was here fifty years ago, and it has been her dream to come back.'

Interest sparked in his eyes. 'Fifty years? And she has not returned in all that time?'

'No. It wasn't possible for her to do so…for several reasons.' Gina spoke with caution, not wanting to reveal the sorry state of their finances. Nor did she wish to confide in anyone but the owner—the only one with the power to help them and grant their wish—the reason why they had made this important trip now.

'So what happened fifty years ago that means so much to her?' Seb probed, and she knew she would have to explain further.

'Nonna Maria was nineteen. She lived in Siena with her family, who took an annual holiday on Elba,' she began, warming to the story as Seb gave her his full attention. 'Matthew McNaught was a twenty-one-year-old ship's engineer. He was enjoying a few days off on the island with some friends while their vessel was under repair in port on the mainland. Both Maria and Matthew escaped for some time alone…and they met and fell in love on the beach by Neptune's rock.'

Seb's eyebrows rose in surprise. 'This beach?'

'Yes. My grandmother said no one lived here in those days.'

'What happened then?' he asked, making no comment about the villa.

'Matthew asked Maria to come to Scotland and marry him. Her family were rigidly opposed to the match, and demanded Maria return to Siena with them.'

'And what did she choose?'

Caramel eyes looked deep into hers, and it took Gina a moment to find her voice. 'She chose Matthew.' Her voice was uneven and she cleared her throat. What was it about this man that affected her so? It had never happened to her before. Aware he was waiting for her to continue, she attempted to rid herself of her wayward thoughts. 'I know the estrangement from her family pained my grandmother— there was no reconciliation—but she never regretted her decision. That life-changing moment led to fifty years of love and togetherness, through good times and bad.'

'You're a romantic.' His smile held the same touch of cynicism as his voice.

'Not really.' Her own tone cooled in response to his attitude, and to the memories of how Malcolm had trampled on her ideals. 'I just know that it worked for my grandparents. I can't imagine how hard it was for Nonna Maria, ripped away from her family and the country she knew, beginning a new life in a foreign land, not speaking the language, with her new husband away at sea for months until he secured a job in Glasgow's shipyards. They survived. They loved each other and were happy.'

Her grandparents' story had been her lifelong fairytale, her dream...a dream she had squashed down when she had lost hope of finding the kind of love they had shared for herself. She'd grown up and headed out into the adult world with those childhood hopes intact, but she had discovered that she couldn't have everything. Malcolm had taught her that. She had been forced to make a choice between her own needs or those of her grandparents. There had been no choice. Since then her own desires had been in cold storage. She had never met anyone who had understood her, and what was important to her, and she had given up believing she would ever find a man who would be to her what Matthew had been to Maria.

'And your grandfather—he is not here with you?'

Seb's question cut through her thoughts, and she gasped as fresh pain seared through her.

'Gina?'

'No,' she managed, meeting his gaze, seeing the concern in his eyes. 'He died several months ago.'

She swallowed down the renewed welling of grief, startled when Seb reached out a hand, resting it on her forearm. 'I am sorry, *cara*.'

'Thank you.' Gina thought of her grandmother, lost without the man who had been husband, friend, lover and confidant for fifty years, and of her own broken heart at losing the grandfather she had loved so much. 'It's not been easy...especially for Nonna Maria. The enforced separation has taken its toll on her. She needed to come here.'

Heat radiated out from the point where Seb's skin

touched hers. She struggled to ignore it, to fight against an awareness that was at once overwhelming yet exciting and unexpected, as if some internal thaw was beginning to reawaken the sensuous woman she had hidden away. His fingers lingered a moment longer, and when they were withdrawn she let out a shaky breath, both relieved and disappointed, unnerved by what was happening to her.

'I want to meet your grandmother.'

Gina's eyes widened in surprise. 'You do? Why?'

'I would like to hear about her history with this place, to know what it is that brings her back and why she wants to contact the villa's owner.' He paused, his gaze turning enigmatic once more. 'Unless there is some reason you do not wish me to speak with her?'

Gina realised this was a test—that Seb didn't yet believe her. Why was he so sceptical? What did he imagine she was doing here? For her grandmother's sake she had to convince him she was telling the truth.

'Not at all. I am sure Nonna will be delighted to talk to you. My concern is not to raise the hopes of a fragile old woman only to dash them if you then withhold your help,' she finished, issuing a challenge and a warning of her own.

'Gina—'

'I came alone today because, whilst Nonna's spirit may be strong, she is too frail for all the walking and waiting around. The journey from Scotland was tough on her,' she pressed on, ignoring the note of chastisement in his tone, unable to mask the protectiveness she felt for her grandmother. 'I don't want her upset—' She broke off and bit her lip, trying to rein in a sudden rush of emotion. 'We only have a few days here, and I want to make her happy.'

To her surprise, Seb's hands captured hers. 'I can promise you, Gina, that I will listen to what your grandmother has to say, and I will do all in my power to help her fulfil her wishes.'

'All right.' She couldn't say why, but she believed him. Relief flooded through her at the realisation she might not have failed her grandparents after all. 'Thank you.'

Gina wished she could excuse the unsteadiness of her voice and the rush of relief at Seb's guarantee, but she knew it was more due to the effect of his touch. Her skin was tingling, her heart racing. She was in real trouble. Her gaze clashed with his once more and she saw the speculation in his eyes—but also the answering heat and flare of masculine interest.

This kind of instant desire and feminine recognition was new to her. She was impossibly attracted to Seb. But she was only on Elba for a short time, and—more to the point—this trip was all about her grandmother, not herself. The last thing she should be thinking about was a man! Yet she couldn't prevent the rush of inner excitement that came with feeling like an attractive woman after a long spell in the dating wilderness.

'You will allow me to show you and your grandmother some Elban hospitality?' Seb asked now, his thumb tracing a tantalising caress across her palm.

'I don't know.'

Gina felt ridiculously flustered. She couldn't think when he touched her. Bemused at the speed of what was happening between them, she withdrew her hand from his. Her resolve was shaky, and it crumbled further under the warm appeal in his slumberous gaze. A short time in this man's company and she felt like a giddy teenager.

'Let me take you both to dinner,' he continued, his voice persuasive. 'We can talk more about your reasons for being here, and how I might help your grandmother.'

Gina wavered. It was important that this trip was a success, and Seb had played the one card guaranteed to make her weaken. This man could be all that stood between them and the agreement they needed to complete their mission on Elba.

'I'll have to ask Nonna Maria.'

'Of course.'

'In fact, I ought to go now.' Feeling an urgent need to remove herself from the temptation of Seb before she lost her head and did something crazy, Gina rose to her feet and picked up her bag. 'I don't like to leave her alone for too long, and she will be anxious for news.'

Something flickered across his face, but he masked it swiftly before she could assess what he was thinking. 'I shall escort you back. Then I can meet her and ask her myself.'

'You don't have to do that,' she protested, concerned at spending more time in his company before she had reinforced her defences, exerted some control over her wayward hormones and given herself a stern talking-to.

'Perhaps not...' He stood, his hand once more resting at the small of her back, sending new shivers along her spine as he guided her across the terrace. 'But I would like to.'

Again there was that edge in his voice. He might find her attractive, but he was still unsure whether or not to believe her story. She didn't understand his misgivings, but the fact that he had them at all could affect the outcome for her grandmother. She had to do all she could to keep him on side—even if it did mean walking on dangerous ground herself. He only had to look at her or touch her and her common sense evaporated.

'All right.'

Before she knew it, he had taken a bike from the garage, she had told him where she was staying, and they were cycling west towards the village. Conscious of him every yard of the way, she wondered what her grandmother would have to say when she brought Seb home.

Gina couldn't help but feel nervous. This man was a

stranger. A handsome and charismatic one—one who attracted and excited her like no other—but still a stranger. And now he had the power to make or break her grandmother's heart.

Would he help them?

Or would they be returning to Scotland disappointed?

CHAPTER THREE

As HE showered, Seb thought back over the afternoon. Maria had enchanted him from the first moment he had met her. Much like her granddaughter…but in a very different way.

For someone who usually remained detached, he had been deeply moved by Maria's story, and fascinated by her memories of the part of Elba he knew so well. The love and affection between her and Gina had been evident in every word and look, and although neither had yet revealed the reason why they wanted to contact the owners of the villa, his doubts about their genuineness were fading. Just listening to Maria talk had confirmed how important it was for her to be on Elba. Despite the emotional and physical upheaval of the trip for someone of her age, it was a final pilgrimage she obviously needed to complete. He wanted to help Maria—and to learn more about Gina. The opportunity to begin that process had presented itself when Maria had accepted his invitation to take them both to dinner.

Knotting a towel around his waist, he sat on his bed and reached for the phone to call his cousin. Now thirty-three, he and Rico were only a few months apart in age, although their early upbringing had been very different. Rico was more outgoing, more trusting, but as a top allergist and immunologist, with his own successful clinic, he was just as dedicated to his career in medicine.

Rico answered promptly, and Seb filled him in on Maria's story and the connection to the family villa.

'You're lucky that Mamma is away on business with the charity, or she would be over there in a flash to investigate,' Rico suggested with wry amusement.

Lovely as Zia Sofia was, Seb was relieved she was not around to interfere. He wanted to handle this situation on his own. Which brought him to his reason for calling his cousin. 'Why does the name Strathlochan mean something to me?'

'It's the county town near the village where Nic di Angelis lives,' Rico reminded him. 'I worked with him in Milan a few years ago—and I went over to Scotland for the wedding when he married his GP partner, Hannah.'

'How strange.'

'Is that where these women are from?' Rico asked, sounding as surprised at the coincidence as he was.

'They moved there from Glasgow. Until a few days ago Gina worked in the A and E department at Strathlochan Hospital.' Seb hesitated a moment. 'Are you still in touch with Nic? Would you be able to make some discreet enquiries for me?'

'Tell me what you need and I'll talk to him.'

'Thanks, Rico. I want to make certain everything is above board.' He paused, still feeling the flicker of guilt he had experienced when Gina had introduced him to her grandmother as the caretaker. 'At the moment they don't know who I am, or what my connection is to the villa.'

There was a long pause. 'Seb, what are you doing?'

'I need to be sure there are no ulterior motives. I've said I'll do what I can to help when I know what it is Maria wants,' he pressed on, ignoring the warning in his cousin's voice.

'I'll check things out with Nic, but my hunch is the same as yours. These women are genuine.' Rico was silent a moment, and his voice was solemn when he spoke again. 'I know what Antonella did to you, that it's made you cautious and untrusting. And I know how difficult things have been with the press intrusion. But Maria and Gina are not media people out to get you. Don't you think you should tell them the truth?'

Sighing, Seb leaned back against the pillows and closed his eyes. He didn't want to think about Antonella and her deception. Or the press. Or his so-called celebrity status. How could he explain to Rico that he had enjoyed being treated as an ordinary person? He didn't want Gina and Maria to judge him on his name or his money.

'I'll tell them when the time is right.'

'On your head be it.' His cousin's disagreement at the decision was plain. 'Before I go, you need to know there are still reporters sniffing around your apartment. A couple have been here, to the clinic, and Papà took no nonsense from one who went to the house.'

Seb ran the fingers of one of his now less able hands across his brow, biting back his annoyance at the way the press were hounding his family. 'I'm sorry.'

'It's fine. I just wanted to fill you in on the official line.'

'And that is?'

Rico chuckled. 'That you have gone overseas. Well, it is kind of true, no?'

'Thanks.'

'No problem, *cugino*. Hang in there. I'll be in touch. Enjoy your dinner tonight with the lovely ladies…and tell them you're not the caretaker.'

Seb set down the phone and rose to dress, trying to ignore Rico's advice. Instead, he thought of the evening ahead. He had been surprised to discover Gina and Maria sharing a small room in a cheap bed and breakfast—but, combined with a few other clues, he had guessed that money was tight and it had been a financial struggle for them to come to Elba. Despite the luxuries his career had brought him, he had not forgotten what it was like to live from hand to mouth, to be thrifty, to go without. As he tended to wear casual clothes on the island, he ignored the handful of designer suits hanging in his wardrobe and dressed down, wanting to put them at ease.

Having learned that they both enjoyed seafood, he had chosen a restaurant that was inexpensive and friendly but had a reputation for excellent food. He'd not been there before, and he hoped no one would recognise him—or, if they did, that they would be discreet. He had not forgotten Rico's warning, but he was not yet ready to reveal his true identity to Maria and Gina.

Gina. Anticipation gripped him at the thought of seeing her again. He had never felt such an instant attraction to a woman before. She was only here for a short time, so it would be crazy to act on the searing desire that charged through him whenever he was near her. But, fool that he was, whatever the consequences, he couldn't keep away.

Picking up the keys to the basic runabout his uncle kept for driving on the island, he headed for the door, tension and expectation tightening inside him. It was time. Time to meet Maria again. Time to be with Gina.

Gina dressed for the evening, conscious of the fact that she was taking far more care over her appearance than she had in ages. It was a long time since she had felt feminine and desired—just as long since she had spent any time thinking about a man. But meeting Seb this afternoon, experiencing an attraction the depth of which she had never known before, made her feel as if she was awakening from a long slumber. A self-imposed hibernation sparked when Malcolm had delivered his ultimatum. She had made her decision then and had stuck to it, never feeling tempted…until now.

She thought of her grandmother's words of concern that she had put her life on hold. She didn't begrudge a moment of the time she had spent caring for her grandparents, but between them and the pressures of work there had been little time for an active social life. She saw her girlfriends when their shifts allowed, but she had neither the time nor the interest in dating, would never take the risk of someone trying to come between her and her family again. It had never crossed her mind before today just how long it had been since she had given any thought to her own needs as a woman.

Seb was the sexiest, most compelling man she had ever met. And potentially the most dangerous to her resolve. Just being with him brought long-forgotten wants bubbling to the surface, and she tried to remind herself for the umpteenth time that she had to continue to set her own wishes aside and remember that this trip was all about her grandmother. She couldn't risk letting her desire for a man jeopardise that. On the other hand, Seb could be the one to help them gain the villa-owner's permission for what they had come to Elba to do. They needed him. She very much feared she needed him in a very different way.

After moisturising her skin following a bath, she applied some mascara to accentuate her eyes and a touch of colour to her lips. Leaving her hair loose, she dabbed some vanilla-scented perfume on her pulse-points and behind her ears, then stepped back to take one last look at her reflection in the mirror. Not knowing where Seb might be taking them she'd put on the best dress she had brought with her. It had capped sleeves and a scooped neckline, which revealed rather a lot of her generous cleavage, while the rich red fabric clung to her curves before fanning out at the hips, the skirt rippling to her knees. Flat shoes, a black wool wrap and her bag completed the outfit. She was ready. If only she didn't feel so nervous. Her heart scampered fit to burst, and a shiver of delicious anticipation tingled down her spine—warnings, if she needed any more, of just how fast and how deep she was falling for this man.

'*Che bellezza!* How lovely you look,' her grandmother praised with a delighted clap of her hands as Gina stepped out of the tiny bathroom and into the bedroom they shared.

'Thank you.'

'Seb will be a man much envied tonight.'

Gina flushed at the gentle teasing. 'He is doing this to help you,' she reminded her, trying to push away her own edgy excitement at the thought of seeing him again.

'I believe his reasons are much more basic. You are as attracted to him as he is to you,' her grandmother stated with uncanny perception.

'We're only here for a few days—' Gina struggled to keep reminding herself of that fact '—and seeing to your needs is all that matters.'

Her grandmother waved her hand dismissively. 'Nonsense, *ragazza mia*.'

'Nonna—'

'I cannot stop caring and worrying, Gina. Despite your protests, I know you have given up so much for your grandfather and me. We never intended to restrict your life by coming to live with you.'

'You haven't,' Gina protested, knowing for the first time that it was not entirely the truth.

Her grandmother took one of her hands in both of hers. 'You are a beautiful woman, but I think you have forgotten this. Today, for the first time, I can see you blossoming again, and it pleases me more than I can say.'

'We are here for a reason—'

'Which does not mean you should not enjoy yourself also,' her grandmother interrupted. 'Have some fun, enjoy the romance. Who knows where the attraction you and Seb share might take you?'

'Nonna…' Her protest died as confusion racked her. Could she really indulge in a holiday romance? 'I don't know.'

'Live your life, *ragazza mia*. Had I listened to all the doubts, I would not have had my special lifetime with your grandfather. I would always want you to follow your heart,' her grandmother insisted, the expression in her hazel eyes serious.

But could she trust her heart? Gina worried. How could she yearn for Seb after such a short time? Was it just lust? Did that even matter? They were both adults. If they were both free…

'I've only just met him, Nonna. We live in different countries. How can I know?'

'You say this to *me*?' Tutting, her grandmother shook her head. 'I knew in that first instant when I met Matthew McNaught. Time means nothing, Gina…not when it is right. When you meet your soul mate, you *know*. Do not put obstacles in the way. Do not let concern for me sway you. I would never want that. Your happiness is my happiness. Do not be afraid to go for what you want.'

Tears stung her eyes as she absorbed her grandmother's advice—what was tantamount to her blessing to explore the incredible connection she had felt with Seb from the instant she had seen him. But she couldn't help but be cautious. Nothing like this had ever happened to her before. She had never met anyone like Seb, had never reacted to anyone the way she did to him.

'I like Seb, Gina,' her grandmother continued, drawing

her from her thoughts. 'I have always had good instincts about people. I believe we can trust him. We must confide in him our reasons for being here.'

Fresh concern welled inside her. 'Are you sure? We need the permission of the villa's owner.'

'Maybe not. Seb has already said they will not return to Elba for some time. We don't have time. I need to do this, *ragazza mia*, and I trust Seb to help us.'

Before she could formulate a reply, or gather her thoughts together, there was a knock at the door. Her wayward heart skittered alarmingly, and a tremor ran through her, a whole flight of butterflies fluttering inside her.

Her grandmother cupped her cheek, understanding behind her smile. 'Open the door, Gina. And don't shut the woman you truly are away again. What will be will be.'

Filled with a mix of confusion and excitement, Gina crossed the room, her hand shaking as she turned the handle. Then the breath locked in her lungs and her heart threatened to stop beating altogether before rampaging on again at an alarming rate. And all because Seb stood there, looking even more amazing than she remembered him. Dressed in dark grey trousers and matching short-sleeved shirt, he was dangerously, deliciously handsome. Her gaze clashed with his. Caramel eyes held warmth, appreciation, and a smouldering awareness that made her burn and threatened to strip away any remaining shred of common sense or resistance. And then he smiled, a slow, private smile that turned her insides molten.

'Good evening, Gina,' he greeted her in English. The smoky, accented voice caused her knees to weaken further. A blush tinged her cheeks as his sultry gaze made a leisurely journey over her, lingering at her chest, an approving gleam in his eyes. 'You look stunning.'

'Thank you.'

Flustered, she stepped back and allowed Seb into the room, thankful when he turned his attention to her grand-mother. She needed a couple of moments to recover her composure.

'Maria, it is lovely to see you again,' he said, with the easy smile and smooth charm that appeared so natural to him. He held out a bunch of flowers. 'These are for you, *cara*. Signora Mancini is finding a vase to put them in.'

'They are beautiful. Thank you so much!'

Gina saw the flush of pleasure warm her grandmother's cheeks and was grateful for Seb's thoughtfulness.

'*Prego*. You are welcome.' Turning, he closed the distance between them and held out a single, fragrant bloom—a pure white rose. 'For you, Gina.'

She couldn't halt her own blush, nor the welling of emotion at the simple but meaningful gesture. 'Thank you,' she murmured, her voice unusually husky. She had forgot-ten what it was like to be romanced, she thought, breathing in the delicious scent of the perfect flower before setting it next to her grandmother's bouquet.

He held her gaze for a long moment, but glanced away, his attention sharpening as her grandmother smothered another couple of coughs. Her unease returning, Gina stepped forward.

'Are you all right, Nonna?'

'I am fine. Just tired. If you don't mind, I shall decline dinner this evening,' she added, shocking Gina to silence. 'Signora Mancini and I have become good friends. She is making me her special recipe ravioli, and then we are going to play a game of chess before I have an early night. You must go and have fun, Gina. Do not always allow me to slow you down. This is your holiday, too.'

'But…'

'Go, *ragazza mia*. Please. You can explain to Seb what is needed.'

Outwitted, Gina hesitated again and glanced at Seb. She had the most terrible feeling her grandmother was matchmaking in the most unsubtle way. Part of her yearned to spend some time with Seb, but the rest of her was reluctant to leave her grandmother, her anxiety increasing over the cough she had been developing in the last couple of days.

'If you are sure that is what you want, Maria, then I will be honoured to escort Gina for the evening and bring her safely home again,' he reassured her, taking a notebook from his pocket and tearing out a piece of paper. 'I will write down the name and number of the restaurant, and of my mobile phone, then you or Signora Mancini can contact us at any time if necessary.' He turned to glance at her. 'Is that all right with you, Gina?'

'OK.'

Heat flashed in his eyes at her whispered reply. All her defences were stripped away. She was grateful for his understanding, his care with her grandmother, and for his consideration of her own feelings. The decision made, the three of them walked to the front hall, where Signora Mancini waited, assuring them again that all would be well.

'Remember what I said, *ragazza mia*,' her grandmother whispered as she hugged her. 'Think of yourself for a change. And trust Seb with our request. Have faith.'

Then Gina found herself outside. Alone with Seb.

'You don't have to do this,' she began, offering him a way out even as he took her hand and led her towards the small Fiat that was parked at the roadside. 'It wasn't the arrangement.'

'Maybe not. And I truly would have enjoyed Maria's company. But I cannot say I am sorry to have you to myself.'

Taking a deep breath, she looked at him, unable to doubt his sincerity. 'If you're sure,' she murmured, realising how close they were as she breathed in the subtle woodsy scent of him.

'I am very sure, Gina.'

The certainty in his voice matched the desire in his eyes and sent a fresh tingle down her spine. The charge of electricity between them was unmistakable, the attraction intense, scary, exhilarating. She waited until she was settled in the car and Seb was walking round the other side before she drew in a few deep, steadying breaths.

At just twenty-eight kilometres long and nineteen kilometres at the widest point, the island was compact, and they did not have far to travel.

'Where are we going?' Gina asked, the gathering dusk masking the scenery of a part of the island she had not yet seen.

'I booked a table at a small seafront restaurant in Marciana Marina.' Seb smiled across at her. 'It's a picturesque fishing harbour, with a Pisan watchtower overlooking the shingle beach. The town is ancient, the smallest *comune* in Tuscany, and although an elegant resort is growing, the old quarter of the village—Cotone—is being carefully maintained.'

'It must be wonderful to live here. I've read so much about the island and its fascinating history. Has Elba always been home for you?'

'No.'

Surprised at the shortness of his reply, she glanced at him out of the corner of her eye. But before she could question him further they had reached the town, situated at the end of a valley, and Seb was parking the car. He came round to open the door for her, all smiles again.

'All right?' She nodded, distracted from her moment of uneasiness by the sights around her. Seb took her hand again, his touch increasing her awareness and firing her blood. 'Come, Gina, The restaurant isn't far.'

They walked a short way along the promenade before they came to an intimate-looking restaurant tucked away from the busy bars and tourist trinket shops. The smiling owner led them through the main dining area to a secluded terrace, settling them at a table where the muted lighting created a romantic atmosphere. The ambience was heightened by the clarity of the evening, the play of moonlight across the gently undulating waters, and the expanse of stars in the darkening sky.

'It's lovely,' she sighed, her gaze taking everything in before switching back to look at Seb. 'Have you been here before?'

He shook his head. 'A friend recommended it. Let us study the menu. What would you like?'

Despite the attraction zinging between them, Seb made her feel comfortable as they discussed the mouthwatering choices available. Eating out was a rare treat for her these days, and she considered all the dishes with enthusiasm, finding an array of exciting ingredients she would never have at home.

'I think I'll have the red mullet cooked with tomatoes, garlic and parsley,' she decided, embarrassed when her tummy gave an audible rumble in hungry anticipation.

'I think that is my sign to hurry and order,' Seb teased, selecting the shellfish risotto for himself and handing the menus back to the discreet waiter. 'What would you like to drink, Gina? You must try an Elban wine while you are here.'

'What would you recommend?'

She found herself distracted by the movement of his lips as he told her about the local wines, the husky cadence of his voice washing over her, warming her. He really was the most incredibly handsome man. All this could so easily go to her head...being wined, dined and charmed after so long in dating limbo. She—

'Gina?'

'Sorry?' A blush tinged her cheeks as she shook off her mental meanderings and noticed Seb watching her with an amused smile. 'What did you say?'

'Perhaps you will trust me to choose the wine for you?'

he suggested, and she realised she had been so busy looking at him that she hadn't taken in a word he had said.

She cleared her throat. 'Yes, please do.'

Usually she would have a glass of rosé Lambrusco with her friends while sharing a pizza, but she was happy to take Seb's advice, listening as he gave the order for a local dry white wine for her. He, she noted, kept to mineral water.

'Your grandmother is a delightful lady,' Seb praised as they enjoyed some antipasti while waiting for their main courses to arrive.

Gina smiled with affection. 'She is.'

'You are very close.'

'Yes. And with my grandfather, too,' she agreed at his observation.

'I am sorry, Gina.' His fingertips brushed her bare arm and she shivered in reaction to the empathetic touch. 'You must miss him very much.'

'I do. I still find it hard to believe he's gone. It's been worse for Nonna, of course.'

Seb's smile was gentle. 'It is good that you have each other.'

'Thank you.' She felt a moment of real closeness with him, feeling that he truly understood the bonds of family— unlike Malcolm.

'Tell me about Strathlochan,' he invited as their plates of aromatic food arrived. 'You enjoy it there?'

'Very much so. After growing up in quite a rough part of Glasgow, it was like paradise to find myself surrounded by lochs, hills and forests,' she explained with a smile. 'It's a beautiful region, and a great place to live. Although the town is growing, it has kept the community feel.'

Whether it was the wine, or the way Seb had of making her feel interesting and important, Gina found herself revealing far more about herself than she had intended. He was attentive, warm, funny and intelligent—and he made her feel special, the only person who mattered to him. It was a heady experience, and she felt the hidden woman she had buried inside coming back to life.

As they lingered over the delicious meal, they talked about books and music, films and politics, finding much in common and a few things they disagreed about, enjoying a good-natured teasing debate. She hadn't laughed so much in ages, Gina realised, taking a sip of her delicious wine, or felt so appreciated as a woman. When Seb encouraged her to talk more about the things that mattered to her, she told him about her grandmother, her home, her nursing and her best friends…quiet, studious nurse Holly Tait, and over-achieving, single-minded GP Ruth Baxter.

'Ruth is keeping an eye on Montgomery while we're away.'

'Montgomery?' Seb questioned, and Gina couldn't help chuckling at his wary uncertainty.

'My black Labrador.'

A flicker of relief crossed his expression. 'You have a dog?'

'I do. I love animals. I'd have a whole menagerie if I had the time and space.' And the money, she added silently. 'Monty was found abandoned at six months old, and we were delighted to give him a home. He's lovely—a year old now, and wonderful company for Nonna when I am at work. Like me, she's a big fan of old films, and we chose the name because she was reading a biography of Montgomery Clift at the time. Nonna said he was dark, handsome and had a flawed upbringing—like his namesake.'

Smiling, Seb nodded. 'And you say you start a new job when you go home?'

'Yes.' Finishing her meal, she set down her knife and fork. 'I'll be working at Strathlochan's new multi-purpose drop-in centre. I enjoyed the trauma work, but there was a lot of pressure and long shifts. I want more regular hours so I can care for Nonna. I could have gone to a higher grade at the hospital, but it would have meant I lost the hands-on work with patients, and that's what the job is all about for me. You have to do what makes you happy and maintain your principles, don't you?'

Seb remained silent. Unlike Gina, he hadn't held firm, but had given in to the lures and inducements to go against all he had believed in. The realisation that he should have stayed true to himself and his roots was sobering. He thought of Rico's advice to tell Gina who he was, but after listening to her speak with such dedication he feared she would think less of him for what he had been and had done.

'Goodness!' she exclaimed with embarrassment as the silence between them lengthened. 'I've been very boring, talking so much about myself.'

'You could never be boring.' He watched her thoughtfully for a moment. 'You speak with such loyalty and love about your family, your friends and your work. But what of you, Gina?'

'Me?'

She looked surprised, as if she didn't think she mattered, confirming his suspicions that she put everyone else before herself. 'Yes. When is Gina time? What do *you* want? What are *your* dreams?'

'I don't know.' She frowned, her fingers fussing with the stem of her glass. 'It's a long time since I've thought about it,' she admitted then, her gaze lifting to reveal the confusion in dark eyes. 'I suppose I've defined myself for so long by family and work. They're important to me.'

He reached out and took her hand in his, relishing being able to touch her again, enjoying the feel of her soft skin against his own. 'As they should be. There is nothing wrong with that. But you are important, too. You should be happy, content, fulfilled.'

As he said the words, meaning them, it dawned on him that they applied equally to his own life. When had he bothered about his own needs? He'd thrown his whole self into his career, needing to succeed, covering up for the fact that it no longer brought him the satisfaction it once had…not since the hospital board had cajoled him into cutting back on the reconstructive work he did for those with birth defects or accident injuries in favour of the celebrity nip/tuck work that brought money and kudos for the hospital as well as himself. It was only now, talking with Gina, that he'd really opened his eyes and his mind to that. It gave him much more to think about regarding the future direction of his life.

'And is there a man waiting impatiently for your return to Scotland?' he asked, his voice less steady than he wanted. But he needed to know.

Spending this time with Gina had reinforced his desire for her, and confirmed how much he liked her as a person. He couldn't remember when he had last enjoyed himself so much, nor when he had been so interested and entertained talking with a woman—one who was not fixated on her appearance, her quest for fame, or what his money and contacts could do for her.

'There's no one,' Gina replied, lifting an anxious weight from his chest. 'I—'

Still holding her hand, he stroked her wrist, feeling the acceleration of her pulse. 'Tell me.'

'I've not really dated in a while,' she admitted, becoming colour staining her cheeks.

'Why not?' Were the men in Scotland blind? 'How long is "a while"?'

She shrugged, her gaze sliding from his. 'About four years.'

'Four years?' he repeated, staggered at the information.

'I guess I've been so busy caring for my grandparents and doing my job. There was someone, but…'

'But?' he encouraged, seeing her frown, sensing this was important.

She paused, nibbling at her lower lip in a way that sparked a fire in his gut. 'My last relationship didn't survive my grandparents coming to live with me. I made a decision then about my priorities, and there hasn't really been the opportunity since.'

It wasn't hard to read between the lines. The man she had been dating at the time had been unwilling to share her attention, so Gina had devoted herself to the needs of others to such an extent that she had forgotten about her own. Seb admired her loyalty, her thoughtfulness. It made him like and desire her even more. But he wanted to help Gina remember just how much of a woman she was.

Before he could voice his thoughts, the waitress arrived and asked if they wanted dessert. Seb declined, ordering a coffee and chuckling at Gina's eagerness to sample the restaurant's home-made ice cream. Reluctantly, he relinquished her hand.

Midway through savouring her sweet treat, she glanced up, the expression on her face making him smile again. She looked self-conscious, but wryly amused.

'I'm being a pig, aren't I?' she bemoaned.

'Not at all. Honestly. It's a pleasure to dine with someone who enjoys their food and has an appreciation for what they are eating…and for the chef who prepared it.'

He thought of women like Lidia, taken to the finest restaurants, who made a fuss over every course, who picked at the food and refused to touch more than a few salad leaves. They cared little about the wastefulness, thought nothing of those who had less than they did, nor gave a mind to the people who had worked hard to deliver the food. Their selfishness and unnatural thinness were unattractive. Gina, on the other hand, was infinitely more sexy and enticing and head-turning for her true feminine curves. And she was natural, honest, completely uninterested in artificiality. It was wonderfully refreshing.

Seb watched her as she finished off her dessert, finding himself aroused by her almost sensual enjoyment of the taste and texture of what she was eating. She wasn't classically beautiful, and bore none of the carefully manufactured polish and sophistication of his rich patients, or the women who had vied—usually unsuccessfully—for his attention. But it was Gina's very naturalness that appealed to him and brought home how fake and unattractive all those other women were. Gina's was an inner beauty. Here was a woman who was comfortable with herself and who was not trying to impress or be something or someone else. His desire for her intensified.

There had been a few women in his past. He had been attracted to Antonella, but any interest had died when he had discovered she was an undercover reporter doing a kiss-and-tell story on him. That had hurt. He had never let anyone into his life again. There had been other women who wanted to be seen with him to further their own careers, to get their pictures in the papers, their names known. They were never interested in him as a person. His career had been pressured and time-consuming, the most important thing to him, and he'd had no time for a relationship.

Gina was the kind of woman he would once have run away from at full speed, but now his feet were planted firmly on the ground and weren't moving. Despite his initial caution, he'd known from the first that Gina was different. He had never been so instantly drawn to a woman. Not just her looks, but everything about her—her manner, her humour, her quiet intelligence, her sense of fun, her caring nature. Her loyal affection for her friends and the fact that she gave so much of herself to her grandmother said a lot about her, too.

He wanted to spend time with her—wanted to know everything about her. And he most definitely wanted to make love to her. He sensed hidden passions, an untapped sensuality he yearned to explore—a side of her she freely admitted she had selflessly restricted due to her responsibilities at home. While she was here on Elba he hoped to encourage the real Gina out to play.

CHAPTER FOUR

SEB was sorry when it was time for them to leave the restaurant. He had hoped to spend longer with Gina, to stroll along the harbour front, fringed with tamarisks, or go back to the villa and talk some more. But he knew she was anxious to return and check on Maria.

'You're sure you don't mind?' she asked as he called for the bill, although her relief was clear, too.

'Of course not.' Her sense of family and her thoughtfulness for others were two of the many things he admired so much about her. 'I understand.' He watched as she opened her bag and took out her purse. 'Gina, what are you doing?'

'Paying my share,' she stated, her eyes widening as he reached out and closed his hand over hers.

'Absolutely not.'

Doubt registered, and she hesitated. 'It's what I do at home,' she explained, and he wondered at the kind of men she had dated in the past.

'It's not what *I* do when I ask a woman to dine with me.' He stroked the back of his fingers down the smooth perfection of her cheek, touched by her generosity. 'Please, this is my treat.'

'OK.'

He drew her hand to his mouth, pressing a kiss to her palm, hearing her breath hitch. 'Thank you, Gina.'

The question of the bill settled, they left the restaurant and drove back to the hamlet in which Signora Mancini's house was situated. While he had enjoyed learning more about Gina, he realised that they had still not discussed the purpose of her and Maria's visit to Elba.

'Tell me more about your grandmother's wish, and this request she wants to make of the villa's owner,' he suggested, glancing at Gina and noting the way she nervously toyed with the hem of her wrap. 'She is hoping to revisit the beach?'

'Yes.' A deep sigh escaped her. 'That was the plan.'

'You realise there is no way Maria is going to be able to use the cliff steps?'

'I know. It was obvious from the first moment I saw them,' she admitted with resignation, and he regretted dampening her spirits.

All too soon they arrived outside the bed and breakfast. He walked round and opened the car door for Gina. Taking her hand, needing to touch her, to keep her close, he went up the path towards the open veranda that ran along the front of the building. He halted at the top of the half dozen shallow wooden stairs so they could have some privacy and talk.

'Is there any other way down the cliff to the beach?' she asked now, hope in her voice.

'No. I'm afraid not.'

Her shoulders slumped in apparent defeat. 'I guess that's it, then.'

He turned her to face him, the light from the porch combining with the moonlight to cast a gentle glow over her skin, illuminating her pensive expression. 'Tell me, Gina. Trust me. What is so important?'

'My grandparents made a vow to each other...and I promised to help.'

'Go on,' he encouraged when she paused, still puzzled by her reticence.

'The place where they met was always special to them.'

He knew this, but he waited for her to get to the point in her own time. Ducking her head to avoid his gaze, she drew her wrap more tightly around her shoulders, and he stepped closer, rubbing his hands lightly up and down her arms.

'Nonna didn't want to tell anyone, to ask anyone but the owner, because…' Again she paused, taking a deep breath before she rushed out the final words. 'I'm not sure it's legal.'

'Not legal?' For a moment Seb froze. 'What do you mean?'

'Nonna promised she would scatter my grandfather's ashes on the spot where they first met. I did some research and, while the law banning the practice in Italy changed some years ago, you need official permission, and some places still don't allow it. We don't have a permit. It isn't something we could do without asking the people who own the beach, and Nonna doesn't want anyone to get into trouble for helping her.' She sucked in another breath, her voice little more than a whisper. 'She wants me to bring her ashes here, too…when the time comes.'

He heard the wobble in her voice, knew how much her grandparents meant to her and how hard this must be for her. Taking her in his arms, he held her close, knowing he would do anything he could to make her happy and help her deliver on her promises. Cradling her against him, he buried his face in the thick lustrous waves of her glorious hair, breathing in the subtle and arousing scent he was coming to know as uniquely Gina.

'We can do it, *tesoro*,' he told her, turning the possibilities over in his mind.

'But how? You said yourself there is no way Nonna can make it down the steps.'

'That is true,' he agreed, but an idea had taken root. 'I have another plan.'

He allowed her to draw back enough to meet his gaze, and saw the dawn of cautious expectation in her dark eyes. 'You do? What is it?'

'We can take Maria to the cove by sea. I have a friend who will help us. He has a boat he uses for tourist trips and to take out divers. We can both go with her to keep her safe. It can be done, Gina. If Maria wishes.'

'But what about the owner of the villa? And the permit? Time is running out,' she fretted, continuing to talk around the fingertips he'd touched to her lips to silence her. 'What is their name?'

It would do no harm to tell her that much. 'The family's name is Linardi. I know them well enough to be certain that they would be happy to help you. I promise you it will be all right.'

'You're positive?'

'One hundred per cent,' he stated, seeing tears spiking her lashes.

'Thank you.'

Taking him by surprise, she threw her arms around him in a spontaneous hug and pressed an all-too-quick kiss to his startled mouth. Instinctively his arms tightened around her, holding her close, but she was pulling back before he had the chance to savour or extend the kiss.

'Sorry about that,' she murmured, sounding shaken, her voice uneven.

'I'm not.' He saw the flame of awareness in her eyes, and something else she could not hide…a yearning need that matched his own. Smiling, he dropped his gaze to her luscious lips. 'Let's try it again. Together this time.'

Without giving either of them a chance to reconsider, he leaned in and touched his mouth to hers, swept along on a tide of passion more immediate and intense than he had ever known. At once he was engulfed in her heat, her sweetness, the scent of vanilla and woman exciting and ensnaring him. She moaned softly, her lips opening under his. He made full use of the invitation, startled by the way the desire between them flared out of control in an instant. That had never happened to him before. He had never lost control, never absorbed himself in a woman, yet just kissing Gina stripped away all his reserve, exposing his base instincts, his raw need. Her taste, her scent, the feel of her soft curves against him, drove him wild.

Madre del Dio! Another few moments and he would forget himself, forget where they were, and take this whirl-wind to its inevitable conclusion. He couldn't do that. Not here. Not now. When the time came—as he hoped it would—he wanted Gina in his bed, where he could take his time and spend all night savouring her, loving her as she deserved. Until this inexplicable storm of desire spent itself. And if it didn't? He tried to ignore the inner voice telling him that the passion between them would only burn hotter and hotter. Gina only had a few more days on Elba. He wanted to make the most of them.

Breaking the kiss, he looked at her, lips plump and rosy from his kiss, her body shaking, her arousal evident in the flush of colour staining her cheeks, dark brown eyes almost black with passion.

'Perhaps we've both spent too long being serious and re-sponsible,' he suggested, hearing the roughness in his own voice. With the fingertips of one hand, he explored the contours of her face, amazed anew at the softness of her skin. 'Together we will have some fun, yes? Take time to be carefree.'

'Seb...'

His name whispered from her parted lips. He groaned,

unable to help himself as he returned his mouth to hers, sparking off another storm of passion. Gina kissed like an angel. Or maybe that should be a sorceress, given the way she had bewitched and beguiled him. He had lost his head from their first meeting on the beach.

Sweet mercy, the man could kiss.

Gina was carried away by the rush of desire charging through her. Seb's slow, deep kisses were consuming and heart-stoppingly sexy. She met and matched every demand…every stroke and glide as their tongues teased and tasted. The magic of Seb was awakening her from her slumber, making her aware for the first time in years of her own body, stirring long-ignored needs inside her. It was four years since she had been kissed, but she didn't remember it ever being like this! Every particle of her skin tingled, her nerves hummed, the blood sped through her veins. Inhaling his masculine scent, she felt drunk on him. She couldn't get close enough, and was oblivious to everything, focused solely on Seb and how incredible he made her feel.

When he drew back a second time they were both breathing raggedly, their hearts thudding in unison. She barely had time to think, much less gather her scattered senses, before he sank his hands in her hair, tilting her head so his mouth could trail a sensual path of fire down her throat and along her neck.

'Seb.' His name escaped on a whimper—appeal, not protest—and she tightened her hold on him, her legs like jelly, unable to support her much longer.

His breath was hot against her skin as his teeth nipped one earlobe before he salved the tiny sting with his tongue. 'You feel it too.'

'I do.' How could she deny his husky declaration? 'But I'm only here for a couple more days.'

'So were Maria and Matthew all those years ago. Don't you think we owe it to ourselves to see where this might go?'

Gina didn't know what to say. She had no idea what was happening between them, but meeting Seb had opened her eyes to the way she had disregarded her own wants. It had taken this man, in this place, to bring her back to life. No one else had ever affected her as Seb did, no one had kissed her as he did, or set her on fire with a single touch. Seb made her feel sensual, desirable, feminine, strong. She would never let anyone come between her and her grandmother, but Seb was no threat to her responsibilities at home. Here on this magical island, steeped in romance, could she indulge herself for a few days, free the woman within, the woman who had only come alive again for Seb?

'My grandmother…'

'I know. I want to spend time with you, but Maria is important, too,' he assured her, and his understanding, his care, his willingness to include her grandmother eased any lingering concern. 'Let me take you sightseeing tomorrow. Both of you. We can discuss with Maria how to put our plan into action.'

She felt overwhelmed, light-headed, wondering if she had the courage to take a risk and see where this mutual attraction took them. She looked into Seb's eyes, his intense expression almost melting her on the spot, and knew she had never wanted anyone or anything this much in her whole life.

'It would be a shame not to experience everything the island has to offer while you are here, Gina.'

She dragged in a steadying breath and tried not to get carried away by the sultry suggestion in his voice. 'I—'

'Tomorrow we will take Maria on a special outing, yes?'

'Yes.' The joy of being with him overrode any remaining fragment of common sense she still possessed. 'I'll talk to her in the morning.'

'I shall call for you after breakfast and learn of your decision.'

'Thank you. And for this evening,' she added, feeling melancholy at having to say goodnight. 'I've had a lovely time.'

'So have I.'

He took her hand, re-establishing the physical connection and re-stoking the passion inside her. That he felt it, too, was apparent by the heat burning in his eyes. A tremor rippled through her as he held her gaze, raising her hand to his mouth and pressing a tantalising kiss to the inside of her wrist, his tongue-tip stroking teasing circles on her skin. He only had to look at her, touch her, kiss her, and she was gone. Everything about him was so sensual, so intense, and yet he had a gentleness and inherent caring that made him even more appealing and impossible to resist.

His fingers combed through her hair again, as if he couldn't stop touching her, while under her own hands she felt the play of muscle across his back, firm, supple, exciting. It had been so long since she had felt wanted, desired…and she had *never* experienced this kind of physical and emotional connection with a man before.

'I should say goodnight,' he murmured, nibbling at her lower lip, which remained full and sensitised from his kisses.

'I suppose,' she whispered back, her fingertips skimming down his spine.

Neither of them let go. Neither moved back. Their gazes locked. Endless moments passed. Then Seb surrendered. Her lips parted in welcome, meeting his in another searing kiss. She had no idea what the future held, but she couldn't stop the onward rush of whatever was happening between them. Didn't *want* to stop it.

She moaned in protest when he began to pull back again. If only she never had to stop holding him, kissing him. 'Seb?'

'You must go indoors, *tesoro.*' His voice was uneven, thick with desire. 'Now—while I can still let you.'

She wanted to step back into his arms and throw caution to the wind, but Seb was opening the front door and encouraging her inside.

'Until the morning, Gina.' His fingers whispered across her cheek and down her throat to the hollow where her pulse beat a crazy tattoo. 'Dream of me...as I will of you.'

Gina had no idea how she forced her legs to move, but she found herself inside...alone. She sagged back against the door that separated them, breathless and trembling, one hand pressed to her chest. There was a long silence before Seb's footsteps carried him away, and she had to fight the urge to run after him and stop him from leaving.

She couldn't imagine how she would ever sleep. She was buzzing. The feel and taste of Seb lingered.

When she could force herself to move, she tiptoed along to the ground-floor room she shared with her grandmother. She couldn't wait to tell her the good news—that Seb was making plans to help them scatter Nonno Matthew's ashes in the villa's private cove near Neptune's Spear. For now she was thankful to find the older woman asleep, although she was restless, her breathing less regular than normal, stirring concern that all was not well.

Careful not to make a sound, Gina readied for bed and slipped beneath the light duvet. Her gaze lingered on the beautiful white rose Seb had brought her, which now sat on the table beside her bed in a narrow vase, courtesy of Signora Mancini. She leaned across and inhaled the scent, a smile on her face, her fingertips brushing the silky softness of the petals. Worry for her grandmother took some of the gloss off her fairytale evening, but Seb continued to dominate her thoughts. *Dream of me*, he had said. Asleep or awake, she knew her mind would be full of red-blooded images of the man who stirred her as no one else ever had.

A cough and an incoherent murmur drew her attention to the figure in the other bed. Hugging her pillow, Gina frowned, lying so she was facing her grandmother, ready to go to her should she need anything. Listening for breathing problems and further coughing, she closed her eyes, reliving every moment with Seb. She might be the biggest fool imaginable, but she could not wait for the night hours to pass— because when the morning came she would be seeing him again.

Seb strode through Elba's hospital in Portoferraio, a mix of emotions churning inside him. When he had arrived at the bed and breakfast that morning, eager to see Gina, to spend the day with her and her grandmother, he had been shocked to be greeted by an anxious Signora Mancini with the news that Maria had been taken ill during the night. Gina, he'd been told, had taken the older woman to hospital in a taxi at dawn.

His first concern had been for Maria's health. Then, on his drive to the island's main town, he had worried for Gina, knowing how upset and alarmed she must be. Even though she was a nurse, when something happened to someone you loved it was hard to hold on to the professional balance. But he also couldn't help the sting of hurt that Gina had not turned to him for help—had not thought to ring him so he could drive them to the hospital. OK, she had no idea about his medical knowledge, but given everything that had passed between them, albeit in less than twenty-four hours, he would have liked her to trust him, to want him with her.

Leaving her the night before had been the most difficult

thing he had ever done. Back at the villa, unable to settle, thinking about her, wanting her, needing her, he had discovered a message on the answer-machine from Rico. His cousin had informed him he had the information he wanted from Scotland. He had phoned back right away.

'Everything checked out,' Rico had confirmed. 'Nic knows them—something to do with their dog and Gina's new job. He says they are one hundred per cent genuine in every way.'

It hadn't been a surprise—not after meeting Maria and spending the evening with Gina—but the relief after his experience with Antonella had been huge. 'Thank you.' In his heart he had known, and he had felt guilty for doubting her, disgusted with himself for being so cynical, especially when Gina herself was so open, so giving.

'How was your evening?' Rico had asked, and Seb hadn't been able to halt the smile that had spread across his face.

'Great.' He'd filled his cousin in on Maria's mission to scatter Matthew's ashes. 'I thought Zio Roberto and Zia Sofia would have no problem with me helping her.'

'Count on it. Do what you think is right, Seb. No one but us will know if there isn't an official permit—and it's our private beach. It's a really touching story.'

He'd been glad to have Rico's backing and understanding. 'It is.'

'So, what's she like?'

'Frail, not in *bad* health for seventy—although she has arthritis and a few niggling problems. Especially with her breathing. She didn't feel well enough to come to dinner.'

Rico had laughed. 'I meant the *granddaughter*—Gina!'

'Oh.' Seb hadn't been able to make sense of his reaction to Gina himself, let alone try to explain them to his cousin. 'She's…'

'…got to you,' Rico had finished for him when he'd hesitated. 'If she's a tall curvy blonde I'll come over to Elba and check her out for myself.'

'Well, she's not. So you can keep away.'

Seb had cursed the tell-tale snap in his voice, the defensiveness he had been unable to mask. As much as he loved his cousin, he didn't want Rico here, exuding his renowned charm, good-looks and sex appeal on Gina!

'Message received. But now I am even more curious,' Rico had teased. 'Gina must be something else if she has you, always so cool and uninvolved, all possessive and tied in knots after a couple of hours!'

'I'm not possessive—or tied in knots,' he had lied.

'Right!' His half-hearted protest hadn't fooled Rico. 'I can hear it in your voice *cugino*. And you had a cosy dinner for two! Tell me you told her the truth about your identity?'

'I'm not ready to say anything yet.'

'You mean you're worried how Gina will react if she finds out you have money and fame,' Rico had interjected, with alarming insight.

He hadn't known how to explain. 'Being with Gina today made me realise that I don't like what I've been the last few years. I'm not sure I'll ever come to terms with losing surgery, but I never should have moved so far from my roots.'

'It's clear she's made an impression on you.'

'I've only known her a few hours.'

'Sometimes these things happen that fast,' Rico had counselled. 'Just don't leave it too long to tell her, Seb. Not if you want to take things further with her. Or this is going to come back to bite you.'

There had been genuine worry in his cousin's voice, and Seb had experienced a few lingering doubts that he was doing the right thing. 'I'll think about it.' But he was scared that the truth would change Gina's view of him.

Now, at the hospital, as he found out where Maria had been taken and went in search of Gina, he knew he was walking a fine line. People here knew him, and it was a risk if he wanted to keep Gina from finding out. Of course he could tell her himself, but this was not the time or place— not while Gina was sidetracked and troubled about her grandmother's health. He *would* tell her…when they were both ready. For now he had to negotiate his way carefully through the minefield ahead, and his main focus was on how Gina was coping and on Maria's well-being.

Turning a corner, he spied Gina sitting alone in a stark corridor, wearing faded jeans and a short-sleeved, button-fronted red top. One trainer-clad foot was tapping in agitation and her hands were knotted together in her lap. A wave of tenderness overwhelmed him. She glanced up as he closed the gap between them, surprise in her anxious dark eyes, swiftly followed by a gratifying expression of welcome relief. With a tremulous smile, she rose to her feet and stepped into his waiting arms. Seb gathered her close, wanting to shield her, protect her, comfort her, grateful that she clung to him as if she trusted him and found solace with him.

He drew back a fraction to examine her face, finding her pale and strained. With the fingers of one hand he brushed away some stray strands of hair that had escaped her hurried ponytail.

'Are you all right?'

She nodded, still leaning against him. 'Yes. Thank you for coming.'

'You should have called me,' he chided softly, stroking her cheek.

'It happened so quickly.' She shook her head, worry reflected in her eyes. 'Nonna deteriorated suddenly, and rather than waiting for an ambulance or bothering you, Signora

Mancini called the man who lives next door to her, who runs the taxi. I'm sorry.'

Seb cursed himself for letting his selfish feeling of rejection add to Gina's concern. 'You did the right thing. I just wish I had been there for you both. Tell me what happened,' he instructed, sitting her down, then taking the place beside her, keeping hold of her hand.

'You heard my grandmother coughing last night?' she began, and he nodded, recalling Maria's moments of discomfort and her disturbed breathing. 'That only started in the last couple of days. She assured me she was just tired after the journey from Scotland. When I got back last night—' a becoming flush warmed her cheeks, and Seb's own blood heated; he knew she was thinking of their passionate kisses '—she was asleep, but restless, her breathing irregular. She worsened near dawn and complained of chest pain, breathlessness, and the cough was more persistent.'

'And have they told you anything?' Feeling her shaking, he slipped an arm around her and drew her close.

'No. Nothing.' She gave a wry laugh. 'I know what hospitals are like, but it's different being on the other side.'

Seb knew that all too well after his experiences the last couple of months following his knife-wounds. 'I'll see what I can find out. I know it is easy to say, Gina, but try not to worry. Maria is in good hands here.'

Cupping her face, wishing he could do more to ease her burden, he placed an all-too-brief kiss on her parted lips. He hated leaving her alone again, even for a few minutes, but hoped he could quietly use his influence here to get some details about Maria's condition and bring Gina some reassuring news.

Gina cursed herself for failing to alert Seb about what had happened and cancel their arrangement for the day. He had been on her mind, but she had been so overwhelmed by her anxiety for her grandmother that she had delayed calling him. Had she secretly hoped he would follow them to Portoferraio? She honestly wasn't sure. But when she had looked up and seen him walking towards her, casually dressed in jeans, black T-shirt, and a cream jumper that highlighted his dark good looks, the rush of pleasure at his presence, followed by the relief of being held in his arms, had been indescribable. She was grateful for his support, and his concern for her grandmother. Language was no barrier, but she was a stranger here, and having Seb on her side made her feel immeasurably better and no longer alone.

The wait seemed endless, and yet it could not have been long before Seb was striding back towards her, the smile on his face lifting a massive weight of worry from her shoulders. She rose to meet him, allowing him to take her hands, needing the contact, warmed by the comfort his touch brought.

'Did you discover anything?' she queried, eager for news.

'Maria is doing well. I have seen her, Gina, and I will take you to her now.' A welter of emotions assailed her—relief, gratitude, impatience to see her grandmother, and puzzlement that Seb, exuding a calm control over the situation, seemed to have gained such swift access to her grandmother. 'Maria has a chest infection. They are doing an X-ray, then tests to see if it is viral or bacterial and whether she will need antibiotics or not. In the meantime she is having fluids to rehydrate her, and paracetamol to lower her temperature.'

'There's nothing wrong with her heart?' she asked, voicing her secret fear.

Seb shook his head. 'Nothing at all. Her heart is strong. I promise.'

'I was so scared.' She bit her lip, trying to stop her voice from trembling. 'I couldn't bear to lose her, too.'

'I know, *tesoro*.'

She sank against him as he wrapped his arms around her once more. It felt so good to have someone else to lean on for once. For so long she had been the strong one, shouldering all the responsibility at home, coping with a stressful job, scared after Malcolm's treachery to allow any man into her life. She buried her face against Seb, breathing in his scent, absorbing his strength. It had all happened so quickly. While the initial attraction remained, and physically she wanted him, she already cared about him, felt an emotional bond she couldn't explain. She was moved by his innate goodness, affected as much by his tender touches as his fiery passion.

'Come, now,' he murmured, stroking her hair, making her feel safe and cared for. 'The doctor is waiting to talk with you.'

'Thank you.'

She fought back tears of relief, feeling bereft when he released her. Scrambling to gather up her bag, she wondered how she could have missed the signs that her grandmother had been brewing a worrying chest infection. She never should have let her make this journey. If only—

'Gina, stop.'

Seb's gentle admonishment interrupted her self-recriminations, and she glanced at him with a frown. 'Sorry?'

'You are blaming yourself,' he challenged with frightening insight. 'Don't, *cara*. It is not your fault.'

'But I'm a nurse. I care for her. I should have *seen*,' she protested.

'Maria didn't want you to see.' He cupped her face. 'This trip meant so much to her that she hid from you how she was feeling.'

Gina's eyes widened in shock. 'Nonna told you that?'

'Yes. She feels guilty now for any trouble and worry she

has caused you.' Seb rested one hand at the small of her back as they walked along the corridor. 'Soon she will tell you so you know this for yourself.'

When they stepped into the small room, Gina's gaze flew straight to the figure propped up in the bed. Her grandmother looked frail, but much more comfortable than when she had last seen her. Oblivious to the doctor and nurse in the room, Gina hurried across to give the woman she loved so much a hug, careful of the drip in her arm. For a moment she experienced a strange mix of emotions…feeling both the responsibility of an adult and yet almost like a little girl again.

'I am sorry, *ragazza mia*. So sorry. But I knew you would make me stay at home, and I *had* to come to Elba to do this for my Matteo…whatever the consequences.' Gina saw regret mix with determination in the wise hazel eyes. 'Forgive me.'

'Oh, Nonna…Of course I forgive you. I just want you well,' she reassured her, trying to smile and hide how frightened she had been.

She sensed Seb moving up behind her, and instinctively she reached for his hand, grateful when he linked his fingers with hers, making her feel stronger.

'Gina, meet the doctor who is looking after Maria.' Seb drew her attention to the small grey-haired man who politely dismissed the nurse and then moved towards the bed. 'This is Dottore Franco Vasari.'

She shook hands, relieved that the kindly doctor immediately inspired confidence. Slipping easily back into Italian, she questioned him about her grandmother's health.

'As you can see, Signora McNaught looks much better than when she came to us this morning.' Dottore Vasari's smile encompassed them all. 'Soon we will have the results and know the nature of the infection, and then we will decide which medication to choose, and whether antibiotics are needed.' He seated himself on the edge of the bed. 'We will continue with intravenous rehydration for the time being. I would like to keep her in for twenty-four hours, for rest and observation.'

Although her grandmother looked disgusted at the idea, Gina nodded. 'Whatever you think is best. But we are only booked to stay on Elba for two more nights,' she explained, noting the doctor's frown and feeling the way Seb's fingers momentarily tightened on hers.

'I would not be happy for Signora McNaught to travel so soon,' Dottore Vasari insisted, glancing at the notes. 'Flying home in two days would not be sensible. I recommend you extend your stay for a little longer. I will write a letter for your own doctor that you can take home for follow-up care.' He rose to his feet and handed cards to herself and Seb. 'I will leave you now to talk things over. I shall be checking on your grandmother regularly, *signorina*, and hope to discharge her at midday tomorrow. If you have any questions or concerns, please call me.'

'Thank you. I'm very grateful,' Gina told him, shaking hands again.

She was confused at the older man's almost deferential nod towards Seb, but her grandmother was reclaiming her attention, and she had no more time to ponder on Seb's authoritative and knowledgeable manner.

'Gina, if I must stay in this place I will not have you sitting here fretting all day,' her grandmother insisted, recovering much of her spirit. 'You have dreamed all your life of seeing Elba. I will be cared for here. You must go and explore the island.'

'But—'

'No arguments, *ragazza mia*! Do it for me. Please? Besides, there will be arrangements to make if we must stay longer,' her grandmother pointed out.

Already Gina was making a mental list. She needed to find an internet café to contact the airline and change their tickets. Then she needed to check with the insurance company about health cover, plus e-mail home with the news. Thank goodness she had another week before starting her new job at the centre.

'I'll sort things out, Nonna,' she promised.

Her grandmother shook her head. 'You will have to find somewhere else for us to stay, Gina. Signora Mancini has already told me that our room is booked for other guests the day we were meant to leave. She has no more vacancies.'

'Don't worry.' Gina smothered a sigh, trying not to think of how depleted her small contingency fund might be at the end of this unexpected change of plan.

'Scusi.' Seb stepped forward, addressing them both. 'There is no question but you must come to stay at the villa for your extra days on the island.'

Gina's eyes widened. 'What about the owners? Won't they mind?' she protested, both relieved and concerned at the prospect of staying with Seb.

'The Linardi family will be pleased to help. Indeed, they will insist on it. There is no problem, Gina, I assure you,' he promised, wearing down her shaky resistance.

With funds low, it would be a great help not to have to move to a more expensive hotel. But she was determined to pay for their keep at the villa, whatever Seb decreed. It would be dangerously tempting to live in the same house as him, and it put wickedly improper thoughts in her mind. And in Seb's, if the sultry expression in his eyes was anything to go by. A shiver of sensual excitement rippled through her.

'That would be marvellous!' her grandmother exclaimed, more colour returning to her cheeks. 'I would be closer to the special place I shared with Matteo, no?'

Smiling, Seb took her grandmother's hand. 'Exactly. And when you are well, Maria, we can take care of the task you came here to accomplish.'

'Thank you.' Her grandmother's whispered words and the longing on her face brought tears to Gina's eyes. 'You are both so good to me.'

'Then it is settled. Gina and I will see to the necessary arrangements and have things ready for you to come home tomorrow afternoon.'

'That sounds like so much work for you both,' her grandmother worried.

'Not at all.' Seb turned to Gina, a private promise in his eyes that fired her blood. 'It will not take long. Then I will show Gina the island. Whatever she wishes. And later we will come back to see you, Maria. How is that?'

Her grandmother all but clapped her hands in delighted acceptance. 'Perfect!'

The decision made, they said their goodbyes and left the older woman to rest. Gina's mind was buzzing—not only with the tasks ahead of her, but with delight at spending time alone with Seb and nervousness at staying at the villa. She didn't know how she would resist temptation. Should she even try?

Seb took her hand, his fingers linking with hers, his touch spiking her pulse. Once outside in the sunshine, he turned her to face him, his hands resting on her shoulders as she leaned against the car.

'Gina, I need you to understand something.'

Her heart beating crazily beneath her ribs, she gazed into molten caramel-coloured eyes. 'What is it?'

'The invitation to stay at the villa comes without strings,' he told her, his hands moving until his palms cupped her face. 'There is no pressure, Gina. No obligation or expectation. I will help you and Maria, whatever happens between us.' He paused a moment, his eyes darkening as his gaze dropped to her mouth, his voice turning huskier. 'Yes, I want you. I want you as I have never wanted anyone before. But only if it is what you want, too. It is your choice…if and when you are ready.'

His honesty, reassurance and understanding made her respect and care about him even more. Electricity hummed between them. She felt strong, centred, yet giddy with excitement, alive with desire, feeling her true power as a woman in a way she never had before. Seb was changing her. She was growing in confidence because of him. She wanted him…badly. No matter what the future held for them, she knew she would forever regret not taking this chance with Seb. She might live the rest of her life and never experience anything this amazing again. The time she had with him might be short, but there was nothing casual about the way she felt for him.

Reaching up, she kissed him. The passion was there, but so was something much deeper—an emotional connection that took them to a whole new level. Pulling back, she rested a palm against his jaw.

'Thank you.'

Seb nodded, seeming to understand without the need for words. 'Let's go and take care of business, then we can enjoy our day together and see where it takes us.'

CHAPTER FIVE

'I COULDN'T eat another thing,' Gina protested, rejecting Seb's offer of more fruit and flopping back on the grass with a sigh. 'That was the best picnic I've ever had.'

Chuckling to himself, Seb packed away the remains of the food he had bought in Portoferraio, while Gina had been at the internet café changing travel arrangements, dealing with the insurance and checking her e-mails. Afterwards, they had briefly explored some of the interesting places in Elba's capital town before he had brought her to this quiet beauty spot for their lunch.

Enjoying being close, he lay on his back beside her and reached for her hand, curling their fingers together. 'What do you do to relax at home?'

'I read. And I love walking, swimming and cycling. My friends and I go ten-pin bowling or to the cinema. Sometimes we stay in with pizza and wine and just chat.'

'But no dating?' he murmured, turning on his side and propping himself on one elbow so he could study her.

'No dating.'

Her eyes were closed, long lashes fanning her cheeks, and the dappled sunlight filtered through the trees, kissing her face. 'What happened? With the man you were seeing four years ago?' he added, as her lashes lifted and he found himself looking into solemn dark eyes.

'Malcolm was in hospital management. He was charming, persistent…I was flattered. We'd been together nearly a year, and I thought things might go somewhere between us,' she admitted, and he felt a strange tightening inside him.

'You were in love with him?'

Gina looked thoughtful, but shook her head. 'I cared about him, and before all this happened I thought I could come to love him. But afterwards I was more hurt and angry at what he did than heartbroken that we had broken up. I could never have stayed with or loved someone like that— not when he showed his true colours. In the end, he wasn't the person I thought he was.'

'I see.'

Seb hesitated, feeling guilty because he hadn't told Gina the full truth about himself. What would she think of him when she discovered that? As he wrestled with his conscience—liking her, wanting her to like him, needing to be with her, but scared that if he told her it would drive her away—she continued with her story.

'My grandparents were becoming increasingly frail, and their Glasgow house was unsuitable, so I persuaded them to move in with me. Malcolm didn't like it. He turned surly, rude and demanding—to them as well as to me.' She shifted restlessly and he brushed his thumb across her wrist as her fingers tightened on his. 'Then he issued an ultimatum. He'd gone behind my back and made enquiries about residential homes. He called my grandparents horrible names, referred to Nonna as "the old crone", and said I either put them in the place he had found or he walked.'

'*Bastardo*,' Seb swore, hating the man for hurting Gina and disrespecting her grandparents, for his selfishness and lack of understanding.

A ghost of a smile curved her mouth. 'I said something similar. There was no choice at all—not for me. My grandparents meant everything to me, and no way was Malcolm, or anyone else, coming between us.'

'He had no idea of the importance of family.' Leaning down, his lips whispered softly over hers. 'I'm sorry, Gina.'

'It was a long time ago—we weren't meant to be. Things were unpleasant at the hospital for a while. Malcolm made remarks about me. But support was on my side and thankfully he got a job elsewhere soon afterwards and moved away.'

No wonder she had been wary of getting involved again, and had put that part of her life on hold, unsure who she could trust, concerned that whoever she dated wouldn't understand her loyalties and responsibilities. As far as he was concerned they only made her more attractive, more special.

Gina sat up beside him, wrapping her arms around her knees, affording him a tantalising glimpse of the small dolphin tattoo at the base of her spine. Unable to help himself, he reached out and traced the shape of the leaping form with his fingertips, feeling her response to his touch in the ripple of her skin.

'This is pretty,' he murmured.

'Thank you.' A mischievous smile curved her mouth as she looked down at him, and he didn't know what he wanted most—to taste her kiss or set his lips to her tattoo. 'I had it done when I was eighteen.'

'Why a dolphin?'

A reminiscent look crossed her face and her smile faded. 'I think I heard nearly as many stories about my grandfather's time at sea as I did about Elba when I was growing up. He often saw dolphins—they were his good luck symbol—joy and spirit and freedom. He took me to see them off the Scottish coast once. It was amazing. I'm a Pisces…I love the water. I love dolphins and I love my grandfather. Instead of the fish of my star sign, I chose this.'

'I like it.' It was symbolic of her—her loyalties, her loves. His fingers lingered a moment more, then he moved, sitting up before he gave in to temptation and drew her down to the grass again, to spend the next few hours kissing her all over. 'We have the afternoon ahead of us. If you could do anything you wanted, go anywhere on the island, what would you choose?'

'I want to see *everything*,' she confessed with a laugh. 'I've been in love with the idea of Elba all my life, and have read everything I can find about it—from the many invasions over the centuries to Napoleon Bonaparte's exile here in 1814.'

His insides knotted when she smiled at him, her dark eyes sparkling with interest and delight.

'I want to see Napoleon's country villa at San Martino, the island's mineralogical museums and old mines, the Medieval and Renaissance fortresses, the Roman villas, the hidden churches and shrines, and to explore the unspoilt landscape.'

'I don't think we'll squeeze all those in before returning to see Maria this evening,' he teased, enchanted by Gina, her freshness and natural beauty.

'Spoilsport,' she accused with a mock pout, which focused his attention back on her delicious mouth.

He clenched his hands to fists to stop himself reaching for her and forgetting all about sightseeing. 'Pick one,' he requested, hearing the roughness of desire in his voice.

'Marciana Alta.'

The oldest settlement on Elba, with origins dating back to 35BC, the medieval village was perched on the mountainside. Seb was unsurprised by her choice. Rising to his feet, he took her hand and drew her up, unable to resist one more kiss, lingering as she moaned, her response eager and immediate. He had meant everything he had said to her earlier. Anything further that happened between them would be Gina's choice. But he couldn't help grasping these stolen moments when they came his way. Before things got out of hand, he set her away from him. Her cheeks were flushed, her lips rosy and plump. Smothering a groan, he dredged up every atom of control he could muster and led the way back to the car.

Before long, they had reached the picturesque village. Gina's enthusiasm was infectious, and sharing this with her was like seeing it all again through fresh eyes. They visited the archaeological museum, with its Paleolithic, Etruscan and Roman finds, walked the narrow alleyways and cobbled lanes of red-tiled houses, their doorways festooned with colourful flowers, and saw the crumbling remains of the Pisan fortress.

'Are you scared of heights?' he asked a while later.

'No. Why?'

'Would you like to take the cableway to the summit of Monte Capanne? It's the highest mountain on the island at over one thousand metres. On a clear day you can see as far as Corsica from the top.'

She looked almost childlike in her delight, her eyes wide, her smile broad. 'I'd love that. Can we go?'

'Of course,' he agreed, happy to indulge her.

He had never spent time with a woman like this, and he was amazed at how much he was loving it. His desire for Gina was ever-present, but the longer he was with her the more relaxed he felt, the more he liked her, and the more he came to realise how false the life he had been living—and the people in it—had become. He could also now admit how much he hated it...and himself for ever getting caught up in it in the first place. The reconstructive surgery he'd used to do full-time might not have paid so well, but it had been more emotionally and professionally rewarding.

Seb had decisions to make about his future. The loss of money didn't bother him, nor did he care about the ending of a fame he had never wanted, nor the loss of the hangers-on, the so-called glamour, the women who had used him for their own ends. What he *did* care about was the loss of his ability to perform surgery. The enlightenment that he had taken a wrong turning had come too late—he had been too caught up in the moment to recognise it. Having to take a step back due to his injuries, combined with meeting Gina, was opening his eyes, making him reassess his life and his priorities.

'Are you all right?'

Gina's soft query drew him from his dark thoughts. He saw the confused frown on her face and the concern in her eyes. What would she think of him if she knew? He couldn't tell her. Not yet. He didn't want to spoil this special time with her.

'I'm fine,' he reassured her with a smile, pushing his self-doubt to the back of his mind. 'Let's take that ride up the mountain.'

The base of the cableway was only a short distance from the village, and they were soon climbing into one of the yellow open-framed metal cradles which held only a couple of people. Gina stepped in first and Seb followed.

'This is cosy!' She glanced over her shoulder and smiled at him.

'Mmm.' Standing behind her, he wrapped his arms around her waist, relishing the feel of her snuggling back against him. 'Perfect for two.'

They journeyed upwards, suspended precariously over crags and crevices, chestnut and holm oak woods, ancient vineyards and a wide array of native fauna and flora. Encouraged by Gina's interest, he pointed out places they could spot across the island.

'The view is amazing,' she exclaimed, her gaze focused on the rugged coast and across the sea far below to other islands in the chain.

'It is,' he agreed softly, captivated by the graceful curve of her neck, her profile, the expression of wonderment on her face.

Dipping his head, he nudged the satin fall of her hair aside and nuzzled against her neck, hearing her soft moan as his lips worked their way to the sensitive hollow beneath her ear, his tongue-tip tasting her skin. She smelled of vanilla, sunshine and Gina. He didn't think he'd ever get enough of her. As she leaned back into him, he flattened his palms on the rounded curve of her belly, nibbling her ear as he inched up towards the tempting jut of her breasts.

Glancing down, he could see her nipples had beaded to tight peaks. Her breathing turned ragged and she gasped when he finally skimmed the rest of the way up her body and cupped her fullness, shaping gently, grazing across her taut nipples. Her hands tightened their grip on the cradle railing. Arching to his touch, she dropped her head back, and his mouth took advantage of more exposed skin, gently biting at her, salving with strokes of his tongue. He wanted more. Wanted to see her, taste her.

Then a noise from above reminded him where they were and he groaned, sliding his hands back down to her waist, holding her steady as they both fought for control in the few moments before they reached the mountain top and exited the cradle. For a while they lingered to enjoy the view, arms around each other, then rode the cableway back down to the village.

'It's time to head back to the hospital,' he told her as they returned to the car. 'Will you come to the villa for a meal afterwards?'

'Thank you. But I'll have to go back to Signora Mancini's tonight.'

Her words dampened his hopes. 'Are you sure? You're welcome to stay.'

'I know.'

'I don't like to think of you being there alone,' he commented, knowing that was partly true, but equally that he just didn't want to let her go.

She met his gaze, a small smile playing at her mouth. 'I'll be fine. There are things I need to do before tomorrow.'

'OK.'

He tried to be satisfied with that, to tamp down his disappointment. He had promised not to rush her, and he wouldn't, but that didn't mean he wouldn't miss her. All he could hope was that Gina would come to want him as much as he wanted her.

Gina wriggled onto a high stool at the counter in the villa's impressive kitchen, watching Seb move around with casual ease, gathering things together to make them a quick meal before taking her back to Signora Mancini's. Having promised the woman by phone that she would return with news and stay a final night, Gina felt obligated to keep her word. She also needed to do the packing for herself and her grandmother. But she had sensed that Seb's unspoken reluctance matched her own. She didn't want to leave him, but the timing and the circumstances weren't right. Not until her grandmother was safely out of hospital and settled in the guest suite Seb had shown her on a quick tour of the large, single-storey villa.

'Maria was looking better, *tesoro*, no?'

'Much better. It's a big relief to know there is apparently

nothing more serious going on than a mild flu-like virus and some pleural inflammation,' she continued, feeling a big weight of worry had been lifted off her shoulders.

Her grandmother had been in much better spirits, her breathing easier, and with more colour in her cheeks after a restful day. The X-ray had revealed a small amount of fluid on the lungs, but tests had shown the cause was not bacterial so no antibiotics would be needed. Instead she had been prescribed diuretic tablets to help clear the lungs and prevent any increase in the oedema which was starting to show in puffy ankles, the skin pitting when pressed and slow to return to normal. She had also been given some anti-inflammatories to ease the pleural discomfort that had caused the chest pain and made breathing painful lying down in the night.

'We'll get things checked out with our own GP when we get home.'

Nodding, Seb stroked one hand over her hair as he passed her. 'A good idea to follow things up,' he agreed. A small frown creased her brow as she recalled how unfazed he had been at the hospital on their second visit at the end of the day, how interested in and understanding of what was happening to her grandmother.

Gina bit her lip as she thought over the various possibilities that could lie behind her grandmother's symptoms. 'Dottore Vasari suggested it might be poor circulation that's causing the water retention and leading to fluid on the lungs.'

'A few days rest here, where we shall watch over her and pamper her, and Maria should be much improved,' Seb promised with a smile.

And then they would be able to return home. Gina didn't want to think of that part, much as she wanted her grandmother well again. Smothering a sigh, she folded her arms and leaned on the counter, watching Seb work, already enjoying the aromas that were starting to emerge from the dish he was preparing for them. He seemed so proficient, and it made her realise how little she really knew about him—how seldom she could encourage him to talk about himself.

'Have you always liked cooking?'

'It's something I've come to enjoy more and more in recent years,' he confided, starting to chop fresh tomatoes and local, seasonal porcini mushrooms.

Gina noted the intermittent trouble he had with the function of his right hand, his chopping action awkward. She wanted to ask him more about his injury, wanted to offer to help with the chores, but she refrained from commenting, knowing that he wouldn't talk about it and would resent her fussing. The grimace on his face as he wielded the knife attested to his own annoyance and impatience with his limitations. So she remained silent, allowing him to concentrate on his task while her own thoughts turned to the events of the day.

She had no idea how they had crammed so much into a few hours. But they had covered a great deal of ground, and she was exhausted but happy—especially since finding her grandmother in such good form. Sightseeing with Seb had been a wonderful experience. He had been a patient and knowledgeable companion, and being with him had made the day so much more special—particularly given all the kissing and hand-holding and touching. A flush warmed her cheeks as she remembered those stolen moments on the cableway, and how incredible it had felt to have him caress her.

What had begun as basic attraction and physical desire had turned into so much more. The more time she spent with Seb, the more she cared about him. He was warm and funny, intelligent, and unfailingly kind. He mixed exquisite gentleness with intense passion. She felt comfortable with him—could talk to him, share with him as deeply, if not more, as she did with her close friends. She could explain her feelings and concerns in a way she couldn't with her grandmother for fear of worrying her. Seb made her feel like a real woman again, desired and feminine, and being romanced by such a stunning and sexy man was incredibly exciting. That he was so understanding and good to her grandmother made him more irresistible.

Seb slid a plate in front of her, adding cutlery and a glass of chilled spring water, his warm smile sparking a new tingle of awareness inside her.

'Thank you for this,' she said as he served her a generous portion of pasta and an aromatic sauce topped with freshly grated Parmesan cheese. 'Mmm—it looks wonderful.'

'Tell me more about your new job,' he requested as he sat opposite her.

'With all the new investment in our area, the local council and health authority are taking advantage of private and charitable donations and opening a new drop-in centre,' she began, pausing to take a sip of her water. 'The plan is to provide a wide range of health and social care, bringing services, advice, support and information together under one roof for those who have difficulty coping or accessing mainline health facilities.'

With an impatient sigh, Seb switched his fork from his uncooperative right hand to his left and resumed attempts to twirl his spaghetti around it. 'Who has difficulty getting health care from the hospital or local doctors, and why?'

'You'd be surprised how many people can't or won't use the services provided—and for a whole variety of reasons: fear, suspicion, lack of knowledge. The centre is designed to help the homeless, migrants and refugees, people with drink and drug addictions, those with HIV/AIDS.'

'What does the centre offer?' Seb queried.

Encouraged by his interest, her enthusiasm for what they were trying to do in Strathlochan bubbled through. 'We have clinics for minor injuries, wound care and dressing changes, vaccinations, TB screening, contraception and sexually transmitted diseases. We offer clean needles, also drugs, alcohol and AIDS awareness, and dentistry for those having difficulty accessing NHS dental care. Counselling, chiropody—all kinds of health and social advice... Whatever problems are presented by those who come to us we try to tackle—medical and social. There is a small hostel attached with washing facilities and short-term beds. And we also have a mentoring scheme, where one-on-one help is offered to those making an effort to get off the streets, off drugs, off alcohol and into work and a safe place to live.'

'It sounds excellent,' Seb praised, genuine admiration in his voice.

'I think it's a worthwhile project,' she admitted, looking up to find him studying her intently. 'I want to feel I am helping to make a difference, even in a small way.'

'You are doing a good thing—an important thing.'

'Thank you.'

She followed his lead and continued with her meal, puzzled by the unidentified edge that had been in his voice, the look of sadness and regret that had briefly crossed his expression before he had masked it.

'What about staffing?' he asked after a moment.

'The regular team consists of Dr Thornton Gallagher, who is the clinical director in charge of the centre, a specialist psychologist, a counsellor, and two other nurses besides myself,' she told him, savouring the last bites of the delicious meal. 'For the time being we don't have the funds to employ full-time doctors or a dentist on staff, so we rely on the goodwill of numerous doctors and other local health-care professionals from the hospital and surrounding GP and dental practices. Everyone has joined forces to back the project, and they volunteer their time to run our clinics. If the centre is a success, we hope funds will be available to expand the full-time medical team.'

Listening to Gina speak with such passion about her work gave Seb even more to think about in terms of his own situation. When had he last felt that real fire in his belly, or had the satisfaction of knowing he was helping people who really needed him? In recent years that genuine fulfilment had only come with his *pro bono* patients. As much as he loved surgery, he had lost his enjoyment and gained little professional or personal gratification from vanity work. Gina, with her honesty and dedication, stripped it all down to the basics, to the things that really mattered most. Need and care. It made him ashamed of the way he had wasted his talents. Perhaps he had deserved to lose them.

His physical scars were fading, and daily exercise was helping his injuries to heal, although he still experienced reduced function plus some numbness and discomfort. He probably always would. But the mental scars at losing his surgical career were harder to come to terms with. What was he going to do with the rest of his life? Was he going to stay in medicine? If not, what else *could* he do? These were the questions he had escaped Florence to answer. Alone on Elba, away from press intrusion, and the understandable but smothering concern of Zio Roberto and Zia Sofia, he had sought privacy to face his future and make decisions.

Maybe things were not as hopeless as he had feared. True, he couldn't operate again, and the knowledge still grieved him. He'd worked so hard and for so long to prove himself that it felt like failure to give in. But meeting Gina, hearing her speak with such passion about her work, posed new questions, and made him look at things in a different way. There were other areas of medicine open to him—other things he could do to make a difference. He could still help people, still heal them. Rico would give him a post at his clinic any time he asked, but that line of work was not for him. What he had to do was find a new niche for himself…and Gina was helping point him in a new and more promising direction.

'How do you feel about people who live on the street?' he found himself asking, playing devil's advocate, shocking himself that he was stepping out on a limb, touching on something he never discussed. 'Many would say that those with the kinds of problems you've mentioned are beyond help, or are taking funds away from others.'

'Well, they'd be wrong. People end up in those circumstances for all kinds of reasons, and they deserve our care and attention the same as anyone else,' Gina riposted, her dark eyes full of sincerity and fire as she met his gaze. Pushing aside her empty plate, she leaned her forearms on the counter. 'It can really narrow your world—make you feel you have nowhere to turn, no choices, no one who is interested in you. We're all one bad break away from needing help and understanding, and everyone is entitled to the care we can offer them.'

'That's true.' He hesitated, wondering whether to take this further, and then Gina herself continued, surprising him anew.

'Both my father and grandfather were made redundant from the shipyards during a time of recession. The industry was being run down. Life was hard. We lost our home, and Mum, Dad and I had to go and live with Nonno Matthew and Nonna Maria. No one had any money. I was ten, but I remember the worry, the adults' constant search for work, the struggle for food, clothes and basics, the feeling of exclusion.'

Seb's heart turned over as she drew in a shaky breath and ducked her head. He took one hand in his, linking their fingers, moved by her story. How stupid of him that he had never once asked about her parents. He had been so focused on Maria—sidetracked by Gina's devoted care of her grandparents—that he had never thought to look more deeply into her motivations, her childhood, her mother and father.

'Gina…'

'Word came of possible jobs on Tyneside, in the yards there. My parents went there but things didn't work out. They were returning to Glasgow when they were killed in a train crash.'

'I am sorry, *tesoro*.'

She shook her head, her voice soft and sad, and his gut tightened. 'It was a long time ago.'

'So your grandparents raised you from the age of ten?'

'Yes. They took me in, cared for me, loved me, were always there for me,' she explained, a sheen of moisture shimmering in her eyes.

No wonder she felt so close to them, needed so badly to feel she was giving back. 'You're amazing.'

'No, I'm not. I told you because it shows that things can happen to anyone—we have no right to judge, to condemn. We don't know what it is like to walk in another person's shoes.'

'I spent a few years living on the streets.'

Seb didn't know why he was telling her. He certainly didn't want pity. Maybe he was testing her convictions, seeing how she would react—if she treated him differently, knowing of his past. He was used to people latching onto him because of who he was now—people who would despise him if they knew what his life had been like back then. Thankfully the reporters who had dug into his background had never discovered the full circumstances of his upbringing. Zio Roberto and Zia Sofia had surrounded him with their protection as well as their love.

He felt Gina's fingers tighten on his and he looked into her eyes. There was concern, understanding, sorrow…but no pity.

'What happened, Seb?'

Affected by the genuine interest in her softly voiced question, he found himself responding, telling her about his mother and those crazy years—things he had never told another living soul. Except Rico. But even his cousin didn't know all of it.

'My father died when I was young—an aortic aneurysm. Knowing his family disapproved of her and their marriage, thinking they would take me from her, my mother ran away with me the same night.' He paused a moment, closing his eyes as he recalled that confused flight from all that had been familiar. Swallowing, unable to look at Gina, he pressed on. 'My mother was unbalanced. Paranoid. Depressed. She drank too much. Took drugs. We lived hand to mouth and she dragged me around after her, moving from place to place…selling herself to buy us food and her next fix.'

'Oh, Seb.'

Gina's words were a mere whisper, but he nearly choked up at the depth of feeling they contained. He didn't stop her when she slid off her stool. Instead, he turned on his as she came around the counter and stepped up to him, hugging him tight. Burying his face in her hair, he breathed in her intoxicating scent, lingering a moment to absorb the comfort.

'Where did you go? How did you live?' she asked after a few moments.

'She'd shack up with a man for a while—usually someone who was dealing drugs and could get her what she needed. Mostly they tolerated having me around—sometimes not. Now and again we'd stay longer in one place, then things would go wrong and we'd move on again. One day, about three years after we had left home…' He hesitated as the events of that morning came back to him, as crystal-clear as if it had happened yesterday and not twenty-two years ago. 'She had one drink too many—one drug too many. I woke up and found her dead on the floor of the abandoned house we were squatting in.'

Gina's arms tightened around him, her cheek pressed to his so he felt the dampness of her tears. 'Oh, God. How old were you? What did you do?'

'I was eleven. And I was scared, alone. I didn't know anyone—didn't know where I was or what to do. So I ran. I knew how to survive on the streets, how to take care of myself, where to find restaurants who'd let me do some dirty jobs in return for leftover food or an outhouse to stay in overnight. I knew which market stalls wouldn't miss a few pieces of fruit, which bakeries threw out bread, where to go to scavenge discarded pizzas to fill my stomach.'

'No one helped you?'

He shook his head, touched that she sounded so scandalised on his behalf—like a fierce lioness about to go into battle to protect her cub. 'I didn't want help…I didn't trust anyone. But, unlike many street kids, I kept away from gangs and drugs. I spent hours in libraries devouring books, sneaking around museums, using their rest rooms, keeping warm and dry on bad days, using my brain.'

'And in the end?' Gina drew back a few inches, and he saw the residue of her tears spiking long sooty lashes. The fingers of one hand stroked along his jaw, firing his blood. 'How did you get out of that?'

'I got sick. Food poisoning. A priest found me on the street, barely conscious, and took me to a clinic run by the nuns. All I could tell them was my name.' Shaking his head, he took both Gina's hands in his and pressed a kiss to each palm in turn, feeling a quiver run through her. 'Unknown to me, my father's sister and her husband had never given up searching for me, and they had circulated my name and photograph. A nun recognised me and called them. Zio Roberto and Zia Sofia came to fetch me, and took me to their home to live with them and their son, Riccardo, who was my age. I was wild, scared, aloof, but they didn't give up,' he told her with a smile, recalling the endless patience, firmness and love that had finally turned him around.

Ever since then he had wanted to repay their generosity and acceptance by making something of himself, making them proud. Rico, the cousin who had befriended the suspicious, unruly boy, had been his rock, his confidant, his best friend, helping him catch up with school work. They had done everything together, including going to medical school. He'd felt driven to succeed—to prove to his aunt and uncle, and to Rico, that they had been right to invest their time in him. And to prove to himself that he was strong, that he could survive, could *be* something, that he was worthy of having people care about him. He hadn't realised quite how deeply his past still affected him until just now, telling Gina things he had never shared with anyone, including Rico.

'So there you have it—the grisly details of my life,' he said, trying to pass off the acute feeling of vulnerability he was experiencing with a false bravado.

'Don't make light of it,' Gina chided gently, curling her fingers with his, warmth and understanding in her expression. 'It can't have been easy to tell me, but I'm honoured that you did. Thank you. Your past is part of you, it's helped shape you, and you should be proud of yourself—of all that you have achieved.'

If confiding in Gina *had* unconsciously been a test, then she had passed with flying colours…and she had turned the tables on him. He felt uncharacteristically emotional. Needing a few moments to regain his equilibrium, he let go of her hands and rose to his feet, his voice husky and unsteady as he turned away from her and reached for their empty plates.

'You go out on the terrace and enjoy the view,' he suggested, praying she wouldn't argue. 'I'll clear up these things, then we can go to Signora Mancini's.'

She hesitated for an endless moment, and he held his breath, waiting. Then her hand briefly rubbed his back before it was withdrawn.

'OK.' He closed his eyes at the soft understanding and edgy emotion she didn't try to hide. 'Thanks for the meal, it was delicious.'

When Gina had left the kitchen, Seb poured himself a glass of water and drank it down. He'd thought he needed time alone, but already he missed her. And he sure as hell wished he had never agreed for her to spend the night at the bed and breakfast. He needed her here.

What was happening to him? He'd never experienced this kind of immediate rapport with anyone. Yes, he desired her. But it was so much more than just the physical, as important and urgent as that was. Gina accepted him. To her he was just Seb. His past didn't colour her view of him—she simply saw the person he was now, saw all that had gone before as making the whole. Yet he was horribly aware that he still hadn't told Gina the entire truth. He had held back because he was scared that when she knew what he had done with his career these last years she would see him differently, think less of him, judge him harshly—as he did himself. And he feared, too, that the reality of his fame and his money would irrevocably change things between them.

Confused, troubled, yet needing to be close to Gina every moment he could, he finished up and walked out to the terrace.

Gina leaned on the balustrade wall at the edge of the villa's expansive terrace, her mind buzzing with thoughts of all Seb had revealed to her about his past. Dusk was fading to the darkness of night, and moonlight played over the softly un-dulating surface of the sea beyond the cliffs. Neptune's Spear was a brooding shape, silhouetted offshore from the crescent of beach far below.

She ached for what Seb had borne as a young boy, ripped away from all that was safe following the death of his father, scared and confused by the erratic behaviour of a troubled mother on drink and drugs who'd flitted from man to man. And then to find her dead, to be left alone so young, trying to survive on the street... Thank God for the aunt and uncle who had searched for him and taken him in, given him a loving home and a secure future.

A proud and private man, it must have cost Seb to confide in her. And he'd been affected by the telling, she knew. She sensed he'd needed time alone to gather his thoughts...just as she'd had to stem her tears for the boy he had been. It seemed so unfair, given all he had been through in his youth, that he now faced what could be life-changing injuries to his hands—all due to a selfless act, helping someone in trouble. How worried he must be about being able to paint again. She wished she knew more about the damage to his nerves and tendons, the possible long-term effects, wished he wasn't so unwilling to talk about it or allow her to help him. There was so much she didn't know about him and his life...including how he had come to be on Elba, painting and acting as caretaker for this villa.

Gina felt rather than heard Seb approach behind her. A shiver of awareness rippled down her spine as he stepped up close and personal, his hands coming to rest either side of hers on top of the wall, his body brushing against her, trapping her in place. Flames of desire uncoiled inside her as the warmth of his breath fanned her skin. Soft, stolen kisses were followed by the teasing lick of his tongue, and when his teeth grazed against her, indulging in a gentle bite of possession, she whimpered, close to melting on the spot.

Succumbing to the urge, she turned in his arms, intending to… Well, she wasn't sure what she intended because the sultry intensity in his eyes banished every single thought from her brain. Seb raised a hand, his fingers whispering across her cheek before they glided along her neck, cupping her nape, holding her in place. She barely had time to draw in a shaky, fractured breath before his lips met hers in a bone-weakening, passionate kiss that instantly flared out of control. Her response was instinctive, inevitable, swamping her under a tidal wave of desire. His free arm wound round her waist, drawing her tight against him, while her own rose to link around his neck. He groaned, changing the angle, deepening the kiss, taking more, giving more, his tongue exploring, twining with hers, drawing her back into his own mouth, sucking on her. Gina lost herself in Seb, in heady passion, the ache of need deep inside her increasing and craving satisfaction.

They broke apart, just far enough and for long enough to drag oxygen into parched lungs, their panting breaths mingling, heartbeats thudding in a frantic dual rhythm. His voice was little more than a rough murmur when he spoke. 'I know this is fast.'

'It's crazy,' she murmured back.

'This thing between us is incredible.'

Gina couldn't deny it. 'Yes.'

'It is not a line, *tesoro*.' He switched to Italian, as if needing his first language to express the depth of his emotion. 'I have *never* felt like this about any woman before. I cannot explain it, to you or to myself, but from the first moment I saw you I was lost. There was an inner recognition, a meeting of souls.'

It was heady stuff, and she was unable to resist him or her own yearning. 'Seb.'

'Kissing you is wonderful. You're honey-sweet…' He punctuated his praise with tormentingly brief caresses, nibbling her lips, teasing the corner of her mouth with his tongue-tip until she was frantic for more. 'But it's not enough, Gina. I need to see you, to touch you, to taste you everywhere, to fill you completely.'

'Oh, God.' The words trembled out of her as her mind filled with erotic images.

He lifted her so she was sitting on the terrace wall, his fingers skimming her jean-clad thighs, which parted of their own volition so he could step between them. She moaned, unable to stop herself wriggling closer, rubbing against the hard evidence of his arousal, desperate to ease the pressure that built within her. He continued to tease her with half-kisses and devastating strokes of his tongue, until she was forced to bury her hands in the thickness of his hair and take what she so urgently needed. He met and matched her hunger, his kiss pure sin. She couldn't get enough of him.

Seb was busy with the buttons of her top, and she quivered involuntarily at the exquisite touch of his fingers on her bare flesh. The pads of his thumbs were stroking circles around her navel, making her muscles tauten, and then his fingers skimmed her ribs, before his hands moved on to explore and caress her back. Lost in a slow, deep kiss, she was vaguely aware of him unsnapping the fastening of her bra, but it was only when he brushed the lacy cups aside and the fullness of her breasts spilled into his waiting palms that she gasped, her head dropping back, her hands leaving his hair to clasp his shoulders for support. He continued to torment her, tracing the outline of each breast, circling inwards, but never quite touching where she most needed him.

'Please,' she begged, unable to wait another second.

Seductive, heavy-lidded eyes watched her as she arched to his touch. Then his hands cupped her fully, firm and sure, and she cried out at the terrible joy of it, awash with sensation after sensation as he shaped her, caressed her, driving her crazy with want. Taut, sensitised nipples demanded attention, and darts of fire speared through her as his thumbs brushed over and around them. When she felt the cool evening breeze against her flaming skin, she opened her eyes, finding him watching her.

He waited endless moments, ignoring her pleas, feasting his gaze on her, then he lowered his head, and finally his mouth was there, warm and moist, teasing and tormenting her swollen nipple with lips, teeth and tongue. Just when she thought she couldn't bear it any longer, he closed his mouth around her and suckled her strongly inside, nearly sending her into orbit at the searing pleasure.

'Oh, Seb!'

It was too much…not enough. She writhed against him, seeking relief for the waves of ecstasy crashing over her. Her hands dragged at his jumper and the T-shirt beneath, needing to feel his skin. The fire threatened to consume them both. His own hands cupped her rear, pulling her tighter, and she locked her legs around his hips, pressing herself against him, wishing for all the world that two pairs of jeans were not separating them. Her flesh burned, her body craved fulfilment.

Slowly, noisily, reluctantly, his mouth released its prize,

a rough moan escaping him as she dragged her fingernails along his spine.

'Gina, you are so beautiful, so responsive,' he murmured against her skin, working his way to her neglected breast at such a lingering pace she wanted to scream with frustration. 'Feel what you do to me,' he demanded, rocking more insistently against her, making her sob with the force of her desire. 'Making love is going to be indescribable for us.'

She had never felt so wanted. Had never been so out of control. Had never needed anyone with such desperate urgency. His mouth claimed her nipple, conducting the same sensual torture as it had to its twin, and she closed her eyes, arching to him, feeling the heat radiating off his skin, his muscles flexing under her fingers, the earthy, masculine fragrance of him making her light-headed.

'Stay with me. Please, Gina.'

'I can't. Not tonight,' she whispered, tempted almost beyond endurance. 'I have to go, Seb. We agreed.'

Seb cursed under his breath, trying to get his raging body back under some semblance of control. He could seduce Gina into his bed in an instant. They both knew it. Both wanted it with a desperation that was painful. But, foolishly, he had promised, so he had no one to blame but himself. With her grandmother on her mind, Gina was understandably distracted. If and when she came to him, he wanted it to be completely, knowingly, willingly, with nothing else to think about but the special magic between them.

Smothering a groan, he wrapped his arms around her and held her close, giving them both time to bank down the flames of passion that burned so fiercely between them. When he felt strong enough to behave, he drew back and reluctantly fixed her clothes back into place. It was a crime to cover up such voluptuous beauty, but he wanted no one seeing her or touching her but him. His task completed, he cupped her face in his hands, seeing the regret and the remaining sparks of desire in her soul-deep eyes.

'I'll drive you back.' He managed to force the words out, stepping away and helping her down off the wall, steadying her as she swayed. A draught of breeze rippled across the terrace, and he felt a shiver run through her as the heat of their passion subsided. 'You are cold, *tesoro*.'

Without waiting for her confirmation, he peeled off his jumper and helped her put it on, his body responding instinctively to the way she wrapped herself in it, closing her eyes and burying her face in the fabric, as if breathing in his scent. Lashes lifted and dark eyes looked into his. His breath lodged in his throat. *Madre del Dio.* He couldn't help himself. He *had* to kiss her again.

Eventually he did the right thing, and drove her the short distance off the Cape to Signora Mancini's. So why did it feel so much like the *wrong* thing?

'I don't want to leave you here,' he complained, linking his fingers with hers as they walked hand in hand to the front door.

'Signora Mancini will be worried. I need to speak to her about Nonna, and to settle up for our stay—I promised her I would be here. And I have the packing to do.'

Seb was disappointed, but he knew Gina's mind was made up. 'If you are sure that is what you want. But you will promise me one thing,' he demanded, turning her to face him, noting that her lips were still plump from his kisses.

'What is it?'

'You will phone or text me at any time of the night if you want to talk or you want me to come and pick you up?'

For a moment she hesitated. 'I—'

'Promise me, Gina,' he insisted, and his urgency, his

need, must have registered, because a sweet, understanding smile gentled her expression, and the palm of her free hand brushed soothingly across his face.

'Yes. I promise.'

'Thank you.'

'Thank *you*,' she stressed. 'For today, for Nonna...for everything.'

He cupped her cheek, needing to feel her silken skin against his own. 'There is nothing to thank me for. I will do anything I can for you, and for Maria.'

'Seb...'

She reached up to kiss him, and he had to force himself to release her. 'Go. Before I change my mind. I will be here to collect you first thing in the morning.'

'Tomorrow,' she whispered with throaty promise.

His gaze clashed with hers. Electric tension sizzled between them...and then the door closed softly, with him on the wrong side of it. For a moment he rested a palm against the solid wooden barrier, the caveman in him wanting to break it down to get to Gina. Then he turned restlessly away and headed home, certain neither of them would sleep that night.

Their sensual chemistry and magnetic connection had left them suspended on the cusp of something extraordinary—scary and wonderfully exciting. He could only hope that tomorrow Gina would make her decision, and they would explore and discover the extent of their combined passion.

CHAPTER SIX

EVERYTHING had gone according to plan, Gina acknowledged with a satisfied smile, sitting for a moment beside the bed as her grandmother, settled and contented at the villa, enjoyed an afternoon nap, propped up on pillows to ease her breathing.

After enduring a sleepless night, cursing herself for being all kinds of a fool for spending it alone, Gina had been thankful to welcome Seb's obscenely early arrival that morning. From the look of him, his night had been no more restful than hers. His urgent, demanding kiss in greeting had robbed her of breath and set her pulse racing.

Having said farewell to Signora Mancini, and moved the luggage to the villa, they had returned to Portoferraio and the hospital, where Gina had been delighted to discover her grandmother had enjoyed a peaceful night and was feeling considerably better. Dottore Vasari had been more than happy to discharge her to their care. A stop at a pharmacy in town to fill the prescription he'd given had followed, which had allowed Gina to buy some things she wanted for Seb, while pretending not to notice as he purchased condoms. She had been crazy with anticipation as it was. Now she was wound up tighter than a bowstring.

She wasn't sure when she had made the final decision to

go for what she wanted and take this chemistry she shared with Seb to its natural conclusion. Her grandmother had encouraged her to grasp happiness when it came her way, not to be scared to acknowledge her feelings. Was this how the older woman had felt fifty years ago, meeting Matthew? All Gina knew was that Seb had changed her, awoken her, made her feel alive, special, confident in herself as a desirable woman. Elba's magic combined with the warmth of Seb's romancing of her made her feel free to explore the side of her she had ignored for years. Yes, it had happened quickly, but the way she felt about Seb was far from casual. Desire had grown to so much more.

Now, leaving her grandmother to sleep, Gina collected the bag of items she had bought that morning and went in search of Seb, finding him in the villa's airy living room. Sitting on an expensive leather sofa, a sports magazine discarded beside him, he had a frown on his face as he flexed his right hand. Gina hesitated, her nerves tightening as she wondered how to broach the subject of his injuries. As if sensing her presence, he looked up, and a smile chased away the frown.

'How is Maria?'

'She's settled and asleep. Her breathing sounds much better,' Gina informed him, stepping closer, aware of the edgy tension between them. Taking a deep breath, she sank to her knees in front of him and set down her bag. Gently, she took his right hand in hers. 'May I? Please?'

For a moment she felt his resistance, but although he remained wary, his expression guarded, he nodded. Struck by the strength of his hand in hers, the feel of his skin, smooth and supple but slightly coarser than her own, she tried to ignore her body's reaction, her awareness and shiver of desire. Opening the bag, she took a moment to prepare the things she had selected for him.

'Gina, what are you doing?' he queried, his uncertainty evident.

'I bought some essential oils,' she explained, concentrating on her task, mixing them with a base oil and then pouring some into her palms to warm it before taking his hand again. 'I'm using chamomile and lavender, both of which have anti-inflammatory and soothing properties. The carrier oil is calendula, which has anti-inflammatory and antispasmodic properties, vitamins, and is also good for healing wounds and bruising.'

As she talked, she carefully began a light, gentle massage of his right hand, paying special attention to the areas affected by the slashing cuts across his wrist, palm and the mound at the base of his thumb. She knew this was where he experienced most sensory and motor problems, with discomfort, tingling and locking in his thumb and forefinger. After several minutes she took some more oil and switched to his left arm, working down from the scar by his inner elbow to where some numbness lingered along the side of his hand and into his little finger.

The aroma of the oils scented the air around them, and she heard his breathing change as some of the anxiety drained out of him. She was far from relaxed herself, struggling to focus on her task and not on the sensuousness of gliding her fingers over his bronzed olive skin. Appreciating the benefits of massage and essential oils, she had done this often before, for her grandmother and for friends, male and female. *Never* had it affected her like this. Biting her lip, she shifted restlessly, returning her attention to Seb's more troublesome right hand, using the pads of her thumbs to work gently across his palm and into the heel and wrist.

'Gina.'

Seb's smoky voice vibrated along her nerve-endings. Looking up, she met his gaze, saw the fire in his eyes, the consuming desire. She couldn't breathe. Her heart was thudding. She felt warm and buzzingly alive. Then his fingers closed around hers, his left hand cupping her cheek as he drew her closer, his lips parting as they captured hers in a slow, thorough kiss. *Oh, my!* But just as she was losing herself in Seb's magic touch and taste, they were disturbed by the sound of the front door closing and someone calling his name.

'*Dannazione!*'

Cursing the interruption, Seb reluctantly released Gina and moved away, giving her a moment to compose herself. She had taken him by surprise with the essential oils, and her bold insistence on confronting his injuries head-on. When she had begun the massage he had been doubtful about its effects, but he couldn't deny how good it had felt. Whether that was just her touch, or whether the oils really worked, he couldn't say—and he had no more time to ponder on it, as Evelina Gilletti bustled into the room.

Short and rotund, with curly salt-and-pepper hair, the sixty-year-old had been part of the villa for as long as Seb could remember. She lived locally with her vast family, had a kind heart and a ready smile, and, despite her propensity to talk incessantly, she was the soul of discretion. She came in a couple of days a week to clean when any of the family were on the island, and checked up on things every day when the villa was empty. Knowing Evelina would be anxious to help, and the perfect person to keep an eye on Maria should he and Gina want to go out or have some time alone, he had phoned to brief her the night before.

'Evelina, how are you?' he asked in Italian, because her English was limited.

'I am good, thank you.' She glanced past him, brown eyes

twinkling with mischief as she studied Gina with curiosity. 'You must introduce me, Sebastiano.'

Evelina was one of the few people who got away with calling him by his full name. He just hoped she would remember his request of the night before and not make any comments to Gina or Maria about who he was. Giving her a warning frown, he introduced her to Gina, thankful that the two very different women took to each other from the first and chatted comfortably…or rather Gina listened with a smile as Evelina talked twenty to the dozen.

'Gina, I thought that Evelina would be able to keep Maria company sometimes,' Seb said, when he could get a word in, explaining the woman's position at the villa.

'That would be very kind. I am sure Nonna will enjoy that. Are you sure it is no bother?'

Evelina gave a dismissive wave of her hand. 'But of course not! Your grandmother and I will have a fine time discussing Elba and life in general. How is she feeling?'

'She is much better. In fact, she's having a nap at the moment,' Gina informed her, and Seb was relived to see that the anxiety shadowing her eyes had vanished now Maria was out of hospital.

'*Bene*. You young ones must go off and enjoy yourselves,' Evelina insisted. 'I will be here for Maria. And I will prepare something for you all to eat later.'

Keen to have Gina to himself, Seb was happy to agree. 'A good idea. Gina, we shall go to the beach for a swim, yes?'

'Yes.' A tinge of pink stained her cheeks as her gaze darted to his and away again. 'I'll get my things. Thank you, Evelina.'

Seb went to his room to change into swim shorts and collect a towel, waiting impatiently for Gina to join him. He could still taste her. Every touch, every kiss increased the tension between them—the last days had been a lingering foreplay that was going to rage out of control when they couldn't stand the waiting any more.

At last she appeared, fresh-faced, her magnificent hair tied back in a braid, a robe wrapped around her delectable body.

'Ready, *tesoro*?' he asked, reaching for her hand

'Ready.'

The word whispered out of her and carried such a wealth of meaning that he hesitated, his fingers locking with hers as he sought her gaze. The expression in her eyes left him in no doubt that she wanted him as badly as he wanted her. And that the waiting was becoming too much to bear. His own body tightening in response, he smothered a groan of needy frustration and led her out of the house, away from prying eyes, and across the terrace to the path that marked the way to the cliff steps. He remembered the last time they had been here together...the day they had met—the day he had caught her when she had slipped and he had held her in his arms for the first time.

Keeping hold of her hand, he ensured she was safe on their descent to the private crescent of beach. Once there, he dropped his towel and kicked off his shoes, letting go of her hand as he walked to the water. Turning, he waited for her in the shallows, sensing her moment of shy hesitation before she unfastened the tie of her robe and slowly slid it off her shoulders, allowing it to fall to the ground.

Dio!

His body sprang to instant attention at the sight of her voluptuous curves encased in a red halter-neck bikini. It wasn't skimpy or revealing, but it set off her womanly form to perfection, heated his blood to fever pitch and made his mouth water. His gaze began a leisurely journey up shapely legs to her soft thighs, smooth and golden in the sunshine. For a moment his focus lingered on the red triangle of cloth that hid the heart of her femininity from his view, then he forced himself to move on to the rounded swell of her belly and navel. How sensitive was she there? He wanted to explore *all* of her with his mouth, to seek out all the secret places that would drive her mad with pleasure.

His thought was cut off as he noticed the way Gina lowered her arms to try and cover her belly, as if self-conscious about her body shape. No way was he having that. She was perfect in every respect—something she would be in no doubt about by the time he had thoroughly loved every inch of her.

In the meantime his gaze continued up to the lush fullness of plump breasts, his heart hammering against his ribs as he remembered how it had felt to caress them and taste them last night. He ducked lower in the water, wishing it were several degrees colder to take the edge off his raging desire. Maybe coming to the beach had been a bad idea. He'd thought it might cool them off, but instead he was hotter for her than ever. The temptation of Gina was going to be impossible to resist.

Gina felt Seb's intense gaze on her as she walked the last steps to where he waited for her in the shallows. Her bikini was entirely decent, but she was very aware that he hadn't seen quite so much of her flesh before, and she was anxious she might have a few too many curves and extra pounds for his taste. But, given the flare of hunger in his eyes, maybe he didn't find her too lacking. The self-confidence that had been returning since she had met him expanded inside her, allowing her to acknowledge that Seb liked what he saw, that she was all woman and desired by a sexy man.

The sea was surprisingly warm, and crystal-clear. Once Seb had assured himself that she was a comfortable and competent swimmer, he stroked away from her, as if needing to burn off some excess energy. She knew the feeling. She enjoyed herself in the water, then floated for a while near the rocky outcrop of Neptune's Spear, watching him moving effortlessly back towards her. Her eyes closed briefly as she soaked up the September sunshine, then she started in surprise as Seb's hands closed around her ankles.

His fingers glided slowly up her legs, drawing her with him nearer to the shore, until they were able to stand rib-deep in the water. Her skin quivered from the sure, confident touch of his hands as he helped her upright and urged her closer to him. Droplets of water glistened on his skin, reminding her of the first day she had seen him here. Her sea-god. Neptune was also associated with horses, dolphins and earthquakes, she recalled. Indeed, he was called 'the earthshaker'. Gina thought how apt that was in her own case. Seb had most definitely shaken the very ground beneath her from the second she had seen him, making her feel alive, changing her.

His wet hair was swept back from his face, and a hint of stubble darkened the masculine line of his jaw. Her fingers locked with his. She looked into his eyes, unable to halt the tremor that ran through her at the expression of sultry intent in them seconds before his mouth claimed hers. Her lips parted in welcome, and instantly she was swept away on the now familiar tide of passion that swelled so rapidly between them.

Their kiss deepened and flared out of control. Her hands glided up the corded muscles of his arms and over strong shoulders, until she could wrap her arms around his neck. Seb's hands stroked down her back, cupping the rounded cheeks of her rear, flexing sensuously in her flesh as he rocked her hips with his, making her excitingly aware of his arousal. Her breasts pressed into his chest, the thin bikini no barrier at all, her sensitised nipples grazing against him as their bodies brushed together in the gentle swell of the water. She moaned, trying to get closer, consumed by the potency of his kiss, his taste, his scent. Their tongues teased and twined. As his retreated, hers followed, need spearing through her as he sucked on her, drawing her into his mouth. Every part of her craved more, and she pressed her thighs together in a desperate attempt to ease the ache.

'That won't stop it,' he murmured huskily as his mouth abandoned hers and journeyed around her jaw to her ear, nipping at her lobe before his tongue tormented the hollow beneath. 'Let me help, Gina. I can make you feel so good.'

He wrapped her braid around one wrist, tilting her head to give his seductive mouth better access to her throat as he literally swept her off her feet. As she clung to him for support his other hand glided down her body, lingering to trace teasing circles around her navel before moving on and easing between her thighs. Shamelessly, they parted to give him better access, and she moaned as he cupped her. For a second she tensed, realising where they were.

'Seb…'

Molten caramel eyes looked into hers. 'No one can see, *tesoro*. This is just us.' Bold, clever fingers dipped beneath the waistband of her bikini briefs, creating magic as they explored and caressed.

'Oh, God,' she moaned.

Her breath coming in ragged gasps, she gave herself up to the impossible pleasure of his devastating touch. She had forgotten what this was like…except nothing had been this incredible, nothing had prepared her for the glory of Seb.

When he eased two fingers inside her, unerringly finding the sweetest spot imaginable, he began a rhythmic stroking that threatened to slay her in an instant. Combining that with the teasing, circling rub of his thumb on and around her most sensitive place, Seb sent her straight to paradise. Gina buried her face in his neck, her hands tightening on supple skin and solid muscle, allowing him and the water to support her as she surrendered totally to him and lost herself in exquisite, torturous bliss. Uninhibited, she soared to her release.

Seb drew her head back, watching her face, fiery passion in his eyes. He held her trembling body tightly against him, gentle strokes of his hands slowly easing her down from the incredible pinnacle she had ascended.

Shaking and shaken, she wrapped herself around him. 'It's been so long.' She scarcely realised she had whispered the words aloud as she regained her breath, her heartbeat slowing to its normal rhythm.

She had never felt this amazing, but her release had in no way dimmed her urgent desire for more of Seb. If anything, despite the delicious glow and wonderful languor, her body felt primed and ready. Wanting Seb to feel as good as she did, Gina pulled back a fraction, uncurling her legs from around him. Standing, she saw his surprise and momentary uncertainty as her own hands caressed down his sumptuous body and freed his erection from the confines of his shorts. She loved the feel of him, velvety soft over the hardness, and a moan of excitement escaped as she imagined what it would feel like to make love with him.

'Gina—'

'Please,' she whispered, silencing his warning.

Allowing Gina the same liberties she had granted him, Seb gave himself to the moment. He had never meant things to go this far, but he hadn't been able to stop himself from touching her. She was so incredibly responsive. Watching and feeling her come apart for him had been beautiful. The way she'd reacted so spontaneously to his caresses had excited him, and sparked his imagination about all the different ways to please her. Knowing it had been some time since she had acknowledged the needs of her body and that, like him, she had been on the point of exploding with frustration, he had hoped to take the edge off without spoiling her hunger for later. Now she had turned the tables on him. He should have known. Everything about Gina had been unexpected from the moment he had met her.

His thoughts hazed as his body reacted to her touch. He had never felt this good. *Madre del Dio!* He had no control around this woman. He was already breathless, shaking, tensing, his heart racing, every part of him rushing past the point of no return. She pressed her mouth to his chest, her lips, teeth and tongue caressing his skin, exploring, driving him insane. But not nearly as insane as her hands. Or her throaty murmurs of encouragement as she took him rapidly over the edge, blurring his vision, destroying his reason, making him groan aloud as he was spun into an intense vortex of pleasure.

Afterwards, he hugged her close, and they rolled into the water, soothing overheated skin and trembling bodies. He'd never known anyone like Gina. She was so unselfish, so giving, so sensual. He couldn't wait to know her fully. Never before had he experienced the explosive passion and intensity of need he did with her. But it wasn't just physical lust. There was an over-arching warmth, a deep connection and affection—and a level of trust he had not shared with anyone else. He had only known her a short time, but already she had changed him. He felt a better person when he was with her—happier, more settled, grounded. He couldn't begin to think what life would be like when she left—wouldn't think about it. They had to make the most of every moment.

'I can't wait to make love with you.' He felt a quiver ripple through her at his words. 'I want to explore and devour every inch of you.'

'Seb…'

'I want you, I need you—but only if it's what you want, too,' he told her, his voice low and raw with need, breathing in the scent of vanilla and sea on her damp skin. 'Will you come to me tonight, Gina?'

'Yes.'

The word was torn from her. All too soon it would be time for her to return to the real world, to put the sensual side of her back into hibernation. Whatever the future held after she left this island in a few days' time, she couldn't say no to the magic she and Seb made together. It felt right. He had re-awoken the woman within her, and she craved affection, fulfilment, closeness. She needed this. Most of all she needed Seb…the man who had set her free, who had captured her imagination and, she very much feared, her heart.

They finally made their way off the beach and back up the cliff to the villa. Her grandmother was resting on the terrace, looking both amused and bemused as Evelina chattered at full speed. Gina went to her room to have a bath and get dressed. Every part of her tingled with excitement and anticipation. She wondered how she was going to bear waiting the hours until she could be with Seb.

It proved as difficult as she had imagined. For both of them. Every look, every casual touch ratcheted up the tension and the expectancy until Gina thought she was going to burst out of her skin.

Evelina went home, leaving them to enjoy the meal she had prepared, after which the evening ticked by, each minute passing with agonising slowness. Seb was wonderful with her grandmother, listening to her fondest memories of Elba and meeting Matthew McNaught, and then playing a game of chess with her.

Her heart soared as she watched them together. Seb treated her grandmother with respect, gently teasing her, and under his attention the older lady blossomed, her cheeks pink, laughing with delight for the first time since being widowed. Tears stung Gina's eyes. Seb had given them so much in such a short time. He had given her grandmother hope, his time and his care.

For herself, his gentle touches and small kindnesses, combined with his passionate nature, had made her feel special. She had wondered in the beginning if she could indulge in a holiday fling, but this was so much more. It was no longer about attraction and desire. Her heart was involved. She cared about Seb, felt connected to him in an elemental way, and it was going to be impossible to walk away in a few days' time. But she had never felt anything this incredible before, and she had to live the fantasy while she was here in case she never experienced anything like it again.

'Well, I think it is time I went to bed,' her grandmother announced, and Gina almost jumped out of her chair.

Blushing at the knowing laughter in Seb's eyes, she managed to rise with more decorum, waiting while her grandmother said goodnight to their host. 'I'll come and see you settled, Nonna.'

First she stopped in her own room, wondering what to change into before going to Seb. Just thinking about tonight sent a tremor of excited awareness down her spine. She had nothing to wear, she fretted. The oversized Winnie the Pooh sleep T-shirt Holly had given her for her birthday was hardly alluring! She stifled a giggle, nerves fluttering inside her. The only item of clothing vaguely sexy was the lacy black slip she had worn under her red dress the other night. It would have to do.

Pulling it on, she fastened her robe over the top, then

padded barefoot down the corridor to her grandmother's room, finding her already in bed and propped up on the pillows.

'Is there anything I can get for you, Nonna?' she asked, ensuring she was comfortable and had fresh water nearby.

'No, thank you, Gina.' One papery hand cupped her cheek. 'It is good to be here and not in hospital. I am comfortably settled and I feel very well cared for.'

'There's a buzzer beside you if you need to call me for anything in the night.'

Smiling, the older woman tutted. 'You must not worry about me.'

'I can't help it.' Gina gave her a hug and kissed her cheek. 'I love you.'

'I love you, too, my precious girl. You are the most selfless person I have ever known. You give so much of yourself. Now it is your time. It is wonderful to see you so happy—I think Seb is responsible for that, no?' she added, hazel eyes twinkling.

'Yes,' Gina admitted, smiling back.

'Reach for what you want, *ragazza mia*.'

Gina fought back the emotional sting of tears. 'Sleep well, Nonna.'

'I am sure I will.'

For a few moments she sat in the armchair beside the bed, but her grandmother swiftly dozed off, and Gina rose to her feet, content to leave her. Anticipation made her heart race and her legs tremble. She tiptoed from the room and closed the door before turning to walk back down the corridor, and then…

She froze when she saw Seb ahead of her, leaning against the doorway at the end of the guest wing. A towel around his waist was his only covering, and her throat closed as she looked at him—perfect, masculine, breathtakingly gorgeous. Hesitant footsteps carried her closer. Her gaze locked with his, the sultry expression in his eyes making the flames of desire burn ever hotter inside her. He held out his hand, waiting for her. Knowing there was no other decision she was going to make, she placed her hand in his, seeing his sexy smile, the quiet flash of relief as he straightened, then drew her with him out of the guest wing to his own room in the main villa and closed the door.

'You haven't changed your mind, Gina?'

'No.' As if she could. She wanted him more desperately than her next breath. 'You?'

'Never.'

The smile, the promise in his eyes, the certainty of his desire for her, nearly stopped her heart. 'Seb…'

His hands, warm and gentle, cupped her face. 'Nervous?' he asked, surprising her with his understanding.

'A little,' she admitted truthfully. She glanced back towards the door. True, she had her grandmother's blessing, but she still felt a bit awkward. 'I—'

'Do not feel inhibited or embarrassed.' Seb tilted her gaze to his. 'I promise you that Maria will hear nothing.'

She felt reassured—then stupidly wondered how he knew that, if he did this often.

'No.'

'Sorry?' She frowned at him in puzzlement. 'No, what?'

'You were wondering if this is a regular thing for me.'

How did he read her mind like that? 'Seb…'

'The truth is that I have never brought a woman here before. Only you, Gina.'

For a moment she was speechless with surprise, but, looking into his eyes, she believed him. It gave her confidence and courage. 'You know it's been a while for me. I want to be enough for you.'

'*Tesoro*, you are so much more than anyone I have

ever known,' he said with a simple sincerity that took her breath away.

He stood behind her and gently unfastened her braid, his fingers combing through the freed waves of her hair with a sensual touch that had her sighing and leaning into him. When he turned her round again she bit her lip as he released the tie holding her robe closed, then she heard his indrawn hiss of breath as he eased it off and his gaze swept over the silky black lace that covered her lush curves.

'You're beautiful, Gina,' he told her hoarsely, drawing her with him as he backed up towards the bed.

She quivered with sensation as his fingertips grazed her thighs and he slowly, slowly drew the slip up her body and over her head before tossing it away, his eyes dark, his breathing uneven as he looked at her, exposed and vulnerable. Her own fingers fumbled with his towel. Releasing it, she let it drop to the floor, running her hands over him, revelling in the texture of his supple skin and the ripple of toned muscle beneath. Her gaze strayed to his impressive arousal, tension coiling inside her. Soon she would know him fully.

Seb's hands explored her with equal thoroughness, driving her insane with wanting. She needed more…so much more. Craved everything. Impatient, she gave him a push, tumbling with him as he fell to the bed, any thought of waiting and teasing gone in the growing urgency of their mutual passion. Despite their sensual play in the sea that afternoon, the days of longing had led them here, and the desperation remained acute. She wriggled on top of him, even more aroused at the rub of her bare skin on his, heat coursing through her at the skilful caress of his hands, their mouths meeting in hungry desire.

Taking advantage of her position, she set off on a journey of exploration, hands and mouth paying homage to his magnificent body. She laved the bronze orbs of his nipples with her tongue before kissing down to his navel, allowing the fall of her hair to caress him. He shifted restlessly beneath her, his muscles tautening, the ardent press of his arousal exciting her.

'Not this time, Gina.' His voice was low and raw as he caught her arms and pulled her back up, giving her a short but very sexy kiss. 'I'm too close to the edge. I need you so badly.'

'Me, too.'

She gave him room to reach for the drawer in the bedside chest, watching as he took out the bag he had brought from the pharmacy that morning. He tipped it up, catching one of the boxes and impatiently tossing the other aside. Filled with unbearable urgency, she took the box from him, wrestling with the outer wrapper, tremors running through her as his hands stroked her heated, sensitised body. Finally she managed to extract a foil packet. Opening it, she evaded him and skimmed down to roll it on, her fingers lingering to caress him.

'Enough,' he groaned, rolling them over, settling her under him and fanning her hair out on the pillows.

Never had she felt so desired, so wanted, so cherished, as Seb's kisses and caresses brought her to a new fever-pitch of need. She sank her hands into his hair, arching to him as his mouth worked its magic on her breasts, drawing each nipple in turn deep inside and suckling strongly, spearing sensation straight to her womb. On fire, desperate to assuage the terrible empty ache within her, she writhed beneath him, inviting, begging, pleading. She needed release *now* and yet she wanted the most incredible experience of her life to last for ever.

'Seb, please,' she demanded, pressing her pelvis to his, rubbing her softness against his hardness.

His fingertips grazed up her thighs, tormenting her, and she wrapped her legs around him in blatant encouragement. Catching both her hands in one of his, he pinned them above her head, setting his mouth to the hollow of her throat where her pulse rampaged wildy.

'Gina, I want to explore you, savour you, love you for hours. But I am too impatient to wait now.'

'I don't want you to wait!' She couldn't last another second.

He buried his free hand in her hair, eyes dark and fiery with passion as he held her gaze. 'We'll slow down—next time we'll do this properly,' he promised roughly, moving against her, uniting them with one searing motion.

Gina gasped at the blissful wonder of being joined completely with Seb. This wasn't *properly*? She had never felt anything so shatteringly beautiful. His body filled hers almost beyond bearing. It was incredible. Perfect. Frantic, immediate and amazing. She wanted everything.

Freeing her hands, she moved them over his back, instinctively meeting and matching his moves, her body totally in tune with his. The delicious friction and sense of impossible fullness as they moved together was mind-blowing. Wave after wave of ecstasy built inside her. Her heart thundered, her lungs were on the point of bursting, but she wanted more, needed everything, couldn't bear for this to ever stop. She pressed her face into his shoulder, breathing in his seductive scent, tasting his warm flesh. She'd forgotten what it was like…and yet it had never, ever been like this.

Seb praised her in Italian, telling her how beautiful she was, how unbelievable she felt, urging her on, taking more, giving everything in return. She relished their blaze of passion. The searing rhythm rushed them both to the point of no return. Drawing her legs higher, she opened more to him, crying out as he sank deeper still, his free arm curling under her hips to keep her tight to him. The pressure was so intense she couldn't stand it.

'Now, Seb. Please.'

His hand in her hair fisted, his breath hot on her neck, his mouth urgent as he bit and sucked at her skin. 'Now.'

Together they soared off the precipice, swirling into oblivion. She feared she might faint from the sheer ecstatic pleasure of it. Sobbing, she clung to him as he masterfully extended and prolonged her shattering climax, binding her to him as he rode out his own. She had no idea where she ended and he began. They were one, sharing something so intense, so incredible, she wasn't sure she would survive it.

They collapsed together, gasping for breath, hearts thundering. Every part of her was shaking, and ripples of sensation continued to undulate through her. Rolling them to the side, Seb drew her leg over his hip and held her close. She felt the tremor in his hands as he gentled her, his fingertips brushing the tears from her cheeks.

'You are mine, Gina *mia*. Mine,' Seb proclaimed over and over, possessive, determined. '*Sempre*…always.'

Wrapping her arms around him, burying her face in his neck, she never wanted to let him go.

Seb had never experienced anything so incredible in his life as the storm of desire he had shared with Gina. He had no idea how much time passed in a haze of fulfilment until some semblance of normal thought processes were possible again. He nuzzled closer to her. The scent of vanilla clung to her skin, the familiar aroma mingling with her own unique womanliness—warm, sexy and intensely arousing. Just a short while ago he hadn't thought he would ever be able to move again, but he was gaining a second wind, and he needed to kiss her, explore her, taste her…do all the things he had not done properly the first time as they gave themselves to the urgent demands of their passion.

'Don't go.'

Gina's husky protest came as he eased her onto her back and tucked a pillow more comfortably under her head. He had no intention of going anywhere—as she would soon discover. Taking a moment to enjoy the way her hair tumbled around her, unrestrained and luxuriant, he knelt back, smiling as he looked her over. A smile of possession. Because spread out beneath him, eyes closed and skin flushed, she looked the picture of abandonment…a woman completely and thoroughly satisfied.

His woman.

Needing to touch her, he ran one palm slowly from her throat, down the valley between her delectable breasts, over her navel—noting how her stomach muscles spasmed in reaction—then lower, to rub his fingers back and forth just above her pubic bone. He added enough pressure to have her arching beneath him, giving a throaty moan of pleasure. Sooty lashes fluttered open to reveal dark, slumberous eyes.

He leaned down to kiss her. 'Hi.'

'Hi.' She skimmed her fingers along his forearms, her breath catching as he worked his mouth down her throat and licked his way to her breasts. 'Seb…'

'Mmm?'

'I can't yet,' she protested half-heartedly, making him chuckle because her body was betraying her and responding to his touch, her nipples swelling and tautening.

'You can.' Reluctantly relinquishing one delicious prize, he whispered his lips down to her navel, loving the way she moaned and bowed into him as he kissed, licked and sucked on her skin. 'I intend to do all the work this time.'

Starting at her feet, he continued his journey of discovery, leaving not a fragment of her untouched or unexplored, finding and exploiting the places where she was most sensitive, learning what made her come apart, where and how she most loved to be touched. He inched his way all over her until finally settling himself between her thighs, his hands curling over her hips and belly as she writhed beneath him, whimpering as he set his mouth to the core of her femininity, relishing her taste, her uninhibited and instinctive reactions to his caresses.

'Seb!' She shifted restlessly, clutching at him as he took her up a plateau at a time, then kept her balanced precariously on the edge of release. 'Please!'

'Patience, *amore mia*.'

He teased her, drawing out the delicious torture until she was crazy with need, before allowing her to crash over the edge, holding her close as she spun through the vortex of pleasure. And then he started all over again, welcoming her eager participation as she gave back just as readily and explored him with equal endeavour.

It was a very long time later when they finally fell into an exhausted, sated sleep, locked in each other's arms.

Seb woke with a feeling of incredible contentment. Gina was spooned against him, and his arms were closed possessively around her. For a man who had never before brought a woman to his home or his bed, who had never spent the whole night with a woman, he had made a remarkable discovery in the last hours. He could not now imagine *ever* sleeping another night without Gina in his arms.

Brushing her hair back, curling the silken mass up on the pillow, he softly moved his lips over the back of her neck, careful not to wake her. He smothered a sigh, horribly aware that he had still not told her the full truth about himself. The more he knew her, the more he cared about her, and the harder it was to own up, to risk ruining the most special thing he had ever experienced.

She was the most amazing woman. Incredibly responsive and receptive to his touch, she gave herself so generously, abandoned and without inhibition. The hours learning her body had been blissful, discovering her most sensitive places…the insides of her thighs, her navel, her breasts, the hollows below her ears, the backs of her knees, the base of her spine near the tattoo. He had discovered how to send her straight to orbit, and how to keep her on the edge of pleasure for ages. He loved it. Loved everything about her, every part of her. Loved nothing more than pleasuring her. It wasn't sex. It was making love.

And it hit him. No way were a few days and nights going to be enough. In a short time Gina had changed him— opened his eyes, given him hope, a sense of purpose for his future. His injuries had brought him to Elba. Elba had brought him Gina. And Gina had given him back his own reality and sense of self. He was angry at the way he had wasted his surgical skill, angry at what felt like the temporary loss of his very soul, sacrificed on the fake altar of money and success. He didn't like the person he had been, the kind of doctor he had become, but Gina had led him out of the darkness and into the light.

Maybe the new life ahead opened the way for him to have a proper relationship—the chance to make a real commitment to something other than his job. Not long ago such thoughts would have scared him. Now he was filled with an increasing excitement and awareness that Gina could be *the one*. All he knew was that he couldn't let her go. Which meant that somehow he would have to stop her leaving…or go with her.

He had no idea about her feelings. He could only hope this meant something to her. At some point they needed to have a serious talk. Knowing how important Gina's nursing was to her, Seb would not insult her by suggesting she give it up. True, he had enough money that neither of them needed to worry much about work again—not that she knew that yet. But he could never sit back and do nothing, and he knew Gina would feel the same.

Sighing, he glanced at the clock, surprised at how late they had slept. He needed to check on Maria. And it wouldn't be long before Evelina arrived. With regret, he gently eased away from Gina, tucking the covers around her and leaving her to catch up on some of the sleep he had denied her through their long night of loving.

He had two main problems to solve and answers to find…

What was he going to do with the rest of his life?

And how would Gina react when she knew the full story about him?

CHAPTER SEVEN

'NONNA, are you all right?' Gina asked, watching her grand-mother stand on the harbourside at Marciana Marina and gaze out to sea, as if miles away in the past.

She turned and offered a teary smile, one that pulled at Gina's heartstrings. 'I am just feeling sentimental. Remembering.'

'Oh, Nonna.' She slipped an arm around her frail shoulders. It was the third morning of their stay at the villa, and although her health had improved rapidly since leaving hospital, Gina couldn't help but worry. 'Are you sure you're up to this?'

'It was always going to be emotional.'

'I know, but…' Gina paused, biting her lip in indecision, looking across to where middle-aged, balding Paolo Benigni, a former fisherman who now ran chartered boat trips, was talking to Seb. 'You can change your mind at any time.'

Her grandmother shook her head. 'This is right, Gina. I must do it—I *want* to do it.'

'OK.'

'It is time to do what we came here for…time things went full circle.' One frail hand cupped her cheek. 'Do not be sad, *ragazza mia*. It is the way of life. Think of all the happy years. Were it not for the life I have been blessed with—including having you as part of it—I would not be here at all.'

Blinking back tears, Gina let out a shaky breath, keeping her misgivings to herself. A lump in her throat, she struggled to come to terms with what was about to happen. Yes, this was the reason they had come to Elba, and she supported her grandmother, had promised to carry out her grandparents' wishes, but… She closed her eyes. It was still hard to let go, to face saying goodbye again to the grandfather she'd loved so much.

'There is a heavy storm coming later in the day,' Seb announced, coming up beside them. 'Paolo says we need to go now…if we're going.'

'We are going,' her grandmother stated with her customary determination.

Gina managed a shaky smile as Seb glanced at her, then turned away. 'Come, Maria. Let me help you.'

Together, Seb and Paolo guided her grandmother on board the boat and saw her comfortably settled, the precious urn clasped protectively in her lap. Gina tossed her braid over her shoulder and looked away, needing a moment to get her emotions in check. Familiar hands settled on her shoulders, thumbs caressing the nape of her neck, and Gina turned, wrapping her arms around Seb's waist, pressing her face against him. One of his hands rubbed her back, and the other cradled her head as he gave her the comfort she needed, letting her absorb his strength.

'How are you doing?'

'I'm fine,' she fibbed, feeling selfish for her doubts and reluctance when this was what her grandparents had planned and so desperately wanted.

She burrowed more fully into his embrace and turned her thoughts to him. The last days with Seb had been the happiest of her life. And the nights had been incredible.

They had quickly fallen into a comfortable routine. The three of them would spend their mornings on short sight-seeing trips, with Seb an entertaining and patient escort. Then after lunch Evelina would come to the villa and keep a resting Maria company while Gina went out with Seb, walking or cycling in the national park, exploring the island or swimming at the private cove.

The previous afternoon they had visited an old mine and its museum, where Seb had bought her a glorious piece of mineral, a classic example of the 'Elbaite' commonly found on the island. The subtle colours and shapes in the smoky quartz with its pieces of tourmaline and beryl intrigued her, and she would cherish it always.

In the evenings, after Evelina had gone home, the three of them ate together, then relaxed until her grandmother went to bed. Then it was time for her and Seb to be alone, to explore the passion that only seemed to burn hotter between them.

Gina shivered in reaction as she thought of those nights with him. Seb was an amazing lover. Intensely sexy, he seemed to know even before she did what her body needed—how to maximise and prolong her pleasure. He was demanding and hungry, but incredibly generous. Sometimes she thought she would expire as he devoted hours to her pleasure, teasing and tormenting her until she couldn't bear it another moment. At other times it was hot, wild, excitingly rough as they gave in to their raging desire. Seb was full of contrasts, adventurous and deliciously naughty. Being with him was the most fantastic experience of her life.

Seb had set her free, releasing the sensual side she'd kept hidden...not that she had ever been as alive and uninhibited with anyone as she was with him. She'd surrendered to him totally, her body glowing and humming from his lovemaking. All she could think about was being with him. She craved his touch, the unbelievable sense of fullness and rightness as she welcomed him inside her, the indescribable pleasure only he had ever given her. His own body was exquisite, and she enjoyed every opportunity of exploring him and bringing him pleasure in return.

'Ready to go?'

His question cut through her reverie and she drew back with a sigh. 'Yes. Let's do it,' she agreed, hoping she sounded more certain and together than she felt.

On the journey west, around the coast and back towards the villa's secluded cove on Capo Sant'Andrea, Seb chatted to her grandmother. But Gina was grateful for the comfort and support of his fingers curled with hers.

All too soon they arrived at their destination. Paolo was discretion itself and he gave them privacy, ducking below while Seb assisted her grandmother.

'What do you want to do, Maria?' he asked, helping her to stand and steadying her on the gently swaying deck. 'Do you need to be nearer the shore? Or do you wish to scatter Matthew's ashes here, by Neptune's Spear?'

'I had meant to go to the beach, but I think the water would be a lovely idea—given my Matteo's love of the sea,' her grandmother decided, her voice shaky with emotion, tears shimmering in her eyes.

Gina had to struggle to hold back her own. 'Are you sure, Nonna?'

'Yes, *ragazza mia*, I am.'

'Whatever you want,' she conceded.

She felt choked as her grandmother made a short but emotional speech about meeting her true love here and their love together. Then Seb helped her to the side of the boat. The breeze was behind her as she uncapped the urn and tilted it, the ashes floating away on the water.

'I want to come here, too, when my time comes.' Cheeks moist, but her expression determined, her grandmother faced her. 'Promise me, Gina.'

'I promise, Nonna.'

Gina barely got the words out before she had to turn away again, the tears she had tried so hard to hide now escaping. It was difficult enough being here to say goodbye to her grandfather, the man she had loved and admired so much. She couldn't bear to think of repeating this in time to come for her grandmother.

Seb came up behind her, one arm wrapping around her waist, one around her shoulders, cocooning her in his warmth. She leaned back against him and he pressed a kiss to her temple, giving her strength and comfort without voicing any unwanted platitudes. There was nothing anyone could say to make this easier to bear. It was enough that he understood, that he gave her his support.

With the wind picking up and the sea turning choppy, the atmosphere increasingly thick and airless, it was time to head back to the harbour. Paolo was respectful, maintaining silence as he guided the boat towards Marciana Marina. Gina glanced at her grandmother. She looked pale and tired, but she exuded a peaceful serenity that implied this had, indeed, been the right thing for her to do.

Back at the port, Gina walked down the gangway and watched as Seb and Paolo aided her grandmother safely to the shore.

'Thank you for all you have done for us.' Gina shook Paolo's hand in gratitude. 'I really appreciate you helping my grandmother like this.'

'It is my honour to assist, *signorina*. Besides, my family owe Seb a huge debt after all he did for our daughter,' he announced, taking her by surprise.

'Paolo.'

Gina heard the warning in Seb's voice, but was unable to decipher the silent message that passed between the two men. Curious, she bit back her questions...for now. They said their goodbyes, leaving Paolo to secure his boat to ride out the coming storm.

Back at the villa, her grandmother went to her room to replace the now empty urn and have a quiet moment alone before lunch, while Gina followed Seb to the kitchen.

'Thank you again for what you did today, Seb.'

'I promised,' he replied simply. 'It was what Maria needed... But it upset you, and for that I am sorry.'

'It was what my grandparents wanted.' She paused a moment, thinking of all that had happened in a few short days. 'I wish I could thank the Linardis for their help and hospitality.'

Seb looked awkward. 'They would not have had it any other way.'

Gina remained silent for a few moments, uncertain whether to press him further. Then she remembered what had happened when they had come off the boat.

'What did you do for Paolo's daughter?' The words bubbled free, and she saw Seb stiffen, his back to her as he opened the fridge and took out some fresh fruit juice. 'Seb?'

'It was nothing, Gina,' he excused, clearly uncomfortable.

'Paolo doesn't think so.'

Pouring two glasses, he pushed one across the counter towards her. 'His child had an accident. I just happened to be in the right place at the right time.'

His tone told her that the subject was closed. A flicker of unease rippled through her, one she couldn't explain, but shadows darkened Seb's eyes and she knew something was troubling him. Something he refused to discuss with her. It hurt to be shut out. And it made her realise how little she knew about him and his life, despite their intimacy...an intimacy that, for her, had gone far beyond the physical.

Before she could try to find out more, her grandmother joined them in the kitchen and the moment was lost.

The predicted storm hit the island during the afternoon. Torrential rain kept them inside the villa. Thunder rocked and rumbled across a blackened sky, streaks of lightning casting unpredictable flashes in the unnatural darkness, the wind battering the trees and threatening to carry off anything not well anchored down. But the freak weather passed within hours, leaving the air clearer and fresher, fragranced with the warm dampness of the earth, and the foliage glistening and beaded under the moonlight.

After she saw her grandmother settled later that night, Gina went out onto the terrace, alone for a few moments with her thoughts. Niggling doubts and unasked questions continued to prey on her mind. Her grandmother spoke romantically of history repeating itself, of Gina meeting Seb on the same spot where her grandparents had found each other fifty years ago. But could she trust her feelings, the speed of it, the fairytale nature of what had happened these last days? What of the things she didn't know about Seb? Why was he so reluctant to talk about himself?

It had been an emotional day. Maria had retired earlier than usual, and Seb stopped off to see her, anxious to ensure that she was not suffering any reaction. He tapped on the door of her room.

'I am awake.'

Smiling, he went inside, pleased to see good colour in her cheeks as she rested against the pillows. '*Buonasera*, Maria. I wanted to check that you were all right.'

'Seb, *buonasera*!' she greeted him, patting the bed and waiting for him to sit down beside her. 'Thank you for thinking of me, and for all you have done for me. I am very grateful.'

'I was glad to be able to help. It was obvious how important it was for you to lay Matthew to rest here. But it can't have been easy,' he acknowledged, taking her hand.

'No. Not easy. Yet now it is done I feel a real peace and rightness.' Hazel eyes shimmered with tears, but her smile was strong. 'Wherever I go, whatever happens, my Matteo will always be with me.'

Seb found himself uncharacteristically affected by the depth of Maria's love and inner contentment. 'You are a very special lady.'

'A lucky one, I think, for having lived a happy life. Today I was more worried for Gina than for myself,' she continued after a moment's pause, her smile fading. 'She has supported me always, but I know this was hard for her. Her grandfather meant the world to her.'

'As do you,' Seb pointed out, continually struck by the deep relationship the two women shared.

'For Matteo and me, Gina has been a joy. We have always been proud of her. I don't know what we would have done without her. But I worry she takes on so much responsibility for me, feels she has to protect me. I know money is more of a problem than she will admit, that she struggled to get us here at all, and I know that she goes without things for herself to make sure I am comfortable.'

'Gina loves you.'

Maria's smile was wide and warm. 'I know. And I love her. But I don't want her giving up her own life for me. She hasn't dated at all since we went to live with her.'

Yet Gina had come to him with a freshness, honesty and eagerness that continued to take his breath away, blooming like a flower feeling the heat of the sun after a long winter.

'You are very professional doing that, Seb.'

Maria's words hit home, and he looked at her in confusion. 'Sorry?'

'You're taking my pulse. Gina does the same thing all the time and she thinks I don't know,' she confided with a teasing smile.

Startled, Seb glanced down, realising that unconscious force of habit had indeed led him to do as Maria claimed. 'I—' He broke off, unsure what to say, but as he went to remove his hand, Maria's fingers closed around his.

'A little advice from an old woman. Do not leave it too long to tell Gina whatever you need to.'

'Maria…'

'You are not simply the caretaker of this villa, are you? Or an artist?' she asked softly, and there was no judgement in her tone, just understanding and gentleness.

Seb sighed, unable to tell her anything but the truth. 'No.'

'I'm sure you have your reasons for keeping things to yourself.'

'I did. In the beginning,' he admitted, running a hand through his hair in agitation. 'Now things have just become complicated, and that's my fault.'

Maria patted his hand. 'I believe you care very much for my Gina.'

'I do. For the first time in my life I've met someone who sees the me inside, Maria. The real person, not the outer trappings.' He hesitated, trying to put his feelings into words. 'I am scared that what I have to say will change how Gina feels about me, that she will judge me harshly and find me wanting.'

'As you do yourself?' she queried with stunning perception.

'Yes.' Taken aback, he looked away, unable to meet her gaze. His own fell on the scars on his right wrist and hand where Maria's fingers rested. 'Meeting Gina has caused me to re-evaluate things and see where I was going wrong. Now I have to decide how to put things right…with her and my life.'

'I know her, Seb, and I have never seen her so happy as when she is with you. My heart tells me you belong together.' A note of warning crept into her voice. 'Gina has a big capacity for understanding and for compassion—but she does value honesty. Whatever it is you are holding back, it will be better coming from you. Tell her yourself—soon.'

He nodded, but Maria's words filled him with anxiety. She was right, but that didn't make telling Gina any easier. How much time did he have left? Now that Maria was well enough to travel, and they had achieved what they had came to Elba to do, what more was there to keep them on the island? They were booked to return to Scotland in a couple of days, and Gina would be starting her new job the following week—unless he faced up to the truth and devised an alternative plan. Never before had he allowed himself to need anyone, to trust and depend on anyone but himself. He had even kept a part of himself detached from Zio Roberto, Zia Sofia and Rico. In an impossibly short time Gina had come to be as important and essential to his very existence as air and water. He couldn't let her walk out of his life— but would she want him when she knew the truth?

'Think on what I have said,' Maria advised now.

'I will. Thank you.' Full of affection for the elderly lady, he leaned down and kissed her cheek before rising to his feet. 'Is there anything I can get for you?'

'No, I'll be fine, *caro*. *Buonanotte*.'

'Goodnight, Maria. Sleep well.'

Troubled by his thoughts, he left Maria's room, returning to his own to make a few preparations before going in search of Gina. He was uncomfortably aware that he hadn't handled things well earlier, that he had upset her by cutting off her understandable questions. But he hadn't wanted to talk about Paolo's daughter. That would have meant explaining the corrective surgery he had performed for free on the little girl after her nasty accident…and how could he do that when he had still not told Gina about his former career?

Maria's advice and her blessing of their relationship took root inside him. He knew what he had to do. Tonight he would show Gina in every way he could how much she meant to him. Tomorrow he would sit her down and tell her everything.

'What are you thinking, *amore mia*?'

Gina stifled a gasp of surprise, a tremor running through her as Seb moved up behind her and wrapped his arms around her, nuzzling into her, his lips, teeth and tongue tormenting her lobe and the hollow below her ear. Her body reacted instinctively the moment he touched her. It was hard to believe that anything else mattered when he made her feel like this, devoting himself to her pleasure, cherishing her as no one else had ever done.

'Nothing,' she whispered, unable to voice her nagging worries about the way he evaded talking about himself.

It was magical here, and she was caught up in the romance of the island. The enchantment of being with Seb, his nearness, was affecting her powers of thought and her concentration.

'Come, Gina, I have a treat for you.'

She allowed him to lead her indoors, finding a bubble bath awaiting her, with scented candles casting their flickering light around the room. His thoughtfulness touched her. Her physical need of him obliterated the unasked questions in her mind, and her fingers went to work dispensing with his clothes, as his did with hers. After she had wound her braid into a knot and pinned it up, he took her hand, balancing her as she stepped into the large corner tub. With a contented sigh, she sank down into the water, making room for Seb to join her before resting back against his chest, sighing as he nibbled the back of her neck. He took the soap, his hands enjoying a leisurely journey over her body before allowing her to turn and do the same for him.

A while later, her skin tingling and her pulse scudding through her veins, they were out of the bath and patted dry. Then Seb surprised her again, leading her naked to the bed and spreading out a dry towel.

'Lie face down for me,' he instructed huskily.

Trembling with anticipation, she did as she was bid. The bed depressed under his weight as he knelt over her, straddling her thighs. His body brushed against her as he leaned down and kissed the back of her neck, before running lips and tongue slowly down her spine to linger over her tattoo. She shivered in reaction. When contact was withdrawn and he paused, she turned her head on the pillow to see what he was doing.

'Seb?'

'I borrowed some of your oils,' he told her, reaching out to a bowl on the bedside chest and pouring some of the contents into his palm.

'That's fine.' She had been massaging his hands and arm every day. The thought that he was now going to reciprocate— all over—made her body hum with feverish expectancy. As she had already discovered, he had amazing hands. A subtle waft of her favourite fragrance stirred her senses. 'Vanilla…'

Moving back into position, he leaned down again, making her squirm as he sucked her earlobe into his mouth. 'It always makes me think of you…makes me hot and needy.' His voice was a rough, sexy murmur, and he deliberately rubbed himself against her, letting her feel his arousal before he moved away again.

'Seb…'

His hands settled on her back and began to glide over her with just the right pressure, the sensuous strokes making her sigh with pleasure. When his thumbs sank into the cheeks of her rear and set up a circular rhythm it was so unexpectedly arousing that she buried her face in the pillow to smother her moans. He moved on, journeying down each leg in turn, and she wriggled as he hit the most sensitive spots, hearing him chuckle as he lingered to torment her.

'Turn over, *amore mia.*'

Wicked fingertips tickling the soles of her feet made her hasten to comply with the demand. Gentle light spilled across the bed, allowing her to see the raw desire in Seb's eyes as he looked at her, and she sucked in a breath, not sure she was going to survive whatever else he had planned for her. All she could focus on was Seb, and how amazing he made her feel. She wanted him…*now*.

'You are so beautiful,' he whispered, the emotion in his voice almost making her heart stop. His reverential appreciation of her made her feel supremely confident in her power as a woman—a power only Seb had given her.

Taking more oil, he started at her feet, driving her insane as he worked slowly up her legs, skimming the insides of her thighs but stopping short of where she most craved his touch. His knee between hers prevented her pressing her legs together to try and stop the terrible ache of need building inside her. Then his hands moved on to stroke and massage her belly, circling her navel, dipping to press just above her pubic bone, making her hips lift in involuntary response, begging him to fill the emptiness.

'Please,' she whimpered.

'Soon.'

Her protest was choked off as he turned his attention to her breasts, his firm, clever caresses almost too much to bear. Her muscles felt boneless, relaxed, yet her body was wound up like at top. There was no way she could wait any more. Sitting up, she caught him by surprise, and he laughed, his arms closing round her as she tumbled him to the bed and settled on top of him. His mouth opened hotly under hers as she kissed him with all the pent-up desperation coursing through veins.

'Are you that hungry?' he teased, fingers skimming her heated, trembling flesh.

'Yes.'

The fire in his own eyes matched that which burned inside her as he reached out for a condom and handed it to her. 'Then take what you need, Gina. I am all yours.'

How she wished that were true—at least beyond this moment. She knew without doubt that she loved him. But she didn't know what he felt—if anything. In a couple of days she and her grandmother were due to go home. She couldn't bear the thought of saying goodbye to him…knew that when she did she would never see him again. As much as she loved her grandmother, her friends and her work, home would mean responsibility, an end to the freedom and romance she had found here. Seb was the only one with the key to unlock the sensual woman inside her.

Unable to say the words aloud, she gave everything to show with her body what he meant to her.

Seb let Gina take the lead, giving himself up to the indescribable joy of making love with her, hoping it meant as much to her as it did to him, that what she might feel for him was strong enough to survive what he had to tell her tomorrow.

They finally fell asleep, bodies tangled together—only to be woken at dawn by the incessant ringing of the telephone.

Frowning, Seb struggled awake, reluctantly releasing Gina as he reached for the receiver.

'What is it?' he demanded in Italian. The shocking news imparted to him brought him to immediate alertness. *'Madre del Dio.'* He listened a moment longer, aware of Gina stirring beside him, then fired off some rapid questions. 'How many? What about supplies? Yes, of course. I will be there as soon as I can.'

Seb hung up the phone and flung back the duvet, reaching for his clothes. 'Gina. Wake up, *tesoro.'*

'What's happened?' she asked sleepily.

'There has been a building collapse at a tourist resort not far from here. There are many injured and missing. All medical help is needed, as well as blood donors, translators, and men to help dig. I have to go.'

'I'm coming with you.' Without hesitation, Gina was up and hurrying to dress.

'Put on layers,' he advised her.

'What about Nonna?'

Seb sat down to pull on his boots. 'I'll ring Evelina. She'll come to be with Maria.'

'Thank you.'

Already he was on the phone and making arrangements. By the time they were ready to leave, Evelina was hurrying up the drive, urging them to take care as they drove off with no idea what awaited them.

'Do you know what caused it?' Gina asked, and he was thankful for her calm.

'All I know is that this new development was built recently by a foreign company who brought in their own workers. There were rumours of corners being cut in the construction, safety regulations not being complied with,' Seb informed her, concentrating on negotiating the cliff road as safely but as rapidly as possible. 'The storm yesterday and the sudden large amount of rain caused a collapse of the unstable hillside ground and brought the building down. There are still many tourists on Elba, and this new complex of holiday apartments was nearly full.'

'How many people does the building hold?'

'Possibly two hundred. Maybe more.' It didn't bear thinking about. 'Men, women and children.'

Minutes later they arrived on site, to a scene of devastation. For a few seconds they both sat in silence as the enormity of what lay before them sank in.

'Oh, Seb,' Gina breathed, her dismay obvious.

'I know.' He shook his head, trying to focus on what needed to be done. 'For now we must do all we can to assist those most in need, until more help arrives.'

Another more personal problem reared its ugly head, and Seb swore aloud.

'What's wrong?' Gina asked, turning to him.

He took her hands in his. 'Before we become swallowed up in this emergency, I need you to know that I care about you—that I never meant it to happen like this,' he told her urgently, the words rushing out in his need to try and limit the damage.

'I don't understand.'

'I know, Gina. And that is my fault. It is *all* my fault. And it is about me, not you, OK?' He glanced out of the window and saw the policeman who had phoned him hurrying in their direction. Desperate, he turned back to Gina. 'I am sorry. When this is over I need to tell you things about me— things I should have said ages ago and was going to tell you today. Just remember how I feel about you and what we are to each other. Please.'

'But—'

'Dottore Adriani—thank goodness you are on the island. We need your expertise at once,' the policeman exclaimed, pulling open the driver's door.

Gina's eyes widened in shock. 'You're a doctor?'

Dio! He should have listened to Rico. And to Maria. If only he had swallowed his stupid pride and his fears, told Gina the truth from the beginning. But he had kept putting it off as it became more and more difficult. And now Gina had found out in the worst of ways.

'Later I will explain. I promise.' He cupped her face and gave her a quick, heated kiss, knowing this was not the time or the place. 'Come, Gina. I need you to be my hands. For now we have to help others.'

Withdrawing, she stared at him for a long moment as if she didn't know him at all, her eyes dark and wounded. 'All right,' she agreed, her voice cool and distant.

As she opened the passenger door and climbed out, Seb hurried after her. He had to focus on why they were here. The injured needed them, and that had to come before his own selfish concerns. But he didn't think he would ever forget that look on Gina's face—incomprehension, followed by disbelief, only to be replaced by hurt betrayal as realisation dawned. It drove a stake into his heart.

How was he ever going to make things right between them again?

CHAPTER EIGHT

CONFUSED and hurt, Gina battled to put her shock at the revelation about Seb aside and focus on what needed to be done. Her years of experience working in A and E, as well as being part of a trauma response team for major incidents such as serious accidents on the motorway, would stand her in good stead now. Even so, she surveyed the chaotic scene in front of her with bemusement.

It was almost impossible to believe that a modern four-storey building had stood here such a short time before. More than three-quarters of the curving structure cut into the hill had been brought down. The part of the end block still standing looked as if it had been sliced through by some giant axe, sheered away to reveal the remains of the rooms inside. Furniture balanced precariously on the edge. Clothes and possessions, dust and debris, were strewn everywhere. At least people in that section would have had the opportunity to get out. What chance would the holiday-makers in the rest of the now demolished building have had to escape, sleeping in their beds and unwitting of the disaster about to befall them?

A few survivors milled around in a daze, bleeding, bruised, concussed, crying…searching for missing loved ones. They were being comforted by a handful of early risers who had been away from the building, walking on the beach or swimming before breakfast. Local men and firefighters continued to arrive, working to clear and search the vast expanse of rubble for trapped tourists, awaiting specialist teams with heavy-lifting equipment, search dogs and heat-seeking cameras.

Moments after she and Seb arrived on scene an advance party of two more doctors and several nurses came from the hospital in Portoferraio, over half an hour's drive away, bringing much-needed supplies with them. Seb took charge, his quiet authority unquestioned by anyone present as he organised teams and assigned them tasks. He also appointed a dedicated triage officer, responsible for the classification of the injured. Following standard procedure for incidents with a large number of casualties, patients would be placed into one of four groups: life-threatening, urgent, minor, and—sadly—dead and beyond help.

'I know what we face seems overwhelming, but we must do the best we can with what we have,' he told them in Italian, succinct and efficient. 'There are up to two hundred people injured and trapped—this could go on all day, even longer, as people are found and freed. More emergency medical personnel are on the way, but the first casualties need our help *now*. Watch for shock, crush injuries and crush syndrome, internal bleeding, fractures and head wounds. If you are unsure, or anything worries you, ask for advice. Those casualties beyond hope we will make as comfortable as possible, but we must concentrate resources on those with the chance of survival. The most severely injured will be taken by helicopter to the mainland—we have to stabilise and evacuate them as quickly and safely as possible. The walking wounded not requiring immediate care should be watched by volunteers until they can be dealt with. The police will record names, nationalities and details of the missing. Any questions?' There was silence. Seb nodded, his expression solemn. 'OK—let's get on.'

Everyone dispersed to their allotted tasks, and Gina found herself working alongside Seb. She still couldn't believe that he was a doctor, that he had never said a word despite all they had talked about. What else didn't she know about him? Could she trust anything he had said and done? Shaking her head, she forced away the painful questions and anxious doubts. People needed her, and she couldn't let them down. There would be time when this was over to get some answers.

'Are you all right, Gina?'

'Fine,' she murmured, unsure if his softly voiced question referred to what they now faced professionally or to the overwhelming shift in their personal situation.

She busied herself preparing instruments, drugs, oxygen, dressings and sundry supplies, so that everything they might need would be to hand. After they had both pulled on some hospital scrubs over their clothes, Gina took two pairs of gloves from the box and handed one to Seb.

'It's a while since I have done this kind of thing,' he told her as put them on, his vulnerability surprising her. 'Let us hope for the patients' sake that I am up to the task. And that my hands will hold out.'

In spite of her mental withdrawal from him, a wave of concern assailed her at his doubt over the decreased physical dexterity that so troubled him. Before she could reply, however, their first critically injured patient arrived—an unconscious man with a depressed skull fracture, broken shoulder and chest injuries.

It was the start of what seemed an unending stream, as more and more casualties were pulled alive from the rubble. As Seb had predicted, there was a predominance of crush injuries, fractures and deep-tissue wounds. Care had to be taken with crush syndrome, because prolonged pressure, when relieved, could cause shock, vascular problems, renal failure, even death. A doctor was on hand for each extraction, and difficult decisions had to be made—occasionally to sacrifice a limb to save a life.

Specialist search and medical teams soon arrived from the mainland, bringing further supplies and equipment. As the hours ticked by, she and Seb worked side by side on patient after patient, and she instinctively took on extra clinical tasks under his direction, to compensate for his reduced physical capacity.

Amongst the many people they treated from a variety of countries were a middle-aged woman with a severely fractured femur and extensive blood loss, two men with serious head injuries, a young woman with a dislocated shoulder, broken collarbone and two broken arms, a teenage boy with flail chest, a woman with extensive facial fractures and tissue damage, who had needed a cricothyroidotomy to re-establish her airway, and an older man with multiple lower leg fractures who was also complaining of chest pain which turned out to be cardiac.

They had all been stabilised and evacuated to hospital. And still the injured kept coming. Each case affected Gina, but it was the frightened, injured children who broke her heart.

Fighting weariness, she changed her gloves between patients and took a drink of the bottled water provided for them, allowing herself a glance at Seb. Over the years she had worked with many doctors, of varying abilities, and Seb was the very best of them. Despite the problem with his hands, his skill was extraordinary, and he was calm, compassionate and thorough. He had said he was rusty at this, so what kind of medicine did he normally do? Frowning, she noted the way he flexed his hands, grimacing with pain as he massaged his right wrist, thumb and forefinger. She loved him, but she was angry and confused, feeling betrayed, hurt, unsure. She needed time to think—but there was no chance of that at the moment.

Their next patient was a young man with chest injuries and breaks to the radius and ulna in his left arm, with the displaced bones piercing the skin. Confused and in pain, he was cold and pale, his skin clammy. While Seb carried out an initial assessment, Gina set to work inserting a cannula into the uninjured arm, and began running a crystalloid drip to replace fluids and ward off the effects of shock and blood loss.

'His breathing is distressed and he's tachycardic,' she told Seb, giving him details of blood pressure, respiration and pulse-rate.

'A couple of ribs are broken, and there are no breath sounds on the right side.' He paused a moment. 'There is tracheal deviation and he has distended neck veins.'

'Tension pneumothorax?'

'Yes.'

While Seb explained to the distressed young Italian what was happening, she busied herself preparing a local anaesthetic and the equipment he would require to aspirate the chest.

'Gina, I need your help.'

She looked up, trying to block out the regret and the plea for understanding in Seb's eyes. 'What is it?'

'I can't do this with my hands as they are,' he explained, his frustration evident.

She ached for his wounded pride and the loss of his full abilities. But with all the other medical teams as rushed as they were, there was no one else to call on. 'All right.' She moved around the makeshift treatment table to Seb's side.

'Have you ever done this before, Gina?'

'Once,' she admitted, remembering how terrified she had been, knowing there was no doctor on hand and that the woman in her care at the time would die if she didn't act fast. She'd later been commended for her actions, but it wasn't something she had ever wanted to do again. 'It was a long time ago.'

'I'm right here with you.' Seb's throaty reassurance rippled through her, and the inevitable but inappropriate awareness caught her off guard. 'We can do this...together.'

Gina sucked in a deep breath, trying to control both her nerves and her reaction to Seb. With the local anaesthetic having taken effect, she followed his detailed directions and inserted the needle into the second intercostal space in the midclavicular line, the aspirated air that escaped confirming his diagnosis. She was more scared than she wanted to admit as Seb talked her through the next step...making an incision in the fifth intercostal space, anterior to the mid-axillary line, and inserting a drain. He was with her every second, praising her, boosting her confidence, inserting a gloved finger into the incision to check the positioning, finally fitting the seal when the tube was correctly sited in the chest cavity. Relieved, her fingers shaking, Gina fixed it in place and checked the drain was working.

There was little time to think as they turned their attention to the badly fractured arm. After administering a top-up of analgesia through the intravenous access, she helped Seb straighten, dress and splint the damaged forearm, ensuring blood circulation, keeping the open wound sterile and applying support to the limb.

'Well done, *tesoro*, that was a great job. You were fantastic.' He smiled as their patient was taken to a helicopter for evacuation. 'We make a great team, no?'

A shaft of pain lanced through her and she turned away, hiding her emotional reaction as she cleared up and prepared for the next casualty. How could he act as if nothing had happened? As if lying to her didn't matter?

'Gina…'

'Not now,' she managed, knowing she would never get through the rest of this ordeal if she allowed thoughts of his deception to play on her mind.

They should have gone home hours ago, Seb acknowledged, but both he and Gina had needed to see it through for as long as they could be useful. It seemed impossible that anyone left buried under the rubble all these hours later could be alive and saved, but miraculously more *were* found, and they worked on to the point of exhaustion to give them the best care and the best chance possible.

The pain and seizing in his hands had increased, and now he could do less and less. His reduced ability made him impatient and angry, and confirmed that he would never be able to do surgery or trauma work again. Not on a regular basis. Thankfully he had kept up to date with emergency procedures, so he had been of some use at least, but as his hands had failed him, he had needed to rely more and more on Gina.

She had been incredible. A tower of strength. Calm, skilled, outwardly unfazed by anything thrown at her—although he could tell that some of the things they had dealt with had affected her, as they had him. She was totally professional and a terrific nurse, attuned to the patients' emotional need for reassurance while being efficient in attending to their clinical needs. They had worked so well together. It had restored some of his confidence, given him new hope for his future career. He *could* still be a doctor—*could* still make a difference and help people. It was a matter of finding a new niche. One which kept him true to himself this time. One which gave him the kind of self-respect that shone through in everything Gina did.

She had taught him so much about himself, had made him look with fresh eyes at his life, and she didn't even know it. He wanted so badly to share it with her, to explain his fears, his mistakes, to discuss where to go from here…but it could already be too late. He might have blown his best chance with the only woman to ever touch his heart, who had ever made him think of for ever. He could see and feel her doubts, her mistrust of him, and it pierced his soul.

It was early evening before they finally left the scene. Replacement medical teams from the mainland had relieved them, and search-and-rescue personnel were using heat-seeking cameras and a dog to locate the dozen people still missing and believed trapped in the lower layers of the collapsed building. The journey home was completed in a tense silence, and once back at the villa Gina walked inside and headed towards her own room in the guest wing.

'Gina, please. I—'

'I'm really tired, Seb.' She wouldn't meet his gaze, and fear clawed at his gut. 'I need to shower and sleep.'

'Of course. Thank you for all you did today. You were amazing.'

With a weary nod, she turned away. Reluctantly, Seb let her go, cursing himself for his stupidity. He had never meant to hurt her. And she *was* hurt. The pain in those big brown eyes broke his heart. Now he had no idea what to do to make things right—whether to go to her, or give her the space she asked for. How could he make her understand? Filled with uncertainty, he sent Evelina home, then checked on Maria before going to take a shower of his own, finally returning to the kitchen to force down a little of the food Evelina had left ready for them.

Some while later, exhausted and aching, he followed Gina's example and had an early night, lying in a bed that now seemed too big and empty. He was restless. Alone. He couldn't sleep without Gina in his arms. Succumbing to temptation, he got up and went to check on her—but she was not in her room. His anxiety increasing, he looked in on a sleeping Maria and found Gina curled up in the armchair beside the bed. Even in the dimness he could see the tracks of tears on her cheeks. Unable to bear her hurt or the separation between them a moment longer, he scooped her up in his arms and carried her back to his room.

'Seb…'

'Shh, *amore mia*,' he whispered at her soft, raw protest. 'Let me take care of you.' Tucking her into bed, he slid in beside her, gentling her, kissing her, licking away her tears. 'I'm sorry, Gina. So sorry.' Wrapping his arms around her, he kept her close. 'Please forgive me.'

He held her through the night, watching over her as she slept, but he was upset and concerned to wake up the next morning and find her gone from his bed. His alarm increasing, he hurried to dress and went in search of her. The villa was empty, but he found Maria and Evelina on the terrace. Evelina excused herself and bustled off to the kitchen to put on more coffee.

'Gina has gone for a walk,' Maria told him, understanding mixed with a hint of censure in her expression. 'She said she needed some time alone to think.'

Dannare! He didn't want Gina thinking…not until he had been able to talk to her, to explain, to tell her everything himself. That he had caused her hurt and had dented her trust in him was too painful to bear.

'Has she gone to the cove?' he asked Maria, his gaze straying down the cliffside to the crescent of beach far below.

'No, *caro*. She didn't say where she was going. And she didn't take her phone.'

Edgy and restless, he paced the terrace. He wanted to

go after Gina. But how could he when he had no idea where she was?

'Sebastiano!'

Evelina's call had him turning towards the villa. 'Yes?'

'There is a call for you. They say it is important,' she informed him.

'Thank you.' Sighing, he faced Maria again. 'I am sorry. I should take this.'

'Of course. Try not to worry,' she added, patting his hand.

Seb knew her reassurance was well meant, but he couldn't help but worry. Concern for Gina and what this distance meant for them preyed on his mind as he headed indoors. The unexpected news he received only added to his tension.

'Is something the matter?' Maria asked as he returned to the terrace.

'That was the police in Florence. They have arrested the man believed to be responsible for the knife attack in July,' he explained, sitting down to drink the coffee Evelina insisted he make time for. 'He was known to the police, but had gone into hiding after the incident. Yesterday he was picked up in Turin and returned to Florence. They want me there today to identify him, before he appears in court and is charged. It is the worst possible timing.'

'You must go, Sebastiano,' Evelina fretted.

'I know. There is a flight arranged for me. But I don't want to leave Gina. Especially now, with things unresolved between us.' He ran a hand through his hair in agitation. 'Where *is* she?'

Maria reached out and touched his arm. 'Perhaps Gina will return before it is time for you to leave for the airport.'

Seb could find little comfort in the words. More than anything he wished he could take Gina with him to Florence. But, even were she here to ask, he suspected she would decline—especially now, with the distance between them and so much unexplained. Besides, he knew she wouldn't leave Maria. He could only hope that time apart would help clarify things, that they could clear up their misunderstandings when he returned to Elba.

Going back indoors, he called for a progress report on yesterday's emergency. All casualties had been released from the rubble, and no one was missing, but the death toll had risen to fifteen. Still a miracle, he thought, given the enormity of what had happened. Next he phoned Rico and arranged for his cousin to meet his flight.

'It is good news that they have this man in custody at last,' Rico declared with satisfaction. 'Of course I will come for you, *cugino*. I will be happy to see you—you have been silent for days, and I am intrigued to hear all about the delectable Gina, who has obviously been keeping you very busy! Will she be with you?'

'Rico.' Seb growled the warning, in no mood for the teasing.

'What's wrong?'

'Nothing,' he lied. 'Not now, OK? I'll explain when I see you.'

He could tell Rico was worried, but thankfully his cousin didn't push the subject further on the phone. There would be enough of a lecture when Rico found out he had ignored his advice to confide in Gina straight away. Instead he had made a mess of everything, and he had no one to blame but himself.

Seb waited until the last minute, but Gina did not return to the house. Now he had to go, or he would be late for the private plane that awaited him at the island's small airport near La Pila, sited on the only flat land Elba had to offer, between Marina di Campo and Poggio. Filled with bitter disappointment, and an aching anxiety that things were falling apart, he said goodbye to Maria and Evelina and went out to the car.

But as he reached the bottom of the drive, he spied Gina walking along the road back towards the villa. Coming to a halt, he climbed out of the car.

'Gina!' The sad wariness in her dark eyes as she looked at him ripped out his heart. 'I did not want to go without seeing you.'

'You're leaving?' she asked, in surprise and confusion.

Cursing at the wobble in her voice, he took her in his arms, burying his face in her vanilla-scented hair. 'Only briefly. Maria will explain. The police have arrested a man for the knife attack. I have to go to Florence to identify him.'

'Of course.'

'We will talk when I come back, Gina. I hope that will be tonight, but it may be tomorrow. It depends on whether this is the man and if I have to attend court.' He cupped her face in his hands. 'I hurt you, and you cannot know how much I regret that. I am so sorry. I held back because of me, Gina, not you. Please give me the chance to explain when I return to Elba.'

Her nod was reluctant, and scarcely the promise he needed. Drawing her closer, he kissed her, putting everything into it, feeling the resistance drain out of her as she succumbed to the chemistry between them. He could only hope that their special connection would work in his favour.

With a monumental effort of will, he forced himself to release her and returned to the car. He drove away feeling deeply uneasy…and already terribly lonely without her.

The time passed with interminable slowness. Gina felt physically restless and emotionally unsettled, confused by all the doubts, worries and suspicions creating turmoil in her mind. Seb claimed he wanted to explain, but what excuse could there be for not telling her he was a doctor? Why had he deceived her?

She tried to occupy herself by devoting time to her grand-mother, avoiding the subject of Seb and the pressing issue of returning home. They were due to travel the next day. The knowledge hung between them, unspoken. She couldn't bear the thought of leaving here, even with things the way they were, but Seb had not asked her to postpone her return to Scotland, and he had given no indication of his feelings— if he even had any. He had only claimed to want to set the record straight about why he had misled her. And then what would he do? Wave her goodbye?

Alone for the evening, the villa feeling empty without Seb's presence, she and her grandmother prepared and ate a simple pasta dish, and then settled down to watch television before bedtime. Gina had hoped there would be something interesting to distract her, but although her grandmother became absorbed in a documentary, Gina's own mind drifted. She was snapped from her reverie when the national Italian news came on, and she found herself staring at Seb's face on the screen. With a gasp, she sat up straight.

'Nonna?'

'I see him, *ragazza mia.*'

They watched in silence as the images unfolded, and Gina felt her blood chilling as she listened to a report of the knife attack and the arrest of the suspected assailant. The pictures showed Seb leaving the police station in Florence late that afternoon. He looked annoyed and frustrated at the intrusion of the journalists bombarding him with questions, at the press of microphones and cameras. The handsome man with him appeared equally irritated, bundling Seb through the crowd to where a sleek black Ferrari awaited.

Gina's mouth dropped open as the reality of what she was seeing and hearing sank in.

'Sebastiano Adriani, who dropped out of sight a few weeks ago and was believed to be convalescing overseas, returned to Florence today at the request of the police, to identify the man arrested for the assault in July. Dr Adriani went to the aid of the woman being attacked, and as a consequence suffered injuries to his hands that appear to have ended his high-flying career. The reconstructive plastic surgeon, renowned for his celebrity clients and equally famous girlfriends, was rumoured to have been dating young actress Lidia di Napoli at the time of the incident.

'Lidia di Napoli—seen here with her new beau, the recently divorced director of her current production— declined to answer questions. It is believed that the starlet abandoned her former boyfriend after his injuries threatened to bring an end to his celebrity status. But Dr Adriani has never been lacking female company.'

The words were accompanied by brief images of the stunning Lidia pouting at the camera, followed by library footage of Seb with a series of beautiful women on his arm. Then there was a short interview with the grateful victim of the knife incident, who praised Seb for his bravery and the way he had protected her. Gina wanted to shut out the pictures and the words, but she couldn't prevent herself from watching and listening as the report continued, breaking her heart in the process.

'Questioned when leaving the police station today with his cousin, Riccardo Linardi, whose parents are wealthy corporate attorney Roberto Linardi and Sofia Linardi, known as a tireless charity campaigner, Dr Adriani refused to comment on where he has been, or discuss his career plans for the future. It is believed he will be staying overnight at the Linardi family's impressive Florentine mansion, rather than returning to his own luxury penthouse apartment in the city, which has remained unoccupied since July's incident.

'*One report claims that Dr Adriani was seen on the island of Elba, giving medical aid to the casualties who survived yesterday's collapse of a block of tourist apartments that claimed fifteen lives. Neither hospital officials in Portoferraio nor the island's police will confirm or deny these rumours, and Dr Adriani's possible involvement, along with his whereabouts these last weeks, remain a mystery.*

'*Tomorrow Dr Adriani will appear in court, when the accused will face his first hearing. Bail is widely expected to be refused, given the accused's history of absconding.*'

Gina stared at the screen in disbelief. Not only was Seb a doctor, he was a wealthy and famous surgeon with an impressive list of celebrity clients. A renowned bachelor, he had a string of beautiful women at his disposal—women who were slim, sophisticated and polished...the complete opposite of herself. The Linardis, who owned this villa on Elba—the villa Seb had allowed her to believe he was caretaking—were actually his family, the aunt and uncle who had rescued him from the streets as a child. The Linardi family were rich, and part of Florentine society, with a lifestyle she couldn't even begin to imagine.

'Gina?' Her grandmother's voice held evident concern.

'He lied to me about *everything*!' She rose to her feet, switching off the television before pacing about the room. 'Not only about who and what he really is, but about the kind of world he comes from. He's Ferraris, Armani suits and champagne. I'm public transport, charity shop seconds and cheap Lambrusco!'

How he must have laughed at the naïve Scottish girl, taken in by an impossible fairytale. She felt hurt, angry and betrayed. And viciously self-critical of her own stupidity. She couldn't stay here. Couldn't face him again. She was so embarrassed. And so out of his league. He had his pick of beautiful women who fitted into his life as she never could. How could she have believed for a second that he could be attracted to and satisfied by her rounded curves, her lack of sophistication, her modest background? No wonder he hadn't wanted to let her into his world—not with the impossible chasm between them in terms of career and social status.

'Seb never cared about me, Nonna. He couldn't even be truthful.' She paused, battling emotion. 'We did what we came here to do. You are well enough for the journey. So we'll go home tomorrow, just as we planned.'

'But—'

'Please, Nonna. I can't stay here. Not now. I just *can't.*'

Ignoring her grandmother's protests, unable to hold back the tears, she retreated to her room, falling to the bed to cry out her hurt. Her foolish heart was shattered into tiny pieces. She had allowed herself to be caught up in an impossible dream, beguiled by Seb's charm, the magic of Elba and the romance of her grandparents' story. But there would be no happy ending for her as there had been fifty years ago for Maria and Matthew. Her brief re-awakening was over.

Her grandmother came quietly into the room. Sitting on the bed beside her, she gathered her into her arms, rocking her just as she had when she was a child.

'Oh, Nonna, I've been so stupid!' she sobbed.

'No, Gina, it is not your fault.' One hand stroked her hair as she soothed her. 'Seb should have told you sooner.'

Gina sniffed and wiped at her tears. 'Did you see the kind of women he dates all the time? He's not remotely interested in someone plain and ordinary like me.'

'You are not plain and ordinary,' her grandmother rebuked. 'My advice to you is to listen to what he has to say.'

'You're taking his side?' she accused.

'It is not a question of sides, *ragazza mia*. It is obvious you love him, and I don't think you should give up on something so right without fighting for it,' she cajoled, her hazel eyes wise and sad.

'But it's not right! I don't even know him. It's all been a lie from the beginning.' She took a tissue and blew her nose. 'It was a holiday fling—nothing more.'

Pain lanced inside her and she closed her eyes, trying to block out images of her days with Seb. He had never asked her to stay, had never told her he felt anything or asked if she did. From the first he had said she should experience the things Elba had to offer *while she was here*. Temporary. Short-term. She had done so. And now it was finished. She had fallen in love with a man she could never have beyond this unforgettable interlude.

Sucking in a ragged breath, she met her grandmother's anxious gaze. 'The fairytale is over, Nonna. It's time to return to real life.'

'What do you mean, they've gone?' Seb stared at Evelina in shocked disbelief, his heart threatening to stop entirely before resuming at a frantic beat. 'Gone where?'

'Home to Scotland.'

'When? Why?' he demanded, unable to get his head round the fact that Gina had left without waiting to hear what he needed to tell her.

Evelina looked both sad and accusing. 'This morning. I arrived after breakfast to find the taxi already here. Maria and I tried to persuade Gina to wait, but she was adamant...and distressed.'

'Distressed? Why? What happened?' The questions came in quick succession.

'You should have told her the truth when you had the chance, Sebastiano.' Placing her hands on ample hips, she fixed him with a speaking glare. 'Gina saw the report about you on the television news last night...the pictures of you with all those fancy, insincere women. Including that actress Lidia—*il sfacciatella*. The hussy. It was a big shock to Gina to find out that way who and what you are.'

'*Dio!* No.' Shaken, Seb sat down and put his head in his hands.

He should have expected the media circus in Florence, but it had never crossed his mind that Gina might see him on TV—nor that the news would run some tabloid piece of gossip and innuendo that held scarcely a scrap of truth. Not that Gina would know that, because he'd never told her. All she knew was that he'd kept so much from her, and now she believed he had tricked her, made a fool of her, used her. And it wasn't true.

'Gina left you a note.' Evelina handed him a sealed envelope, shaking her head as she walked away, muttering to herself at his foolishness. '*Uomo stupido!*'

Evelina was right. He was a stupid man. He opened the envelope and a wave of fury washed over him when he found the money Gina had left to cover the cost of her and Maria's stay at the villa. Now he was mad! Then he read the note, her thanks for what he had done for her grandmother and for making it possible to succeed in what they had come to the island to do. The final sentences had him clenching his hands around the paper and swearing viciously at himself.

He should have told Gina all about himself from the beginning. But, as he had tried to explain to Rico, when his cousin had predictably read him the Riot Act last night, by the time he'd known she was genuine he'd been enjoying being accepted for the person he was, and not for his name or position or reputation.

'It's a lie, Seb. Albeit by omission,' Rico had protested.

'What are you afraid of—that she'll turn out to be a gold-digger like the rest of them?'

'Gina's the least materialistic person I've ever met,' he'd defended, thinking of her enjoyment of the most simple things. She was so refreshing, not to mention fun to be with, and he had never felt so relaxed and light-hearted with anyone as he did with her. 'But I thought it would change things. And I didn't want money or anything else to affect what we have. I'm a different person with her. I *like* me when I'm with her. And I wanted her to know the real me before the other stuff got in the way.'

'But she doesn't, does she? You've kept an important part of you back. Now she's found out by default that you're a doctor. It will be even worse if she discovers you've not been honest with her about the rest,' his cousin had warned, with what now turned out to be startling presentiment. 'If she means something to you—'

'I love her, Rico.'

Saying the words out loud for the first time had cemented the truth in his mind. These last days with Gina had been the best of his life. The feelings were new to him, and he was scared but determined—and falling more and more in love with her by the hour. All other women seemed fake and uninteresting compared to her. He wanted Gina. She was the one. A few days, weeks or months with her would never be enough—he needed her in his life permanently.

Missing her like crazy, he had tried to phone last night from Florence, but her mobile had been switched off and there had been no reply from the house phone. It had been later than he had intended, because he had been delayed having dinner with Zio Roberto, Zia Sofia and Rico, so he had not worried unduly at being unable to speak with Gina. He had guessed that she and Maria were having an early night. It was only now he realised that she had seen the news and had been avoiding him.

He considered trying her mobile phone, but then thought better of it. He needed a proper strategy. If he rang or texted her now she would reject him. And it was all his fault. He had misjudged the situation from the first, and he had driven Gina away in the process, hurting her and destroying her trust in him. Unlike any other woman he had ever known, rather than seeing his money and his name as an advantage, to Gina it was a barrier, making a relationship between them impossible. He read again the final lines of the note crumpled in his hands...

I understand why you didn't tell me—I could never fit into your monied world or compete with the beautiful women you are used to. But I'll never forget my time with you on Elba. It was a lovely fairytale while it lasted. Now I have to face reality and go back to my own life. I wish you well with yours. Gina.

Dio, she had it all wrong. He had never for a second imagined that she was not good enough for him. It was the other way round. *He* didn't deserve *her*. And no other woman held a candle to her. Somehow he had to make her understand. He'd been a fool, and now he risked losing the best thing that had ever happened to him because of it. His innocent subterfuge had backfired on him in a major way. It wasn't a mistake he would make again.

He was used to getting what he wanted. And he wanted Gina. No way was he giving up on her. She was the only woman he had ever loved, and it was time he fronted up and told her how he felt about her. Momentary doubt assailed him because he had no guarantee of her feelings for him. Yet if Gina didn't care, surely she wouldn't be so upset. The magic between them was special…the fairytale *was* real. He was the one who had messed up, so it was up to him to sort it out—to win back Gina's trust, to claim her heart and prove to her how much he loved her.

His mind made up, he reached for the telephone, ignoring the noisy banging of pots and pans from the kitchen as Evelina made her displeasure at him known. Renewed determination fired inside him as his call was answered.

'Rico, it's me.' After updating his cousin on the latest events, he waited for the berating he deserved to come to an end, then, 'I need your help, *cugino*. Again. I have a plan.'

CHAPTER NINE

'There—that's the dressing done. We're all finished, Tam.' Gina pulled off her gloves, discarded the remains of the sterile wound pack, and smiled at the elderly man sitting on the treatment table. 'How does it feel now?'

'Much more comfortable, lass. I'm obliged to you.'

With painful dignity, over-long strands of straggly grey hair falling around his rugged face, the man leaned forward, pulled up his threadbare sock and rolled down the leg of his frayed trousers. Everyone in Strathlochan knew Old Tam. Of indeterminate age, he lived rough. He found it impossible to accept help from anyone, and got by doing odd jobs and living off scraps. His was a sad story of a lost job, lost home and lost family. He could be irritable, and he indulged in a drinking binge once or twice a year, but Gina knew he had a good heart. She wished he would accept the other things they could do for him, but he refused to go to hospital when poorly, rejected charity, and declined to take a place in a hostel, preferring the way of life he had become used to, suspicious of anyone who tried to interfere.

It was miracle enough that Tam had come to the centre to have the bad cut on his leg cleaned and treated. It had developed a nasty infection—not helped by the poor state of his living conditions. At least now they could keep the

wound clean and dressed…and provide him with something hot to eat and drink. Given the way he had demolished
a bowl of vegetable soup, a meat pie, a whole plateful of
biscuits and two cups of tea, Tam clearly appreciated what
the more informal and less pressured conditions of the new
multi-purpose drop-in centre had to offer.

'Will you come back and see me in a few days?' Gina
asked now, helping him to his feet and walking with him
towards the front door, where his fiercely protective and
constant companion Jock, a Jack Russell terrier, awaited
him, barking noisily as he spied Tam returning.

'Aye, lass. Maybe I will.'

Gina knew it was as much of a promise as she could
expect. Certain Tam would never take a course of tablets if
she offered them, she had taken the precaution of giving him
a broad spectrum antibiotic injection, along with a tetanus
shot. She could only keep her fingers crossed he would
return to have his dressing changed.

Smiling again, she held the door open for him. 'We're
always here, Tam, so pop in any time that suits you.'
Mentally crossing her fingers, she gave him a bag of fruit,
and a couple of treats for Jock.

'Thank you, we'll enjoy these,' he allowed, and Gina let
out a sigh of relief that he had not rejected the gift.

'Anything else I can do?'

He shook his head, untying the piece of bailer twine that
served as Jock's lead, and bending to give the white and tan
dog a gentle stroke. 'We'll be all right. You could tell Doc
Gallagher that I'll take care of that gardening job for him.'

'I'll do that.' Bless Thorn for realising that Tam needed
to feel useful, and to believe he was giving something in
return. 'Take care.'

She watched him walk away, wondering where he went
and how he managed. It made her ashamed of herself. She

had so much to be thankful for, but all she had been able to think about this last week was the pain and desolation of losing Seb. Not that she had ever really had him. But leaving him and Elba had been heart-wrenching. A distraught Evelina had begged them to wait for Seb's return, but, aside from being unable to face him, Gina had felt awkward knowing the kindly woman had been party to his deception.

The taxi had dropped them at the hospital in Portoferraio, where Dottore Vasari had given her grandmother the official all-clear to travel. Then they had taken the ferry back to the mainland and caught the train to Pisa for their afternoon flight back to Scotland. Arriving home had brought mixed feelings…familiarity, warmth at her effusive welcome from Montgomery, but always the ceaseless ache of missing Seb and knowing that she would never see him again.

One day had passed into another, the nights dragging slowly as she found it hard to sleep without Seb, and when she did, his image filled her dreams. Everything made her think of him. Even starting her new job and catching up with her friends couldn't block the memories and her pain over Seb from her mind.

Trying to push the disturbing thoughts away, she went back inside the welcoming reception area, where Lesley Stuart claimed her attention. The centre's secretary turned her hand to anything that was needed, and had an uncanny knack of handling anyone from the fearful to the obstreperous with tact, compassion and firmness—a skill she claimed she had acquired raising three irrepressible boys alone. Gina had no idea where Thorn had found Lesley, but thank goodness he had, because everything ran like clockwork when she was around.

'Gina, Thorn asked if you could stop by his office before you leave,' the older woman informed her with a smile.

'Of course.' Gina tried to hide a flicker of anxiety as she

wondered why the clinical director wanted to see her. 'Thanks, Lesley.'

After she had tidied the treatment room, written up her notes and finished her final tasks of the day, she went to the staffroom to collect her things and say goodbye to a few of her colleagues who lingered there, sharing a chat over mugs of tea as they changed shift. A few moments later Gina stood outside Thorn's office and knocked on the door.

'Come in.'

Gina did as she was bid. Her boss was on the telephone, but he smiled and waved her to a chair, mouthing, "Won't be long," before returning his attention to the call. She sat down and waited, picking up from Thorn's end of the conversation that he was talking with Nic di Angelis, an Italian GP who worked locally. Thoughts of Italy inevitably brought images of Seb to mind. To prevent herself lingering on them, she tried to focus her attention on the man across the other side of the desk.

Thornton Gallagher was an enigma. There was an edge about him—something a bit dangerous and unconventional. He had not been in town long, but he was an excellent doctor, having proved himself during a six-month stint in Strathlochan's busy A and E department, which was where Gina had met him. In his early thirties, he was tall, with a rangy body and a leanly handsome face. He had unusual amber eyes and untamed, just-got-out-of-bed hair, its shade somewhere between dark blond and light brown.

Gina had always found Thorn good to work with, and he had been the perfect choice to run this centre. Experienced beyond his years in various areas of medicine, at home and abroad, he was full of exciting, often radical ideas for getting care delivered where and when it was needed. He was also not averse to bucking the system and going out on a limb for what he wanted.

As her boss said goodbye to Nic and hung up the phone, Gina found herself subjected to the full force of his enigmatic amber gaze.

'How have you found your first days here? Any problems?' he asked, leaning his elbows on the desk and steepling his fingers under his chin.

'No, it's been good. I enjoy the work.' Despite her personal issues, she maintained her enthusiasm for her job, but Thorn's intense assessment made her uneasy. 'Why? Have I done something wrong?'

'Don't be silly, Gina.' He dismissed her question with an impatient wave of his hand. 'You're the best nurse I know. Why do you think I was determined to have you as part of my team?'

'Oh! Well, thank you,' she murmured, flattered and taken by surprise.

'How's Maria?'

Thorn's change of tack momentarily wrong-footed her. 'She's fine in herself. Our GP is keeping her on a maintenance dose of the diuretics, and monitoring her for any further fluid on the lungs and oedema…and investigating the cause.'

'It must have been a worry, her being taken ill while you were away?'

'Yes.' Pain lanced through her as she recalled Seb's arrival at Elba's hospital, his care and concern for her grandmother. 'Thankfully, all was well.'

Veiled amber eyes studied her, a pout of consideration shaping Thorn's mouth. 'And what about you?'

'What about me?'

'You've been pale and quiet,' he remarked, demonstrating once again that little escaped his notice. 'And sad since you came back from Italy.'

'I'm OK,' she lied, struggling to hold onto her composure.

She wasn't OK. She feared she never would be again. It was foolish, hopeless, but she loved Seb with every fragment of her broken heart, and she tormented herself over the way things had ended. Was her grandmother right? Had she made a mistake not waiting to see him? They were questions that plagued her in the darkest hours of the night. She had run because she had been hurt and scared. Scared she hadn't known him at all. Scared she could never be good enough for him. Scared Seb would explain why he had deceived her and then ask her to leave—tell her it had been fun, but... And it wasn't as if he had made any effort to contact her. Not that she expected him to. But a week's silence confirmed she had made the right decision. He was likely relieved to have it over without further awkwardness and embarrassment. But that didn't stop the welling of pain and disappointment.

'You met someone.' Thorn's uncanny insight spooked her. 'Your heart is still in Italy.'

Gina forced back an unwanted sting of tears. 'It wasn't to be.'

How could it be, when Seb was used to dating beautiful, rich women? She wouldn't fit in his world and they both knew it...that had to be why he had misled her and hidden the truth about himself from the beginning.

'You're in love with him.'

'Yes,' she found herself admitting. She huffed out a breath, wishing Thorn wasn't so adept at zeroing in on people's emotions and getting them to confide in him, even when they didn't mean to. 'But there's nothing I can do about it.'

Thorn remained silent, continuing to watch her, his expression unreadable, a small, mysterious smile pulling at his mouth.

'Anyway, you asked about work. I've just seen Old Tam,' she said, determined to divert the conversation away from herself. 'Whether he comes back to have his wound re-dressed remains to be seen. He asked me to tell you he'll take care of the job you asked him to do.'

Knowing amusement sparked in Thorn's amber eyes. 'Thanks. Are you off home now?'

'Yes.' Thankful to be let off the hook—because he had most surely sussed out her ploy—she rose to her feet. 'After a stop at the supermarket on the way back. Holly and Ruth are coming round later.'

'I'll walk you out.'

Puzzled, because it wasn't a normal thing for him to do, she watched as he gracefully eased his athletic frame from the chair and walked across to open the door. She might not be attracted herself, but she could understand why many other women were. It wasn't just Thorn's looks, it was the bad-boy edge he had about him.

'Thanks. But you don't have to bother. You're busy,' she added, not wanting to be impolite.

'I'm about to show someone around the centre. He's inter-ested in making a donation...of both money and expertise. A skilled doctor, he could be on board full-time.' He paused, his unfathomable gaze watchful. 'Let's hope we can satisfy his needs and give him all he wants to stay in Strathlochan.'

'The additional help would be welcome,' Gina agreed, thinking of the benefit to the centre of having an extra full-time doctor on staff with Thorn, rather than relying so much on the voluntary efforts of local GPs and hospital staff. 'Is there anything I can do to help?'

Thorn's mysterious smile widened as they stepped out of the building and into the small car park. 'Later, no doubt. But I have this end covered for now.'

'OK.' She fastened the zip of her jacket against the kiss of the cool autumn air, hooking the strap of her bag over her shoulder. 'I hope it works out.'

'Me, too.'

She frowned at the amused edge to his tone, sensing there was something he wasn't telling her. 'Goodnight, Thorn.'

''Night,' he answered. 'Give my love to Maria.'

'I will.' She was about to step away when Thorn tugged gently on the long braid hanging down her back. Halting, she turned and faced him again. 'Yes?'

For a long moment his gaze searched hers. Then he nodded and smiled again. 'You never know what waits for you around the next corner. Good luck, Gina.'

More confused than ever by Thorn's curious comments, she walked away, feeling his gaze on her until she turned out on to the street. Shaking her head, she switched on her mobile phone, finding two texts awaiting her—both Holly and Ruth cancelling their evening. Disappointed, she rang her grandmother to ask if she needed anything from the shops, and to let her know she was on her way home.

Home. She loved it here, but she had felt so restless since returning from Italy. Her time on Elba with Seb had been a fantasy. Now she was back to earth with a bump, with only the memories of a few snatched days and nights of happiness to sustain her...memories of a magical passion she knew she would never experience again.

Seb watched from his hire car as Gina left the building, his breath catching and his heart kicking as he drank in his first glimpse of her for far too many days. Then his eyes narrowed as he noted the man who followed her out. From where Seb was sitting, the guy was being far too familiar with Gina—a fact borne out when she turned to walk away and the man reached out a hand to catch her braid.

'Who the hell is he?' Seb growled, overcome by a wave of possessive jealousy.

Nic di Angelis, his companion in the car, chuckled. 'No one for you to worry about, *mio amico*. That's Thorn.'

'Thornton Gallagher?' he exclaimed, unable to hide his shock.

'The one and only.'

As Gina disappeared from view, Seb returned his attention to Thorn, watching as he sauntered in their direction. He had spoken to the clinic's director several times by phone in the last days, and he had formed an image in his mind of an older man—a no-nonsense and deeply committed doctor. Yet Thorn was around his own age. Needing to be open about the reasons for his interest in the centre, and where Gina fitted into his plans, Seb had uncharacteristically taken Thorn into his confidence, finding a willing ally.

Even with Rico, Thorn and Nic pulling strings for him it had taken several days to get his papers in order and make the necessary arrangements for major changes in his life— the success of which rested on seeking Gina's forgiveness. He didn't know what he would do if he couldn't talk her round, if she didn't love him even a fraction as much as he loved her.

Nic and his lovely wife Hannah had welcomed him to their home the previous night, after his arrival from Italy, offering him a place to stay. They had been friendly and helpful, and Nic had also shared his experiences of living and working as a doctor in rural Scotland.

'I've been here nearly five years to the day, and they have been the happiest of my life,' he had told him with obvious sincerity. 'It's a great place to live.'

'What about the weather? The cold winters?'

'It's not that bad. And there is much to be said for cuddling up in front of a log fire with the woman you love,' Nic had responded, warm amusement in his dark eyes.

'I would be happy anywhere with Gina by my side,' he'd agreed, filled with renewed determination. 'Now I have to make it happen.'

Earlier that day he had visited Maria and won her support. She had invited Gina's friends Holly and Ruth for lunch and, after their initial reticence, he had been able to bring them on board, too. All that remained now was to meet Thorn in person, look round the centre...and then face Gina.

'I can see why you told me to dress casually,' he commented as Thorn, wearing jeans and a sweatshirt bearing the centre's logo, approached the car.

'Thorn doesn't stand on ceremony. But don't be fooled by his relaxed, lazy air...he's as sharp as they come,' his new friend advised. 'He's a first-class doctor, and his maverick nature makes him perfect for this job.'

As Nic opened the passenger door and climbed out, Seb followed suit, slipping from behind the steering wheel and exchanging a firm handshake with the man he hoped to be working with in the very near future.

'Good to meet you, Seb.' Thorn smiled as Nic introduced them. 'The coast is clear. Gina's heading home via the supermarket, so you have a while.'

'She doesn't know I'm here?'

'She has no idea,' Thorn confirmed. 'But I wanted to test the waters. Even I can be subtle when needed.' A wry smile curved his mouth before he sobered. 'If I didn't think this was in her best interests, we wouldn't be here. Come on in and have a look around.'

* * *

Gina pushed open the front door, juggling keys and carrier bags as she was greeted by an enthusiastic Monty, his wagging tail beating a tattoo against the hall radiator. 'Let me put the shopping down first.'

The dog trotted after her to the kitchen, where she found her grandmother putting the finishing touches to an evening meal. Surprised at this change to their normal routine, Gina halted and stared at her.

'Gina!' The older woman smiled. 'Good—you are home.'

'Is everything all right?' she queried, setting her bags down on a free piece of worktop.

'Yes, of course. As Holly and Ruth are not coming, I wanted to make you something special for supper,' she informed her, turning back to the counter. 'I have done your favourite apple and blackberry crumble for pudding!'

'Nonna, it's kind of you, but I'm really not that hungry.'

'Nonsense. You must start eating properly again,' her grandmother chided.

Sighing, Gina put the shopping away. 'How did you know Holly and Ruth had cancelled?'

'I talked to Ruth earlier.' Her grandmother's cheeks were stained pink, and Gina's gaze sharpened in suspicion. 'She was telling me the latest news about that Julia—Holly's awful sister. Holly's so upset. How Gus Buchanan—'

'Nonna,' Gina interrupted, confused and frustrated.

'I just wanted to do something nice for you,' her grandmother explained, making her feel bad for her lack of appreciation. 'I know you are tired. And sad.'

Gina closed her eyes, trying to shut out the pain. 'I'm fine.'

'We both know that isn't true…and why.' Shaking her head, her grandmother tutted again. 'Go upstairs, now. Have a shower and change into a nice frock.'

'But…'

'Make the effort for me, *ragazza mia*,' she requested firmly. 'Please?'

Anxious to escape another discussion about Seb, and their disagreement over leaving Elba so suddenly, Gina escaped the kitchen and went upstairs to change. It was unlike her grandmother to be so dogged, or so tactless—yet she gave her no peace, seeming unable to understand why she was so hurt by Seb's lies. Her heart aching, she sat on her bed, feeling listless and very much alone.

She missed Seb so much. How could she have fallen in love with him in such a short time? She would never feel again as she had with him. Not just the spectacular experience of making love with him, but everything...just being with him, how he made her feel, the way he listened to her. Yet he had shared so little about himself.

Her gaze strayed to the bedside chest. Apart from memories and a broken heart, she had taken only three things from Elba. The beautiful piece of Elbaite Seb had bought her, with its delicate colours and intriguing textures. The white rose, pressed now between the pages of a book. And she had kept his jumper—the one he had taken off and pulled over her head that night on the terrace. She had never given it back. Now she tortured herself, sleeping in it, keeping it, a small part of Seb, close to her. She picked it up now and buried her face in it, breathing in his lingering scent.

'Gina! I can't hear the water running!'

As her grandmother called impatiently up the stairs, Gina choked back a fresh welling of tears. Setting the jumper aside, she rose to her feet, taking off her trousers and the sweatshirt with the centre's logo that constituted their informal uniform. After a quick shower, she stared at her wardrobe. Her red dress caught her eye and new pain lanced inside her. She couldn't wear it—not without remembering her night out with Seb at the restaurant in Marciana

Marina...the night he had kissed her for the first time. That sensuous, confident woman had been put back under wraps again. There was no room for her here—and no Seb to set her free.

Drawing in an unsteady breath, she pulled out a floaty skirt and a button-through top, her fingers shaking as she dressed. Her grandmother was behaving very oddly. Gina just hoped she was not to be subjected to another lecture about Seb, or she would never survive the evening with her emotions intact.

'What do you think?' Thorn asked, closing his office door and bringing their tour of the centre to an end.

Seb had met the staff on duty, and found the place and the whole philosophy behind it exciting and intriguing. 'I'm really impressed. And enthusiastic.'

'You are vastly over-qualified, but if you are sure this is what you want, I'd be delighted to have someone of your experience on the team here.'

'Thank you. I might be unable to perform surgery again, but Gina helped show me that I can still be useful—still be needed,' he told Thorn, having already confided in him about his background as a child on the streets. 'I'll need to brush up on some areas, and I will be happy to take any courses you recommend. I've heard so much about this place from Gina, and I share her belief in what you are doing.'

Thorn nodded, his amber gaze assessing. 'And now you need to see her.'

'Yes.' Anxiety rippled through him at what still lay ahead. 'The final decision on whether I stay or go rests with her.'

'I wish you luck.' Thorn shook his hand, his expression serious. 'As a friend to Gina—and I hope soon to you—get this right, Seb. You hurt her once. Don't do it again.'

Admiring the man, and appreciating his genuine concern, Seb nodded and went outside to join Nic. Hannah had arrived to collect her husband, and they wished him well on the next stage of his venture. He watched them leave before crossing to his hire car and making the short drive back to Gina and Maria's cottage.

He planned to win Gina back—to prove to her that he was worthy of her and not some flash surgeon who had lost his soul and forgotten why he had become a doctor. Having Gina in his life had opened his eyes and his heart to where he had been going wrong. It wasn't too late to get his career back on track. He just hoped it wasn't too late for him and Gina.

As agreed with Maria, he used the key she had given him and slipped in through the back door of the small but homely cottage situated in a quiet, leafy road. The views of the hills and woods appealed to him—he loved what he had seen of the region in his first hours here, and he couldn't wait to explore with Gina. He hunkered down in the kitchen to greet Monty, having bonded with the dog earlier in the day. Maria cracked the door open and peeped round it.

'Gina will be down any moment,' she whispered, hazel eyes sparkling with conspiratorial delight. 'I'll lure her into the living room. You come along when you are ready.'

Seb nodded. The door closed again, and his heart lurched as he heard Gina's footfall on the stairs and Maria's voice calling to her. He'd give them a few moments—and himself time to try and steady his nerves. He was more scared than at any time in his life. He had support from Maria, Rico, Thorn, Nic and Hannah, even Ruth and Holly. Now it was all down to him. Could he persuade Gina to forgive him and grant him a second chance? He *had* to succeed. Life without Gina was unthinkable, unbearable.

Leaving a disgruntled Monty in the kitchen, and closing the door behind him, he walked quietly along the corridor. Any moment now he would face the most important test of his life. Female voices became clearer, and Gina's words temporarily shocked him to immobility…

Gina stood in the living room, her hands tightly clasping the back of a chair as she faced her grandmother's latest challenge.

'Have you given any more thought to what I said about Seb?' Hazel eyes reflected fierce determination. 'It's been a week, Gina.'

She knew how long it had been—was aware of every painful second. 'Seb lied to me, Nonna.'

'Did he tell you he was caretaker of the villa?'

'No. But he knew that was what I thought, and he did nothing to correct me. He never told me he was a surgeon, that he was rich and famous, or that his family owned the place. He deliberately deceived me.'

'And why do you think he would do that?'

Gina shrugged, upset that her grandmother was pushing her like this. 'We've been through all this before, and it isn't going to change anything. It was stupid of me to ever believe in a fantasy,' she stated, hurting inside at the thought of Seb's duplicity and her own foolishness.

'You don't think there may be other, more understandable reasons, *ragazza mia*?'

'What reasons could there be?' Her hands tightened their grip on the chair as she battled her emotions. 'Seb didn't respect or care about me enough to be truthful, to trust me. And I'm nothing compared to the women he's used to dating.'

Her grandmother tutted in annoyance. 'That's rubbish.'

'Anyway, it was different when I thought Seb was just a normal guy. I—'

'Exactly.'

With a cry of shock, Gina spun round as Seb's voice sounded behind her. Her heart thudded wildly at the sight of him. He looked divine…casually rumpled, the thickness of his hair tossed by the early autumn breeze, the beginnings of a five o'clock shadow darkening his jawline, that delectable body encased in dark-grey chinos and a chunky black jumper. For a moment she swayed, certain she must be hallucinating. But when she closed her eyes and opened them again Seb was still there. She glanced accusingly at her grandmother, whose expression was one of defiance mixed with guilt.

'Do not blame Maria,' Seb intervened. 'I am the one who needs to explain things to you. I was desperate enough to follow you here as soon as I could arrange it, and to appeal to your grandmother and your friends for their help.'

'Why?' she whispered.

'Will you listen to what I have to say?' Warm caramel-coloured eyes she had never expected to see again looked deeply into hers. 'Please, Gina?'

Racked with indecision, Gina hesitated. She was aware of her grandmother exiting the room, but when Seb tried to close the distance between them she backed up, keeping out of his reach. If he touched her now, all her defences and common sense would crumble. The front doorbell rang, startling her, and her eyes widened as her grandmother opened it and both Holly and Ruth stepped into the hall, conspiratorial smiles on their faces. Holly gave her a thumbs-up.

'What's going on?' Gina demanded.

'I'm staying the night with Ruth.' Smiling, her grandmother picked up a small overnight bag. 'You and Seb need to be alone. Supper is ready in the kitchen—it will keep until you want it.'

Gina's mouth dropped open. She couldn't believe any of this. But before she could find her voice to protest, the girls had ushered her grandmother outside. The front door closed. She was, indeed, alone with Seb.

'What's going on? Why are you here?' Her hands were shaking badly, so she clasped them tightly together. Unable to help herself, she let her gaze drink in the sight of him, but the pain inside her couldn't be denied. Pent-up tears stung her eyes. 'You lied to me from the beginning. I wasn't good enough for you.'

'No!' Gina's accusations cut through him, and seeing the mistrust and tears bruising her dark eyes made him realise just how deeply he had hurt her, how badly he had misjudged everything. 'It was never that, Gina. It was *me*, not you.'

'I don't understand.'

He cursed the wobble in her voice, desperately needing to hold her, but knowing he had to give her space until he had explained. 'I know, *amore mia*, and that is my fault. I was ashamed. I so admired your passion, your goodness, your principles. I feared that when you found out how shallow my life and career had become you would be disappointed in me, reject me.'

For long moments she stared at him in silence, and he waited, hiding nothing from her. 'You're serious,' she whispered, confusion, disbelief and wonder all layered through her voice.

'I am. Will you allow me to explain from the beginning?' He held his breath, knowing how important her answer was, uncaring that he was begging. 'Please, Gina.'

She bit her lip, and desire flared inside him. He couldn't wait to taste her mouth again, to taste her all over, hold her, make love with her. Finally, when he thought he couldn't stand the wait another second, she nodded—although she remained too far away, regarding him with suspicion. Not that he could blame her. He had this one chance...he couldn't blow it.

Leaving nothing out, he told her all about Antonella, about the people who'd used him, the way he had been en-

couraged to change the direction of his career. He talked of
the Linardis, even of how he had operated free of charge on
Paolo's young daughter when she had been badly injured in
an accident on Elba, and how he'd only felt fulfilled doing
the *pro bono* work.

'I was attracted to you the second I saw you,' he continued, searching her face, hoping she understood and believed
him. 'But I was wary—suspicious of your presence because
of past press intrusion. At first I thought there was a possibility you were a journalist, looking for a clever way
in…that's why I was cagey and didn't tell you who I was.'
Her mouth opened in protest and he rushed on before she
could interrupt. 'As soon as I got to know you it was clear
you were totally genuine. By then my feelings for you were
escalating and I was overwhelmed by how natural you were.
I'd never met anyone like you, Gina. You treated me as a
normal person. I liked it—liked that you saw *me*. The intention was never to trick you or deceive you—I just wanted
some time, so you would know the real me, in the hope that
the other things would no longer matter when you knew.'

'Seb…'

Scared in case she stopped listening, he held up a hand.
'Wait—please. I need to tell you it all, to explain what you
did for me.'

'What *I* did for *you*?' she repeated, a stunned expression
in her eyes.

'Yes—in so many ways.' To resist the temptation of
reaching for her, he sat on the edge of the sofa, his elbows
resting on his knees. 'You've taught me so much about
myself, Gina.'

Sitting opposite, she looked at him in confusion. 'How?'

'I've never told anyone else the things I told you about
my past. Not even my cousin Rico. Talking to you, listening to you, I realised how much I have been unconsciously

striving to prove myself worthy of the faith and love the Linardis showed me when they took me in. I never felt good enough—I needed to belong. I had some success in my surgical career, then I was guided down a road I should never have agreed to travel. But I did. And that responsibility rests with me,' he admitted, making no excuses. 'As I became known, all people saw was what I could do for them—and the money and the fame. You are the first person to see who I am on the inside, without all the trappings. You made me like myself. And hearing you speak of your work with such passion and dedication showed me how far I had come from my roots. I had forgotten why I had become a doctor in the first place.

'I feared you would hate what I did—would judge me for having wasted my surgical skills—' He broke off and looked at his hands. 'Having these injuries may have been a blessing in disguise. Without them I would never have gone to Elba and I would never have met you. Learning about your values, your down-to-earth goodness, made me reassess my life and find it wanting. I had taken that wrong turning for the wrong reasons. Now I want to believe in something again, to use my medical knowledge to do good. I don't care about the money. I never have. And I hate being recognised. Those things are not important. I want a second chance with my work—but most important of all I want you.

'In such a short time you have opened my eyes to what was wrong with my life. I was at a turning point, coming to terms with losing surgery. I didn't know who I was or what I wanted to be. For years I have been used for my name and my position. But for you, Gina, I was just Seb. I was myself with you. I know I should have told you everything from the first, but I was already in so deep and I cared so much that it became harder and harder to find the right moment. I was frightened it would change things between us—

change how you saw me.' A wry, self-deprecating laugh escaped. 'I was right, no? It did make a difference. It opened that gulf and spoiled everything. You no longer saw *me*.'

Seb looked up, and the sincerity tinged with fearful doubt in his eyes brought a lump to Gina's throat.

Yes, he should have told her about himself. But she had some understanding now of why he hadn't. She was also uncomfortably aware that he was right…at least in part. She *had* reacted to the news by forgetting all she knew him to be. Her attitude towards him *had* changed. She had seen only the differences between them, believing there to be an unbridgeable chasm. Would her reaction have been more measured had he told her when they had first met? She wasn't sure, but she feared that had she known at the start that Seb was a rich and famous surgeon she would have withdrawn, put up barriers, never become involved with him despite their attraction and sexual chemistry. She would have judged him—not harshly for the work he did, but believing she wasn't good enough for him.

'Seb…' She paused, struggling for the right words. 'I was frightened by the truth. Scared of everything I imagined came with you,' she admitted, knowing she had to be equally honest. 'But I would never have judged you about your work. And money means nothing to me.'

'No, but it came between us just the same. Instead of seeing what it would do for you, as others have done, you saw it as an obstacle, and it changed the way you saw me—us. You mistakenly decided that we couldn't fit. But we can—we *do*.'

'What about all those women? They are beautiful, thin, sophisticated—'

Again he interrupted her, edging closer, his fingers on her lips silencing her protests and sending shivers of sensation zinging through her body. 'Gina, the truth is that I have *never* taken a women to my home, in Florence or in Elba, until you. The women I was seen out with were all using me to further their names and careers. They liked to be seen on my arm, to meet people who could help them, and I had convenient escorts to official functions. I wasn't "dating" them, I had no relationship with any of them, and there was no romance, no emotion—and ninety-nine times out of a hundred no sex. My career was everything to me. I wasn't interested in a relationship...until I met you.'

'But—'

'But nothing,' he chided softly, cupping her face in his hands. 'Those women are vain, artificial and uncaring, interested only in themselves. I am not attracted to any of them. You are so much more beautiful in every way, Gina. You are real and honest and generous, the most natural, giving person I've ever known.' The pad of one thumb brushed across her trembling lips and she couldn't look away from the raw expression in his eyes. 'You are the only woman who has ever stolen my heart, who I have ever needed, who I want to spend the rest of my life with. I've missed you so much. I love you, Gina. I don't want to live another day without you by my side, or another night without you in my arms.'

Tears escaped, squeezing between her lashes and trickling down her cheeks. Seb was a proud man, independent, unused to needing or trusting anyone, and yet here he was, vulnerable and open, laying his heart on the line—for her. There was much to talk about, and to understand, but she knew she wanted to face whatever life threw at her with him. She loved him beyond bearing. Stifling a sob, she melted into his embrace.

A shuddering breath of relief rushed out of him as he wrapped his arms around her and held her tight. She absorbed his strength, breathed in his familiar scent, knowing she was truly home...at last.

'We'll work everything out, *amore mia*.' His voice was

shaky, his breath warm against her skin as he whispered in her ear. 'I love you more than life itself. Never leave me again. Promise me.'

'I promise. I love you, too.'

He pulled back a few inches and for endless moments their gazes locked, silent messages and reassurances exchanged. Then he was kissing her with all the devastating skill and desire she had come to know so well and had missed so terribly these last lonely days. She took everything and gave it back with enthusiasm, swept along in a whirlwind of passion and love. Until, that was, they were interrupted by Monty, who pushed his way between them. Laughing, they tried to hold off the exuberant dog.

'I come as a package, Seb,' she reminded him, seriousness underlying the humour. 'Not just Monty, but Nonna, too.'

'I know that, *amata*. And I wouldn't have it any other way. Monty and I are already good friends, and Maria is very special to me,' he reassured her, one warm palm cupping her cheek. 'Her place will be with us—always.'

Closing her eyes, she rubbed her face against him, revelling in his touch. 'So what do you plan to do...for the future, I mean?'

'I've been making arrangements with Thorn. Today I looked round your wonderful centre,' he admitted, laughing at her gasp of shock.

'It was *you*!' That was why her boss had been behaving oddly, asking her those questions. 'Thorn knew all along!'

'He did. My cousin Rico and Nic di Angelis have also been helping me.'

Startled, she pulled back and looked at him. 'How do you know Nic?'

'I didn't...not until recently.' He smiled and ran the fingers of one hand through her hair. 'The name Strathlochan struck a chord when you mentioned it, but I couldn't remember why.

Rico reminded me. He worked with Nic for a time in Milan, and they have remained good friends. Rico came over here for his wedding. He put me in touch with Nic.'

'I see,' she murmured, feeling dazed.

'Everything is in order for me to come here. I want us to be together, Gina, and I'll be happy anywhere you are. We can live here in Strathlochan and have holidays on Elba. If you will have me, we can work side by side during the day…and love each other every night.'

It was a shock to realise how much organising and ma-noeuvring had gone on behind her back. Her grandmother, Holly, Ruth, Thorn, even Nic and Hannah, she discovered, had all joined forces to help Seb plan all this. She might have been disgruntled if she hadn't been so blissfully happy that Seb was here, that he loved her, wanted her, had followed her to Strathlochan. She loved the idea of working with him at the drop-in centre—loved even more his plans for their nights together.

'What about your family?' Doubts and insecurities assailed her. 'Maybe they won't approve of me.'

'Rico has demanded to meet you from the first day,' he told her, shocking her anew. 'He's been your champion, telling me I am an idiot for keeping things from you. He wanted to come straight over to Elba to see you and Maria, but I wouldn't let him.'

'Why not?' she queried, concerned despite his arguments to the contrary that he had been ashamed of her.

'Because Rico is charming and handsome and outgoing. I didn't want to risk you falling for him instead of me.'

The admission, so obviously sincere, revealing his vul-nerability, stunned her. 'You shouldn't have worried. I would never have seen anyone but you…not from the instant I met you on the beach,' she vowed, laying her own hand against his stubbled jaw, seeing his eyes heat and darken.

He gave her a hasty but delicious kiss before drawing back. 'As for Zio Roberto and Zia Sofia—they are equally enthusiastic,' he reassured her. 'They are eager to meet you. Eager, too, to meet Maria and hear her memories of Elba. They are fully supportive of what you came to the beach to do. Zio Roberto built the villa as a fifth anniversary present for Zia Sofia thirty years ago. It is a special place for all our combined family.'

'It is.'

The familiar burn of heated desire flaring inside her, she met his gaze, her fingertips exploring, relearning the contours of his face. He caught her hand, his lips and tongue teasing her palm, causing the ache of need to knot deep within her.

With Monty curling up in front of the fire, Seb drew her down with him on the sofa. 'I love you. You are my life,' he murmured huskily, moments before his mouth met hers. '*Per sempre*, Gina *mia*…for ever.'

Fresh tears, joyful tears, stung Gina's eyes. Just a short while ago she had been in despair. Now she was the happiest woman alive. How could she be this lucky? Wrapping her arms around him, wriggling on top of him, she showed Seb in every way how much she loved him.

History had repeated itself after all, and Elba had worked her magic a second time. The fates had smiled on them as they had on Maria and Matthew, leading them to meet and fall in love in the same special place half a century later. Gina smiled and gave thanks. Like her grandparents before them, she and Seb had found togetherness, a secure bond, and a love to last a lifetime. They were blessed indeed.